Also By Edward Rand

Non-Fiction

The War of Sober: Fight For Your Life

Horror

Lizzie

The Traveler

and

The Chicken Man

Edward Rand

The Traveler and The Chicken Man

Copyright © 2024 BloodChuckles Press

All rights reserved.

http://bloodchucklespress.com

Available in these formats:

eBook ISBN: 978-1-954019-06-5

Paperback ISBN: 978-1-954019-07-2

Hardback ISBN: 978-1-954019-08-9

Editing: E.K. Hamilton

Cover Design: 100Covers.com

Library of Congress Control Number: 2023914318

Publisher's Cataloging-in-Publication

(Provided by Cassidy Cataloguing Services, Inc.).

Names: Rand, Edward, 1972- author.

Title: The traveler and the chicken man / Edward Rand.

Description: Jacksonville, Arkansas : BloodChuckles Press, [2023]

Identifiers: ISBN: 978-1-954019-08-9 (hardback) | 978-1-954019-07-2 (paperback) |

978-1-954019-06-5 (ebook) | LCCN: 2023914318

Subjects: LCSH: Serial murderers--United States--Fiction. | Revenge--United States--Fiction. | United

States. Federal Bureau of Investigation--Fiction. | Nebraska--Fiction. | Diners (Restaurants)

--Nebraska--Fiction. | Small cities--Social aspects--Nebraska--Fiction. | Family secrets--

United States--Fiction. | Evidence (Law)--United States--Fiction. | Suspense fiction. |

LCGFT: Thrillers (Fiction) | Detective and mystery fiction.

Classification: LCC: PS3618.A486 T73 2023 | DDC: 813/.6--dc23

BloodChuckles Press

North Little Rock, Arkansas

This one's for Grandma.

Her name was Ruby, and she was the best grandmother a kid could ever have, although I wasn't smart enough to know it until it was too late to tell her so.

Monday

1

Mrs. Jacobson swayed up to the order window with a knowing twist to her full, pink lips; I could see my warped self in her mirrored sunglasses, and I looked as nervous as I felt.

"Hello, Jack."

"Uh, hello Mrs. Jacobson."

Her beige-leather purse was slung over one shoulder and a pair of open-toed Spanish sandals encased her shapely feet. She'd painted her toenails and fingernails glitter banana yellow, like a girl half her age, and her tan was seamless; a ninety-dollar spray job if I'd ever seen one, and I've seen my share. Her neon-orange bikini comprised half a dozen strings and four itty-bitty triangles.

I swallowed, hard, and shot a look past her and found her white Escalade sitting in my parking lot, glittering under the hot summer sun. Her three kids were behind the windshield with their heads down and their minds buried in their smart phones. I didn't see Mr. Jacobson.

I breathed a little easier.

"You look good, Jack. Still working out, I see."

"Um, yeah. I mean, uh, thanks, I have been. You look good too, Mrs. Jacobson." Still no sign of Mr. Jacobson; he traveled for business. A lot. Mr. Jacobson was also an avid target shooter and gun collector, and he didn't like me. Not one bit.

I took in her body with its joke of a bikini and realized my vast understatement about how good she looked; I don't think she'd aged a day in three years. Maybe she had Frodo's ring stashed in her purse. A sunburned fat guy in cargo shorts and a faded Yankee's cap standing behind her in line pretended to mess with his iPhone while ogling her ass.

She undulated closer. "Now Jack, don't you think we know each other better than that? Please, call me Miriam."

Donnie was passing behind me as I was bent over with my face pressed to the little screened-in view port, and out of the corner of my eye I saw him jolt to a halt.

"Shit, look at that!" he said. Loudly. "I *love* this fuckin' job!"

I elbowed him away, and he went, laughing. I didn't think Miriam could see him past the tall menu board, or the signs advertising Crazy's floats and shakes, or the carved driftwood plank that announced SHIRT AND SHOES, NO SERVICE, but I had no damn doubt she'd heard him because one corner of those glossy lips twitched higher.

"Can I get you something, Miriam?"

"Sure, Jack." She gave me the order for her and her kids, and when I told her the total, she handed me two crisp Andrew Jackson's, then held on to them, stroking her Ultra-Tan index finger over the long bones in the back of my hand. "I was so sorry to hear about you and Jenifer."

I pulled the money free. "Thanks." I made her change and handed it out the window; it had been ten months since Jen left—over ten months—but it still stung. Maybe it always would. "We'll call the number on the ticket when your order's ready."

"I know," she said. "I've done this before." Her sculpted eyebrow-twitch made the double entendre clear. She reached into her purse and set an embossed card on the stainless-steel shelf under the window and slid it towards me with a yellow-glitter nail. "My number hasn't changed. Doug is out of town this week. Maybe we could get together and talk about Jenifer, or about old times. Or about whatever you want."

By reflex I picked up the card and then wished I hadn't. The fat Yankee's fan leaned around her and gave me thumbs-up. I ignored him. The card was expensive and elegant—just like Miriam. It was her business card; she owned a high-end dress shop in downtown Indian Head. I've never been inside, but my mom says it's nice.

"Uh, well, I'll think about it." What I wanted to say but couldn't was, "No fucking way, lady." I'd had a run-in with her gun-happy husband already and staring down the little black hole at the end of a Glock 9mm once was once too much.

Miriam said, "The kids are going camping Saturday, Jack," still with that smile, and then she swayed back to the Escalade. I wasn't the only one that watched her go; Yankee's cap and every other male over the age of ten joined me.

Donnie punched me on the shoulder and I jumped. Occupied as I was, I hadn't noticed him slink up beside me. "Dude! You are the fuckin' Mack Daddy!" He laughed and punched me again. "The Mack Daddy *Jack!*"

"Get back to work, Donnie."

"Yessuh, boss!" Still laughing, he went over to the dungeon window and wrapped and bagged the rings and burgers Miguel had just shoved out and carried them to the pick-up window past an oblivious Tiffany, who wore a dire frown as she worked an ice cream scoop over an Extra-Large Crazy Coke Float. Donnie snatched up the old CB mic I'd rigged to the sound system and clicked the button.

"Order ninety-eight is up, people!" He twirled the long, loopy cord, even though I've told him not to do that ten thousand times. "Cooooome aaaaand get it!" The bullhorn speaker mounted on the corner of the awning outside whined and crackled when he clicked off. A young woman burping a newborn got out of a powder blue Toyota Camry and headed for the pick-up window, ticket in hand and yellowish goo glopped on the striped dish towel draped over her shoulder.

I spared one more scowl for Donnie and then relented, making allowances. I did that a lot with him; Don is nineteen—at least physically. I jammed Miriam's card in my pocket and turned to Yankee's cap, who had motivated up in front of the window and was standing there not-so-patiently waiting for me to acknowledge his sunburned corpulence.

"Welcome to Crazy's. May I help you, sir?"

"You bet, kid."

Kid.

I had turned twenty-nine in June, and big boy there didn't look like he'd rolled out of his mid-thirties yet.

Kid.

Yankee's screwed around on his fancy phone as he ordered one large Coke and enough Crazy's fare to feed three people, but when I handed him his ticket and credit card and a red Crazy's pen and the receipt to sign, he glanced over at Miriam sitting in her running Escalade, then scribbled on the receipt and shoved it back and said, "Fuck 'er for me, kid."

I didn't answer, and he took his card and order ticket and waddled away like he hadn't expected one. He also stole my pen. A woman in her fifties wearing a dry one-piece beneath a billowing purple-and-blue tie-dyed Bahama Mama tee-shirt stepped up to the window, and any hope that she hadn't heard flickered and died when she shot a glower at Yankee's sweaty back. She turned and put that glower on me, and I smiled at her through the mesh.

"Welcome to Crazy's, ma'am. May I help you?"

She ordered three Crazy's Kid Meals with cheeseburgers and fries and two Crazy's Bacon Cheeseburger Baskets with rings and root-beer floats in a clipped, icy tone, and when I handed back her change, she leaned closer to the screen and peered in at me like The Judgment personified.

"That woman is married, young man. God won't approve of you fornicating with a married woman."

God. Fornicating. Wonderful. "Yes, ma'am. Your order is number one-oh-three. We'll call when it's ready."

"You remember what I said. Jesus is watching, and His Day is coming."

Jesus. "Yes, ma'am."

Unfortunately, Donnie had caught the tail end of that conversation—if conversation it could be called—and when I turned around, he was glaring past the menu board at the lady as she marched back to her car, where an older man and a gaggle of grandkids awaited.

"Fuck her! Like Jesus cares where Jack Ross gets his little Johnson wet. Stupid bitch. She ever hear of wars, or starvation, or any *real* problems? I'm sure *Jesus* has. Fuckin' self-righteous cunt."

No one else was in line so I slid the glass shut on the mesh; any chance to cut the electric bill—and keep Donnie's rants from floating out to the customers—I took. "Chill, Don. Who gives a shit what she thinks? C'mon, we've got orders to fill." I was using the Calm Voice on him. I do a lot of the Calm Voice with Donnie; for his sake, and for mine. "Besides, even Jesus freaks have a right to go to the lake and eat bacon cheeseburgers."

He went back to work after giving me the "Yessuh, boss" again, but his heart wasn't in it; sometimes bipolar didn't begin to describe Donnie. As if to prove my point, a bright, toothy smile flashed through the sulk: "So, you gonna bang the hot milf? If you don't, I will!"

"You're a pig, Donnie."

We turned, surprised. Tiffany stood by the ice cream cooler, glaring at both of us; those were the first words she'd spoken since she'd come in late this morning and I'd informed her she had to work the Fourth; she'd been in Full Silent Pout Mode ever since. She finished with the scoop, stalked over to the fountain gun, squirted Coke on top of the vanilla ice cream, then snatched a big red straw and stabbed it into the foamy mix and slammed a lid down over the straw. Tiff then thumped the results of her efforts on the counter below the pick-up window and stamped back to the cooler and began the process all over again.

Donnie grinned at me and winked; the Van Dike he was attempting to grow framed teeth nowhere near as even or as white as Miriam's.

"It speaks!"

"You're an asshole, too!"

"It speaks again!"

Calm Voice. "Guys…"

He favored me with a quizzical look. "I knew it was still here, Jack, but I thought it'd gone mute. I was wrong. Hopeful, but wrong."

"You're a fucking asshole *pig*, Donnie!"

Here we go. "Guys, let's just—"

"Ooooooooh! Such language! What would Mommy and Daddy think?"

"You have no respect for women!"

"That's not true! I looooove women! They're my sun, moon, and stars! They're the center of my universe and the bull's eye of my loins! Who says I don't respect women?"

"Guys, stop it." Other than his mother, I doubted Donnie had ever been closer to a woman than whatever image his brain could project onto his right palm. But I had to keep the peace. "Let's get these orders filled and then stock up. We'll probably get hit by another wave or two before the dinner rush." At least I hoped so.

"You've never gotten any, Donnie! I bet for all your big talk, you're still a virgin!"

His acne scars flushed purple beneath the skimpy Van Dike. "I've gotten plenty, just not from stuck-up little—"

"Yeah, right! That inflatable doll in your closet doesn't count!"

"Guys, enough, we've got—"

She rounded on me, clutching the silver cross that hung above her generous breasts. "I don't have to stand here and listen to him badmouth God *and* women, Jack!"

"You gotta be fuckin' kiddin' me! An ice princess *and* a Jesus freak?" Donnie covered his face with his hands. "This is too much…"

"One more word, and both of you are cleaning the bathrooms. I was going to do it, but I'd be happy to let someone else have all the fun."

That did the trick; nobody wanted to clean the restrooms out back, especially if a wave of campers had just crashed onto Crazy's shore. I let some sullen silence hang, then said, "C'mon, let's get these orders out, then stock up."

They got back to work, each now trying to out-sulk the other. I cranked the radio to cover the heavy quiet; I keep it tuned to the local classic rock station, WROK: We Rock Your World, despite Donnie's assertion that all their music was "lame". Right then, WROK was jamming Aerosmith, ol' Stevie Tyler busy telling everybody about his big ten-inch.

I glanced into the dungeon. Miguel was looking at me out the service window, iPod wires dripping from his ears, metal fan up in the corner blowing his short hair sideways. He put his tired brown eyes on the teenagers that worked with us, then looked back at me and shook his head before getting back to cooking, bobbing to the Mexican hip-hop blasting into the sides of his brain; maybe he'd let me borrow the iPod if I asked nicely.

When all the greasy grub was bagged, I retrieved the cleaning supplies and snuck out the side door opposite the parking lot while Donnie called the numbers. The restrooms weren't that bad, not today, but I stayed in there as long as I could so Miriam and her brood and her Escalade and her libido would be gone by the time I got back. Maybe aliens would abduct Donnie and Tiffany as well, replacing them with post-lobotomized, post-anal-probed docile workers who silently followed directions; one can always hope.

My master plan worked. A lone car still sweltered on the gravel; the zealot and her family munched away on the World's Greatest Cheeseburgers and Bacon Cheeseburgers and looked content doing so, despite my impending damnation. Leonard Skynyrd was on WROK, chiding us about not asking them 'bout their bizness. Donnie carried the last of the straws and bags and napkins and Styrofoam cups out of dry storage, saw me, then stopped and raised the scant armful and waggled his bushy eyebrows meaningfully before shoving stuff onto the wire shelving against the back wall.

I could only shake my head. Two weeks ago, when I had filled out the order for the current holiday week, I'd neglected to check dry goods. Who orders burgers and hot-dogs and cheese and chili and bacon and tomatoes and pickles and ice cream but forgets straws and bags and napkins and cups? You can't serve the former without the latter—not without making a gargantuan goddamn mess, anyway. So yesterday, when I'd realized my mistake, I'd tried to call in an emergency order. But emergency or not, Metro won't deliver until the end of the holiday week—not for *my* tiny operation, at any rate—so the plan was to catch a break between waves today and race up to town and hit Marcie's and pick up what I could, no matter the cost (and it will hurt), as a stopgap. But now with Tiff and Donnie at each other's throats, I hesitated to leave.

I had no choice, however, which meant I needed to ensure this current temporary armistice lasted—at least until I got back. Tiffany had finished stocking her station and was now standing in the farthest corner of Crazy's, plum-colored nails flying over her phone. Tiff is always texting. Always. I figure she texts on the toilet, and almost certainly in her sleep. She'd probably text in the shower if she had a waterproof phone; I may be a kid to Yankee's, but Tiffany makes me feel old. I glanced into the dungeon; Miguel was nowhere to be seen.

I walked over to her as something sent from the texting ether elicited a laugh; she saw me coming, and the phone was hastily shoved into her front pocket. For a moment I wondered if she'd been texting about me, then decided I wasn't that interesting, especially to a sixteen-year-old girl. When she'd first started at Crazy's, I'd gotten the impression from the big-eyed looks that Tiff had developed some sort of silly crush on me. But in the six weeks since, it seems to have faded—or maybe I'd misread the situation from the jump. It wouldn't surprise me; I've never been able to understand teenage girls, and I'm not sure I want to start.

She eyed me sideways, a little wary, then switched gears and faced me full-on, giving me a sexy pout; I think she's been practicing.

"I'm sorry about earlier, Jack, but Donnie is *such* a prick."

"It's glandular, he can't help it." That got a conspiratorial giggle. "I just wanted to say I'm sorry too, for making you work the Fourth. I know it sucks, but I really need you here, Tiff."

"It *does* suck. I'll miss my family's cookout! I've never missed it before! Plus my friends and I are—*were*—going to Deek's party. It'll be so sween!" Her lower lip pooched out. "Or at least it *would* have been."

Sween. I wasn't sure what sween meant, but I could infer. I looked at her: long, dark hair and big dark eyes and pretty enough to make a daffodil jealous—and not a thought in her head except what she wanted, and wanted right now. Her parents had made her get a summer job, and Crazy's was her first experience in the workforce. No doubt she'd harbored dreams about seeing all her friends, partying and hanging out down by the lake; I'm sure hard work had never reared its ugly head in those fantasies. Despite that, she was a good kid, and she did bust her pert little butt—when I could get her off the goddamn phone, anyhow.

Sixteen. Did I remember sixteen? I thought so, but it might as well have been five hundred years ago instead of thirteen:

Prison will do that to you.

I glanced over my shoulder to clock Donnie; it was a coward's move, but I did it anyway. He was done stocking and gone, probably out back smoking. *Good.* "Listen. Work for me on the Fourth until the last big rush is over, and then you can go have fun with your friends. Donnie and I can handle closing." Sixteen. What the hell had *I* been doing on the Fourth at sixteen? Something stupid, I'm sure.

She squealed and bounced and then hugged me before snatching the phone back out, plumb nails blurring. "I've got to tell Becca! You're so sween, Jack! Thank you thank you thank you!"

I turned away, flustered and attempting to hide it. Tiff was sixteen, sure, but I still felt the press of her heavy breasts on my chest as I leaned my elbows on the order counter and looked outside. The holier-than-thou lady had snarfed her bacon cheeseburger and was polishing off her root-beer float…and suddenly I was glad Jesus wasn't back yet; if He showed up now, I would be judged and judged hard, no pun intended. Sixteen. Still, I was only thirteen years older than her, old enough to be her, well, big brother. *Yuck.* Okay, besides that, thirteen years wasn't *that* bad; Tiff and I would be a perfect match in one of those ubiquitous Stan's that made up the USSR before it circled the bowl—after our families arranged the union and forced her to marry me, at any rate; and I was sween, too.

Can't discount the sween factor.

I glanced over and watched her gleefully text Becca, imagining what that tight little body would look like in bed. Better than nice, I'm sure…but then, after the fun, I'd have to talk to her.

Or worse, listen to *her* talk.

I shuddered and looked away. *Never mind.* It was time to run up to town while I could, before the next wave hit. I straightened and stuck my hand in my pocket and felt Miriam's card and pulled it out along with my truck keys; ten months since Jen left.

Ten months *plus.*

I was still staring at the card and remembering Miriam's enthusiasm for her husband's long trips while trying to forget what the business end of a 9mm looked like when Donnie pushed through the side door, cloud of cigarette smoke wafting after.

"Shit. We got a wave crashing, people."

I stuffed my keys and the card back and looked outside just as a flock of SUVs invaded my lot. Sleek, shiny soccer uniforms were bursting the seams of every Tahoe, Suburban, Yukon, and Escalade crunching across the gravel; the Park Service maintains a field down by the campground, but you have to bring your own nets.

The mob piled out and rushed our way, screaming, cleats pounding. I said, "Look sharp, guys, here they come," and then we were paddling for our lives.

2

We shot the curl and were nearly home free when something knocked us off the board—well, me at least. I'd seen the black-on-black 328i Beemer park between two SUVs, a sleek kraut shark among domestic whales, but I didn't realize who'd gotten out until she was at the front of the line, and even then it took me a second.

She wore the requisite flip-flops and faded and frayed cutoffs rode her hips; the top of her black bikini consisted of more material than the sum of Miriam's. Her golden hair barely brushed the lobes of her ears, but it looked good set against her tan; not a spray job, just old-fashioned radiation. She clutched her purse in front of her pierced bellybutton; an anxious posture, yet she was smiling below dark shades as she stepped up to the window.

"Hey, Rossie."

No one had called me Rossie in a long, long time…

Her smile faded.

"*Angie?*

The smile came back, though a bit uncertain, now. "The one and only, but it's Angela these days. Nobody calls me Angie anymore."

I did some gaping, and then I clicked my teeth together and gathered myself; I hadn't talked to Angie Beaumont in over ten years. "Um, sorry, Angela. Yeah, it's been a stretch since anybody called me Rossie, too. It's just Jack now."

"Just Jack." She sounded wistful.

"Yeah, just Jack." I strove mightily to keep my eyes up and on her face, but then Donnie appeared at my side, and he had no such qualms.

"Jesus fuck, dude. You *are* the Mack Jack. You go, dog!"

I cleared my throat and stood up, using the motion bump Donnie away as she took her sunglasses off; I'd forgotten how blue her eyes were.

"It's good to see you, Jack."

"It's good to see you too, Angela."

Three years my junior, Angie Beaumont was kid sister to my best friend throughout grade school up through high school, Chris. The last time I'd seen her in person she'd been a stunningly beautiful, utterly annoying, and stuck-up fifteen-year-old; I'd glimpsed her on television since then, of course, but the small screen didn't do her justice.

A matron wearing a white golf visor leaned around Angie. "Could we hurry this along? My kids are starving."

"What can I get you?" I asked Angie. Angela.

She ordered two Crazy's Bacon Cheeseburger combos with fries and root beers, and when I glanced a question at her, she pointed over at the Beemer and the smoked window rolled down and I was confronted with yet another blast from the past; Chris considered me, face neutral beneath the wrap-around Ray Bans, then gave a curt nod; the Beemer's window slid back up.

I looked at Angie. Angela.

She seemed disappointed by my reaction, or perhaps by Chris's—or maybe both—but what the hell did she expect? Chris and I were ex-best friends for a reason. It'd been over ten years since I'd talked to him, too, even though we still lived only a few miles from each other; it made me wonder why he'd dropped by now, and if she'd had anything to do with it. At that thought, hope budded in my chest (and regions lower), and I knew I was an Idiot of The First Order; that didn't stop the bud from blooming, though.

Idiots got needs, too.

I took her money and made change and wrote her ticket, the whole time watching her but pretending not to. She had her face tilted toward the menu board, but it seemed she was doing the same thing; maybe that was the hope talking. I handed everything out the window, glancing at her left hand; no wedding ring. So the divorce rumors were true.

"Thank you, Rossie." Then she grimaced and laughed a little. "Sorry. Jack."

"No problem. And you can still call me Rossie if you want."

The visor lady leaned again and gave me impatient.

Angie smiled, eyes warm on mine, then slipped her shades back on and walked away.

The Ping woman bulled up to the window. "Honestly! We could just go to McDonald's, you know."

"Sorry, ma'am. Welcome to Crazy's. What can I get for you?"

She gave me a huffy order and paid and got her ticket; she was the last in line, so I shut the glass and turned around to help; we were all nearly running, but Donnie still had time to punch me on the shoulder.

"You da *man!* Jack gets more ass than a toilet seat!"

I ignored him, my hands busy with work but my mind occupied with golden hair and sky-blue eyes; I'd heard she was back from Chicago, just like I knew Chris had been selling million-dollar estates over in Lochmore Heights for that fucker Richards. He and the old man's son, that date rapist Zane Richards, were good buddies again, too; another fine reason not to hang with Chris. My teeth flaked enamel until I got hold of myself; Zack and Zane and Bob Jr. had been eons ago—just not long enough.

I shoved those assholes from my brain and replaced them with Angie. Angela. Had she stopped by just because she was hungry, or had she made Chris pull in for other reasons? It wouldn't have been *his* idea. Maybe I really was an idiot; she'd dropped in to grab some chow and say hi, that's all there was to it.

I'd been helping Donnie bag orders, but Tiffany had gotten backed up so I checked the hanging tickets and started scooping ice cream into cones; she threw a frown at me sideways.

"Wasn't that Angela Beaumont?"

"Yeah." I didn't bother to tell her that Angie's last name wasn't Beaumont any longer, although for all I knew she'd changed it back. Who *was* that guy she'd met at art school? Brian…Brian Something; oh well, didn't matter now; Brian Something was out of the picture, and I truly *was* a fucking moron. Horny is an uncomfortable gear to be stuck in; I felt like Donnie.

Speaking of Donnie, evidently he had his ears peeled over the R.E.O. Speed Wagon: "No shit? That was Angie Beaumont? God *damn* she's fine! Wasn't she Miss Wyoming a few years back?"

"Yes." I offered no more, hoping Donnie would let it go, but that was like hoping gas would drop back under a dollar a gallon.

"Holy shit! You dippin' your wick in a beauty queen?"

Tiffany scowled at him. "She's not *that* pretty. She only got third runner up at Miss America." Her eyes cut back to me, then flicked away. "*Are* you dating her, Jack?" The sparkling scent of jealousy wafted into the air, like someone had just sliced open a tangerine.

"That's the first time I've spoken to her in over ten years." Spoken, not seen; I'd watched the pageant like every other inmate in F-Pod, drooling on the concrete-and-steel picnic tables in the day room. I'd told no one I knew her, though; volunteering info about your life to the foreskin that populated a place like Torrington wasn't smart. "I hung with her older brother a long time ago, and she used to tag along and spy and tattle on us."

I handed double scoops of mint chocolate chip on plain waffle cones to Tiff. She smiled at me as she took them. "Oh," she said, and turned to the window and gave someone their ice cream.

I sighed.

Sixteen.

Donnie wasn't satisfied, naturally. His voice went falsetto: "Oh, *Roossssie!* It's so good to see you, Rossie!" He grinned when I gave him a look. "Dude, from now on you're Rossie. That's such a bitchin' name. Why don't you still go by it?"

I shrugged, playing it cool, trying not to show how uncomfortable the nickname made me; it would only egg him on. "Call me whatever you want, man, just get those orders filled."

"Yessuh, Boss Rossie! Iz on it!"

We worked in blessed silence after that, if you didn't count the Kiss song blaring through Crazy's. "Detroit Rock City", baby; I caught Donnie jamming to it and was going to rib him about "lame", but decided to enjoy the quiet while it lasted.

And then Donnie handed me two sacks, along with two root beers in a cardboard drink carrier and a shit-eating grin. "I'll let you call this one. It's your girl's."

"She's not my girl." But I took the food and drinks.

"Whatever, *Rossie.*" He turned away, playing air-drums with Peter Criss as I stared at the white-paper bags; grease had already spotted their bottoms and sides. Then I went to the mic and called the number. I watched Angie climb out of the passenger side of her brother's Beemer, and my stomach had two squirrels brawling in it when I headed for the side door.

"I'll be right back."

Donnie said, "Oooooooooooooooohhhh!" Tiff stayed quiet, but particulates of tangerine began filling the air again as I stepped out into the heat; maybe this would convince her to fixate on a boy her age.

Whatever the hell *this* was.

Angie stopped, surprised, when she saw me walk around, and I swallowed; the squirrels had invited some friends for a cage match. We met near the picnic tables. Chris lowered the Beemer's window and gave me a big frown; I smiled at him before focusing on his sister.

"Here you go."

"You didn't have to do this, R—Jack. I could've come to the window."

"It's no problem. I hope you like everything."

"I'm sure we will."

Then we stood there, facing each other. I cleared my throat. Six centuries later, she shifted the food and drink carrier to one arm and lifted her sunglasses onto her hair, showing me the blues. "I…I'm sorry it took me this long to stop and say hi, but, well, you know." She shrugged, and didn't quite look over her shoulder at her scowling brother, but she didn't have to; I knew the score.

"Well, I'm glad you did." I heard crunching gravel and glanced over her shoulder and watched a white Silverado Z-71 4x4 pull in next to Chris's BMW. It was towing a ski boat; a spanking-new ski boat; a ski boat I wouldn't mind owning myself; a ski boat I wouldn't be affording in this life or the next. I barely noticed the boat, though, because I knew that truck.

Worse, I knew the driver.

Zane Richards rolled his illegally blacked-out window down and put one of his steroid-inflated arms on the edge of the door and stared at me. I stared back. Angie saw my face and turned.

"Rossie…"

Lake water still dripped off the back of the trailer; I looked at Chris, then at Angie in her bathing suit.

"You guys were out with Zane."

It was only a statement of fact, but my tone was a *biiiig* mistake.

Her eyes flashed. "Yeah? So? He invited me, and since I hadn't been on the lake in like forever, I went. What's it to you, anyway? Why do you care what I do?"

"You're right, I'm sorry. It's none of my business."

She didn't seem mollified, but she sniffed and let it go, then tossed her head and glanced over her shoulder, following my gaze again; Chris had lowered his passenger window and was leaning over the console to talk to Zane. They laughed, both turning to look at us as they did, which is probably why I was dumb enough to say what I said next:

"Just be smart and don't drink anything he hands you, 'kay?"

Her face turned to stone. She flipped the glasses back onto her nose. "You're an asshole, Rossie." She stalked away.

Fuck. I am an asshole. But I couldn't let it go like that. "I'm glad you came by," I called after her. "It was good to see you, Angela."

She just kept trying to stamp my gravel through to China; the squirrels had called it quits and gone back to the tree; they knew I'd blown it. I was turning to head back inside when she spun around so fast her shades fell off, and she almost dropped the drinks; she plopped everything on the nearest picnic table, which earned open-mouthed stares from the kids sitting there, then snatched up her sunglasses and jabbed an earpiece at me.

"You're not just an asshole, Rossie, you're a stupid, *stubborn* asshole!" She turned and jabbed that earpiece at her brother and Zane; their grins dropped into their laps. "Just like *them*. You're all stupid, stubborn, assholes!" She stalked back to me in a blue-eyed fury, jabbing harder: "None of you can let the past go. It's *done*, don't you get it? You can't change it, but you dumb-asses got to keep it front-and-center all the stupid time. God, I'm so *sick* of all of this *shit!*"

Angie trailed off, breathing hard. Then she glanced around; everyone was watching: the soccer mob; the parents who'd retreated to the AC in their SUVs; even the littlest kids swinging their cleats at a picnic table two over who hadn't a clue what was going on except that the pretty lady was mad and saying bad words.

She blushed, then leaned towards me and lowered her voice: "I'm glad I came by, too. It really *is* good to see you, stubborn asshole or not." She glanced over her shoulder at Chris and Zane, and her full lips somehow firmed into a grim line as she pulled her phone from the faded cutoffs. "Give me your number. We'll go get coffee sometime and talk where it's more private." She cut her eyes meaningfully.

I stared at her. Angie Beaumont wanted *my* number? Call me a fool, but I hesitated; maybe it was the tone she'd asked for—demanded—it in, like a man making plans to complete a job he didn't want to do with people he didn't particularly like.

I guess I hesitated too long; she lowered the phone and straightened, frowning: "You don't have to give me your number if you don't want to, Jack. I just—"

Turns out the squirrels were alive and well and line dancing. "Uh, no." *Shit.* "I mean, yeah, I think it's a swell idea." *Swell?* I pushed ahead; sometimes it's all you can do. "Coffee would be great. My number is…" I drew a blank, a gigantic and sucking black hole where my phone number used to be. Angela stared at me with those eyes, waiting; one of the soccer brats under the striped umbrella closest to us snickered. Then I remembered and rattled it off and she punched it in, and we stood there roasting in the sun, staring at each other while somewhere glaciers melted and flowed into the sea.

"Um…" I glanced down, patted around, felt my phone's rectangle shape, pulled it out. "Maybe the call dropped. They put those two new towers up, but the signal down here is still iffy somet—" It vibrated and then rang in my hand: "Uh, there, got it."

Smooth.

So smooth.

"Good," she announced briskly; a job of work. Angela strode away, hipbones twitching beneath the cutoffs, and snatched up her Crazy's fare, earning more open-mouthed stares from the kids. "Call me!"

Chris scowled harder; Zane sneered.

So that was the game. Would she even answer? And if she did, what would the excuse be? Angie climbed into her brother's car; Zane said something to her, and she snipped something back without looking before slamming the door. *That* made me feel better. He looked back up at me as the Beemer's engine turned over, and we engaged in a staring contest that I wanted to end by dragging the big date rapist out of his pretty truck and making him eat some Crazy's gravel.

For Zane, it would be free.

But two things stopped me. One was Angie. Angela. I already looked like a douche; on the off chance she really wanted to get coffee and wasn't just tweaking her brother, kicking the shit out of Zane would put the kibosh on that, and quick-like; I didn't know her anymore, true, but I instinctively knew that.

Number two was common sense: If I thrashed Daddy's little rich boy on my property, Daddy's lawyers would own me before sunset.

So I turned my back on Zane and went inside, no matter how much it hurt.

The Ping matron and her starving multitudes had just picked up their grub; Donnie slammed the window on them, almost crushing the last Crazy Coke Float.

"Well?"

"Well, what?"

"What the fuck do you mean, 'well what'? I'm trying to live vicariously through you, Rossie baby. You gonna nail the beauty queen, or what?" Tiffany was sweeping her station vigorously and very much not looking at me.

"I just wanted to say bye," I told him. "No nailing involved."

I looked outside. Chris and Angie were long gone, but I watched Zane pull across the highway and up to the closest pump island; that Shell station and I share a lot of customers back and forth. Zane got out and swiped a card and started gassing, then faced the front of Crazy's; his short black hair and tan muscles contrasted with his tight white tee-shirt as he yawned and stretched and flexed. Zane's always been an inch or two taller than me, but now he was about six inches wider than the last time I'd had the misfortune of seeing him; the wonders of pharmaceuticals never cease.

Tiffany stepped up beside me, lips parted, broom forgotten in her hand.

"Hell-lo," she said.

I wanted to tell her to grab a napkin and wipe her chin, but I kept it zipped. Donnie frowned at her, then snorted like Seabiscuit as tangerine scented the atmosphere once more; I pretended it was only coming from Donnie.

"Isn't that Zane Richards?" he asked me.

"Yep."

"Thought so."

I felt him take in my stony expression, and then he wisely said nothing else before turning away. It took Tiff a few seconds, and then she glanced at the other side of my face with big eyes before prying herself away from the yummy vision across the road; she got back to sweeping.

They knew, of course. Everybody knew. Nobody talked about it, but in a town like Indian Head, everybody knows everything; knowing isn't the worst, though.

The worst thing is, nobody forgets.

Ever.

Zane replaced the nozzle and then stood there staring coldly across the road. I stared back until he got in his truck and pulled out, gorgeous boat following, and then rolled down his illegal coal-black window and looked over and raised his middle finger just before a wall of blackjack pines hid him.

I decided to let him have that one; Zane hates me, perhaps for excellent reason. I don't hate him, though: I *despise* him. Is it just jealousy of the looks and the money? I hope not. I want to think I'm better than that. I want to think it's for the way he treats the people of Indian Head, the unthinking arrogance; we're all just serfs for the Richards' family. His clan had built this town. And the lake. And the resort and the golf courses and the condos; and now there was Lochmore Heights. After I was paroled, I'd heard the rumors about Zane and the roofies…and about Daddy's payoffs; supposedly, Daddy had made the pending charges *and* the sorority girl's civil suits go away before anything could become official.

Supposedly.

I, for one, having unfortunately known Zane and Bob Jr. for a long, long time, didn't doubt the rumors one little stinking bit. Despise? Loathe would be nearer the mark; but even with all that, Zane had a better reason to hate me.

After all, I killed his twin brother.

Outside, the kiddos were finishing up, and some of the little bastards were even throwing their trash *in* the cans, not just toward them. Some. Then they saddled up and roared away, giant SUVs flocking in strict formation; we'd survived the wave, surprises included. I turned around to tell the guys to stock up for the next one but there was no need; they were doing it already, not looking at me and not looking at me hard. The merest whiff of my murderous past will do that. I glanced into the dungeon; Miguel bobbed to his iPod, oblivious to the tension.

I leaned my elbows on the counter and pursed my lips; Angie had changed, and not just her name and her hair; there was a new sadness in her blue eyes, and for some reason it was a turn-on. I don't know why having life knock someone around would be an aphrodisiac to me, but there it was. She wasn't just a spoiled little look-at-me anymore; maybe that was it. Little Angie had grown into a woman. I smiled, remembering her outburst; a woman with firm opinions about how the world should be, and about how the people in that world should act.

I snorted. *Is there any other kind?*

I decided then that I would call her and hope for the best; if she turned out to be playing games, well, there was always Miriam.

I knew the games *she* liked to play.

I pulled out my keys, and Miriam's card; so Doug was out of town, and the kids were going camping Saturday?

Hmm.

"Miguel's in charge 'till I get back."

I expected a squawk from Donnie, but he just waved me off. I felt their eyes on me as I headed out to pick up the trash that the shit parents hadn't made their lazy brats throw away, then hopped in my beater F-150 and fired the old girl up. I tried to think about tiny orange triangles as I rumbled up the mountain, but visions of wounded blue eyes and short blonde hair rode with me all the way into town.

3

"Shut up, Chris!"

"I'm just saying; don't get so mad at me."

Her brother downshifted and flew around a curve, not bothering with the brakes, and Angela braced herself as her hair swayed against her ears. Had Ros—Jack liked her new bob? She hadn't worn it this short since middle school.

The g-forces lessened, and she crossed her arms beneath her breasts: "If I want to have coffee with Jack Ross, I will have coffee with Jack Ross anytime I damn well please; what I do—or who I do it with—*is none of your business!*"

"All right, all right, jeez." Another downshift, another curve, and then a long, steep straightaway; Chris glanced over at her. "So now he's 'Jack', huh? Whatever he calls himself these days, he's still a killer. You're going to sit down and have coffee with a *killer?* Really?"

"That was a long time ago, and he paid for it. Besides, he's different now." Angela was still marveling at *how* different. "He's grown up, Chris." She looked out her window, not seeing the wall of green needles flashing by. "I guess we all have."

"Yeah, sure." Another downshift and corner; they'd be back to town soon at this rate. "Just promise me that coffee is as far as it goes, sis."

She slowly turned her head, and he shied into his door. "Okay, okay, it's none of my beeswax, don't hit me." When she relaxed and turned away again, he barked a laugh. "Boy, that cup of coffee is gonna piss Zane off."

Angela didn't bother to answer while she attempted to enjoy glittering glimpses of lake vistas flashing between pine-studded slopes; but it was no use: Zane Richards *liked* her, and he was very handsome—not to mention very, very rich.

He also gave Angela the creeps.

Oh, she'd caught herself staring at his sculpted body today, but the problem was he'd known she was looking; she'd finally grown tired of his preening and ignored him, even though it had been almost four months since she'd been with a man. She didn't think about sex much anymore anyway (a rough divorce would do that), but since seeing Rossie—Jack—those months seemed like years.

Angela blushed and shifted in the seat; Rossie was different, true, but he still had those melting brown eyes, and he was still in great shape…but really?

Get a grip, girl.

Chris spoke into the silence. "He likes you, you know that."

Angela resisted the urge to quip if he meant Zane or Jack; she knew whose case her brother was pleading. No, the important question was, had Jack liked her? She couldn't decide. He'd seemed more astounded to see her than anything, as if he hadn't thought about her in years, even for a second.

Angela slapped at a vent until it blew on her suddenly hot face; she had never stopped thinking about *him*, especially since she'd moved back; knowing he was so close, guessing what he looked like now, and how else he'd changed. Jack wasn't on Facebook—or any other social media she'd searched—so she'd been left wondering.

Well, she thought wryly, *now I know.*

She couldn't *believe* she'd made Chris stop, with her all sweaty and no makeup, after months of planning how to oh-so-casually drop by to say hi to his mom and dad. *Oh, by the way, is Rossie here?* So much for that brilliant idea. But after only a quick bite early this morning followed by a day trapped with Chris and Zane, she'd thirsted for decent company *and* she'd been starving. And Crazy's had been right there, along with Ros—Jack, so...

Angela sniffed hungrily, then frowned at the food and drinks resting between her feet before putting that frown on her idiot brother; she could smell French fries—and it was driving her crazy!—but Chris had forbidden her to eat or drink anything in his new toy.

Chris paid her no mind as he cursed and hit the brakes; an older pickup pulling a flat-bottom boat was trundling along dead ahead, with two more rigs in front of it, all negotiating the switchback curves at about thirty. She'd forgotten how bad Fourth of July traffic got around here; at least there would be no more racing, for now.

Angela eyed him sideways; she and Rossie—Jack—had changed, sure, but in some ways Chris had changed the most, and she wasn't sure she liked what she saw; she wasn't even sure she liked her brother anymore, period.

She pushed that uncomfortable thought far away; he was all she had left, so she'd just have to accept this new Chris. That's what family did: acknowledge each other's foibles and love each other unconditionally.

He sighed at the delay, then pulled his sunglasses off and looked over at her with eyes as blue as hers. "You could do worse than Zane, sis. A *lot* worse," he added. Pointedly.

Love them no matter what, but Angela was at her breaking point; she spoke through clenched teeth:

"Who I date is none of your concern."

"I'm just saying."

"Stop *saying* and drop it. Please."

"All right."

A few more curves, some blessed quiet, then: "Have you decided about Bob's offer?"

Angela stared at him; he'd handled her with kid gloves those first few months, because of Brian she supposed, but lately it was poke-poke-poke, like he was trying to take Dad's place. "I told you already, just like I told Zane: *I'm still thinking about it.*"

"What's to think about? Christ, it's been over two months! Do you know how many people would kill for an opportunity like this? And you, with no experience? Do you know how lucky you are to get this chance?"

She glared out the side window, arms folded, and watched needles crawl by.

"I mean *c'mon*, sis! Tell Bob Jr. yes, take the classes and get your license, Zane and I will set you up with leads, and with your looks and intelligence, you'll be pulling five figures the first year; six within three. Those lots out at Lochmore are selling like heroin cupcakes, I don't give a fuck what the rest of the country is doing. And Bob just tied up the north side of the lake. Finally. He's been after that deal for *years*. That means there'll be three more developments, all three with championship golf courses. Indian Head will be hopping for a long, long time, sis. You can be a part of it, like me." He jiggled the ebony-and-chrome shifter knob. "How do you think I pay for this car, or the condo? I'm not spending *my* inheritance, that's for sure. I'll be a made man within ten years, maybe less. Think about *that*, sis; after just a few years, you could do whatever you want. Hell, sit around and draw all day, whatever, but right now you need to do *something*; you can't hide in Dad's house and sketch and live off what he left you forever."

Angela didn't answer because she knew he was right; and even if it was the twentieth time he'd made that speech, perhaps she'd needed to hear it again. And working for Bob Jr. would truly be a great opportunity—financially, anyway. But there were problems, like the minor fact that making money off bulldozing pristine mountain forest repulsed her on some basic level.

And then there was the other…difficulty.

She looked over at Chris. He peered back hopefully; he thought he was finally getting through to her. Poking and pushing and prodding; it was time to poke back.

"Tell me something, big brother. You and Zane talked to Bob Jr. and got me this job already, right?"

"Riiiight." Wary.

"Would *keeping* the job be contingent on my sleeping with Zane?"

He shoved his wrap-around shades back on and looked out the windshield, jaw tight: "I don't care who you sleep with, little sister, and I don't even think Zane cares that much." He laughed, a grim rasp: "It's not like the guy's hard-up. He gets so much pus—uh, so many women throwing themselves at him…believe me, he doesn't need you. So Zane? No Zane? Don't care. And Bob Jr.? You know he'd do anything for you. You *know* that. And I guarantee you he doesn't care who you sleep with, either; make that man money, that's what he cares about."

"Oh, I know very well what Bob Jr. cares about."

Chris snatched his shades off again. "What the hell's that supposed to mean?"

"You know what it means."

"What, you don't like money? You don't like nice cars, nice things? Don't like Dad's house? Don't like *food?* Well that's too bad, little sis, because Mom and Dad invested in Bob a long time ago, and you've been reaping the fruits of Robert Richards Junior's efforts your whole life. Still are, as a matter of fact, so don't get all sanctimonious on me now."

Angela seethed; he was right about that, too, but now she was too mad to care. "Yeah, and he's such a wonderful father. That's why Zane's so kind to his fellow human beings."

Chris didn't back down. "Bob's a hard charger, no doubt about it, and he rubs people wrong sometimes, but he's a good man, and I'm lucky to work for him. Zane…well, Zane's Zane, what can I say. He's got his issues, but he works hard for his dad, and for Indian Head."

"I might take the job, but Zane Richards can go jump in Daddy's lake. 'Issues'? Do those *issues* include slipping girls roofies?"

Chris frowned. "I don't know anything about that."

"What, he never bragged about his *conquests?* He sure did enough bragging today." If Angela had to hear one more word about how much Zane's boat or his house or his convertible Porsche cost, she would scream herself silly.

"Of course not. Don't be stupid."

Stupid!? Angela opened her mouth, then forgot to be furious as Chris edged out to see if there was room to pass, then whipped it back as a red truck pulling a pontoon boat blew by going the other way; the Silverado's driver laid on his horn and flipped Chris off.

Angela swallowed, then glowered at him; how this new Chris drove his new toy upset her, too—especially while *she* was in it.

"Besides," he continued, "I don't believe all that crap about Zane and roofies. Those cu—those *girls* just saw an opportunity to scam for cash. Why would he need to drug anyone? He's loaded, and judging by the way you were drooling today, the guy's not bad looking."

He smiled over at her, and she wanted to slap it off his smug face. Why *would* a man with Zane's resources and looks stoop to that? Maybe Chris was right.

"Let's just drop it," she said. "I'll make my decision soon, and when I do, I'll tell Bob, not you or Zane."

"Fine."

"Fine."

She hesitated, then said, soft: "Besides, me and Zane? That would be just…too weird."

Chris was silent. Then: "Yeah," he sighed. "I know."

After a few morose seconds, her brother turned up WROK, the same station that'd been playing at Crazy's. *Why in the world did Ros—Jack name it* that? She would have to ask him—if he even called…

No.

She was done obsessing about Ros—Jack! Or Zane. Or Bob Jr. Or that she really, really, really needed to do something with her life. What Angela needed right now was to eat these yummy smelling French fries, first off, before she fainted from hunger; then she would hop in the shower and change and pull weeds in the little garden she'd started in the same spot her mother had planted hers long ago, on the south side of the detached two-car garage, where it got the most sun.

Unfortunately, that was the only way Angela's efforts resembled her mother's; for an activity that boiled down to sticking a seed in the ground and watering it, who knew gardening would be so much work? Or so hard to get right? But her tomatoes and cucumbers and yellow squash were doing well (Angela refused to think about the green beans; God, what a disaster), particularly her tomatoes, and after one taste-test against Marcie's tomatoes, hers had won hands down, so she must be doing *something* right.

And after the garden she would draw, of course; whatever Chris said, with all the practice, she was getting better. She knew what she would sketch tonight, too. Angela's lips twisted; how many times had she drawn him when she was younger? Too many to remember, or count if she could; she'd had *such* a pathetic little-girl's crush on her big brother's friend. *Had?* Maybe crushes never really went away, just festered; judging from the way she'd acted today, she thought that might be true.

No. No more Ro—Jack! *Not until tonight.* It would be a good sketch, her best yet. She was still thinking about it when they rolled into what passed for downtown Indian Head.

On the right was the post office, triple flags flying, and a block down on the same side was Habersham's Barbershop, red-white-and-blue striped pole spiraling up and up forever. Don Habersham had cut hair in downtown Indian Head for so long, some joked he'd trimmed the original Indian's feathers. Har har. Chris still went there, just like her father until he became too sick to drive. Angela had vivid memories of her dad and brother getting their hair buzzed while she swiveled around and around in the empty chair with a lollipop in her mouth from the glass jar that never ran out of lollipops; it never even got low.

She scrubbed leaky eyes and looked across the red-brick street at TJ's Hardware; Tom Jonas had been in business nearly as long as Mr. Habersham. Next to the hardware was an empty storefront with a "For Rent" sign in the window; Angela tried to remember what used to be there but couldn't; she hardly ever came to this part of town. Next to the empty space was The Dress Shoppe, Miriam Jacobson's place.

A ludicrous worm of jealousy bored into Angela's brain; she'd heard whispers about Miriam, including some connecting her to Ros—Jack, whispers she refused to believe, but other whispers linked Miriam to every handsome young man in town, so it was hard to dismiss them all as just small-town gossip. *Surely he's too smart to get tangled with a married woman, especially a big ol' slut bunny like that one.*

Chris abruptly shot over—without using his blinker!—into one of the diagonal spaces marked on the brick in white paint.

"What are you doing?"

He killed the engine and threw open his door. "Getting a haircut." He saw her expression. "Wait out here. This won't take long." He jabbed his keys at the bags and drinks between her feet. "Just don't eat in my car."

Angela grimaced at the food, sighed, then opened her door.

Mr. Habersham was stooped now and a little slower, but the same wry amusement shone from his kind face as he ushered

Angela to the unused chair. He gave her a lollipop from the same bottomless jar, which still glowed like a multi-hued jewel in its spot before the mirror; he even remembered her favorite, green, so she put her feet up and swiveled back and forth and ate her lollipop like she was seven again as she breathed in the evocative aromas of menthol shaving cream and spicy aftershave and Mr. Habersham's cigars; they made her think of men in general and her dad in particular. By the time she'd crunched the lollipop away, she'd had to fight off tears at least twice, but when Mr. Habersham saw her spin around and throw the loop in the little can under the wash sink, he just fished in the jar and gave her another green.

To distract herself from the ghost of her father (a specter that loomed here even worse than the house she'd inherited), Angela checked out the antique gewgaws and plaques and signs and jokes and the faded and framed Old Glory and the sixty-something-year-old yellowed newspaper articles about the Korean Conflict (which Mr. Habersham happened to be a veteran of) hanging on the paneled walls, but soon she was listening to Mr. Habersham and her brother chat.

At first they talked about Dad, which didn't help, but then they talked about sports. Of *course* they talked about sports. When men got together, they had to talk about sports; Angela figured it was some sort of unwritten law only they knew about. But when sports ran dry, the discussion inevitably turned to Indian Head's rapid growth; Chris did the holding forth: Bob Jr. this and Bob Jr. that, putting Indian Head on the map, wonk wonk wonk. Mr. Habersham's contributions shrank to noncommittal grunts, and his kind expression turned grim as he hovered behind Chris's chair, scissors snipping and trimmer buzzing; apparently Angela wasn't the only one who harbored reservations about Indian Head's new prosperity.

When the haircut was over, she hugged Mr. Habersham and pulled him down and planted a kiss on the smooth, spotted crown of his head. That brought his smile back. Then he tried to give her a green lollipop for the road, which nearly caused a fresh flood of tears because as far back as Angela could remember, Mr. Habersham had always offered her one for the road, always, but she'd always had to ask Daddy's permission. The answer had most often been yes (unless she'd been particularly bad), but *not* having to ask only drove it home that her father was gone, and that he wasn't coming back. Her melancholy was absurd, and it wasn't what Dad would have wanted her to feel, but that didn't make it go away.

And then her temper flashed:

I'm a grown woman, and I can have a stupid green lollipop for the road if I want!

She took three.

4

It took less than a minute for downtown's flaking red bricks to vanish from the BMW's mirrors.

Most of the growth had been to the north and east, and before long they passed the gleaming new fire station on the right and then a shiny mini-mall on the left; Indian Head even had a McDonald's now, and a Subway, and a Chinese restaurant, Mr. Wang's (not a chain, thank God), but Pat's Diner was still sitting over on Third St. right where it had always sat across from Indian Head's lone and now-shuttered bowling alley, The Injun. Pat's Diner had been Angela's favorite place to eat when she was a little girl and a teenager, and it was *still* her favorite; Pat's Diner was hanging tough against all the fresh competition; Pat's Diner would never die…or at least Angela fervently hoped.

They came up on Marcie's Family Supermarket. Marcie's had been an Indian Head fixture for longer than Angela had been alive; her grandparents and mom and dad had shopped there, and she knew the Washburn clan that owned and ran it; the store was named after the Washburn's beloved-but-long-dead great-great grandmother. Unlike Pat's, though, Angela harbored no illusions concerning Marcie's survival; the market was convenient to Indian Head residents, sure, but it just couldn't compete with the big-boxes in price or selection. She'd heard rumors that the Washburn's wanted to sell, but the only potential buyer was Bob Jr. and he wouldn't offer them anywhere near what it was worth, so they soldiered on.

Angela sadly took in the almost empty parking lot and wondered how much longer they could make it. She still shopped there twice a week out of grim loyalty, but even she found herself sneaking down to Sheridan two or three times a month.

Suddenly she focused on a vehicle parked in a slot close to the electronic doors, one not designated for the handicapped; an older-model F-150 4x4. Dingy and red, it had a wide, dinged-up chrome toolbox behind the single cab, chrome aftermarket wheels, and off-road tires to shoe them.

That's Ros—Jack's truck.

Angela fought the urge to tell Chris to pull in so she could run inside and say hi. *Sure, chase him down the tuna aisle even though I just talked to him forty-five minutes ago.* Not gonna happen. Still, Angela was tempted to do it just to annoy her know-it-all brother…and then they were beyond the turn into Marcie's.

Probably just as well.

Traffic soon grew even worse, and they slowly rolled past two new multi-national bank branches and a new tanning salon and a new miniature-golf course with dozens of laughing teenagers and a few families with grandparents and little kids playing spirited games of putt-putt and Angela slumped into the leather bucket seat and closed her eyes, unwilling to see any more changes, telling herself to stop thinking about Ros—Jack! Whatever his stupid name was, he would call or he wouldn't.

I'll be fine with it either way.

She would!

The enticing aromas of crisped bacon and grilled meat wafting up from between her flip-flops also reminded Angela of Rossie/

Jack, and that she hadn't eaten a bite since breakfast. She snatched a white bag and held it up: "I'm *starving*, Chris! I promise I won't get anything on the seats. Don't be a jerk."

"No way, put that down. Besides, you're almost home; you won't die if you have to wait a few more…" He suddenly laughed and pointed. "Check *this* freak out!"

She looked, then sat forward, squinting in disbelief: a giant chicken stood a few feet back from the stoplight spanning the upcoming intersection; the chicken faced the junction, holding up a crude cardboard sign to passing traffic.

Angela blinked rapidly, but the giant chicken really was wearing a black-leather motorcycle jacket; it even had little round hipster sunglasses balanced on its beak.

Chris said, "Is that thing wearing a fucking *biker jacket*, or am I hallucinating?"

"You're not hallucinating."

Angela immediately thought of the San Diego Chicken, but other than the chicken part, this getup bore no resemblance to that iconic mascot whatsoever; for one thing, this chicken's feathers weren't yellow. Beneath the leather jacket they were a blazing mix of red and orange, with bright crimson dominating the head and face. For another, there was no trace of the San Diego Chicken's trusting blue eyes; this outfit had no eyes at all, only those round, black glasses perched on its beak—and speaking of that beak, it wasn't open in a friendly smile, oh no. *This* chicken's beak was blood red with a pointed hook at the end; wide, dark nostril holes flared below the hipster shades.

That's where you see out, she realized.

A waist-high river-rock-and-concrete wall separated the lot to her right from the lot the chicken stood in, so Angela could only see its top half, but new details registered as they crept closer: long, arching tail composed of fluttering crimson feathers; the jacket's chrome zipper was fastened at the bottom, creating a rising V of red-and-orange feathers, and its collar was raised stiffly around the chicken's ears—*Do chickens even* have *ears?*—framing that harsh, feathered face.

Ears or no ears, the collar wasn't high enough to be called Napoleonic, like one of those glittering monstrosities Elvis had strutted around in, but it came close. *A cross between Elvis and James Dean*, she decided. The comb wagging on its head only reinforced her idea; it was thicker in the front, almost bulbous, falling across its forehead like a pompadour hairstyle. The tiny orange-red wattle beneath the hooked beak only added to the notion; to Angela, it looked just like a soul patch.

The light turned red, and they stopped as a jacked-up Tahoe pulling tandem Jet Ski's crossed through the intersection heading east, windows down all the way around and stuffed with teenagers. They pointed and laughed and yelled and waved, and the chicken waved back. The kids hooted, and one girl in back turned and lifted her bikini top, breasts bobbling; the teens cheered, and the chicken lowered the sign and gave her a black-gloved thumbs-up before raising the message, whatever it was, to passing vehicles again.

Chris laughed and slapped the steering wheel. "I fuckin' *love* this place in the summer!"

And then the light switched again and the BMW cleared the low wall and Angela discovered two things: one, it was a man in the costume, and two, he was only wearing half of it; the orange and red feathers ended just below the black-leather jacket; faded jeans covered his muscular legs and tight butt; battered steel-toed work boots encased his feet.

The light flickered yellow and went red, and Chris cursed and hit the brakes; they were now first in line, and Angela was now less than thirty feet from the giant chicken; tufts of red-orange feathers stuck out of the jacket's cuffs, and wide hands covered by black suede gloves stuck out of the feathers, still holding that crude sign, whatever it said; the chicken was turned away, the cardboard edge-on to her.

"Man, he's gotta be burning up under all that shit," Chris opined.

Angela concurred; it had to be ninety out there, even at Indian Head's elevation, but the man didn't seem to notice. Then he turned toward them, black-gloved hands holding up the homemade sign with a two-part message neatly printed in blue magic marker: HAPPY BIRTHDAY USA above, and below, WE BUY GOLD AND SILVER. Behind him squatted the rectangular building that belonged to the small, rectangular parking lot; dark yellow letters stenciled onto its plate-glass front windows announced: "RAWL-ING PAWN AND GUN"; other than that, the structure appeared dusty and forsaken.

Chris said, "Huh, that's weird. Mr. Rawling closed that place down six months ago."

Angela didn't respond as she stared at the man wearing the top half of a giant chicken costume; she supposed she should have seen him as comical, like Chris did, but to her he wasn't funny; to her, he resembled an enormous and bloodthirsty half-man, half-poultry Aztec god who'd foolishly been re-awoken by some mad scientist and then plopped down in the 1950s, where he had then disguised himself to fit in with his unsuspecting prey.

A nervous giggle formed, but before it could escape, Angela realized he had stopped waving his sign around and was now look-ing right at her. *Why is he staring?* Those round, black sunglasses, and those dark, flaring nostril-holes that he *had* to be looking out of—where else?—were portholes into forever, giving nothing back.

He lowered the sign then, a quick, violent motion, and rocked onto the balls of his feet, as if he wanted to charge, but he only stood tensely while looking straight at her. He couldn't *really* see her, though; the window tint ensured it was impossible to make out anything but her silhouette...

Didn't it?

She was breathing in fast little hitches. *Why are we just sitting here? How long is this stupid light?* A pickup rolling through the intersection honked, and the driver yelled; the chicken never took those flaring nostril-holes from her.

Chris said, "What's *his* problem?"

Angela yanked her eyes away and glanced up just as the light turned green. "Go!"

"God, you're shaking. What—"

Someone behind them laid on their horn.

"Go! *Go!*"

"Asshole. Guess he doesn't like BMW's. *Yeah!*" Chris rose in his seat, sneering at the giant chicken as another horn blared: "You like this? You *like* it?" He dropped back down with a laugh and sped off, but Angela's eyes stayed glued to the man in the half-suit, turning to watch out the back glass as the chicken swiveled his feathered head to track them, then his whole body, arched tail swinging behind, fat red comb flopping to the other side; the cardboard hung beside one blue-jeaned leg, forgotten.

And then, behind him, Angela spotted something that made her forget all about the angry man in the weird half-costume; a pickup was parked beside the pawn shop. She hadn't seen it before because they'd been coming up from the lake side. The older-model red Ford 4x4 was a single-cab, jacked up with chrome wheels and off-road tires; a battered chrome toolbox was snugged up behind the cab.

It was Rossie's truck.

That's impossible. She'd just seen it parked in front of Marcie's, and with the crazy traffic, he would have had to literally fly to get ahead of them. But there it sat, no mistaking it; nobody else in Indian Head drove a Ford like it.

Angela's stunned gaze drifted back to the man wearing the top half of the almost-sorta-Elvis-chicken costume; he was still watching them drive away, cruel, feathered face framed by that stiff collar, and his bottomless stare seemed to go right through her.

Then a dip in the road hid them from each other and she blew out a shaky breath and turned around, mind a jumble: *That can't be Rossie's. It just can't.* Angela knew his truck (not that she was a stalker or anything), and even if it wasn't his—and it wasn't, she was sure of it—it was still a dead ringer; perhaps there'd be differences if you compared them side by side, but not many.

Chris was frowning at her. "You all right? You're still trembling." He glanced into the rear-view. "You know that guy or something?"

"N-no. No." Angela clasped her hands in her lap to stop them shaking. Why *had* he stared that way? And who was he? And why was he so angry? And why did he have a doppelgänger to Jack's Ford parked back there? Was it even his? *Who else's could it be?* Chris said Mr. Rawling had closed that place months ago; she looked at her brother sideways.

Had *he* seen the Ford?

No, she decided. *He would've said something.* Chris would recognize Rossie's truck, too.

"Well, whoever he is, I bet he's just pissed because he's making a buck like that while we're riding in a car like this." He patted the shifter knob. "Too bad so sad. Fuck him."

Angela shot him a disgusted look, then winced and rubbed her temples; her head was killing her all of a sudden. She should've felt sorry for the man, having to stand in the sun like that to make a living—not that it seemed to bother him much—but God, her head was *splitting.*

"You got any ibuprofen or aspirin in here?"

"No."

"Morphine? Heroin? Anything?"

"Are you sure you're all right? You're so pale it's like your tan washed off; I thought you laid out, not paid for that spray shit."

"Just take me home, funny guy. And you're right, I don't feel so good. I might even throw up."

Behind the wrap-around shades, his eyes went wide with horror: "Don't! If you gotta, tell me and I'll pull over."

They made the two miles to her house in what Angela was sure was record time; despite the jarring race, she felt somewhat better by the time Chris pulled down the long, pine-shaded drive. He stopped next to her white Camry, which sat out by the front porch, glittering in the sun.

"All right, we're here."

"Thanks, Swami. Never woulda figured that out."

"Sorry. Just don't puke in the car."

"Your concern is touching." She retrieved her purse and the bag with her lake supplies from the back seat: sunblock and spare tee-shirt and spare shorts and tampons, just in case. Angela tried to hand him one of the white Crazy's sacks and his root beer: "Here."

He made a face. "No thanks. You eat it."

"What, you think Jack would do something to it? He wouldn't do that."

"I don't think that, I just refuse to eat from the hand of a murderer."

"You…*augh!*" Angela got out and whammed the door closed.

Chris rolled down the window. "Hey, easy on the—"

"He was never convicted of *murder*, Chris. It was involuntary manslaughter; it was an *accident*. If you're going to be a dickhead, at least get your facts straight. And you were his best friend. Don't you care about that?"

"That was a long time ago."

"He was still your friend. Your *best* friend."

Chris pointed his shades at the dash and didn't answer.

Angela had just reached the porch steps when he called out, "Wait!"

She stopped, but didn't turn around. "What?"

"I was wrong earlier."

Now she turned. "About what?"

"When I said Bob doesn't care who you sleep with. If he finds out you're fucking Rossie, you can forget about that job. Hell, you can forget about working in Indian Head, period. Jack Ross is poison in this town; he might as well have a skull and crossbones tattooed on his forehead. Remember that, little sister."

Angela stared, then simply turned away again; he was her brother and the only person she had left in the world, but she was on the verge of saying things that couldn't be taken back. Chris zoomed off down the sun-dappled driveway as she unlocked her front door and slammed it behind her.

Hard.

5

The rest of Monday passed in a blur of pouting Tiffany and bitching Donnie; Tiffany because I'd taken Angela's food outside. I think. Maybe sullen is just the natural state of sixteen-year-old girls. Donnie was another matter; when he found out I'd promised Tiff she could take off early on the Fourth to party with her friends…

Yeah.

But I endured as we rode wave after wave of campers and boaters, serving up corn dogs and bacon cheeseburgers and fries and Crazy Shakes and rings. Some hefty gal wearing an unfortunate black-and-white polka-dot one-piece told me I needed to add tater tots with cheese to Crazy's menu, like Sonic; they were her favorite.

I smiled vaguely at her through the mesh and said I'd think about it.

I should've been paying more attention, I guess; this is my summer livelihood, after all, and Rossie's gotta eat, but why had Angela given me her number? Was it just to piss off Chris, or did she really want me to call? My skull felt like it was stuffed with cotton balls; even Miguel stopped bee-bopping long enough to stare a question at me out the dungeon window.

Miguel's wife Maria showed up at six like clockwork, with their four kids in tow; I can never remember their names. My cook emerged from the dungeon carrying three greasy bags and held them up, asking silent permission like he did every day even though

I've told him he didn't have to do that at least a hundred times. I nodded, and he nodded back, his weary eyes thanking me, although his face held a touch of shame as he headed out to his family, where they promptly sat under a white-and-green striped umbrella. The kids inhaled their hamburgers and rings while Maria, face an unforgiving hammer, spouted a river of Spanish and waved her free arm around when she wasn't jabbing a finger at her husband; Miguel just nodded as he ate, shoulders slumped. At least the kids were smiling. The eldest is about nine, I think; she's about the size of a six-year-old, so it's hard to be sure.

We were between waves, so I was watching them out the order window when Donnie glanced outside and shook his head. "Man, you're such a sucker. Do you know what this daily feed is costing you? Have you done the math? *I* have."

I only looked at him, that's all, but he raised his hands and backed away: "Easy thar, big fella. I pay for *my* meals."

"Just drop it, okay?" I like Donnie. I really do. He's smart, way smarter than me (not that that's hard), but he hasn't learned when to shut up; maybe it was time to teach him. "Or do you want to work the dungeon until close?"

"Nosuh, Boss Rossie. Iz just a sayin', dats aw. Miguel is taking you for twenty bucks a shift, though. That's not rabbit feed."

"Let it go, Don." I went back to watching the kids eat. Marissa. That's the eldest's name. Maybe. The youngest was about two, and he was chomping away and grinning from ear to ear while wearing a saggy Daffy Duck pull-up and no shirt and no socks and no shoes; his dangling, swinging feet were dirty.

Donnie's wrong; it's costing me over twenty bucks a shift, but I wasn't sure those kids were getting any other full meals since summer break had started. Miguel's my rock, though; here at ten on the dot every damn day, and I hadn't once heard him complain about a thing in three seasons; not a single, ever-loving, thing. That's rarefied mana from Heaven, and to be treasured around Crazy's country.

"I still say you're a sucker, but whatever; it's your dough. Speaking of chow…" Donnie patted his belly. "Since we're between waves, I'm gonna make me something—something for which I will pay, of course." I grimaced, but somehow kept my molars together; sometimes a little Donnie goes a long, long way. He headed into the dungeon, voice echoing as he called over his shoulder: "You want anything?"

I sighed and turned away from the smiling kids. "Get out of there, I'll make it." I strapped on a clean white-and-green Crazy's apron as Donnie squeezed past me. I yanked a fresh hairnet out of the dispenser, then did likewise with the disposable gloves.

"Yessuh, Boss Rossie."

"And stop with the Boss Rossie shit or I'll spit on your food."

He leered at me through the window: "Spit makes it sweeter."

I shook my head and gave up. "What do you want?"

He told me, and I glanced out at Tiff; she was as far from us as she could get, over behind the soft-serve machine, hammering away on her phone; I guess she thought we were severely nearsighted and couldn't see her over there.

"Tiffany, I'm making Donnie something. Want anything? It's on me today."

Donnie lit up. "No shit?"

Tiff pried herself from the screen long enough to say, "I'll take some rings, I guess."

Donnie rolled his eyes up to the ceiling. "Big fuckin' surprise. You're gonna turn into a walking onion ring by Labor Day." Rings were the only Crazy's fare Tiffany would eat. I figured it had something to do with not gaining weight, so I'd never told her about the grease we fry them in. I didn't want to squash her illusions; time would handle that just fine without my help.

Donnie said, "Since we're freeloading like Miguel today, forget the puny cheeseburger basket. I want a double-bacon cheeseburger with everything, some rings like the stuck-up Jesus freak there, and an extra-large root-beer Crazy Float; don't worry about the float, I'll make it."

"One cheeseburger basket and one order of rings, coming up."

Tiffany's silver-bell laugh came as Donnie whined, "Aw, c'mon, Jack." But he left it there; he usually knows when not to push. Usually. They appeared side-by-side in the window, looking in at me as I dropped the rings and fries and slapped a patty on the grill.

"So what's the occasion?" Donnie asked. "All those numbers you scored today got the ol' spirits up, among other things?"

"It's just a thank-you for having to work the Fourth. I know how much that sucks when you're your age." It sucked when you were my age, but I didn't bother to tell them; they'd find out.

"Thank you, Jack. You're sweet."

"Thank you, Jack! You're so *sweeeeeet!*"

"Fuck off, Donnie."

"My Lordy my! What would Jesus think about such language, young lady?"

I smiled and listened to them go at it, not bothering to referee; Tiff gave as good as she got, and soon they wound down after reaching a verbal draw. I only wanted a plain double cheeseburger, so we took everything outside and sat in the deepening dusk at the same picnic table from which Miguel and family had only recently disembarked (after wiping it off *and* throwing their trash into the cans), eating and arguing and laughing and slapping at mosquitoes; Tiff even left her phone alone—for the most part.

We finished before the next wave and rode it fine; after that it was sporadic until close, so we got everything cleaned and stocked early and locked up at fifteen minutes after nine. I lowered and padlocked the plywood shutters and padlocked the bathrooms. A billion-jillion stars glimmered overhead; this far from any serious city lights, it's a stargazer's wet dream.

Tiffany said, "Goodnight, Jack."

"Goodnight, see you tomorrow."

"Yep." She walked toward her convertible canary-yellow VW Beetle.

"Goodnight, Tiffaneeee!" She hadn't bothered to say goodnight to Donnie, but that didn't faze him. "Tell Jesus I said hi!"

She turned and walked backwards in the gravel, giving him the finger. Then she hopped in the bug and lowered the top and vroomed away, following her headlights up the mountain, dark hair streaming.

Donnie and I stood side by side and watched her go.

"Ya know," he said, "I think I'm starting to like that chick."

"Yeah." I stretched, feeling the long day. "Oh, I forgot. You can take off early Friday night, to even things with Tiff."

A bushy eyebrow lifted in surprise: "Right the fuck on. I take back everything I ever said about you, Jack."

"Thanks. See you tomorrow."

"Yeah, see ya."

I pulled out my keys and moseyed toward my truck, but Donnie was still just standing there with his own keys, looking at the gravel between his sneakers. "Uh, Jack?"

"What?"

"Hold on a sec, I need to tell you something."

I stopped, still watching him watch the gravel; his mouth opened and closed like a banked crappie.

"Don? Still with me?"

"Yeah, boss, present and accounted for." He finally shook his head, sharp, as if putting paid to an argument with himself, then faced me and said, "You don't have to do that."

"I don't have to do what? What are you talking about?"

He shrugged, then looked away toward the black wall of Ponderosa looming behind Crazy's; their jagged tops pierced the glimmering stars. "You know, make it even. It's not like I have plans for the Fourth, anyway. Or Friday night."

I got the distinct feeling it wasn't what he'd planned to say, but I didn't press him, just looked until he glanced over: "All the same, you can take off early if you want."

"Okay. Thanks, man."

"Not a problem. See you at ten o'clock tomorrow."

"Yessuh, Boss Rossie!"

I chuckled and went to my truck as Donnie ambled to his rust-spotted Accord. I pretended to fiddle with something until his headlights splashed across the Shell, then slid down in the bench seat and blew out a long breath and stared at the monster I'd created:

A monster otherwise known as Crazy's.

I have a dream. Someday, somewhere, somehow, I want to open a real restaurant, a place with indoor seating and waiters and paintings on the walls and steaks and salads and turning a decent fucking profit and everything. I've always loved to cook, but I'm no trained chef, and at the time, I didn't have any experience running a business, let alone a restaurant—so if I had gone to the bank with my dream and my hand out, they would have laughed me right back out the door.

Thus, Crazy's: We're only open from Memorial Day until Labor Day, same as the campground; the rest of the year I frame houses all over the state, and sometimes up in Montana and over in Idaho and even further afield…or at least my ass had, until this whole mess with Dad's stroke. Now I didn't know what I was going to do because Mom and Dad are getting up there, and she can't handle laid-up Dad *and* our place by herself, sure as hell not for weeks and weeks while I'm out on the road, so…

Sigh.

This seemed like such a good idea when Jenifer and I had sat down and hashed it out; make a little summer money, gain some experience, have fun down by the lake. Now Jen was married to a dentist down in Sheridan—*my* (former) dentist, which somehow made it worse—and this was my first season without her. I still sometimes expected to see her smiling in that way she had every time I turned around—I know Donnie missed staring at her ass—but now Jen's banging my dentist, and here I still am, livin' the dream.

Lucky me.

I pulled my phone out and went to the received calls and found Angela's number, but my brain was too tired to process all the implications; I knew I would call her, though.

Even if nothing came of it, it'd be worth it just to piss Chris off.

I put the phone back and felt something else in there, then dragged out Miriam's card. I almost crumpled it and threw it under the seat, but...

Ten months—ten months *plus*.

Kids' camping.

Gun-happy husband out of town.

I slid the card back and waved goodnight to the monster, feeling both worn out and down as I drove home, just me and the pines and the road and the mountains and the stars; a pair of sad blue eyes...

And a smokin' body in a neon-orange bikini.

Ten months is a long goddamn time.

6

Angela set her charcoal pencil down and rolled her stool back and stood, linking her fingers and pressing her palms toward the coffered ceiling; her back and wrists cracked nicely. She lowered her hands and contemplated her latest creation.

She'd meant to draw the new Rossie-Jack, she really had, but *this* had come pouring out of her instead, almost of its own volition: a foot-tall rendering of a man wearing the top half of a 50s-greaser-chicken costume. She'd drawn him facing out of the page, with the jacket and the zippers and the stiff collar, and the blue jeans and work boots on his lower half; the pompadour comb lay over to the left, her right, and the hooked beak had a mean cast; she'd even put the homemade sign in, black-gloved fingers obscuring all but IRTH DAY U and UY GOLD AND SIL.

Angela met the stare from behind those round, black glasses and had to stop herself from looking away. Suddenly she reached out and shut the pad on the image, then thought about what she'd done and shrugged.

Why not? Why not draw it, and why not get freaked out by it after? Maybe it just showed the power of her talent.

Angela grimaced, then laughed. "Sure," she said. "I'm awesome."

She clicked her retractable spot-lamp off, plunging her workspace into darkness. Startled, she fumbled her phone out of the cubbyhole on the side of the inclined desk and woke the screen; it was past ten-thirty. She'd gotten completely absorbed; it went like that when her juices were flowing.

Angela had lost her appetite after the fight with Chris, so she nuked her Crazy's burger and fries and wolfed them down standing by the small kitchen island; it was all good, although she knew it would be much better fresh. Next time she would eat it immediately. That there might *be* a next time brought a smile, and when she realized why she was smiling, Angela laughed again.

"Maybe I'm just horny," she told her kitchen. *Now I'm talking to my kitchen.* She really needed to get out more. Maybe she should get a cat; it would go great with the old-maid image she seemed to be cultivating; just like her friend, the elderly Mrs. Barbary, her neighbor up the slope. The only problem with *that* plan was the teensy-weensy fact that the smell of cat urine made her sick, which is why she begged off visiting Jess most of the time, instead inviting her friend down for coffee. Angela thought the crafty old lady knew why, but no offense was taken—or at least expressed; it didn't hurt that Jess liked her coffee. Angela still had three pounds of hand-roasted Bolivian beans left from the five-pound bag she'd bought from her favorite café in Chicago.

I could get a dog. She'd never had one growing up because Dad and Chris were allergic to dog hair. But *she* wasn't. That first year, she'd tried to talk Brian into getting one of those little froo-froo dogs, maybe a toy Yorkie, but he wouldn't even consider it. Said he was too busy to train it, and that a dog would just ruin the carpet in the condo, but after five years of marriage, Angela now understood the truth: a dog would have taken Brian's time away from Brian; God knew how important *that* was.

Angela shivered and rubbed her arms; the house was freezing. She cleaned her mess up, then turned off the AC and opened all the windows to get the cross-breeze; come August it would be too hot, even this high up, so she did it every night while she could, sleeping with just a ceiling fan going in her upstairs childhood bedroom; she could've never done that fourteen floors up in downtown Chicago, and her ex-therapist would probably say that doing so now was some sort of rebellion against her ex-husband, but Angela was hunky-dory with that diagnosis.

She was done with both of *them*, anyhow.

Angela opened the freezer and filled her favorite black-and-yellow Batman stein with chilled, sweet Italian (yet another thing her ex had never liked: her love of cheap red wine; to Brian, wine had to come from France, the more expensive the better, and never mind that it tasted like feet) and went out to the long front porch and sat in her wicker chair; it had been her mother's chair, but now it was Angela's. She'd left the porch light off so the bugs wouldn't swarm her.

Angela sipped, then set the mug on the little wicker table and looked across it at the matching-yet-much-more-worn wicker chair: *Dad's chair*. How many evenings had her parents sat out here talking, or perhaps just quietly enjoying the twilight scents and sounds? How many sleepless nights had her dad sat over *there* and stared across the table at his wife's empty chair, missing her, brooding over the terrible accident that had so unfairly taken her away?

Now it's just me, sitting in the dark, missing them. She picked up the Batman stein and sipped.

Maybe I will *get a dog.*

Her mind drifted to her sketch. It was creepy, no denying that; good, but creepy. So what on earth possessed her to draw it? But she knew; that bizarre scene today in the pawn shop's parking lot had stuck in her artist's eye, just like the time she'd glimpsed the homeless wino camped out in the alley down the block from the entrance to their building. She'd grabbed her pad and a sharpened pencil from the condo and then ventured down the filthy alley and tentatively asked his permission before rough-sketching him in his stained trench coat and ratty scarf and his shopping cart full of aluminum cans and shopping bags, finishing with the cardboard box he called home slanting in the background. Angela had drawn him staring out of the page as well, gray-whiskered face sad and weathered, yet noble and defiant at the same time; she'd been so *proud* of that sketch, even though it made her ashamed of all that she and Brian took for granted.

Angela sipped the wine; she remembered almost flying back to the condo and redoing it and redoing it until it just about jumped off the pad it was so right, remembered being excited to show it to her new husband when he arrived home from his law firm. She also remembered what had happened when she did: one look, and Brian had wadded it up and thrown it in the garbage compactor, demanding to know if *that bum* had touched her, saying he wanted Angela to stay away from scum like that; she'd told him that she'd only spoken briefly with the man, and that his name was Phillip—doubtful if it was his real name—but Brian had called the cops anyway, saying that a homeless vagrant had accosted his wife. Shortly thereafter Phillip had been removed, and Brian had made her promise not to talk to any more homeless people. You just didn't know what filth like that would do. They weren't safe to be around. And they certainly weren't safe to converse with. The city should just roust them out and round them up and dump them into the lake, and good riddance to bad rubbish.

That had been the last time Angela had shown her husband one of her sketches.

She grimaced and tipped back the stein, then went to the freezer and replenished it and came back out; the warning signs had all been there, but she'd ignored them. *God, I was* such *a fool.* She'd let looks and the charm of joining his well-heeled, Old-Chicago-money family cloud her vision. *Who cares how much money you have if you treat everybody who doesn't have it like dirt?* Brian hadn't always been like that, though; when they'd met in college, he'd been sweet and funny. She'd fallen in love with *that* Brian, but after they were married, the real Brian came out to play.

Even so, she'd hung on for five miserable years, trying to make it work, trying to make the Brian she loved come back, so you couldn't call her a quitter—but in the end you could call her a coward. Angela had filed for divorce while her husband was on a business trip to New York City. She hadn't even called him, just left a note on their bed saying she didn't want anything from him; not alimony, not anything. Her divorce attorney had flat-out told her she was insane, but she'd only taken her clothes in three enormous suitcases, the coffee, and all her sketching materials, including the desk her dad had bought her; Brian would have just sold it or thrown it out.

And the worst part? The absolute *worst*? Angela sat up in the chair and dashed at her eyes; she would *not* cry—not over *him!* Brian had called once—once!—to try to get her to come back. It'd taken him a week to call, too, even though he'd been scheduled back in Chicago two days after she'd left. And when he finally did, his efforts to convince her had been lukewarm at best, so Angela had come to the inevitable conclusion that Brian didn't mind her leaving after all; in fact, he had sounded almost relieved when she'd told him it was over for good.

Relieved!

Angela thumped the stein on the little table and lowered her face into her hands. *Had* he been cheating on her? She'd suspected him for years; she supposed it didn't matter—they were done—but for some reason, it still did.

After a time, she used her tee-shirt to wipe her face. *No more.* No more tears over that selfish, cheating bastard. How could she have been so stupid? She picked up the Batman stein with a shaking hand and took a sip: No. More. Brian! The sketch. *No.* Angela didn't want to think about that stupid sketch, either; she'd gotten it out of her system, and good riddance.

Jack.

Angela smiled. She would draw Jack tomorrow: his short brown hair and melting brown eyes; his muscular frame; the deep dimple that appeared at the corner of his mouth when he grinned; that tight little ass…yes, drawing Jack would be just the thing to drive Brian out of her brain once and for—

A sharp *snap* came from the right of the long porch, and the insects over there gave a final peeping chorus and went silent. Angela stood up slowly, looking that way, trying to pierce the darkness behind the overlapping needles.

That had sounded *big*.

Several vegetable-loving mule deer and a family of adorable raccoons and a few opossum and just about every other critter known to Wyoming shared the four acres of Ponderosa and Limber pines with her, and her dad said he'd seen two black bears over the years—or maybe the same bear twice—but Angela had never even *glimpsed* one, so she'd always thought he was just teasing and trying to scare her. Mountain lions roamed higher up, mostly in the park, but surely they wouldn't come down this far, not in the summer when their food was plentiful.

The bugs hesitantly resumed their song, so Angela sank back down, but she perched on the edge with her knees held together and peered intently toward the tree line off to her right, but saw only clusters of needles and two or three pale, scaly trunks; everything else was lost in the gloom.

Ice crept up her spine; Angela felt watched. Her lips twisted, and she leaned back deliberately. *There's nobody out here but you and a few hungry deer.* She sipped the wine, but the sweetness had turned sour, tainted by her fear.

Abruptly she set the mug on the table and went inside, then slammed the front door and threw the bolt and went into the living room and killed the lights so she wouldn't be backlit. She crept to a window and peered out…but how the heck was she supposed to see anything in the dark?

Angela bounded around the house, flicking all the outdoor floods on while switching the rest of the inside lights off; she rarely used the LED floods, preferring the soft glow of the moon and stars, but now she was grateful for their powerful brightness. When all was dark inside and lit up outside, she stood in the dining room and peeked through her mother's floral curtains toward the tree line on the side where she'd heard…whatever the heck she'd heard; she saw nothing but her side-yard and a green wall of needles.

Maybe it really had been just a buck mule deer moving toward her garden; those could get big, and God knew the mulies liked her garden. She'd staked an eight-foot wire fence around the little plot, strong-arming a grumbling Chris into helping her, just so she could enjoy some of her hard work herself. The pillaging had stopped with the fence, but she suspected some of those deer could jump pretty high—she'd seen it on nature shows—and that the mulies were just working their courage up before—

Angela's breath froze as she heard another, softer snap, and then *crunch-crunch-crunch-crunch*.

Panicked little rasps whistled in and out of her throat as she backed away from the open window. *That's no deer.* She'd heard animals moving through those pines her whole life, and she'd also heard the deliberate, single steps of a person.

Someone was out there.

Angela clamped her throat down on a scream. *Don't panic, girl, don't panic.* She thought her eyes would pop from her face.

Who was out there? What did they want?

She bolted out of the dining room and across the living room and up the staircase and down the hall past her room and Chris's old room to her parent's bedroom and slipped in and eased the door shut, locked it, then yanked open the closet door and grabbed the soft case from where it leaned in the corner and unzipped it and snatched out the double-barrel Coach gun and broke it open to see if it was loaded—it was. The reliable old-west shotgun had belonged to her grandfather, a towering, smiling, gentle man she barely remembered, and it was the only gun Angela had ever shot in her life. Her dad had made her learn when she was a little girl, even though it had been big and scary to her then (still was), and the first lesson Dad taught her had been as simple as it was true:

Guns don't work unless they're loaded.

She snapped the breach closed and stood on tiptoes to feel around on the shelf for the rest of the shells, but couldn't find the box. She pawed faster, frantic; had Chris moved them? Why? Then she grabbed it and promptly dropped it; red-and-brass shells clattered on the hardwood, some rolling under her parent's four-poster.

"Shit!"

Angela snatched a handful and stuffed them in her pockets; then, carefully keeping the barrels pointed away, she pulled both big, pointed hammers back with her thumb; they locked into place with a comforting *clack-clack*. She tiptoed over to the window and peeked out; it was shut, and she wanted to open it, but she *didn't* want whoever was out there to hear and know exactly where she was. She couldn't see anything moving in the yard. She needed to *hear*; she needed to go back down and find an open window.

Angela was moving past the foot of her parent's bed when the *thump* came from downstairs.

She froze.

Another *thump*, louder—and right underneath her! Someone was in the house! Hadn't she locked all the doors? This wasn't the city, and she sometimes forgot to secure the back door, but this time she could *swear* she'd—

The windows are open, dummy!

Angela trembled from head to foot. Her phone! Where had she left her stupid phone? Then she remembered: it was still in her desk.

Downstairs.

Someone was in the house with her.

What was she going to do?

And then she straightened her spine and gripped the shotgun so hard her knuckles ached and opened her mouth, and what came out was not a wail or a cry, but a voice she almost didn't recognize:

"I HAVE A GUN!"

Angela stamped across the room and unlocked the door and jerked it open and stepped into the hall with both barrels leading, then moved to the top of the stairs and looked down. Nothing.

She listened.

Nothing.

"Whoever you are, if you want to keep breathing, GET OUT OF MY HOUSE!"

She slammed down the stairs, coach gun up, trigger finger held outside the guard, just like her daddy had taught her; if she curled that finger in and let loose with both barrels, anything short of an M-1 tank would be obliterated. So Daddy had told her, and so she'd seen with her own eyes; those watermelons he'd propped on that old stump out back hadn't stood a chance; it had been years since she'd held the shotgun, but it felt right in her hands—felt *good*. She reached the bottom and peeked left into the kitchen, nothing, then right, into the living room, barrels leading.

Nothing.

She stalked through the rest of the first floor, checking both doors and all the windows; the back door was locked, just like she'd thought, and no one had forced their way through a window screen, so Angela retrieved her phone, stood in the kitchen, held her breath, and listened:

More nothing.

Those thumps had to have been caused by *something*. Maybe a deer had tried for her garden and scraped up against the garage, and then her yell had scared it off...but those thumps had come from below her, not outside—or so she'd thought; the garage was on the same side of the house as Mom and Dad's room, and she'd been freaked out big-time, so maybe…

Angela unlocked the front door and walked out and downed the wine in one gulp; the stein's edge rattled against her teeth. She sank into her mother's chair and rested the coach gun across her knees and carefully dropped both hammers; another lesson from Daddy: always keep the hammers down unless you're going to shoot something.

She blew out a long, long breath. *All my imagination.* She'd worked herself into a tizzy over a deer…*but those footsteps: crunch-crunch-crunch.* That hadn't been an animal; *that* had been a person walking back under the boughs, she would *swear* it.

Angela looked out at the night.

She still felt watched.

She popped up again and went back inside, bolting the door behind her, then checked all the window screens and the back door once more—still locked—then went into the kitchen and stood by the island; it was now almost a quarter past eleven, but she wasn't sleepy, not the least little stinking bit.

I don't feel safe here.

It was a surprising and uncomfortable thought; Angela had grown up in this house, had lived in it the past seven months by herself, but tonight she didn't feel secure; there was a weird charge to the air. She didn't know if she'd spooked herself or she was just craving human company that bad, but she couldn't deny the feeling:

I don't want to stay here tonight.

Chris.

She raised the phone, then hesitated; he would make fun of her forever for this, and it would just add fuel to his argument that she should sell the house and get a condo near his over in Shady Cove. Angela didn't *want* to sell; she loved it here…

Just not tonight.

Chris didn't answer, so she hung up when she got his voicemail and tried again; after the fourth time, she put the phone down. Was he still mad about this afternoon? He didn't have anything to be mad at *her* about; he was the asshole. She started to text him, then stopped; if he was pouting, why would he respond to a text? Maybe he was asleep. Oh wait, no, that's right, he'd bragged to Zane that morning about the woman he was seeing—that *married* woman; she was staying at his condo tonight.

Angela grimaced; so either he was ignoring her, or her brother was busy.

Who else could she call?

It hit her then, maybe for the first time, how alone she was in the world, now. And after all the friends she'd had back in Chicago…her jaw tightened. No, they'd been Brian's friends; his *family's* friends—or more correctly, his family's *money's* friends; they'd never really been *her* friends, that's for sure, something she'd painfully realized before she'd left. And she had no real friends here, not any longer. Oh, at first she'd gotten together with three or four high school chums for a girls-night-out every month or so to laugh about old times, but those women were married with kids now and would not enjoy hearing from her this late; besides, no matter what she'd told them about her ex, they'd seemed both envious and utterly mystified by her decision to leave the high-life in Chicago; after the last awkward dinner-and-wine gab session, Angela had decided it would be her last.

In short, who she had was Chris.

Zane.

She picked up her phone and just as quickly set it back on the island; Zane would welcome her over to his palatial condo quick enough, even this late, but there would be a price; Angela wasn't ready to open that particular Pandora's Box, not yet. Perhaps not ever; what she'd said to Chris in the car was true: way, *way* too weird. After their mothers had died in that awful crash, she and Chris and the twins had grown close—not brother-and-sister close, no, but their dads had been best friends, just like their mothers, and even if they weren't all that close now…

Still too weird. Ugh.

So who *could* she call?

Angela contemplated her iPhone; she could just dial 911…she snorted. *No way.* Chief Rogers would have to come out—or more likely, one of his full-time officers. Four months ago, she'd had the poor judgment to have a fling with one of them, Rick "Tommy" Toms. Tommy and Angela had gone to school together, and he'd always liked her, so in a moment of extreme loneliness she'd finally given in; it had only happened the once, though, and she'd broken it off the next day.

So Tommy coming out in the middle of the night would be kinda awkward, to say the least, but worse would be Chief Rogers' other full-time flunky, that creep Ryan Fleming. Officer Fleming had never said a word to her, not a single, solitary word, but every time he saw Angela he stared with his cold, hungry eyes. She shivered. *Forget that.* And she just *knew* that whoever responded would then find nothing, or maybe just some frightened animal. Besides, if she had the police out here, all of Indian Head would know by lunch tomorrow; Angela would *not* be known as the hometown girl who'd done got citified and couldn't hack it in the mountains anymore, not if she could help it.

But there were those thumps; she hadn't imagined them. And those footsteps. And now she had that itchy feeling on the back of her neck, like someone was about to touch her there…and all the stinking motels and cabins were booked for miles and miles around because of the holiday.

So who can I call, damn it? Think, girl!

Angela picked up her phone and scrolled through her dialed calls until she found the number. *No.* He would be asleep, and today was the first time they'd spoken in over ten years; what would he think, her calling this late? She blushed; what anyone would think, that's what.

Damn Chris!

Angela screwed up her courage. *This is crazy.* Her heart was pounding harder than when she'd thought someone was in the house with her. *This is nuts.*

She pushed send.

7

I bounced down our rutted driveway and immediately knew something wasn't right, because Jezebel didn't bark.

I'd had the Ford for over three years, and she still issues her ropey, raspy alarm at the rumble of its small-block 351. Every time. But not tonight. Another clue that all was not well in the Kingdom of Ross: the bare bulb hanging over Mom and Dad's screened-in porch was blazing; more evidence surfaced when I killed the engine and slid out. The dog scurried from her spot in the crawlspace and headed my way while watching the lit porch over her shoulder like it might detach itself from the house and leap on her. Mom's old navy blue Le Baron was snugged in the carport; at least that was as it should be.

"Hey, Jezzie!" I gave her scratchy-scratches when she waddled up and hid behind my calves; she was trembling. "What's wrong, pretty girl?" She didn't answer, just looked up at me with those liquid eyes, the rings of silver fur surrounding them even more pronounced in the dark.

I got my answer when a deep voice rasped from the recesses of the porch:

"Well, lookie who it is! It's the *man of the house!*" A belch, and then a can crunched, and then the dull, metallic clank and clatter as it hit the pile; a cooler lid creaked and then closed with a thud; next came the *crack* and the *pssssst*. "'Bout goddamn time you got home, boy."

I stared at that burning bulb with a lead weight in my gut, then walked across the yard and opened the screen door and stepped up and into the light; Jezebel had already slunk back to the crawlspace. She's the smart one.

He was kicked back in his ratty green-corduroy recliner, footrest extended and ankles crossed. Mom had bought him new socks; they just about glowed under the bare bulb. He'd stacked his slippers by the chair and propped his cane against the armrest. I let the door whap shut and opened the scarred red-metal Coleman at his elbow; still quite a few in there, more than I'd expected, but his tolerance isn't what it used to be.

"I thought Doc Swanson told you to cut this crap out."

"What's that faggot know? Man can't enjoy a cold one on his own goddamn porch, might as well already be worm food." He belched again, long and loud. "You ain't my mother or my doctor, so mind your own goddamn business or I'll take you out there and show you who's the *real* man. I won't let you win like last time, neither."

"Sure, Dad." I shut the Coleman and opened the front door.

"That's right! And don't forget it! *'Man of the house.'*" He snorted, then took a glug as I stepped inside and closed the door and leaned my forehead against the jamb and squeezed my eyes shut.

A reedy voice floated to me: "Jackie? Is that you?"

"Yeah, Mom."

I pried my lids up and turned around and motivated down the short hall to the master bedroom. She was lying on top of the coverlet with a damp floral-print washcloth folded over her eyes. When I stepped in she lifted the cloth and smiled wanly; she wore a pair of Dad's plaid boxers and a pink Care Bears rainbow tee-shirt, ready for bed.

"There's my handsome Jackie."

"Where'd he get all the beer, Mom? Did Angus bring it?" Angus snuck beers to Dad on occasion since the stroke, but there was way more than a beer or two out there tonight.

She put the cloth back over her eyes. "No."

I stared at her lying there, and then the implication hit me like a paving brick. "*You* gave it to him? For God's sake, why? He's out there piss drunk! Shit, Mom, what about what Doc Swanson said?"

"Don't cuss me, Jackie. I get enough of that from your father."

"Sorry, but…*why?*"

Mom blew out a breath, cheeks puffing, then lifted the cloth away and struggled to sit up. I stepped over and helped; her long, straight hair, now more gray than the dark brown I'd inherited, rippled like a muddy waterfall in the soft glow from the lamp on the nightstand.

She patted my cheek, then put her bare feet on the hardwood and used both hands to steady her balance on the edge of the coverlet: "Your father fell off the tractor today."

"*What?* What the hell was he doing on the tractor? Is he okay?"

"His ego's bruised, along with his hip and ribs, but Dr. Swanson said that's all, thank God. Fool man decided to pull that rotting gatepost out and put a new one in. Over on the far corner of your barn?"

"Yeah," I said. The gatepost I kept meaning to replace and never getting around to replacing; Mom had the grace not to mention that, though.

"Well, he used the Farmall and the stump chain to pull it out, along with twenty feet of fence after the tractor got away from him and he fell; said his foot slipped off the clutch and it bucked him off. Fred White and I managed to prop the fence up, but if his cows figure out it's not attached to your barn anymore, we'll have them all over the yard again come morning."

"I'll secure it before I go to bed." It wasn't just tractors Dad wasn't supposed to be operating. "How'd he buy the new post?"

She rolled her eyes. "He didn't think that far, just decided to do it and did. He's going stir crazy around here, Jackie, which is why I got him the beer."

"Christ, Mom."

"Don't you take the Lord's name in vain! Not in *my* presence!"

"Sorry, but I don't think beer will help anything."

"Don't you take that smart-alecky tone with me either, mister." She dabbed her face with the cloth. "The beer wasn't for him. It was for me."

She caught my expression and laughed quietly. "Not to drink. Just for some peace. He'll be out there until he passes out, then I'll dump the rest. He'll think he polished them off." She reached up and squeezed my elbow. "Get some rest. I know it's a big week for you. We'll be fine. Go on, Jackie."

Considering what the doctor had said—and considering what we'd both been through over the years—I still couldn't believe she'd gotten alcohol for him. I sat on the bed next to her; the springs creaked. "You can't give him any more to drink, Mom. Doc Swanson said—"

"Shh-shh-shh, now." She took my left hand in both of hers and stroked the back of it with her velvety fingers. "You're a good boy, Jackie, but you're selfish, like most young people; you don't understand. You *can't* understand. That job was all he had. And now with you having to do everything around here…" Mom patted my hand and let it go. "The beer helps him forget, is all, and it gives me a little break. Perhaps I was wrong; if so, God forgive me, but I'd do it again." She paused. "God forgive me for that, too."

"What do you mean, the job is all he had? He's got this place, and you, and Jezzie and Angus…and me, I suppose…" She was looking at her hands, which were folded in her lap. "Mom, what is it?" Silence. "Mom?"

She sighed. "Your father and I haven't been intimate in over three years."

Every smidgen of blood in my body was suddenly pumped up and into my face.

"Uh…"

"Oh, grow up. It happens with old married coots sometimes. Point is, maybe we both needed the beer tonight."

"Okay," I said. It wasn't, but another revelation like that and I just might join the old man in hoisting a few. *Christ!* "Did…did Dad have an affair?"

I knew they'd had their problems—to say the least. I'd nipped one in the bud the day Mom picked me up outside the halfway house sporting a black eye and a busted nose, but I couldn't fix everything. Not that way.

Mom said, "Nothing like that, Jackie," but her voice was strange, and she peered off into the corner of the bedroom.

"Did…did you…"

She looked at me then, but without the outrage I'd expected. She just seemed…drained; the delicate crow's feet that had appeared around her beautiful dark eyes the last few years had become a road map to Wornoutsville.

"I don't think that's any of your business," she said, firm but quiet; I flushed again. "Oh, we have our issues, like anyone else, but I said the words: to love and to cherish, for better or for worse, in sickness and in health, unto death do us part—and Mary Elizabeth Ross doesn't take her vows lightly."

"All right, but that's not—"

"Go *on* now, Jackie. I've got to work tomorrow, same as you. Mr. Greer wasn't happy when I had to leave the bank and rush home; poor Fred was at wits' end, finding your father like that, next to a stalled tractor and with half his Hereford's wandering all over creation."

"Mom—"

She planted a dry kiss on my cheek. "Goodnight." She climbed under the covers and folded the cloth back over her eyes. "Click that lamp off on your way out, please."

The door was almost closed when I heard her voice from the darkness:

"Jackie?"

I stopped, fingers resting on the knob. "Yeah?"

"I know you're not seeing anybody—which is a shame, handsome man like you—"

"Mom…"

"But I wanted to tell you I was wrong when I scolded you for fooling with that flip-skirt Miriam Jacobson."

"Oookaay." Mom's a lot of things, but "wrong" has never been high on the list.

"I mean it, son. Life's too short to be alone; take what comfort you can find, when and where you can find it. Just don't marry a woman like that, for God's sake. Fool around with who you want, but be careful." The bedsprings creaked, and when she spoke again, I knew she'd turned to the wall; her voice was barely audible. "For better or for worse; that's what you're signing up for, Jackie. They just don't tell you how bad worse can be."

I waited; nothing else seemed forthcoming, so I shut the door and stood there thinking about the surprises this Monday had offered up, and the women who had authored them: first Miriam, then Angela, and now Mom. I finally shook my head and zombied back down the hall and tiptoed out.

The old man was sawing logs, glowing socks still crossed and square chin tilted toward the blazing bulb; a Pabst Blue Ribbon lay on its side below his big, slack hand, amber contents puddling and dribbling through the cracks between the boards.

I picked it up, wrinkling my nose at the smell, then started to gather the crushed pile, intent on throwing them in the barrel out back—something Mom wouldn't have to worry about tomorrow—but then I stopped.

She bought the shit, she can clean it up.

I chucked the can into the loose pile and went down the steps and into the night; neither the clatter of cans nor the screen door whapping shut behind me fazed the sawing. Mom's right, it's time for bed; tomorrow, the 3rd of July, would be chaotic, with families flocking from miles around to enjoy the lake and dropping by Crazy's for a bite and sip. I hope.

Jezzie waddled after me as I dodged three half-fresh cow pies—great—and unlocked the wide, left-hand door and fired up the air-conditioner and cranked open the twin skylights above the loft bedroom to let some steam escape, brushed my teeth, triple-scrubbed the stale-beer reek from my fingers, scratched Jezzie in her sweet spot as she lay on her doggie bed next to the stove, climbed the ladder to the loft again, and flopped face-first across my comforter.

Then I remembered the gatepost.

Son of a bitch.

It took me twenty minutes to secure it so Fred White's cows couldn't escape and frolic about the yard; said inmates stood around and watched me work with the flashlight and the pliers and the bailing wire and the maul; they seemed amused at my efforts, but maybe I'm just bitter. I stored the wire and tools in Dad's shop and washed my hands and went back to barn and loft and bed; at least Jezzie got an extra scratchy-scratch.

My body was exhausted, but my mind was wide awake, so after fifteen minutes of wiggling I slipped into my cotton workout shorts and hung the bag from the crosspiece that supports the loft and moved my meager furniture and small flat-screen up against the wall; I would *pound* myself sleepy. It wouldn't be the first time. Or likely the last.

I had wrapped my hands and was almost done with a light stretch when my phone rang; the tone was neutral, a stranger.

Who the fuck is calling this late?

I shot up the ladder and snatched the phone from the end table just as the ringing stopped. I didn't recognize the number, but it was local, which had me scratching my head…

But then I did.

Holy crap.

I hesitated about four nanoseconds, then sat on the edge of the bed and called her back; she answered on the first ring.

"Jack?"

"Hey, Angie. I mean, uh, Angela. You called?"

"Yeah, sorry it's so late. Did I wake you?"

"No! No, I, um, I was just about to work out."

She laughed. "*This* time of night, and your working out? Suddenly I feel lazy."

"I couldn't fall asleep, so I figured I'd wear myself out. Sometimes it goes like that."

"Oh. Well, I'm glad I didn't wake you."

"No, no problem, you didn't."

"Good."

Crickets.

"So you called because…?"

"Oh! Uh, yeah." She cleared her throat. "You're going to think I'm so stupid…I tried to call Chris, but he won't answer." A prim note entered her voice: "I think he's with that woman he's seeing, the one from down in Sheridan. That *married* woman."

"Oh," I said. "That's bad of him." I hurried on. "Why did you want to talk to Chris?"

"This is where you'll think I'm stupid. I heard something in the woods." A pause. "Or someone."

"Some*one?* Are you sure?"

"Yes. No. I don't know! I just got a little creeped out, I guess. I wanted someone to talk to, or maybe somewhere to go."

I pulled my phone away and looked at it before putting it back to my ear; I had to speak around a gargantuan lump in my throat. "Do, uh, do you want to come over?"

More crickets; I felt like the world's biggest shit-for-brains. "Or we can just talk on the phone if you—"

"No, that'd be great. Just give me a few minutes." Angela laughed again; she has a great laugh. "I think I remember the way, but it's been a long time." Something in her voice had changed—some unidentifiable *something*—but in truth I hardly noticed and didn't care:

Angie was coming over.

"Yeah." I attempted to wipe the smile from my voice, but gave up on my face. "It has."

More crickets.

"Well, I guess I'll see you in a few."

"Okay. Bye."

"Bye."

I was about to hang up, when: "Jack?"

I crammed the phone back to my ear. "Yeah?"

"It's sweet of you to do this, you know, let a friend come over and talk when it's so late. Thank you."

Friend.

My grin melted. "Sure, no problem."

"Okay, bye."

"Bye."

I grimaced at my phone…then sat bolt upright; a girl was coming over—just a *friend*, true, but still a real, live girl.

I threw a shirt on and made the bed and picked up the pile of dirty clothes and dumped it in the basket and picked up the basket and then cursed myself for a moron; she wouldn't be coming up *here*—friends, Jack, remember? I tossed the overflowing basket into the corner and blasted down the ladder and began an attempt at composing order out of bachelor chaos.

Jezzie raised her head from her paws and watched me frantically clean my kitchen counters, silver brows bunched together.

"Don't start."

I compressed the trash into the full can and slammed the lid back on. Where had I put the damn broom? Do I even *own* a broom? That's right, I borrow Mom's broom. *Shit.* Jezzie wagged her tail cautiously and lowered her head, still watching.

"She's just a friend," I told her; more uncertain wag. "I mean, I saw her today for the first time in ten years, and now she's coming over in the middle of the night." *And won't Chris love that.* No wag, but her eyebrows twitched. I dug a dated *Black Belt* out of the trash and used it to sweep as best I could. She'd been creeped out by something—or some*one?* Someone walking out in those pines behind her dad's place?

Is *that* what she'd said?

And was it true, or was it just an excuse to—

No, no, just friends.

"You're right, old girl. We're all fucking nuts."

Wag-wag-wag.

I cleaned faster.

8

The purr of the Camry's exhaust had long since faded when there was a stir and the closet near Angela's workspace opened.

He ducked low, then stepped out and straightened and closed the door with the black-gloved hand that didn't hold the ax; it was the kind firemen preferred, with a pointed pick balancing the wide, heavy blade. The long and slightly curved handle was stained and splintered, the head and pick pitted by rust, but both the bit and the tip of the pick gleamed with fresh metal.

He peered around, listening to the still house, then stepped to the inclined desk, boots clumping, and turned on the retractable lamp and adjusted it down and opened the pad, bending at the waist, and flipped through charcoal renderings of deer and skunks and rabbits and flowers and vegetables as well as portraits, both common and famous, until he got to the last sketch.

He studied it in the bright light, then closed the pad and pushed up the lamp and clicked it off and clumped into the darkened living room.

He stopped, feathered head swiveling, then stepped over to an antique hutch behind the couch and passed the ax to his other hand and opened a glass door and removed a framed family portrait and held it up so he could see; the boy and girl were young and blonde and blue-eyed, their parents positioned behind them. Smiling. Happy.

The frame trembled. He placed it back in the hutch, and it rattled on the glass shelf before he let it go and gently shut the cabinet door.

He stared at it through the glass a moment longer, then suddenly moved, carrying the ax back across the silent house, clumping faster, faster, and burst into the kitchen. He looked at the six red shotgun shells lined up brass-down on the island. He looked at the old Coach gun leaning against the wall next to the stainless-steel refrigerator. He stepped forward and reached to pick the gun up, but his gloved hand shook violently; he stared at that betraying hand, then stood tall and made a fist, leather squeaking.

He left the shotgun there and went to the front door and unlocked it, stumbling as he bent to clear the lintel, and stepped onto the wood-railed porch. He shut the door, considered the Batman stein resting on the wicker table, then turned and peered down the long, empty driveway.

He clumped down the steps and into the yard, his gaze drawn to the steep slope north of the house; a security light shone through the needles up there, ocher glow illuminating a small dwelling with shake siding along with a gleaming metal outbuilding.

He stood looking for a time, then passed beneath the sharp-scented boughs and started up the hill, shifting the ax from hand to hand and flexing his fingers as he weaved between the tall, straight trunks.

9

Angela crept down the pitted drive, worrying that her car wouldn't make it through the deeper ruts, then smiled when she finally exited the tunnel of tall Ponderosa and her headlights illuminated Jack standing in the yard, waiting for her.

He wore black gym shorts that showed off his muscular thighs and a plain gray tee-shirt and white ankle socks and blue New Balance running shoes; he looked good. He also looked tired, and Angela immediately felt guilty; it was almost midnight, he'd worked all day, and he had to work all day tomorrow, too. A small, fat, short-haired dog barked furiously at her car while hiding behind Jack's legs. He said something sharp to it, but the white-and-brown mutt kept voicing its raspy protest. She pulled up next to his truck and shut the engine off, and through her open window she heard him hiss-whisper, "Cool it, Jezzie!"

The little dog looked up at him adoringly, wagged its stubby tail, and resumed barking. Jack glanced over at his parents' house; Angela followed his worried gaze but saw nothing to get excited about, just the house. *God, it looks exactly the same.* She got out.

"Hi," he said.

"Hi."

The dog bobbled toward her and growled; those teeth looked sharp, but Angela figured she could outrun the little butterball if push came to shove.

Jack saved her from finding out. He whispered, "Jezebel, stop!" and picked the dog up and walked over, still whispering: "Sorry about that. She's protective."

"I see that," she whispered back, then extended the back of her hand; the dog sniff-sniff-sniffed, then licked it. "*Jezebel?*"

"Dad named her," he whispered, as if that explained everything, and Angela supposed it did. He glanced toward his parents' house again. "Somebody dumped her while I was…while I was away. She was all beat to hell and half-starved, so Mom got her fixed up." He scratched the dog's ears. "She sorta adopted me." He put his nose down near Jezebel's wet black one and squeaked, "Didn't you, pretty girl?"

Lick-lick-lick, wag-wag-wag.

Angela smiled, a little ruefully; rough, tough Rossie, high-school football stud, Gold Glove boxing champion, and karate black belt, squeaking at a dog.

He shot another anxious look at the house and then put the dog down and started towards the red-and-white barn in the field behind the house. "I'll show you my place," he whispered. "C'mon."

"Why are we whispering?" she whispered. He lived in the *barn?* Jezebel waddled at her feet, grinning up at her, tongue hanging; Angela smiled at her.

He whispered, "Dad's asleep on the porch."

"Oh."

"He, uh, he does that sometimes."

Angela recalled the gossip she'd heard around Pat's; Hank Ross was infamous in some Indian Head circles, and five months ago he'd suffered a stroke to go on top of his other…issues. "Um, how's he doing, anyway?"

Jack swung open the left side of the big red-and-white double doors. "He's been better."

"I'm sorry, Jack."

His face softened. "Not your fault." The dimple flashed, and he bowed and swept one arm out: "Enter, milady."

"Thank you, kind sir."

The interior was wide open—it was a barn, after all—with a minuscule kitchen to her left and a huge living area to her right, with a ladder leading to a deep loft. A window air-conditioning unit had been installed into the back wall, and three ceiling fans hanging from thick beams swirled the cold air around.

Despite all that space, a small flat-screen and a black-leather recliner were the only furniture; a Blu-Ray player and a rack of movies occupied a wall-mounted shelf above the television. She raised her eyebrows at a duct-taped punching bag hanging from the crosspiece supporting the loft. Eight-foot stained-pine shelves covered the near wall, running the length of the barn, full of books. Midway down was a single gap in that army of books; a digital clock and a picture frame occupied the lonely breach. The photo was of his mother, a black-and-white head shot from a time long before Jack was born.

One picture; there were so many photos in Angela's house it took her an hour to dust them all.

The kitchen was tiled in dark green, but the rest was smooth, unstained pine plank, without even a single rug to soften it. The walls had all been paneled in that same pine plank to about fifteen feet up, and then eggshell wallboard above; except for the shape, the interior didn't resemble a barn in the least. It reminded her of a bare cathedral—bare being the operative word; no posters or paintings, and no windows; no animal heads either, she was thankful to see. The first thing Angela had done after moving into Dad's house was put his trophies on eBay, cheap. Chris had been mad at her for a month, but it'd been worth it to get rid of all those creepy dead glass-eyes staring at her.

Angela's gaze followed the ladder up to the loft. *That must be his bedroom.* She flushed and glanced away.

"This is beautiful," she told him. *A painting wouldn't hurt, or maybe a rug. And how in the* world *does he live without windows?*

"Thanks." He pulled the left-hand door shut with a thud and a clank. Jezebel waddled into the kitchen and circled a dog bed by the stove and flopped down with a little doggie sigh. Jack walked over to a bulky beige over/under refrigerator with a chrome handle and opened the bottom half; raised chrome letters on the freezer door spelled out "Air Stream" in flowing script; the thing looked like a refugee from an old black-and-white *Leave It To Beaver* episode.

"You want something to drink?" His sudden laugh echoed in the open box: "I've got water and water, your choice." He looked over his shoulder: "Or I could make green tea?"

Stop staring at his butt! "Water's fine." He brought her a bottle and twisted the cap for her. "Thank you." She took a drink, then waved the bottle around: "Did you do all of this yourself?"

"Dad helped with the electric and the plumbing and the septic. He's good with stuff like that. Or at least he used to be. Jen…Jennifer, my ex, helped with the floors and…and other things."

Angela blushed, took a sip to cover it, then set the water on the counter and wandered over to the bookshelves, conscious of his eyes on her. She pulled down a small, beaten-leather volume and held it up: "*The Hagakure: The Book of the Samurai.* By Yamamoto Tsunetomo?"

He nodded and shrugged, and she put it back and pulled another: "*The Yojokun; Life Lessons from a Samurai Doctor.* By Kibara Ekiken." She arched an eyebrow at him. "I'm not going to find *Eat, Pray, Love,* am I."

He laughed. "Probably not."

"It's good. I'll let you borrow it sometime."

"All right."

Boxing training, and Jujitsu, and Krav Maga (whatever that was), and military knife-fighting tactics; something caught her eye, and Angela stopped and pulled the *SAS Hand-to-Hand Combat Guide* out and showed it to him. He shrugged again. She put it back. There were several outdoor survival guides, and a few home-repair manuals; plumbing and wiring and other such yawn-inducing topics; there were even books about gardening.

She brushed a spine with the pads of her fingers: "I started a garden in the old spot Mom used."

"How's it doing?"

"Better now that I put a fence up. The critters were eating it all." She motioned to the gardening books. "Did you start one?"

"No time. Maybe next year. Of course, that's what I said last year."

Angela waved down the long line of shelves. "Got any *real* books? You know, like with stories and stuff?" She smiled to say she was kidding, and he smiled back, but in truth, after sampling his collection, Angela expected him to say he didn't read fiction anymore; her dad had been of the same ilk. But Jack surprised her when he wordlessly led her down the wall.

Angela whistled. There were many, many authors she didn't recognize, and some she did if hadn't read—and even a few she had; she grinned as she pulled down *The Hobbit.*

"I think I was like seven when Chris talked me into reading this. God, you guys were totally nuts for elves and dragons and all that stuff back then."

"Yeah." His jaw flexed, but his dark eyes were unreadable. "I remember."

She put the book back. *Maybe I shouldn't have mentioned Chris.* "What are you reading now?"

He walked to the recliner and bent to grab something off the planks and held up a thick novel: "*The Passage,* by Justin Cronin."

"What's it about?"

"Well, did you ever read *The Stand,* by Steven King?"

"A long time ago."

"It's like that, end-of-the-world stuff, except with vampires."

She made a face. "Cheery."

He grinned, flashing the dimple. "Yeah. It's good, though." The grin dropped away, taking the dimple with it. "You said on the phone you thought someone was in your woods? What happened?"

"Um, do you mind if I borrow your bathroom first?" She smiled. "You *do* have a bathroom, right?"

Dimple. "Over here." A narrow door was hidden on the other side of the bulky fridge, so small she figured Jack had to turn sideways to get his shoulders through. He opened it for her and flicked on the overhead light and stepped back.

"You, uh, you gotta hold the handle down. I keep meaning to repair it, but, well, you know. Sorry about that."

"I don't mind." Angela stepped through and stopped, surprised. "This is nice." When she'd seen the size of that door…but the green tile from the kitchen had been repurposed here, and there was a matching green-tile shower stall with a green curtain, but no tub—a *big* minus in her book, or any woman's. Angela would've insisted on a tub, wondering why his ex hadn't; perhaps this Jenifer had known by then that she wouldn't be around for the long haul.

He was still holding the door.

"I can handle things from here, Jack."

She got the pleasure of seeing him blush.

"Sorry." He closed the door.

Angela smiled a little as she pulled her cutoffs and panties down and did her business and held the handle, as per instructions, then washed her hands while resisting the urge to peek the medicine cabinet; Jack didn't seem like the type to have a bunch of illegal scrips, but you never knew. She dried her hands on a green (more green!) towel and stepped out.

Something struck her funny then, and she stood there and looked until she had it; the narrow doorway had been cut out of the barn wall—which meant the bathroom had been built onto the outside.

Angela said as much while noting that Jack had put a kettle on the stove; packets of green tea sat on the green counter, waiting for the water.

"Yeah, it was easier; no tearing everything out and then rebuilding walls to add plumbing." He motioned to the tea. "How do you like yours? I've got honey and yellow stuff."

"Honey is fine, but you didn't have to go through all this trouble. I was great with water."

"It's not for you. I need a little pick-me-up. You can have some if you're nice, though."

Angela frowned. "I didn't mean to keep you up so late. I know you have to work tomorrow…maybe I should go."

"I was just kidding. And I couldn't sleep, anyway."

"Are you sure?"

He looked into her eyes. "If you want to go, well, then of course you can, but I wish you wouldn't."

A little shiver went through her; he was the first to look away.

"I'll stay," she said softly.

"Good."

"For a little while," she added.

He blinked and frowned. "That's what I meant, for a little while, not the night." He stared hard at the kettle.

"I know."

Silence.

Face flaming, Angela retreated to the nonfiction section and pulled down an illustrated Korean cookbook; there were three shelves dedicated to nothing but cookbooks.

She turned and held it up. "I *love* Korean! There was this little mamasan-and-pop place in Chicago that had *to-die-for* pepper beef. Do you still cook, Jack?" She laughed before he could answer: "God, I remember all that stuff you used to whip up for us in your mom's kitchen!" It had usually been him and Chris cooking together, but she didn't mention that: "Tacos or spaghetti or scrambled eggs with cheese and onions, but I think my favorite was always macaroni and cheese with hot dogs; after a day chasing you two around in the woods, nothing hit the spot better than mac n' cheese with hot dogs."

He glanced at her sharply, and she knew he was thinking about Chris again, but he only said, "I remember. I also remember how much trouble I got into if we didn't clean Mom's pans." The dimple reappeared. "And my mac n' cheese has come a long way. I use sautéed pancetta instead of hot dogs now, and I mix diced Roma tomatoes into my homemade sharp-cheddar cheese sauce. Cover it with another layer of extra-sharp and pop it under the broiler and wallah; comes out all crusty on top and gooey underneath."

"That sounds amazing."

"It is. I'll make it for you sometime." He frowned at the kettle again. "I mean, I will if, you know, if you have time someday."

Angela squashed her smile before it could peek out. "I'd like that."

He cleared his throat. "Okay."

Silence. She glanced at the book in her hands. "Do you make pepper beef?"

"Uh, no. I haven't opened that one yet. Hell, I haven't cracked three quarters of them. Jen bought me most of those, and I, uh, I used to fix us something new about twice a month, you know, experimenting, but it's not worth the trouble or the mess cooking for one."

"Oh." *Us.* Angela shoved the cookbook back on the shelf; she was sorry she'd asked.

The kettle mercifully started whistling then, and he poured—and not into dainty cups, she was glad to see, but into a pair of tall, thick steins advertising some construction supply company. He led her into the living area carrying the steaming mugs and handed Angela hers and then offered her the recliner.

"Where will you sit?"

"Watch." He set his tea on the planks and went to the wall at the back of the alcove beneath the loft where a green exercise mat was folded on the floor; it reminded her of P.E. class long ago, except this mat was firm, not mushy. He dragged it still-folded over in front of the chair and plopped down crossed-legged and picked up his stein and motioned to the recliner; Angela perched her butt on the edge and rested her elbows on her knees, tea steaming between her hands:

"Maybe I should use that. I don't want to take your chair."

"Not gonna happen. You're my guest, so you get the One and Only Chair." Angela opened her mouth, and he held up his hand: "Sorry. Barn Rules. Not negotiable."

Angela smiled. "Okay." She tasted her tea; just the right amount of honey. "This is good."

"Thank you. Now will you tell me what the hell happened?"

She hesitated. "You'll think I'm an idiot. It was probably just some animal."

"Tell me."

It didn't take long, and Angela found herself looking around just to avoid his intense gaze; what she saw made her a little sad: the single chair; the books; no plants or artwork. *Portrait of a lone male.* But she was surrounded by furniture and photographs and mementos galore at her house—and just as alone.

"…so it was likely just some mulie buck trying for the garden," she finished. "*I have a gun!*" Angela laughed and shook her head.

"Maybe," he said. "But maybe not. You grew up in those pines, and you can tell the difference between a person and a deer."

It wasn't a question, but Angela nodded and licked her lips; she had *really* wanted to think it'd just been some scared woodland creature.

"And these 'thumps'? Are you *sure* they came from downstairs and not outside?"

"They sounded like they were right under me, but I was in Mom and Dad's room, and I had the door closed." She shrugged. "It's hard to remember; I was kinda freaked out by that point."

Jack nodded, sipping his tea thoughtfully, then suddenly locked onto her again; Angela knew then that she would draw him sitting cross-legged and staring out of the page at her, serious as death; she might even put the Cheyenne Lumber Co. stein in. No dimple, though; this new Rossie didn't flash it quite as often.

He said, "I think you should call Chief Rogers and have him or one of his boys check everything out before you go back."

She didn't hesitate. "No. If I do, it'll be all over Pat's by the end of lunch. They'll say little Angie Beaumont went and got herself citified and can't hack it in the mountains anymore. You know how everyone in this town is."

Jack's smile was a slash; no dimple in sight. "I'm aware."

Angela stared at the mug between her hands; she only looked up when he spoke again.

"Then call Chris, get him to check."

"He's with that married woman, remember? Besides, I think he's mad at me. We got into it about…"

"About me? About stopping at Crazy's?"

"It's none of his business who I'm friends with, but he thinks it is; always the big brother, that's Chris."

"Yeah, that's Chris. Tell you what, I'll follow you home and check everything. That way you can get a good night's sleep."

"It'll be way late when you get back, and you have to work to-morrow."

He chuckled. "All I gotta do is flip some burgers; no rocket science involved."

"Jack—"

"It's no problem, I promise."

She said, "I could just stay here tonight."

They stared at each other.

Angela's mouth worked, but nothing came out; she dragged her eyes away from his and spoke to his bookshelves. "Never mind, I'll just go home. It was just some stupid deer anyway, and I don't want you to—"

"You can stay."

She looked at him again; it was a surprisingly difficult thing to do. "Are you sure?"

"I'm sure."

"Okay."

"But I want you to promise me something."

"What?"

"When you get home tomorrow, if there's any sign that someone's been there, you'll call Chief Rogers."

"I promise."

"Okay," he said, then put his mug down, hopped off the folded mat, and shot up the ladder. Angela blinked; she'd forgotten how *fast* he was. "Let me change the sheets and pillowcase." His voice echoed weirdly from overhead: "Mom has an extra set I can bum. I've got an old sleeping bag for me. It'll just be a few minutes while I run over…"

He's giving me his bed.

Angela jerked to her feet, stood there fidgeting, then finally yelled up the ladder: "Jack, I can't take your bed! I'll be comfortable down here!"

Rossie's bed.

His face popped over the ledge; there was no railing. "I insist. I won't have a guest sleeping on the floor."

"I'll be all right; it *has* been a long time since I went camping, I admit, but I'm a tough girl."

A smile played with his lips. "I remember. Even so, you take the bed."

"Jack—"

"Unless you want to drive out to your place and let me scope everything? Then you could sleep in your own bed."

Angela scowled up at him. "I'm remembering a few things about you, too. Like how goddamn stubborn you can be."

The dimple flashed. "It's good to be remembered." He disappeared again. "I'll strip these and go grab clean—"

"All right, fine." Angela set her stein on the planks next to the recliner and started up the ladder. "But we aren't waking your parents just for stupid sheets." Her head breached the lip, and she saw him standing by a queen-sized bed with gleaming brass head-and-foot boards, a green comforter wadded in his arms and green sheets piled at his feet. *More green.* He watched her uncertainly as she stood up and looked around.

"But these aren't clean," he protested.

"They'll be fine. Like I said, we're *not* getting your mom and dad up for sheets."

"You mentioned something about stubborn?"

"Ha ha."

Angela found herself swatting away a preposterous surge of jealousy; up here, she'd finally discovered a woman's influence. There was actual artwork on the angled walls; floral Monet prints, mostly, but nice. An overflowing green (of course) laundry basket sat in the corner; that was all male. A plain computer desk rested against the flat wall that marked the far end of the barn—not green, thankfully. A laptop (not green) was open on it, screensaver rotating and flashing; his iPhone, brown-leather wallet, and keys lay next to the computer, along with a cream business card with gold lettering. Clean clothes occupied hangers in a wide armoire that took up the rest of the back wall. Skylights had been cut into the sloped ceiling above the bed; well, those were *kinda* windows.

Jack was still just standing there, holding the blanket with the sheets and pillowcase piled at his feet.

"Put those back," she commanded.

He gave a pointed sniff to the blanket: "All right, can't say I didn't warn you." He started re-making the bed.

Angela walked past him to the laptop. The tumbling screensaver, stark black letters against a silvery background, shouted: HAPPY IS THE MAN WHO FINDS REFUGE IN HIMSELF.

"That's profound."

He came up beside her and closed the laptop, then picked up the business card and stuffed it into his wallet and placed the wallet in a desk drawer, then shut the drawer.

She flushed and stepped away. "I'm sorry. I didn't—"

"It's okay," he said quickly. "I just…I'm not used to having people up here." He chuckled; it sounded forced. "It was something I got in a fortune cookie once. I guess it stuck in my head."

"Oh."

They stood there looking at the laptop.

"I'd better—"

"I guess I'll—"

He faced her, smiling, but not enough to bring the dimple. "You first."

"Let's go to sleep. I don't want to keep you up any longer." Angela reached out, hesitated, and then touched his arm; his skin was warm and smooth. She pulled her hand back. "Thank you. You're a good friend."

Jack nodded; Angela thought he glanced at his arm where she had touched him, but couldn't be sure. "Hey, what are friends for?" He walked over to the ladder and started down. "If you need anything, let me know. Goodnight."

"Goodnight."

Angela surveyed the loft again, then considered the bed; she'd never felt so *not* tired in her entire life. She thought about her purse—she'd left it in the car, along with her phone—then decided it would keep until morning.

Angela glanced at the bed again:

Jack and Jennifer's Big Green Bed.

Nope, soooooo not going there!

She stripped to her panties, set her bra on top of the pile, then eased between the sheets; they smelled like a man, like Jack. She stretched out and sighed, then faced the drop where normally there would be a wall; good thing Jack—or Angela, for that matter—wasn't a sleepwalker. She listened to him moving around in the dark; there was a thud, and a muttered curse.

She sat up, holding the sheet to her breasts. "Are you okay?"

"Yeah, just stubbed my toe."

"Well, turn on a light, dummy. If you're stumbling around in the dark for my sake, I'm still wide awake."

"Yes, ma'am."

A dim light clicked on, likely from the stove in the kitchen, or the bathroom; he didn't have any lamps. Jenifer must have taken those; they had probably been green. Angela lay back and listened as he brushed his teeth; then the light went off, and then the brief but intriguing rustle of clothes hitting the planks, and then the sleeping bag's zipper…

Silence.

Angela gazed out of a louvered skylight; stars winked and blinked up there in the black. She wondered what it would be like to make love while they glimmered and watched.

"Jack?"

"Yeah?"

"I feel safe here. Thank you."

"You're welcome."

A charged quiet settled, and Angela grinned up at the stars: he *liked* her! It would be so easy to speak the words, and he would climb the ladder. And then…but as tempting as the idea was—and it *was* tempting!—it scared her more.

She put her back to the missing wall, hugging his pillow between her breasts.

If she did—if *they* did—what then? It was way too soon for her to be in a serious relationship.

So what did she want?

Angela sighed as the late hour began to take its toll; she didn't know what she wanted, not really, but she'd told him the truth: she felt safe. But it wasn't just the place; she felt safe with *him*. Jack would never try anything without her starting it, and she knew in her heart that he would never let any harm come to her, and that was enough for tonight. So Angela pushed aside the image of making love to Rossie under the stars…

For now.

"Goodnight, Jack."

"Goodnight, Angela."

She was asleep in seconds.

10

"Little shits."

A last stroke of sleek fur, head to tail and through the tip, and Jess Barbary dropped the cat on the rough boards. It immediately hopped up on her potting shelf and stuck one back leg in the air and went to town.

Jess huffed through her nose; the nameless cat was getting more action than she'd seen in years. Not that she missed it much; once you arrived in the bizarre country known as your late seventies, you didn't think about sex. Much.

The other four nameless cats purred and meowed and twined her bare ankles as she surveyed her dusty and needle-strewn yard under the glow of the tall security light; nothing there, so she peered nearsightedly into the darkness under the pines, but saw only just that; blurry, piney darkness.

So what riled these fool cats?

She let her right thumb play over the revolver's cocked hammer, and then, with the naturalness of long familiarity, eased it up.

Probably just a raccoon. Jess had lost several cats over the years to the big coons who lived hereabouts. Still, even Big Mike had hissed at the front door as Jess had sat in her recliner with the remote in her lap and a Dewar's rocks in her hand. She hadn't seen Big Mike that fired up in ages, so she'd levered herself up and retrieved her late husband's Smith & Wesson from the nightstand and moseyed outside to see what all the damn fuss was about.

Jess glanced back through the open door; Big Mike rarely stirred from the house anymore, and who could blame him? He was even older than Jess. Mike's shredded ears and scars and faded calico fur were familiar and comforting, but the sight of him now gave her pause; crouched, ready to spring, what was left of his ears up and alert, long tail twitching.

"What is it, boy? One of them mean ol' coons?" More than one set of Mike's scars had come from raccoons, but now he was just fooling himself. "Well, you can forget it, mister. Some big, bad coon will make a meal out of—"

Mike suddenly stood up and *hissed*. The others got up a caterwaul too before darting past her ankles and inside.

Jess squinted out into the yard again but saw even more blurry, piney nothing. Damn her eyes. They'd been slowly failing her, and now she needed her prescription glasses just to read; she should've grabbed them up when she'd gotten up. Her ears were still hunky dory, however (well, for the most part), and she easily heard something moving around over behind her shed.

Jess looked at Mike again. "Hold the fort, big boy." He ignored her, hackles raised and back arched, fierce yellow-green eyes fixed on the darkness beyond the porch. Jess shut the door in his fool face.

All her babies were secure; now it was time to deal with whatever had come to call.

Jess pushed out the screen and down the steps, the thin door whapping shut behind her as she cocked the pistol again and held it down by her leg. Her late husband, the original Big Mike, had been fairly useless, but at least he'd taught Jess how to shoot. She still went out behind the shed about twice a year and plunked Campbell's soup cans from twenty feet; she used to shoot from forty, but her eyes. Jess stalked over to stand under the light and peered toward the shed, but saw only a dim, metallic rectangle with a peaked roof.

"Go on, now! *Git!* I don't wanna have to make no raccoon kits orphans! *Git!*" She slapped the wooden pole with her free hand and listened, but she heard only night peepers. She turned a full circle but saw less than she heard. Jess figured the noise and her people smell had scared it off already, but she marched over to the shed and looked on either side and around the back, just to make sure; the light was poor this far from the pole, though, and Jess saw nothing but even darker blurry and piney dark.

She stomped back over to stand under the light again with an edgy feeling crawling through her. Jess wore only panties under the half-done housecoat, and if somebody *was* out here, then they were getting an eyeful of something they probably didn't want to see.

Not that she thought there *was* anybody.

It's just some old coon...

Jess was tempted to fire a coupla rounds into the air—that would scare whatever it was off—but didn't; little Angie Beaumont down the hill might get all worked up. The girl had married and moved away, but now she was back sans hubby and living all alone in her mom and dad's house, God rest their souls. Good people, the Beaumont's; more importantly, good *neighbors*. Jess turned and squinted down the hill, then frowned; it was lit up like a damn airport down there. Now why would Angie have all those lights on *this* time of night?

Pretty as a sunrise in the mountains, Angie Beaumont could've had every man within twenty miles between the ages of ten and seventy sniffing 'round her tail, but she didn't carry on that way; she was one of those beautiful women that acted as though she wasn't, which only made you hate her more—if you were that type. Jess was beyond all that silliness, now; she liked the girl, even though she wasn't cat people.

Jess snorted. The girl kept telling Jess to call her *Angela*, as if changing your name could change who you really were. But Jess did so enjoy visiting with her—and her coffee—so she didn't hold that foolishness and not being cat people against her.

Well, not much, anyway.

Jess turned another full circle, listening, then gave another snort; there was nothing out here. Stupid cats had rousted her for nothing.

"Little shits."

She eased the Smith's hammer up again and marched back to the porch, put the hook on the screen door, locked the storm door, and then slammed and locked and bolted and chained the front door and went back to her chair and scotch. The television was running without sound, the way she liked it, moving pictures she could watch and think about or not as she chose. She thumped the Smith down beneath the lamp, within easy reach, then settled back in the recliner with a sigh and picked up her Dewar's.

One or two or six more of these honeys and maybe I can sleep tonight.

Jess glanced over at Big Mike, where he puddled on top of her sewing machine; his long tail curled and swished as he stared out the kitchen window.

"You're getting old."

He yawned, displaying fangs that were still impressive.

Jess sipped her drink. Maybe those blasted fireworks still had them flustered. Earlier, the white trash down the road who just couldn't wait for the Fourth had shattered her evening's peace with booms of thunder accompanied by green and purple and red and every other color blooming in the sky; she'd also heard and felt the bone-jarring *thump* of some mighty big ones down by the lake. The cats hadn't liked those *at all*. Jess hadn't much, either. Oh, she'd enjoyed shooting fireworks when her kids were young, but Susie and John both had kids of their own who had kids of their own now (Jess could remember all their names if she tried), and she was over fireworks. She was just grateful she had this holiday to herself, though both her daughter and son had made noises about Thanksgiving and Christmas.

Jess sipped the scotch and settled deeper into the recliner and hoped that's just what they'd been, noises.

She didn't take to a whole heap of company anymore, family or not. The last time they'd all trotted across her doorstep, the subject of a care home had floated around the room like a fart; something everybody knew about, but nobody wanted to bring up. So she'd aired it out herself and told them to forget it. Jessica Barbary could still clean her house and tend the yard and do her own marketing, or even drive down to Sheridan if she got up the notion; for now, Jessica Barbary could take care of herself *just fine.*

She sipped the scotch.

And when the inevitable day came that she couldn't?

Jess glanced at her late husband's revolver shining beneath the lamp's yellow light; there would be no sitting around with the other old wrecks, pissing themselves and watching television with the goddamn volume turned way up.

Nor for Jess Barbary, there wouldn't.

One of the nameless cats hopped into her lap, and she stroked it while it kneaded her thigh and turned circles before curling up. Jess never named them. She would start keeping them if she did, and Jess Barbary was no goddamn hoarder, no matter what some fools down to town said. She had them all fixed and kept them free of fleas and mange and ear mites. Doctor Watkins at the Sheridan clinic sent her a card and a fruitcake every Christmas, but the cheapskate bastard should've sent her something naughty from Victoria's Secret, as much money as she spent with him. Jess lifted the bottle from the floor next to her chair and refilled her glass and swirled it and took a sip, then glanced into the kitchen; too far to get ice.

Neat worked just as well. Hoarders should be shot; she took care of *her* animals. Jess put the bottle down and scratched the little female and leaned back.

But if she *did* name them, this one would be Blackie. Blackie was a wiry short-hair with jet fur except for one white sock on her left hind leg, and she had spunk. Once a year or so, or about five or six strays—half-a-dozen was her limit; any more and the hair got too bad—she would put free-cat ads in all the local free rags. Jess made those who responded come to her so she could judge them and had turned more than a few away; some people were trash, plain and simple, and Jess had learned the hard way that not all who wanted a free cat wanted it for the right reasons. It was just about time to run the ads again.

She took a sip, then leaned back again and rested her eyes. Maybe she'd find sleep tonight. Sleep was like sex; both were luxuries the young took for granted. What had those fool animals so worked up? Even Big Mike had got in on the act. She'd named him after her late husband, a big, handsome man with a big voice and big dreams. Jess snorted softly without opening her eyes; Big Mike had turned out to be a big man with a small imagination, small work ethic, and a small penis. What a naive idiot she'd been to marry him, but regrets were for fools, so Jess Barbary harbored none. And dumb or not, she'd stuck it out with Mike, raised two kids, and buried him twenty-two years ago this spring; all in all, Jess thought his namesake was better company.

She missed her kids, though; not her own children, but the classrooms full of fresh faces she'd taught English to for forty-odd years until the school board forced her to retire. She'd also been Head Librarian of Inglewood Elementary; dead and gone now, just like Big Mike. They'd closed it in the consolidation fifteen years ago and tore it down three years later; there was a half-vacant strip mall there now, and a do-it-yourself car wash.

She woke herself up long enough to sip the warm scotch. *Little shits.* She missed them so…well, most of them; some had only grown up to be big shits, but a handful had turned out all right. Jess had more of the scotch, then grimaced; those that had been given a chance to grow, at any rate. A depressing number hadn't, taken by auto accidents or the Big C or that useless war over in that godforsaken jungle or what have you, leaving only her memories of smiling and eager little faces.

Jess shook her head and reached down and poured herself another dollop. She was wide awake again; it went like that nowadays. She stared at her bulky Zenith, where a man and a woman were trying to sell her a blanket with sleeves; their smiles were bolted to their pretty faces. She snorted and looked away. Thank God for the mute button; the greatest invention since fire, as far as Jess Barbary was concerned.

Her eyes fell on a framed picture high on the living room wall; she couldn't see it well, but she knew what it showed: her, angry and not bothering to hide it, twenty-five years ago or thereabouts, accepting her forced-retirement plaque before an assembly of bored kids.

Conan the Librarian; that's what some little shit had christened her long ago, a play on her last name; she'd pretended to hate it, but she'd secretly been pleased. Those trashy, musclebound *Aaaanold* movies had come out in the early eighties, but she could've told the little shits that Robert Howard penned those stories decades before—not that they cared. Conan the Librarian: Her Ruler was Her Sword; woe betide the child that didn't return a book on time—or worse, lose it and then have the temerity to not pay for it.

Jess's head nodded. *Little shits.* She'd burned that insulting plaque, yes indeed, but she still kept her ruler in her panty drawer, and Jess dug it out now and then and swished it around, nostalgic for the snap as it connected with little knuckles. She even sniffed it sometimes, and its heavy, dull-green plastic still smelled like glue and chalk and pencils and musty hallways.

Like fear.

Like children.

Her chin touched her chest, and she fell asleep with a bitter half-smile.

Jess came awake with a yell as the cat dug its claws through her robe.

"Ow! You little—" She tried to dump it off, but by that time it had already jumped. That's when it penetrated through the fog; *all* the cats were going bonkers, including Big Mike. He was atop the sewing machine, back arched, fur stiff, facing the front door and hissing up a storm.

"Oh, for Pete's sake. There's nothing—"

A crash shut her up. That was no coon; it sounded like her screen door had just been ripped off, but that was impossible. Maybe a limb had fallen on the house; several of the big Ponderosa needed trimming, but Jess would be damned if she paid some tree service when she had a son and three strapping grandsons. If they wanted to eat her ham and cranberry sauce on Thanksgiving, by God they could—

A sound came then, one Jess had heard thousands upon thousands of times; the latch on the storm door rattled.

Her old heart managed to reach a gallop. "Who the hell's there, by God? Don't you know what time it is?"

There was an awful silence; her heart was still whamming along, and Jess could feel blood pushing into crannies it hadn't visited in quite some time.

Then there was a crash that made her jump as her storm door went, and something pointed and sharp blasted through her front door, between the bolt and the jamb, and was withdrawn. Cats yowled and scattered as her hand drifted toward the Smith; maybe she was dreaming all this.

She fumbled for the revolver, spilling fragrant single malt in her lap as the pointed and sharp thing blasted through again, splinters flying, and then someone shouldered her compromised front door open, tearing the chain like linguine, and stepped inside.

Jess's mouth dropped open; now she *knew* she was dreaming. She brought the revolver around, but she'd grabbed it up up-side-down, and both the open sight and the hammer caught on the arm of the chair and tore it out of her hand; it landed on the carpet next to the Dewar's with a dull thud.

Jess looked over the edge at it—*damn*—then straightened and considered her unwelcome guest; he stood tall and still, staring down at her from on-high, holding an ax in both black-gloved hands; somehow she found her tongue. "Well hi-ho, daddy-o. That's some getup. I don't know what you're selling, but part of your pitch better be fixing doors."

He only stood there, looming tall and strange, looking at her silently; waking up from this dream was sounding better and better. "Don't just stand there like a lump. You wanted in bad enough, come sit a spell." *Was* this a dream? It had better be; those blank, round sunglasses made the blood thrumming through her heart turn slug-gish. Just in case it wasn't, Jess dropped her hand and oh-so-casually pawed for the Smith; when she had it again, this feathered fool would find he'd brought an ax to a gun fight.

He suddenly kicked over her coffee table and sprang forward and pressed the eye into her chest, *hard*, rocking the recliner back against the wall. She gasped, then found the comforting weight of the revolver and brought it up and around, but he snatched it away lickety-split; still pinning her in the chair with the ax, he lifted the stainless-steel revolver and studied it.

Jess was having trouble breathing with the ax head in her bread-basket, and black leather and chrome zippers and a hooked, red beak filled her vision; a long tail arched behind him, thin crimson feathers hanging over her silent television; those round glasses were solid black pits.

"Wha-what do you want?"

A hissing yowl, and then Big Mike flew in and latched onto his leg. He reached down and ripped Mike away and flung him into the kitchen. The cat cartwheeled through the air and crashed into the edge of the Formica counter next to her refrigerator and slid to the linoleum, and at the sight of his crumpled form, Jess Barbary knocked the ax away and lurched out of the chair and flung herself on him, fingers clawed like her Big Mike's.

"*Don't you hurt my babies goddamn you you sonofabitch!* Get out! Get out of my house!"

He had backed away and bumped into her overturned coffee table when she'd scrambled up, and she almost had him when he reversed the ax and swung, quick as lightning; white light, as if someone had taken her picture, and then darkness, swimming up like heat from desert hardpan.

That hot dark took Jess far away.

A noise brought her back.

It was loud, and right over her head, and reminded her of that time she'd been silly enough to get talked into riding one of those awful roller coasters; it had come from underneath them as they'd climbed that first big hill: *clack-clack-clack-clack-clack-clack*. This racket had pauses in it, though, unlike that horrible climb: *clack-clack-clack*-pause, *clack-clack-clack*-pause.

Then Jess realized her arm was being raised over her head, and she had to go up on her toes to ease the pressure. The clacking stopped, and labored breathing replaced it; the sonorous breather moved behind her, and then more ratcheting, clacking noises as her other wrist hoisted into the air.

What in the world?

Jess lifted her head and opened her eyes.

Pain blasted through her skull, almost blinding her, but slowly the agony eased and her vision cleared as her second hand came even with the first; the noise stopped. She had to stand on the balls of her feet to keep her shoulders from popping out of joint. A bright light shone in her face, making it hard to see straight ahead, so she squinted down at herself.

She was buck naked.

He stepped around in front of her; the light put his feathered face in shadow, but that plump comb had a blood-red corona. Her head throbbed, and her wrists and shoulders and lower back and calves were on absolute *fire*.

Nonetheless, Jess worked moisture into her mouth and then spit it at him; it fell well short, but the gesture was what mattered. "Like what you see, boy? Too bad you didn't visit me forty years ago. Wouldn't've found any better 'round here, I guarantee *that*."

He just stood there and looked while she panted and shifted and tried to ease the pressure on her shoulders and wrists. Abruptly he turned and walked away.

She squinted past the light, watching as his giant, wacky outline moved past her riding mower and vanished into the night. That's when Jess knew she was hanging in her own blasted shed. Big Mike had used it to work on his junk cars—his fool "projects." All his tools and gewgaws were still out here, gathering cobwebs and dust, and the only thing she used it for was to store the mower and the snowmobile and the ladder and the occasional tool when she needed it. She squinted at the light source and saw that her own metallic-green LED Maglite had been propped on the snowmobile's cover to shine right in her face.

"Christ A'mighty," she whispered.

Jess squinted up at what held her and then understood the ratcheting; her husband had liked to yank the engines out of his junk right here in this shed with his homemade "cherry picker". She wasn't sure—too many years and too much Dewar's—but she thought that's what he'd called the contraption. It was bolted to the shed's metal rafters, and one chain held her wrist while another chain held the other.

She squinted harder and discovered that two of her own dish-rags had been used to fasten her to the chains. *Now that's just too much.* She gave a few weak jerks, but she was in an awkward position and tied tight, so Jess quit that useless crap and thought about scream-ing for help. But who would hear her? Angie? She was the closest, but what could that sweet girl do except get hauled up beside her? Jess's next closest neighbors were a half-mile in the other direction on the other side of the highway, and white trash to boot. Still, she wasn't just going to give up like some craven milksop.

Jess took a deep breath and screamed for all she was worth.

She had just sucked in her fourth lungful and was hitting her stride when he appeared before her again. Jess panted, glaring, re-fusing to show fear; Conan the Librarian wouldn't give this sono-fabitch the satisfaction.

"Well, here we are, big boy. I gotta say, you sure know how to show a girl a good time."

He moved closer and stared down at her, blocking the light, and then held up something in his black-gloved hand. Jess thought it would be the ax, so she blinked in astonishment when she saw her own green-plastic ruler hovering a foot from her nose; it and his hand shook, as if he had some sort of palsy, but Jess barely noticed.

My ruler?

He moved to the side and presented the trembling ruler in the light, making sure she could see it; making a *point* of showing it to her. His breathing was labored and loud, as if he were about done in, but he still said nothing as he turned the ruler; he hadn't said a single word since he'd chopped through her door.

"W-what do you want? Who are you?"

He gripped both ends and snapped it, then held the jagged pieces for her to see, expressionless feathered face directly above hers now, round sunglasses twin holes into the abyss.

"Please," Jess whispered. A tear rolled down her cheek. "*Please.*"

He didn't answer. He only began.

Tuesday

11

I didn't sleep a damn wink.

What I did was lie in my musty sleeping bag and stare up at the lip of my loft and listen to the woman in my bed breathe; sometimes she would snore. Not bad, though; it was a cute little rasp of a snore.

It was also pure torture.

On the plus side, I had the entire night to think about important stuff—you know, stuff like how if I didn't make bank this week I might have to close Crazy's; stuff like what the hell were we going to do with Dad if he couldn't be left alone? But mostly I thought about Angela's stuff. I thought about her stuff a lot.

No. We're just good friends; I'm pretty sure I thought about that particular word more than anything else; *the eff-word.* Not the right eff-word, especially with a beautiful woman in my bed, but there you go.

It was a long night.

Angela woke as the cockcrow bled through the skylights and sharpened the interior of Casa Jack. I could hear her getting dressed, and I pictured each article as it slid on; things have to go in a certain order, right? That fun mental exercise ended when she climbed down and then stood there looking at me.

I played possum. I don't know why; maybe I was scared she'd tell me what a good eff-word I was again. I watched through slits as she finally tired of staring at me and walked to the kitchen and squatted to pet Jezzie and whisper she was a good girl and to take care of me. Then she stood up and looked at me one more time before slipping out. I laid there until I was sure she was gone, then unzipped and sat up and glanced over at the dog.

"Eff me."

Jezebel smiled her toothy smile and waddle-wagged to the door and snorted and bounced on her front paws, impatient to take care of business. I dragged my ass out of bag and let her out, then brewed coffee; my head felt like someone had blown insulation up my nose, but the bean water helped—to some extent. It was the third of July, we would (hopefully) be swamped, and here I was running on zero sleep; it had been a long night, sure, but it would be a longer damn day.

I carried a steaming mug up, then stood and sipped and surveyed; nothing seemed disturbed, but there was only one thing up here I didn't want her to see; it had been a damn close call last night. I went over and opened the desk and got my wallet out and removed Miriam's card; I thought about ripping it up…and then put it back.

The kids are going camping Saturday night, and Angela and I are just eff-words.

I stood next to my bed and held the coffee out to the side and bent down; a wondrous whiff of woman came to my nose, and, greedy for more, I peeled back the blanket and sheets and lifted the pillow to my face; *there* she was: lotion or body spray or shampoo or perfume or whatever, it was pretty darn neat. I covered it back up to preserve the scent and then scooted down the ladder.

I know, I know, kinda creepy and sad, but when I finally get to sleep tonight, I want company; eff-word or not, Angela smells incredible.

I showered and shaved and then took a long gander in the mirror over the bathroom sink: five-eleven, brown, brown. Average. Who was I kidding? Why would a woman like Angela Beaumont want anything to do with a guy who framed houses three-quarters of the year and ran a roadside burger shack during the summer? Don't forget convicted felon and broke; Jenifer sure hadn't. She'd jumped the fence for greener pastures—also known as my thrice-divorced dentist with four kids down in Sheridan, whom she'd married after only two months of courtship; a whole two-and-a-half months out from *me*, the man she'd supposedly loved. But I wasn't the least bit bitter about it.

Yeah.

In short, I was prime eff-word material for a woman like Angela, and that's all I would ever be. Against my will, an image of Zane formed: jet-haired, buff, and handsome. Sneering. Don't forget rich. He obviously liked Angela, too…but did she like Zane?

No.

I would *not* do this to myself. I turned away from my brown mundaneness and squared my shoulders, even though I really wanted to crawl back up the ladder and take a ten-hour nap.

Time to go to work.

I locked up and scratchy-scratched Jezzie and told her to monitor the fort and started my truck, then glanced over at the porch; Dad wasn't in his chair. If he'd noticed Angela's car, I would hear all about it. Mom's car was in the carport because she was still getting ready; I didn't need to go in this early either, but if I let myself lie down, I wouldn't get up until the Fourth or the fifth, or maybe even the sixth.

I put my old beater into gear and rumbled down the long, rutted driveway and drove through a sleepy Indian Head and wound down to the lake. The whole way, I tried to stop thinking about Angela and her stuff, but I might as well have attempted to quit breathing; however, when I crunched into Crazy's lot, I discovered something new to focus on.

"Mother *fucker!*"

The plywood barriers were still lowered over the front and side windows, and neither of the heavy-duty Master Lock all-weather padlocks had been tampered with, nor the steel hasps, but someone had spray painted "KILLER" in drippy maroon letters two feet high on the front board beneath the awning; I ventured around to the side and saw "MURDERER".

I stood there and took several deep, careful breaths while a black Z-71 pulling a white-on-blue ski boat drove past on 269; I could *feel* the occupants staring. How many people had seen this since the sun came up?

Goddamn-mother-fuck!

I unlocked the padlocks, but before I raised the plywood, I studied the tags; "Killer" had been underlined three times in descending length, like an upside-down pyramid. It sure wasn't the artwork I'd seen tagged on freight cars, but it got the message across. I secured the heavy boards and unknotted my jaw and hopped in the truck and glanced both ways before blasting across to the Shell.

I didn't know the kid slumped on the stool behind the counter; Auschwitz thin, he'd shaved his hair in back, but he had to brush his bangs aside just to see me. He also sported several earrings and a chrome hoop through his left nostril and a double-handful of piercings across both eyebrows. *Ouch.* The badge on his red-and-yellow Shell Polo had been pinned crooked below the little shell, and informed the world he answered to "Eric". Eric looked like he was seventeen max, but since he was by himself I knew he had to be at least twenty-one to sell beer; the knobs of his spine were outlined through the shirt.

"Hi," I said. "I own Crazy's." I pointed across the highway, just in case Eric didn't know where or what Crazy's was; he didn't follow my finger, only looked at me, holding his bangs with one translucent, tattooed hand: "Someone vandalized my place last night," I informed Eric. "I need to look at your security recording."

That got a reaction; he hunched to the end of the counter and squinted through the plate-glass, swishing his bangs up to do so. "No shit? Man, that sucks." He ambled back to his stool. "Why don't you call the fuzz?"

"I will in a minute." That was a lie; there would be no fuzz-calling. Oh, if we'd been inside city limits, I would've called Chief Rogers because I knew he'd be fair with me. But down here we were in Sheridan County, and I knew Sheridan County's finest would do nothing for Jack Ross; they knew it too, even if Slouching Boy Eric didn't. "But first I want to see for myself. Mr. Wright's my landlord, and he has a camera, the one over on the south end of the far pump island, pointed across to keep an eye on his property."

A furrow appeared between the piercings, but otherwise Eric didn't respond; maybe I'd been yammering away in Etruscan and just didn't know it. I tried again:

"You guys record to disc for seven days, so it'll be on there."

"Man, I don't know…" Then Eric got a bright idea; I could tell because he shifted a fraction of an inch on his stool and straightened two vertebrae. "You could ask Donna, she'll know about that stuff. She comes in at noon. I just hired on last week, and now I gotta work the fuckin' Fourth. Don't that suck?"

"Just call Mr. Wright, he'll tell you it's okay." I started around, aiming for the tiny office; I was almost twitching, I was so eager to find out who had paid me an artistic visit.

"Whoa, you can't come back here." Eric slid off the stool and held out a tattooed stick-arm; I stared at him, then spoke carefully, making sure I hadn't slipped back into Etruscan.

"Call Mr. Wright. He'll tell you it's fine." Eric fidgeted, and I thought about just pushing past him; what could he do, remove an eyebrow ring and scratch me with it? "I'll wait until he gives the all-clear. Okay?"

"Hey man, I believe you're righteous, but the big guy's over in Jackson Hole with the fam. I got the number, sure, but we're not s'posed to call unless we get held up or somethin's on fire; this is his vacay, know what I mean?"

"Yeah." *Shit.* "I know what you mean." I pulled my phone. "I'll call him. That way it won't blow back on you."

Eric plopped on the stool and assumed a relieved slouch. "Hey, that's cool."

I stood between a display of cheap, overpriced sunglasses and a rack of magazines and found Darryl Wright's number and hit the button just as an SUV and trailer hoisting tandem jet skis parked at the pumps. A man and a woman and two sleepy kids got out and the woman and kids came inside and browsed and yawned as Darryl's cell rang and rang and rang; I left a brief message outlining the situation and apologized for bothering him during his vacation.

After the family left, I stepped up to the counter; Eric was back on his stool, slumping away. "I left a message. Mr. Wright should call soon, and then I'll be over to look at the recording. I appreciate your help, Eric. I'm Jack." I stuck out my hand.

Eric brushed hair out of his eyes and considered my hand as if wondering what it was, then shook; his grip was as limp as the rest of him, and if aliens swept the planet with a giant magnet he was screwed, but at least he was trying to do right by Darryl.

"Thanks again for the help. I mean it. There's a free cheeseburg-er in it for you. Just pop over any time."

Eric sat up maybe an inch; pure and exuberant joy. "Sure thing, bro. Hey man, me and my girl stopped at your place coupla weeks ago. It was good shit."

"Thanks."

The bell *ding-dinged* as I yanked open the door; perhaps I should stencil "Good Shit" on the menu board. I hopped in my truck and slammed the door so hard the glass rattled; anorexic Eric of the face jewelry and wet-spaghetti spine had landed a girlfriend, but I was just eff-word material. The world is a wondrous, mysterious, and shitty place sometimes.

I drove back across the highway and got to work.

12

Miguel and Donnie arrived at ten, right on time, but Tiff was late; not unusual, so I thought nothing of it at first. Donnie told me I looked like shit. I told him I looked better than I felt; I didn't mention our artistic visitor, not yet. We got the place prepped, and by twenty 'till, still no Tiffany.

Donnie said, "Where *is* that Jesus freak?"

"Good question."

No text saying she'd be late. Darryl hadn't called me back, either. I'd also secretly hoped for a call or a text from Angela; I wouldn't even mind her telling me I was a good friend again…well, not much. But right then I needed to call Tiffany; at the last second I decided to send a text, since I wasn't sure she actually talked on her phone.

Where are you? It's 10:43.

I slid the iPhone back in my pocket and went about my business, fully expecting a text back saying she was right down the road, but when 10:58 rolled around and still no yellow convertible bug, I began to worry; there'd been two bad wrecks already that summer on the sharp curves coming down the mountain, and I'd seen the way Tiff zoomed around in that bug.

At the stroke of eleven, three pickups pulling boats crunched into the lot just as I flipped to "Open". I took the first order and then my phone rang, the neutral tone. I motioned Donnie to cover the window and ducked around the ice cream cooler.

"Hello?"

"Is this Mr. Ross?" It was a woman, and her tone was frosty enough to rival the box next to me.

"Yes. Who is this?"

"This is Mrs. Downing. Tiffany's mother."

"Okay."

I closed my eyes because I knew what was coming, but I said what was expected of me even though it was a waste of breath; sometimes you just gotta play the game out.

"Do you know where she is? Tiffany was supposed to be here by ten, and—"

"Tiffany will not be working for you any longer, Mr. Ross. She informed us of your…history…last night, and I will not have my daughter employed by a murderer. In fact, if we had known that's what you were, her father and I would never have allowed her to work there in the first place."

The phone's case creaked in my hand, and somehow, *somehow*, I worked my jaw free enough to say, "I see."

"I'm sorry if this inconveniences you, Mr. Ross, but Tiffany's father and I have made up our minds."

She didn't *sound* sorry. "It's fine, Mrs. Downing." Things could get hairy with three, and undoubtedly would at some point, but we'd survive: "I'll mail Tiffany's last check. Tell her thanks for me, and that she's welcome to drop by anytime." The right thing to do would have been to tell me to my face, not get Mommy to call, but sixteen-year-olds are a lot like politicians in that regard; they know the right thing, but getting them to actually do it is tough.

"My daughter will not be 'dropping by', and thank you, Mr. Ross, but either her father or I will pick up Tiffany's last check. I do not want a convicted murderer to have our address."

The line went dead, and I wanted to call the hypercritical cunt back and tell her I already knew where she lived; the address was on Tiffany's application. But, as much fun as that would've been, I didn't; she would likely call the fuzz, as my new buddy Eric would put it, and Sheridan County's finest would race here a helluva lot quicker than they would have if I'd called them about the vandalism.

I knew the score; it wasn't hard to add up. Mommy and Daddy had made Tiff get a summer job, and like a good girl she had, and Mommy and Daddy had been happy and proud of their good girl. Now she'd done what Mommy and Daddy wanted *and* she didn't have to work the Fourth *and* she would have the last six weeks of summer free.

It was kinda slick. Hell, I almost admired her for it.

Almost.

Had this move just occurred to her, or had she planned it all along? I suppose it didn't matter. I shoved my phone away and got back to work.

Donnie said, "Well?"

"Well what?"

"Is the silly bitch coming or not? For craps' sake, Jack, you let her get away with—"

"She's done, man."

"What?"

"She quit. It's just us three."

I expected an explosion, so when Donnie stayed silent, I looked over at him; he was just standing there with a greasy bag dangling from each hand and orders piling up in the dungeon window behind him and a lost, hurt expression.

I rested my hand on his shoulder. "You all right?"

He shrugged me off and turned away. "I'm fine."

I watched him for a few seconds, then looked in at Miguel, who gave me the patented Miguel-Shrug and went back to bee-bopping to his iPod. Tiffany, no Tiffany; didn't make two green shits to Miguel. Almost five minutes went by before Donnie said a word; it was some kind of record, but I wasn't happy about it.

"She didn't even…"

That's all. But I understood: no goodbye or lick-me; not even a measly fuck off. That's hard to take when you care for someone. When I saw Donnie swipe at his eyes with the sleeve of his dark-blue Crazy's tee-shirt, I pretended not to notice.

Donnie isn't the guy who lands girls like Tiffany; I figure he's smart enough to know it, too. But that hadn't stopped him from dreaming. I wanted to tell him that it wasn't all it was cracked up to be, that he really wasn't missing anything, but I kept my mouth shut because I doubted that tidbit would comfort him.

It was a long, quiet lunch.

All day we got hit with wave after wave, but we bailed hard and stayed afloat. Still, I was beginning to worry about supplies again; I'd snagged enough dry goods from Marcie's yesterday to last the week—or so I'd thought—and I'd originally ordered what I'd *thought* was enough food to get us through 'till Saturday, when Metro would next deliver, but at this rate we'd run out of fries around Thursday night and burgers Friday afternoon. Not good. And no way would they deliver sooner, not with the holiday; not to *my* little account.

We finally caught a break around three. Donnie was out back smoking. Miguel was in the dungeon doing Miguel things. I leaned my elbows on the stainless-steel order counter and let it hold me off the floor as I watched seventeen carloads and four crowded picnic tables snarf my fare. That's when a familiar white Camry flashed its blinker and pulled in.

The side door blasted open, smoke billowing: "Miss Wyoming in da *house*, y'all!"

My stomach did a slow jig. "I see her."

Donnie and his cigarette reek came up beside me to peer around the edge of the menu board as the car door opened and a white Adidas cross-trainer with no sock emerged. Attached to the shoe was a perfect tan ankle, and attached to the ankle was a shapely calf, and above the calf was a long, tan leg; then the rest of Angela shut the door and headed our way. I swallowed. Today she had on khaki shorts and a sleeveless white tee-shirt and no makeup, and she was still knock-down gorgeous.

Donnie whistled low, then turned and gently bopped me on the shoulder:

"The Mack Daddy Jack."

I should've told him that Angela and I were just eff-words, but I didn't. She stepped beneath the awning and lifted her sunglasses onto her hair as I slid back the window, offering me a blue-eyed smile that would've stopped birds in flight had any been lucky enough to witness it.

"Hi."

"Hi."

"I just wanted—"

"Did you sleep—"

She laughed and said, "You first."

"Okay. I, uh, I guess you left kinda early; I don't know, I was out. Did you sleep all right?" The smooth operator, pretending he hadn't pretended to be asleep when the woman left. *Like silk, I am.* "Was the bed comfortable?"

"It was fine, and I slept like a baby."

"I'm glad."

She frowned. "You look tired. Did *you* sleep okay?"

"I slept great, but the girl working for me quit, so now it's just the three of us and we've been slammed, that's all."

"Oh."

I became aware of Donnie, jaw resting on chest; I glanced at him, and he blurted, "She spent the night? You *dog!*" He raised a palm: "Skin from the Mack Daddy Jack!"

Angela leaned, trying to see past the board: "*What* did he say?"

"Um, excuse me for a second." I slid the window closed and stood up.

Donnie backed away, hands in the air. "Whoa, whoa, take it easy, I was just—"

"Keep your goddamn voice down. Better yet, just shut the fuck up, okay?"

A nasty grin did unpleasant things to Donnie's acne scars, but he whispered, "Holy shit! You really *are* the Mack Daddy!"

"Shut. The fuck. Up. It's not like that, okay? We're..." I glanced out at Angela, who was reading the menu with her head tilted; I forced it out: "We're just friends." It hurt to say, but I had to be honest with him, and myself.

"Whatever, dude. And I thought *I* was dumb about girls."

"Go away, Donnie."

"I'm gone, man."

I waited until he'd moved toward the dungeon before opening the window. "Hey, sorry about that."

"Everything all right in there?"

"Yeah, I just had to, ah, take care of something."

"Oh. Well, the reason I came by was to say thank you for letting me stay over last night. I know I sounded like a nit, scared of the dark and all that—"

"Not at all."

"—but I appreciate it. You're a good friend, Jack."

"No problem. Hey, what are friends for?"

"Yeah." She frowned at me again. "You *really* look tired. Are you *sure* you slept okay down there? That whatchamacallit you slept on, that..."

"Tatami."

"Tatami. That couldn't have been comfortable, even with the sleeping bag. You should've let me sleep down there, and now you have to work so hard today—"

"Wasn't gonna happen. Barn Rules, remember?"

She smiled, though a little sadly this time, I thought. "I remember. Thank you, Jack. You're sweet."

"One tries."

Our eyes held, and then we both looked away; she studied the menu board again, blonde head tilted in that cute-as-hell way. "I want to try something fresh. I didn't eat until late yesterday, and I had to heat it up."

"What can I get you?" Past her hip, a young couple fought in the bench front seat of an older Dodge pickup; the woman gesticulated toward Angela, wielding a handful of my cheese fries like a weapon. Her boyfriend appeared sheepish, but that didn't stop him from glancing at Angela's legs again.

Busted.

"I think I'll have a double-bacon cheeseburger with mustard and jalapenos only, and a small Crazy root-beer float."

"Done and done, and it's on me. If we're not too busy, I'll bring it out to you, too."

"You don't have to do that, and I want to pay."

"Nope, I insist, Barn Rules. And Barn Rules are enforced at all Crazy's locations worldwide as long as I'm CEO."

That blue-eyed smile again; I didn't *see* any stunned birds hitting the ground, but that didn't mean there weren't some.

"Thank you, Jack."

"You're very welcome."

I closed the glass and wrote her order and stood up. Donnie was in the dungeon whispering with Miguel, who stuck his head out the window and watched Angela walk back to her car. Miguel then jammed the buds back and gave me a Groucho Marx eyebrow wiggle and got back to work; even legs like *that* couldn't throw Miguel off his stride for long.

Donnie came out…and froze.

"What? What did *I* do?"

I sighed. "Nothing." I clipped Angela's order to the wheel and spun it.

Donnie's palm shot up: "Miss Wy-fuckin'-*oming!* Skin!"

Our palms cracked together; I can dream, too.

I stopped counting after six vehicles pulled into the lot following Angela's order. Donnie called her number, and she came to the window, every male eye over the age of twelve following her; most of the women's, too.

"Here you go, ma'am." Donnie wore a silly grin.

"Thank you."

I pressed the double scoop of mint chocolate chip into the plain waffle cone and crowded Donnie out of the way and leaned to look at her, balancing the cone to the side so I wouldn't dump it. "Sorry I couldn't bring that out. We got slammed again."

"So I see." She stared at all the people. "That girl left you guys in a bind. If you want, I could help out."

Donnie, on his way back to the order window, jerked around so fast I thought his neck and spine might separate.

I said, "Uh…"

"What, don't think I'm qualified?" She said it with a smile, but this wasn't a bird-killing smile; *this* was one of those all-female and thus extremely dangerous I'm-only-sorta-kidding smiles.

"It's not that, but, um…"

"But *what?*" The line at the order window was ten deep and growing.

"I appreciate it, Angela, I really do—"

Donnie had been carving something into the order pad, and now he tore a ticket off and slapped it on the counter by my hand and *tap-tap-tapped* it with a red Crazy's pen:

IF YOU SAY NO, I WILL BEAT YOU TO DEATH WITH A BASEBALL BAT.

I looked at him; I think he meant it. I looked back out at Angela. What would it be like to spend all day with her in close, sweaty quarters?

Let's find out. "All right, but go finish your meal first. You can—"

"I'll eat when I get a chance. The door's over there?"

And with that, my new employee walked around and waited to be let in; out of the corner of my eye I witnessed Donnie doing a gleeful soft-shoe by the register, and then I was escorting Angela Beaumont into the glorious environs of Crazy's.

The first thing she said was, "You won't have to pay me, either."

"Wrong. I'll pay you what Tiff was making, eight-fifty an hour."

"You don't have to, Jack."

I pointed over her shoulder at the still-open door. "I do, and if you don't agree, back out you go. We'll manage."

"Fine, whatever." She plunked her burger and float and purse on a back counter. "Show me what to do."

I introduced her new coworkers; Donnie only nodded, tongue-tied, but Miguel stared at her, then gave me a slow head-shake. I wanted to go in there and ask him just what the hell *that* had meant, but I was afraid he'd tell me. Then I trained Angela to serve fountain drinks and Crazy cones and shakes and floats; she had it down in three minutes.

After that, we were a team. Donnie was as shy as a seventh-grade boy at a ninth-grade dance, and almost as silent; it was beautiful. Angela worked hard, and she was funny and sweet and called numbers and served grub at the pickup window with that smile; I'm pretty sure a handful of guys came back and ordered something else, just to talk to her again. I couldn't blame them.

As for me, by the end of the day I was head-over-heels in love. So was Donnie. Hell, Miguel probably was, too.

Tiffany *who?*

And for that matter, *Jennifer* who?

13

Angela never had so much fun in her life.

Part of it was getting to know the new grownup-serious Rossie; oh, he still joked around, but when a customer seemed determined to find fault with everything her family had ordered—and Angela noted the woman waited to complain until the food was almost gone—Jack flashed that dimple, but refused to give a refund; he did give her a coupon for two free Crazy Kid Combos, good for a year, and the grifting bitch went away almost happy. And when teenagers began tossing a football, Jack went out the side door without hesitation. He gave it back after they promised to move away from the picnic tables and the cars, and then he proceeded to show them how it was done; that dimple was in full force when he came back in.

Yes, the new Rossie was an improvement, even though Angela had enjoyed the old model quite a bit. But she'd been a girl then, with a girl's foolish tastes; now she was a woman.

So, how much do I like this new *Rossie?*

"Excuse me, Angela."

Donnie stood behind her gripping the push broom; his eyes roamed everywhere but toward her.

"Sure."

She pressed against the ice cream freezer, and Donnie pushed around the corner as Angela pinched her tee-shirt away and blew down her front; sweat trickled between her breasts, and *God*, her feet hurt! Jack and Donnie didn't seem to notice their feet, but they were used to this. She puffed down her front again.

"You okay?"

Jack was peering out the kitchen—*dungeon*—window. She'd gone in there to watch Miguel during a lull around five, after Jack asked her to park her car over by his truck, and Angela could totally understand why they called it that.

"I'm good." Sweat streaked his face, and there were deep bruises under his eyes. "You look like hell, though."

Dimple. "Thanks."

His exhausted features dropped away and scraping sounds ensued; Jack had taken over the dungeon when Miguel clocked off at six. Crazy's quiet day-cook had then sat outside with his wife and four adorable kids and chowed down; Angela wasn't sure, but she suspected that Miguel had failed to pay for his family's food. *None of my business.* Miguel's wife Maria had spotted her in the window and had done an almost comical double-take, then sniffed so hard it had been audible over the music.

Angela tried to be nice to everybody, but with some, that was easier said than done.

"Excuse me again," came from behind her, and she turned, but didn't move.

"You know, Donnie, you could just say, 'Get the fuck out of the way.'"

He blinked at her. She'd heard him say those exact words to Jack earlier, when they'd been slammed. Jack had cussed him right back, but there'd been a bantering ease to it; Donnie treated *her* like she was still in Montessori school and it was on her last nerve.

Jack laughed. "Yeah, Donnie, just say, 'Get the fuck out of the way!'"

Angela put her hands on her hips; the cloth she'd been using to wipe down the freezer tickled her thigh. "Well?"

"Um…get the fuck out of the way?"

"You can do better than that."

He cleared his throat, crimson flooding his cheeks: "Get the fuck out of my way!"

"Better." She patted his shoulder, then crouched to wipe the side of the gleaming freezer as Jack laughed again and went back to scraping and Donnie pushed by with this sort of dreamy, stunned grin.

They finished stocking at five minutes until nine, then lined up at the front window and looked out at the customers still eating. Angela would've liked nothing better than to sit down, but there was nowhere to do that in the cramped interior of Crazy's.

Then Jack faced them and said, "We had a great day. I didn't think it would turn out that way, considering what I found when I got here, and all that crap with Tiff, but it did." He focused on her. "Donnie and I would've gotten our asses handed to us after Miguel left. Thank you, Angela."

"Yeah, thanks, you were great!"

"You're welcome, guys. I had fun today." Well, except for her feet; she would soak them for an *hour* tonight before bed. *Two* hours. What did he mean, what he found when he got here? He wouldn't tell her, though, saying it was nothing. But then Donnie jumped in.

Angela listened, outrage driving away thoughts of her feet. "Why didn't you call the police and file a report?"

"I didn't tell you about that so you could blab it to the world," Jack told Donnie.

Donnie wilted, pinned under that look, and no wonder; apparently, a big ol' slice of original Rossie still lurked in there. "Easy, man, she works here now. She deserves to know what's going on."

Angela said, "And it's just me, not the world."

Jack sighed, cut those eyes one last time at Donnie, then relented: "I didn't file a report because the cops wouldn't have done anything but just that, file some report; there wouldn't have been any follow-up investigation."

"Why the hell not?"

"Because it's what they think of me, anyway."

Donnie put his gaze on the floor. Angela wanted to reach out and gather Jack to her and hold him when she saw the pain that flooded his face, but didn't; not because of Donnie's presence—well, not entirely—but because there was anger there to more than match the pain.

Bottom line, that expression didn't invite holding.

So they stood and waited for nine o'clock; a car turned its headlights on and backed out and drove up toward town, then another; the last two soon followed, and Jack checked his phone and at the stroke of nine, flipped the "Open" sign to "Closed".

He said, "You guys take off. I'll clean the lot." Grease-spotted white bags and Styrofoam cups and clear-plastic straws and lids and used white napkins dotted the gravel around the three big green trashcans; even more were scattered between the picnic tables.

Angela said, "I'll help." Donnie said he would too, and they all trooped outside and soon had it done.

"Okay, thanks, I'll see you in the morning." Jack awkwardly stood there, not looking at them, and Angela's heart went out to him. Even so, she made her voice firm; firm but gentle:

"Show me." An idea flickered, but she needed to *see*, first.

"Yeah man, show us what that puke did."

He gave them each a long look, then shook his head and trudged over and lowered the boards and locked them down with giant padlocks. He stepped away, and they all just stared for a few seconds.

Then Donnie grated, "Fucking asshole."

"What will you do about it?" she asked Jack.

"Dad has spray paint in the shop. I'll steal some in the morning and cover this up. I'd do it tonight, but it's not like anyone comes down here after the ramp closes, anyway."

Angela could tell he didn't like leaving those hateful terms blaring from his place for even a millisecond longer than necessary, and she was about to share her fledgling idea, but Donnie beat her to it:

"Fuck that. I've got wall candy in the ride, man. We'll blob this bullshit lickety-split." He dug his keys out and crunched toward his Accord; he must've felt their stares, though, because he stopped.

"What?"

"Why are you carrying spray paint, Don?"

"Hey man, don't judge. Just be happy I roll prepared."

Angela shared a shrug with Jack, and then Donnie was showing them the can: "It's Navy Blue." The ball rattled. "Time to make that happy horseshit like it never was." He stepped beneath the awning.

"Wait." They looked at her. "I've got an idea."

Jack listened, then said, "That's a lot better than blue blobs." Donnie hesitated. "Go ahead, give it to her. She's an artist."

Angela took it, a warm flush spreading through her body; she wanted to kiss Jack right there and then, but shook the can instead. They watched as she sized the boards up, then stood on tip-toes; when she was done, she stepped back.

Donnie said, "Holy crap." Jack said nothing, but when Angela looked over, she was greeted by that dimple.

She said, "I'll need a stepladder to finish the top, but that should do for tonight."

The long front board now read: *Our Shakes Are* **KILLER!!** She'd added blue curlicues in the corners she could reach; they were supposed to be waves. The side board now read: *Our Burgers Are* **MURDER!!** She'd covered the last two letters with extra-thick exclamation points; it wouldn't win any prizes, and she needed to do some touch-up in the daylight, but Jack was right: it was better than blue blobs. She handed the can back to Donnie.

He said, "You're awesome, Angela. You really *are* an artist."

"Thank you." She stretched up to peck his whiskery cheek. "You're pretty cool, too."

Donnie stood stock still, then touched his cheek and looked at his fingers before stumbling toward his car. He jumped in and started it up and peeled gravel onto the highway; they waved, he waved back, and then he was gone.

Jack's grin stretched from ear to ear, showing *both* dimples.

"What?"

"I think Donnie's finally met his match; the Beast never could stand up to the Beauty, as I recall."

"Oh." Angela blushed a little. "He's sweet."

Jack laughed. "You might be the first person on earth to call Donnie sweet, but yeah, he's a good kid under all the crap. Smart as hell, too. He's a structural engineering major down at UY, full ride. He'll be a sophomore this fall." Suddenly he frowned at something she couldn't see.

"What is it?"

He glanced at her and blinked; he looked so *tired*. "Nothing, really, just that he's been acting weird lately, even for Donnie."

"How so?"

"Oh, I don't know. Just…weird, I guess." At her raised eyebrow, he said, "It's like he wants to say something, but he's worried how I'll react; I think he wants to tell me this will be his last summer."

"Oh," she said.

"And that'll suck, big time, and not only because he's a good worker; he's been with me since Jen and I…since our first season, three summers ago, when he was just sixteen. I think we've even become friends—although sometimes it's hard to tell with Donnie. Hell, with him starting college, I didn't think he'd come back *this* season, but he did. I still don't know why."

"He worships you, that's why."

"I guess."

Silence, and then more silence; Angela shifted from sore foot to aching foot and pretended to study her work on the boards.

Then: "It's funny how life works, you know?"

"What do you mean?"

"Well, I envied you and Chris because Bill did all the stuff he was supposed to, like fishing and camping and ball games and cookouts, and he was always there for you guys, especially after your mom died. On the other end of the spectrum, you have Donnie; his dad took off when Donnie was little, left his mom to raise him by herself. And then you have *my* dad; he's never gone anywhere, but I think it would've been better if he had."

"Oh."

"Life's just fucked up sometimes, I guess is what I meant."

"Yeah."

There was a sudden pop and crackle, and they turned to watch purple, silver, and red sparkles bloom above the jagged pines; when the early fireworks faded, he faced her again.

"Uh, look, I really appreciate today, but you don't have to come back. We can handle it if, you know…"

"You're firing me already?"

"No! No, I just thought…I usually hire kids, like Donnie and Tiffany, and—"

"Did I help or not? Was all that earlier about 'Oh, thank you, Angela, we wouldn't have made it without you, Angela' just bullshit?"

"It wasn't bullshit." He squinted at her. "You *liked* it, didn't you."

"I told you, I had fun." She winced and leaned against Crazy's and lifted an ankle to rub. "My *feet* didn't, but they'll adjust. Seriously, Jack, I've been cooped up in that house for almost eight months. I think I need this."

"If you say so."

"I do." She set her foot down. "Besides, Chris has been on my case about getting a job."

"I'm pretty sure working for me isn't what he had in mind."

"You let me worry about Chris. Deal?"

"Deal."

More fireworks popped over the pines; they watched for a minute, Angela extremely aware of how close he stood.

"Tomorrow night will be the big show over the lake; we'll be able to catch most of it from here."

"I'm glad. I think I was about seventeen the last time I saw it."

"Good. Hey, uh, was everything okay at your place when you got home this morning?"

Angela hesitated, then said, "Yeah, but I left without bolting the front door. How schizoid is that? Freaking out and thinking someone's outside, then I go and leave the door unlocked."

Jack frowned. "That doesn't sound like you. Did you check the whole house?"

"Upstairs and down. Nothing missing or disturbed."

"Okay," he said, but that frown lingered.

Then more fireworks…and more silence. He cleared his throat and half turned toward her, then told the parking lot, "I guess I'll see you in the morning. We get here at ten to prep, but you don't have to come in that early if—"

"I'll be here at ten, Jack. You don't have to treat me special." Her feet were going to *fall off* tomorrow night, but she would tough it out.

"All right, see you at ten. Goodnight.

"Goodnight."

Angela followed him across the lot to the accompaniment of more fireworks; they were popping in all directions now, eager kids (and no doubt a few adults) getting a jump on the Fourth. He opened his door and looked over at her as she opened hers.

"Thanks again. I don't know how we'd have made it through today without you."

"You're welcome." Angela smiled, and he smiled back; maybe she would draw him standing on the other side of his truck, smiling across the toolbox at her like that; she would leave out the raccoon circles etching his eyes, though.

He got in and shut the door and started the engine, and she yelled, "Wait!"

He rolled down the passenger window and looked a question at her.

"Don't leave yet. I want to follow you." Those bruises under his eyes worried her; had the idiot slept *at all* last night?

"You're staying over again?"

Angela felt her face heat. "No, I meant I'll follow you and make sure you don't fall asleep and wrap your truck around a pine tree. You look worn out, Jack."

"Oh. I mean, uh, okay, I knew what you meant. That's probably a good idea," he finished hastily.

"Of course it is."

"Okay." He rolled up the window, and Angela fought a grin until she shut her door, then let it break through. She started her car, and he backed out and pulled onto the highway. Angela followed.

He'd thought that she wanted to stay the night again.

The question is, do I?

She trailed him up the mountain as fireworks flashed in her mirrors, and Angela decided that yes, yes she did; he wanted her, and she knew what would happen when she eventually *did* stay over again…but not tonight. Timing was everything, and tonight didn't feel right. And she enjoyed this new Rossie way too much to rush into anything.

But someday…

She kept her eye on him, but he drove perfectly. When he reached the junction where they would have to go separate ways, he turned and then stopped. Angela slowed, and she had to fight the urge to turn after him; instead, she flashed her lights and honked, and after a pause he honked back. Then he was gone.

Angela drove the rest of the way home with a tiny upward curve to her lips.

She was fantasizing about that foot soak as she pulled down her driveway, but when she saw what was sitting on the porch steps, Angela forgot all about it; a small black cat with one white foot stared into her headlights, green eyes flaming. Its tail twitched as she parked and shut off the car, and she heard it meow, a plaintive sound. She recognized it; one of Jess's nameless strays. She got out but left the headlights shining.

"Kitty-kitty-kitty."

Four more padded around the corner of the house, eyes luminous, tails waving; two came on, twining her ankles.

"Meow!"

"Mrow!"

What were the old lady's cats doing down here? A worm of worry burrowed; Angela had cell phone numbers for Jess's son and daughter pinned to her fridge. The son, John, had given them to her last Christmas, just in case something happened to his "stubborn-as-stone mother."

Angela peered up the hill; Jess's security light was a radiating orange ball on top of its pole; beyond it, yellow rectangles glowed through the needles.

She picked up a cat. Its fur was calico, but its stomach and legs were tacky and dark. It licked her hand with a raspy tongue as she brought it to her nose and sniffed, and her eyes widened. Angela stepped over and studied its belly and legs in the headlights. She dropped it. It shot away.

"OhmyGod."

She peered at the lights upslope again as she went around the porch and unwound her hose and washed her hands; cats circled like meowing sharks.

"You guys're thirsty, huh?" The implication sank Angela's heart, and she thought about fetching a water bowl but just sprayed the hose around, soaking the yard, then shut it off and sprinted to her car, leaving cats lapping wet grass as she tore around and back down the driveway; when she got to the highway she barely looked both ways before shooting out. An eighth of a mile later, she made the turn up Jess's steep drive, but Angela's heart sank further at the white envelopes poking from the battered mailbox; Jess Barbary retrieved her correspondence from the bottom of her driveway every single mail-day, without fail.

"OhGod."

Down and to the right, Angela's living room windows shined through the needles as she caromed to the top, and then she gasped and slammed the brakes.

There was Jess's little shake-sided house, but its screen door hung on one hinge, its storm door had been ripped completely off, and its front door had been broken open, almost shredded; the lamp was on, though tilted and throwing funky shadows; Angela spotted the coffee table and recliner lying on their sides. Jess's old Dodge Ram was snugged in the stand-alone metal carport, big wing mirrors folded in so it would fit.

Angela swallowed her heart back into her chest, hesitated, hesitated some more, then shut the car off and got out, gripping her keys so tight she thought she might crush the fob.

"Jess! It's me, Angela! Are you okay? *Jess, answer me!*"

Jess didn't answer.

Angela looked at the only other structure besides the house and carport; the shed. It had a high, peaked roof, and Jess stored her mower and snowmobile in there—or so Angela thought. She'd never been inside, and the double sliding door had been pulled shut every time she'd visited, but tonight the right side door was open about four inches.

Angela stared at that black crack and then turned away.

"*Jess!* Can you hear me?"

She popped her trunk and dug under the rug and rattled around until she freed the four-way; its iron weight felt heavy and deadly in her hand—but, oh, what she wouldn't give for her shotgun right about then. Angela patted her pocket and felt the reassuring rectangle of her phone, then shut the trunk and held her breath; she couldn't hear a thing over her galloping heart.

"Jess!"

No answer.

Angela took a deep breath and walked toward the house.

What could've done that, a bear? But the screen door looked like it'd been *pulled* off its hinges, not clawed. She squeezed around it and stepped up; bloody cat prints covered the porch and the carpet inside.

"Jess?" Angela hefted the tire iron and stepped in and immediately spied the crumpled form on the kitchen linoleum.

"Oh no, Big Mike."

His pink-gray tongue protruded through sharp teeth, gold-green eyes half open and dull. Angela looked around wildly then, and, tire iron leading, sprinted through the remaining rooms; they'd been ransacked, drawers pulled out and closet doors standing open and clothes and sundries scattered, but no Jess.

"Jess? *Jess, where are you?*"

Angela spared one last pitying glance for poor Mike and hurried back to the porch and pulled her phone; it was almost ten. She needed to dial 911. She *needed* to dial 911, now, immediately. Instead, she inched past the hanging screen door, eyes fixed on the peaked shed across the yard; she seemed to float toward that black crack.

Call someone! Don't go in there!

Angela ran the door open with a bang.

The smell hit her first, and then flies smacked her face, her neck, her chest, her arms, her legs; she dropped the four-way, *clang-clang!*, and flapped them away and gagged and spit, and all hope for Jess died.

She spit again, snatched up the four-way, covered her mouth and nose with the pit of her elbow, then stalked into the darkness, pushed a button on the side of her phone, and raised it high.

The Fourth of July

14

Chief Ron Rogers stood with his thumbs hooked into his duty belt, facing east. A burnt-rose false dawn had ventured above the spear-tip Ponderosa, but he wanted the real thing; he wanted the big, golden ball to burn away what he'd seen in the shed behind him.

Rick "Tommy" Toms crunched up and stopped, head swiveling between Ron's face and the brightening sky. Ron didn't help him out, though, just soaked in the quiet while it lasted; Tommy didn't disappoint:

"You ever seen anything like that, Chief?" Tommy hiked his thumb toward the shed. "I mean, back in the day?"

"No." Not a lie, exactly; while Ron hadn't encountered this specific atrocity, he'd seen rage before, and that's what was hanging back there: pure rage.

"Really? I figured in a big city like Seattle, there'd be wacky stuff like this happening all—"

"Go relieve Ryan at the bottom of the driveway and tell him to secure the Beaumont place until the Sheriff's team gets there."

Tommy scuffed from boot to boot. "Aw, c'mon, Chief, I just came up. It's his turn. Let me secure Angie's place."

Ron considered his officer; behind Tommy, yellow crime-scene tape wrapped the dead old lady's porch and carport; earlier, Tommy had ducked under it like it was a partition rope at the county fair. "I want it *undisturbed*, which means you sit at the end of the drive and keep people out. You pull another stunt like before, you'll be at the station writing reports the rest of the summer."

Tommy's face darkened, but he met Ron's eye; the kid was dull as opera, but he had sand, Ron had to give him that. "I learned my lesson, Chief. I won't let you down."

Dumb or not, Tommy deserved a second chance. Everyone did. "All right, go on. Sit on it until I call you or SID gets there."

Tommy hesitated. "Who's Sid? I thought Sheriff Neal—"

"Go, before I change my mind."

"Sure, Chief."

Ron didn't watch him walk away; he was thinking about his slip. SID: Scientific Investigation Division. In the old days, that's who he'd be waiting for, technicians whose sole job was to systematically gather and photograph and video-document evidence; and not only to help solve the crime, but to preserve the chain so some skunk lawyer couldn't rip apart the prosecutor's case on a technicality.

But that was Seattle. This was Sheridan County, Wyoming, and in Sheridan County, Wyoming, Ron was waiting for Sheriff John Neal and a couple of deputies with a fingerprint kit.

He grimaced. Not entirely fair or accurate, but the DCI in Cheyenne should have already been notified, early hour and holiday be damned. Ron and his little department didn't have the resources to deal with this, and neither Neal nor his men had the training—or frankly, the experience. Ron had considered dropping a line to the DCI himself, maybe even the Bureau's field office, but things would be testy enough with Neal as they stood; best to let the man make those calls himself.

Ron pursed his lips at the now turquoise-and-amber layered sky; surely Neal would call for help. Even *he* wasn't egotistical enough to think he could handle something like this on his own. Neal had proven he could diffuse domestics without getting anybody killed—always a tricky proposition in a place where machismo, alcohol, and firearms were equally prevalent—and that he could set up DWI stings and bust pot dealers and root out back-room gambling dens, but in all Neil's years on the job, Sheridan County hadn't had a true whodunit; even the four murders he'd fielded had been gimmes, smoking guns that made it easy to book the bad guy and smile for the cameras and then make it home in time for dinner.

This was another order of magnitude.

"I think she's asleep," Tommy stage whispered. Ron turned, and his left eyelid fluttered before he got it under control; an old tell. The officer he'd just ordered to go guard a potentially important and most definitely unsecured crime scene was standing by Ron's patrol car and grinning at a fluff of blonde hair pressed against the glass. "Man, when we were dating, she had hair down to *here*." Tommy reached around and thumb-tapped his lower back. "Why'd she cut it?"

Ron waited. Tommy finally looked around at him, and the grin faded. "I'm going, Chief." He hustled to his ride and opened the door, then said, "Do you think she's right? She's one lucky little filly if she is."

"That's why we're securing the scene, to find out." He shouldn't have had to say it, but this was Tommy. "Go on, son."

"Going, Chief."

The IHPD cruiser's tail lights vanished over the lip of the driveway, and Ron glanced at the sleeping woman in his car, then looked at his watch and smoothed out an irritated scowl before it could form; the thought of turning this investigation over to a man like Neal made Ron's acid reflux flare, but Indian Head's normal forty-eight hundred plus souls had more than tripled this week, what with the resorts and rental cabins and high-end condos down in the coves filled to bursting, and he and his men were already working twelve-hour shifts with no days off, including his two reserve officers.

I should be happy county's taking lead.

Maybe if Ron kept repeating it, he would believe it.

He watched stars wink out over South Dakota as the Bighorn's loomed unseen behind him; that storied and weathered range had been the reason he'd stopped drifting east after Seattle, though he rarely had time to enjoy it, now. Its snowy caps and abrupt granite slabs would stand revealed, an awesome display that never got old, but Ron waited for the golden ball and Neal, mind churning the case; might as well bat it around while he could.

The victim would point the way to the killer; they always did, the dead reaping justice from the beyond: Jessica Louise Barbary, seventy-nine Y.O.A., cat lover and retired elementary English teacher; two kids, a son and daughter, and several grandchildren and two great-grandchildren, all of which lived out of state. Husband deceased twenty-odd years, and no family staying for the holiday; in his one cautious walk-through before he'd sealed it, Ron had seen no sign of anyone occupying the house but Mrs. Barbary and a herd of felines.

That reminded him; Angela Beaumont had stated that she could provide contact information for the son and daughter; shit detail, they'd called it back when, before letting it ooze down the totem. But even if he was resigned to Neal taking over, Jess Barbary had been one of his:

Ron would notify next-of-kin.

But who was old Mrs. Barbary pointing at? With a woman, you clear the spouse first, then the ex-spouse, and then the other ex-spouse, so on and so forth; then current boyfriends and/or girlfriends and jilted ex-lovers; after them came family and close friends. Strangers were always last, because despite all the ridiculous shows and pop-culture mumbo jumbo, you were much more likely to be bumped off by someone you loved or liked, or at least knew to look at.

That was all well and not-so-good, but Jessica Barbary had been a seventy-nine-year-old widow, so unless she'd been part of a jealousy plagued elder swing-group, that meant—

His radio squawked. "Chief?"

"Go ahead, Flemming."

"The Sheriff's here."

About damn time. "Okay, have him park and walk up. We've got to preserve—"

"Ah, Chief? He's already on his way."

"Of course he is. Head back to the station and start that prelim and keep an eye on things."

"On it, Chief."

Ron hooked the hand-held back on his belt and watched the sky unfold as he listened to the big diesel chug up the driveway; when it rattled to the top, he turned.

Sheriff John Neal pulled the new Chevy 2500 to a halt beside Angela Beaumont's Camry; pearl white, with a star on both front doors and the tailgate, it was spotless. No doubt several trustees down at the county lockup had spent an hour detailing it yesterday. The clatter stilled, and Neal lifted his white cowboy hat off the passenger seat and tamped it on his head before sliding out.

Ron didn't walk over to greet him.

Beneath the hat, Neal's long face peered about, dark eyes missing nothing—or at least giving that impression. His walrus mustache was streaked with gray, and he sported cowboy-cut Wrangler's and down-the-heel cowboy boots and a shiny belt buckle roughly the size of Ms. Beaumont's Camry; the spittin' image of a Wyoming cowpuncher, even though the only things John Neal had ever ridden were barstools and the occasional female county commissioner, the latter being where he'd secured the funds for the new truck; tall and lanky, and throw in the 'stache, people said he looked like Sam Elliot. Ron didn't care what the man looked like as long as Neal served the people of Sheridan County as best he could.

That thought made Ron's acid reflux surge; he knew who John Neal's true master was, and it wasn't the people.

Sheriff Neal eyed Angela Beaumont's car, and then the comatose woman herself in the back of Ron's cruiser before turning a slow, full circle, as if by doing so great insight could be gleaned. Ron suffered through this show in silence. Finally, the mustache pointed his way, and the hat brim bobbed a quarter of an inch.

"Chief."

"Sheriff."

The 'stache twitched toward the shed. "She in there?"

"Yes."

The hat dipped toward the house. "What about there?"

"Porch and storm doors ripped off, so some size, or at least strength, and the front door hacked and pried open at the jamb; an ax pick or crowbar. Something sharp, anyway. Not a sledge. Ransacked, but her purse is still in a pulled-out dresser drawer, with her checkbook and credit cards and a wallet with two hundred and thirty-seven cash. Maybe some jewelry was taken, but if so, I can't tell. We'll…you'll have to ask the family or check her policy. There's a big, dead cat in there with its neck or back broke, maybe both, and she put up a struggle. Officer Flemming was first-on-scene; I was second. I sent him to write up the preliminary. I'll go over it when I get back to the station and then have Mindy email it to you." Ron unhooked his pen and pulled a folded sheet of notebook paper from his uniform shirt pocket and held it out toward the Sheriff: "We marked and cordoned off clear prints at the northwest corner of the metal outbuilding—Men's steel-toed work boots, if I've ever seen them; size 12, or maybe 13—and since I had so much time, I plotted where everyone walked and drove, so they're for sure not—"

Neal strode off on long legs to the aforementioned metal out-building; Ron slipped the folded page back, hooked his pen beside it, and followed. The Sheriff waited as the flies buzzed in and out. Ron stepped up and lifted the ribbon, and Neal ducked under; no thanks were offered. Ron ducked after; the smell was worse.

"Jesus God!" Neal recoiled, then fumbled a crimson handker-chief from his back pocket and covered his mouth and nose. "Give me your Mag," he mumbled. "I left mine in the truck."

Ron twisted his mini on and passed it to the taller man. Neal pointed its bright LED beam into the recesses and held it there for maybe five seconds, then ducked back under the tape, unaided this time. Ron followed.

"Ho-lee shit-on-a-shingle! Is that a *ruler* hanging out of her?"

"Believe so." Hard to tell for sure with all the blood. And the flies.

Neal pushed the mini back at him and stood bent over with hands on knees, swaying and gulping air past the mustache. Ron twisted it off and hung it back on his duty belt and waited. He felt a tinge of disappointment when no puking ensued, but Neal didn't lack for toughness; it was the man's competence and integrity that concerned Ron. The Sheriff scrubbed a forearm across the mus-tache and stood straight.

"The girl found her?"

"Yes."

"You record her statement?"

"Fleming did. I'll have Mindy attach it to the prelim."

The 'stache motivated toward Ron's cruiser. "Let's wake up Sleeping Beauty. I want to talk to her."

Ron followed.

Neal tapped a big knuckle by the blonde fluff, and when it didn't stir, Ron opened the far door and ducked in; she'd propped her cheek on folded hands, just like Lisa when she was little. He pushed away the bittersweet memory and jiggled her foot.

"Ms. Beaumont?" He jiggled harder. "Ms. Beaumont!" She stirred and opened deep blue eyes, then groaned and sat up, hair roostered on one side. "The Sheriff wants to ask you a few questions."

"O-okay." She glanced around, muzzy. "God, what *time* is it?"

"About five-thirty."

"What…" She covered her mouth with a hand. "OhmyGod, Jess." Then the tears started up again; she'd bawled in his arms for an hour last night.

Whap-whap-whap: "Ms. Beaumont? Please step out of the car." Like he was ordering some drunk out for a field test.

Ron kept his face smooth with an effort.

Angela looked big-eyed out at Neal, then at him, and Ron nodded encouragingly, so she scooted and climbed out on his side. Ron shut the door and hooked his thumbs in his belt; this was Neal's show. The only reason he was still around was this girl; she was his people, too.

Angela dug at her eyes with her knuckles, then blinked up at the Sheriff; she was average height for a woman, five-five or six, and Neal towered over her. The 10-gallon hat gave him even more height, which was why Ron suspected the man wore the silly thing.

"You found the body?"

"Yes."

"Your place is right down the hill?"

"Yes."

"Why did you suspect something was wrong? Did you hear anything?"

Ron curbed his impatience and a big dollop of irritation; all this was in the statement, but Neal had to prove he was in charge.

When she finished—again—the Sheriff's eyes held an unpleasant gleam. "Jack Ross? You work at his grease trap? And you spent the *night* with him?"

Angela Beaumont's spine seemed to grow three extra vertebrae; she sure didn't look muzzy anymore. "Yes, I do. And yes, I did. What business is it of yours? Shouldn't you be focused on finding the maniac who did this to Jess, Sheriff?"

"Thank you for your cooperation, Ms. Beaumont." Neal's voice had turned to February up on Cloud Peak. "You can go, but let me remind you that this is an open investigation; there will be no gory rumors spread to frighten the citizens of my county. That's an order. God help us if those media jackals get wind of this."

Angela said nothing, but Neal's mustache should've sprouted blue flames.

"Is that *understood*, Ms. Beaumont?"

"Yes, *Sheriff*, I understand perfectly."

"You'll likely need to come in and record another statement at some point. Will you be comfortable with that, or will your career at your killer boyfriend's burger shack interfere with doing your civic duty?"

"Jess was my friend. I'll do whatever is necessary to catch the sick-o who did this to her."

"That's nice to hear. Go on home now, or back to that murderer's bed, I don't care which."

Ron jumped in before Angela exploded. "I had Tommy lock down her property until your men can get to it."

Angela rounded on him. "You mean I *still* can't go home? I need to shower and change clothes!"

Sheriff Neal eyed Ron sideways past the mustache; he should've thought of sealing the Beaumont property, and they both knew it.

"All right, good work, Chief." Although he couldn't help but add, "Probly a waste of time. It'll turn out she heard a ki-ote or a deer or some other critter."

Angela flung an arm toward the metal shed. "Does it look like some *critter* did that, Sheriff? My, my, selling cars must teach outstanding investigative skills."

The mustache bristled; John Neal had sold used cars for Bob Jr. before running for Sheridan County Sheriff thirteen years ago. Bob Jr. had financed Neil's entire campaign under the table, and every four years since. Neal was Bob's man: root, fruit, and bough; it was such common knowledge who pulled Neal's strings that Ron figured even the squirrels knew what was what in Sheridan County. The tourists currently bursting Indian Head at the seams probably didn't know, but they were from Nebraska, so you couldn't expect too much.

"Now listen here, you little—"

Ron stepped between them. "I need to speak to you, Sheriff." He pulled the taller man away, and Neal shrugged his hand off but followed. "Ms. Beaumont, do you have someone you can call? I don't know how long the Sheriff's men will take to clear your place."

"I'll call my brother." An impressive blue-eyed sneer at Neil: "Or maybe a *friend*." She dug in her purse until she came up with her phone.

Neil halted and intoned, "Remember my order, Ms. Beaumont. No detail of what's in that outbuilding leaves here."

"Oh, I remember, Sheriff." She bared her small white teeth in what passed for a smile—if you were a badger.

Ron tried to lead Neal further away, but the man shoved his hand off again. "What do you want, Rogers? I've got an investigation to conduct."

Ron glanced over his shoulder, but Angela was occupied with her phone; he lowered his voice anyway. "Have you called the DCI?"

"No need. Doc Watkins does all our COD certs." Ron shook his head in dismay, and Neal smiled. "Does that bother you, *detective?* Is that not how things were done in Sea-at-tale?" His laugh grated. "I'll handle this investigation how I see fit. Besides, Cheyenne leaks like me after a twelve pack. The last thing we need is the media up here, stirring folks up, scaring people."

Normally Ron would have agreed, at least about Cheyenne; if word got out about the sheer cruelty of Mrs. Barbary's murder, there would be a mass exodus back to Nebraska. Bad for business, that, and Indian Head relied on the summer tourist season to make it through the slow times, which happened to be the rest of the calendar other than the brief mid-winter ski season. But it was better to be alive and broke than rich and dead, and all his experience and instincts told Ron that whoever committed this crime would do it again; a mind that could conceive and execute such brutality towards another human being wasn't a one-timer.

He explained it all patiently to Neal, then finished with, "We need to warn people. If they run, we'll lose tourist dollars, but the tourists will be alive to spend their dollars next year." *And the DCI will catch wind and take this over, no calls or stepping-on-Neil's-toes necessary; the damn sooner the damn better.*

Neal leaned back on a boot heel. "Well, well. The big, bad detective isn't so big and bad after all. What do you know about Jess Barbary, Rogers?"

Ron understood then that the Sheriff had information he didn't and was enjoying that fact immensely. He wanted to know what it was, though, so he played along, reciting the basics of Mrs. Jessica Louise Barbary, retired English teacher slash widow slash cat enthusiast.

The mustache twitched almost gleefully: "Ah, but do you know the significance of that broken-off ruler?"

"It's the murder weapon. Her injuries are consistent with a jagged object, not necessarily a sharp one. And unless the perp was carrying a schoolhouse ruler around for some reason, I'd say it's what he—or she; always that possibility—tossed the house for."

"You don't know dick, detective. Ha ha, get it? I'll tell you what that ruler means. It means as soon as I saw it shoved up that old lady's twat, I had a suspect pool, not to mention motive. You would've too, if you were lucky enough to grow up 'round these parts."

Ron kept his cool; his left eyelid fluttered, but he kept his cool. "Tell me, Neal."

"Well, glory be! Do I know something the Great Detective doesn't?"

"What does the ruler mean?"

"Now, don't trouble yerself, Chief; I'm sure you've got parkin' citations to issue. Wouldn't want ta distract ya from those."

Ron heard a motor and turned with the gleeful Sheriff to watch three Sheridan County radio cars breach the driveway and park in a row next to Neal's truck. The men inside eyed Angela as she fiddled with her phone; she seemed embarrassed by their attention and put her back to them.

Ron looked up at the Sheriff once more when Neal spoke in an iron tone: "What I told the girl? That goes double for you and your boys. Any leaks, and I'll come down hard. Not a one of you will work law enforcement in the great state of Wyoming again if I have any say."

"I answer to Mayor Ford and the people of Indian Head, Neal, not you. Or Bob Jr."

The mustache darkened. "You want to know what that ruler means, you can follow the trial in the paper like everyone else. Now get yerself gone and take that slut with you. Me and my boys got work to do."

Neil strode off then, waving his arm, and the Sheridan County deputies, six in total, boiled out. Ron headed toward Angela, who saw him coming and ended her conversation; his left eyelid was going good, but he got it under control by the time he reached her.

"Was that your brother?"

"No. We had a big fight the day before yesterday, and he's still sulking. I'm going over to Jack's."

"All right."

Her face clouded. "Don't you start, too, Chief. I don't care what happened in the past. Jack's a good man."

"I wasn't judging, Ms. Beaumont."

Privately, he thought it was a bad idea, but telling her so would get him exactly nowhere. Besides, his long experience sizing up ex-cons told him Jack was a decent sort, and had likely learned his lesson; that didn't make him any less dangerous, though. Ron had met plenty of men who could handle themselves and others, and Jack Ross was definitely one of those men.

"Good." Angela blinked, seemed to steel herself, then faced the yellow-tape-wrapped metal building; big, glistening tears cut down her cheeks. "Goodbye, Jess." She stumbled toward her car, then turned back, swiping at her eyes. "What about the cats?"

"The county will find homes for them." A lucky few might make it; strays were a problem, and the shelter was always full.

She looked at him, then scrubbed her face with the tail of her shirt. "You're a terrible liar, Chief. Anybody ever tell you that?"

"My ex-wife."

"Don't call the county. I'll take care of them. It's what Jess would've wanted."

"Yes, ma'am."

She glared at Neal where he was directing his deputies near the shed; the Sheriff should've keeled over doorknob-dead from the acid in that look. "Don't let *him* call them, either. And please let me know as soon as his men are done. The cats will need food and water."

"I will, Ms. Beaumont. Ah, those numbers for Mrs. Barbary's children? Where are they, exactly?"

"On my fridge, under the Batman magnet."

Ron would've figured her for a ladybug magnet, but he knew people could surprise you, and usually did. "Okay, Ms. Beaumont. Thank you for your cooperation this morning."

She glanced wet-eyed at the shed again before climbing into her car. Ron watched her start it up and back around and go down the driveway, and he wasn't alone; four deputies who were supposed to be searching for evidence watched, and one elbowed another and said something that made the others laugh.

Ron turned back to the sky, but a molten glow now spilled through bunched needles and scaled trunks at ground level, shooting golden rays past the house and carport, making him squint.

Sunrise. He'd missed it.

He glanced at the fly-ridden shed.

And it doesn't help a damn bit, either.

Ron strode to his cruiser and opened the door, then rested his forearms on the window frame and turned his eyes up and breathed deep; those crisp, slab-sided peaks were better than any cheap Chinese fireworks. Much better.

"Happy Birthday, America."

He dug in his uniform shirt pocket and retrieved the folded crime-scene map, then tossed it underhand out into the middle of the drive, where it wouldn't be misconstrued for anything other that what he wanted it construed for.

Ron hopped in the car and drove down the hill.

Despite Neal's wishes, he wasn't heading off to write parking tickets just yet. He intended to warn his people that there was a maniac on the loose, starting with Mrs. Barbary's immediate neighbors. Neal wouldn't like it, but Ron couldn't have cared less; he just prayed to God he didn't find the neighbors in the same state.

And, while he was warning and checking on people, Ron decided that asking a few questions about Mrs. Barbary and a certain green plastic ruler might be in order.

A yawn split his jaws. It had been a long, long time since he'd gone without sleep—Seattle, in fact—and it reminded him of a line from his favorite cheesy movie, *Road House*. Maybe Neal had made him think of it; Sam Elliot starred in it, along with Patrick Swayze, who was dead now. The line came when someone told Elliot's character, Wade Garret, that he needed to get some sleep.

Ron said it out loud: "I'll sleep when I'm dead."

He was powering out onto the highway when his radio crackled. "Chief?" Jennings again.

He snatched the handset. "Here."

"Got another body. Mindy just got the call-out. It's bad, Chief."

"Ah, Christ." Ron took his finger off the button and let his hand sag into his lap.

"Chief? Chief, you there?"

He raised the set back to his mouth. "Tell me."

15

I was halfway through my third kata when the cell rang; the plain tone.

What stranger would call *this* early? It wasn't even six o'clock.

I shot up the ladder and crossed the loft and snatched it from the desk just as it quit; the tone had been a stranger's, but the number was Angela's. One of these days, I need to put her in my contacts and give her a cool ringtone. I called her back and tried to ignore the twisting in my gut; I just knew she'd changed her mind about working at Crazy's. Not that I could blame her.

She answered, "Oh Jack, thank God," and in a tear-clogged voice told me about her neighbor. I sat on my bed and dripped on the comforter, thinking, *Why would someone kill old Mrs. Barbary?*

Then a jolt shot through me. "Did you tell Rogers what you heard Monday night?"

"Yes, and now they've got my house locked down as a potential crime scene. They won't let me in until Sheriff Neal's 'boys' are done with it. That's why I'm calling. I need a shower and a change of clothes."

She let that hang there, but I barely noticed.

"Neal." I eased my grip on the iPhone before the case cracked.

"Yes. He doesn't like you much."

"Yeah, well, the feeling's mutual."

Neal.

"I don't care what he thinks. He's an asshole."

"No argument here."

Teeth-grinding silence.

"Jack? Still there?"

"Yeah, sorry." I pushed Sheriff John Neal away; he didn't go easy. Then what else she'd said whopped me upside my thick noggin. "Uh, did you want to come over and get cleaned up? I think Mom has something you could wear; you're about the same size." She didn't say anything; maybe I'd misread her. "Unless you're staying with Chris. I didn't mean—"

"No, Chris won't answer. I think he's still pouting. And that would be great. Thank you, Jack."

A grin bloomed; Angela was coming over again. To take a shower. "No problem. I'll run to the house and grab something for you to wear. I need to tell Mom about Mrs. Barbary, too. She knew her."

"I don't want to put your mom through too much trouble. Did… did your ex leave anything? Jenifer? Was she about my size?"

I pulled the phone away, looked at it, then put it back. "Yeah, she was about your size, but she didn't leave any clothes."

"Okay," Angela said quickly. "I'll see you in a few minutes. Chief Rogers is headed this way again. He's probably going to remind me to keep my mouth shut, like Neal did."

"Um, you just told me."

"I mean *details*, Jack. Whoever did this didn't just kill her. They…" She sobbed. "I can't talk about it. Just count yourself lucky you didn't see it."

"Okay." *Holy crap, what had been done to that old woman?*

"Thank you so much, Jack. You're a good friend."

"Sure."

She hung up. I sighed, then skimmed a semi-clean towel off the top of the mound and dried most of the sweat and went down the ladder and out the door and quick-trudged across the yard. Jezzie met me, and I scratchy-scratched her ears and told her she was a good girl. She trotted at my heels, but stayed outside when I stepped up on the porch. Dad's ratty green yard-throne was present and accounted for, but the battered Colman and the pile of empties were MIA. I knocked, but didn't wait for an answer; they'd be up.

"Good morning, Jackie." Mom had her back turned as she plated something and clicked the stove off and carried the plate to my father, who was watching the early newscast out of Cheyenne. The cane was propped at his elbow, and Mom moved it before setting the plate on the TV tray that covered his lap, then leaned it back. Dad didn't thank her, or even look at her, just dug in. "Do you want an omelet, or some bacon?"

"No thanks. Um, I've got some bad news."

Mom listened, eyes going wider and wider, then let out a little scream and pressed her hands over her mouth; Dad went so far as to click the TV off. He growled, "I'll be goddamned. Somebody finally did for that mean old whore."

Mom whirled on him. "*Harold Ross!* She was my friend!"

Dad clicked the tube back on and cut a slice of omelet and stuffed it into his mouth; he didn't bother to stop chewing before responding: "Your knuckles bled from that bitch's ruler too, so don't tell me how much you loved her."

"That was a long time ago. I've gotten to know her since then, and she's a fine woman...*was* a fine woman. Dear God!" She turned to me. "You say Angie's coming here, and that she needs some clothes?"

"Yeah. She can't get into her house until the Sheriff's men are finished with it."

"Why? Do they think something happened there as well?"

I explained, and Mom said, "So that *was* Angie's white car out there the night before last. I thought I recognized it. That's so sweet, you two becoming close again." She shook her head. "Little Angie Beaumont. You boys used to bedevil that poor girl, but she'd follow you around like a puppy. I hear she got divorced."

"Yeah, she's divorced, but we're just friends, Mom."

Dad grunted and kept chewing. Mom said, "Ah. Well, let me see if I can…my goodness! I don't have a *thing* fit for a beauty queen!" She bustled down the hall and into her room.

"She just needs a pair of shorts and a tee-shirt, nothing fancy!"

Mom didn't answer.

I sighed and watched the weather. Dad chewed and watched the weather. Highs in the low-nineties and lows in the mid-sixties; perfect for the show over the lake tonight, but a thirty percent chance of scattered thunderstorms on Saturday as a fast-moving system barreled over the mountains. It didn't have much juice to work with, though, which was why only the thirty percent—but if that thirty hit, it would kill traffic on the lake, and I needed Saturday to be busy.

I could hear Mom rummaging in her closet and talking to herself. The seven-day forecast ended and some actor from a sitcom that had gone into syndication around the time I was born began telling me about the life-changing benefits of a home equity line of credit.

Dad muted him and scraped his fork across the plate: "Ya know, son, a rich, spoiled beauty queen is the worst kind of woman to get hung up in." The last bite of mushroom and cheddar omelet disappeared; Dad didn't look away from the aging actor as he offered this wisdom.

"Sure, Dad."

He grunted again. Dad has an entire language of grunts. This one said I was a fool, but he'd done what he could to set me straight, so I was on my own. The news came back, and he put the volume on and we watched a story about construction on I-90 until Mom appeared with both arms so full she could barely see to walk down the hall.

"Mom, she only needs one change of clothes."

"Don't take that tone with me, mister. How do I know what she needs?"

"Because I just told you."

"Well, Angie can pick from these, or just have all of them. I haven't worn any of this stuff in—"

Jezebel started raising hell, and Dad flicked one of Mom's lace curtains aside.

"Miss Wyoming's here."

Mom's glare should have fused him to his brown-leather Lay-Z-Boy; she stamped past me and I hastily opened the front door for her, and then we stood on the porch and watched Angela park her Camry next to my truck and step out.

"Oh!" Mom gasped. "She's so *beautiful!*"

Hard to disagree, even with puffy eyes and no makeup and hair bunched punk-rock style and wearing the same rumpled outfit from yesterday. Angela knelt and loved on Jezzie; the dog's tail was going so fast I thought she might helicopter away… Mom was watching me.

"What?"

"'Just friends'?" She butt-bumped the screen door open before I could formulate a response. "Angie Beaumont, as I live and breathe! Come here, girl! I haven't seen you in *ages!*"

I caught the door and followed her out as Angela stood up; that megawatt smile was short a few watts this morning.

"Hello, Mrs. Ross."

"You poor thing!" Mom turned and pushed the clothes into my arms, and then I stood there like a giant laundry hamper and watched them hug. Angela's face suddenly contorted, and Mom stroked her back and hair, murmuring; I felt about as useful as, well, a big laundry hamper.

Mom said, "Have you eaten, dear?"

"No, Mrs. Ross." Angela hiccoughed and glanced at me and scrubbed tears away and tried to repair her hair with her fingers, then visibly gave up.

"Well, come on inside and I'll whip you up something." Mom put her arm around Angela's shoulders and guided her past me.

"Hey," I said.

"Hi."

"There's no time for that foolishness, Jackie. Take those to your place. I'll send her over when she's freshened up. I hope you like what I picked out, dear. If not, I still have a closet full of things I'm too old to wear now, but they'll look wonderful on you."

"Whatever you chose will be fine, Mrs. Ross. Thank you so much."

"My pleasure. And I was so sorry to hear about your dad, Angie. William Beaumont was a fine man; one of the best I ever knew."

"Thank you, Mrs. Ross."

"It's Mary, dear."

"Thank you, Mary."

"That's better. Now, let's get you…"

The front door shut with a thump, and I stood there some more; when that got old, I looked down at Jezzie.

Wag-wag-wag.

"Something just happened," I told her. "Not sure what, but I know it did."

I walked to my barn, carrying the clothes and shaking my head.

There was a knock about a quarter to nine, and then my left-hand door clanked and opened and Mom poked her head in. Angela stepped inside behind her, and I took one look at her damp hair and scrubbed face and understood through my keen powers of observation that the shower had already been taken care of; she wore a fresh pair of khaki shorts and a dark-blue Crazy's tee-shirt.

"Hi."

"Hi."

Mom gave me a hands-on-hips glare; those are never good. "Why didn't you tell me Angie was working at your place?"

"I didn't know myself until yesterday."

"Oh. Well, you can't expect this poor thing to work today, not after what she's—"

"Please, Mary, it's all—"

"I *don't* expect it. She can just hang out here 'till Neal's people are done."

Angela said, "But I *want* to work today."

Mom patted her arm. "Don't be ridiculous, dear. You can stay with Harold and I until—"

"No, I can't just…just sit around and think. I need to keep busy."

I said, "Are you sure?"

"I'm sure."

"Okay, then."

Mom was harder to convince. "Jackie and his crew can handle it; you need to rest while—"

Angela clutched Mom's hands in both of hers. "Please, Mary, I need to stay occupied, so I don't dwell on—" She blinked and swallowed. "Besides, they would've gotten their butts kicked if I hadn't been there yesterday."

I nodded. "It's true."

Mom appraised me for a long moment, then pulled Angela into a hug. "Don't push yourself."

"I won't."

Mom released her and pointed at me. "And don't you work her too hard."

"I won't, Mom."

"All right, then. I'll leave you young people be." She pulled the door shut wearing a tiny smile, for some reason.

We looked at each other, then looked at each other some more; Angela hooked a stray strand of hair behind her ear; damp, it resembles ripe wheat instead of sunshine. I seemed to recall that from swimming when we were kids; ultra weird seeing her in a Crazy's tee-shirt.

"Do, uh, do you want some coffee?"

"No thank you. Your mom brewed me some. She's so nice." Then the wheat-brows lowered, and those full lips pursed. "Your dad's kind of a dick, though."

"Some things never change."

"I suppose not."

"So…I guess you don't need that shower."

"Nope. All taken care of."

"I also couldn't help but notice that you still let her call you Angie."

"And *I* noticed she still calls you Jackie."

"Point taken." Shower and fresh clothes and coffee aside, she didn't appear ready for eleven plus hours on her feet; not even close. "Look, I know you want to help, but—"

"Don't start. I meant what I told your mom; I need to keep busy. You'd understand if…" She shuddered, then the hands were jammed on hips; still never good. "The subject is closed. You're not getting rid of me."

"Okay, okay. I have to warn you, though; we might be even busier than yesterday."

She sagged and went a little hollow-eyed. "I know. Let's sit while we can."

"All right."

Angela walked over and looked at my chair. "You *really* need to get more furniture, Jack." Then she plopped crisscross applesauce onto my planks and patted a spot in front of her. "Join me."

"You can sit in the chair. That's what it's for, you know."

"I'm not going to look down at you like I'm perched on some stupid throne. Will you do that to me?"

"I guess not."

"Good." She patted the floor again, so I folded my legs under, then almost jumped back up when she laced her hand into mine.

"Uh…"

"Shh." Her fingers were warm, and fit between mine perfectly. "I want to tell you something, so just don't say anything and listen. Ready?"

I nodded.

"I don't want to stay by myself tonight."

I stared at her.

"Jack? Earth to Jack, come in, Jack."

"Um, sure. I mean, okay."

"Um, sure, okay, what? What does *that* mean?"

"Well…" I blinked. Her blue eyes were steady on mine, and suddenly less than a foot away. "I mean…"

"I should've stuck to you not saying anything." She seized my right hand with both of hers and stroked the knuckles with a fingertip; it sent delicious little shocks through me. "Life is short, Jack. I guess that's also what I want to say. After seeing Jess strung up like that…"

Strung up?

Angela pressed warm fingers against my lips. "Don't. Forget I said that." The fingers left my lips and trailed across my cheek, up into my hair, then down the back of my neck and held there. "I don't know what I want long-term. I don't even know if this is the right thing to do. I know life is short. I know I can't stay at that house by myself tonight. I want to stay here with you. Do you want me to stay?"

"Yes." *God, yes.*

"Good." She studied me, then leaned forward. We kissed, tongues swirling, and then she broke it off and studied me again, darted back in for a peck on the lips, then abruptly stood and moved toward the door. "We better get going, I need to finish the boards. Grab that stepladder. Oh, and see if your dad has anything besides Navy Blue; I have some more ideas."

"Okay," I said.

"Jack."

"What?"

"Are you coming?"

"Yeah, I'm coming."

"Then you should probably get up off the floor."

"Right." I stood. Work. I sold burgers. And fries. And shakes sometimes.

Angela said, "Are you all right?"

"I'm good. Time to go to work."

"That's right." She frowned. "Are you *sure* you're okay?"

"Never better." Keys. Pocket. I pulled them out, showed them to her. "Keys."

"I see them." She took my arm and guided me outside. "Now go get the ladder and see about that different-colored paint. We'll take your truck. I'm too tired to drive."

"Okay."

"Jack?"

"Yeah?"

"Ladder and paint?"

"Right." Ladder and paint. I looked back once and found Angela watching me with this tiny, knowing smile, just like Mom's; maybe women hung out and practiced those.

I made it to the shop, but for the moment I didn't have a clue where the ladder was, let alone if there was any different-colored goddamn spray paint; the only thing I knew for sure is that life is pretty fucking amazing sometimes.

The dog wagged her tail when I looked down.

"It's going to be a *great* Fourth of July, Jezebel. The best *ever*."

She grinned her sharp little toothy grin and wagged harder.

Ron stared at the gaunt and whiskery old man seated on the other side of his desk, then tossed his favorite Mariners' pen, the Ken Griffey Sr., onto his battered notebook and clicked off the digital voice recorder. He scrubbed his face with both hands; it was barely ten o'clock in the morning, but it was already the longest Fourth of July of his life.

"Smitty…"

The old man hunched forward in the steel-legged chair and started jabbing a big, gnarled finger over Ron's desk. Despite being somewhere past eighty, Smitty's hands still looked like they could crush walnuts, as Ron had heard they could when the former cow-punch and lumberjack was younger. Ron noted that enormous hand was trembling.

"Goddamnit, Chief, I know what I seen, and I'm tellin' ya, that freak-show sonofabitch killed old Bill! Chopped 'im up like a rick o' stove wood!"

"I know it's what you *think* you saw, but—"

"I don't *think* I seen it, I damn well *seen* it!"

"Bill was your friend, Smitty. Don't you want to help us catch his killer?"

"A'course I want ta help! And I know damn well who my friends are! A sight bettern' you!"

"Calm down, Smitty."

That knotty finger jabbed faster: "I know what you're a thinkin'! I know what *ever'body* in this piss-ant town thinks, and I don't give a cross-eyed shit! It weren't the booze, Chief. I saw 'im plain as day, with poor old Bill's blood drippin' off that ax. It was spattered all over 'im, too, all over those feathers and that damn leather jacket! No one's a bigger fan of the hooch than me, but it'd have to be Grade-A rocket fuel to make me see somethin' like that! I'm tellin' ya, Chief, I *seen* 'im, and I don't care what you or that boot-licker Neal thinks!"

"Stop yelling at me or you're going in the tank to cool off."

Sam "Smitty" Smith dropped his giant finger and collapsed back into the chair like a sullen spider, glaring at Ron from under bushy silver brows. The old drunk blinked at his trembling mitts, then curled them into slab fists and set them upright on his knobby knees, where they continued to boogie.

"Okay, Chief, okay, that Neal just got me riled." His red-veined eyes glinted across the desk at Ron: "He had yer goat too, I could tell."

Neal had split his deputies as soon as he'd heard about the new murder, then interviewed Smitty at Bill Napier's gore-spattered cabin and told Ron to take him back to the Indian Head police station and see if he could get anything coherent out of the "old souse". Ron had offered his own officers, now that Neal had three crime scenes to deal with, but the Sheriff had told him to interview Smitty and then go direct traffic, since that was what he and his men were cut out for.

Ron's left eyelid fluttered, but he got it under control before he thumbed the recorder. "Okay, Sam, we're back on the record. I want you to go through it from the beginning. What time did you say you walked home from The Nest?" Maybe something new would shake loose from the old man's pickled memory, something besides the insanity he insisted he'd seen walking out of Bill Napier's cabin last night.

Smitty jerked as straight as his osteoporosis would allow. "*Again?* I done told that shit pile Neal once and you twice already, and neither o' you know-it-all sumbitches believed me! What's the goddamn use—"

Ron turned the recorder off and stood up and pulled his key ring from his belt. "I warned you. Let's go to the tank."

Smitty held up his massive, trembling hands. "A'right, a'right, don't get yer panties in a twist." Ron sat back down, and the old man licked his lips. "I'm hurtin', though, Chief, and bad. Now ya know I don't norm'ly partake in the daylight," Ron somehow kept his face straight, "but after what I seen, I could sure use a bracer."

"Let's just get through this one more time and then you can—"

"Aw, c'mon, Chief, just one. I know ya got that bottle in here someares. It'll straighten me out so I'z can sing to ya again. It's gonna be the same goddamn song, but ya said ya wanted ta hear it."

Ron stared at him and let the silence stretch. Smitty finally wilted.

"Guess I'll live 'till—"

"How do you know about what I supposedly have in here?"

"Shit, Chief, ever'body knows you like a belt at the end o' shift. Not more'n one, mind you, as befittin' a proper gentleman, but—"

"*Everybody* knows?"

Smitty's grin displayed all five of his yellow teeth. "Hell yeah, ever'body knows. This ain't Seattle. This is Indian Head. People in this town know what color drawers yer wearin' and if they're smudged, but I ain't all judgy. I just need one to straighten me out, and then I'll go through the whole thing again, even though it's a big waste o' time." Smitty ducked his head modestly and used one of his colossal hands to smooth his thin shock of silver hair. "Ya probaly don't think an old fart like me has plans for the Fourth, but I do, and I cain't be sittin' here all day—"

"Shut up. You can have *one.*"

"Yer a peach, Chief, I don't care what they say."

Ron slid the bottom right-hand drawer open and lifted out a bottle of Jack Daniels Black Label and a short, heavy glass and poured a finger while the old man followed the proceedings like a dog watching his master dangle raw sirloin. But when Ron nudged the glass his way, Smitty only looked at him.

"That wouldn't wet a virgin's whistle, let alone satisfy an old campaigner like me. Have a heart."

Ron glugged another finger and spun the cap on the bottle and put the whiskey back in the drawer and ran it closed with a bang. "That's all you get. Now talk."

Smitty downed the whiskey in one gulp and smacked his lips. "Jack do a body good, it does!"

"Start talking about last night or you're going in the tank."

The old man eyed him speculatively, then held up the glass. "Words'd come easier if—"

"*Smitty…*"

He hastily plunked the glass on the desk, and Ron snatched it and put it with the Jack, slamming the drawer again. Smitty whined, "Just funin' ya, Chief. Cripes! That Neal's got yer back up good, ain't he?" The old man sighed. "Ya want it again? Welp, here goes…"

"So after I walked home from The Nest—that was 'bout ten, like I said a'fore—I jumped in my truck, and…I know, I know, don't look at me like that, Chief. I shouldn'ta drove in that condition, but Bill ain't got no cell, and he wouldn't answer his house phone, and he didn't show for the bones game, and 'sides, he still owes me a ten-spot from the other night, and I've got bills ta pay…I'm real sorry, Chief, but it's a long walk out to Bill's place, 'specially for an old man like me, and, well, that shit bird Neal said he was gonna write me up for a DUI, and I just got my dangburned license back! Maybe ya could git in 'is ear fer me?"

"Don't worry about it, Smitty. Neal's got bigger fish to fry. Just keep talking."

So Smitty told of his drunken drive across Indian Head—"I kept 'er 'tween the lines, Chief, I swear"—and down State Highway 15 and around to the east side of the lake to old Bill Napier's two-room cabin (shack) in the woods. The driveway was over a quarter-mile long, and the nearest neighbors even further, so Smitty hadn't thought anything was wrong—"figured old Bill'd had a nip or five and fell asleep"—until his headlights shone on the open front door.

Smitty paused there and swiped at his mouth with the back of a giant, shaking hand; the tremors had calmed somewhat after the Jack, but Ron didn't think DTs were the problem, now. "I could tell somethin' wuz up, cuz old Bill never leaves that door open, even when we're kicked back and enjoyin' a few sips on the porch, and all the lights wuz dark, and so I shut my truck off and was just climbin' out, worried-like—thought maybe Bill had fallen and couldn't get back up, ya know, like in them commercials—when that freak stepped out and stood on the porch, big as life and five times as strange. Thought maybe I was dreamin', then I spotted Bill's leg stickin' out behind 'im—or the bottom half of it, anyway. It'd done been chopped off at the knee."

"Well, I screamed like a little girl, I ain't ashamed to admit it; some crazy sumbitch in a goddamn giant chicken suit carryin' a blood drippin' ax wuz starin' at *you*, you'd scream too, Chief. Then I hopped back in my truck and cranked it and slammed that fucker inta reverse and peeled backward, and that freak show come off the porch and took after me. When I lipped off'n the driveway and hit that big pine and stalled, I figured I was a gonner, like poor old Bill, but he just strolled up to the driver-side glass." Smitty stared at something that wasn't in Ron's office with bulging eyes and raised his wide hand and let it hover two feet from his whiskery, haunted face: "He was *this* close, Chief. I was shakin' so bad I couldn't start the truck again, so I pawed 'neath the seat for my Smith and Wesson; keep me a snub-nosed .38 loaded with Mags under there, but

I couldn't find it, and then I remembered I'd taken it out to clean it and never put it back, but I kept pawin' cuz I didn't know what else to do, and I couldn't take my eyes offa his face…" Smitty blinked, then looked at Ron. "And then the crazy sumbitch just moseyed off inta the pines, headin' toward the lake, right where I showed that turd Neal. Guess I passed out then, cuz I woke up 'bout daylight. My cell couldn't get a signal down in that little dell Bill lives in…*used* to live in…" Smitty covered his face with his pancake hands and sobbed: "I…I had to go inta Bill's place and use his phone, and I seen…ah, God, poor old Bill…"

Smitty cried, and Ron watched him do it; the old man had told the same story four times, nearly word for word. After a minute he got up and snatched a handful of tissues from a box on the bookshelf and went around to the front of the desk and handed them to Smitty.

"Thankee, Chief."

"You're welcome." Ron went back around and sat and waited for the old man to blow his nose. "Look at me, Sam." He did, with eyes even redder than before. Ron reached out and deliberately turned off the recorder, then leaned forward and spoke in a low voice while glancing out his office window at Mindy, where she sat at her station behind the long reception counter. *Everyone knew about the bottle?* Ron could guess how. She was staring at her flat-screen monitor, probably playing Solitaire as usual, or maybe Hearts—although with this morning's excitement, perhaps not. "The man who killed Bill wore the top half of a *giant chicken costume?* Tell me the truth, now."

"I swear ta Almighty Jesus God and the Holy Everlovin' Ghost, Chief. I ain't no church man, never have been, and I'll probly be headin' the opposite direction real soon, if'n ya know what I mean, but—"

"I believe you, Smitty."

The old man stared in amazement, then spluttered, "Ya do? Well, I'll be damned fire! Ya oughta go tell that fool Neal that cuz he said I wuz a—"

"I've got everything I need for now. You want me to call Daisy for you? I don't think your truck is going anywhere anytime fast, even if Neal releases it."

Smitty slumped. "Yeah, I bunged up the back pretty good." He waved a platter-sized hand: "Nah, I'll call 'er m'self; she ain't at work on accounta Pat's is closed fer the holiday. She'll have 'er hands full with them brats and 'er no-count husband, and she'll be mad at me for buggin' 'er, but that ain't nothin' new."

"Well, if she can't give you a ride, I'll drop you at your place on my way out."

Sam gave him a haunted look. "I 'preciate it, Chief, but if ya think I'm goin' home after last night, yer a bigger fool than Neal."

Bill's murder would be all over Indian Head by noon; the Sheriff sure wouldn't like that. After a little thought, though, Ron decided that was just fine by him.

Sam unlimbered his cheap flip phone and was squinting at the tiny screen, tree-branch finger hovering, when Ron shot him a question:

"You got any more guns besides that snub?"

Smitty's head lifted like a hound catching a scent; he stared at Ron keenly before saying, "'Course I do. What's up?"

"I want you to tell everybody down at The Nest—and your great-granddaughter, and her husband; and while your at it, her mother and his mother, and tell them to pass the word to all their people as well—to arm themselves and don't let anyone stay alone tonight, especially the elderly, and *especially* if they live out in the woods."

"Hell, Chief, that's half this burg."

"Goddamnit, I know that. Just go do as I say."

The old man gathered his feet under him and stood up slowly with fire in his eyes. "We gonna get that sumbitch! That the plan, huh Chief?"

"No, that's *not* the plan. Just pass the word that Chief Rogers said to arm yourself and don't let anybody stay by themselves tonight. Got it?"

"Yeah, yeah, I got it." The fire hadn't left Smitty's eyes, though; he reached over the desk and clutched Ron's forearm; Ron decided the stories about the walnuts were true. "We gotta get this freak, Chief. Old Bill was my friend, and a good man besides. Oh, he wuz a washed-up drunk at the end, but whatever he ended up, he didn't deserve that." Tears coursed down Smitty's lined cheeks. "Bill worked hard his whole life, first out at that school before they closed it down, and then with me at the mill before Bob Jr. shut *that* down, but wherever he drew a check, Bill took care of his family first, just like he shoulda. And then his Emma up and died on him, and now his girls won't have nuthin' to do with him while sayin' all that mean stuff 'bout him to boot. Just 'bout broke his heart, that, but—"

Ron raised his free hand. "Bill worked at Inglewood Elementary?"

"Said so, didn't I?"

"What'd he do there?"

"Why…" Smitty got a faraway look and let go of Ron's arm and stood as straight as he could and scratched his gray stubble with a crooked banana finger. "He was a janitor, the head custodian of the whole shebang—or so he told me. Didn't know 'im then, not 'till he hired onta the mill. Said he mopped up after those snooty teachers and those snot-nosed brats for over twenty-five years. Not that they ever 'preciated—"

Ron rubbed feeling back into his arm and hopped up and walked around and put his hand on the old man's knobby back and propelled him out the door. "Thank you, Sam. You be sure and let me know if your great-granddaughter can't give you a ride."

"What's old Bill workin' at that school got ta do with anyt—"

Ron shut the door in Smitty's face and almost ran back around the desk, fresh current jazzing through his limbs; he believed in a lot of things, but coincidence wasn't one of them. He snatched up his desk phone; he needed to talk to the Sheriff.

His index finger froze over the last number, however, and then Ron lowered the handset back into its cradle. He considered that hand, the one still gripping the receiver; by not informing Neal of this potential development, he was maybe stepping over a line that he couldn't jump back across so easily.

Ron's jaw firmed, and then he let the phone go. *So be it.*

The charge was all through him now, singing in his blood. He flipped his notebook open and clicked the Griffy Sr. ready and fast-wrote everything he knew about both murders—and what he didn't know, a much longer list—adding to the notes he'd jotted by pure habit at Mrs. Barbary's earlier that morning. They were rough, and not in order, but he would flesh them out and sort them later; he needed to get it all down while it was fresh. Ron was only partially aware of Daisy arriving to pick up her great-grandfather with a long-suffering expression that turned to wonder as Smitty regaled her with his story.

The portable standing in the charger on the corner of his desk crackled:

"Uh, Chief?"

Tommy. Ron had forgotten about Tommy; more important-ly, he'd forgotten what Tommy was guarding. He stretched and grabbed it up. "I'm here. Have the Sheriff's men gone through the Beaumont house yet?"

"I ain't seen hide nor hair of a single one, and I'm starvin'. You 'spose Ryan could bring me—"

"I don't think they're coming now, Tom, but I am." Ron needed the girl to show him where she'd heard what she'd heard, or he'd be out there all damn day. "But first I'm going to fetch Ms. Beaumont, so I'll pick you up something from Jack's place." He stood and folded the battered notebook lengthwise and stuffed it into his back pocket. Mindy snatched the mouse and minimized a window as he came striding out. "We'll be there in about forty, forty-five minutes," he told Tommy. "Hold the fort until then."

"Crazy's? Hey, I love that place. Get me a bacon cheeseburger basket with rings, would ya? And one of those Crazy Floats with root beer—"

"You'll get whatever I bring back."

"Uh, yes sir. Over and out."

Ron shook his head and hooked the hand-held on his belt and addressed Mindy. "Forget that stupid game. Get online and find out all about Inglewood Elementary: when it was built and opened, when it was closed and torn down, and who worked there and who attended it. And when."

"I wasn't playing any…that place has been gone forever. What's it got—" Mindy's plump fingers flew to her mouth. "Mrs. Barbary! You figure whoever—"

"Just find out what I told you to find out and leave the figuring to me."

"Yes *sir*, Chief."

He was across the lot and opening his cruiser when Mindy pushed the station's glass door open and stuck her head out. "I don't know how much will be online, Chief! That school got tore down before Al Gore invented the Internet! I could call district records, I guess, but with the holiday and all, it'll have to wait 'till tomor—"

"Just do the best you can! Anything will be better than the nothing I know now!"

Ron yanked his notebook free and chucked it in and climbed in after it and slammed the door, vaguely aware of Mindy making a face at him before letting station's door ease shut. He grabbed the notebook up and started flipping, looking for Angela Beaumont's cell number, found it, and called her and told her what he wanted. She agreed, saying she needed to get some stuff and take care of the cats, anyway. Ron said he wanted to order some food for him and his deputy, and after a muffled conversation, she said they'd make it even though they weren't open yet, and that there wouldn't be any charge. He thanked her and told her to thank Jack and hung up and fired the car up and turned his lights and siren on as he sped across Indian Head and down Highway 269.

If the killer *had* visited the Beaumont place, did that throw a wrench into his theory? Angela most likely wouldn't have been born yet, or just barely, by the time Inglewood was a memory. Had her parents attended? If so, wouldn't a local perp know they were already dead? And don't forget Smitty; letting a witness live made no sense, unless…throw in that wacky costume, and it spelled trouble for everyone, big trouble, especially for Ron and his normally sleepy little town; as soon as the media caught wind…maybe that's what the killer wanted…but if so, why? The hoopla would only ensure that the powers-that-be threw every resource at this until he was caught…was Ron painting reason onto a demented, attention-seeking madman who preyed on random, isolated victims? That sent an icy-hot shot down his spine; no motive meant no pattern and no handle to catch him with. The victimology was similar, true, but two wasn't a sample size you could trust, and Ron was determined to take this perp off the board before the body count grew enough for certainty.

He shook his head; too many questions and not enough answers, as usual, but right now Ron knew three things for absolute sure: one, his people were dying, one each of the past two nights;

two, his head and heart and gut told him a third would die tonight; and three, he wasn't going to just sit around and hope that Sheriff John Neal kept them all safe.

A giant *chicken?*

What fresh hell had come to Indian Head on Ron's watch?

The tires squealed as he took the corners too fast, but he didn't slow down; whoever was slated to die tonight didn't have time for him to slow down.

Ron drove faster.

17

The disillusion of my dreams for a wonderful Fourth began early, but even as the evidence mounted, pointing to what a truly shitty day it would turn out to be, I kept on hoping—more fool me.

Angela was outside, on Dad's ladder, adding finishing touches to the front *and* back of the boards, so they'd be advertisements when we were open as well—I would have never thought of that, obviously—and Donnie and Miguel and I were inside prepping and staring at her legs when her phone rang. She climbed down to answer, and the big blue eyes got even bigger as she made an urgent motion for me to come out, so I wiped onion off my hands and hit the side door. She put the phone on her shoulder when I got to her.

"What's going on?"

"It's Chief Rogers. There's been another murder." Dark saddles under those eyes showed last night's ordeal was taking its toll. "The Sheriff's men are spread thin, so he's checking my house. He wants me to walk him through Monday night; you know, what I heard, and where I thought I heard it. I need to feed and water Jess's cats anyway, and get some stuff for tonight. He's coming to pick me up. Is that all right? I should be back before the end of lunch rush, but I can have him run me back faster."

I heard myself say, "We'll be okay, take as much time as you need." *Another murder? Holy crap.* "Who was it?"

"He didn't say. Are you sure? I don't want you guys to get swamped."

"Do what you gotta do, we'll be fine."

"Thank you, Jack." She went up on tip-toes and kissed me on the cheek and then raised the phone back to her ear. I touched my cheek and looked above the order window, where Donnie had his face pressed to the mesh, listening and watching uneasily.

"*Another* one?" Angela had told them about Mrs. Barbary earlier.

"Yeah."

"Shit."

"Yeah."

"Who was it?"

"Don't know."

"Jack?" The phone was back on her shoulder. "Chief Rogers wants to order some food for him and his deputy. I know we're not open yet, but—"

"That's okay, we'll fix them up. I won't charge them, either. What do they want?" Rogers told her and she told me, and I motioned for Donnie to write it down. He scowled ferociously, but did it after I scowled back. I could hear him bitching to Miguel, something about "fucking pigs getting special treatment", but I was watching Angela.

She said, "All right, Chief, see you in a few." She ended the call. "He said thank you." Unshed tears made her eyes shine. "Jack, what's happening? Who would do that to poor Jess? And now there's another one…"

Angela put her face in her hands, and I wrapped her in my arms. She hugged my ribs and cried into my chest, and I let her because I knew she'd held tough through last night, but this new shock had eroded the fragile glue sticking her together. Donnie and Miguel were peeking around the menu board; Donnie gave me dou-ble-thumbs up. Miguel gave me the same head shake as yesterday. I still didn't know what the fuck it meant.

After a minute, Angela pushed away and scrubbed her face with the neck of Mom's blue Crazy's tee-shirt. "I'm sorry."

"Don't be. In fact, I think you should have Rogers take you back to my place after he's done. Mom will take care of you, and you can get some sleep—"

"Don't start that again. You need me and you know it."

I gave her a slow smile. "Yeah, I know it."

Angela looked at me hungrily then, making my breath catch. She snuck a glance at the window, then positioned me so my back was to Crazy's and stood close, real close, right in front of me, hidden from Donnie and Miguel's view, and I thought she was going to kiss me. Instead, she let her hand trail down my stomach…and then lower.

She whispered, "I want you so bad, Jack."

My heart pounded, and my penis swelled against her hand; she squeezed, making me shift. I was thinking, *Holy smokes, from crying over two murders to horny in no-time-flat.* Maybe Angela was one of those girls who got hot watching slasher flicks.

I said, "Hey, I've got an idea. Maybe after you get back, we'll tell Donnie and Miguel we're both sick, then we can go back to my barn. Think they'll buy it?" I was joking, but then again I wasn't.

"You can wait until tonight, big boy." She smiled and squeezed again, then let go of my dick and patted my chest and turned and climbed the ladder and picked up the paint from the shelf sticking out the back and shook it; the ball rattled. "I want to finish before Rogers gets here. What do you think? Do you like it?"

"Yeah, I like it."

"Jack." I raised my eyes from her ass, which was head-high and five feet away and perfect. "I'm talking about the board." Despite her tone, she didn't look mad. "Seriously, what do you think?"

"It's great, Angela. I mean it."

And it was, and I did; she'd transformed two words filled with vitriol into works of art that happened to advertise my burgers and shakes, and all with a little imagination and some spray paint. "You're amazing," I told her. "You're a damn good artist, too."

The smile I got from the top of the ladder, dark saddles and all, would've powered a Nimitz-class carrier for six months. "Thank you, Jack." She turned back to the board and eyed it critically. "I know you're not the Facebook type, but you should set up a page for Crazy's, get the word out, maybe even do some advertising. Your food is great, and this place would really take off if more people knew about it."

"People go to the lake," I said. "Then they stop here when they're hungry. Or they don't. I'm pretty sure advertising won't change that either way. And how do you know I'm not the Facebook type?"

"Because you're not on Facebook."

"And how do you know I'm not on Facebook?"

"Because I looked, dummy." Angela was still facing the board, but I thought the back of her neck was a little pinker than usual. She shook the can again. "There are some final touches I want—"

We both heard it then; a siren, distant but rolling down the mountain, and fast.

"Rogers," I told her.

"I guess he's in a rush." She eyed the board again, then sighed and climbed down. "I'll finish between waves, or after close."

"It looks great now. You don't have to do anything else. You've done too much as it is."

"You're a sweetheart, but don't argue with the artist. I can make it better with—"

"Hey, *sweetheart*, you gonna help us make this piggy food, or what?" Donnie rammed the glass home and stomped out of sight.

Angela and I exchanged a wondering glance.

"What's *that* all about?"

"Not a clue." I headed for the side door. "Gonna find out, though."

Angela cocked her head in that ultra-cute way she had, listening to the siren wailing closer. "He sure is in a hurry. Hand me my purse, I'll wait out here."

"You bet," I said, then went inside and did just that, receiving another tip-toe peck on the cheek as Miguel passed baskets of rings and bacon cheeseburgers to Donnie. I made the floats and watched from the corner of my eye as he jammed the food into bags. I clamped the lids down and took the bags he almost threw into my hands, and then inquired, as mildly as I could, "So, Don, something you'd like to share?"

"Not really. If you want to go all gratis-chow with your pal the Nazi, it's none of *my* business. I'm heading out back to smoke." He unlimbered a box of Marlboro Red shorts and a gleaming new Zippo and whammed the door open, then slammed it shut.

Miguel and I looked at each other, but just then Chief Rogers whipped in with a wail and a blue flash and a crunch of gravel; across the highway, several people were gassing up at the Shell, and they were all definitely watching. I stuffed a fist-full of napkins and a pair of scoop-straws into a random bag and joined the party outside as Rogers killed the siren. He left the blues strobing as he hopped out. Late fifties, medium build, about three inches shorter than me with a slight pot-belly and receding, skull-gripping, gray-ish-brown hair, Chief Rogers was about as unimposing as you could get—until you saw the hazel eyes. He has the cop-peepers: the eyes that weigh and measure everyone and everything to the teaspoon; today those peepers were razors.

"Ms. Beaumont. Thank you for this."

"Anything I can do, Chief."

He nodded to me and stuck out his hand. We shook. Angela took the food and the floats. Rogers said, "I'll have her back as quick as I can."

"No problem. And take your time, we'll be fine." Rogers was aware of my felonious past, but he had never mentioned it. What's more, he'd always treated me with courtesy, and even a guarded respect. I kinda liked him for that. Sort of the polar opposite of my feelings for Sheriff Neal, you could say. "Can you tell us what's going on?"

He eyed me, then said, "Two people are dead. Two elderly and isolated people. Do your mom and dad have any guns?"

A quiver went up the back of my neck. "A handful of hunting rifles and a Colt .45 semi, but Dad hasn't shot since before the stroke, and it's been ten years since Mom held one, or longer. Why?"

"Make sure they load some and keep them handy."

"That bad, huh?"

"That bad." And then a smile appeared; it didn't touch the cop-peepers. "And I assume that you do *not* have a gun, correct?"

I spread my hands in a gesture of total innocence. "I'm a convicted felon, Chief. That would be breaking the law."

He nodded, peepers pinned on mine: "That's good." Suddenly he shot those razors over my shoulder. "Hello, Mr. Straus. How are you this morning?"

I heard a mumbled, "Fine", and turned in time to see a cloud of cigarette smoke disappear around the corner. Rogers grinned—a bit sardonically, I thought—then quick-strode back to his car, motioning for Angela to follow and then to climb in the front. "Thanks again, Jack. I'll have her back as soon as I can."

"No problem. Happy hunting, Chief."

"Thanks."

Doors slammed, the siren came back on, and Rogers peeled my gravel onto the highway as he floored it back up the mountain. I caught a last glimpse of Angela's face before they disappeared behind a prickly screen of needles.

She looked scared.

Ten minutes and two short-but-frustrating phone conversations with my parents later, we finished prep and opened Crazy's for the Fourth of July. There were already four SUVs full of wet, hungry boaters waiting when I flipped the sign. As we worked and Donnie sulked and the parking lot filled, I thought about Mom and Dad's differing reactions to the news.

I wasn't worried about Dad. I figured that should this psycho make the mistake of showing up while Dad was awake and sober, I could almost feel sorry for the poor bastard; the old man was mean and bored and currently cleaning and loading every rifle he owned in eager anticipation of company; Dad couldn't prep the .45 because it was presently resting on the shelf above Crazy's register. Mom was who I was worried about. She had pooh-poohed my suggestion that I run it up to her so she could stash it in her car, saying she'd be safe at the bank during the day and that she had Dad and me there at night. She'd also heard who the second victim was, old Bill Napier, and that someone had sectioned him into a hundred pieces with a machete.

I passed grub out the pick-up window and studied the faces of my customers because, frankly, I was anxious. Oh, I suppose I should've been worried about some nut job running around stringing and/or chopping up old people, or the fact my mom seemed disinclined to take her own safety seriously, but what I was concerned about was Crazy's; if the tourists fled the mountains, I was sunk. I know, I know, but a man has to worry about his own nest first. So I watched and listened. Everyone in line was talking about the murders, and when WROK did its noon news update, they were the lead story. All and sundry got quiet and peeled their ears; all the adults, anyway. The kids just kept laughing and eating and grab-assing around the picnic tables.

When the news was over, everyone started talking again, but I was relieved to see few worried faces; to these boaters and campers—men and women in their prime, most with small children—two old people getting whacked out in the woods seemed far removed, even if it was only half a mountain away.

We were blessed with a small break around one o'clock, and I was rapid-fire stocking and worrying about supplies while Donnie and Miguel cranked out the remaining orders. Then my phone rang. I had been thinking of Angela—when I'd had a chance to think—and wondering when the heck she would be back, so I snatched it out.

I blinked at the screen. Twice. Maybe he was calling to wish me a happy Fourth, although I couldn't remember Tuck Ritter ever doing that before.

"Sup, boss. Happy Fourth of July."

Tuck Jeremiah Ritter owned the construction company I worked for the other nine months of the calender. He'd known Dad forever, and Tuck had offered me a job the day after I'd sprung out of Torrington. He'd also put up with me disappearing on him during the summer to run Crazy's for the past three years, something I doubt many (or any) other bosses would do.

"Hey, Jack. Happy Fourth. You stayin' busy up there?"

The forced joviality in Tuck's voice made my abdomen tighten. "Just got our butts handed to us for lunch. You and Deb and the kids flee Sheridan and go somewhere fun for the holiday?"

"Nah, just hangin' in the backyard. I'll grill up some burgers later, then the kids'll set firecrackers off and scare the holy hell out of the dog."

"Sounds good."

"Yeah." Tuck cleared his throat. "Uh, look, Jack, I don't know how to say this, so I'm just gonna say it. I came to a verbal agreement with Bob Jr. yesterday to build Phase Three and Phase Four of Lochmore Estates."

Shit. The air whooshed out of me. I saw Donnie frowning at my expression, so I zombied over to Tiffany's old hiding spot.

"Jack? You there?"

"I'm here."

"Man, I know this sucks, but, well, business has been slow, you know that, and this contract is for six hundred units, minimum. I hate that bastard as much as you do—"

"No, you don't."

"Goddamnit, you know I don't like this! You're the best crew leader I got, but this deal…look, Bob Jr. or no Bob Jr., I got three college educations to pay for soon, cuz God knows there ain't gonna be any fuckin' scholarships."

The reeking undercurrent of the conversation wasn't being aired, so I pulled it out and waved it around so Tuck could smell it, too. "So no go if I'm on a crew, right? Is that part of the 'deal', Tuck? I could stir up some shit about that, and you know it." I regretted it before I said it, but I said it anyway.

Tuck was quiet, then said, "I wish you wouldn't. This'll keep me afloat for the next three years, and, well, I ain't gonna work for that motherfucker forever. When I'm through with him, there'll always be a job for you on my crew. Always, Jack."

My throat tightened. "I know, Tuck, and I'm sorry I said that. You've been good to me and Dad. And don't worry, I'm just pissed. I won't raise a stink."

Tuck's breath whistled in and out, in and out, and then a clatter and a crash as he threw something: "*Goddamnit!* That mother*fucker!* If I didn't need his…*fuck!*" Another crash, more cussing off-phone, then: "I hate this, Jack, but it's just business."

"I know." Tuck had to watch his own nest. "How the hell did he finally talk the guy into it?"

It was common knowledge that Bob had been after the prime acreage surrounding the north side of the lake for years, but some high-roller lawyer from New Jersey had scooped it up in a land-speculation deal, and then wouldn't sell it for anything less than outrageous—especially to one Robert Richards Jr.

Bob had that effect on people.

"I don't know, not for sure, but if I had to guess, I'd say Bob's a mite poorer these days."

"He's still doing better than me."

"Yeah," Tuck said. "Me, too."

Something else was bothering me; it wasn't technically my business, but Tuck had just laid me off, so fuck it. "I didn't know you were in the habit of submitting bids to Bob, Tuck." I left the rest unsaid; Tuck didn't do business with Bob Jr. for any number of reasons, the largest and thorniest of those numerals being me and Dad.

He hesitated, then said, "Well, truth is I didn't. The sonofabitch called me out of the goddamn blue yesterday afternoon and offered me a contract."

"Huh," I said.

"Yeah," Tuck said. "Called me his own high-and-mighty self, and on his personal cell phone, too, if you can believe that shit."

"Huh," I said.

"Yeah," Tuck said. "Said he wasn't happy with Blakeley and Sons anymore, said they'd been holdin' out for more money and then layin' down on him when he wouldn't shell it out, and I said I believed it because Dan Blakeley is a shit stain and his sons are piss-poor enough to make their daddy look good. Then he said that he'd heard for years that my outfit was the best around, but…"

"But."

"Yeah," Tuck sighed, "but." Then my former boss brightened. "Don't you worry about finding another job, Jack. Tell 'em to call me, and before I'm through, they'll think you shit platinum and piss champagne. You'll be a crew leader somewhere before you know it." Tuck laughed; it sounded strained. "Hell, I'll probly have to fork over the big bucks to get you back."

"Count on it. Gotta go, Tuck, we're getting busy again. Tell Deb I said have a happy Fourth and hug the kids for me."

"I will." Then he groaned. "Ah, hell, your old man is gonna auger me a new asshole. How's he doin', anyway?"

"He's still kicking. See you, Tuck."

"Good luck, Jack."

I slid the phone into my pocket. Tuck was right; with his glowing recommendation, I could land any framing job I wanted. But there were three problems, and the first two were Mom and Dad. I would have to travel around the state for the good money, and probably out of state. How could I be gone for weeks at a stretch with Dad in this condition? Mom couldn't take care of him *and* our place, not by herself. As for the third problem, I was standing in it. Tuck had allowed me to pursue my dream of someday owning a proper restaurant, but what were the odds of finding another boss so accommodating? Somewhere between zero and zip, I was sure.

In other words, that phone call might have been the death knell for Crazy's, not to mention my dream.

Donnie poked his head around the ice-cream cooler. "You takin' a nap back there?"

I went to the pick-up window and looked out at those enjoying my fare. *Eat up while you can, people.* "Nah, man, just resting a minute." Donnie whistled a snappy tune as he stocked napkins. "Glad to see you back in good spirits. Now will you tell me what's up with you and Rogers?"

"Maybe. Will you tell me what that call was about? You look like someone just ran over your dog."

"Maybe."

"Okay, then."

"Yeah."

My phone beeped, and I pulled it back out, hoping feverishly for good news for a change, and was rewarded by a text from Angela:
We're heading your way. Finally.

Did Rogers find anything?

I had time to make three Extra-Large Insane Root-Beer floats and four regular Crazy Coke floats and take two orders and call out three numbers and hand them out the window before she responded:

Yes. He was in my house, Jack. Rogers found a partial boot print that he thinks matches one from Jess's yard. Gotta wait for the Sheriff's people to verify, but he's pretty sure, and now there's no telling how long I have to stay away. Rogers is also reminding me to tell you to keep that to yourself. I had to get PERMISSION to even tell you in the first place. BTW, finally heard frm Chris. He's not happy about where I'm staying 2night, but it's none of his biznus and I told him so.

I read this with a chill. The psychopath that had been killing old people had also been in Angela's house? She was anything but old. If this bastard was targeting everyone that lived in an isolated setting, then three-quarters of the town was in danger, my parents included. Myself included. I read the last line again, and I guess I should've been pleased, but for some reason I wasn't. I was thinking how to respond when the phone beeped again.

Had to stop by the cop shop, but now we're almost there. Talk more L8R. Hope u guyz didn't drown w/o me. :)

Despite the smiley face, I could sense her fear and distress. What would it be like to know that a killer had been in your house, and that you'd come thaaaaat close to meeting him? I sent back an **ok c u soon** and then put the phone up. Maybe now I could talk her into taking my truck back to the barn and getting some rest, but I doubted it. Angela looked soft, but she was tough as rawhide inside, where it counted, and I found myself liking her even more—if that was possible.

Of course, that's when Miriam Jacobson pulled her white Escalade into my lot and parked. She saw me at the window and those ripe lips quirked; today there were no kids in there with her, and definitely no husband. She waved.

I raised my hand in slow motion and waved back from somewhere out among the stars and planets.

"Ah, shit."

18

Miriam swayed up just as Rogers pulled in, sans lights and sirens this time; it was perfect timing, just not for me. I peered at her through the mesh and watched Angela from the corner of my eye as she stepped out of the cruiser. This was not good, not fucking good at all. At least Miriam was clothed; no tiny orange triangles and strings today, but her olive khaki shorts rode high on the back of her tan legs, way high, and the form-hugging white tee-shirt did little to obscure a black-lace bra. One part of my mind noted she looked yummier than anything on my menu board while the rest of me wished her somewhere into New Hampshire.

"Hello, Jack."

"Hello, Mrs. Jacobson. Welcome to Crazy's. What can I get for you today?"

"Jack. Please call me Miriam."

"Uh, sure, sorry, Miriam." Angela said something to Rogers, and then the trunk popped and she walked around; she hadn't looked this way—yet. The wire-cage fan in the corner above the soda station was blowing right on me, but for some reason I was sweating buckets. "What can I get for you?"

The lip-quirk flattened out. She stared at me for a second before saying, "I guess I'll take a small Diet Coke." She took her mirrored sunglasses off and showed me the greens, and her dark hair swayed on her shoulders as she shook her head. "You really need to put a salad on the menu. A girl can't keep her figure eating here." Miriam ran her left hand down her flat belly, and despite everything, my gaze followed it. The ring weighing down her hi-I'm-married finger—a diamond and emerald conglomeration worth three times my truck; okay, four times—winked at me from the shadows under the awning, and the little twist was back on those full, glossy lips when I looked up again.

I swallowed. *Jesus Christ.*

I speed-scribbled something on an order pad and said, "One small Diet Coke coming up. That'll be, uh, $1.27 with tax." The trunk banged, and I cut my eyes and beheld Angela carrying a bulky black suitcase and a blue tote. She bent down to speak to Rogers through the open window again. Maybe I still had time.

Miriam's little lip-twist had lit out down the trail once more; she frowned at me quizzically as she reached into the purse slung over her shoulder and retrieved two one-dollar bills from her wallet and snapped the wallet closed and stuffed it back and handed the bills to me and I made her change as fast as change has ever been made in the history of the change-making world; I wasn't even sure it was correct.

"I'll have that right out to you, ma'am." I dropped the coins into her palm, but Miriam's strong fingers grasped mine before I could pull back.

"You know why I'm here, and it's not for a Diet Coke. I haven't heard from you about Saturday night." Her index finger stroked the back of my hand, shooting little tingles up my arm.

"I don't think Mr. Jacobson would like that. In fact, he seemed quite upset about our, ah, friendship, the last time I spoke to him. Gun-in-my-face kind of upset. I'd rather not go through that again."

She stroked my hand with that finger and leaned one hip against the steel counter beneath the window. "Things have changed, Jack. You don't have to worry about Doug. We came to an understanding. We're still together for the kids, but we're each allowed our fun time." *Fun time.* Of course she would put it that way. "I promise you, if you come over Saturday night, it will be nothing but enjoyable."

"Uh…"

Angela turned and saw my hand in Miriam's, and I finally yanked it free as, behind a frozen Angela, Rogers peeled my gravel onto the highway yet again as he zoomed back up the mountain.

Miriam stood straight and followed my helpless gaze. The greens narrowed as she surveyed Angela standing there holding the suitcase and bag, looked back at me, and then she looked at Angela again and smiled and slipped her mirrored sunglasses back on.

"I, uh, I still don't think it would be a good idea, Mrs. Jacobson," I said, loud enough that Angela could hear. Hell, folks in North Dakota could hear.

Miriam ignored me. So did Angela as she stalked to the side door; she never took those blue slits from Miriam. Suddenly she smiled. Miriam's lips quirked higher. The two women kept smiling and quirking as Angela brought her things inside. Miriam swayed over and tapped on the pick-up window: "Can I have my Diet Coke, Jack?"

Angela dropped her suitcase and tote and slammed the door. "I'll get it for her," she announced.

"Okay," I said, because I didn't have a fucking clue what else to say.

Angela smiled her way through making the Diet Coke; a large, but no one corrected her. She stabbed a straw through the lid and shoved the drink out the window and said, "Here you go, *Mrs.* Jacobson. Thank you for stopping at Crazy's."

"You're welcome, dear." And then Miriam turned to me with that full, glossy quirk. "Remember, Jack, Saturday night. My number's on my card." She undulated away then, and I watched her go; not the smartest move, perhaps, but it beat looking at Angela; her eyes on the side of my face made the one o'clock sun seem like an ice cube. A whisper and a snicker behind me; I turned, and Donnie and Miguel ducked below the dungeon window. I'd forgotten all about them. Miriam climbed into her Escalade and drove away; I had no choice but to face Angela.

"Get a good look?"

"I—"

"You're involved with her." Not a question.

"Not now. A long time ago. She stopped by the other day, just before you did…" I went through the whole story, and finished with: "I told her no. You heard me say I didn't think it would be a good idea."

Her glower softened maybe a hair—maybe—and she folded her arms under her breasts and glared blue death at the people eating in their cars, lips pursed, mulling it over. I glanced over my shoulder, and Donnie and Miguel ducked down again. Hey, at least I was entertaining somebody.

After a minute, I tried again. Calmly.

"I told her no, Angela."

She tagged me with that fiery squint. "She's *married*, Jack. Doesn't that mean anything to you?"

"Hey, I'm not the one who's hitched. Besides, Miriam said she and Doug have an understanding now…"

Bad idea.

Angela uncrossed her arms and stepped close and smiled up at me coquettishly; graft it to the dangerous squint, and it was a frightening combination. "Do you still have her card? You know, the one you tried to hide from me the other night?"

"Angela…"

"Do you or don't you?"

I took out my wallet and pulled the card and handed it to her. She studied it. And then those eyes lifted back to my face. "Were you planning on calling her?"

"No," I lied. "And I was going to throw it away, but I haven't had the chance—"

She jabbed it into my chest. It fluttered to the floor as she yanked her cell phone from her pocket. "Don't. You'll need it. I have to make a call." With that she was out the side door and standing in the sun and talking to someone; I watched woodenly until she hung up and came back in. "Chris will pick me up tonight and take me to get my car. I'll be staying at his condo until the police finish with my house."

I could have explained more, I guess, or pleaded my case again, but I felt the skin on my face draw tight, and my jaw was a rock as I bent and picked up Miriam's card and smoothed and straightened it and slipped it into my wallet and put the wallet in my back pocket, making sure Angela observed the entire operation; her hard, bright smile slipped a notch, but she never turned away.

"That's fine with me," I said.

"Good. I'm glad." Four cars, two pickups, and then a black Suburban pulling a dripping party barge crunched onto my lot, and Angela raised her sweet voice over the fans and air conditioner and REO Speedwagon: "We got a wave crashing, guys!"

Donnie emerged from the dungeon with a sheepish look and slunk to the order window under my stony stare. Angela went to the pick-up window and stood there. I took in her icy profile, then turned away.

Fuck.

The rest of that once-promising Fourth of July passed, and it only took about seven eons. I also somehow became invisible and inaudible, because there was plenty of joking and laughter to go around, just not with me; even Miguel quit talking to me. Around four-thirty, two blond guys in their early twenties sporting no shirts and tan six-packs crunched up in a powder-blue Wrangler with the rag top down. Angela hip-checked Donnie away from the register and took their order, and when she carried their food out to the Jeep, I went around back and cleaned the restrooms.

Six o'clock arrived during the fifth eon, and Maria appeared with the kids, right on schedule. Miguel nodded to me without meeting my eyes and scurried out carrying three bags of food and met his family at the picnic tables and turned them around and herded them back to their ancient Celica while answering Maria's startled inquiries in Spanish and casting hunted looks over his shoulder. I tied a clean apron on and pulled some fresh gloves and a hairnet from the dispensers and retreated gratefully into the dungeon and hoped Miguel showed up in the morning.

We stayed busy, but with no real killer waves. Angela caught me taking peeks at her out of the dungeon window once or twice or thrice, and she turned away with a haughty scowl every time, but the pop and sizzle from earlier was a distant memory; when she could, she leaned on the counter and sighed and rubbed her ankles. I wanted to tell her to call Chris to come get her early, and that Donnie and I could handle it the rest of the way, but I kept my head down and my mouth shut and nine o'clock finally arrived and we finished stocking and Donnie grabbed his keys and fled.

I said, "Thanks, Don. See ya tomorrow."

"Yeah, man, see ya." He wouldn't look at me, either.

I told myself I didn't care as I lowered the newly decorated plywood and locked the padlocks. Final touches my ass; Angela was already standing in the gravel with purse slung over her arm and tote and suitcase at her feet, face aglow with her iPhone's screen as she texted someone.

I crunched up behind her as Donnie sped away while waving to her, not me. She waved back, and then we were standing there, not looking at each other. I opened my mouth to say something, not sure what, and that's when the first sky rocket exploded over the lake, lighting the black with silver streamers that fizzled and faded as they arced toward the water; down at the park, hoots and much cheering and whistles and clapping. More fireworks bloomed over the jagged treetops, and Angela and I tipped our heads back.

After five joyless minutes of that, I yanked my keys free and headed for my truck, and that's when Angela said, "I'm sorry, Jack."

I turned, surprised, but she was still watching bursts of purples and reds and greens with trailing silver sparkles.

"I'm sorry too, Angela."

"You don't have anything to be sorry about," she informed the flaming heavens. "You…whatever you had with her was a long time ago, and I shouldn't judge, but…" She sagged then, almost wilted, and I wanted to go to her and hold her, but I didn't. "Brian cheated on me," she whispered. "Or at least I'm pretty sure he did. I guess that's why I reacted that way."

She watched the sky. I watched her watch for a minute, then said, "I'm sorry that happened to you."

"Like I said, you have nothing to be sorry about." Now she looked at me. "Maybe we rushed things. Maybe *I* did. I don't know. I'm so tired I can't think straight, but I believe I should stay with Chris, at least for now." She hesitated, peering at my face, frowning a little at what she found there—or didn't find. "Maybe we can talk more about us tomorrow."

"Maybe. But maybe you were right about rushing things."

The little frown turned into a full-blown scowl; apparently it was wrong to *agree* with her as well. Then I said, "And you don't have to come back. I can mail your check."

"Don't start that crap. I'll be here. You still need me, right?"

I just nodded and looked back up at the booming display; I didn't trust myself to say out loud that I needed her, not without losing it.

It was her turn to watch me. I felt her want to say something, but she didn't, and we were still standing that way when a car slowed and turned onto the gravel. I didn't look away from the exploding sky because I knew who it was and what his expression would be, and I didn't want to see that and maybe drag the man who'd been my best friend—the friend I'd hunted and fished and cooked with and built forts with and played video games with; the friend who'd cried on my shoulder for hours after his mom died when he was twelve—and kick the living shit out of him in front of his sister. So I watched the heavens erupt until I heard the Beemer's trunk shut and its passenger door thump and its low-profile tires crunch away and hit the pavement and bark as the inline-six roared…and then they were gone.

I stood and watched, and after the crashing climax drifted over the water to cheers and claps and whoops from the campground, I chucked Dad's ladder into the bed of my truck and drove home; when I slid between the sheets, the lingering scent of Angela was the perfect piss-icing on the shit-cake of this day.

"Happy fucking Fourth of July, everybody."

I rolled over and tried to go to sleep. It was a long time coming.

19

The grand culmination ensued, thundering stars of red and white and blue, the calm mirror of the lake doubling the patriotic display as they faded and trailed toward the water, replaced by more partisan bursts above and below.

Tiffany supposed it was amazing and beautiful and spectacular and all that, but she was having a hard time paying attention. The reason for her distraction moved closer and put an arm around her shoulders, and she rested her head on his chest. He was so *tall*. She couldn't believe this was happening! Her shoes should've been floating two feet above the dock!

She'd crushed on Mike Hawkins since that first breathtaking glimpse outside Chem lab in ninth grade, but back then Tiffany had only been some pimply freshman and he'd been a senior and a star pitcher on the baseball team—and dating that ho-bag Courtney Nells besides. But they'd broken up after Courtney cheated on him, and then he'd played baseball at Ohio State the past two years and Tiffany thought she'd never see him again, but he'd posted on Instagram last week that he would be at Deek's 4th party, and she'd just *had* to go, just to see him. She'd worked all summer anyway, like her parents wanted, gotten "experience in the work force" (as her dad had so boringly put it), and now she only had, like, five weeks left, no time at all, so she'd told her parents about Jack's past because she'd known how they'd react.

A wave of guilt crested inside Tiffany and then was blasted to foamy bits as Mike smiled down at her and hugged her closer. When she and Becca had arrived at Deek's, Mike had told Sean to tell Becca to tell her he thought she was cute, and so she'd wound her courage up and started talking to him and they'd been hanging out all night and he was so sweet and *God he was gorgeous!*

He held her eyes, and then his lips parted and he leaned down and was he going to kiss her? Oh my God, he was going to kiss her! She would just die or faint or both. Tiffany went on tip-toes and their tongues darted together, swirling, and she thought her heart would rupture from pure joy.

Then, with a crashing crescendo that hurt her ears, the fireworks were over for another year. Whoops and yells and cheers, and Mike broke the kiss and chucked under her chin with a knuckle before raising both arms: "Go USA!" Beer sloshed from his red plastic cup and splashed her shoulder, but Tiffany didn't mind. Then Chucky Deerpoint threw his head back and howled. Everyone laughed because Chucky was crazy; everybody knew it, too, especially Chucky. He screamed, "Fuckin' a USA!" More laughter, and soon a chant rose toward the stars, replacing the fireworks:

"Fuckin' a USA!"

"Fuckin' a USA!"

"Fuckin' a USA!"

"Fuckin' a USA!"

Tiffany joined in even though she was one of the few sober people, maybe the only one; she had to drive Becca home later, and later was coming up fast because Tiff had a midnight curfew which was *soooo* not fair, but her mom would be up watching the clock, and she would also be on the lookout for the least sign of drunkenness. Tiff would have to spray perfume on her shirt to cover the beer stench, but her mom would still probably smell it and lay into her.

The chant died down amid more laughter and more whoops and cheers, and Mike gulped his beer and snaked his arm around her shoulders again, pulling her close.

I wish this night would never end!

Crazy Chucky Deerpoint howled again and flung his red cup into the air, showering Tiffany with more suds, and then took off down the dock and ran pell-mell to the end and dove into the lake fully clothed. Four idiots howled, threw *their* beer, and then followed Chucky in; even two girls did it, high-pitched howls and all, though at least they had sense enough to slip their shoes off before jumping. Soon the sounds of a serious splash fight came from the dark water. Thankfully, Mike had stayed with her. Tiffany wrapped her arms around his ribs and snuggled close.

Chucky popped up at the top of the dock's ladder, dripping like a wet rat, tee-shirt clinging to his muscular arms and chest and distended beer-belly. "Hey, Deek!"

"What?" The host of the party was pumping the tap; they'd dragged the keg out of the house and down to the shore because apparently you couldn't watch fireworks without beer.

Chucky squished up. "Let's take the fuckin' boat out, man!" He pointed at the forty-foot cabin cruiser moored to the long dock; it rocked in the waves generated by the splash fight. The name on the side said *Sea Foam*, which Tiff thought was stupid since it was floating on a lake.

There were several cheers, but Deek said, "No fuckin' way. I spent the whole next day cleaning puke out of it last year. Hungover. 'Sides, my old man said not to touch it."

Chucky said, "Don't be a pussy! We'll load the keg and just take it out into the cove and dive off the back and swim and shit!" Most of the morons in the water had made their way up the ladder, and now they dripped around Chucky, adding their two cents about not being a pussy.

Mike hadn't joined in. Tiffany glanced up at him, but he was looking over at Sean, and there was major silent communication going on there. Tiff caught Becca's eye, and her friend gave her an inebriated grin and hugged Sean closer; those two had hooked up last year, and Tiffany knew Becca wanted to screw him again even though he had a girlfriend at college, now—maybe even *because* of it.

All of a sudden there was cheering and high-fiving, and Tiff caught Deek saying, "…but I'm driving."

"Aw, c'mon, man."

"Fuck you, Chuck. No way am I letting your insane ass drive. You'll take us all the way around the fuckin' lake. I know you, man."

Everybody laughed, including Chucky. "Whatever, man. Let's get the keg loaded and *go!* The keys up in the house? Where are they? I'll go snag 'em!"

Deek produced a pocket-sized purple-foam life preserver and held it up, key dangling: "You think I'd leave this lying around with *your* ass in the house? Forget that shit. Grab the keg."

"Hey, Deek." It was Sean, and Tiffany felt herself propelled toward where he and Becca stood wrapped around each other; her friend grinned again, but Tiffany couldn't smile back because her heart was *wham-whamming* and her palms had suddenly turned clammy.

"What?"

"I think we're gonna skip the boat ride and head back up."

Mike said, "Yeah, man, think we'll pass."

Deek scowled at the four of them as a chorus of "Oooohhhs" and a "Fuck 'er for me, Sean!", and then an "I already did!" that got some laughs; a whiplash, "You wish, Stevie!" from Becca that got even more. A pack of older girls glared at Tiffany while *reeking* of jealousy, just like they had all night; she batted her eyes and smiled sweetly at them, though now there was sweat trickling from under her bra and down her ribs.

Deek shook his head in disgust, then pointed at Sean. "All right, but stay out of my room, and my parents' room. I find any cum on those sheets, I'm gonna get my dad's 3-wood and wail on somebody. Capiche?"

Tiffany blushed so hard she thought her face had caught fire. She shifted her gaze away from the jealous skanks to Rebecca and found her friend had lost her grin and was peering at her worriedly.

Sean said, "Got it."

Deek's finger shifted, and Mike raised his cup. "Got it."

"You better." Deek then let one regret-filled glance linger on Tiffany before he and two other guys hefted the gray trashcan packed with ice and silvery keg and lugged it down the dock; Deek was really cute, even though he was way old, like twenty-three or four, but he was no Mike Hawkins. Not even close.

Soon they stood alone, watching the others pile onto the white boat. Sean said, "Christ, what's that thing rated for? They're gonna capsize and drown."

Mike said, "Good thing we're not going, huh?" They exchanged grins over the girls' heads and slapped high-five, and then Sean and Rebecca left the dock and walked across the pale, narrow strip of rocky beach and started up the concrete footpath that led to the manicured grounds surrounding Deek's parents' gargantuan lake house. Mike released her shoulders and grabbed her hand and took a long pull from the red cup and threw it off the dock. He squeezed her hand. "You okay?"

Behind them, the boat's engines burbled to life, and everyone cheered. Tiffany swallowed, hard, and smiled weakly up at Mike Hawkins. *Mike Hawkins!* "I'm fine."

"Good." He pulled her off the dock and up the walkway.

Ahead of them, a whispered conversation was taking place, and then Sean stopped dead and said, "No shit?" Then he looked back at *her.*

Tiffany blushed again.

Mike said, "What the fuck's that all about?"

Tiffany didn't answer. Then Becca slipped from Sean and came back down and pushed Mike away from her with a smile. "Go talk to your butt buddy. I need to have a confab with my best girl, here."

"Ooookay." He looked at them both, then shook his head and walked up to Sean, who grinned and threw an arm over his taller friend's shoulders and said something too low to catch; Mike's groan was so loud they probably heard it out on the boat. He said, "You gotta be fuckin' kiddin' me." Sean laughed and shoved him up the walk.

The girls watched them go, and then Becca looked at her. "You okay with this?"

Tiffany wiped her palms on her shorts and observed the tall, lithe body of Mike Hawkins as it moved up the concrete stairs and then vanished into the landscaped backyard. She swallowed again. "I'm fine."

Becca grimaced, then put her arm around her as they started up. Tiffany could hear Sean and Mike goofing off, maybe wrestling like they'd done earlier. Behind her, the boat's motor burbled louder, and then music came on; she glanced back to see the big white cruiser covered with people and lights move out into the cove and drift to a stop. Someone, probably Chucky Deerpoint, yelled something and jumped into the water. Several people followed. Tiffany fought the wild urge to run down to the end of the dock and scream for them to come back and pick her up.

Deek would do it in a heartbeat.

Becca squeezed her shoulders. "Hey." Tiff looked at her. "Are you *sure* you're okay? You don't have to do this, you know. But, I mean, you gotta—"

"Lose it sometime," Tiffany finished for her.

"Yeah, you do." Becca gave her another gentle squeeze as they mounted the steps, and then she turned Tiffany to face her; over her friend's shoulder, Sean and Mike whispered while glancing their way, and then Sean took something out of his back pocket and tore something small and square off and handed it over; they high-fived after Mike slipped it into his own back pocket.

Tiffany swallowed again.

Rebecca said, "Baby girl, look at me." Tiffany did. "You-don't-have-to-do-this-if-you-don't-want-to. Just hang out with him, and I'll be back soon." She rolled her eyes. "Believe me, Sean won't take long. Then we can split. Okay?"

"No, I want to. I think."

Becca gave her a look. "Well, you better figure it out soon. I made Sean give him something, you know, for protection, but if you don't want to, then don't. But if you *do*, well, it'll hurt, at least at first, and then it'll be——"

Tiffany finished for her: "Wonderful. Incredible. Amazing."

They'd had this conversation about a zillion times over the last year. Rebecca was almost eighteen, a year and four months older than Tiff, and she'd been with, like, four guys not counting Sean, and always said the same thing about sex: the first time would hurt, at least initially, and then she'd *love* it. Tiffany had broached the subject with her mother and gotten basically the same spiel, except her mother had tried to extract a promise to wait until she was married, or at least engaged. When Tiff had countered with whether *she* had waited, her mother hemmed and hawed, and then would only say that she *wished* she had. Whatever. Same old do-as-I-say, not-as-I-do bullshit; Mom would have a holy frickin' *cow* if Tiffany showed up drunk, but she'd be plowed on Crown and Sprites by the time Tiff got home tonight.

Rebecca hugged her. "That's right, it will, but if you want to wait, just tell him. He'll understand. Okay?"

"Okay."

The guys had been sidling closer while pretending they weren't listening; suddenly Sean darted between them with a quick "Pardon me, Tiffany" and scooped Rebecca up and threw her over his shoulder and sprinted toward the house. Becca shrieked and laughed before swiping blonde hair from her face and raising her head to look at Tiffany. She mouthed, "I love you." Tiff mouthed, "I love you." Despite all that, Becca still looked worried for her when Sean got to the front door and jerked it open, darted inside with Tiff's friend, and then slammed it closed.

And then Tiffany and Mike were alone on the lawn.

He looked at her—a trifle uncertainly, she thought—then took her hand. "Let's give them some space. We'll go hang out in the pool house."

Tiffany tried to swallow again, but she had no spit to go down. "Okay," she croaked.

He led her around the kidney-shaped swimming pool, sapphire water glimmering in the lights shining below the surface; the reek of chlorine replaced the natural lake-smell. The massive main house loomed over the hedges and banks of flowers on her right, and Tiff tried not to think about what Becca and Sean were doing in there; what *she* might soon do in the pool house.

Tiff shook her head. *Pool house*. It was almost as big as *her* house, and her house wasn't small. Deek's mom and dad had flown their private jet to San Francisco to attend some Fourth of July charity ball and auction benefiting the homeless or global warming or something, and, as always, they were cool with Deek throwing a party as long as no one took off after they'd been drinking. Tiff and Becca had to leave because their parents weren't as cool as Mr. and Mrs. Simpkins, but everyone else was eighteen, or their parents were righteous—or their parents just didn't care.

God, I can't wait to turn eighteen!

They were nearing sliding doors when hip-hop suddenly thumped from the main house, the base line so deep and loud that it shivered the glass in front of them. They turned, startled, and then Mike laughed. At her questioning look, he said, "That's Sean. He likes to crank the tunes when he's…you know."

Tiffany blushed again. "Oh."

"C'mon," he said softly, and scraped the door open. Tiff cast one last glance back; she couldn't see the boat from here, and she couldn't hear the music over the booming rap, but she could imagine them gathered around the keg, pumping the tap and laughing and dancing in the lights above swimmers splashing in the dark water.

Then Mike tugged on her hand and Tiffany followed him inside.

He let go to close the door, and she moved deeper into the room and stopped by the nine-foot pool table and let her fingertips trail over the pearl-white felt. Then she turned and stood, fidgeting. Mike kept his beautiful brown eyes on her as he lowered the blinds and turned the rod, blocking the blue glow and leaving them with only twin spotlights crossed on the ceiling behind the wet-bar. He weaved through the low-slung white furniture and then halted ten feet away to look her up and down. "My God. Little Tiffany Downing. You used to be a skinny kid, but you're so *hot* now."

Tiffany preened a little; Mike Hawkins wasn't the first guy to tell her that, just the cutest. Some girls, like Becca, bloomed early, but Tiff had finally caught up—and then some. She'd even noticed Jack looking once or twice, but even as fine and well-built as *he* was, he was really too old for her, and Tiff didn't want to even *think* about all the petrified Donnie drool she'd had to chip off her boobs the last seven weeks.

Thinking of Jack and Donnie made the guilt come back, though, and suddenly she realized she missed Crazy's. She even missed sparring with that pig Donnie! It was a strange feeling; she'd *hated* getting up early during her summer vacation to work every day— Tiff would bet Deek's parents didn't make him work during the summer!—and if she hadn't done what she'd done, she and Becca would have arrived at the party late and Mike would have probably already hooked up with one of the skanks and she would have missed this opportunity.

So why do I feel so awful?

And then Mike swooped in and scooped her up and sat her on the rail of the pool table and kissed her. He was so *strong*; he'd handled her like a doll. His kiss was urgent, and he pressed into her as his hand cupped her left breast. But even lost in the rising heat, Tiffany felt a moment of pure panic; she pushed at his chest, but he didn't budge. She pulled away from his mouth and said, "Stop."

He squeezed her breast, hard, and tried to kiss her again, and then Tiffany slid off the table and braced her bottom against it and *pushed*. He staggered back a step and just looked at her, panting.

"*Stop*. I said stop."

Mike shuddered and turned away. "I'm sorry. I know that you haven't…that you're a…"

"Virgin." For some reason, saying it calmed her even as her blood and the panic still surged from his touch.

He swiped his mouth with the back of his arm, then jammed his hands into his back pockets and walked over and leaned on a white sectional twenty feet away. "Yeah, I know. I'm sorry. I guess I went too fast. We don't have to—"

He was so sweet, even though the words didn't go with the sulky frustration on his face. "Just shut up and come back over here." The realization that she was in charge, even if Tiff didn't know exactly what she was in charge of yet, had brought her confidence back. He hesitated, then came to her; she wrapped her arms around him and put her head on his chest; his heart throbbed against her ear, fast and strong.

Tiffany looked up at Mike Hawkins' beautiful face then and had a moment of woman's clarity. He was almost four years older than her; she would be a senior in high school this year, and he would be a junior in college. He was going places in the world, maybe even turning pro next year; he'd talked about little else all night, the possibility of pitching in the major leagues. How many girls had he been with in college? She knew roughly how many Mike Hawkins had gone through in high school, and it wasn't a small number.

I'm just another girl to him, another piece.

And what did she feel about him? Tiff didn't love him, that's for sure; for all his looks, there wasn't much rattling around in that pretty head except baseball. But that didn't matter. What mattered was that they were here, together, in this moment, and that he wanted her. Mike Hawkins *wanted* her! And Becca was right; she had to lose it sometime.

It might as well be to Mike Hawkins.

Tiffany reached up and touched his face; he kissed her knuckles. She would probably never see him again—except on Instagram— and she was okay with that. Then she tangled her fingers in his hair and pulled him into a kiss; before their lips touched, she whispered, "Just take it slow, okay? Go easy with me."

"I will," he whispered.

Then, as their tongues swirled together and his hand went to her breast again, gently this time, they heard the scream.

Mike jerked up and back, looking around. "What the fuck was that?"

Tiffany cocked her head. "That sounded like Becca."

She hopped off the pool table and pulled up the blinds as Mike slid the door open…and then another shrill scream laced through the rap, followed by a crash from inside the main house.

"Oh my God, that *was* Becca!"

They stood by the rippling blue pool and stared at the immense house, but now they heard nothing besides thumping hip-hop. They looked at each other, and Mike shrugged and gave her a weak grin. "Maybe he's givin' it to her hard."

"That didn't sound like a *fun* scream. We should check on them."

"Are you serious? Would *you* want to be interrupted? They're fine." He took her hand and tried to pull her into the pool house. "Let's go back inside."

Tiffany shook him off. "Wait." When they'd had one of their talks about sex, Becca had confessed that she liked it when guys were gentle and went slow and not just jack-hammered her, so Tiff doubted Becca would be into the rough stuff. But he was right about the interrupting.

"C'mon, let's—"

"Shhhh!"

Tiffany stepped up onto the low diving board. She could see over the topiary now, and lights blazed from almost every down-stairs window, plus a few upstairs; the rap still thumped. Why *had* Becca screamed? Her friend had sounded terrified—and if it *was* just rough sex, why would she be terrified? Mike steadied her with a hand on her elbow; up on the board, she was even a little taller than him.

"I might buy screaming during the rough stuff," she told him, "but what was that crash?"

He shrugged. "Maybe they got a little wild and knocked over a lamp, I dunno." He tugged on her sleeve. "Come back with—"

Tiffany shook him off again and pulled out her cell phone. "I'll text her."

"Man, Sean's gonna be *piiiiissed...*"

"I don't care. And if Becca doesn't answer, I'm going over there. Something's not—"

The thumping from the main house suddenly lowered to a sane volume, and then a progression of windows went dark on the lower floor. Tiffany frowned and lowered her phone and watched as Mike said, "They just broke something, that's all. Deek's gonna have a cow, but fuck 'im. He don't want shit broke, he shouldn't throw a party." He tugged again. "Come back inside with me."

Tiffany looked at him, and then back at the main house, and that's when an indistinct form moved behind the drawn curtains of a triple-bay window just before it went dark; that had been too big to be Becca.

Mike had seen it, too. "See? That's Sean. They're fine."

The last glowing window on the lower floor went dark. Tiffany said, "But why is he turning off all the lights?"

"How should I know? Maybe he's walking around naked, or maybe she wants to do it downstairs but doesn't want anybody sneaking up and peeking at her. Chucky would do that sick shit, I bet, if he thought of it. C'mon, let's go inside!"

Tiffany took in the naked desire on Mike Hawkins' gorgeous face and felt some of her own enthusiasm return. He was probably right. Tiff let herself be handed down from the diving board and led back to the open sliding doors. She glanced at the main house one last time, then Mike scraped the door shut and locked it and dropped the blinds again.

He grabbed her hand and tried to lead her down the hallway, but she pulled free. "No, out here."

He grinned. "Right on." He stepped toward her, and she held up a hand, palm out.

"Wait."

Tiffany took a deep breath, then grabbed her courage and the bottom of her tee-shirt and lifted it over her head and tossed it on a white chair. She reached behind and unhooked the double clasp on her bra and shrugged out of it and threw it on top of the shirt; her breasts swung free in the slashes of dim blue leaking through the now quarter-open blinds.

Mike's eyes rounded. "Wow."

He stepped toward her, and Tiffany backed up. "Over here." She kept backing up, and he followed, pulling his own shirt off, all lean muscle and long arms, and then her butt thumped into the pool table and she slid up onto it and then he was between her legs and kissing down the side of her neck, and then along her collar bone, and then across the top of her breast. He took her nipple into his mouth, tongue swirling, and she moaned as a heat so hot she couldn't believe it washed through her. She reached down and grasped the swelling in his shorts, and then it was her turn:

"Wow."

Tiffany moaned as he put the other nipple in his mouth. She gasped and shuddered as he nibbled on it, then whispered, "You've got what Sean gave you, right?"

He took her breast out of his mouth long enough to look up at her. "In my pocket."

"Get it."

He stood up and reached around into his pocket as she unbuttoned his shorts to get that wonderful swelling out and into her hand; past his elbow, she saw motion at the window.

Tiffany looked, and then screamed.

Mike jerked backwards. "*What?* What's wrong *now?*"

The insane figure outlined by the blue glow walked away from the window.

Tiffany pointed, finger trembling. *I have to be hallucinating.* "There was someone looking in at us!"

Mike spun. "Where?" Then he spat, "Sonofabitch! I see him!" He bounded to the window and craned to the left: "He went around back! He's wearing some kind of weird feathered motorcycle jacket! That's fucked up."

Tiffany crossed her arms over her breasts. "No," she whispered. "He's wearing a giant chicken costume."

Mike's dark eyebrows scrunched over his aquiline nose. "What?"

"A *chicken* costume, with feathers and a long tail and a black jacket. And sunglasses." Maybe she *was* hallucinating.

Mike scowled in disbelief, then shook his head. "The light from the pool had to be playing tricks, or—"

They both jerked as a *thump* came from the rear of the pool house; a door back there opened onto a long porch that looked out over a sloping bank of colorful flowers; Deek had given her and Becca the tour earlier, saying it was his mom's favorite spot.

Then Mike snapped his fingers. "That's gotta be Chuck! That *fucker!* He's messing with us! Or he wants a peek at *you.*" His face twisted. "I'm gonna kick his crazy ass!" He stalked over to the hall-way. "Stay here." He vanished down it, and Tiff snatched her shirt off the low white chair and pressed it to her breasts.

A minute passed, and then another, and Tiffany held her breath and listened, but heard only Mike cursing as he checked the back door and the windows in the bedrooms. Then he stalked back into the main room. "He's still out there. I saw him. And you were right. The crazy bastard's wearing a giant chicken costume with a leather jacket and fucking *sunglasses.* What a tool." He went past her to the sliding glass doors.

"Wait. Don't go out there. Stay here with me."

Mike's grin was feral, and he clenched his fists and showed them to her. "This'll just take a second." He scraped the door back and stepped out. Tiffany went to the window as he shouted, "Chuck, ya fat fuck! I'm gonna kick your sorry ass! Where are ya, man? Don't be hidin', ya pussy! Come get ya ass whoopin'! You shoulda stayed on the fuckin' boat!"

Mike turned full circle, waiting, but there was no answer. Now that the rap was at a normal volume, snatches of music drifted up from the cove: Beyoncé. Tiffany knew if she walked out to the far edge of the pool, she would see couples slow dancing on the deck and making out in the—

And then, with a shock of icy dread, Tiff remembered the old people, the ones that had been murdered. Her parents and everyone else had been talking about it all day, but she'd barely paid attention because…well, because it was just two geezers way out in the sticks, and *her* grandparents lived in Michigan! Now a trill of terror went through her. *OhmyGod.*

She crept over and poked her head out. "I don't think that's Chucky," she hissed. "Come back inside!"

"Don't be stupid," he snapped without looking at her. "Of course it's that crazy bastard. Who else could it be?" He cupped his hands around his mouth. "All right, ya pussy motherfucker! Ya know what's good for ya, you'll stay in hiding! I see your fat face, I'm gonna stomp it!" He tromped toward her, motioning angrily for her to get inside, and Tiffany scowled.

Stupid?

She walked stiff-backed over to her bra and picked it up. *Stupid?* This from a doofus who probably didn't know anything about anything except baseball and getting girls to drop their panties. Tiffany took AP *and* Honors courses; if she pushed hard next year (and if that egghead Alvin Dansbury had a stroke), she might even be valedictorian!

STUPID!?

Maybe Mike Hawkins wouldn't be her first.

He saw her glare and stopped in the open doorway. "What's wrong?" He frowned at the bra in her hand. "What are you doing?"

"Getting dressed, moron. What's it look like?"

Then he tried to act all sweet again, but it was too late. "Hey, look, I'm sorry, okay? That asshole riled me up. We can lock the doors and he won't be able to bother us."

Tiff shook her head. "This was a bad idea. I'm going to get Becca and then I'm heading home. If she's not done, I'll leave without her." She doubled her hands behind her back and hooked her bra, then shook her shirt out.

Those heart-stopping features had turned all sulky again. "Aw, c'mon, Tiff…"

She paused, tee-shirt stretched between her hands. *Now he's whining.*

Maybe her contempt was plain, because Mike drew up to his full height and sneered down that perfect nose at her. "Whatever. You don't deserve a piece of the Hawkster."

The Hawkster?

She snorted a laugh, and he scowled. "I fucked this gorgeous twenty-six-year-old grad student last week! You think I wanna waste my time on some little high-school tease? A *virgin?* Please."

Tiffany was staring at him while feeling sorry for herself because of her own stupidity (or maybe just feeling sorry for *him*), when motion over his shoulder widened her eyes.

Maybe Mike saw her look, or maybe he heard something, because he tried to turn as an ax flashed through the open sliding door and slammed into him. He staggered, then went up on his toes and made a gurgling sound and tried to reach back and touch the ax as a booted foot came through the door and kicked him off. He fell to his hands and knees, blood spurting from the wound like a grisly fountain. The doorway behind him filled with a black leather jacket, and then a man wearing the top half of a giant chicken costume and blood-splattered faded jeans and brown-leather work boots stepped inside the pool house and looked at her with round, bottomless sunglasses perched on a hooked red beak.

Then Mike made a half cry, half gurgle, and the man brought the ax up, reversed it, and drove the long, curved point between his shoulder blades. Mike sprawled on the white carpet, eyes open and legs spasming. Then those beautiful, long legs went still and a horrible sound and stink filled the pool house as the Hawkster voided into his shorts and died.

The man yanked the ax free and looked at her again; Tiffany stood motionless twenty feet away, shirt clutched to her chest and mouth hanging open. Then, moving in slow motion, like a nightmare she couldn't wake from, the man wearing the top half of a bizarre biker-chicken costume leaned the bloody ax against the wall, head down and handle up, then started around a blood-splattered white chair toward her with his black-gloved hands outstretched.

The scream finally came, a shriek that hurt her own ears as Tiffany lurched backwards, dropped her shirt, then turned and ran across the room, but she instantly realized her mistake; she should have run down the hall to the back door, and now he was between her and *both* exits. She darted around the pool table, sure she would feel hands clutching at her, but when she turned, she saw the man in the bloody half-suit down on one knee beside the long white sectional with his elbow resting on its cushioned back, as if he'd tripped and fallen and gotten halfway back up, then paused to rest. He watched her, labored breath chuffing inside the costume, audible even over the music.

Music!

Tiffany cupped her hands toward the open door over his shoulder: "Help me! *Help me! PLEASE!*" She lowered her hands and spat, "You *killed* her, didn't you? Becca. You *killed* her, just like Mike. And Sean, too!" *Becca! Oh, God!*

He didn't respond, just watched her while down on one knee, puffing like he'd run a marathon. Suddenly he pushed up, staggered, then swayed as he raised his hands in front of that hooked beak; his black-gloved fingers shook.

And then he slowly drew his hands into fists, leather creaking, and started for her again.

Tiffany snatched a ball from a woven-leather corner pocket and flung it at him. It missed by three feet and crashed tinkling into the glass cabinets above the bar, but he stopped as Tiff snatched another. She missed again, but she kept grabbing into the pocket and throwing as fast and as hard as she could, yelling, "You sick, crazy *fuck!* You *killed* her!" He raised an arm to ward them off, but the fourth one, a striped green, scored on his beak, and he grunted; the first sound she'd heard out of him besides breathing. "Yeah! You like that, you fucking sick bastard?"

Then the pocket was empty, so she switched to the other corner, but he pulled a cushion from the sectional and held it up like a shield and advanced on her, the balls bouncing off and rolling away on the pale carpet. She aimed the last ball at his knee but it went wide, and then he lunged for her and she grabbed a cue from the wall rack and gripped it two-handed on the top half of the narrow end and swung, the cue cutting through the air in a deadly arc; Tiffany had played softball since she was ten, and she was always the best hitter on her team.

The man jumped back, though, so that the butt swished just in front of that beak. And then he stood there and eyed her; they were both panting now, she with her teeth bared and cue brandished, he still using the cushion as a shield. Then he started toward her again, cushion held high, and Tiff readied herself to sprint around the pool table to the open door.

He seemed to realize his mistake then; he changed course and went and faced her from the far end of the table, blocking her from both exits once more. But now they were at an impasse; if he came around either side, he would leave a path to one door or the other. Tiffany's phone was in her pocket, but she doubted he'd give her time for a 911 call. Her gaze flicked past him to the bloody, terrible ax, where it leaned against the wall above Mike's corpse, and then back to those black sunglasses staring at her out of that feathered, expressionless mask.

Why isn't he using the ax? If he'd kept it, she might've been dead already. *Why?*

He slowly came around from her left side, so she moved right, and he threw the cushion at her and lunged over the table, black-gloved hands reaching as she took her stance and swung with everything she had and connected solidly with his shoulder and arm.

He grunted again, but he tore the cue from her grasp and slid off the table, leaving crimson streaks on the otherwise pristine felt as Tiffany backed away, frantic as he braced the cue against his knee and heaved, snapping it. He tossed the smaller end to the floor.

Tiffany feinted toward the still-full rack of cues. He moved to cut her off, and she dashed through the small opening between him and the long bank of windows overlooking the pool, the sliding-glass door beckoning beyond the sectional and the glass coffee table, but something crashed into her hip and she staggered into the blinds, grabbing them and ripping them down, and then he was on her. She fought and kicked, but he pulled her up and swung the broken cue at her head. Tiff ducked, and it snagged in the blinds as she drove her heel into his knee, making him stagger. He let go, and she fought free of the blinds and scrambled up and hopped away on one foot—her hip was on *fire*—and over Mike's long, still legs and outside, screaming "Help me! Help me, please!" She hopped past the diving board and then past the bend in the pool, and now she could see the boat out in the cove, its lights reflecting off the ripples, so beautiful, and people were dancing, and she screamed, "*HELP ME!*", and heads turned. A few people pointed at her, and someone shouted something she couldn't make out.

They hear me! They see me!

Running steps behind her, and then his weight drove her to the paving stones, blasting her breath away. He got off of her and her head was yanked back by her hair, and something smashed into the side of her face. Her vision doubled, and then he hit her again and she went limp, coughing and gasping and crying as he tightened his gloved hand in her hair and dragged her caveman style back toward the pool house.

From far away Tiffany heard more shouts, and then the music cut off, and then the boat's motor grumbled and burbled. She gripped his wrist to ease the terrible pressure on her scalp, and she could feel his hand and arm trembling. He yanked her inside the pool house and dropped her right next to Mike, and Tiffany tried to crawl away as he slid the door shut and locked it, but then a heavy boot smashed between her shoulder blades, driving her to the floor and blasting her breath away again.

He grabbed her by the hair once more and pulled her up and ran her across the room, and she didn't know where she was until the rail of the pool table smashed into her middle. He pressed her face into the blood-streaked white felt so hard she turned her head to the side to keep her nose from breaking. She got her breath back and *screamed* as he yanked her shorts down, the buttons popping, and then her panties were around her ankles, and then the jagged, splintery end of the broken pool cue was held before her bulging eyes, as if he wanted her to see. It disappeared from her vision as he kicked her feet apart, and then Tiffany found out why he didn't want to use the ax.

Thursday

20

Tiny waves lapped near Ron's steel-toed Interceptor's as he stared out over the deep, clear water. Thumbs hooked behind his duty belt, he watched the false dawn chase stars from the pine-studded horizon. The eastern faces of the Bighorn's would be spectacularly lit above and behind him, but he didn't feel like taking in their splendor this morning.

Directly behind him, up at the Simkins' lakeside estate, the Division of Criminal Investigation's Regional Enforcement Team and criminalists from the State Crime Laboratory and technicians from the Sheridan County Medical Examiner's office were processing the scene, conversations hushed; even the squawk of their radios seemed subdued. A ragged puff of cloud drifted across the lake, shell pink and burnt orange on its leading edge, wispy gray tentacles dangling below. It floated along as if it hadn't a care in the world. Ron envied it.

The first call to 911 had come in at 2209. It had taken Ron and Tommy and Sheriff Neal and two Sheridan County deputies almost fifteen minutes to race around to the west side of the lake from where they had been set up on the back roads north and east of downtown. That was where most of the poor and isolated elderly people were congregated, nearly all of whom had attended Inglewood—or at least had relatives that had. Three troopers in the area had responded as well, one arriving first-on-scene, but even so, they'd had all they could handle corralling freaked-out kids and securing three separate crime scenes in two different buildings. Several wits had taken off already, afraid of charges for minority drinking and probably drugs (or just plain freaked out), and Ron had spent most of the night identifying the runners and tracking them down and hauling them back—or trying, at least; some had been friends of friends, and two or three were known only by first names or even silly nicknames; it had all been a futile attempt to keep a lid on the situation for as long as possible, but they'd at least had to go through the motions.

Ron grimaced. Every wit that had stayed had been on their phones when he'd first rolled up, texting or updating Facebook or Twitter or Instagram or God knew what else. He'd ordered all phones confiscated, ignoring their outraged protests, but ten minutes after he'd gathered everyone sulking and sans phones out in front of the main house, frantic parents began arriving, calling out desperately for their children.

The lucky ones had gotten answers.

He spit into the pebbled sand by his boot and checked it for blood again—clear, finally—and then fingered his swollen lip. Mr. Downing looked like the corporate accountant he was, but his right cross would make Sugar Ray jealous. Ron had kept hold of him even after Downing had decked him, not letting him inside the pool house, but Mrs. Downing had made it past while he was occupied with her husband, dashed inside, taken one look at her only child sprawled face-down across the once-white felt of the pool table, and then screamed and fainted right on top of the Hawkins kid. Mr. Downing had screamed his wife's name, then his daughter's, and then collapsed sobbing into Ron's arms.

The man didn't need to go inside; like all of them, he could see past the shredded blinds and into the pale interior of the pool house, all illuminated by the spotlights behind the wet bar.

Mr. Downing could see what had been done to his little girl just fine.

Ron spit again—still clear—then glanced up and down the shore at the colossal estates marching away in both directions, some as large or even larger than the death house behind him. A little over a mile away, near the end of the southern reach of the lake, the emerging light had revealed a long peninsula jutting into a wide cove, with tennis courts and a gargantuan pool set amidst a sprawling stucco-and-tile Spanish-style complex; dual boat docks with two massive lake cruisers tied up alongside them; Bob Junior's mansion. Or one of them.

It makes the rest of these spreads look like log cabins. The only thing missing was a place to land the family helicopter. Bob was infamous for his fear of flying, however, so no helipad, although Ron knew the man made up for it with a stable of classic cars that would make the most rabid collector bite his or her tongue.

Cowboy boots clopped on the railed concrete walkway that led down to the shore; the muted squelch of a radio accompanied them as the boots left the walk and approached him and stopped, but Ron didn't turn around; he wasn't the only one that had escaped down here for a few moments' respite over the long course of this night. Several of the men who made up the Regional Enforcement Team had daughters, too.

A throat cleared. "Chief?"

It was one of his own, but he still didn't turn. "What is it, Tommy?"

"Rife wants you up at the house."

"Which one?"

"The big one."

"I'll be there in a minute."

The RET had been assigned its own frequency, a necessity with the hodgepodge of agencies on scene, but Ron had turned his radio off—hence Tommy as gofer; he said nothing else, and Tommy hesitated before clumping back up the walkway. After the allocated minute, Ron sighed, then snapped his hand-held back on and turned away from the coming dawn.

When he stepped up into the Disneyesque backyard, however, he stopped; every man in sight was facing the pool house, hat in hand, head bowed. Ron faced the same way, but he didn't have a hat to doff, and he did not bow his head.

The ME had made the preliminary pronouncements—not that there was much mystery—and then hightailed it back down the mountain, leaving his flunkies to wait for the criminalists to finish before loading the meat wagons; through unspoken agreement, the Downing girl had been saved for last. Ron had excused himself and walked down to the lake when the state's techs had begun preparations to remove the pool cue.

A man and a woman wearing light-blue coveralls and matching cloth face-masks and booties appeared from the wide-open sliding-glass doors. Between them they wheeled a gurney upon which lay a dull-green body bag, zipped tight. They made their way around the diving board, and the rumble and squeak of wheels on granite pavers and the agitated twitter of swooping Chimney swifts disturbed from their lodgings high up on the main house were the only sounds.

Ron had seen too many bodies wheeled by in his time, but he kept his focus on this one as the ME's people left the pool and squeaked their way past sculpted banks of red and pink and yellow blooms and out of sight; then wide-brimmed hats were tamped back atop shaved heads, and quiet conversations resumed. The white jump-suited techs that had come out to watch now went back inside the pool house, heads bent together, murmuring through their clear-plastic face shields.

"Chief."

Ron turned.

DCI Special Agent Rife waved him over impatiently, then gathered the rest of the TFOs with a barked command here and a curt gesture there and led them through the topiary. Ron was at the tag end when they mounted wide flagstone steps and entered propped-open double-front doors. Rife stopped in the foyer, and everybody halted with him; there was room enough for the eight men to spread out and not crowd each other in its tiled and mirrored expanse, and the chandelier hanging over their heads gave plenty of light. Past Rife, part of a cavernous living room was visible, the back half cordoned off with yellow caution tape. Ron glimpsed the long blood stain soaking the beige carpet in front of the river-rock fireplace, where the Coulsin girl had been found; most of her, at any rate.

Rife addressed the team. "Gentleman, I have no goddamn doubt that the media is about to descend upon us like the pack of heartless jackals they are, so we need to steal a march on 'em. Chief, you and Sheriff Neal call a press conference. Schedule it for eleven hundred hours. Now this goes without saying, but considering who I'm talking too, I'll by God say it anyway: You'll feed *them* only what the AG gives *me* the green light to feed *you*. Understood?" Rife didn't wait for a response. "Matter of fact, you two will handle the media until this shitty ride is over. Your mission is to keep them out of my hair so the RET can catch this animal."

Three men ahead and to the right of Ron, Neal hitched his shoulders, which made his white cowboy hat bob close to the chandelier, and unwisely spoke up:

"Let Rogers handle the media. My men and I can help catch this bastard."

Ron's eyebrows twitched before he could control them; Neil backing away from a chance to get the mustache on camera was the last thing he had expected.

Rife swiveled his square head and put gray eyes that resembled steel rivets on Neal. Beneath his off-the-rack charcoal suit, Rife was only medium height and build, but he was as hard as you would expect from an ex Force RECON Marine and the former Deputy Commander of the Wyoming State Police before jumping to the DCI. Rife commanded great respect in the Wyoming law-enforcement community, and from what Ron had seen over the past few hours, it was well deserved.

Rife held that unflinching gaze on Neal for several heartbeats, then spoke quietly, at least at first.

"So be it, Sheriff. Your men will salt the roadblocks I plan to set up tonight, and we'll use your knowledge of the territory hereabouts to coordinate the locations of said roadblocks, but after that I will kindly allow you to take two of your deputies and scamper back to Sheridan or I don't give a good goddamn where and conduct Sheridan County business to the extent of your limited abilities, unless called upon by Chief Rogers to blabber to the vultures about this giant fucking mess you two have engineered for the rest of us to mop up. Are my orders clear on this, Sheriff?"

Neil stiffened with every word until the crown of his hat set the chandelier tinkling and swaying. "What about those prints at the two previous scenes? And the tracks on that dirt road out beyond Napier's place? My men worked hard to gather that evidence, Rife."

"Three scenes," Ron said, which got a turn of the hat and a glare over the mustache.

Rife held up rein-and-rope-calloused hands. "Enough. You're right, Sheriff, that was good work. Cheyenne is running with them now, and we should have boot and tire makes any minute. But we should've been called in *immediately* after the English teacher was discovered. Now we're playing catch-up."

And four families just paid for it.

But Neil didn't know when to shut up, or seem to share an ounce of Ron's guilt. "It was before dawn on the goddamn Fourth of July, Rife. I called as soon as—"

"You called only after that reporter from the Casper Star-Tribune told you he'd already contacted us for a comment and that we didn't have a single, fuckin', *clue* what he was blaberin' about!"

"Yes," Neil said, swiveling the mustache Ron's way again, dark eyes blazing. "And it's pretty obvious where he got his—"

"*Enough.* The Monday-morning quarterbacking will commence just as soon as we put this animal down, believe you me, but putting him down is the priority. Sheriff, you are dismissed until the meeting about the roadblocks. I will value your opinions and knowledge during that meeting, but until then, vamoose the fuck out of my sight."

Neil quivered, then spun and shoved through the gathered TFOs without a word; he glared at Ron the whole way out.

When Ron turned back, the angry rivets were fixed squarely on him. The DCI Special Agent had pulled him and Neil aside about three-thirty that morning after the underage wits had been released to their parents and the parents who no longer had children left to be released had been either told to go home, or driven home in the case of those in too deep of a shock to get behind a wheel—or in the case of Mrs. Downing, sedated and taken to the hospital down in Sheridan for observation. And then the RET leader proceeded to rip him and Neil up one side and down the other. Neil had tried to argue, but Ron had just nodded along: The DCI should have been called in at once, early on the Fourth of July or not. After Neil stomped away, Rife had looked Ron square in the eye and said it best:

He doesn't know any better, but you do, Chief.

Rife finally put the rivets up and rubbed his face wearily. Several of the TFOs had dragged on-scene with bloodshot eyes, either from lack of sleep or the depredations of the holiday or both, but even the good-natured grumblings had dried up and blown away upon seeing the girl in the pool house.

Rife dropped his hands and didn't look at Ron again. "All right, back to business." He hiked his thumb at the only other man in the foyer wearing a suit, but this one wasn't off-the-rack. "This is Special Agent Kinsley with the FBI. He's spoken to his superiors, and they have graciously offered to process our evidence through Quantico on the highest priority. I declined his offer just as graciously. I believe our rats have a handle on things."

More than a hint of tired irony laced Rife's voice as the team glanced at the Federal agent in their midst, most with guarded curiosity and some with open hostility. The Big G bullied its way into any case it wanted, especially if the spotlights were shining, but so far Special Agent In Charge of the Wyoming Field Office Brad Kinsley had only offered what assistance he could while observing from the periphery. Kinsley had popped up around two that morning with a pair of dapper agents in tow, and no one had questioned how he'd heard of the murders; it was just assumed that after sixteen years in the Wyoming FO, he had the law-enforcement community wired.

Bullies or not, Ron was glad to see the Bureau; like Rife, he knew Kinsley by reputation, and also like Rife, that rep was good. The FBI called places such as Wyoming "hardship postings", and the agents who were stuck there had the stigma of being the dregs of the Bureau, but after working with several over the years, Ron knew that that was mostly undeserved. D.C. was the cherry chased by the movers-and-shakers, followed by New York or L.A. or Chicago; the agents in the hinterlands had usually run afoul of internal politics—or better yet, didn't care to play politics. Despite the stigma, Ron knew they were nearly all dedicated and top-notch investigators with the weight and resources of the Federal government behind them.

But Ron also knew Kinsley wouldn't shy from seizing the reins if he could manage it. That was how the game was played. This was Kinsley's ticket out of Wyoming, if he wanted to punch it. Especially since multiple wits had confirmed what Smitty had seen. Kinsley, a big man with curly salt-and-pepper hair and a wide, hard gut hanging over his belt—that had probably kept him out of D.C. all by itself—only nodded to Rife, expression neutral, disdaining the sarcasm and the hostile looks equally.

"Next order of business: Those tourists are sitting ducks, so I'm sending Thomason to coordinate with the Park Service and shut down the campgrounds."

Someone up near Rife cleared his throat; likely Thomason, although Ron had only caught a few of the flurry of names that morning and wasn't sure.

"Um, they're not going to like that, sir."

"Who, the Park Service or the tourists?"

"Probably both, sir."

"Well, tough titties. This maniac has proven his vics are random; the only thing we know for sure is that he kills every night." The DCI Agent shot Ron a withering rivet-glare; he had filled Rife in on his Inglewood theory—Ron had even managed to convince a skeptical Neal, for a time—but given the kids' murders, kids that hadn't even been born before Inglewood had been reduced to scrap and carted away, Rife had drawn his own conclusions. "That means we know *when*, but we don't know *where* the hell he'll strike next. We don't have enough resources to protect everyone, so we reduce his targets as much as possible. Get with the Service and close those campgrounds pronto, Thomason."

"Yes, sir."

"*Now*, Thomason. I want those people cleared out by fifteen hundred hours at the latest. The *very* latest."

"Yes, sir."

Thomason passed grimly through his fellow TFOs and was gone. "Now," Rife barked, "as I said before, every goddamn smart-ass scribbler on the planet is about to descend upon my investigation, and one is bound to be bright enough to sniff out our freek. So from now on, we'll keep everything 10-21 unless it's a by-God, all-hands-on-deck, somebody's-gonna-be-fuckin'-dead emergency. I want everyone to write their cell number on a master list that I'll keep, and then we'll have to spend a few minutes updating our contacts, but it'll be worth it if we can spike—"

The radio in Rife's right hand squawked. "Rife? Helm."

The DCI Special Agent looked around with a stern expression and said, "10-21 from now on after *this*." He raised it to his mouth. "Go, Helm."

"We got him coming and going, sir, two sequences, almost four-minutes total vid."

The team stirred and exchanged excited whispers and even one or two low-fives, but Ron only waited; Helm's voice had been far from happy. Helm and another man he didn't know, both staties, had been sent to canvas the exclusive neighborhood on the off chance they could pull any surveillance video of the killer from one of the high-end systems. They had started at the north entrance because the wits had said the killer took off that way, two of the boys even following until the subject turned around and menaced them with the bloody ax. *Idiots.* Copping video was a longshot because most owners had learned to turn their systems off for the fireworks display; and some, like the young man who'd thrown last night's ill-fated party, disabled theirs because they didn't want rowdy guests to set it off—and, as Ron suspected with Deek Simpkins, so his parents wouldn't see the shenanigans.

Longshot or not, Rife had sent the men because he'd've been negligent if he hadn't, but everyone had figured it would be a lengthy process to learn well-heeled absentee owners' names, probably even a search in the property records and subsequent requests or even warrants for video; steps Rogers was sure they—and the people the killer would target tonight—didn't have time for. But now Helm was calling in a hit after only forty-five minutes; it was a break worth a few low-fives.

Rife could hear the caution in Helm's voice as easily as Ron, however; he shared the rivets around until everyone fell silent before keying again: "How's the quality? Can we get a still for distribution?" Everybody looked at each other as the silence dragged out. Rife keyed again. "Goddamnit, *talk to me!* What's your twenty?"

Helm came back with a squelch. "Twenty is…" He recited an address, then added, "Eighth house from the highway on the woods' side, sir. Uh, about that still… You should look at this first. I think you need to see it."

Rife slowly lowered the radio while staring at Ron. All the TFOs in the foyer stared too, including FBI Agent Kinsley. He'd told Rife what Smitty had said, and a dozen wits at the party had reported the same, but almost none of the jaded law-enforcement personnel on the RET had really believed it—or perhaps *wanted* to believe it.

Rife raised the set and keyed while still staring at Ron. "Inbound. Hold position, Helm."

"10-4."

Rife squared his shoulders and marched outside; the team parted for him or they would've been run over.

"C'mon, boys. Let's take a gander at this piece of dog shit."

Ron let everyone go first while he looked past the caution tape at the rusty blotch in front of the wide river-rock hearth, then followed the last man into the red and slanting sunshine.

Dawn. He'd missed it again.

21

The owner of the security video was named Rockingham. He was a lawyer with receding silver hair, bleached teeth, a heavy golf tan, and the overdeveloped upper body of a gym rat north of sixty trying for forty. He was from Los Angeles, and this was his vacation home—one of two, actually. The other was out in Big Bear, California. Rockingham used to defend scumbags for pocket change until he got wise and started suing doctors. That's why the state-of-the-art security: rapists, murderers, and drug kingpins were one thing, but a doctor from whom you'd just taken reputation, career, and then home…well, that's a whole other level of dangerous.

"Never end up in the hospital, that's my advice. People die in hospitals. And you wouldn't *believe* some of the ways—"

"Can I offer any of you gentlemen coffee?"

Mrs. Rockingham appeared from the restaurant-ready kitchen and stood in the arched native-stone entryway to the cathedral living room. It was early, and she was barefoot with no makeup, yet Mrs. Rockingham was lithe and buxom in black athletic shorts and a sleeveless white tee-shirt and black sports bra. She had long, lustrous dark hair and big dark eyes, and if she was thirty yet Ron would eat his badge.

Crickets. Rife finally cleared his throat and said, "No thank you, ma'am. I believe we're all good."

"All right, then." She turned, hips twitching, hair swaying, and disappeared back into the kitchen.

The lawyer grinned like a wolf and shrugged. "She's wife number four. By six or seven, I figure I'll have the knack of picking them."

The toothy grin faded as they all just stared at him, and then Rife said, "Sir, could you please play the two video sequences you showed Lt. Helm a few minutes ago?"

Rockingham straightened and donned a solemn expression; Ron figured it was his courtroom face, although the vast majority of lawyers never saw the inside of a courtroom—or wanted to.

"I'd be happy to, Special Agent. Tragic situation, just tragic. Those poor children." He raised a black remote about the length and width of a professional wrestler's forearm and squinted at it, then said, "Ah, here we are." He pointed it at an eighty-inch HD flat-screen that hung high on a natural-stone wall, and the TV flickered to life, glowing bright blue. "Incidentally, Special Agent Rife, this system has a fail-safe that instantly downloads a copy of real-time footage to an off-site server, and both the original and fail-safe footage are archived to the cloud every twelve hours as a second tier of redundancy. I keep six months before I dump it, so if you think this madman came around here before, you won't need to get a warrant; I'll cooperate in whatever way necessary."

"Thank you, sir, but let's see what we have first and then we'll go from there."

"Of course. Tragic, just tragic…" The lawyer pushed another button, and the blue turned into a black-and-white nighttime view of forty-foot lodge-pole pines and thick undergrowth.

Rife said, "Pause it, sir, if you would."

"Of course." The image stilled, and a counter appeared in the upper-right corner; it read 11:13:36 p.m. 03/JUL/2015.

Silence, more silence, and then Rife growled, "Sonofabitch!"

He waited, Ron thought. *He hid inside the house all day and all through the party and waited for his opportunity.* 11:13. *He must've come straight from killing old Bill, or near enough. But that was risky;* anything *could have happened, could have gone wrong. Why risk everything?* That led Ron down a path he didn't want to walk, but his mind went anyhow: *Unless he knew just where and when he was going, and why. And* that *means—*

"Yes," the lawyer said, interrupting Ron's stunned thoughts—and every other team member's, judging by their faces—on why the killer had camped out the entire Fourth inside the Simkins' estate. "My wife and I flew our Cessna in late last night to catch the fireworks from the air, like we do every year. Spectacular. Just spectacular. Have you ever watched fireworks bloom from the darkened earth in every direction, Special Agent Rife? I recommend you do so at least once before—"

Rife scowled; he didn't look at the lawyer when he cut in, saying, "Which direction are we facing here, sir?"

The shyster's eyes narrowed, but his voice was still courtroom-smooth when he said, "Ah, yes. I believe that's—"

Helm spoke up. "It's a camera on the north wall; specifically, this is the view north from the compound's northeast corner, sir." The Trooper glanced at the lawyer. "Sorry to interrupt."

Rockingham gave Helm a wry grimace. "Of course."

Helm turned back to Rife. "There are eight boxes, two on each corner, deterrents, but this one is below those, set flush. It's not exactly a pinhole, but you gotta get close and know where to look."

"Yes," Rockingham intoned. "A smart doctor can avoid or disable cameras he can see. These are for them, although you'd be surprised at how dumb even the smartest…" They were all staring at him again. "Yes, well, please continue, Lt. Helm."

"That's the best view of him we have, sir; him and his vehicle."

"*Vehicle?*" Rife whipped around. "Sheriff, call some of your men up here and—"

Helm broke in. "There's a utility access road just beyond that line of trees, sir. Runs behind the whole development on the mountain side. I cordoned off a wide area, well away from where he parks and walks. Unless they drive in and jump the tape, nobody will mess around back there." Trooper Helm ostentatiously cracked his wide, knobby, and chapped knuckles. "Or at least they *better* not."

Rife relaxed; a fraction. A tiny fraction. "Good work, Lieutenant. Mr. Rockingham, will you please continue the video?"

"Absolutely."

The black-and-white footage resumed. Mrs. Rockingham came out of the kitchen and weaved through the officers, who made way while tipping their hats. She stood next to her husband with her arms crossed under those full breasts, hugging herself and frowning up at the television. Ron figured it couldn't be easy for her to know that a mass murderer had been just outside her home, even if he had stayed on the other side of multiple safety barriers that only a pile of money could erect.

After twenty seconds of nothing but pine trees, Neil shifted and whispered to the man next to him, "What the hell are we—?"

Rife snapped, "Be silent!" just as headlights shone through the needles before going dark, and then the square, bulky form of a pickup halted on the utility road. Even through the intervening trunks, it was clear the truck was a boxy Ford F-150, mid-nineties model, single-cab four-wheel drive with gleaming chrome aftermarket wheels, jacked up with knobby off-road tires and tinted windows.

Ron recognized it instantly; if the footage had been in color, he knew the truck's paint would be a dull, dusty red.

Sheriff Neal recognized it, too.

"Son of a *bitch!* That's—!"

"*Be quiet!*" Rife roared.

"But that's Jack Ross's truck! I'd bet my left nut on it!"

Special Agent Rife swung around as Mr. Rockingham paused the video without being asked. "Sheriff, if you continue to discuss my investigation in front of the public, then not only will I have you escorted from these premises and remove you from the RET entirely, I will make it my everlasting mission in life to see that you are never elected to trouble the people of the great state of Wyoming again."

Neil opened his mouth, glanced at the Rockinghams', and then closed it. Rife didn't need any more; he turned back to the screen, and the lawyer continued the video, again without being told.

Ron could feel Neil's glare, but didn't acknowledge it; the Sheriff wanted him to confirm the ID on Jack's truck, since he was the only other man in the room who would recognize it. But his mind was in turmoil:

Jack Ross?

It didn't make sense.

And then the Ford's driver-side door opened and a fever dream rose from the cab.

You could've heard a cat whisker hit the deep-pile carpet as everyone watched the man wearing a giant chicken costume shut the door and reach over the bed rail and pull out a long fireman's ax. And then Ron caught his breath as the man swiveled his little round sunglasses toward the Rockingham's wall; it felt as if he were looking at them even as they were watching him; more than one team member shifted, and Mrs. Rockingham squeezed her eyes shut.

Then the bizarre figure turned away and walked down what Ron assumed was the utility road; after a few seconds he reappeared in a break in the pines off to their left, and they saw he wore jeans and boots below the bulky feathers and black jacket. Ron strained to make out details of those boots, but in black-and-white and at night and so far away—it had to be over forty yards at that point—it was only possible to tell they were boots and not sneakers. Three more glimpses of him swaying between the tall, straight trunks, carrying the ax in his left hand, long, feathered tail arching behind, and then he was gone.

Utter quiet as the lawyer pushed buttons, and the screen went solid blue once more. Mrs. Rockingham buried her face in her husband's shoulder, and he patted her back absently as he pointed the club remote at the television and it filled with the grainy black-and-white woods behind the wall again, but now the time stamp had jumped to 10:25:46 p.m. 04/JUL/2015.

The Ford sat there, and then suddenly there was motion on the far left of the screen and the nightmare reappeared, striding and swaying through the pines, and even from fifty or sixty yards away and in grainy black and white, the dark blotches on his pants were plain.

Blood.

Someone cursed, and several muttered, but all eyes were on the man as he swayed closer and casually tossed the ax into the bed, opened the door, and climbed behind the wheel, bending nearly in half and scooting forward to do so.

And then they all watched in silence as the Ford backed around; seconds later the faint shine of headlights appeared and then swung toward the highway and freedom.

Mr. Rockingham stopped the video.

Rife hung his head. Two or three seconds of total silence went by. Then the DCI commander straightened and turned around; Ron had never seen so much fury constrained inside one face. "Thank you for your cooperation, Mr. Rockingham. If it's all right with you, I'll have our techs make—"

"Rife, *listen to me*. I know who—"

"In a minute, Sheriff. They'll eventually need to work through what's stored in the cloud, but for right now—"

"I recognize—"

"*In a goddamn minute, Sheriff!*" Rife took a deep breath and blew it out. "The technicians will need to make a copy of this for the investigation. Is that fine with you, Mr. Rockingham?"

The silver-haired lawyer peered at Neil like a bird at a worm, then looked at Rife and spread his hands, tree-branch remote waving to the side. "Anything I can do to help, Special Agent."

"Thank you." Rife hesitated, then added, "I'm afraid I must also ask for your discretion, Mr. Rockingham. Yours, too, Mrs. Rockingham. If the press catches wind of this…well, let's just say I don't need all that mess. I need to catch this murdering piece of weasel shit—pardon my French, Mrs. Rockingham—before he kills someone else's kid."

The lawyer and his wife looked at each other, and then she nodded and Rockingham said, "Of course, Special Agent Rife."

And then he smiled.

Behind Rife, two extra-wide staties exchanged a glance.

Rife shook his head, but only muttered, "Thank you. Those techs will be here soon."

Neal was shifting from boot to boot like he had to pee and shooting Ron glares over the mustache. "Rife, I recognize that truck. So does Chief Rogers, even though he's not—"

"Everyone outside! *Now!*" Rife pushed past Neil and walked out of the Rockingham's considerable front door, followed by the team. Ron was last, and he looked over his shoulder to see the lawyer already with a cell phone pressed against his jaw. Mrs. Rockingham met Ron's eyes, and her bee-stung lips curled slightly.

He pulled the heavy door shut with a thud.

Rife stalked around the circular driveway and past the silver convertible BMW 540i with the pink California vanity plate that said "Hers 4.0" and past their squad cars and plain-wraps and up to the wrought-iron double gate. Ron figured "His" was still in L.A., or maybe behind one of the quadruple doors of the detached garage, although he didn't make the lawyer for a BMW. A Mercedes or a Jaguar would be a better fit; probably a Jag.

Rife stopped between the wide-open gates and waved everyone close, then fixed Neil with the rivets.

"Who the hell is Jack Ross?"

"He's a murdering son of a bitch, that's who he is. Ten…no, eleven years ago now he got drunk and beat Zack Richards to death at a high-school graduation keg party down by the lake, way out at Hawk's Point. Plead MS with intent and served five out of ten. Ross drives a '94 F-150 four-wheel-drive piece of shit that looks a helluva lot like the one our freak-show was driving." Neal turned to Ron and smirked. "Chief Rogers here knows it, but he ain't sayin' nothin cuz he's 'ol Jack's buddy." Neal faced Rife again. "There's somethin' else. Ross has a connection to the Downing girl. She worked for him."

Rife's face didn't change, but the rivets darkened, and the energy of the men listening became charged, just as Ron had known it would when the link between Jack and the girl came out.

Neil picked up on it and pounced. "Let's go hook this bastard up and see what he has to say for hisself. Hell, I bet he's good for it. I always knew that son of a bitch would—"

Rife held up his hand, shushing Neil, and turned to Ron.

"Chief, tell me about Jack Ross."

Neil's lips writhed like mating worms beneath the mustache, but he kept them pressed together as Ron said, "Jonathan Eugene Ross, twenty-nine YOA. Resides out on the south slope of Crow Ridge with his parents. Frames houses all over the state and sometimes the surrounding states, except from Memorial Day to Labor Day, when he operates Crazy's, that hamburger stand off Highway 279, just outside the gates to the Rocky Branch Rec Area. The Downing girl started working for him there this summer."

"You see? Even his pal admits—"

"Be quiet, Sheriff. Now, Chief, tell me what everybody *doesn't* know about Jack Ross."

Ron met the Special Agent's unyielding gaze, then nodded. "After serving his five, Ross stayed clean and completed a three-year tail in eighteen months; early termination for GB. After I took the job, I wanted to know about him, so I contacted his PO and she only had good things to say: doesn't drink or drug, works hard and takes care of his parents and that place out there. His father had a stroke seven months ago." Ron glanced at the glowering Neil.

"What else?" Rife's growl was soft—if iron could be called soft.

"Some say Ross got drunk and murdered Zack Richards, but the truth is they were all drinking at that party, and the twins jumped him."

"Now wait just a goddamn minute! That's—"

Rife spun on Neal like a cat, and the taller Sheriff snapped his teeth together and backed away two steps. The DCI Agent kept that stare pinned on Neil and rolled his hand at Ron, telling him to continue.

"During the fight, Zack Richards stumbled over an old deadfall and the back of his head rammed down onto about three-inches worth of broken branch sticking out of a dry Ponderosa log; just enough to shred his brainstem, unfortunately. Ross and the boy's twin tried to help him, so did others, but they had no medical training and it took the ambulance almost forty minutes to get around to the north side of the lake over those old logging and fire roads. Long story short, the Richards' boy was DOA. Sheriff Neil was called to the scene, and he arrested Ross on suspicion of murder one, though the DA later reduced the charges to manslaughter. The boy's court-appointed lawyer convinced him to plead after the prelim found enough probable cause for intent, but plea or no plea, some say Ross shouldn't have gone to prison at all, and that the twins had a history of violence, and that in a way, Zack Richards got what was coming to him. Some also say Bob Jr. not only muscled the judge and prosecutors' office into imposing the maximum sentence, but also into sending Ross to a stew like Torrington instead of a minimum security facility as should have been done, considering the mitigating particulars."

He looked at Neil.

So did everyone else.

"*Some* say," Ron added.

Neil's face was a red thunderstorm under the hat brim, and his mustache was almost jumping, but he somehow stayed quiet. Rife studied the Sheriff, then looked at Ron.

"Do you think Jack Ross could be good for this?"

"It doesn't matter what I think; Neil's right, that pickup is a dead ringer for Ross's Ford. There's also the connection to the girl. He needs to be questioned."

Rife nodded sharply. "I agree." Then he squinted at Ron. "*But...?*"

"The man who did what was done to the Downing girl... Sir, we're talking about rage. Add the English teacher, and you've got pure fury directed against women. I don't believe Ross has that in him." Ron shrugged. "But, like I said, he needs to answer some questions. Oh, and he has an alibi witness for the teacher."

Ron caught more than a whiff of disappointment from Rife. "Who?"

"His girlfriend. Angela Beaumont. She was with him that night, over at his place. His parents may vouch for him, too."

Neil's cell phone rang then, and he shot a sneer at Ron before stepping away to answer. Rife's cell began to play classical music, and then every man's phone rang or sang or beeped or vibrated, including Ron's; Fleming's cell. Ron had ordered Ryan to stay in Indian Head and mind the store. The team split in nine directions to answer nine calls.

Nine at once. A tingle began in the back of Ron's head. "Rogers."

"Chief, we've got a big problem." Ron could hear the desk phone buzzing in the background.

"What is it? I'm busy here. And answer that damn phone. You don't have to wait for Mindy."

"Um, I don't know if that would be such a good idea, Chief."

"Why not? Tell me what's going on."

Fleming told him.

Halfway through, Ron looked at the other team members and saw them getting the same news. Rife had his eyes squeezed shut and gripped his iPhone so hard it was a wonder the thing didn't crumple. Neil was cursing and yelling at someone, and FBI Special Agent Kinsley said something and hung up and then deliberately moved away from the team, calling a new number as he went. Rife hung up and watched Kinsley with a resigned expression, then met Ron's eyes.

"Goddamn cell phones. I hate 'em."

Neil hung up and then pointed the mustache at the ground, not saying anything for once. The rest of the team ended their calls and waited silently until Rife blew out a long breath, then squared his shoulders before plowing back toward the mansion.

"Okay, boys, let's go borrow the goddamn egg-sucking lawyer's giant TV again and see how deep the shit is."

When he was far enough away, a plus-sized statie muttered, "Should we tell 'im we can watch it on our phones?"

"Be my guest," another statie said. Glances were exchanged, and then the RET trooped after Rife; nobody said a word.

Ron waited until the final man went by, but this time he wasn't last. FBI Special Agent Kinsley stood not very far from the fender of "Hers 4.0", free hand cupped over his outside ear as he listened to someone on the other end of the line; Kinsley's gaze tracked Rife until the DCI Special Agent disappeared inside.

22

Angela stood in Chris's living room with her purse and keys and sunglasses in one hand and the remote in the other. It was almost nine-thirty, and she needed to go if she was going to make it to Crazy's by ten, but they would show it again at the half-hour and she wanted to watch; it would be the tenth time she'd seen it, but, like the entire nation it seemed, she couldn't get enough.

She was watching CNN Headline News, but the shaky cell-phone video had first broken on Fox. Now even the networks were running it—all showing "Courtesy of Fox News" on a tag line at the bottom—and even flagship morning programing like *The Price is Right* had been preempted by talking heads. An icy dread pulsed through Angela, but she did her best to ignore it as she waited for the commercial for flavored coffee creamer to end. When the spinning red "Breaking News" graphic filled her brother's fifty-inch Sony flat screen, she un-muted it.

A handsome man in his late forties with a distinguishing white dash peeking from his dark hair looked grimly out of the television at her. "We have breaking news this morning," he informed her. "A murderer has been caught on camera, and the bloody ax in his hand isn't the most horrifying thing about him—apparently, this killer is also wearing a *costume*." He turned to his co-anchor, a stunning thirty-something blonde with large green eyes. She took the hand-off smoothly.

"Yes, Tom, and this is sending shock waves around the country as Americans wake from their Fourth of July celebrations to the scene of a massacre. We're going to show you the footage—the parts we *can* show you—but first some background for those of you just joining us. This cell-phone video was captured in the resort mountain town of Indian Head, Wyoming. Indian Head is on the eastern slopes of the Bighorn Mountains, in Sheridan County, the north-central part of the state."

As the blonde talked, a satellite map of Wyoming appeared over her left shoulder and then swelled, zooming viewers below and to the right of the long, inverted comma of the mountains to Indian Head, and Angela felt a sense of unreality; her flyspeck hometown had made the national spotlight, but in the worst possible way.

The map vanished and the male anchor picked up the thread. "Special Agent John Haskins of Wyoming's Division of Criminal Investigation confirms that four are dead from this terrible attack, but when asked about reports that this same killer has also struck the previous two nights in a row, murdering two elderly residents of Indian Head on the second and third of July, Haskins had no comment. He also had no comment about the ages of the victims from the Fourth of July slayings, although as stated before, this network has received word that the four were juveniles or young adults attending a lakeside party. At the top of the hour CNN also reported that an unnamed suspect has been identified and is being sought for questioning, but again the DCI spokesman had no comment. Haskins did announce a joint press conference to be conducted by the Indian Head Police Department, the Sheridan County Sheriff's Office, Wyoming's Division of Criminal Investigation, and the FBI, who are assisting with the investigation. The conference is scheduled for eleven a.m. Mountain Time, one o'clock p.m. Eastern, and will be held inside Indian Head's downtown square."

The camera pulled back, and both anchors folded their hands on the electric-blue desk as the blonde took over. "Now we're going to the video. From CNN's family to yours, we must warn you that even this heavily redacted version might not be suitable for young children. We'll give you time to remove them from the room before starting."

Then they sat there staring out of the television with somber frowns and an eager glimmer in their eyes because a third of America was watching (at the very least). Five seconds went by—Angela assumed this was plenty of time to shoo an inquisitive six-year-old—and then her stomach fluttered as a familiar jouncing, chaotic scene filled the television.

Angela had never gone in for the whole home-video movie fad, ala *The Blair Witch Project*, or any of the ubiquitous *Monster-Eats-New-York-City-Except-For-The-Teenager-Running-Around-With-The-Video-Camera* movies, although she'd suffered through a couple with Brian, but this was different:

This was real.

Panting. Running. Bare feet flapping and shoes scraping on concrete. Pine trees and then darkness and then white and blue sneakers on sock-less feet above hairy male legs and then landscape lighting and then darkness and then white and yellow flowers and then the camera steadies on a concrete path running beside a three-story French Colonial.

More panting, more running, then a male voice, the timber deep but young: "Holy BLEEP! Did you see that?"

The camera swings to the left and there's a glimpse of a barefoot muscular shirtless guy wearing sopping-wet cargo shorts with his face blurred and then back to the path as they round the corner of the Colonial into a vast, sloping yard filled with manicured mature pine trees spaced well apart. Off to the right is a long and winding driveway marked by more landscape lighting and lined by more shaped pines. Cars and pickup trucks are parked grill-to-bumper along the far edge.

Another adolescent male voice, this one from behind the camera: "No, man. See what?"

And then the sound of running stops:

"BLEEP!"

"BLEEP BLEEP BLEEEEEEEEP!"

"What the BLEEP is that?!"

"Holy BLEEP!"

The camera swings wildly and then steadies on a large figure striding across the yard; caught in a patch of illumination from the lights shining at the edge of the nearby driveway, the image is of a man wearing the top half of a wacky leather-jacketed giant chicken costume. The ax in his black-gloved hand is clearly visible. So is the blood splattered on the man's jeans, and the suit's reddish-orange feathers, and the leather jacket, and the ax head; the long handle glistens wetly in the lights.

"BLEEEEEEEEP!"

"Oh my BLEEPing God!"

The camera holds steady as the figure stops next to a tall pine and turns slowly to face them. The bulbous red comb lays over to the right as it dangles down his feathered forehead, and the round black sunglasses perched on his hooked beak seem to bore into Angela's brain. He grips the wet handle in both gloved hands and stares at the camera for at least five long seconds. The boys say nothing, but their breathing is fast and loud.

Angela knew what was coming next and winced in anticipation.

A shrill female scream shatters the tableau, wailing on and on like a tornado siren. The camera jerks around to point back toward the big house.

"What the—"

Another young woman's voice, in the distance: "OH MY GOD! OH MY GOD!"

The barefoot shirtless guy appears again as he takes hesitant steps back down the walk, face still blurred. More piercing screams join the first, male and female. The shirtless guy bleeps again and runs toward them. The guy with the phone starts to follow, then stops and swings back to point the camera toward the yard, steadying the shot on the pine tree, but the blood-splattered man in the bizarre half-costume is gone.

Turn again and running back down the concrete path between the flowers, bare feet slapping, shoes scraping, panting, more screams, more yelling, oh-

my-God's every two seconds, pure pandemonium, following the shirtless guy, bleeping every two steps as the bouncing view shows bushes full of white and yellow blooms, and then the back of a smaller house appears on the right. The shirtless guy skids to a halt with a bleep as two teenage girls in bikini bathing suits run across the path from right to left in front of him, screaming with their hands pressed over their faces. The shirtless guy takes off again and rounds the corner and vanishes and the kid behind the cell camera bleeps as he sprints to catch up. He turns the corner and the shimmering blue light of a swimming pool comes into view as he says, "What is it? What the BLEEP's going—"

The screen went blank.

The anchors reappeared, grave and silent. The blonde looked pale beneath the makeup and had to swallow before speaking. "I'm afraid that's all we're allowed to show you. The rest is too gruesome for national television." She opened her mouth to say more, but nothing came out.

The camera hurriedly swiveled to cover the male anchor; *he* still had that gleam in his eye. "To summarize, four are confirmed dead in the resort mountain town of Indian Head, Wyoming, in what was apparently an attack by a man dressed in the top half of a gi-ant chicken costume. Authorities are not releasing the age or name of the victims, but a source has told CNN they were teenagers or young adults attending a Fourth of July party being thrown at a lakeside estate. There are also unconfirmed reports that this attacker has killed two other people the past two nights, also in or around the town of Indian Head. The multiple law-enforcement agencies on scene have scheduled a joint press conference for eleven a.m. Mountain Time, one p.m. Eastern. That's all we know for now, but of course CNN will bring you any breaking developments."

The camera switched to the double view again, and the blonde took over, full mouth pressed into a grim line, green eyes deter-mined. "We're joined now by Dr. Roger Whittier, a Professor of Criminal Psychology at the University of Maryland. Dr. Whittier worked for twenty-five years as both a field agent and as a profiler in the FBI's Behavioral Analysis Unit before retiring nine years ago to teach at UM, and during his time with the FBI he played a part in catching dozens of this country's worst killers." The anchors swiveled their stools to the left, and the camera angle expanded to show a man seated at the end of the long oval desk. He was balding, and wore rimless spectacles and a conservative dark-gray suit and a subdued maroon bowtie, but those things did little to disguise wide shoulders, a deep chest, and an erect bearing. "Welcome, Dr. Whittier."

"Thank you."

The male anchor leaned forward; the white spot over his temple was incandescent under the hot lights. "Dr. Whittier, what can you tell us about the mental state of someone who would dress up in a costume and kill four people—with an ax, no less."

"Not being part of the investigation, and thus not privy to the details, I can only speculate from a distance on the pathology of such—"

Angela shut the television off and tossed the remote on the couch. Her steps wobbled as she left the condo and locked it behind her with Chris's spare key and then made her way to her Camry. She cranked the air and adjusted the vents to blow on her and gripped the wheel with both hands and squeezed her eyes shut.

That psycho *had been in her house.*

He had been *stalking* her.

And if I hadn't decided to go to Jack's…

Jess Barbary's nude, hanging, and desecrated body appeared on the back of her eyelids and Angela hurriedly opened her eyes. She shuddered, then groped in the passenger seat until she found her water bottle. She wiped her mouth and spun the lid on and backed out of Chris's guest spot and drove to work.

Angela thought about her sketch as she wound her way up from the cove. She and Chris had argued about whether to call Chief Rogers and tell him they'd seen the man in the Elvis chicken costume on Monday; her annoying brother had pointed out that several hundred people had probably seen the guy that day, and that the cops were no doubt getting more calls than they could handle, and Angela had conceded the point—but she also doubted anyone else had drawn a picture of him. Chris had agreed with her—about that, at least—and had left it up to her to call. She'd ultimately decided to wait, but she would eventually tell Rogers about the sketch and hope that it would help. Somehow.

What they'd really argued about was whether Angela should go back to work for Jack. She'd finally told her brother to mind his own damn business, but in truth he'd been distracted by worry over how several of his wealthy clients—wealthy clients who were considering relocating their families to Lochmore Estates—would react to the murders, and his heart hadn't been in the fight. A hasty Skype meeting had been scheduled with Bob, who was out of town somewhere on business, as usual, and Chris had been in a rush to meet Zane at their office; before he left, however, her arrogant brother *had* conceded that she was a grown woman (thank you!), and that she could work for whom she chose (thank you!), but when he'd added that comment as he'd grabbed his keys and hurried off, that snide little snippet about her burgeoning relationship with Jack...

Angela eased her double grip on the steering wheel; hateful remark or no hateful remark, she hadn't had the heart to tell Chris that there was no relationship because she'd already screwed things up.

She dug in her purse one-handed to retrieve her fourth antacid of the morning; between video of the psycho who had stalked her and the memory of how she'd acted yesterday, her stomach was a hot knot. *How could I have been so stupid?* So Jack had slept with Miriam Jacobson, so what? It had been a long time ago, and he'd tried to explain that Miriam had been the one to invite him over, and that he'd told the slut no because of Angela, but she'd been so *furious* when she'd saw that hot-bodied whore grinding her hips against the order counter…and holding Jack's hand…

Angela eased her death-grip on the steering wheel again and blew out a long breath.

And who was she to judge? There'd been that married GD professor in college, the dreamy one with the eyebrows, but she'd broken it off after she'd realized he wouldn't leave his wife for her, that he was just stringing her along for sex. But she'd been so *tired* yesterday and still traumatized by finding poor Jess strung up like that—and then finding out that *freak* had been inside her *house*—that her temper had gotten the best of her.

She'd always had a bad temper, and after seeing that dark-haired hussy *throwing* herself at Jack…Angela eased her grip again. Jack had been hurt at first, and then seemingly as mad at her as she was at him—which had just made her even madder. But by the end of the day she'd been so tired and Jack had gone so cold that all she'd wanted to do was go back to Chris's condo and sleep for two weeks. And now all she wanted was for Jack to hold her again, like he had yesterday morning in Crazy's parking lot.

God, she was so *stupid* sometimes. How was she going to make this right?

I'll just have to apologize and hope he accepts. She could blame it on the shock of finding Jess and the lack of sleep and everything else, and then pray things went back to the way they'd been before she'd lost her idiot temper. Then she could stay at Jack's barn for the next few nights…yes, that would be *much* better than staying with her holier-than-thou brother…

Angela frowned and hit the brakes, jarred away from Jack's hard arms and soft lips under the starry skylight over his bed; traffic had ground to a halt. The drive up to town had been slower than usual and the congestion heavier, but just how slow and heavy she'd missed while agonizing over what a mess she'd made. She glanced at the flood going the other way; SUVs and pickups loaded with gear and kids and pets, most pulling boats or personal watercraft, interspersed with campers and big RVs.

The tourists are running.

Through breaks in the pines on a switchback curve above and to her right, Angela glimpsed a news van complete with satellite dish poking from the roof; the media was invading Indian Head. She checked the dash clock and scowled, annoyed; her house was another mile or so, and she'd planned on ducking under the stupid yellow caution tape and feeding Jess's cats again, but now it would have to wait until tonight or she would be *really* late. The thought of going home after dark with that maniac running loose made her scalp prickle. Maybe she could ask Jack for an hour off during the afternoon lull, drop by and feed them then.

Yes, that would be better…

Angela suddenly growled at herself in disgust. *Sitting in line like a tourist.* She waited for a crack in the flood and punched a U-turn, eliciting a honk from a guy in a tan Ford Explorer pulling a collapsible camper. She rolled down the window and flew him the bird and then left the highway a quarter mile later and proceeded to make her way around town on the lake-side, passing disgruntled locals doing the same. She pulled out her phone and called Jack, discarding the sudden and cowardly urge to hang up.

"Hello?"

"Hey," she said. "It's me."

"Hey."

He didn't sound mad; he sounded…well, calm. Not at *all* what she'd expected after how she'd treated him yesterday. He said nothing else. She looked at the screen to make sure the call hadn't dropped; that happened up here sometimes, but a lot less since they'd put up those two new towers.

"Hello?"

"Hello? Can you hear me?"

"Yes. I thought the call dropped."

"No, still here."

"Oh. Well, uh, I was calling to let you know I'm going to be late. There's a bunch of traffic, what with all the commotion because of the murders." Then she remembered all those books and realized he might not know yet; Angela doubted he watched much television. "Did you hear what's going on?"

"Donnie and Miguel are watching the video on Donnie's phone. For about the hundredth time." In the background, Donnie told Jack to eat him.

"Anyway, I'm running late, but I'll be there as soon as—"

"You don't have to come in. We can cover it."

"Jack…" She swallowed, forced it out: "I'm sorry about yesterday." Silence. "I really, really am. I was wrong. It's none of my business who you've slept with, and I'm in no position to judge." Nothing. Angela frowned, but kept her tone smooth. Barely. "Besides, I promised to help you guys, and I don't go back on—"

"It's not that. Hold on." She heard a door open and shut, and then him walking across the gravel. Then he spoke, voice low and tired. "The Park Service evacuated the campgrounds. You don't have to come in because I'm thinking even opening Crazy's today will be a waste of time." He sighed. "But we're here, so we'll finish prep and flip the sign, and then if lunch goes the way I think it will, I'll send Donnie and Miguel home in the afternoon and close up shop."

Angela's heart went out to him; this was his make-or-break week, and it was turning up break. "Send them home if you want, but I'll stay and help with whatever you need. Besides, I want to talk to you. Face to face."

There was that silence again. Then he said, "Okay. That's good. I want to talk to you, too."

"Good," she said…but she was frowning again. The sparkle was gone, that was it; he sounded like he was talking to his insurance agent, not her. Angela shrugged it off. *He's just upset about his business.* "I'll be there in a few minutes. I'm trying to make my way around town to the west, but it's been *years* since I've been down this way." She forced a laugh. "Hope I don't get lost."

"See you when you get here."

The line went dead.

Angela slowly lowered the phone into her lap.

A *wump-wump-wump* both felt and heard brought her head around as a helicopter swooped over the scattered farms and houses dotting the pines before darting out over the lake like a giant dragonfly and streak toward three others hovering over the southwest end.

News choppers. Maybe it really *was* an invasion.

Angela raised her phone and looked at it. Jack had hung up on her. Was it just worry about Crazy's? *No. It's more.* She could feel a gap between them now. Her little tantrum yesterday had done this.

She had done this.

Angela blinked back tears. She'd created this chasm, so she'd just have to bridge it no matter what it took, because she was just realizing that her feelings for Jack Rossie Ross went way beyond like.

Way, *way* beyond.

It was ten twenty-three when she pulled in next to Jack's truck and walked around to the side door, aware of Jack and Donnie and Miguel peering out at her past the menu board. The exodus of tourists droned just a few dozen feet away; Crazy's lot was empty—except for the employee vehicles parked off to the side, of course—but the Shell across the highway was beyond packed.

Angela spied a Wyoming State Trooper car sitting in the shadows next to the drive-through spray wash, facing across the road. Two extra-wide cops hulked inside, the outline of their flat-brimmed hats distinct against the crosshatched safety cage. She figured they were there to keep an eye on the flood, but at that moment they were both watching *her*. The driver pressed a cell phone to his ear.

She opened the door. "Hi, guys. Sorry I'm late. And, um, sorry about how I acted yesterday." Best to get that out of the way.

Donnie gave her a shy grin. "Hey, no problem. Everyone has a bad day now and then."

Jack didn't respond, or even look at her; instead, he turned from the onion he was slicing and looked at Miguel. Miguel looked at Angela, and then *he* looked at Jack and shook his head and dropped back below the dungeon window.

Angela stifled sudden irritation. *What was all* that *about?*

Irritation flared to anger as Jack *still* wouldn't acknowledge her, so she thumped her purse onto a wire shelf and stamped into dry storage and snatched cups and straws and napkins and began to stock with a vengeance. *So* that's *how it is. Two can play this game!* She helped where she could while keeping up a conversation about the murders with Donnie and ignoring Jack and Miguel; after a few minutes, Jack reached up and cranked the volume on the radio.

Talk with Donnie petered out, so she worked and fumed and watched them and noted Miguel and Donnie seemed fixated on the flow of trucks and SUVs and boats and campers; coupled with their sidelong glances at Jack, it was easy to understand their concern. But Jack hardly seemed to notice the fleeing tourists, and she finally figured out he was watching the extra-wide Troopers. Each time he glanced at them sitting over there in the shade beside the auto-wash, his brown eyes seemed resigned, almost sad…but also unquestionably sullen. And she didn't understand why.

After about ten minutes of that crap, she'd had enough; either he would talk to her, or Angela would hit him with something. She dipped the last onion ring in the batter and placed it on the end of the row and covered the tray with Saran Wrap and shoved it through the window at Miguel and then wiped her hands on the towel hanging from her back pocket and marched over to Jack and stared up at him until he finally blinked at her with mild surprise, almost as if he'd forgotten she was even there!

She jabbed him in the shoulder with her index finger. "You." Jab. "Outside." Jab. "Now."

Angela stomped to the side door and held it open. He stared at her and didn't move, and she eyed a steel napkin dispenser—*that would make a nice dent, even in Jack Rossie Ross's titanium skull!*—but then he sighed and wiped his hands on his own towel and tossed it on the counter next to the cash register and walked past her and out. Donnie and Miguel were very much not looking at them. Angela let the door bang shut; she didn't care what they thought.

She didn't!

Jack waited for her in the shadows beneath the awning, directly under the speaker. He had his thumbs hooked in his front pockets and was staring across the road with that resigned, angry look again. He didn't turn when she stepped up beside him, so she took his hand and made him face her.

"I'm so sorry. I was wrong to judge you. Like I said on the phone, I don't care who you've slept with, and it's none of my business besides." His skin was warm, his fingers callused. "I know she's the one who…who…" Threw *herself at you. Slut.* "…came to see you, and that you turned her down because of me. I should have listened, but after seeing Jess, and finding out that weirdo was in my house, and I was so tired…I lost my temper, Jack. I do that sometimes. I'm sorry."

He just stared down at her, regret now filling those clear brown eyes. Angela caught her breath as he gently brushed a strand of hair from her forehead.

And then he pulled his fingers from hers and looked across the road again and spoke in a monotone: "You have nothing to be sorry about. You were right. I've been thinking a lot about it. We took things too fast. Besides, you deserve better than me."

She reached for his hand again. "Jack—"

He took a fast, smooth step away, like a dancer. "*Don't.*" That face was a mask of pain, but then calm resignation replaced it so quickly Angela wondered if she'd imagined the other. "I'm a nobody, Angela, a nobody going nowhere fast, and an ex-con to boot. My boss fired me yesterday. He's starting a project for Bob, and me not running a crew was an unofficial part of the negotiations. So that's that. And now, with Crazy's failing…so much for owning a real restaurant someday. I'll have to find a job now, somewhere local because there's no one else to take care of Mom and Dad, maybe down in Sheridan…Christ, I'm *never* getting out of here." He looked at her then, and Angela almost wished he hadn't; his eyes were fully dead now, like muddy ponds with all the life choked out. "You need someone like Zane, who can give you an amazing life." Lightning flashed across those muddy ponds. "Okay, maybe not Zane, but someone that can be there for you and only you, that can provide the things that a special person like you deserves. That's not me." He put the mud-dead eyes back across the road. "Maybe Miriam is all I deserve, someone who just wants a toy. That's the only kind of woman a man like me needs in his life."

Angela trembled. All the sorrow and pain, along with the ten thousand things she wanted to say to refute his self-pitying gibberish, washed away in a black tide of rage.

Miriam Jacobson.

Words seared into Angela's brain in lines of ruby-red flame:

The kids are going camping.

Remember, Jack, Saturday night.

So much she wanted to say…so much she *needed* to say…and what pops out of her stupid mouth?

"Will you see her on Saturday?"

If he says yes, I'll…I'll just…augh!

He didn't answer her question, though. Instead, he nodded toward the highway and spoke, voice both wry and resigned.

"They're here."

Angela's head whipped around as five vehicles crunched into Crazy's lot, one after the other after the other. Chief Rogers led in his dusty brown-and-green Indian Head patrol car, followed by an unmarked navy-blue Crown Victoria with a chrome spotlight mounted above the driver's mirror. Behind that were two Wyoming State Troopers and a windowless white Chevy van that had State Crime Lab stenciled on the side in big black blocky letters. The Trooper that had been sitting at the Shell turned on his party lights and chirped and bulled his way across the highway, then crunched up behind Jack's truck sideways, blocking it in, making the count six; the Crime Lab van blocked *her* in.

As Chief Rogers and two men in suits and a herd of uniformed officers opened their doors and stepped out, Angela realized that Jack hadn't sounded the least bit surprised to see them.

23

They stared at my Ford when they got out, and then I watched them exchange glances and shut their doors and come, all but Chief Rogers with expressions that said I'd already been tried, convicted, and sentenced.

Angela said, "What's going on? Why are they here?"

I ignored her.

They stepped under the awning and spread into a semicircle with me at the axis. Two wore suits, and I keyed on the shorter one in the gray pinstripes, mostly because he'd zeroed on me like a hungry eagle and I was the rabbit. But whoever was in charge, Chief Rogers was the one who extended his hand and said, "Morning, Jack."

We shook. "Morning, Chief. What can I do for you?"

"I suppose you've heard about the situation we have?"

"Yes, sir."

"Son, some questions have come up, and we need to get answers from you."

"Am I a suspect?"

Rogers nodded. "For now."

Two guys wearing blue latex gloves and carrying clipboards slipped from the Crime Lab van. One wore an honest-to-God pocket protector overflowing with blue, black, and red pens. They went to my truck, conferred in low voices, and then circled it in an intent, professional manner; they didn't touch it, not yet, but they glanced our way every two seconds, impatient to get to work.

My scalp prickled. "Should I get a lawyer?"

Rogers shrugged. "I told them you might talk voluntarily. Up to you."

"This is so stupid!" Angela burst out from beside me. "Jack didn't hurt anybody!"

Everybody looked at her except the one I'd marked as the lead dog. He had buzz-cut gray hair, an outdoorsman's mahogany tan, and the build of a drill instructor under the cheap suit. He said, "Jonathan Eugene Ross, I'm Special Agent Steven Rife with the Wyoming Division of Criminal Investigation." He didn't offer to shake hands. "As Chief Rogers' said, we have questions for you, and you will continue to be a suspect until you answer those questions to my satisfaction. You can answer those questions the easy way or the hard way, but you *will* answer. And just so you know, the Chief vouched for you, or you would already be under arrest. Now, son, I'm aware of your past and your present, and I have to agree with his assessment; you don't seem like the type of man who would commit these crimes. But we have evidence that points to you, and I'm here to either clear you and take this investigation in another direction, or arrest you for murder."

Above stunned-to-speechlessness me, Night Ranger's "Don't Tell Me You Love Me" faded and WROK went to commercial break and a man who sounded like he'd ingested too much caffeine or crack or both squawked about a mattress liquidation, low-low prices this Fourth of July holiday week only. Rife glared toward Crazy's and pointed up at the speaker: "Hey! Turn that crap off! I can't hear myself think!"

A wide-eyed Donnie and Miguel were pressed up against the inside of the order window. I nodded to Donnie, and he reached up and clicked off the radio; the speaker over my head whined before going quiet.

"*Thank* you," Rife barked. He squared on me again. "Now, what's it gonna be, son?" He produced an iPhone three incarnations newer than mine and showed me the darkened screen. "I've got a judge on standby. She's ready to issue warrants for your pickup, your place of business, and your barn, as well as your parent's house and property."

Rogers said, "Talk to us, Jack. Let them look at your truck. We can be done with this in just a few minutes."

I stared at him, and he just nodded. So I nodded back and then opened my mouth and said something to Special Agent Rife that was probably pretty fucking stupid:

"I'll talk to you."

Rife continued to hold the phone out. "What about the truck?"

"You have my permission to search it, but I don't know what you're looking for."

"Let us worry about that."

He stepped around a barrel-chested Trooper and scribed a fast circle in the air with one finger, and the Crime Lab dweebs sprang into action. One whipped out a tiny digital camera and click-click-clicked, mostly focusing on the tires. *The tires?* The other squatted next to my driver-side front tire and produced a small set of gleaming chrome calipers from his giant pocket protector and measured something and then jotted more something on his clipboard.

I swallowed.

Angela twined her small fingers into mine. I glanced down at her in surprise, but she kept those fierce blues pinned on Rife. Unlike before, I didn't pull away; I just squeezed gratefully, and she squeezed back.

"Mr. Ross." Rife was now planted three feet in front of me with fists crammed on hips, suit coat spread, the butt of his matte black semi-auto—an HK Tactical .45, very nice—sticking out of an underarm combat holster; the German hand-cannon hung on his right side. Rife was left handed. "Tell me where you were between nine-thirty and ten-thirty last night."

And then he looked at Angela.

They all did.

She flushed a beautiful pink as she shook her head. "I stayed with my brother." She explained, and a new tension entered the group, even Rogers, but I kept my focus on Rife, the man with the key; the key that would either set me free, or lock me up again.

Rife scowled. "'A little after nine'? Can you tell me the *exact* time your brother picked you up, Ms. Beaumont?"

She glanced up at me worriedly. "I think the dash clock said 9:13."

"You *think?* We need specifics, young lady, not—"

"It was a few minutes after nine, Special Agent Rife. Ask my brother. He might know the *exact* time."

"Oh, I will, Ms. Beaumont." He faced me again, fists planted on hips, feet spread. "Tell me where you were last night."

So I did, making an attempt to appear forthright and innocent; you know, not lick my lips or shuffle my feet, maintain eye contact, so forth and so on. But the teensy-weensy fact that I *was* innocent didn't make me confident of anything because I knew from hard experience that innocent or guilty didn't mean squat; our justice system is a machine, and once the powers-that-be decide you are deserving of being ground within its gears, that machine is loathe to spit you out.

"Can your parents back your story? You said they were there when you got home."

"Yeah, but I'm pretty sure they were already in bed. Dad has an appointment with his stroke specialist down in Buffalo this morning, I think at ten, and Mom took the day off to drive him. I heard them leave around six-thirty, when I was working out, and they saw my truck then, but as for last night, I'm not sure. Mom said something about going shopping, after, so they won't be back 'till late this afternoon. But you can call and ask."

I rattled off Mom's cell number and Rife made the circle-move with his finger and the heftiest patrolman fished a dinky spiral notepad from his uniform shirt pocket and clicked a tiny pen to life with Kielbasa fingers and asked me to repeat the number. I did.

Rife stared at me without blinking through the second recitation, then inquired, "What boot size do you wear?"

"Twelve. Why?"

The men behind Rife exchanged glances—*not good*—but before I could further ponder the implications, George Jones started crooning about the bottle in his hand. The other suit—a big man with curly salt-and-pepper hair and a heavy, hard gut—pulled a phone from his hip, rudely cutting off George; "Special Agent Kinsley." Kinsley's caterpillar eyebrows shot up his forehead. "Yes, *sir*." He placed a palm over his free ear and walked out into the sun and kept going, putting distance between his conversation and the other men.

Rife watched Kinsley with a hard scowl, then planted that scowl on me. "Size twelve, huh?"

"Yes, sir."

Rife produced his own little spiral notebook and licked his thumb and flipped back two pages: "Do you own a pair of Red Wing Heritage Men's work boots? Specifically, the model 8146 six-inch Moc Toe Lug Boot?"

The hope I'd been clinging to, the hope that said this was all a big, silly mistake, detached itself from my tenuous grasp and disappeared into the darkness on a greasy slide to hell.

"Yes."

Angela's hand clenched mine, almost to the point of pain. I felt her looking up at me, but I kept my gaze on Rife, the man with the key.

"Where are they?"

"Uh, I think they're in my armoire, up in my bedroom…no, I put them in my toolbox." I pointed at my truck, where the techs were comparing clipboards and nodding like dweeb bobble-heads. "It should be open. I never lock it unless I'm carrying a bunch of tools."

"Helm."

The smaller (smaller being relative) patrolman standing behind Rife stepped forward.

"Sir?"

"Go ask the boys to check."

"Yes, sir."

Helm trotted past my green trashcan and out into the sun, bulk jiggling under the uniform. Everybody watched him go except the largest Trooper, who kept alert on me. Helm relayed the orders, and the dweebs lifted the lid on my scratched chrome toolbox with their blue-gloved hands, peered inside, reached in and eased stuff around for a bit, then glanced up and shook their heads.

I said, "Then I guess they're in the armoire."

Rife nodded. "We'll need to examine them." He sized me up for a second. "Will you still cooperate, or should I bother the judge?"

"Yeah, you can look at my boots. Hell, you can search my barn, my business, my truck, or any other goddamn thing you want."

"Calm down, son."

"I'm calm, Special Agent Rife. Don't I fucking *look* calm?" Angela squeezed a warning. "Look, I don't know what 'evidence' you have, but I closed Crazy's at nine and stood in my lot and watched fireworks until they were over and then I drove straight home and went to bed. I don't know if anyone *saw* me do it, but that's what

I did, and if you don't believe me, you can take a flying fuck at a rolling—wait a minute." I jabbed my finger at the Shell across the highway. "Their security footage will show you *exactly* when I left."

They all looked at the station and then back at me.

Chief Rogers said, "Security footage?"

Rife frowned at him as I explained my arrangement with Darryl, singed hope scrabbling back up the greasy slide, but the Special Agent only sent it wailing back down again with, "That'll just tell us when you supposedly left, not where you went. Speaking of that, what were you doing Tuesday night? Say around eleven-fifteen?"

"I did the same damn thing, minus the damn fireworks. And by eleven-fifteen, I was in bed, sound asleep. What—"

Angela said, "I followed him to where he turns toward his place, after we left here. Before I found…" She blinked and cleared her throat. "So I can attest to that much." Her sudden and indignant blue-eyed sneer was a thing of beauty. "You can't think Jack would—"

"And you were both here all day the Fourth?"

"Yes," I said. "Well, except when Angela went with Chief Rogers. But what's that—"

"You have an employee named Tiffany Downing. Age sixteen. Correct?"

And then I finally got it; a faint buzzing started in my ears, but I still heard myself say, "She's dead, isn't she."

Angela let go of me to cover her mouth with both hands. "Oh my God!"

"Answer the question."

"She…she used to work for me. She quit the day before yesterday. Well, she didn't exactly quit, she just didn't show up. Her mom called and told me she wouldn't be back, though."

Something changed in Rife's expression, and it spelled bad news for my future. "How did that make you feel? Did it piss you off?"

"No, it didn't piss me off. And no, I didn't kill Tiff. She was a good kid, Rife. I'm sorry she's gone. I'm sorry for what her parents must be going through."

"Holy shit! Tiffany's *dead?*" Donnie's moon-face was pressed to the screen above the order window, jaw slack and skin three shades pastier than usual.

Rife wheeled on him like a wolverine in a suit. "Young man, that hasn't been released to the public, and if I hear even a *whisper* in the media, I guess I'll know who to come down on with both boots, won't I?"

Donnie just stared through the mesh, then turned and stumbled deeper into Crazy's. Rife muttered something before rounding on me again.

"That was a nice speech, Jack, but—"

"Special Agent Rife." The tech with the pocket protector stood by my furthest picnic table; the other geek was still by my truck, scratching eagerly on his goddamn clipboard. "I need to speak with you, sir."

Rife growled, "Stay put!" and marched over and snatched the clipboard and read while the dweeb whispered and pointed helpfully with a blue finger. Everyone went with the lead dog, crowding around to listen…everyone except the biggest cop, who stared at me from beneath the flat brim of his tilted-forward hat. By that expression, he was watching a large, erect turd, a turd that he sincerely hoped might make a break for it.

"Jack." Angela took my hand again; she looked almost as scared as she sounded. "What's going to happen?"

I never got the chance to answer because that's when Rife shoved the clipboard into pocket protector's hands and stamped back over to me, followed by the whole gang; I sought out Chief Rogers, and what I saw in his face frightened me.

Rife said, "Son, we got us a big problem. We can now connect your pickup to five of the six murders."

"This is so *stupid!*" Angela erupted. "Is Jess one of those? Well, that's impossible, because I was *with* him that night!"

"I am aware, young lady. It's one reason your boyfriend isn't in cuffs."

"He's not my boyfriend. We're just friends."

I knew it had to be so—had told her myself that it had to be that way—so hearing her say it shouldn't have hurt…but it did.

Bad.

"Be that as it may—"

"There's more." Angela found Rogers with pleading eyes. "Chief, I wanted to call you this morning, but I knew you'd be busy. Chris and I saw him. We *saw* him. And I sketched him."

She launched into her story, finishing with, "So it *couldn't* have been Jack. And I bet you've had other people calling, saying they saw a giant chicken waving signs around on Monday while standing smack in the middle of town. I *also* bet you can find witnesses—witnesses like Zane and me and my brother and Donnie and Miguel, not to mention the dozens and dozens of customers who ate at Crazy's Monday afternoon, and the video from across the road Jack told you about—and every *bit* of it will prove he was right here all day!"

That got the gang out under the baking sun and into a sweaty, muttered conference. The other suit, Kinsley, was still out there on the phone, and he watched the gathering, too, even as he nodded and responded to something said on the other end of the line.

Angela squeezed my fingers and smiled up at me, and I smiled back while pushing down thoughts of the concrete and steel, baby, not the fucking concrete and steel again, Jesus Christ, anything but that; and just friends, only friends, but boy oh boy, how I wished it could be different.

And then Rife led everyone back beneath my awning.

"Did you also happen to see Jack's Ford parked at this pawn shop?"

Angela glanced up at me uncertainly. "Well, yes."

I opened my mouth, indignant (and more than a little scared), but Angela squeezed sharply and said, "But that's not the *only* place I saw it," and told them about glimpsing it at Marcie's just before the hock shop. Rife raised an impatient eyebrow at me, so I hastily confirmed I'd slipped up to town on an emergency dry-goods run; Donnie and Miguel and Tiff could…Donnie and Miguel could back me up.

Rife frowned for a moment, but all he said to Angela was, "I have to follow the evidence. And that evidence—*hard* evidence, mind you—is pointing straight at your 'friend'. I'll watch the gas station video, if there is any, and question witnesses to find out who was where when—but I believe it's time for the judge to dash off those warrants. We need to take an official gander at those boots, then go from there." Rife saw my expression. "That should be good news, Jack. If you didn't do this, then more information will only prove it, and sooner rather than later." He made the goddamn finger move again. "Advise him."

Trooper Helm tweezed a white business card from his uniform shirt pocket and read me my rights and asked me if I understood those rights.

"Yes."

"But Jack *didn't hurt anybody!*"

"Be quiet, Ms. Beaumont. This is just a precaution. He's not in cuffs. Yet."

Concrete and steel and no sunshine and stale air and bad food and worse company. Fuck me. But even as I signed the back of the little card on the nearest picnic table and handed Helm his fucking pen back, there was this whisper running through the back of my head:

My tires, my boots, my truck somehow in two places at once…

"I'm being set up."

They considered me with faces that said they'd heard that from a thousand cons, and would hear it from a thousand more… all except Chief Rogers. He squinted somewhere into the middle distance, pursed his lips, and nodded slowly.

That got the hope scrambling back up the slide, yes indeedy it did, but before I could do more than open my mouth, sirens chirped and wailed out on the highway. We all turned to look as traffic pulled to the shoulder just before two Sheridan County cars crunched onto my lot, followed by Sheriff Neal's pearl-white Chevy 2,500 diesel; two more county mounties brought up the rear. They all had their lights going, even Neal's blue dash bubble and the flashers behind the chrome grill. People pumping gas across the road gathered in excited clumps to watch as they shut the sirens down, but kept the lights strobing. Rife cursed.

As Neal ducked beneath the awning, the Special Agent snapped, "What do you think you're doing, Sheriff?"

"My job."

He planted his shiny cowboy boots in front of me and straightened to his full height. "Jonathan Eugene Ross, you are under arrest for six counts of first-degree murder. Lace your fingers behind your head, spread your feet apart, and stand still while my deputies search you."

"You can't do this!" Angela fumed. "Jack didn't hurt anybody!"

"Goddamnit, Neal!" Rife shoved his way between us. "I said *what the hell do you think you are doing?*"

"And I told you: my job."

"Your *job?* Your *job* is to help coordinate those roadblocks, not arrest my suspect! Now take your boys out of here and let me conduct this investigation!"

Neil sneered. "And while you're *investigating*, a murderer is walking free and endangering the good people of my county. I won't stand for it one second longer." He glared down at me over the mustache. "I said hands behind your head and spread 'em!" He turned to his deputies and bobbed the hat brim in my general direction, and five of Sheridan County's finest started for me.

Angela said, "No, you can't do this!", and clung to my arm. A beefy deputy seized her by the other arm and jerked her away.

She cried out.

Beefy's eyes shot wide, and he let go of Angela to raise one hand to fend me off and grope for his gun or pepper spray or both with the other. I snatched the raised hand, and there was a loud *crack-crack-crack*. He shrieked and dropped to his knees in the gravel in front of me.

"You don't touch her."

Helm fumbled out a Smith & Wesson roughly the size of an ICBM and dropped into a shooter's stance and put the business end of the giant revolver on me:

"Let him go and step away, hands in the air! *Now!*"

Neil's stunned deputies put their hands on their holstered butts and looked at Neil; I flexed my wrist, and the asshole at my feet moaned.

Angela had her fingers pressed over her mouth; her frightened whisper came from behind those tented fingers: "Let him go, Jack. Please."

I drank in the sight of her, then released the shattered digits and stepped away and raised my hands over my head…and then tucked into a ball, but they still drove me into my own rocks; rough points pressed hot and hard into my cheek as someone in a brown uniform put a knee on my head and another knelt in the small of my back and yanked my hands behind me and cuffed me while I had my rights read to me for the second time in five minutes.

"Angela, call my mom and tell her not to—"

A boot toe slammed into my ribs. "Shut up, dirtbag."

"*Stop it!* You can't treat him like that! Tell her not to what, Jack? Jack! Tell her not to what?"

"…work in law enforcement in the state of Wyoming again, I promise you!"

"Do what you have to do, Rife. I answer to the people of Sheridan County, not the DCI. And sure as hell not *you*."

"…broke my fingers! The sonofabitch broke my *fingers!*"

Another boot toe landed, this time in the kidneys, where it hurt the most.

"Ya like that, tough guy?"

"*Stop it!*"

"Neil, tell your people to back off!"

"Stand 'im up! Did you advise 'im? Good."

"Goddamnit, Neal!"

"*He broke my fingers!*"

"Shut the hell up, Dorsey! I *told* you he was dangerous. Maybe next time you'll listen. We'll have that hand looked at shortly. *I said stand that piece of shit up!*"

Two deputies grabbed me by the elbows and yanked me to my feet. My vision swam, but I glimpsed a crying Angela off to one side and a disappointed-looking Chief Rogers to the other before Sheriff Neil filled my world.

"You're under arrest for assault with bodily harm against an officer *and* six counts of first-degree murder, shit-for-brains. Your ass is grass this time, and I'm the fuckin' Lawn Boy. Jennings, get Dorsey down to Doc Swanson so he can look at those fingers."

"Yes, sir."

"Neal, this is my last warning!"

"Hathaway, search Ross and then stick 'im in the back of B-ride and watch 'im."

"Yes, sir."

They felt me up and patted me down and emptied my pockets and put my stuff into plastic baggies and then hauled me stumbling across the hot gravel. Angela kept up off to the side, wringing her hands; tears poured down her cheeks.

"Angela…"

"I'm here, Jack."

"Tell Mom not to put anything up for a lawyer."

"…there'll be hell to pay for this, Neil! Mark my words!"

"What do you mean? You *need* a lawyer!"

"Bring it on, Rife. We'll see who standing in the end."

"She'll want to hire someone, and the only thing we have that's worth anything is the land. Don't let her sign it over. I'll get a public defender."

"Are you sure that's smart?"

"I'm innocent, you know I am. I'll work with a PD. I'll be fine, I promise."

Hathaway laughed. "Yeah, he'll be *just fine*, sweetheart. Now stand back." Angela moved away as they opened the back of B-ride and shoved me in; my right ear smashed into the top of the door frame.

"Oops! Watch your head, tough guy."

"*Hey!* I saw that! You can't—!"

The door slammed, muffling Angela's protests. Pain flared from the tightness of the cuffs; sitting on them wasn't helping. I was forced to lean forward, and my knees were already smashed up against the hard-plastic backing; the crosshatched safety cage loomed inches from my face. Also, the cruiser was running, but the air wasn't, and it was beyond stifling.

Claustrophobia and, yes, a bit of panic closed in, and I took deep, slow breaths:

I will NOT scream. I won't give them the satisfaction!

I breathed and not-screamed and turned my head to see the end of Angela's fruitless argument as Hathaway walked back toward Crazy's; the other deputy stayed by the car. I heard several curses in Angela's sweet voice, and then she looked in at me and stretched out a hand and said something, but I wasn't a lip reader so I couldn't tell what the hell it was.

Impotent rage burned in my throat.

I'm innocent as a lamb this time, but I'm still going back behind the fucking concrete and steel!

I gave her a ferocious grin, and she furrowed those slim golden eyebrows uncertainly. It was so hot in the cruiser. I couldn't breathe. I couldn't breathe. I breathed anyway and grinned from ear to ear and my eyes slipped past her to Neil, who said something to a beet-faced Rife and then they were piling in, Dorsey cradling his ballooning hand as he climbed into the passenger seat of the other lead car, two more asshole pigs into *my* car, Hathaway driving, and the good Sheriff into his truck. I stared at him until I couldn't see him anymore, and then I imagined him removing his hat and wiping the sweat away and turning a vent to blow cold air on his mustache as he watched the back of my head in satisfaction.

Fuck you, Neal.

Hathaway said, "Comfy back there, tough guy?"

He and his buddy laughed, but I didn't deign to answer. Hathaway cranked up the air, and I forced myself to not strain toward it; they might see and turn the vent away.

We pulled onto the highway, and Angela stretched her hand out to me again and said something; it looked like "I love you", but that was probably just wishful thinking. Or delirium from having my skull slammed into the gravel. Or the rabid claustrophobia. Then the green wall of needles hid her, and I leaned back on my tingling hands and closed my eyes and just rode.

The last Sheridan County radio car vanished behind the pines, and Ron shifted his thoughtful gaze to the clumps of people over at the Shell as they yakked excitedly both to each other and into their phones; meanwhile, Rife was busy having a stroke on his own phone while he informed someone at the DCI what Neil had done.

This play makes no sense.

Oh, sure, this was Neil's jurisdiction, and the man could arrest anyone he chose as long as he had probable cause—and even if he didn't. But preempting the DCI's Task Force, especially like this, was tantamount to career suicide; the Sheridan County Sheriff's Department didn't exist in a vacuum. There was cooperation on myriad levels, such as multi-agency training in new tactics and equipment, not to mention budget supplements for purchasing that much-needed equipment—a budget the Director of the DCI if not controlled, then had a heavy hand in steering; Neal was burning bridges he couldn't afford.

And then there was Rife. Neil had just made a lifelong enemy, and a bad one; bottom line, even if Sheriff Neil convinced the people of Sheridan County to let him serve another four-year term next election season, he was done in the state of Wyoming; it was only a matter of time.

"Chief?"

Why had he done it? Had Neil's loathing for Jack Ross clouded his judgment that far? *No, I can't believe it.* Neil wasn't the brightest bulb, but when it came to self-preservation, the man always had a wet finger in the breeze; the Sheriff would understand the consequences.

So why?

"Chief!" Someone grabbed his uniform sleeve and shook it. Ron looked down into the tear-streaked face of Angela Beaumont. "You have to do something! Jack wouldn't hurt Tiffany, or those other kids! Or anyone else! I *know* he wouldn't, and so do you!"

"Tell that to Deputy Dorsey."

She flushed prettily. "He was just…being protective of me. We're friends, and that jerk shouldn't have grabbed me."

"Well, he sure didn't improve his situation with that little stunt."

"You *know* he didn't do this! What about Jess? He couldn't have killed her, he was with me!" Her face twisted. "*Neil.* He's had it in for Jack forever! You *can't* just let him—!"

"It's out of my hands."

"But—"

"Do what he asked and contact his parents. He'll need a good lawyer."

"He doesn't want them to put up the money. He says he'll make do with a public defender."

"That's up to him, but—"

"*Chief!*" Rife stalked under the green awning. "Why is she still here? Get her gone." Rife jabbed a finger at Crazy's. "Them, too. They're all stinkin' up my crime scene—and it's still *my* crime scene, I don't care what that idiot Neil thinks he's doing. As soon as Judge Haskins' clerk faxes those warrants to my car, we're gonna tear this place apart."

Angela flared, "How *dare* you? And *crime scene?* This isn't a stupid *crime scene!* It's Jack's business, and he didn't—!"

"Right away, sir." Ron propelled Angela toward Crazy's. A brawl between these two could turn bad, and fast; enough blood had already been spilled.

"He has no *right* to talk about me like that! And he doesn't have the right to tear Crazy's up! *And stop pushing me!*"

Ron kept his voice low. "As soon as those warrants come through, he does, and that was just a figure of speech." *I hope.* "They have to search for evidence. Get in touch with Jack's parents, it's all you can do. And go easy with Rife. Neil's already put a twist in his shorts."

"Why, because that asshole arrested him first? Like I give a damn. Let go of me!"

Ron did, since they were around the side of Crazy's by then and out of Rife's laser sights; the door was propped open, and Don Straus and the Mexican cook, Miguel Rodriguez, watched them uneasily: "Just contact his parents. That's all you can do right now."

Her face crumpled. "I don't know their cell numbers, and I don't think they have a land line. I guess I'll head out to their place and wait until they get home. Oh God, I don't know *how* I'm going to tell Mary. She's such a sweet lady…"

A throat cleared, and they turned to see Don standing in the doorway. Rodriguez hung well back, and when their eyes met, the thin brown man jerked his to the floor; illegal, but Ron already knew that. He wondered if Jack knew. Ron also wondered if Jack had a glimmer of what young master Straus had been up to lately; he doubted it, because the boy was still working at Crazy's. Jack wouldn't tolerate that nonsense…or at least Ron didn't *think* he would; after that crap with Deputy Dorsey, Ron wasn't as confident in Jack's judgment as he had been.

"I've got his mom's number," Don said, and held up a cell phone. "Jack made me save it in case…in case anything ever happened and he couldn't call."

Angela stumbled over and hugged him, still crying. "Thank you, Donnie."

The boy turned seven shades of red, but he met Ron's eyes even as he patted her awkwardly on the back. "Jack wouldn't do what they said, Chief. He wouldn't hurt Tiffany."

Ron sighed. "I don't think so, either. But it's not up to me."

Rife's snarl appeared at the mesh above the register. "*Why are they still here, Chief?*"

Rodriguez ducked and scuttled into the kitchen as Don said, "Hey, man, we gotta turn off the grease so this place don't burn down, and put all this food in the walk-in. Give us five minutes."

Rife glared, then relented: "Five minutes. But my men will search you before you go. No evidence leaves this scene." He spun and stomped away.

Don said, "Prick. What, does he think someone's gonna stuff a fucking giant chicken costume in their back pocket?"

Ron said, "Hurry up. The man means five minutes. Does anyone have a set of keys?"

Don said, "Sure, I do."

"Give them to me and I'll lock up when they're done."

The exchange was made, and then they put away food and powered the kitchen down as Ron walked back around and crossed his arms and leaned against the wall near the window where you got your food. Rife and the state patrolmen and the lab rats milled around Jack's truck without touching, impatient for the warrant. Ron pretended he didn't see Donnie pull Jack's .45 Colt off the shelf above the register and hand it to Angela, who secured it in her purse. He also pretended not to hear a whispered conversation concerning Rodriguez's wife, who was also illegal, and who didn't want to pick her husband up with so many *policia* around. Ron couldn't blame her.

Special Agent Kinsley of the FBI had finished his phone call, but he was still standing out there in the sun. He, too, had his arms crossed as he watched Rife and his men, and then the fed looked straight at Ron; after a second, he nodded. Ron nodded back. Kinsley uncrossed his arms and motivated through the picnic tables and under the awning and wiped glistening sweat from his broad forehead with a sleeve and put his back up against the wall on the other side of the steel counter holding the napkin dispensers and mustard and ketchup and mayo squeeze bottles and crossed his arms again.

The whispers from inside dropped even lower.

"Chief."

"Special Agent."

Rife stormed up. "Well. Don't you two look comfy. Are they gone yet?"

Angela's voice floated from inside: "We're leaving!" All three then trooped out the side door; it slammed before they came up front.

Rife pointed at their feet. "Halt right there." They froze. He whistled, and two state boys trotted across the gravel. "Search 'em for anything pertinent to this investigation."

Don Straus scowled ferociously, but stayed quiet; Rodriguez was equally silent and kept his eyes down; they took the most time with Angela, of course, but she didn't seem to mind. Helm even wore a little appreciative grin until Rife's glare wiped it away; however, all hell broke loose when they dumped her purse onto a picnic table. Ron had to separate Angela and Rife again before the Troopers finished pawing through the contents, but they let her keep "her" gun, which she told them she carried for protection, and had since she'd lived in Chicago. The techs had to move their van so Don and Angela could back their cars out; Rodriguez rode with Angela. Ron chuckled when she rolled her window down and thrust her arm out, middle finger flying.

Rife shoved that square, leathery face into his: "Something funny, Chief? Because I sure as hell see nothing funny about chopped-up kids. Do *you* find anything funny about chopped-up kids?"

"No, sir, I do not."

Rife stomped away.

Ron went back to the shade and leaned and crossed his arms again; Kinsley hadn't moved.

"So."

"So."

"When's the Bureau taking over?"

"Who said we are?"

"C'mon, Kinsley. I was watching when you answered that call."

The fed glanced at him appraisingly. "Chief, I keep forgetting you're not just some hick." Kinsley pushed off the wall and uncrossed his arms and put a hand on his hip and cracked his back, first one side then the other. He folded his arms again and settled against Crazy's tall menu board; the FBI Agent spoke softly, watching Rife the entire time: "That was Deputy Director Knots on the phone. Met him?"

"Haven't had the pleasure."

"Believe me, the pleasure would be all his. DD Knots just informed me that the Kansas City FO got a call right after that video broke this morning. Some enterprising chap who owns a chain of fast-food chicken joints in and around KC called, get this, Rocky's Rockin' Chicken, says that's his suit, ol' Rocky the Rockin' Rooster himself—the top half of him, at least. Rocky, by the way, seems to be missing his inflatable electric guitar as well as his legs. He and his guitar disappeared three weeks ago to the day, along with the employee who was wearing him, twenty-two-year-old Miranda Leigh Keys. Miranda was outside the Overland Park location on Cavanaugh Rd. while strumming the guitar and waving at traffic— part of some promotion for bigger, tastier nuggets—and she and Rocky and his guitar vanished somewhere between 1545 and 1600, just before Keys was scheduled to hand Rocky off to the next lucky employee in the Rocky-rotation and cool off and take a restroom break; can't stay in those things long without cooking, apparently, at least in this heat; broad, sweet-summer-daylight abduction, in other words. Overland Park PD confirms." Kinsley turned his wide head and looked at Ron. "Four days later, some farmer outside Kershaw, Iowa found Keys' body on the edge of one of his giant corn fields. She'd been dead for over forty-eight hours, so the farmer followed his nose, obviously. She was also nude, and she'd been tied up, gagged, sodomized, and then raped to death with a foreign object. Did her right there in the black Iowa dirt, between two rows of golden tassels. Quantico says the bastard's partial to orange-plastic mop handles for his fun time, generic brand, and that it likely took the unfortunate Ms. Keys upwards of six hours to die."

"He tortured her to death. With a mop."

"Yep. The fate of the inflatable guitar, however, is still unknown."

They stared at each other across the squeeze bottles while something more than electricity jolted through Ron's limbs. Kinsley nodded slowly before looking back at Rife. "Anywho, the interstate thing gives us an in, Chief, and we're taking it."

Three weeks. And the Kansas City field office "getting a call" and all that about "Overland Park PD confirms" notwithstanding, the feds had been in on it from the get-go, or close enough, if Quantico was involved. Kinsley didn't seem to notice his slip, however…if slip it was; the man shouldn't be telling Ron any of this.

He studied the SAC's profile for a long moment before probing:

"At least this should be good for your career."

Kinsley's sardonic grin showed teeth. "You'd think so, right?" He didn't look away from Rife, who was cursing and waving off a Channel 5 News van trying to turn into Crazy's. They gave up and honked their way back through traffic and began setting up at the Shell, the talent checking her hair and makeup in the big wing mirror. "The problem for my career," Kinsley deadpanned, still watching Rife, still grinning, "is that the BAU has pried itself out of the basement and is now jetting this way, along with their own criminalists and their very own Special Weapons and Tactics detachment." A thick, hairy wrist shot out of a suit cuff as he checked his digital Timex: "The profilers land at Sheridan Municipal in twenty-five; the C-130 Herc loaded with all the egghead's equipment—and, I assume, the SWAT boy's toys—will arrive 2130. Or at least it's supposed to. You know how that goes."

Ron whistled before he could stop himself, and Kinsley re-folded his arms and nodded somberly without taking his glittering eyes from Rife: "You're playing with the big boys now, Chief."

As the stunning implications crashed around in Ron's skull, he offered the only thing he could think to at the moment: "Neil's not going to like this."

That got Kinsley's shark-grin to pop out again: "Nope."

Ron grinned for a bit himself, then said, offhandedly, "Do you think Jack Ross was in Kansas City three weeks ago?"

That grin stretched wider; Kinsley didn't stop tracking Rife. "Probably not."

Ron watched Kinsley grin at Rife. "When are you going to tell him?"

The grin melted. "*Me?* Fuck that. I'm waiting for his boss to break the news. And I'm keeping an eye on him because, when he finds out, I might just have to shoot him."

25

We turned into the "Authorized Vehicles Only" entrance, and I stared at the new Sheridan County Jail. Well, it was new to me; it had been built seven years ago, while I was being shelved someplace far worse, and I was getting my first up-close look.

There were three distinct sections: Booking, the detention pods, and the Sheridan County Sheriff's Office—otherwise known as Neil's Lair. The pods loomed in the background, surrounded by chain-link fencing topped by loops of concertina wire, complete with blocky security cameras at each junction; cameras jutted from the roofs of the hexagonal two-story pods as well; it looked more like a prison than a county jail. It looked more like a prison than some prisons I'd seen.

A news chopper flew over the pods with a thumping roar as the lead car stopped at an elevated key pad, but before the cop driving could even lower his window, the gate swung back and the yellow-and-black striped crossbar rose; seems we were expected. We convoyed through, the lead car peeling off, leaving the car I was in to roll into the cavernous cop's entrance to Booking first, and I fought a surge of dread:

I was back inside the concrete and steel.

I was innocent, damn it, but I was back anyway.

Hathaway and the other deputy opened my door. "Hop out, tough guy." I crabbed sideways, my lower back and wrists on fire;

my hands had gone completely numb. I guess I crabbed too slowly for Hathaway because he jerked me out, and when I straightened painfully, Neil was standing in front of me.

"Feels like comin' home, don't it, Jack."

I refused to look at him. Fucking *refused.*

Six strapping Sheridan County Detention Officers (always Officers, never just Jailers; call one that and he'd get all pouty) buzzed out of a steel door that said "Booking" and spread into a foreboding line and watched me with hard eyes; some had their hands resting on their yellow holstered TASER's, as if they thought I would go berserk. A white sign with black-edged red letters was posted next to the door they'd piled out of. It shouted, "NO FIREARMS PAST THIS POINT."

Neil told Hathaway, "Hook him up in front, he's got paperwork ta sign. But we're gonna put the leg chains on 'im, boys. Not gonna have none o' that horseshit like he pulled with Dorsey again, no siree."

Hathaway took the cuffs off and roughly brought my arms around and ratcheted them down on my wrists again. My hands began to tingle, and then they felt like someone had doused them with kerosene and lit them on fire, but at least I knew they were there.

Two Detention Officers buzzed back inside and soon returned with the leg chains, which were actually ankle-and-waist chains attached by a long chain between; a shorter chain fastened my wrist cuffs to the waist chain. The two chain guards approached cautiously and knelt in front of me while keeping their chins tucked and their knees prudently together, just in case I went for a throat or a groin; the other four moved forward and drew their TASER's, ready and more than willing to zap me if I did something they didn't like.

They finished and backed away and Neil said, "I'll take 'im from here, boys. Good job, Hathaway. Good job, Delatorre."

"Thank you, sir."

"Yes, sir. Thank you, sir."

Hathaway's skinny hand left my arm and Neil's long-fingered grip replaced it as another buzz sounded, and a guard swung the steel door wide again. Neil shoved me past his burnished truck, even though I tried to walk on my own; the ankle chains shortened my step considerably, and the good Sheriff seemed to delight in making me stumble.

A bald and knotty Detention Officer in his fifties held up a slab hand. Lt. Smithers was carved into the name tag pinned to the chest of his gray uniform.

"Sheriff, your weapon."

Neil scowled down at him, then pulled his old-school Smith and Wesson Model 10 from its leather holster and handed it over. Smithers nodded us through, and a still-scowling Neil propelled me clinking and stumbling past a bare-bones processing area on our right and through a mantrap's two metal doors that also had to be buzzed open by a faceless someone monitoring a camera.

Now I was *really* back. Fuck me.

Neil stayed by my side through the entire booking process, and I wasn't the only one annoyed by that. Smithers came back from securing the Sheriff's pistol and watched for about three minutes, then went away with a disgusted shake of his big, gleaming head. The other Booking personnel kept their eyes down and did their jobs, but I could tell most didn't enjoy the Sheriff peering over their shoulders.

One fine thing about being me—the only one I could think of at the moment—was that they did me quickly; it took less than an hour, which is lightning speed. Some poor saps slouched in the bolted-to-the-floor, hard-plastic chairs facing away from the Booking counter (the guards don't want a bunch of surly dirtbags staring at them, and I don't blame them) had been slouching there for half a day, or even longer, and would be slouching there for hours more, whether they were being processed in or out; the guards are in no hurry. It's all the same to them, and justice is a slow bitch everywhere.

Those slumped postures and glazed expressions perked up when they brought me in. Everyone in stripes and about to be put into stripes and the lucky few about to be taken out of stripes whispered and elbowed each other as Neil marched me to the counter. Someone eventually barked at them to turn around and shut the hell up, but you couldn't blame them; most of those guys were in for a dee-wee or drugs or losing their cool and smacking their old lady around, or maybe just failure to pay court fines or child support; a real-life mass murderer wasn't something they ran across every day.

They fingerprinted me first, and I discovered that the toys and tools of law enforcement had moved up in the world while I'd been away. Instead of laboriously rolling each finger on the ink pad and then onto a print card, they quick-scanned my prints into some fancy machine that zapped them into a national law-enforcement database stored on an armored server in an underground bunker somewhere where they would undoubtedly be kept until the end of time. *Fan fucking tastic.* Knowing cops, the database probably had some pithy acronym, but I couldn't bring myself to give a rat's ass what it was or what it stood for. They even scanned my palms and the sides and backs of my hands.

Out fucking standing.

Those infamous booking photos sure hadn't changed much, though: stand on the little feet painted on the concrete floor and look at the camera, Ross. Good, now turn to your right and stand on those little feet; head up and look at the spot on the wall. Excellent. Any tattoos or scars? No, sir, no tattoos, which seemed to take the guards aback; several of *them* had tattoos peeking out of their uniforms every which-a-way—but photo-documenting my scars and typing their location and description into the computer took twenty-five minutes.

Neil occasionally made comments such as, "Not yer best side, Jack" or, "Maybe you can get ya some jail-house ink this time, since you'll be down for the rest of yer miserable life." The jailers (excuse me, Detention Officers) eyed him sideways, but I didn't respond or acknowledge his presence.

Then came the shower, and that's where I almost lost it.

I was okay when an awestruck, owl-eyed trustee in green stripes handed me my red stripes and weathered gray boxers and orange plastic sandals, size twelve, and I was still pretty groovy when a guard went into the bathroom with me and took the chains and cuffs off and watched me undress and then put my civvies and shoes into the bag on the hanger he'd brought, and I was still doing mostly all right when he watched me get into the stall before leaving and closing the door...

And then I wasn't.

It was the stink of the industrial lye soap. I'd scrubbed myself with nothing else for five years, and that smell was worse than hand-cuffs and chains, or even Neil. I managed to not-scream as I jabbed the chrome button below the cheap showerhead, but it was a near thing. I washed myself with the hated lye and sobbed for a bit, but then my tears evaporated in a burst of righteous rage:

I'm innocent, damn it, and I will prove it somehow and get the fuck out of this shithole if it's the last goddamn thing I ever motherfucking do!

Then I would find who'd set me up.

And then...

Oooooohhhh, yeah, and then...

I dried with the "towel" the guard had left folded on the metal sink and dressed in my new two-piece red-and-white striped pajamas and slipped my hard-plastic orange sandals on and stepped out carrying my wet scrap and they hooked me back up and then handed me off to a new guard, a big guy with receding dark hair and a soft, heavy gut. I could *feel* the bad vibes oozing from him, but at first I thought it was because of the red stripes. All the guards were eyeing me with amped hostility since my reappearance in the red, and it wasn't hard to understand why:

Regular inmates wear black-and-white stripes (well, black and gray; a million zillion washings turn the crisp white gray pretty quick), and the trustees wear green and white. The runners wear orange stripes to let the guards know that that particular idiot might grasshopper on them again.

Red is for the inmates who'd assaulted an officer.

Neil was at the Booking counter, chatting up some bottle-blonde desk-jailer in her forties. He waved languidly. "Bring 'im, Dorsey."

"Yes, sir," the new guard rumbled, and then grasped the chain attaching the cuffs to my waist and dragged me stumbling and clinking across the room. *Dorsey.* I glanced at his name tag: Sgt. Dorsey. As we neared Neil, I lifted my eyes to someone's face for the first time since they had put me back behind the concrete and steel, and found myself regarded in turn; Dorsey was about ten years older than his little brother, probably seventy pounds heavier, and definitely a thousand times meaner. He also had the use of all his digits, a luxury his little brother didn't enjoy. Not anymore.

Dorsey pushed me into Neil, who caught me before I could fall on his boots and scuff them. The Sheriff laughed and stood me upright, and I faced the bottle blonde over the tall counter and answered her standard questions in a monotone as she alternately poked one hard, mascara-laden blue eye at me around the flat-screen monitor and smiled warmly at Neil:

Did I have any medical conditions that required supervision by a doctor?

No, ma'am.

Did I take any prescriptions?

No, ma'am.

Did I have any communicable diseases, venereal or otherwise?

No, ma'am.

Did I have an emergency contact?

I gave her Mom's information.

Could I provide another, preferably not a relative, in case the first is unavailable?

I was tempted to give her Angela's info, but instead rattled off Donnie's.

Have you ever considered suicide or attempted to harm yourself?

No, ma'am.

Are you currently considering suicide?

I slowly turned and looked up at Neil; his dark eyes shown exultantly down at me from between the cowboy hat and the bristling mustache.

"Not even close."

Dorsey popped me on the back of the head: "Answer the lady, fuck nut."

"No, ma'am, I'm not considering suicide."

The questions eventually ended, and the chains clinked as I signed the copious paperwork and slid it back to her. Neil said, "Alrighty then, Jack, looks like you'll be my guest for a nice, long while, but yer not goin' ta D-Pod with all the reg'ler scumbags, no siree. Yer a *special* scumbag, so yer goin' inta lock-down with the baby rapers and the violent shit-birds just like you. Sgt. Dorsey here is the head screw in E-Pod, where our lovely lock-down cells are located. Ain't ya, Big D?"

Dorsey rumbled a hungry affirmative, but I addressed the blonde lady: "Ma'am, may I make a call, please?" I needed to talk to Mom in the worst way. Four wall-mounted phones were over by the drunk tanks, and several inmates had gotten up from the hard-plastic chairs and made calls, and none of the guards had said anything, so I knew it was permitted.

She leaned around her monitor to frown at me, then glanced uncertainly at the Sheriff.

Neil bent down and breathed in my ear: "You want somethin', you ask *me*, not her."

I suppressed the boiling anger as best as I could: "May I make a phone call?"

Neil straightened and considered me from on high; the long face under the white hat was grave, but the eyes above the mustache were jazzing. "May you make a phone call, what?"

I didn't grit my teeth or even flare my nostrils; I was proud of myself. "May I make a phone call, please."

He smiled, tight and toothless, then jerked the hat brim towards the phones: "Take 'im, Dorsey."

The blonde spoke up: "You'll need your booking number, so the service knows which inmate account to charge." She rattled off five digits, and I memorized them using a trick an old-timer at Torrington taught me; visualize a key pad, say like the kind you'd find on a converted pay phone, and punch them in with your mental finger while focusing on the pattern your finger traces, not the numbers; worked every time.

"…didn't have much cash with you, so you'll need to have someone deposit money into your account. You also must do that if you want commissary. Orders are taken on Mondays and you get the goodies on Thursday, so it's too late this week, but next Monday you—"

Neil broke in. "He knows, darlin'. Jack here's an old pro when it comes to incarceration. Ain't ya, Jack?" He laughed, then jerked the hat brim toward the bank of phones again. "Let 'im make his call and then get this piece of trash down to E-Pod, Dorsey."

"Yes, sir." Dorsey dragged me stumbling and clinking towards the phones—by the arm this time—and I glanced over my shoulder at the nice lady guard:

"Thank you, ma'am."

She nodded absently, makeup-laden gaze fixed on Sheriff Neal, but there was no smile now. I concentrated on not falling as I fast-shuffle-clinked after Dorsey. It was a pleasure to know I'd ruined Neal's play with the blonde—a small pleasure, true, but I'd take what I could get.

Two denizens in black-and-gray stripes were hunched and muttering into the closest phones, so Dorsey took me to the far one nearest the tanks, then suddenly shoved me into it. My shoulder knocked the receiver out of the cradle; it swung inches from the floor on its chrome-armor-plated cord.

The whispers from the chairs died as I straightened.

Dorsey grinned, eyes hot, ham-fists clenching and unclenching; I doubt he even thought of the TASER at his belt, or would bother to use it if he did. Big brother wanted to tool up on the scumbag that had hurt his little bro. I could understand that, so I just turned away, ignoring his sneer of contempt, and bent awkwardly and grabbed the receiver and hung it up, then picked it up again and followed the faded instructions printed on the phone. The inmate on the phone two down from mine eyed me, then Dorsey, then turned his back while hunching harder and muttering lower.

A deep voice thundered across Booking:

"Sgt. Dorsey! Front and center!" Lt. Smithers stood near a large steel door that I assumed led deeper into the jail.

Neil drawled, "Go easy, LT. Dorsey was just—"

"How I discipline my men is none of your concern, Sheriff."

The Sheriff of Sheridan County and the Lieutenant in charge of Booking in the Sheridan County Jail faced each other from a distance of twenty feet, and everyone seemed to hold their breath.

Neil broke the stalemate by turning away, but his face was livid beneath the hat. Smithers visibly dismissed him, then barked, "I said front and center, Sergeant!"

Dorsey shot me a baleful glare before trotting off, belly jiggling: "Yes, *sir*, LT."

I finished following the convoluted instructions and dialed Mom's cell and watched Dorsey get quietly dressed up and down by Smithers and then dismissed back to E-Pod. Dorsey gave me a long stare that held a promise of pain before leaving. The other end of the line rang as Smithers considered me with a frown, and then I forgot all about the Lieutenant or Dorsey or even Neil as someone answered Mom's phone, but it wasn't Mom.

"Hello?"

It was Angela.

"Uh, hey."

"Jack! Thank God! Where are you?"

"In jail. Is Mom around?"

"Yes, but—" A yell, Mom's voice, and then a crash; a deeper voice, Dad's, yelled something back, and a louder crash. "Let me step outside so I can hear."

"Ooookay."

The front door banged, and then the screen door's rusty spring creaked and it whapped shut. "Did you say you were in jail?" Jezebel's bark rasped over and over.

"Yeah, Sheridan County. Why are Mom and Dad fighting? And what has Jezzie riled?"

"Your mom and dad are fighting because your dad's a complete asshole, and Jezebel is barking at the agents searching your barn."

"Did Rife take anything besides my boots?"

"I don't know what they've taken, I've been with your mom." She hesitated. "And it's not Rife. It's the FBI."

I tried to say something. I really did. I even opened my mouth, but nothing came out.

Into that stepped a fresh Detention Officer. He smirked as he took position against the cinder blocks between me and the drunk tank. I glanced over at Neil, and I guess he'd been waiting for me to look at him because he turned to Smithers and declaimed loud enough for everyone in South Dakota to hear:

"Gotta skedaddle, late for the big press conference. Lieutenant, chunk that vile piece of shit inta lock-down until tomorrow. He goes before Judge Haskins at 1100, and I want him polished and shined and waiting in Booking for my men at 1015. Are we clear, LT?"

"Clear, sir."

"I want my weapon back as soon as I step outside. Fetch it for me."

"Yes, sir." Smithers turned away to do as he was told…but the *look* on his face.

Yikes.

"Is that Neil yelling? Jack? Hello?"

Sheriff Neil pinned me with a triumphant, hateful smile—I could tell he'd been waiting to do that, too—then barked at a desk guard to let him out; two buzzes later, he was gone.

"Jack? *Jack!* Are you there?"

"Yeah. Are you *sure* it's the FBI? And where's Rife?" Why would the FBI be involved in this?

Jezebel raised cane in the background as Angela snapped, "How would *I* know where that dickhead is? And they've got FBI in foot-high yellow letters on the back of their shirts, so I'm pretty sure it's the FBI. That guy in a suit who was at Crazy's earlier, the big one that didn't say anything, he's here. I think he's in charge, so I guess he'd have to be FBI, too. Jack…why is the FBI looking through your stuff?"

"I don't know." I had a bad feeling I would find out, though.

A crash, Mom yelling, and then a *creeeak* and a *whap!*

"Here she comes."

"Good, let me talk to her."

"Is that my Jackie?" Then Mom, crying hysterically: "Jackie! Oh baby, are you all right? Did they hurt you?"

"I'm fine. Listen, I don't want—"

"I can't *believe* they think you'd hurt those kids! And poor Jess! This is all that Sheriff Neil's doing!"

"Mom, *listen to me*. We need to talk about—"

The screen door creaked and then Dad bellowed something; it whapped shut again, and then the front door *whammed.*

"What are you guys fighting about?"

"Your father…" Mom's voice, which had been full of fiery wrath, dropped fifty degrees, but didn't lose an ounce of fury: "I've had it up to *here*, Jackie. This is the last straw. I'm leaving him."

I tried to speak, but once again only air puffed out.

Mom suddenly screeched, "I see you there, stealin' my son's things! You! Yes, *you!* March back in there and put that down! You've got no right…" Both Angela and a male voice tried to reason with her, but Mom was having none of it: "I don't give two hoots about evidence! My Jackie didn't hurt those kids, so you just put all that stuff back right this instant!"

"Mom! *Mom!* You *can't* leave him. Dad can't take care of himself."

"What? Oh pooh, he can make his own eggs and do his own damn laundry for once. It'll serve him right. Here, talk to Angie. They're tryin' to take your things, and I won't stand for it!"

"Mom!"

Angela said, "It's me."

"Jesus Christ! Why is she so pissed at Dad?"

"Your dad…Jack, when they showed him the search warrant, your dad told them that you probably *did* kill those kids. He said you had a temper, and that you even beat him up the day you got out of prison. Your mom blew so high I thought she'd bounce off the moon."

Silence.

"Hello? Still there?"

Sigh. "Yeah."

"Is…is that true?"

"Yep."

"For God's sake, *why?* Why would you do that?"

I told her while Mom and Jezzie raised hell in the background. *Good for them.*

When I finished, Angela said, "Oh. Well, he didn't mention *that!*" Fury to match my mom's laced her high voice: "No wonder she wants to leave! She should've left *years* ago!" Confusion replaced the anger. "But she didn't *say* anything."

I leaned my forehead against the cinder blocks. "She wouldn't want strangers to know. Try to get her back on the phone. I need to—"

Beeep!

"What was that?"

"Time's almost up. Listen to me, Angela. Are you listening?"

"Yes."

"I see a judge at eleven tomorrow. I know this is a burden, but if you would, please bring Mom to the courthouse so I can talk to her, after. She can also visit me in here, but I don't know what days or times. That should be posted on the jail's website. Or she can call—"

Beeep!

"It's no burden, I'm happy to help. And she'll stay with me tonight."

"Isn't your place still a crime scene?"

"Neil can kiss my ass. If he's going to arrest *you*, then *I'm* going home."

Beeep!

"Angela, someone has to stay with Dad! He had a *stroke*, for God's sake!"

"I won't make her stay if she doesn't want to, and I'm sure he'll be all right for one night. Don't worry, we'll swing by after court tomorrow to check on the wife-beating cocksu—"

The line clicked dead.

I slowly lowered the battered receiver into its chipped chrome cradle.

My new minder smirked harder. "All done?" He ushered me toward yet another steel door. "This way, tough guy. Time to introduce you to the new digs."

The smirking guard was joined by yet another smirking guard, and they waved at the camera above the door and some faceless someone buzzed us through. They were probably smirking, too. A green-and-white tiled hallway echoed ahead, and the jolly guard told me to keep to the right-hand wall and to stop and face said wall if anyone that wasn't a fellow scumbag approached. Then we set off down the depressing hallway, smirking away.

Dazed, I clinked and shuffled between them.

Friday

26

Ron woke in the middle of the night, bright eyed and bushy tailed after sleeping almost ten hours; it would take days to even out his rhythms again. He padded downstairs and brewed coffee and poured a mug straight up and placed his iPhone on his kitchen table and scraped out a chair.

He cocked an ankle on a knee and sipped while brooding over the current sorry state of affairs in his adopted hometown; every half-hour he listened to the NPR update on the app on his phone; the "Chicken Man" murders, and Jack's arrest, were the leads every time.

After no change in the four o'clock update—and, thankfully, no call-out to a fresh murder—he retrieved his battered notebook and unlimbered his Ken Griffey Sr. and planned out the calls he would make today and what he needed to say to those on the other end of the line.

When four-thirty rolled around and still no change or call-out, he toasted a bacon, tomato, and cheddar-cheese sandwich with mustard on rye and stood by his Mr. Coffee and ate it in four bites, then showered and shaved. Ron creased his uniform carefully before dressing, then drove to work, determined to set things right.

He shook his head as he turned off the one-way street that edged the litter-strewn and newly rutted town square, then motored past the bandstand where Neil had held his dog-and-pony show yesterday and down East A St. one block and parked next to Tommy's restored '86 Silverado; the lot was sunk in early morning shadows, but the mountains soaring over the red-brick station glowed at the tips.

Ron got out and stood next to his cruiser and drank it all in, but didn't linger.

Inside, he found his officer asleep behind the counter, tilted back in Mindy's chair with his boots crossed next to her ergonomic keyboard, straw cowboy hat shading his face like a bit player in a cheesy western. He was also snoring.

"Tommy."

Tommy started, then lifted the hat and peered blearily at Ron. "Chief?"

"Go home. I'll cover until Ryan gets here."

"What time is it?" Mindy's chair creaked as he swiveled to check the duty clock; he glanced at his watch as if he couldn't believe those big red digits. "Five-thirty." He grinned and yawned at the same time. "Nobody died last night." The grin slipped as he took in Ron's expression. "That's a good thing, right Chief?"

"That's a very good thing. Now get some sleep. You did good yesterday, Tom, real good, but I need someone to cover tonight, and that's you."

Tommy tamped that ridiculous hat on his head, then stood with a rap of hard-heeled cowboy boots and adjusted his utility belt. "Is that really necessary, Chief? They arrested Jack, it's over." He studied Ron's face. "It *is* over, ain't it?"

"I hope so, son, but we'll keep someone awake and here at the station until I say otherwise."

"Yes, sir. Uh, is there anything you need 'fore I go?"

"Coffee, but I'll take care of it."

"Okey doke. See ya tonight."

Ron went behind the counter and got the works together for a big pot, but he could feel Tommy looking at him from near the door, and when he spoke again, Ron wasn't surprised.

"I still can't believe it 'bout Jack. I mean, I *liked* the guy. And he just don't seem the kind who'd chop those kids up. Not to mention…ya know…"

Ron glanced back as Tommy took a furtive look around. The fed in charge of the BAU team, one Senior Special Agent Mark Denton, had been firm in expressing his wishes that the details of the rapes—specifically, that they had been inflicted by foreign object—stay out of the media. He'd even explained to Ron's wide-eyed officers and a not-so-wide-eyed Ron about copycat killers and false confessions, and the need to withhold a key piece of information—Denton termed it a "control"—in order to distinguish those copycats from the real deal, and to sift out the attention-seeking nut jobs that would confess to high-profile murders.

Once Tommy was reassured no snooping reporters had sidled near, he continued in a stage whisper: "…what was done to that girl, and to old Mrs. Barbary."

Maybe the kid wasn't as dumb as he looked (or acted or sounded), but Ron only turned back to the coffeemaker. "Get some sleep, Tom. I'll see you tonight."

Tommy hesitated, then said, "See ya, Chief."

Ron watched the coffee stream as Tommy's Silverado rumbled away, and then he went into his office without pouring any; he'd had his fill. Making some was just a routine, a way of bringing normalcy to what would be anything but a typical day—especially if he had to stir the kettle hard, as he suspected he would. Ron checked the incident report from last night and found it blank; another routine. Tommy would have told him if anything had popped.

He fired his laptop and discovered an email from Mindy in the pile. She'd contacted the SCED yesterday about Inglewood (as per his "oh-so-polite" request), but the district had converted to computer storage twelve years ago, and considering that Inglewood had been closed for twenty-two years and gone from the earth for nineteen, the lady Mindy had spoken with—or "grouchy old bat"—said she doubted she could find word one about the place. Mindy's suggestion was for Ron to call and butter the bat himself; maybe he'd have better luck.

He thanked her for trying, but he wouldn't be taking her advice. He'd decided to set another dog on that scent, one that would track better than a glorified secretary who'd rather play computer games than work.

Then he saw the message slip stabbed onto the spike at the corner of his desk.

It was in Tommy's surprisingly elegant hand: Don Straus had rung the department's non-emergency number yesterday evening at 1943. He'd wanted Ron, but since it hadn't been an emergency, Tommy'd had strict orders to let him sleep. Young master Straus had left no message, just a cell number and the boy's request for Chief Rogers to call him ASAP.

Ron grimaced at the asap before pulling his ring from his belt and removing the key to Crazy's. He slapped it on the hot-pink slip and went out to Mindy's so-called workspace and set them next to her Dilbert mug, where'd she'd be sure to see them first thing. He would have Mindy tell young master Straus that he could pick the key up anytime during normal business hours.

The aroma of roasted beans caught him, and he topped off his favorite mug, the white one with the heavy base and black lettering that said, **"I'm the Chief, who are you?"** Mindy had special ordered it for him last Christmas. He sat back down in his office and blew across its top while checking the time: 0620. It was an hour behind on the coast, of course, but if Jerry had kept his routine, then his phone was resting on a stack of 45 lb. plates nearby; Seattle Homicide Detectives were on call even when they weren't on call. Ron wanted to dial right then, but decided to let Jerry get most of his workout in; he'd be in a better mood that way.

While he waited, Ron called a certain Sheridan County Detention Officer who bowled for a rival team in the Sheridan County Law Enforcement League. Said Detention Officer shared Ron's opinion of Neil's competency as Sheriff; Mike would tell him how Jack was getting along down there.

Mike's cell went straight to voicemail, though, which meant he was either on duty, or at home asleep—with luck, it was on duty— so Ron left a message.

He checked the time again, and a burst of impatience wormed him; his ex partner was in good enough shape. The man answered cautiously on the third ring; Jerry wouldn't have his new number.

"Hello?" Jerry's west Oklahoma twang was still strong after decades in Seattle.

"Rock, how's it hangin'?" Tinny pop music thumped in the background, punctuated with clanks and grunts.

"Long and to the right, like always." It took him a couple seconds. "*Roy?* Is that you?"

Ron winced. He'd always hated that nickname—which had only made it stick like high-grade epoxy, of course. "The one and only. You got a minute?"

"I'll be damned. Uh, sure…hold on, I'm cloggin' up the squat rack." Jerry told someone they could take over; the music faded, and then a door closed before Jerry said, "Roy Rogers, King of the fuckin' Cowboys. Ho-lee shit on a shingle. How you doin', partner?"

"Can't complain," Ron lied. "How 'bout you, Rock?"

"Oh, ya know. Some days ya eat the bear…"

"I hear that. How are Abby and Dylan? They both in college now?"

"Abby is. She'll be a sophomore up at Washington State this fall, but Dylan dropped out of Oregon last semester and now he's workin' at a goddamn 'coffee shop'—you know what that shit means—in Portland. Sez he wants to open a bar with some dropout buddies and that he don't need a degree to run a bar. *I* think he's sittin' 'round smokin' dope and playin' video games, but maybe he'll get his shit together someday. Abby's doin' real good, though, straight A's just like always, got a steady boyfriend she informs me she don't intend to marry—and I pray to Almighty God every damn day that they're usin' condoms, Roy." A tinge of wonder, and perhaps fear, flavored the love in Jerry's deep voice. "You should see 'er now, partner. She's still got Susan's dark hair and my green eyes, but she's filled out. Turns *all* the creeps' heads. Makes me sick to even think about it."

Ron smiled wistfully. "I bet, Rock, I bet." The last time he'd seen little Abigail Kirkland, she'd been a gangly preteen with braces. "How's Susan? She still puttin' up with your shit?"

Ron knew the answer in the tick of silence before Jerry spoke: "Nah, we're splitsville. Separated 'bout a year ago. The divorce was final in April."

"Sorry to hear that, partner."

"Yeah, well, so was I. She came down with that empty-nest bullshit after the kids left—or so she said. Judgin' by the way she ambushed me the week after Abby moved into 'er dorm, she'd been plannin' it for a long time."

"Jesus."

"Hey, no sweat off my sack. You wouldn't *believe* how many divorced women are runnin' 'round this city, and all of 'em just wanna fuck. That's my motto now, Roy: no contracts. Turns out they ain't worth the paper they're scribbled on. Got me one now, a sweet little redhead, hooo boy! I can barely keep up with 'er. Best favor Susan ever did me was boot my ass to the curb. 'Sides, we made it damn near twenty years, which is a helluva lot longer than most cop marriages…" Jerry cleared his throat. "You know I didn't mean nothin' 'bout you and Melanie—"

"I know you didn't, partner. And I'm glad you're happy now. Listen, I need—"

"Hey, speakin' o' kids, how's Lisa doin'?"

It was Ron's turn to hesitate. "She moved to Vancouver after the funeral, and she's engaged and living with another attorney, but that was over two years ago, so she's probably married by now. I've emailed her a few times," Ron emailed his daughter once every two weeks like clockwork, "but she won't respond. Her mom's illness hit her pretty hard, and, well, I guess she blames me for not being around to help her and Melanie through it."

Jerry's voice was somber. "Sorry to hear that, partner. It happens, though."

"Yeah," Ron sighed. "It happens. Look, Jer, I need your help."

"What with?"

He started to outline the situation, but didn't get far before Jerry said, "God *damn*. When everythin' blew up, I told my current partner 'bout how The King of the fuckin' Cowboys had settled in Wyoming, but I had no idea you were in the middle of all that shit. You *are* in the middle of it, aren't ya."

"Hip deep, Rock. Just listen."

But it wasn't long before Jerry interrupted again; his ex-partner and onetime trainee had seen straight to the heart of the matter, which wasn't a surprise. Jerry Kirkland was one of the most gifted and dedicated investigators he'd ever had the pleasure of working with:

"Ya want me ta smoke the Big Blue Bear out of 'is cave." He didn't sound happy about it, either.

"Just run the VICAP and see what pops. You don't have to admit anything about me."

"Yeah, sure, they'll b'lieve that horseshit. They already know we were partners—and if they *don't* know, they can find out with a goddamn phone call. But that's what yer after, ain't it? Ya want me ta ping the bastard for ya."

"Yes," Ron admitted. "Denton will think I'm trying an end-around, and he'll bring me in and see what I think I know and what the hell I think I'm doing—and most importantly, make sure I'm not crashing his party. Because it's *his* party, Jer, believe me. He'll flex at me a little, and he'll be pissed we smoked him out, but it's better than going begging. He wouldn't give a small-town Chief the time of day, but this'll at least get me in. I won't be making any decisions, but I need to know what's going on so I can do the best for my people."

"Nobody called 'em? They just showed up?"

"Said they had jurisdiction because of the interstate thing, but if this killer is what I'm afraid he is, then the feeb's been on him for longer than KC." Ron paused. "A *lot* longer."

"Shit fire." Jerry sounded stunned, as well he might. "And they flew in their own rats?"

"Yep."

"And their own fuckin' SWAT team, too?"

"Yep."

Jerry whistled. "You really are hip deep in it, Roy."

"Yep. But don't worry, I've got a plan to keep the G out of our rectums. Let me finish, and then you can decide."

"'Don't worry', the man says." It was Rock's turn to sigh. "Fine, lay it on me."

When he was done, Jerry breathed while the silence stretched. Ron finally said, "Forget it, partner. I'll find someone else—"

"Didn't say I wouldn't. Hell, it'll be fun to poke the G in the eye—ya know, as long as I don't lose an arm doin' it."

"So you're in?"

"I'll get the ball rollin' later this mornin.'" Jerry hesitated. "But is all this necessary, Roy? They're actin' funny, I get that, but this is still be-have we're talkin' 'bout, not some anti-sand-nigger BAM squad wavin' the Patriot Act around."

"Maybe, maybe not, but you know how the feeb's been since the towers, even the ones not in CT."

"Guilt's a motherfucker, ain't it?"

"Yeah. And my read on Denton is that he's a ladder-climbing rat with ambition oozing from his fur follicles. There's no telling what a guy like that will do when a small-town Chief tweaks his whiskers. I think—I hope—that once Denton understands what he's up against, he'll just release Ross into my custody to avoid a messy fight; his superiors wouldn't want that, which means it's the last thing *Denton* wants. But if he plays hardball, this'll make sure we're in a position to pitch and not just catch. You with me?"

"Yeah, I'm with ya. But who's this Ross to you? Why're you riskin' this, Roy?"

"Jack Ross is one of my people; he's also a young man who made a mistake and paid for it—paid more than he should have, in truth— and now someone is trying to make him pay all over again. And it's not much of a risk; I'm already tired of this job, and if Denton or Mayor Ford or the town council or anyone else wants to bum-rush me, I'll happily re-retire and start hiking with my fly reel again."

Five seconds went by before Ron's ex-partner finally said, "All right, then." A metal locker slammed, a male voice said something, and Jerry responded unintelligibly before coming back: "Gotta head out. The new LT will have my balls in a jar on 'er desk if I make us late for the sit-meet again. She's pretty cute, but don't think I'd enjoy that process."

"Thanks again, Rock. I owe you."

"Bet yer cowboy ass ya do. I'll collect someday, too, count on it. And watch yer six out there, Roy. The Big Blue Bear just might be chewin' on it."

"You too, partner."

"Always." Jerry hung up.

Next, Ron called a friend that worked as a ballistics tech in the State Crime Lab down in Cheyenne; acquaintance, at any rate. Amory Sims was a vain and insufferable little prick, but he and Ron shared a love of competition shooting. They'd bumped into each other two-dozen times over the last five years at various ranges and meets and knew each other well enough to talk guns and shooting and shop, but not much else. There weren't any ballistics on the so-called Chicken Man case, though, so Amory should be on the periphery looking in, and hopefully feeling safe enough to talk. Ron only had one question, really, and he could get to it in a roundabout way that wouldn't jeopardize their "acquaintanceship", or rouse Amory's suspicions too much.

His question for Amory was simple: Was the state still processing any Chicken Man evidence, or had the feds scooped it all up? The answer would give Ron a strong indication if his fears about this killer were correct. But Amory didn't answer, so Ron left a message to call him back.

He tapped the phone on his palm as he considered his next call, then blew out a long breath and bit the bullet.

Tony Thompson, the crime beat reporter for the *Casper Star-Tribune*—the journalist he'd leaked the first two murders to—didn't answer his cell either, so Ron left yet another message. Tony was probably angry with him, anyway; he'd sent Ron text after text yesterday and left about twenty increasingly snippy messages after the Lake Shore slaughter and the Chicken Man splashed, but once Tony heard his request and did the sums, Ron doubted the stringer would stay mad long.

Next, he flipped through his notebook for Rife's cell number. Ron wanted to watch the lawyer's security recording again (to see if he'd seen what he'd thought he'd seen), and he doubted the FBI would let him view their copy. Special Agent Rife likely still had a copy somewhere and was also likely still pissed enough to let Ron have a "gander" without much fuss.

He was about to dial Rife when the reporter called him back.

Ron was right. Tony was steamed, but once he heard what Ron wanted, he pelted him with questions. Ron broke in: "Just find out what you can about him and get back to me ASAP."

Christ, now I'm doing it.

"But what does this have to do with—"

"If you don't want it, I'm sure one of your many colleagues leaving slime trails across my town might like to be handed the story of their career." A little much, but with reporters, you sometimes had to hit them upside the head. Mindy waddled in, 0700 on the dot, and scowled at him through the glass. He frowned back as he prodded Tony "The Tiger" Thompson: "I don't need to know Bill Napier's cup size. Just focus on the years he worked at Inglewood Elementary."

Ron thought that might get the Tiger's attention, and he was right.

"Inglewood…waaaait a minute, isn't that where Jessica Barbary taught? Are you saying—"

"I'm not saying anything. I don't know enough to say anything, not yet, but you're going to help me with that. And in return, I'll help you. Deal?"

Tony gave a strangled laugh. "Shit, Chief, I'm on a deadline. There's a lot of newsworthy stuff goin' down right now, ya know?"

"In or out, Tony."

"Fine," Tony growled, as if trying to live up to his nickname. "But there better be something to this."

"There is." *I hope.*

"When do you need it?"

He thought about one of his people, Jess Barbary, tortured, mutilated, and then murdered in her shed:

"Last Monday." Ron hung up.

He was dialing Rife again when Lt. Smithers called him back, and what Mike had to say made Ron forget the bloodsucker's security footage. He grabbed the hand-held off the charger and told Mindy where he was going, and that he wasn't to be disturbed short of the entire town burning down. Ryan could handle anything less.

"What happened, Chief?" The phone rang, and she put it on hold without answering and snatched the pink phone slip and key and brandished them at him. "And what the heck am I expected to do with these?"

He explained quickly, then added, "And two inmates just assaulted Jack Ross."

"Oh my God! Is he okay?"

"He'll live, but the idiots who attacked him are being rushed to Sheridan Memorial."

"Oh." Mindy's brow furrowed. "How could this happen? I thought the Sheriff stuck him in lock-down."

"He did, but Mike said there're a bunch of shenanigans cropping up down there in E-Pod, and he's busy getting to the bottom of the why and the what-for. I don't like it either, so I'm going to see if I can move Jack out of there before it's too late."

He pushed out and hustled to his cruiser. He had to talk to Denton—or, as Jerry Kirkland would say, it was time to brace the Big Blue Bear in his cave. It was sooner than he'd planned, but for Jack's sake—and his own—Ron hoped he'd stocked enough ammo to give them a fighting chance.

He was reaching for the handle when Mindy slung open the glass door and yelled, "Chief, wait!"

"What?"

She held up the phone; its curly blue cord stretched back inside: "It's Darryl Wright. He owns that munch n' gas across from Crazy's."

"I know who he is. What does Mr. Wright want?"

"He says he has a recording from his security system that he thinks you need to see."

"Another one? Well, tell him to contact the Sheriff, that's Neil's jurisdiction. Or better yet, the FBI."

Ron waited with his hand on the handle as Mindy spoke, but she just held the receiver out again. "He says this is something different, from Monday night. He—" Mindy frowned and put the receiver back to her ear, then thrust it toward Ron again. "He says he won't give this to Neil, not for all the tea in China. He wants *you* to see it, Chief."

Ron didn't recall retracing his steps back across the lot, but he knew he must've boogied because Mindy's eyes popped. He had a two-minute conversation with Mr. Wright standing there in the doorway, then chunked the phone at Mindy and flew back to his car and hit the blues and sirens and peeled out on his way down to the lake.

Very Special Senior Special Agent Denton—and Jack—would have to wait.

27

I was doing reverse dips off the edge of my rack when the intercom out in the dayroom crackled:

"Med call! Face the wall next to your bunk with your hands clasped behind your back! If you're not in compliance when I open your cell, then no goodies for you! *Med call!*"

I toweled off with my scrap and went to the window in my door; it wasn't glass—or even a window, really. The six-inch by four-inch opening comprised two plexiglass sheets with cross-hatched steel-wire mesh sandwiched between in case some angry or desperate lock-down inmate managed to shatter the shatter-proof plexiglass; judging by how many gouges and scratches marred the inside pane, more than one had tried. I found a relatively clear spot and peered out. E-Pod's dayroom had been painted a washed-out yellowish-green, both floors and walls; it was the color you'd see if you drank a pitcher of margaritas and yakked it back up. Neil must've picked it out.

Our little slice of puke-green heaven was an obtuse triangle, with the door to the free world—or at least the E-Pod guard hexagon—at the narrow tip to my far left. The single shower and the one wall-mounted phone occupied the slanting wall immediately to my right; the cells ran to the right as you came in, and mine was the last, adjacent the phone. The longest side of the triangle was all re-inforced mirrored glass; the guards had a view of the entire shebang, shower included, although there was a stainless-steel "door" that concealed you from mid-thigh to nipples; all we could see when we stood in front of that long mirrored wall was the picnic table bolted to the floor in the middle of the triangle behind us (its concrete tabletop and steel benches had been painted margarita-puke green as well, because of course they had), and the six cell doors in the wall behind that, and our lovely selves standing there in our stripes. Or at least that's what I *thought* you could see; yesterday, they'd told me I'd arrived too late for a shower or my hour in the dayroom. With the angle, all I could currently see from my murky and scarred little porthole was half the table and the reflection of the door out and the reflection of the two cells furthest from mine.

A sharp buzz-and-clank sounded—the doors in lock-down are controlled electronically, though each has a keyhole and can be opened and locked manually—and then three full-sized Detention Officers trooped in and began escorting med-call prisoners to the middle of the puke-green triangle one by one. They stood them by the puke-green picnic table and frisked them before cuffing them.

The first one they brought out was Tweaker. He'd told me his name was James, but he acted like an amalgamation of all the meth heads I'd ever had the misfortune of knowing, so Tweaker he was; wiry, about my height, mid-thirties probably but looked forty-five, with dark hair and faded soot-colored tattoos scribbled on his forearms and biceps and peeking from the collar of his orange stripes; Tweaker's first jaunt behind bars this was not, and a runner to boot.

Tweaker had gotten his hour late yesterday afternoon, just before chow, and the first thing he'd done was bound over to my door and peer in at me through the scarred little window with roaming and vacant blue eyes and chat me up as if we were best buds; after fifteen times excitedly asking me about killing Tiffany and those other kids, and after I'd told him fifteen times that I didn't do it, he'd shared his drug-and-mistake-filled life story and finally went away with, "Okay, man, be cool, be cool." He then proceeded to twitch his way around and around the yellow-green picnic table like a Jack Russell Terrier on acid before meandering back over and calling someone. Whoever Tweaker rang hadn't seemed happy to hear from him, though, and the conversation ended with Tweaker cursing them out and slamming the receiver back into the chipped chrome cradle and raging up to the mirrored wall and spitting and ranting at the guards until they'd tired of it and came in and bum-rushed him back into his cell.

Good riddance.

The second man they brought out was the yin to Tweaker's yang: fat, balding, mid-fifties, with sagging jowls and a timid, gray-whiskered face. I didn't remember his name, but I recognized him from a series of news reports from six or seven months ago; fat boy there was a former school-bus driver who'd been arrested as part of a nationwide federal sting for downloading and sharing kiddie porn with his sick-o friends. That was bad enough, but two fourth-grade girls on his route had since come forward, saying they'd been molested by fat boy, one of them on multiple occasions over the past three years. Neil, that fucker, hadn't been joking when he'd said I'd be housed with the goddamn baby rapers. During his hour yesterday after dinner, pedo had taken a shower and gotten dressed, and then he'd just sat out there at the picnic table with his face in his hands; he hadn't bothered to call anyone.

The third man they brought out was the Indian.

That's what I called him, anyway. He looked like one, with his long, straight hair, flat copper face, and high cheekbones, but he might've been Mongolian or Peruvian or some half-breed shit for all I knew. Whatever he was, he was tall, with taut muscles covering his long limbs, muscles you earn working hard outdoors and not pumping machines in a gym; early yesterday afternoon, not long after they'd stuck me in here, the Indian had been granted his hour.

I'd watched him, at least at first; it was better than reading the crude graffiti or counting the swastikas scratched into the walls of my new eight-by-six apartment. But the Indian had only paced the triangle, looking neither right nor left, copper face expressionless; he had a smooth, unhurried gait, and an upright bearing. He looked dangerous; going by the red stripes the Indian wore, I figured some-one else had figured that out already.

I'd grown tired of watching him and was unrolling my "mat-tress" on the steel rack bolted to the wall when something made me look up; the Indian was standing at my window, peering in at me with emotionless brown eyes. We stared at each other for what had to be over two minutes, and the Indian never said a word, or even blinked. Then he vanished as silently as he'd come. I watched him pace the triangle some more, but he never stopped again, let alone looked over at me.

Dangerous?

Yeah.

Now, after some delay, they marched the Indian out beside the others, and not only did they put the cuffs on him, they added my new friends, Mr. Leg and Mrs. Waist Chain. Tweaker shied from the big, silent Indian, but quipped something I didn't catch; it's hard to hear anyone out in the dayroom unless they're standing at your door or they yell. The Indian ignored him. Then Tweaker got a querulous look on his twitchy face and said something to the guard standing back with his hand on his holstered TASER while the other two hooked the Indian in the waist chain; to me it sounded like, "He don't take no meds. Why is *he* going?" The screw told him to shut the hell up—I heard that clearly—then glanced over at me. So did the other guards, the kiddie fiddler, *and* Tweaker. The only one who didn't was the Indian; he just kept staring straight ahead like his eerie cigar-store cousin.

Hmmm.

They finished with the chains and then marched them out; the door clanged shut behind the trailing guard, and suddenly I was alone in lock-down.

What the hell had those looks been about? And if the Indian didn't receive medication, why was he visiting the nurse for med call? Prisons (and jails) run on strict procedures; it has to be that way to keep everyone safe—or as safe as they can be kept.

So why the break in routine?

I wasn't sure, but I was already on the lookout for revenge from Dorsey—even though his shit-head little brother deserved a few broken fingers for grabbing and scaring Angela—but I doubted Dorsey would try anything inside lock-down; too wide open, and too many witnesses and cameras. There are oodles of better places to stage such a thing in a jail, hidden nooks and unwatched crannies, and the fine and upstanding Sgt. Dorsey undoubtedly knew them all.

No, Dorsey wouldn't make his move here, like this. I'd have to watch for him and maybe another fine and upstanding guard suddenly deciding to take me somewhere on some pretext—not that I could do much about it. I accepted I had a beating coming, but I'd survived beatings from worse men. Dorsey just better be careful to never get caught alone with me; I'd learned a few things about stun guns—and their limitations—over the years. There are ways around them, such as catching the barbs in your state-issued (or county-issued, in this case) PJ's; that prevented you from receiving the full charge, and anything but a full charge wouldn't debilitate me.

It would just piss me off.

No, the good Sgt. Dorsey wouldn't want *that*.

I put Dorsey and his coming payback from my mind and finished the reverse dips before moving on to military squats, knuckle push-ups, mountain climbers, and then a series of wide-legged jumping-Me's. I pressed my palms together and bowed, then toweled the sweat off again before laying out my "mattress" on the cold floor. I tried to focus on fully relaxing and extending my muscles and joints through each stretch, but the train of worries that had kept me from achieving more than an hour of sleep last night came rushing back into the station.

Would Mom really leave Dad? I mean, c'mon, could she have worse timing? God knows she had enough reason, but sheesh, the man's a stroke victim! How the hell would he take care of himself? No. No thinking about Mom and Dad. I'd just have to talk to her after court, or failing that, call her this afternoon when I finally got my hour.

How had Dad gotten along by himself last night?

Shit. Think about something else. My hour of "freedom" scheduled for this afternoon reminded me of my upcoming criminal-justice field trip scheduled for this morning; there was zero chance of bail, I knew that, but I had a plan:

First, I'll plead innocent (because I am, goddamnit), and second, I'll tell Haskins I'm indigent; pretty much true, and there is no way in hell or New Jersey I'll let Mom leverage the property. They'll give me some drooling baby-lawyer who will no doubt harbor dreams of becoming the next Johnny Cochran, but hopefully the media furor will flush out some criminal-defense mastermind who will work pro bono for the exposure; the promise of the spotlight should be enough blood in the water to lure a big one to—

The intercom squelched: "Ross, get into the dayroom!" A loud buzz and *ta-chunk*, and my door was suddenly unlocked.

I stared at it, then stood up slowly and put my "mattress" back on the rack; yet another break in routine, and I didn't like it.

"Ross! You alive in there? Get your ass out into the goddamn dayroom!"

I pulled my cell door open—it was heavy, but swung smoothly—and poked my head out and shouted toward the mirrored wall:

"My hour is this afternoon!"

"I changed my mind. But if you don't want it, no sweat, just ooze back inside your cage there and I'll lock the door again. Just know this: you won't get another one 'till tomorrow. It's now or never, tough guy." The speaker embedded in the high ceiling whined as it clicked off.

I still didn't like it, but I slipped my orange-plastic sandals on and flapped out and stood by the margarita-puke table and gazed into the mirrored wall; there I was, red stripes and all, hollow-eyed and hair roostered in back. *How many assholes are watching me?* No telling, but the guard on the intercom hadn't been Dorsey; I could *feel* the man's eyes, though. Was this his play? If it was, it didn't make sense; still too many witnesses and cameras. Maybe I was paranoid. Maybe my hour had been rescheduled because of court.

Maybe.

I resisted the urge to fly them all the bird, somehow, and instead waved jauntily. Then I retrieved my almost-towel and took a shower. I left my sandals on in the stall, and there were three reasons for that; one, the pedophile; two, the pedophile; and three, it's just wise-practice in jail. I dried off in my cell and re-donned my stripes and then went to the phone and followed the posted instructions and pushed the smeared chrome buttons, and as their tones beeped in my ear, I wondered idly how much a minute I was being charged; five bucks? Seven? More? I had bigger dolphins to fry, truly I did, but it still rankled how the system was rigged to fleece the incarcerated and their families; some two-bit phone company was reaping a more-than-healthy profit from their captive customers, and all without having to sweat the competition.

Nice setup. I wondered what they'd bribed Neil with to secure the contract.

After a series of clicks, the golden meter whirled as Mom's cell rang three times and was picked up, but it wasn't Mom.

"Hello?"

"Angela?"

"Jack! Are you all right? You sound tired."

"I'm fine," I lied. "Uh, is Mom around? And why are you still answering her phone?"

"She asked me to, just in case you called. Again. And she's upstairs in the shower. We're getting ready to go check on your dad." Her voice had held a tinge of the acerbic at the start of all that, but it faded to concern as she asked, "Are you *sure* you're all right?"

"Oh, I'm just peachy—you know, for a man about to be charged with six murders he didn't commit." I regretted it as soon as it popped out: "Sorry."

"That's okay," she said softly. "I understand. I'll get your mom."

"Thanks."

I listened to her climb the stairs and knock: "Mary? Jack's on the phone!"

Mom's muffled exclamation, and then a door opened; water hissed in the background:

"Jackie!"

"Hi, Mom."

"Are you okay, baby? Is that bastard Neil treating you right? I've been worried *sick* about—"

"I'm fine, I promise. Mom, we need to talk about Dad."

Silence except for the shower, and then Mom said, "I'm dripping all over Angie's beautiful hardwood floors. Here, talk to her while I dry off. You two have a lot to discuss, anyway."

I heard Angela breathing as a door shut. I pulled the receiver away and looked at it before putting it back; more breathing. I glanced at the mirrored wall, feeling all those unfriendly eyes, then faced the swastika-and-profanity-filled puke-green cinder blocks above the phone again.

We have a lot to discuss? Like what?

Angela was still just breathing, so I cleared my throat: "Um, is she drying off?" I rolled my eyes and thumped my forehead against the largest swastika.

"Yeah. I gave her a towel."

"Oh."

More breathing.

"So, uh, what did she mean? Why do we have a lot to discuss?"

She sighed. "She didn't mean anything, Jack. She's just…being Mary." The door opened, and Angela said (a trifle hurriedly, I thought), "Here's your mom."

"Jackie? Are you *sure* you're okay? Because you don't *sound* okay!"

"Yeah, Mom, I'm great. Listen, I know you're mad at Dad, but—"

"My relationship with your father is none of your concern, young man."

"The man had a *stroke*, for chrissakes! Can't this wait 'till—"

"Don't you *dare* take the Savior's name in vain, mister! Not where I can hear!"

"Mom, godda—" Deep breath. "You can't leave him there by himself. Do you even know if he made it through the night? He may have fallen. He may be lying out in the yard right—"

"Your father is just fine. Angie drove me out late last night to check on him, and we're going back before court to make sure he's got everything he needs for tonight. I took both sets of keys to his truck—*and* the tractor keys, *and* the mower keys, *and* the snowmobile keys—so the fool man can't drive anywhere, and I put out food for Jezzie. She's fine too, by the way. *Everything's fine*, Jackie, including your father. As a matter of fact, I think he's enjoying this little break from me as much as I am from him." She sniffed. "He must've called that hoodlum friend of his because there were beer cans on the porch. He's probably hung over as all getup this morning. Serves him right."

"But what if something happens while—"

"The subject of your father and I is closed. And for your information, I'm not *abandoning* him. His appointment with that Hindu fella whose name I've given up trying to pronounce has been rescheduled for next Tuesday, and I'll still drive him." Mom sighed.

"I just need some time away, Jackie. Angie has been kind enough to let me stay here for a few days, but we'll be going out twice a day to check on your dad."

"Mom—"

"That's the way it has to be for right now. As for down the road… well, we'll see."

"But—"

"The subject is *closed*, Jonathan!"

I knew better than to press her when my full name made an appearance. "Yes, ma'am."

"Now, we need to talk about getting you a lawyer. Your father won't sign off on putting up the property, but there are ways around him I think we should—"

"He's right."

"Jackie…"

"Just listen." I outlined my plan to plead innocent (you know, since I *am* fucking innocent) and then take advantage of the hoopla to lure in a big-time (hopefully) pro bono (hopefully) defense attorney. I finished with, "Let's just see who the judge gives me and go from there."

"What about bail?"

"They won't grant bail, Mom, not for this."

Tears clogged her voice: "But that means…that means you'll be in there until the trial! That could take *months!*"

"I know." It would probably be more than a year, but I didn't tell her; the yellow-green walls squeezed in, and I had to take a deep breath: "I'll be all right, Mom."

"Oh, Jackie…" Then she flared, "This isn't *right!* You didn't kill those people! *This isn't right!*"

"I know." It was all I could say. "I know." I wiped my cheeks with the neck of my red-striped pajamas while carefully keeping my back to the mirrored wall.

She was crying full-force, now. "I can't stand it. I just can't *stand* it. I have to get ready. I'll see you at the courthouse. Here, talk to Angie. I love you, Jackie."

Sobbing, and then a door *ka-whammed*.

"I love you too, Mom." I swabbed my face again; the receiver trembled in my grip.

Shit.

"Jack? Still there?"

"Still here."

"I'm so sorry this is happening to you."

"Yeah," I said. "Me too."

"I wish there was something I could do to help you."

"You're doing it. You're helping Mom. I don't know how I'll ever repay you for that, but if I get out…" I squeezed my eyes shut. "*When* I get out, I'll think of something. I promise."

"Jack…you're not all right, are you."

"I'm scared, Angela. I'm scared of…"

Her sweet voice was soft. "What?"

Then it came pouring out because for some reason, I knew I could tell this woman anything; this woman who I could never be more than friends with because she deserved better than an ex-con. Then, despite everything, I almost laughed:

Make that *current* con.

"Torrington was bad, really bad, but I knew they would release me someday; I had that hope to cling to. But if they convict me for this…well, if they don't put me on death row, then they'll lock me away and I'll never see Mom and Dad or trees again except though wire mesh."

"Jack…"

"But let's say I get lucky and they eventually figure out I'm innocent. You can catch some poor schmuck on the news like that every few weeks, seems like; somebody finds some DNA, or maybe an eyewitness recants, and then there he is, surrounded by microphones and his happy family—the ones still alive, anyway—because it's a cause for celebration, right? Everyone's so fucking happy, and there he is, gray now, but free and smiling and hugging everyone… but have you ever looked at his eyes, Angela?" She didn't respond. "Have you?"

"No."

"I have, and they're dead; flat and empty and fucking dead; his body is out, sure, but something inside him will never leave. They took his *life*, Angela. They just flat-out took it, and he'll never get it back."

"Oh, Jack…"

"And even when I'm exonerated—*when*, not if—I won't be able to sue the bastards and get paid."

"Why not?"

"Because Wyoming doesn't have a wrongful-conviction statute. And *that* means the fuckers can lock you up for whatever they want, and when it turns out they fucked up, they just say, 'Whoops, so sorry.' You can sue them all you want, but there's nothing on the books that says they have to pay a goddamn dime."

"God, that's…that's *awful*."

"Yeah, but it's what you get when you put the real crooks in charge and let them write the rules." I scrubbed my face again, fighting for calm. "Sorry. I shouldn't put all this on you."

"It's okay."

"No, I mean it. You've done so much for Mom…for both of us. You're a good friend, Angela, and we're lucky to have you."

Utter and complete silence; I thought we'd lost the connection.

"Hello? Shit. Angela? Hello?"

And then she spoke, low and hard and clipped: "I don't want to be your friend, Jack."

My stomach dropped away. I swallowed. "I'm sorry to hear that."

"Don't be such a moron! I meant I don't want to be *just* your friend. I fucked up, okay? I overreacted to you and that…that *whore*, and I'm sorry; your past is none of my business. It was just… seeing you talking…and I could tell you were still attracted to each other…" She growled, actually growled, then spat, *"But she can't have you."*

"Angela—"

"And don't you *dare* spout that bullshit about not being good enough for me! We've all made mistakes, and none of us can do anything but move forward and try to do better. And if I hear another *word* about it, I'm going to kick your ass next time I see you, I don't care how tough you are or how many stupid martial arts you know! You're a good man, Jack Ross, and *I* know it. We'll get you out of there, and then I'm going to take you up into your loft and make love to you under the stars until your *ears* fall off. Do you understand me, mister?"

My jaw was brushing my red-striped pajamas; I clicked my teeth together.

"Hello? Still there?"

"Uh, yeah."

"Well? Damn it, don't leave a girl hanging."

"Until my *ears* fall off? That sounds…interesting."

Her throaty chuckle made my blood hum. "You have no idea. But I'll show you."

The speaker in the ceiling blasted to life: "Wrap it up and scoot back into your cage, Ross."

I threw a glare at the mirrored wall; perfect fucking timing. "I've only been out for about twenty minutes!"

"To bad so sad, tough guy. Your fellow dirtbags are inbound, and we can't have you wandering out and about when they land. Back you go. Then we can serve your yummy breakfast. I think it's eggs this morning. Well, sort-of eggs."

I ground my teeth; they'd never intended to give me the full hour. I started to tell Angela, but she said, "I heard. What a prick."

"Yeah."

The speaker crackled. "In, Ross. *Now.*"

"I have to go."

"I know. Take care of yourself."

"I will."

"See you in court." She hung up.

So did I, then flapped back into my cell and pushed the door closed just as the outside door buzzed and clanked. I watched the reflection of the guards lead the reflection of the Indian and the pedo and Tweaker in and unlock their cuffs and chains and escort them to the reflection of their cells; I observed the reflection of a whispered exchange between one guard and Tweaker before Tweaker's cell bonged shut.

The hair on my forearms stood straight up.

The guards collected the chains and cuffs and vamoosed, nothing out of the ordinary about that, but there was a missing link in the sequence I'd just witnessed; I couldn't quite pinpoint it, but…

…door opens, guards walk dirtbags in, guards unhook dirtbags, dirtbags go back into dirtbag cages, guards leave…

I lowered my gaze slowly and considered my door, then grasped the handle and pulled it open about an inch.

Son of a bitch.

The locks had never engaged.

I glanced out again and caught the reflection of an open cell down the way; I didn't want to be trapped, so I jerked my door open and stepped out. The Indian stopped twenty feet away; he'd been slinking down the wall to my left, across the faces of the cells, and he had a claw hammer in his right hand, held down low by his red-striped thigh; it had a dark-blue rubber handle, and its head was scarred from long use. I met his brown eyes and beheld the first expression I'd seen in them; excitement. I backed away, and he followed me only with those eyes, taking my measure.

I glanced at the mirrored wall, but there would be no guards rushing in to break this up, just like there would be no warning over the intercom to get back into our cages.

It seems I had underestimated the good Sgt. Dorsey.

Tweaker watched from the safe side of the picnic table; he followed my gaze to the mirrored wall before twitching a shrug. "Hey, man, it's just bizness. Nothin' personal." Tweaker suddenly spun towards an open cell beyond the motionless Indian. "Ya fat fuck! Get out here and help! The man ain't gonna give us what he promised if we don't deliver!"

The pedophile slunk to his open door and glanced at me and then at the mirrored wall before hissing at Tweaker: "I don't like this! We're going to get in trouble!"

"So what? It ain't like they're gonna let your sick ass out this century, anyway. Might as well have the money for your family." Tweaker then favored me with a dank grin: "Hey, man, we ain't gonna *kill* ya. We're just gonna take out a knee or two, maybe an elbow and a wrist. That's all the man wants. Sez the *last* thing he wants is you dead; nah, he wants you alive, bro, but crippled and in prison and *wishin'* you wuz dead." Tweaker laughed, revealing the full ruin of his teeth. "That's harsh shit, I know, but my ma and my sister need the scratch—and it's an *ass load* of scratch, bro. Might even be some left when I get out." Tweaker glanced at the Indian, who was still crouched by the wall, watching me: "Well? Whatcho waitin' for dere, Chief? An invitation? Smash 'im up with that thing so we can get our fuckin' money!"

The Indian suddenly straightened and flung the hammer toward the table; it clattered across the concrete, and Tweaker snatched it up with a, "Hell, yeah!"

And then the Indian spoke in a voice that wasn't deep and resonant, as countless movies had conditioned me to expect; if anything, it was surprisingly high for a man his size. And he sure didn't say, "How, Kemosabe," or anything like that, but his English did hold a tinge of something guttural and tribal.

"You've made a bad enemy," he informed me as he moved lithely to the center of the room. "The kind who will not face you like a man, but pays others to fight in his stead." He spat on the puke-green floor without breaking his gaze from mine: "*That* is what I think of such a man."

Tweaker scowled and stopped swishing the hammer around. "You ain't backin' out, are ya, Chief? We got a *loooootta* money ridin' on this." He snarled over at the pedo, who still hadn't left his doorway: "Get your worthless ass out here! You're in this, too!"

The fat man took two cringing steps and froze. "I don't like this," he whined.

Tweaker snorted in disgust, then came around the picnic table, swinging the hammer in wide arcs. "Enough bullshit. Let's—"

The Indian held out a hand without looking away from me. "I will do this."

"What? I got the fuckin' tool, man. Just hold his ass down so—"

"*I* will do this." The Indian never took his eyes from me. "If you interfere, I will kill you."

Tweaker's pockmarked face twisted, and he opened his mouth… and then he looked at the hammer, as if to remind himself that he still held it. Then he scrambled around behind the table again. "Sure, Chief, sure, whatever, just hurry the fuck up. You heard what that screw—"

The intercom flared over our heads: "Get it done, goddamnit!" Dorsey.

But a dark suspicion blazed through me; Tweaker had talked about money, a lot of money, and the last time I'd checked, Sheridan County Detention Officers made just above shit. So where had

Dorsey gotten the green to motivate *these* guys? And something else; the risk Dorsey was taking. He could end up in a cell right beside me—or someplace worse. Much worse.

This made no sense.

Unless—

The Indian kicked his orange-plastic sandals off and circled to my right. I kicked mine away and circled left while watching Tweaker in my peripheral; even with the big Indian's threat, I knew that hammer would eventually make Tweaker brave.

The Indian circled closer, and I risked a glance at the pedophile. He still hadn't joined the fun, but he was watching us eagerly. In fact, he was almost panting, and with sick dread, I knew I was seeing the face those fourth-grade little girls would forever see.

And then he hissed, "We have to say it! It's part of the deal! If we don't, we don't get the money!"

I addressed them for the first time.

"Say what?"

Tweaker snarled at the fat man. "*You* say it. Not like you're gonna do anything else to earn your share."

"All right." The pedo faced me, blinked and cringed at my stare, shot a fearful look at the mirrored wall, then raised his voice ever-so slightly: "He said to say, 'This is for Zack'."

A red film dropped over my vision:

I knew who had set me up.

I launched into the big Indian.

28

His list was coming along.

He thought about what remained as he walked back behind the Rockingham estate, once more keeping the trees and then the pickup between him and the lawyer's cameras as much as possible without being obvious. He chucked the bloody ax into the bed and opened the door and bent forward and scooted in and laboriously straightened while trying not to get blood on the headliner and failing, then started the engine and backed out and drove down the utility road. When he was far enough away and hidden by a thick screen of needles, he stopped and shrugged out of the gore-spattered half-suit and shoved it crumpled and sticky over into the passenger side of the cab.

He drove on slowly until he was between the third and fourth houses north of the Rockingham's; the same place he'd come in. The adjacent estates didn't employ cameras, only alarms; the lone such arrangement in Lake Shore he'd been able to find, but find it he had. Needles hissed and branches squealed, and then he edged the Ford onto Lake Shore Drive and leaned and took his watch out of the glove box:

Right on schedule.

He lowered both windows and let his sweat-soaked clothes, hair, and skin dry as he wound through the stately residences; ahead, sirens wailed in the distance, coming closer; behind, screams drifted on the warm night air.

He smiled, lips quaking.

He took deserted back roads down to the Splash n' Dash, avoiding the highway crawling with police, and rolled into Bay 3 and yanked the bloody boots off and stuffed them and the rest of the cash into a navy-blue Nike gym bag and got out in his sock feet and hid it in the agreed-upon spot.

He cautiously crossed the highway and took different side roads back up around the lake to the undeveloped northwest quadrant; twenty-five minutes after leaving the self-service car wash, he bumped up to his isolated two-room cabin near Hawk's Point, tamped on his own boots, and got to work.

It was almost three in the morning when he sprayed the last blobs of tan and olive-green paint onto the Ford and stepped back and shook the cans and eyed his efforts critically, then fell prey to a jaw-cracker of a yawn and decided it would do; he was beyond tired, but he also felt mostly all right for a change; he'd done good work this night. The little Downing whore was another nail in Ross's coffin, although a burr of unfulfilled frustration dug at him; he hadn't been able to take his time with her, or that mouthy little fleet-footed blonde, like he liked.

He put the paint away and got his hacksaw and removed the ax handle, then sawed it into smaller pieces and tossed the pieces into the iron half-barrel behind the cabin, splashed a mix of gasoline and two-cycle oil from his chainsaw can, and burned them. He took a shower and changed clothes and then burned his bloody garments and gloves. He opened a new pair of black-suede gloves and drew them on, pulled a pair of heavy work gloves over them, wrapped the tacky, feathered half-suit inside two lawn bags and duct taped them together, stuffed the mass into a backpack, and then mashed and mashed until he could zip the bulging pack closed. He put the taut and swollen backpack in the Ford's toolbox and locked it with a small chrome key.

He started to clean the long bench seat, but that much blood would never come out, not all the way, no matter how he scrubbed, so he blotted the headliner and wiped the inside of the doors down as best he could, then dug around in his cabin until he found an old gray boat tarp and spread it across the seat. He hooked the motorcycle trailer to the Ford's ball hitch just as the first blush of dawn lit the mountains hovering over the cabin.

He stood back and surveyed his work, nodded, then went inside and activated one of his phones and took care of some business. His shaking legs felt burnt out from under him, but he caught Sheriff Neal's press conference on the boxy old tin-foiled rabbit-ear and conducted more business on another phone. Satisfied all was proceeding according to plan, he stretched out on the couch and tumbled into exhausted darkness.

Early Friday morning, rested and refreshed and wearing a bushy fake beard and a L.A. Dodgers cap along with his Oakley's, he drove the still-tacky camouflaged pickup out of the woods, utilizing dirt roads all the way down past Sheridan, where he dropped in on his old friend, Fred Starkly. Fred's wife Amanda wasn't home, which was disappointing, but he and Fred enjoyed a brief yet satisfying chat before he doubled back and got onto I-90 headed north, still right on schedule.

An hour and a half into Montana, near the northern boundary of the vast Crow Reservation, he rolled down the window and tossed the ax head into the Bighorn River as he crossed the bridge.

He turned north on 47 at Hardin; at Kingley, he turned left on Rd. 150 and drove the Ford into hills that would've been termed mountains in any other state.

Forty-five minutes later he rumbled through the sleepy township of Creedmoor, Montana; population 313, according to the bullet-riddled sign he'd just passed; he wasn't sure he believed it. On a dusty dirt road a little less than five miles from Creedmoor, he stopped at a rutted lane that branched up a moderate slope before vanishing between the pines; access to those needle-choked ruts was denied by a Krieg wider than his gloved fist and a 2" titanium alloy chain and a hinged triangular vehicle barrier with a **Keep Out—Private Property** warning bolted to it. The elements had bleached the red notification pink in the five years since he'd seen it, and the barrier's brown paint was flaking over rust blossoms; the chain and padlock had spot-rusted as well, but everything still appeared sturdy—and most importantly, undisturbed.

He produced a key and unlocked the Krieg and unwound the chain with a clanking rattle, then unlimbered another key and unlocked the barrier and swung it back with a squeal of tortured metal and drove the truck and trailer through. He checked up and down the sun-dappled dirt road to make sure he was unobserved, then swung the barrier back and locked it and wound the chain around and locked the Krieg. He climbed back in the Ford and dropped it into four-wheel drive and powered up and into the woods.

A quarter mile later, he discovered a storm had washed a deep rut across the slope and through the trail; no way to get the trailer over that in one piece—or the motorcycle on his way out—so he unloaded the gleaming new black-and-chrome Roadster and concealed it behind a wind-scoured juniper and got back in and gunned it, dragging the trailer over the rut, hearing the crash and clang and bang as it bottomed out, but the thing had served its purpose;

he bashed over another, even deeper storm rut, further ruining it before he reached the old quarry exactly seven-eighths of a mile from the dusty dirt road.

He nosed the Ford onto the granite shelf overhanging the clear, still water and shut the engine off. Three-thousand-foot "hills" bulked all around, silent and sunny and majestic. He paced the shoreline, but saw only deer and raccoon and rabbit and squirrel and an old, dried bear track; a fresh cougar print waited at the far edge of the shelf, a big one, but no human traces. That was good. Hunters were a danger, even though the season was supposedly out, and the Forestry Service had an emergency contingency plan to use the quarry for their chopper dips and drops, but there hadn't been a serious blaze up here for three decades.

He stood by the truck, straining his ears; only the hiss of the wind through needles and the far off *skree* of a hunting raptor. He studied the stunted Ponderosa bunched at the top of the seventy-foot cliff across the water, but saw no movement; the pale, vertical plumb lines, where workers had long ago drilled and set the shaped charges, were stark against the rose-tinted stone, even after all these years.

Satisfied they were alone, he took the bulging backpack out of the toolbox and set it out of the way before climbing in and starting the Ford. He rolled both windows down, revved the engine, and then leaned and shook his guest's shoulder; he wanted the man conscious for this.

The lump on the back of Fred's hard head was impressive, but it had never quite bled; wisps of silver hair stuck up around the purpling bump. Fred's groan was muffled by the duct tape, and his eyelids fluttered before he opened them, focused, and saw him sitting behind the steering wheel wearing the royal blue cap with a bushy black beard spread across his chest; the esteemed councilman's face crinkled in bewilderment. Then memory returned, and anger and fear replaced confusion; mostly it was fear.

Fred's wrists and thumbs were taped together behind his back; his ankles were bound as well, so the soon-to-be-former Sheridan City Councilman had to worm his way inelegantly up and out of the passenger floorboard. When Fred at last sat up, hunched forward because of his hands, he took in the expanse of clear water and the rose-stone cliff and his eyes above the tape got as big and as round as soup bowls.

Fred turned to him and *mumphed* an outraged question, but he was done listening to Fred Starkly in this life. He slammed his gloved fist into Fred's face, bliss enveloping his entire being when he felt *and* heard Fred's nose break; he'd waited thirty years to do that.

Fred's pointy head slammed against the door frame, and then Fred sat there dazedly as he reached across the councilman's lap and secured the seatbelt. Fred recovered somewhat and *mumphed* something else, so he socked Fred one more good one before dropping the truck into gear and sliding out; Fred's red-rimmed eyes pleaded with him above the snot-and-blood-covered tape, but he only smiled at his old friend.

And then Fred screamed a bubbly and muffled scream as he released the emergency brake and jumped back.

The trailer neck caught on the lip, making a grinding racket that echoed from the cliff across the water and sent the pickup swinging into the vertical wall of rock below with a crash, Fred thrashing about and mewling pathetically, but the Ford's weight soon lifted the back of the trailer into the air and the camouflage truck, motorcycle trailer, and Fred made a great splash and froth and disappeared.

He stood at the edge and watched the bubbles churn and waited to see if Fred would manage to unbuckle the seatbelt and wriggle to the surface like an old, annoying seal; after five minutes, he waited to see if Fred's body would somehow break free and rise, but it was just habit; it didn't matter if Fred rotted in the pitch black two hundred and seventy feet down or bobbed to the surface and putrefied in the sun.

It would have mattered before the diagnosis; he'd always taken pride in being methodical, because it was important to keep his true self hidden. He raised his hands and watched them tremble, then clenched them into fists, gloves squeaking.

Was important. Soon he would be done with hiding. Very soon.

He fought off a surge of weakness and checked his disposable phone, but still no text. He stuffed it back into his pocket, where it joined two others, trying to curb his impatience; he'd gotten everything he'd ever wanted in this world by following careful plans step by step; the damnable disease had changed things, but not everything. He would be patient; he only had to suffer this indignity until his list was complete.

And then…

He paced the rock shelf, back and forth, back and forth, faster and faster, fighting against the trembling in his legs that threatened to buckle his knees to the warm stone; for all his resolve and discipline, patience came hard today.

He was so close to completing his list.

The Harley and even Fred Starkly had only been tidbits, much like Mrs. Barbary and her goddamn ruler. That old, mean bastard, Mr. Napier, the janitor—*he'd* been much more than a tidbit, oh yes, but the rest were only afterthoughts to be checked off when circumstances permitted. Even Angie Beaumont was only a morsel, albeit a tasty one, and one that would not escape him again; he had special plans for that little whore.

But the text he was waiting on would tell him whether the one thing—the *only* thing—that truly mattered could at last be crossed off.

He checked his watch; almost ten-thirty. He lifted his chin and used one gloved finger to scratch beneath the beard. Why hadn't he heard anything? There'd been plenty of time to see the deed done and done right. Had something gone wrong? Perhaps, with all the commotion, his man hadn't had a chance to step away and use the phone he'd provided; that had to be it.

That had *better* be it.

A silvery burp roiled up and burst; Fred's last gasp before he'd sucked in the cold, dark water, perhaps. He stared down and down and down, past where it turned lightless, but vertigo seized him, so he stepped back and contemplated the depths from a safe distance.

How many of his whores were down there? He couldn't quite remember; three…no, four. After all the years and all the whores, it was hard to keep track of which whore went where, but he'd brought that tattooed Austin slut up here five years ago; what a wildcat, but by the end, she'd begged him to stop, just like all the rest. That was the last time he'd visited here; the Austin wildcat made four.

Or maybe it was five.

He shrugged. Either way, Fred wouldn't be lonely down there.

A sly grin creased his twitching, trembling face; he hadn't hidden *all* his whores, though, oh no. Perhaps he should have, but, as much as he was singular among men, he also shared a weakness with those lesser than he: the craving of attention; the thirst for acknowledgement of his accomplishments.

He began to pace again. He'd given in to that weakness, yes, but he hadn't announced himself to the ignorant world with bad poems or self-righteous letters or other numbskull moves. He'd simply arranged for a specific set of professionals to know that he was out here, living the life he chose—and now that he'd lured them here, he had plans for those men that hid behind their three bold letters; those men who thought they were so smart—smarter even than *him*.

He would show those men how wrong they were.

But first he needed to receive a text message. After that, he could move on to enjoying the Beaumont whore's screams, and then two or three other tidbits perhaps, if he had time and energy; he would save the FBI for last.

They would be a fitting end to it all.

Weary and increasingly impatient, he lowered himself to the warm stone and crossed his ankles and rested his elbows on his knees. The sun beat on the back of his neck as he scratched beneath the beard again and contemplated the clear water; zero bubbles. The esteemed councilman now rested in the pitch black, slumming with a sample of rotten whores; it felt good to finally cross Fred off his list. The breeze hissed and whispered and muttered, unceasing; the hunting cry came again, somewhere high above and to the north.

What name had those oh-so-smart men come up with for him? What did they write on their casefiles and at the top of their whiteboards when they charted his movements in their vain attempts at grasping his majesty? He'd speculated about it over the years, and now he couldn't help but think he was close to finding out. They always named them, men like him (although there had never truly been a man like him, he was confident of that), and he hadn't been able to stop himself from wondering.

It mattered less than nothing, however; a foolish bit of vanity on his part. Name him what they would, they would never understand the drive and the determination and the sheer genius that was his.

He shook his head in disgust. Whatever it was, it couldn't be worse than what those fools in the press had christened him: *Chicken Man.* Chickens bobbed about laying eggs—if they were lucky enough to live that long—but a rooster treaded his females whenever and wherever he liked, whether they wished to be treaded or not. "Rooster Man" would have been much more accurate, for both the costume and the man underneath; couldn't trust those media blockheads to get anything right; one of the many reasons he'd avoided them until now.

He considered the backpack with the bloody half-costume stuffed inside, then scraped it over and rested his arm on it. When he got the word, he would weight it with rocks and send it down to join Fred, and good riddance…but he would wait, just in case. If the text wasn't what he wanted to hear, he might still need it, no matter how abominably hot the thing was. You'd think someone would design a better way to get air circulating under all those feathers, although he supposed the jacket didn't help; the absurd thing was real leather.

The phone buzzed against his thigh.

He surged to his feet before staggering and catching his balance, then fumbled it out and flipped it open with eager, trembling fingers.

They were waiting for him.

Ron spotted the black-on-black Suburban as soon as he turned off the square. It sat in the station's lot like a dark and ominous whale with government plates. They saw him as well; two men wearing dark-blue blazers over white button-down Oxford's with matching dark-blue ties got out of the Suburban even before he turned in.

Not only were they dressed alike, they were tall and well-built with squared-off jaws, and both sported crew cuts and wore black Ray Bans; they could've been twins except one was a ginger with the freckles to prove it. Even under present circumstances, Ron would've taken them for standard GS-9 drones except for the way they moved; quick and lithe as the carroty agent waved for him to stop. The dark-haired agent swiveled his head this way and that, right hand hovering beneath his left arm; both had their jackets unbuttoned for easy access.

Ron grinned wryly. Denton was classic FBI arrogant, but even he was circumspect enough to hide his tactical squad behind ties and shiny shoes; the slowest reporter in the world might question why a TAC team was needed to "assist the local authorities in gathering evidence." The freckly agent continued to flag him urgently, but Ron drove around him to the glass front door and grabbed his tattered notebook and the two flat, clear-plastic cases from the passenger seat and hopped out, leaving the motor running.

They moved up fast, one on either end, trapping him against the red bricks and the glass; the ginger spoke, waxy face all hard angles and flat planes beneath the Ray Bans:

"Chief, Special Agent Denton would like a word."

"Hello, boys. Be with you in a moment." He slipped inside and shot the bolt just as the dark-haired agent grabbed the handle; the door rattled. Ron waved cheerfully as he turned the rod; the gaps between the wooden slats slowly vanished, shutting out his close-up view of those expressionless faces. He turned around to find Mindy standing behind the counter with one hand grasping her throat and the other covering her mouth; her watery blue eyes hovered big and scared over her thick fingers.

She dropped her hands to the counter and gushed, "Chief, oh thank God, there's so much I need to tell you! They made me call you on your cell, not the radio, and I did, but you didn't answer or call back and I had to give them your number…I *had* to, so don't you *dare* look at me like that! And then when you didn't call them back either, they asked me where you were and what you were doing and why you weren't answering, but I didn't know, not for sure, and then they just…they just stood there watching me! They didn't take those glasses off *the entire time!* They wouldn't even sit down, just stood there! Gave me the jim-jam crawlies, but about thirty minutes ago they finally went back out to their vehicle and I tried to call and tell you they were here, I really did, but you *still* didn't answer, and I didn't want to get on the box for fear they'd listen."

"It's all right." Ron had angled for this meeting, but he'd be dammed if he hopped when Denton crooked a finger. He handed her a silvery DVD-RW disk and kept the other: "Put that in the floor safe when we're gone."

She took it hesitantly…then jumped, heavy breasts jiggling, and almost dropped it when the door rattled in its frame again:

"Chief! Special Agent Denton is waiting!"

"Be right with you!" He passed his battered notebook over. "This, too. Put it all in the safe."

"What—"

"Just do it." The door rattled again and then came a pointed *whap-whap-whap*. "I'll be back this afternoon," he told Mindy. *I hope.* "Where's Ryan?"

"That's another thing I need to tell you! Manda Starkly called around 0900 and asked if we could send someone to check and see if Fred was up here. Manda went for her early morning walk—she's trying to lose weight again, and good for her—but when she got back, Fred was gone. He didn't take his truck neither, cuz it's still sittin' in their garage, and Manda said his wallet and cell phone and keys are on his desk. Sheridan PD sent a coupla uniforms out to poke around, but they only took her statement and left. She wanted to file a missing person's, but they didn't think it was necessary yet. The poor old girl is about at her wits' end, Chief, so I asked Ryan to run out to their cabin, but he called in a bit ago and said the place is shut up tight, no sign of Fred."

"Did she try the Sheriff's Office?"

"Yeah, and they told her to call Sheridan PD. I think they got their hands full this mornin', what with the attack, and Jack's first appearance being postponed, and now Neil's having another press conference." She eyed him speculatively. "You heard about that, right?"

"I heard." It had been Ron who'd tipped the media to Neil's carelessness—if carelessness it was; he had serious doubts about that. Then he smiled a little: "But I don't think this show will go near as smooth as yesterday's."

Mindy smiled a little back. "I expect not."

Whap-whap-whap, rattle-rattle. "Chief Rogers!"

"Tell Manda we're thinking about her, and that if Fred's not back by dinner, I'll file a MP myself and come down there and start looking." *If I still can. Whap-whap-whap, rattle-rattle.* "I better go with these guys before they break the door down. If I'm not back by shift change, though, or if you haven't heard from me by then, call Mayor Ford." Mindy's big eyes got even bigger, and her hand shot back up to cover her mouth, but she nodded. Ron turned toward the closed blinds and the twin silhouettes of Denton's suited thugs beyond. "Wish me luck."

"Chief, wait." He turned back at the urgency in her voice. "You got a call on the non-e line this morning."

"Mindy—"

"It was Donnie Straus. When I told him you were out and weren't to be bothered, he got all upset and said he left a message with Tommy last night, but you never called him back."

"I gave you that key and told you to tell him—"

"I *did*, but he didn't care two friggin' frigs about Crazy's; said he wanted to talk about something else, something important. He demanded your cell, but I informed him I couldn't give that information out. Said I'd relay a message, though, but he's all hot and bothered to talk to *you*, preferably face to face. Wants to give you something."

Whap-whap-whap, rattle-rattle. "Chief!"

"Give me what? What's all this about?"

"I asked, but he only said again—in so many words—to tell you to call him as soon as you could. And then he hung up on me!" Mindy scowled. "That boy sure has some mouth."

"All right," Ron said slowly, frowning, then shook his head. "If he calls back, tell him I'll get to him as soon as I can. If that's not good enough, tell him to come to the station and wait for me."

"I will, Chief."

He reached for the deadbolt with the hand that didn't hold the second disk, then looked over his shoulder: "Remember, find Mayor Ford if you haven't heard from me by shift change."

"I will. And good luck."

"Thanks." He threw the bolt and jerked the door open and stepped outside where the well-dressed drones loomed. "Well, boys, what are we waiting for? Let's go see your boss."

30

Donnie jabbed the start button, pausing the game, and tossed his wireless controller onto the cluttered coffee table; it hit the overflowing ashtray and scattered ashes and half-smoked butts before caroming off the two-foot-tall purple-glass bong; the blackened water filling its globular base sloshed.

"Hey!" Skeeter whined. "Easy on Deep Purple, man! She's a classic." Donnie heaved up from Skeet's sway-backed couch and went to the grimy front window and peeked between the dirty blinds. His car still sat out there, ass end snugged to the peeling porch, only steps from the scabby front door; the Honda's trunk didn't appear as if it had been jimmied open or otherwise messed with.

Good.

He checked the dirt road out past Skeet's needle-choked front yard, but only heat shimmers from a ninety-plus July afternoon moved on the dusty road. He probed the shadows beneath the tall Ponderosa surrounding Skeet's place in endless green-arrowhead rows, but saw only sun-dappled forest fading back and back into impenetrable darkness.

Anybody could be in there, and I'd never know it. Not until it was too late, anyway.

He shivered, then dug for his Marlboro's and packed them on his palm *pop-pop* and tapped one out and stuck it between his lips and freed his shiny new Zippo and opened it with a metallic *schink* and lit the smoke. He took a deep, deep drag, then blew it out; smoke spread against the pane, adding a fresh layer of grunge. When the haze cleared, nothing outside had changed; his Honda still sat there unmolested, the dirt road was still sunny and dusty and deserted, and the darkness beneath the never-ending rows of pines was still, well, *dark*.

The crinkle of cellophane came from behind him: "You sure are wound tight, amigo. Let Miss Purple take the edge off."

"I don't want that shit."

Silence except for Skeet loading the bong, then: "You're freakin' me out, brohime. That's the tenth time you've stuck your nose to that window since I woke up, and that was less than a fuckin' hour ago. What're you lookin' for out there, anyway?" Donnie didn't answer. "Come back over here and let the DP smooth the way through yo' day." Skeeter's matching new Zippo fired and then came the gurgle from Deep Purple.

"I said I don't want any."

"Oh, I get it." Skeeter's voice was strained as he held the hit; then he blew it out, and the reek of ganja filled the room. "You was *beggin'* to smoke with me yesterday, like for the first time in forever, but now you're suddenly too *good* again."

Donnie spun. "I'm not too *good*, motherfucker. I just don't want any today, okay? Back the fuck off my case."

"All right, all right, shit." Deep Purple bubbled again as Skeeter applied flame to her wide bowl, and then he yanked the stem out and took his finger off the carburetor and sucked the two-foot tube of solid white into his lungs; he coughed behind clenched teeth, eyes tearing, smoke trailing out of his nostrils like a dragon. "Wanna tell me what the fuck's goin' on? You been actin' weird as hell." He tilted his head and blew a cloud toward the ceiling; his bloodshot blue eyes were huge behind his Coke-bottle glasses. "I mean, I know your best boy turned out to be a freakazoid killer and all, but—"

"He's not my *boy*. And Jack didn't do it, they got the wrong guy."

Skeeter raised a solemn finger toward the new sixty-inch HD Sony boob-tube hanging on his grubby, off-white wall: "Not what *they* say."

"Yeah, well, they're wrong." Donnie went back around the table and collapsed into the crummy couch, butt sinking almost to the threadbare carpet.

"You bitched about that same shit for a fuckin' hour last night. 'Jack's innocent! They've got the wrong guy!' Thought you'd never shut the fuck up. And you never told me *why* you think that." Skeeter snorted. "Said you'd tell me 'later'. Well, guess what, amigo? It's fuckin' later. Spill them guts."

Donnie only looked at him, thinking, *I can't, he'd freak out. And there's no telling who he'd spill his guts to. He's got other friends now, not like the old days.*

That thought was surprisingly bitter. "Just trust me, man, Jack didn't kill those kids."

Reginald "Skeeter" Rumpke rolled his hugely magnified eyes. "What the fuck ever." He set the bong down, exposing the new forearm tattoo stuffed full of flames and skulls and motorcycles and other dumb-ass shit Donnie didn't care to peer too close at, and grabbed his wireless controller and made an impatient pick-it-up motion at Donnie's. "Just because the boss you have a gargantuan man-crush on turned out to be a costume-wearing freak doesn't mean we can't finish this level."

Donnie glared. "I don't have a *man-crush* on Jack. He's just a good boss. And a good guy, too."

"Sure." Skeeter made the impatient motion again, then scratched around the edges of the glistening tattoo; the Neosporin he kept smearing on the ugly thing made his arm look greasy. "Let's do this. I gotta get ready in like ten minutes."

Man-crush? Four-eyed dickhead. "I don't want to play anymore."

Donnie heaved up, the couch's broken depths releasing him reluctantly, and stubbed his smoke in the overflowing tray on his way back to the window; everything outside was still dusty and hot and quiet.

Good.

Silence radiated from the couch behind him. Then Skeet growled, "What the fuck *ever*. I gotta get ready for work, anyway." The controller clattered onto the table, and then the couch creaked before he passed icily behind Donnie and down the short hallway toward the bedrooms. "You can hang out, I don't care, just lock the door if you leave. I don't want nobody ganking my new shit."

"It's *our* shit, fuck face! I bought it for *both* of us!"

A muffled, "Possession is nine-tenths of the law, *fuck face!* You don't like it, pack it all up and take it home! I'm sure *Mommy* will loooooove to hear how you got the dough for it!"

Donnie's nostrils flared, but he had no rejoinder; after a few seconds, the pipes groaned as the shower started.

He turned back to the filmy window. "*Fuck!*" Skeet was right. His mom *would* freak if she learned he'd blown almost a grand on thirty cartons of smokes and matching chrome Zippos and a Play Station 4 and a sixty-inch HD Sony flat screen, not to mention the steak dinners down at Rufio's; they'd also changed a fist-full of twenties into a basket-full of dolla bills, y'all, and tried to get into Woody's, that strip club way out off 67, but that roided-out bouncer had just laughed and confiscated their fake IDs before reintroducing them to the parking lot. *Asshole.*

No, his mom wouldn't like it at all, especially if she knew the real truth; the "truth" Skeeter knew was what Donnie had made up on the fly to explain how he was suddenly flush with fifteen crisp Benjamins. *Face it, numbskull, Mom won't like* either *truth.* Skeeter thought Donnie's long-gone sperm-donor Phillip, otherwise known as Daddy, had found him on Facebook. Phillip, wracked with guilt over abandoning his wife and young son fifteen years ago, now wanted to buy back Donnie's love with cash, but didn't want his mom to know about it; hence the grand-and-a-half-in-hand. Skeeter had swallowed the lie easily…not that he'd given much of a rat's ass about the particulars once Donnie started buying crap and stashing it in his house.

Phillip hadn't contacted him, and probably never would, but Donnie had easily found *him* on Facebook four years ago. His long-lost Daddy now lived in Eugene, Washington and worked at the humongous Caterpillar plant there. Daddy had a new blonde wife and two new little blonde-headed girls named Marissa and Carissa, age four and six; his half-sisters would be eight and ten, now.

I have sisters, and I'll never meet them.

Donnie grunted sourly and lit another cigarette. *Fuck Phillip. And fuck his shiny new family, too.* He had more important shit to worry about anyway, didn't he?

Oooooh, youz better believe it, muchachos.

He tried to laugh, but couldn't dredge one up.

I am so fucked!

He pulled his phone: 4:27 fuckin' Friday afternoon, and that sonofabitch Rogers *still* hadn't called him back! The Heap Big Nosy Chief had time to *spy* on him and pull him over and roust him about where he'd gotten all this money to throw around, that's for fuckin' sure, but not to return Donnie's goddamn calls!

He puffed angry smoke at the pane and listened to Skeeter get dressed, and when his friend came out wearing his red Rufio's shirt and black jeans and carrying his red apron, Donnie said, "I'm sorry, man. I know I'm acting like a schizoid, but, well, uh, this thing with my dad contacting me out of the blue…I guess it's got me freaked out."

Skeeter studied him with shrewd blue eyes behind the glasses, then moved his wiry frame to the couch and reached under and fished out a green-and-white Reebok size 10 1/2 shoebox and popped the lid and lifted four quarter-ounce baggies of bud and stuffed them into his front pocket, then lifted another baggie to the light and shook it; this one held several tiny blue footballs, all bunched down into the corner. He tied it off and stuffed it in his other pocket. Skeeter was a line cook, but his real income came from slinging pot and Xanax to his coworkers and their friends—and whoever else would buy from him.

Skeet finally looked up. "If my worthless old man suddenly skinned me fifteen-hundred dollars, don't think I'd be freakin'." Then he gave Donnie a sardonic grin. "Hey, you gonna hit the sperm-donor up for another fifteen bills, or what?"

Donnie stared at him. *He didn't buy it, but he still doesn't give a shit where it came from.* He took a drag and numbly turned back to the window. "No. That was a one-shot deal."

"Oh. Well, that sucks."

"Yeah, that sucks."

I have thirty thousand in cash, Donnie could have told him but didn't. *It's sitting in a fucking Nike duffel bag in my trunk, right out there in your shitty yard,* he also could've said but didn't. Donnie understood now that he could never trust Skeet with something like that, let alone *how* he'd come by that much salad.

As for what else he had in that trunk…

No, not even the *first* thought of trust.

That reminded him of Chief Rogers. Again. *Call me back, you oink fuck!* Rogers was the only cop Donnie trusted not to throw the cuffs on him without at least listening first; he wasn't going near that douche bag Neil, that's for fuckin' sure. *I'd end up in jail before I could blink, prob'ly in a cell right next to Jack's. Wouldn't that be sweet.* He wouldn't be going anywhere near Rogers, for that matter, not until he'd explained his side of the story on the phone—preferably from an undisclosed location—and had gotten some reassurances first.

A throat cleared, and Donnie almost jumped out of his skin; he'd forgotten Skeet was even alive. He turned, and Skeeter arched his eyebrows in pure amusement. "Well, gotta hit it, da man's gonna fire my scrawny ass if I'm late again." Despite his professed hurry, Skeet squinted out the window for a long moment, then back at Donnie. "I don't know what the hell's put the twist in yer panties, but yer a college boy now, so you'll figure somethin' out."

Then they slapped hands and exchanged bro hugs, a sacred ritual, but Skeet's eyes slid past him, and his friend's narrow face was blank as he retrieved his apron and wallet and keys from the crowded coffee table, puffed stray ashes away, then motivated to the front door. He paused with his hand on the knob. "You gonna be here when I get home?"

"Nah. I'll hang out 'till six or so, then head over to Steve's. They should be off the lake by then. I'll stay out there tonight."

I'm sure as shit not going home.

Skeet whistled, long and low. "You gonna tell her?"

"Hell, no."

Skeet laughed. "So you leavin' the loot?"

Donnie laughed, too; he couldn't help it. "Yeah, for now."

"Then don't forget to lock the door." Skeet suddenly crouched and shot him the bird, like a gunfighter drawing from the hip, and Donnie did the same. They straightened and grinned, and for an instant they were back in eighth grade, the Dos Amigos ride again— *fuck* all those pansy-ass, preppy-jock motherfuckers, and the whole shit-eating world with 'em!

The moment faded.

"See ya."

"See ya."

Skeeter yanked the front door open and slammed it behind him and hopped down his weathered porch steps and sauntered to his Bondo-spattered four-door '83 Bonneville and backed around and headed for the end of the gravel driveway. The big car's window rolled down, and another bird flew; Skeet knew he'd be watching.

Donnie raised his own middle finger almost wistfully; it'd been a long time since the Dos Amigos had ridden comfortably together, and Skeet had just summed up the reason in five words:

Yer a college boy, now…

Their sophomore year, Donnie had realized that if he didn't slack off the smoke and buckle down and get his GPA up, he would never leave these mountains—and he soooo wanted to get away from these mountains. Skeet hadn't, though, slacked off or buckled down or wanted to leave or any of it, so while Donnie was studying for the SAT and applying for scholarships, Skeet was slinging Mary Jane and getting into fights and finally getting expelled. Skeeter was sharp enough to say fuck it and ace his GED on the first try, but Donnie suffered the rest of the way through high school without his amigo and graduated with honors; they'd hung on the weekends, though, still paramount buds, even as his mom and the guidance councilors and the fucking vice principal, that smug faggot Mr. Montgomery, tried to tell him Skeeter would only pull him down. Donnie had told them all to lick his left nut… well, in so many words. They'd gotten the message, though: Skeet and Donnie had been best friends since fourth grade, and the Dos Amigos would *stay* best friends until the day they died, or the planet crumbled to space poo.

That was then, however.

Donnie had since tasted life outside Sheridan County, and now he couldn't help but think his mom and all the rest had been right, including that poof Mr. Montgomery. Chief Rogers had even sung that same sad tune when he'd pulled Donnie over two weeks ago, saying he better not be slinging like his deadbeat friend, Skeeter Rumpke…

He blinked, then frowned; Skeet was just sitting out there at the end of the driveway. *What the fuck is he waiting for?* Then dust plumed through the needles just as a big fucker rumbled by on a black Harley.

Dude wore wraparound shades perched beneath one of those half-helmets, the kind where if you wrecked face-first, your ears and noggin would make it but your nose and chin would grind off; built like a pro linebacker, he wore tight black jeans, black riding boots with silver buckles, and a flat-black tee-shirt. Below the tee's rolled-up sleeves, serious ink covered massive arms all the way to the black gloves gripping the Harley's handlebars; to go with the ink, a gray beard spread across his deep chest, and a silver-streaked braided ponytail hung behind the half-helmet.

Like one of those cats from ZZ Top, except jacked on juice.

The biker looked over at Skeet and waved, but in the cool way, dropping his black-gloved hand down by his foot peg and holding it palm-flat. Skeeter waved back like an excited little kid, then pulled out and headed the opposite way, down into Indian Head.

Must be one of Skeet's new butt buddies from up the road. Donnie'd heard aaaall about them all summer, and he'd finally met two a week ago; that's when he'd learned Skeet was dealing weed for them—and maybe more than weed.

Both had been big, tattooed, anti-government-white-power types with adjective names, like Big Willie or Smelly Frank or some shit, and they hadn't liked Donnie sitting there on the sagging couch listening to their business almost as much as Donnie hadn't liked it. They'd taken Skeet into the front yard while Donnie peeked out this same window; there'd been much looming and jabbing of thick, tattooed fingers toward the house, but Skeet had faced the larger men confidently, and then he'd left them standing there glowering and came back inside, still with his self-assured grin…but Donnie had seen how much his friend was sweating.

"What's going on?"

"Shit, man, I just talked them out of stomping your lily-white ass, that's what's going on. They think you're a snitch. I had to vouch for you, so you better not turn out to be a rat. And quit staring at them or they're gonna kick *both* our asses. Go sit on the couch and play with your pud. They'll be gone in a minute." Skeeter went into his bedroom to fetch something for his new buds and then scampered back outside.

Donnie'd flashed on Chief Rogers pulling him over just a few days before, and he'd almost said *Hell, man, everybody knows already*, but hadn't. Instead, he sat on the couch; he'd refrained from playing with his pud, but only just.

Two days later, Skeet had invited him to a big Fourth bash out at his new pals' pad; five or six kegs and a band and some wild and naked chicks, Skeet gushed, but Donnie begged off; he had to work. That'd been true, but the truth-truth was that there was no place on earth Donnie would rather be less than at a party with a bunch of drug-dealing, white-power bikers.

No wonder it felt like the Dos Amigos barely knew each other anymore. *If Skeeter's going to hang with guys like that, it's just a matter of time until he's busted again—or worse. I need to cut him loose.* It was a sad thought.

Suddenly he realized just how quiet Skeet's house was; Donnie glanced around uneasily. *Where the hell are you, Chief? Call me back, you snooping fuck!* Restless and on edge, he walked into the kitchen and grabbed two packs of smokes, then counted the unopened cartons piled high in the center of the dirty table. *Only nineteen left; shit, we've gone through almost eleven cartons of cigs. No wonder my lungs feel cashed.* He glanced at the piles of dishes and trash filling Skeeter's sink and swamping the counters and wrinkled his nose. *Jesus, how does he live like this?*

Donnie retreated to the living-room window and lit another smoke. Everything outside was still hot and dusty, but with it going on five o'clock, the long, eerie twilight had settled over the pines. Donnie hadn't really appreciated the protracted dusk's splendor until he'd been away, but right then he couldn't care less about the quality of the light.

He stared at the trunk of his car; a bead of sweat trickled out of his hair and ran down his cheek. Donnie swiped it away.

"Fuck this," he growled. *I'll just scoot on over to Steve's now.* Hell, they might be back already, and they were both probably drunk—check that; after spending the day tooling about on ol' Steve-o's ski boat, they were *definitely* drunk—but chilling on Steve's dock or even dealing with all their mush-mouthed bullshit beat the hell out of sitting here by his lonesome.

He turned around, then stopped uncertainly, looking at Deep Purple there on the jumbled coffee table. He twitched his phone out. "I'll call first, make sure they're back," he told the Purple Lady.

Now I'm talking to the fucking bong. Great.

Mom's cell went to voicemail. He hung up without leaving a message and tried Steve's; same thing. He scrolled for Steve's land-line, but then Steve's cell rang through.

"Hello?"

"Hey, you just call?"

"Yeah, man, I was wantin' to come over, maybe hang with you guys for the night, if that's cool."

"Yeah, bud, you're always welcome, you know that, but your mom's not here. I was hopin' you were her usin' your phone, actually, but, uh, I guess you're not."

Donnie rolled his eyes. *No shit, genius.* He liked Steve, he really did; the guy didn't beat his mom or him, and he had a cool boat and a good job; he even lived in his own place. Most of the losers Mom dragged home didn't possess any of those fine qualities, but *jeeeez...*

Then a tingle of alarm spiked. "If she's not with you, where is she?"

"Well, uh, we got into this big fight last night. We'd been drinkin', you know how we do it..."

Fear seized Donnie by the scrotum and squeezed. "Where the fuck is she? Did she go home?"

Please tell me she didn't go home. Please o please.

"Well, yeah. Where else was she gonna go?"

"Shit!" *Oh, fuck. FUCK!* "She was supposed to be staying with you all week! She was *supposed* to be *safe* with *YOU!*"

"Safe? What are you—"

"Did she make it home last night? Have you talked to her? Shit, I gotta call her!"

"Whoa, whoa, slow down, sport. She made it home; I talked to her this mornin'. She's hung-over to beat all hell and still pissed at me, but she's home. What's goin' on with you, man? What's all this about your mom bein' 'safe'?"

"You talked to her this morning? She was okay?"

"Just said so, didn't I?"

"Yeah, okay, okay." *Early this morning.* "Have you, uh, have you talked to her since?"

Please say yes, please say yes, please say yes—

"No, she won't answer. Still pissed off, I guess. I tried to apologize, but she was havin' none of it."

"Shit!"

"Easy, tiger, she's prob'ly just takin' a nap. You know her and her naps."

"I gotta go, I gotta call her."

"Okay, kid, just take it easy. Tell her I love her and that I'm sorry and that I'll make it up to her, and to call me when she—"

Donnie hung up and hit the button assigned to his mom's cell, but she didn't answer again.

Five calls later, she *still* hadn't answered.

Donnie couldn't breathe.

Mom.

He bolted out the door, skidded on the porch, whirled, pounded back inside and scooped up all the unopened cartons of Marlboro's, hesitated, then tossed two back on the table and started toward the front door again when he heard the motorcycle. He froze for a long moment, then snuck over and peeked around the jamb with his arms full of cartons just in time to see the ZZ Top 'roid freak blat by going the other way, back down into Indian Head. Dude glanced over at Skeet's house, but the Harley's blat never changed pitch.

Donnie warily watched his dust dissipate. *I could've told you your loser-asshole buddies weren't home, shithead.* The whole pack, six or seven strong, had thundered by early this morning, not long after he'd hung up on that fat bitch dispatcher, yelling Skeeter's name and revving their engines and beeping their horns, but Skeet had been dead to the world.

Donnie sprinted out and chunked the cigs in the backseat, jumped up on the porch and locked the front door and slammed it, then flew back to his car.

Oh shit, Mom.

He shot down Skeeter's driveway and out into the dirt road, not even checking for traffic, and pushed the Honda up to fifty; he thought about what was in the trunk and reluctantly slowed to the limit, thirty miles per hour.

Shit!

Two miles later, the dirt morphed into unlined blacktop and the limit increased to forty. Another mile to the city limits, and then two more across town to their place; ten minutes, fifteen tops, depending on traffic.

Mom.

Oh God, Mom.

31

The good news? They busted me out around three that afternoon.

The bad news?

"They" were the FBI.

I'd been back from the nurse's office for about two hours and was fingering my puffy eye in the occluded steel mirror when the intercom crackled:

"Ross!" I recognized a fuming Sgt. Dorsey through the distortion: "Step out of your cage, press your ugly mug against the wall, clasp your hands behind your back, and don't fuckin' move 'till I tell you!"

A loud buzz, and my door *ka-chunked*.

I went to the scratched window and warily peered out; I didn't see anyone lurking, but I still didn't open the damn door.

"*Ross!* Motivate your useless ass! I promise, shithead, you won't like it if I have to—" A man barked something in the background, Dorsey snapped something back, and then a crackle and a thud. Dorsey said, a little whiny now, "Hey, you can't—"

Thud, skronk, screech, *skrooooonk!*

Silence.

Then an unknown male voice scratched down from the ceiling like God from Heaven:

"Jack Ross, this is Special Agent Hawthorne with the Federal Bureau of Investigation. Step out of your cell and proceed as Sgt. Dorsey requested. We'd like to have a word with you."

Not God, but close: federals. I hesitated only another second—if the FBI wanted a confab it was no use hiding—then yanked the door open and gasped, hunching over my right side. I straightened with a long, pain-filled breath, then finished swinging the heavy door in with both hands and stepped out and immediately scanned around, but no Indian—who'd turned out to have a name after all, Thomas Johnson. Tom Johnson was about the most un-Indian fucking name I'd ever run across, so I'd decided to keep thinking of him as the Indian.

The intercom crackled as Dorsey spat: "Face the fucking wall and clasp your hands behind your back!" I did. "Spread your legs and don't goddamn move!" I did that as well.

The steel door to the pod buzzed and two tall, fit gentlemen attired in dark blue suits with monotonous blue ties came into lock-down, followed by two wide-body jailers in drab gray uniforms. I would've known the suits were feds just by the way they carried themselves; well-dressed wolves compared to the jailer's frumpy yard-dog.

The wolves considered my puffy eye and my cut-up knuckles and exchanged coldly amused glances. Neil's flunkies secured me in the cuffs and the waist-and-leg shackles, and I realized (somewhat belatedly) that they were taking me somewhere.

That could be good, or very, *very* bad.

"Where am I going? I thought you wanted to talk."

The carrot-head wolf answered, and I recognized his voice: Hawthorne. "You're going to see the man. His name is Senior Special Agent Denton, and he's the one who wants a word. We don't converse with trash. Isn't that right, Walters?" The dark-haired wolf smirked and nodded. "We just dip the scum and carry it to where the man says dump it," Hawthorn continued helpfully, but I got the feeling neither wolf was much pleased with scum-delivery duty.

The flunkies finished and stepped back and Hawthorne grasped me by the right arm; Walters took the other, and then they frog-marched me toward the steel door. I winced; the county's nurse had informed me my ribs were only bruised, and maybe sprained, not cracked, but I was having a hard time believing her.

I looked up at Hawthorn's stony, freckled visage; both wolves were at least three inches taller than me. "I want to file a complaint," I said as they hauled me past the puke-green concrete-and-steel picnic table bolted to the puke-green floor in the center of the puke-green triangle. "Two lock-down inmates attacked me. That's how I got this eye. The guards were in on it. They even supplied a hammer." I shook my left forearm, rattling my cuffs, wanting to show them the swollen, circular contusion where I'd blocked a hammer blow from Tweaker, otherwise known as James Lee Baxley (I still liked Tweaker better), but neither wolf bothered to glance at my boo-boo. I jerked my head toward a trailing flunky: "That fat asshole back there, Miller, he's one of them. He—"

Miller spluttered, "Hey, that's bullshit!", but he looked antsy.

"—took them out. Two more assholes helped him, one a retard named Salisbury. I don't know the other screw's name, but I can point him out. Sgt. Dorsey, he's in on it, too. He's pissed because I broke his little brother's fingers, but I heard the inmates who attacked me say they were offered a lot of money to cripple me."

Hawthorn droned, "Save it for someone who cares," without looking at me and snap-snapped his fingers at the mirrored wall; a sharp buzz, and then we were leaving lock-down. I glanced over my shoulder; the pedo was peering at me out of his little crosshatched window. Then Miller and the other flunky asshole came out and the steel door slammed *clang!* between us.

Good riddance.

Dorsey hulked at a terminal in the hexagon-shaped pod-control, glaring through the clear bullet-and-shatter-proof barrier. Three other flunkies were standing around in there watching, but they ignored me while nervously eyeing the FBI wolves and trying to pretend they were doing no such thing.

Hawthorne flew them a lazy, two-fingered salute. "Thanks for your cooperation, gentlemen." There were no return salutes. He and Walters turned me and marched me shuffling and clinking away; I could feel Dorsey's glare pressing on my red stripes the entire way out of E-Pod.

At the end of the hall we found another hexagon, this one empty and powered down. We went halfway around it past three other hallways marked A, C, and Kitchen & Laundry, then turned down a long corridor I recognized as leading to Booking; ahead, two laughing, tattoo-festooned trustees wearing green-and-white stripes pushed wide dust brooms towards us over the gleaming floor; their laughter cut off when they saw the suits. They crowded the wall and pulled their brooms out of the way and watched us go by with avid curiosity.

Muffled shouts perked my ears. The Wonder Twins exchanged a wry glance over my head and hustled me faster. Then Walters pulled the buzzing Booking door open and we stepped into the middle of it.

"...telling you this is a mistake! Ross is *dangerous!* You know what he did to my deputy!"

The door clanged behind us.

Neil turned to look, along with every "Detention Officer" and inmate in the place; a dozen of the latter were already craned around in the uncomfortable blue-plastic chairs, and nobody was telling them to face forward again. The guards at the intake stations watched out the corner of their eyes while keeping their faces pressed to their monitors; even the green-striped Booking trustee had ventured out of his closet to gawk, a pair of orange-plastic sandals dangling forgotten in his hand.

The man Neil had been shouting at lurked near the first station, the one closest to the mantrap leading out, leaning against the cinder blocks with his arms crossed; he looked like a guy waiting for the bus (and not happy about it) except for the charcoal suit, cream silk shirt, and yellow silk tie. About my height, with receding steel-gray hair, mid-fifties, and slender as a whip; a little pair of rectangular glasses perched on the long blade that passed for his nose. He straightened when I appeared and gave me the once-over with the coldest, greenest eyes I'd ever seen, paused for a fraction of a second on my puffy eye, then crossed his arms again and leaned and put his green-ice gaze back on Sheriff Neal; he could have been looking at a cockroach that had somehow found the impudence to crawl into his soup.

This cat had to be Denton, no question.

Chief Rogers stood nearby with his thumbs hooked behind his utility rig; he looked tired. I wondered why he was there, but I didn't have time to wonder long because that's when Neil stalked toward me, locked on like an ICBM, a hot one with a bristling mustache. He jabbed a long finger in my face, looming over the twins that still held my arms, white cowboy hat seeming to brush the fluorescents embedded in the ceiling.

"The goddamn FBI may take you and this goddamn case, but I'll see you prosecuted for what you did to Dorsey if it's the last goddamn thing I do! And that's not all." He turned and jabbed that finger at Denton, who had freed one slender hand and was studying his manicured nails as if they were the most interesting thing in the world. "Do you know he put two men in the hospital? One may never walk easily again, and the other has a broken jaw. Last I heard, he hadn't even woken up yet! He might *never* wake up!"

My knee-sagging relief that I would soon take leave of the good Sheriff's puke-green hospitality blew away in a gale of outrage. "That's bullshit, Neal! *They* assaulted *me*, and they're the ones who had the hammer! You should know. Your men gave it to them."

For a second I thought he would take a swing. So did Hawthorne, because he pushed the Sheriff back while Walters moved me away. Neil was shouting at me over Hawthorne's blue-suited shoulder, something about calling him Sheriff or Sir, that I was a piece-of-shit murderer and that I didn't deserve to use his name, when Denton's precise Midwestern non-accent cut through Neil's rant like a hot-buttered sword.

"I've been trying to decide something, Sheriff. Do you want to hear the conundrum I've been weighing?" Denton didn't look up from his nails, turning his fingers over and back and then over again.

"I don't give a good goddamn what you've been *weighing*," Neil mimicked.

"The question before us, I believe, is simply this: Are you as incompetent as you appear, or are you corrupt?" Booking fell into a shocked hush as Denton thumbed his little glasses up his blade of a nose and continued in a soft, deadly voice: "From my observations, I conclude it is both, though not in equal proportions; a sixty-five to thirty-five percent ratio, I'd say. Perhaps sixty/forty."

"You…" Neil's face was a mustachioed red apple beneath the hat. I was grinning from ear to ear, and when I realized it I tried to stop, but not very hard. "How *dare* you—!"

"I have an investigation to conduct and a demented killer to catch, so I was content to let you house and feed the primary suspect, believing you were at least proficient enough to do that; however, it appears I overestimated your capabilities."

Neil's mouth worked as several jailers hid smiles, including the bald hulk I'd seen during my intake, Lt. Smithers; actually, Smithers wasn't hiding his smile at all, and he watched his boss squirm with something close to open contempt.

The good Sheriff found his voice and jabbed that long finger at me again. "*That's* the goddamn killer right there! And you can't talk to me like that, I'm the Sheriff of—"

Denton simply turned away; the most beautiful display of contempt I'd ever seen. I was jealous. "Retrieve Mr. Ross's property and let him get dressed," the Senior Special Agent told a nervous-looking Detention Officer. The man didn't even glance at Neil before leaping to obey. "And remove those ridiculous fetters."

I was gleefully letting my red stripes fall to the bathroom's damp concrete floor when the shouting started up again; Neil had found an easier target. I got dressed quickly and tied my sneakers and stepped out with the now-empty property bag. Hawthorne and Walters were waiting for me, along with the anxious jailer.

Neal was jabbing that finger in Chief Rogers' face, although Rogers only looked up at him calmly; Denton leaned on the wall and contemplated his fingernails.

"…your doing! Somehow I'm goddamn *sure* of it! Well, congratulations, you sprung your murdering pal out of the hoosegow, but don't think this won't have consequences! When Ross finally gets his ass thrown in prison for good and all these fancy Washington bigwigs go home and forget us, *I'll* still be here!"

Rogers said, "You brought this on yourself, Sheriff."

"You smug sonofabitch, I'll…!"

I held the empty bag out to Walters. "Here you go." But the guard reached in and snatched it and fled to the property room, spoiling my fun.

"Funny guy," Walters said, then spun me and cuffed my hands behind my back. I didn't like it, but at least I was done with the damn leg chains; never really appreciate a good, long stride until it's shortened for you.

"Secure him in front," Denton ordered.

Walters sourly re-did my cuffs, and then their boss pushed off the wall and flicked his manicured nails at the steel door to indicate someone should buzz him out. That's when Neal made the grievous error of opening his mouth again.

"I'm tellin' ya, you are makin' a mistake, Mr. FBI Man. *'Secure him in front'?* Maybe yer not used to dirtyin' yer soft little hands out there in D.C., but I'll bet ya my paycheck that even cuffed and surrounded, Ross could—"

Denton spun and stalked toward Neil so fast he was under the bigger man's chin before the buzzer stopped buzzing.

"One more word," he hissed.

The Sheriff started back. Several people snickered—one might have been me—and Neil shared a glare around before stretching to his full height.

"I—"

"A personal pronoun, technically, not a word, so I will give you that, Sheriff. I shall clarify my intent: A pack of reporters is milling outside, waiting for a statement concerning the assault perpetrated upon Mr. Ross. I was content to let you spin some outrage to cover your ineptitude and/or culpability, but if another *syllable* issues from beneath that travesty you no doubt fancy a mustache, I will stand Mr. Ross in front of the microphones and let him share his experience. The assault upon his person in your facility while under your care, whether accomplished with your implicit knowledge, as I suspect, or behind your back due to your ineffectiveness…well, I postulate many individuals will be interested in paying you a visit, specifically state and federal individuals; more specifically, individuals with the power of oversight, and as such, the power to bury you so deep you will never enjoy another Wyoming sunset, at least not as an employed, or perhaps even free, man—and if *they* don't see to it, *I* will. Now, do you have anything to say to me, Sheriff?"

Neil's face was closer to purple than red now, and his mustache twitched, but he stayed silent. Denton stared up at him, waiting, then finally nodded.

"I thought not."

Booking was a tomb as he walked back to the mantrap; three buzzes later, we piled into a classically intimidating black-on-black Suburban. I melted into a second-row leather bucket (still grinning), with Rogers taking the bucket next to me. Walters slid onto the third-row bench, I guess so he could scowl at the back of my head. Denton rode shotgun as Hawthorne powered us out of the open bay doors, and the strong July sunlight flashed through the windshield and bathed me, making me squint.

I've never felt anything so wonderful.

The reporter-swarm swiveled their collective heads when we appeared from the "Authorized Vehicles Only" gate. Some swiveled their cameras as well, but none had any reason to think I was inside the Suburban—the windows were too dark for them to see jack shit, let alone Jack Ross. Several must have been blessed with a good reporter's intuition, though, because they piled into their vans and gave chase.

"Lose them, Agent Hawthorne."

"Yes, sir." The engine throbbed, and after a bit the satellite dishes and antenna sticking out every which-a-way were nowhere in sight.

Hawthorne finally dropped to a sane speed, and only the air blowing on high and the thrum of rubber on pavement laced the loaded quiet. I thought about politely inquiring just where the hell they thought they were taking me, but figured it didn't matter much as long as it wasn't back to Sheridan County. I could guess anyway, from the direction we were going—up; back to Indian Head.

I needed to tell them a few things, though, important things, so I cleared my throat: "Chief, Special Agent Denton, let me just say that I would *never* hurt Tiffany. She was a good kid. And I didn't kill any of those other kids either, or Mrs. Barbary, or old Bill. Someone set me up, and I think I know who."

Denton's seat creaked as he turned and looked at Chief Rogers, not me, and then he swung back around and snipped, "And who might that be, Mr. Ross?"

I scowled a question at Rogers.

"We know you didn't kill them, Jack, but right now—"

"We're *pretty sure* you didn't kill them," Denton broke in without turning.

I opened my mouth, but Rogers shook his head in a warning and cut his eyes toward Denton; I snapped my teeth together, although I thought I might choke.

Denton continued in his arid voice: "And save your 'deductions', Mr. Ross; we'll have a powwow as soon as we get to where we're going. And this foolishness with the Sheriff has set my timetable back, thus I would appreciate some quiet as I plan my next move."

The requested planning-quiet descended. I stared at the back of Denton's ears; they didn't really stick out that far, and they weren't that big, but his skull-gripping haircut made the little pink suckers look like wings.

Powwow? And *next move?* What a fucking tool. "Where the hell *are* we going?"

Denton didn't answer. Instead it was Hawthorne, who peered at me in the rearview through his solid-black Ray-Bans:

"We're going home, tough guy."

Walters laughed, then seized my trap and squeezed. I didn't wince, although I wanted to; fucker had a death-grip.

"Home Sweet Home, tough guy, that's where we're going."

Walters laughed again, then bore down and breathed it in my ear:

"Home Sweet Home."

32

Home Sweet Home turned out to be the old Injun Bowl, Indian Head's lone and currently defunct bowling alley. The Injun had shuttered its lanes for good in '02, a victim of bigger and snazzier competition down in Sheridan, but now it had a new lease on life… if life counted as being taken over by the federal government. A black-on-black Suburban sat across the 3rd St. entrance, blocking access, and another was parked at the end of the long and railed wheelchair ramp that led up to the front doors; now I got Denton's powwow crack.

The Injun had given the PC Nazi's gas, probably still did, but I had great memories of the place from when I was a kid, like watching Dad get plastered and still be good for a six-bagger, or even a clean game; Dad could really knock 'em down, and he was better after a pitcher of beer. Or three. That had been in the late eighties and early nineties, however, which turned out to be both the Injun Bowl's heyday as well as my dad's.

Now the tall sign that had stood proudly at the edge of the lot facing 3rd, the one with the stern and feathered buck-skinned Chief holding a neon-purple bowling ball under his cleft chin with both red hands, like he was about to roll'm heap-big strike, was long gone. Even the mural that some quasi-famous local artist had splashed across the red-brick exterior (the one that had so fascinated me as a kid, showing the Injun sitting Injun style in front of a colossal wigwam and smoking a three-foot-long peace pipe while beaded squaws and stone-hatchet-wielding braves danced around him as a horned moon hovered over the wigwam), had washed out; only bits and pieces of the scene were now visible, ethereal on the chalky brick; the wigwam's door was also the entrance to the bowling alley, something that had delighted me no end at one small point in my life.

We turned into the Injun's cracked and weedy lot and waited for the blue-suited clone in the obstructing Suburban to look up from playing with his phone and then hastily back out of our way; he repositioned the big Chevy across the entrance after we drove through, and I wondered why the blockade until I glanced over my shoulder and beheld two news crews lurking at Pat's, which sat right across 3rd from the derelict Injun. Dueling brunette reporters were doing stand-ups next to the old-fashioned railcar diner, both positioned so that the Injun was framed over their shapely shoulders; the women and their crews were situated well away from each other so as to give the impression that their network's brunette was the only brunette covering the story.

I turned back, but halfway through I spied a scarlet-and-white real-estate sign tilted at the edge of the ditch fronting 3rd. An eight by five, its bold lettering informed the world: FOR SALE OR LEASE, and then the square footage and lot dimensions and zoning and a phone number underneath; what made my good eye pop, though, was the scarlet line beneath the number:

OFFERED BY R&R INVESTMENT GROUP

Holy shit.

I shook Chief Rogers' elbow and pointed at the sign.

"Don't these guys know who *owns* this place?"

Denton answered before Rogers could. "We know very well, Mr. Ross." He emitted a dry chuckle, though he didn't sound amused in the least. "Robert Richards Junior is charging the United States government a not-inconsiderable sum for the privilege of leasing this fine establishment."

"But—"

"I admire your tenacity, young man, truly I do, but if you could exercise a modicum of patience, I believe most of your inquiries will be answered shortly."

I looked dazedly at Rogers. He only nodded, but something grim moved beneath his normally calm disposition.

I collapsed back into my leather bucket.

Sonofabitch.

"Around back," Special Agent Denton ordered. Hawthorne adjusted course, and then we were down the side of the red-brick Injun and into her enormous and pine-shaded rear lot; out front could slot about fifty cars, but in back could hold at least two hundred. I'd always wondered why they'd built so close to 3rd when they'd had all this room…

My musings on optimum commercial-lot utilization died as I spied the vehicles; three more anonymous black-on-black Suburbans, along with a not-so-anonymous cross between a bread truck and a RV on steroids; dark blue, FBI had been stenciled in three-foot-high yellow letters on its side, with smaller renderings on the doors, just in case someone missed the point.

But what really caught my attention was the white Toyota Camry parked next to the Frankenstein bread truck; Angela's car.

And then I spied the black Beemer beside it.

"What the hell are *they* doing here?"

"Patience, Mr. Ross."

Hawthorne brought the Suburban to a stop at the Injun's back entrance, which was a mirror to the front, wheelchair ramp included, but minus the ghostly mural. And then Angela pushed out of the double doors that used to be metal-framed glass but were now covered with fresh yellow plywood and ran to the rail and waved. "Jack!" Mom came out right behind her.

I blinked my eyes (well, eye), and swallowed.

Mom.

Mom was here, too.

Walters hustled out and slung my door open and began not-so-gently urging me to join him just as Hawthorne turned and inquired, "How did a loser like you get a girlfriend like that, anyway?"

"Fuck you," was all I had time for, and then I was out and he was laughing and Denton was ordering everybody back inside the Injun in that irritated little snippy Midwestern non-accent and Walters was shoving me around the grille toward the concrete steps as Angela flew down those steps and enveloped me in a tearful hug. God oh *God* did she feel and smell amazing. Then Mom clamped onto us both. "My poor Jackie! What did they do to you?" She rounded on Denton, demanding that I be uncuffed and that Neil be held responsible for my condition, and I tried to tell her I was all right as Angela rained kisses on my neck and cheeks and Chris came out of the plywood and stood on the Injun's back porch and scowled down at me with his arms crossed.

"Inside! Or he goes back to jail!"

That got everybody moving, especially me, though Angela refused to let go of my arm, and Mom kept haranguing Denton about the cuffs. "My Jackie didn't hurt those kids, so I want those damned things off him right this—"

"INSIDE!"

Then we were up the steps and through the swinging plywood and the empty, dusty foyer, and I discovered that the faded mural was the least of the changes that time and neglect and the FBI had wrought upon the old Injun.

The lanes were still there, albeit gritty and dull where they used to be slick and gleaming. The scoring screens were gone, along with every bit of the ball-return machinery, leaving cobwebby holes between the approaches; some had fresh yellow plywood laid across them, no doubt to save federal ankles; even the horseshoe-shaped hard-plastic seat groupings had been cannibalized, though as I squinted my eye, I saw that lanes thirteen through eighteen, on the far, dim side of the building, still retained their horseshoes.

The arcades down on my right—to the left as you strolled in through the chalky wigwam—were abandoned caves, except for one; the video arcade echoed, and the pool tables were missing from their parlor. The foosball tables had also vanished, but their cubby was now lit up with bright new fluorescents, and a covey of suited agents sat at a long folding table, hammering busily on their laptops; extension cords and power strips snaked everywhere underfoot, most duct taped to the floor. Four flat-screens had been hung about the walls, and they showed the news muted, closed captioning popping up and disappearing on an upward scroll. On one, I recognized a Pat's brunette; the out-front Suburbans and the Injun were visible behind her; too fucking weird knowing I was looking at it as I stood in it. The suits in the foosball room all stopped to watch us pile through the plywood, then went back to hammering.

That vacant video arcade hurt. I'd spent hundreds of hours in there on league nights playing *Centipede* and *Donkey Kong* and *Frogger* and *Galaga* and *Ms. Pac-Man* and *Tron* and all the rest, dodging through a forest of legs back to Mom for more quarters when I ran dry (never Dad; Dad was the anchor, and he had to concentrate). Seeing that rambunctious arcade now silent and forsaken peeled away a strip of my childhood and sent it fluttering into the uncaring breeze.

Us non-federals had huddled unconsciously, I realized, even Chief Rogers; a gloomy bowling alley without "Girls Girls Girls" blasting down from the ceiling or the thunder of the pins exploding into the cages felt kinda eerie. I *was* enjoying the cool air, however; the FBI had apparently prioritized the compressors (our tax dollars at work), although the place still smelled musty.

I could see Chris up ahead. Snazzy in dark slacks and a pale-green dress shirt and a blue-diamond tie and even snazzier Gucci loafers, he stood between the bathrooms (something else I hoped the G-Men had rehabbed), which were themselves between the desolate pool room and the bare video arcade. Arms crossed, he scowled first at me, then his sister, then Rogers, and then at Denton; sharing it out.

I still didn't know what the fuck he was doing here.

Mom rounded on Denton again: "I want those restraints off my son. He's done *nothing* to—"

Angela cut in; she'd been watching me squint and hunch with a worried frown. "Jack needs to go to the hospital. He's favoring his right side, and that eye is just about swollen shut." She pointed at the bruised node that had risen on my forearm like an alien pustule. "And *that* can't feel good."

"I'm fine," I said.

Denton concurred: "He'll live." The Senior Special Agent then addressed Hawthorne, who had just pushed through the swinging plywood after parking the G-ride. "Guard this portal and make sure no one leaves."

Hawthorne's considerable freckled jaw clenched. "Yes, sir." He took a post before the plywood, back stiff and hands clasped at his waist.

Chris liked it even less than Hawthorne.

"*What?*" Angela's brother almost flew towards us, agitating like a pale-green poltergeist in the gloom. "You can't hold me! My sister tricked me into coming, and the only reason I'm still here is she and Chief Rogers ganged up on me and almost *begged* me to stay! I'm an American citizen, I pay my taxes—which pays *your* fucking salary, Denton—and I can damn well leave when I *want* to leave!"

He jabbed a righteous finger at hunched-over, half-blind me. "*He's the fucking murderer! And why the hell is he out of jail, anyway?*" He threw his hands in the air. "And what's this *big secret* I need to hear? Just tell me what it is already!"

Angela looked like she was about to deck her big brother. "Jack didn't hurt anybody! Shut up!"

Mom stalked toward Chris, jaw thrust out; he beat a hasty retreat, which I thought was very wise of him.

"If you think I won't paddle your skinny little be-hind again like I did when you and Jackie shot up my flowerpots, you've got another think—"

"Enough! Chief, take your people over there," Denton pointed at the horseshoe groupings still lurking at the end of the high-number lanes, "and get them settled while I check in with the surveillance team." He pointed at Agent Walters. "You." He pointed at me. "Stick with him." Then he peered at Rogers, pale eyes glinting behind the little glasses, even in the Injun's gloom: "This plan of yours had *better* come to fruition. For your sake, and for your friend Detective Kirkland's."

With that, he spun toward the foosball room. The suits at the laptops all scraped back their folding chairs and stood, then scurried about, ties flapping, as he snipped fresh orders.

Rogers grunted. "*My* plan. It'll be *his* plan if it works."

"Of course," Agent Walters said.

"What else did you expect, Chief?" added Hawthorne.

Rogers looked at them for a long moment, then just shook his head. "Let's go."

Our footsteps raised puffs from the threadbare arcade carpet with the pink-and-green neon squiggles as we marched beside the low wall bordering Lane 1 and turned in front of the abandoned check-in; the registers were gone, and the see-through counter was empty of high-dollar balls and polish and hand chalk and other die-hard bowler's gewgaws, and all the league trophies were missing from the elevated display, and the cubbyholes were empty of ugly rental shoes…but it wasn't *total* desolation back there.

Someone had hung a carved effigy about where the wall phone had blared its bell over the Mötley Crüe, a Lincoln Log cabin with a red-and-green Christmas wreath on the door, HOME SWEET HOME painted in bright white beneath the split-railed front porch; a less-than-artistic hand had added dull-yellow letters spelling FBI in descending order to the river-rock chimney.

These government stiffs are a riot.

Rogers led us through a gap in the low wall and we discovered the ball returns and the scoring screens and the seating might all be MIA, but the long, divot-pocked shelves that kept the army of house balls from rolling willy-nilly about the place were still around. That ball army was missing, of course, but dust and grime and cobwebs had taken over for them; seems the housekeeper G-Man hadn't made it over here yet.

It grew gloomier as we trekked further from the lights, so Rogers pulled his mini and twisted it on, shining our way. He passed a mound of gear resting against the empty ball shelves at the end of Lane 11, sweeping the beam over it too fast for my lone eye to catch. But when I got close, I stopped dead.

Six black duffels, stuffed full and cinched tight; black helmets with clear-plastic face guards; black bulletproof vests with FBI in big yellow uppercase across the chest and back; a rack of black Heckler & Koch machine guns—of what caliber I didn't have a clue, but they'd do the trick. Black ammo boxes; black ammo clips; but what had stopped me were five long, flat cases (also black) stacked on top of each other; a sixth was open on the floor, an empty cut-out in pebbly gray foam inside, and the silhouette was of a long-barreled rifle with a short stock and a great big scope. The dissembled weapon itself rested on top of the ball shelf, a bi-pod holding the silenced barrel up. A pile of rags and a small bottle sat beside the pieces; the citrusy gun-oil drifted through the general dust-and-mold reek of the Injun like a refreshing slap in the face.

That thing has to be .50 cal. A man possessed of some natural talent and a slough of diligent practice could hit a body from a thousand yards with that beauty—and what a .50 caliber bullet would do to a human being's body didn't bear thinking about.

Sniper rifles?

What kind of FBI *are* these guys?

Agent Walters said, "Like those, tough guy? Maybe I'll show you how to shoot one someday. Better yet, I could show your girlfriend." He nodded ahead of us. Angela was using her phone's screen to illuminate where she stepped; her ear-length golden hair bobbed as she kicked disgustedly at a cobweb clinging to her shoe.

I looked up at Agent Walters with my good eye. He grinned, all toothy, then shoved me forward to join the others, who had clustered around Chief Rogers; he'd stopped at the first horseshoe he'd encountered, the one that served Lanes 13 and 14. The jagged hole where the ball return used to sit and rumble hadn't been covered by plywood here, and we all gave it a wide birth.

"Good *Lord!*" Mom proclaimed, fists on hips, then swiped a finger across a seat, dashed it clean on her pants, then snapped at Rogers, who was making as if to sit: "Don't you dare!" He froze, butt hovering, then straightened warily and watched with the rest of us as she marched back to the gear and opened a duffel with a jerk and rummaged. Walters frowned, but kept his peace. I decided he was smarter than he looked.

The Chief pursed his lips at me. "Forceful woman."

"You have no idea."

Mom came back with what I thought were black rags until she shook one out; not rags. Tee-shirts. Each had yellow lettering on the front that said FBI.

On the back they said S.W.A.T.

I surveyed Walters with my good eye again, and once more he favored me with the wide, predatory grin. *Well, that explains a few things.* Mom finished and tossed the grimy shirts aside in disgust, which got another silent frown from Agent Walters, and then we all had a seat except for my minder, who planted me in a contoured chair before taking position at my back.

Angela scowled at the tall agent while taking a conjoined seat next to mine. "Easy, bud. Jack didn't hurt anybody, remember?"

He didn't respond, only smiled, but for her it was anything but predatory. She gave him the dead-eye in return, then deliberately took my hands and kissed them, one after the other. She held them in her lap as she leaned close to examine my bad eye.

I craned around and one-eyed Walters again, but this time he studiously ignored me.

Sore loser.

I leaned around Angela so I could see Rogers across the horse-shoe: "Chief, what's going on? And why are Mom and Angela and Chris here? And while we're at it, can we take these damn things off?" I raised my cuffs.

"Restraints stay," Walters announced from behind me.

Mom hopped up, chin thrusting. "Listen here, mister; my Jackie didn't hurt those kids, your boss said so his high-and-mighty self, so I want those—"

Chief Rogers reached out and caught her gently. "The hand-cuffs remain, Mrs. Ross."

Mom squinted, but said nothing as he drew her back and sat her down next to him. He patted her shoulder, but Mom continued to eye him dangerously. Chief Rogers is a brave man.

Mom left it to Angela to voice the question:

"Why?"

Rogers sighed, then fixed me with a disappointed stare. "We know someone is setting you up, Jack, but—"

"*I* don't know that," Chris chimed in. He'd sprawled directly across from me—I in Lane 14, he in Lane 13—with his arms crossed. He was also glaring with utter contempt while ignoring his sister practically sitting in my lap. It would have caused problems, that glare, ex-best friend or no ex-best friend, handcuffs or no handcuffs, sister or no sister, but I had other issues on my plate; I filed it for later discussion, however.

Rogers was still scolding me: "But after that boneheaded move with Deputy Dorsey, the FBI doesn't trust him, and I can't blame them. Assaulting an officer is no petty offense, Jack, and you'll pay for it, probably with several months in Neil's jail. If you're lucky. But right now, I wouldn't worry too much about it; right now, I'd worry about staying alive."

Silence as we all stared at him; then I cleared my throat: "I know who's setting me up," I said, and launched into what had happened in lock-down before anyone could shush me again. I concluded with, "It has to be Zane, Chief. It all fits: the money, his history with drugging and assaulting women, and his hatred of me for killing his twin." Mom looked poleaxed, but she was nodding; Angela just sat there holding my hands, blues narrowed down thoughtfully. Rogers didn't look surprised, just tired as he gazed at me—a little wryly, I thought. "I mean, I figured he try for *some* kind of revenge *some*day, but chopping people up and framing me for it was, well, a bit more than I expected."

"*Bullshit!*" Chris jumped to his Gucci's. "That's complete fucking *bullshit*, Rossie, and I don't know how you got Chief Rogers or the fucking FBI to swallow it, but you killed those kids and now you're trying to blame Zane!"

Mom popped up again, this time shaking a finger. "Shut your mouth! My Jackie didn't—!"

Chris shouted, "I won't sit here and listen to this! I'm fucking *out* of here!"

He turned around, then jerked back in surprise; Denton had come up on us unnoticed during the commotion, Hawthorne trailing. I was wondering who was guarding the back door (just in case we all made a break for it), but then Special Agent Denton spoke:

"Pleas sit down, Mr. Beaumont."

"Forget it, Denton, I'm leaving. Rossie the Ax Murderer over there is trying to blame his slaughter on Zane Richards, and I won't listen to a good man slandered by a convicted killer!"

Denton nodded to Hawthorne. The big redhead came toward Chris, who suddenly didn't appear so confident. "Hey—" And then Walters appeared out of frigin' nowhere and twisted Chris's arm and locked his hand up behind his shoulder. "Ow! Quit that, you can't—!" They sat him in his chair with a thump.

Walters ghosted behind me again as Chris jerked away from Hawthorne, then worked and rubbed at his shoulder while mustering his outrage. "I'm a tax-paying American citizen!" he managed. "You can't—!"

"Be quiet, Mr. Beaumont, or I will direct Agent Hawthorne and Agent Walters to tape you to that seat—as well as your mouth closed."

Chris's eyeballs bugged so hard I thought they'd pop out and roll down Lane 13 like red-veined blue marbles…but he kept his mouth shut. Unfortunately.

"I apologize for this treatment, Mr. Beaumont, but I fear it's necessary. It's necessary because I require your assistance, and we have little time, certainly not for foolishness." He turned to regard us. "I require *all* of your assistance, which is why you all are here." He looked at me the last and the longest—and more-than-some-what skeptically, I noted.

"Sir, the inmates who attacked me were paid, and they were told to say something before they crippled me." I ran it down for him, then added my conclusions.

Denton considered me; as with Chief Rogers, he didn't seem the least bit surprised.

Finally I said, "You have to arrest Zane before he—"

The greens went scary-frosty behind the little glasses. "I retrieved you from the Sheriff's custody to enlist your assistance, Mr. Ross, and to ensure your physical safety. I did *not* bring you here to direct my investigation. Clear?"

"Yes, sir." The implication that I could easily find myself back in Neal's tender clutches was plain.

Motherfucker.

Angela spoke up. "Why do you need us?"

Those cold eyes shifted to her, then to Chief Rogers, where they narrowed; no love lost there. Denton glanced behind him and grimaced before stiffly lowering himself between Chris and Mom; he fussed with his suit jacket, spine ramrod straight. Finally, he said, "I require your assistance to catch the most vicious serial murderer this nation has ever been afflicted with."

Stunned silence; Denton surveyed us all, then spoke softly:

"We call him the Traveler."

33

As Donnie motored across town—and considering what was in his trunk, he motored carefully indeed—he thought about how he'd gotten into this gargantuan fucking mess.

Blind greed had been his first and worst mistake, he understood that now, although he hadn't thought of it in such harsh terms at the beginning; after all, he was a poor college kid riding a magic carpet of stitched-together scholarships, so when someone offered him fifteen-hundred-fucking dollars just to steal a pair of beat-up boots…yeah.

At first he thought it was a scam; what else was he supposed to believe when a number he'd never seen before suddenly pops with **Do you want to make a thousand dollars?** Donnie'd responded **Fuck off loser**, but the mystery sender just repeated the message. Donnie had replied with **Lick me cum gargler** and other polite gems, but after a half-dozen more monotonous texts, he became curious:

Who is this? Is this bullshit?

No bullshit. I'll give you $500 up front to prove it.

That snagged his attention, and a text negotiation followed. The stranger refused to meet in person, though, saying he/she would leave the cheddar in some hollow tree out in the bum-fuck woods near Hawk's Point. No goddamn *way* was Donnie trekking way the hell out there, though, not for a measly five-hundred clams, so they'd agreed on the Splash & Dash as a neutral drop. The Dash was a twenty-four-hour self-service auto wash near an old strip mall in a wide spot along Hwy. 331, about halfway between Indian Head and Sheridan.

Donnie fretted all that next endless day, waiting to close Crazy's so he could drive down to the Dash, wondering if there would be anything there; wondering if it was all an elaborate practical joke; wondering if it could be Jack or Tiffany or even Miguel behind it. It wasn't Jack's style to play pranks, though, and Tiffany hardly talked to him some days, so why would she bother? As for Miguel, that freeloading wetback barely spoke English, so Donnie doubted he could cobble this together.

So he kept his lip zipped and waited and waited and finally they buttoned Crazy's up and he said goodnight to Tiff and Jack and drove straight to the Dash and pulled into Bay 3. Some cat was hosing off his twenty-thousand-dollar ski boat over in Bay 6, mist billowing and gleaming under the sodium lot lights, but dude didn't even glance up when Donnie got out of his Honda and went to the garbage can sitting against the brick wall between Bay 3 and Bay 4 and lifted the lid and pulled the half-full liner out.

He paused then, fully expecting Skeeter to jump out and say, "Ha, gotcha!" or some shit (although admittedly this setup was a little involved for Skeet), but the only thing that happened was he spotted a plain white envelope resting at the bottom of the can. Heart pounding, he bent and grabbed the envelope, dropped the half-full liner in, slammed the lid, then scuttled back to his ride.

Five Benjamins, baby.

He drove home in a happy daze and sat on his couch and stared at the spray of crisp bills in his hand, sniffing them occasionally, reveling at their new-money smell (and also wondering if they were fake), all while keeping an eye on Mom's bedroom door, but she was fast asleep by that time, past eleven.

He was also waiting for a text from the mystery number.

He didn't have to wait long.

Are you ready to make $500 more?

The implications weren't lost on him. Either this dude (Donnie was thinking of the sender as a guy by then, even though it could've been anyone; something about the tone told him it was a man, and one used to getting what he wanted, too) had been hiding somewhere in the pines around the Dash, or maybe over behind that strip mall—or he'd just assumed Donnie would go for it.

Either way, it creeped him out more than a little…but hey, a thousand bucks was a thousand bucks.

What do I have to do?

The stranger told him.

What in the everlovin' fuck?

What could be so goddamn important about *Jack's boots* that someone would pay a thousand bucks for them? He posed that very question; the stranger answered (reluctantly, it seemed), saying they were for a practical joke, and that Jack would think it hilarious.

A grand was a helluva lotta scratch to lay out for a gag. Who the fuck *was* this guy? Jack's construction buddies swung by two or three times a season to inhale bacon cheeseburgers and rib him about being a culinary master, so forth and so on, ha ha; they all seemed a mite hard-up for doling out a grand for a joke, though. Stealing all the toilet paper from the job site's Port-a-Potty right before a guy went to take his customary mid-morning-break shit, sure…but dropping ten Cs for *boots?*

No fucking way.

So Donnie said he'd do it for another grand, $1,500 total, thinking dude might just call off the whole thing, or that more text negotiations would ensue. But the response came back instantly:

Done.

That no-hesitation made him even more leery (who didn't shy at paying $1,500 to set up a one-shot joke? Ashton Kutcher maybe, but nobody Donnie knew, that's for goddamn sure); despite his misgivings, the next afternoon he found himself nonchalantly tell-ing Jack that, since they were between waves, he was heading out back for a smoke.

Jack only waved him away, and then Donnie was flaming a cig with his old cheap Bic and strolling over to Jack's truck and lifting the toolbox lid and pulling out the worn leather work boots, and then he was opening his Honda's trunk and putting the boots in.

He banged it shut and meandered back over to Crazy's and leaned his shoulder against the pale blue wall and proceeded to have him a little smoke. He thought, *I just stole my fucking boss's fucking boots and made fifteen-hundred fucking dollars* and wanted to laugh, but didn't.

That night he drove back to the Dash and parked in Bay 3 again. The whole friggin' shebang was a ghost town, the highway dark and empty except for his dumb ass, so he hurried over, breathing hard, goosebumps prickling, to the same trashcan while wondering if the stranger was watching and pulled off the lid and yanked out the bag (empty this time), and there it was: another white envelope. He snatched it out, feeling its satisfying thickness, then booked it back to his car, grabbed the fifteen-fucking-hundred-dollar boots, flew to the can and chucked them in, stuffed the bag back, slammed the lid, then made like a tree and got the jumpin' Jesus out of there.

That'd been over three weeks ago, and he'd waited and watched for some mind-blowing prank, one involving a pair of worn, $1,500 steel-toed boots no less, but it never happened—or at least Jack never *said* anything about his construction buddies pulling anything epic. Donnie thought about confessing at least a hundred times a day, but a little voice would always pipe: *It's just boots. I'll buy him another pair. And so what if nothing's happened yet? Jack's crew is probably just waiting for the season to end and for Jack to go back on the road with 'em…*

Rationalizations and justifications; that's all they'd been, he saw that now, but he'd clutched them like a drowning man clings to a scrap of hull in the ocean—until Sunday, July 1st, anyway, because that's when he'd received another text, this time at work…and somehow he'd known who it would be, even though it was a fresh mystery number:

Would you like to make $10,000, Donnie?

So he'd zoomed home after close and plopped on the couch (Mom'd already lit out for Steve's for the holiday week, so he didn't have to worry about her) and once again opened text negotiations with a stranger who seemed to know him, yet didn't want to be seen and who wanted to pay him ass-loads of green to transport a pair of shitty boots from point A to point B—but now he was to pick the boots *up* from the can at the Dash on the 5th (way in the early ass morning, too), and put them *back* into Jack's toolbox. So he guessed it was from point B to point A, this time.

He should've been asking questions, he really should have; questions like how did the guy get Donnie's number in the first place? And how did he know Jack kept his boots in his toolbox? *Donnie* hadn't even known that shit, even though Jack had sent him out to fetch a screwdriver or some other damn thing from it at least a dozen fucking times over the past three summers; Donnie'd *seen* the crusty fuckers in there, though he'd barely registered their existence—and yet somehow this guy knew all about them?

And, of course, the most important question: Why was he willing to fork over so much damn bread to move a pair of fucking *boots* around?

Sooooo many questions he should have been asking…but what had he done?

He'd talked the guy up to thirty Gs.

Thirty-fucking-thousand dollars—ten up front, twenty on the back end—to transport a pair of boots.

Hello? Red flag, anybody?

So once more he dashed down to the Dash and looked in the garbage can against the wall between Bay 3 and Bay 4, and this time there wasn't a white envelope, oh no; *this* time there was an orange-and-white Nike shoebox, Size 12 Wide, and when he ran back to his car and jumped in and opened that Nike shoebox…

Surprising how little space ten grand used; less than a quarter of the box had been taken by the rubber-banded stacks of hundreds; ten of ten, a thousand clams each.

That jaunt home was now a blur, but Donnie knew his head had been full of what he could do with ten grand—and eventually thirty grand; his idiotic skull had *still* been stuffed with such fantasies when he'd went back to the Splash & Dash at 2:30 on the morning of the 5th of July to pick up the boots which would be waiting for him inside that lovely and oh-so-generous trashcan, along with his remaining twenty thousand buckaroos.

The Dash had been dead-creepy deserted again, but Donnie knew he had been almost skipping (or maybe he'd actually skipped, he couldn't remember) as he went to the can and pulled out his twenty grand with a grin, although it hadn't been in a shoe box that time, but in a black Nike duffel bag, and he'd even unzipped the damn thing right there in front of God and anybody who happened to drive by on the fucking highway, eyes popping at the sight of *twenty-fucking-thousand dollars*; only *after* he'd snatched out the black-plastic lawn bag that wrapped the boots and put the can back to rights and hustled to his car did he realize anything was wrong:

An…odor…wafted from the lawn bag.

He listened with sick dread to the sticky ripping as it peeled away from the boots, and then he turned the dome light on and held them up—and sure enough, the fuckers were *covered* in gouts of semi-dried blood, from the leather laces to the steel toes.

That drive home hadn't been so much fun.

Donnie pounded the Honda's wheel with the heel of his hand, then grabbed it in time to make the turn onto 3rd. "I'm a goddamn *idiot!* FUCK!"

He drove the exact speed limit past Pat's on the left and saw two smokin' dark-haired reporters holding phallic microphones while talking to cameras operated by lucky-as-shit camera guys, and then he swiveled his head and looked at the old Injun Bowl across the street and saw the ominous black Suburbans—those fuckers screamed "Government" like nothin' else.

Goddamn F mother B fuckin' I. He swallowed convulsively. *It's bad enough I'm in deep shit with Neil and Rogers and prob'ly that supreme asshole Rife; what will the goddamn FBI do to me for holding back a trunk-full of evidence in a mass murder investigation?*

What could *they do?*

A lot, he figured.

Donnie puttered along and stewed and sweated until he turned off 3rd onto Sycamore, and then off Sycamore onto Ash, and then off Ash…and *punched* it down their driveway; relief blasted through him when he shot out of the pines and saw not only Mom's beat-up Outback parked in front of the small guest house they rented from Mrs. Holly, but Mrs. Holly's burgundy Cadillac CTS sitting in the open garage of the main house.

He slewed in next to his mom and killed the engine and waited, but she didn't come to the door, like she always did when she heard his tires pop on the gravel; maybe she really was taking a nap. Steve had nailed it; Mom *was* a world-class nap-taker.

Donnie drummed his fingers on the steering wheel, eyes darting, then craned and looked out the back glass; Mrs. Holly was eighty if she was a day, and she'd been a widower longer than Donnie'd been alive; as such, she had an old-lady-widow's point of view about the world—i.e. it was ready to pounce. That garage door was *never* allowed to stay up…but there it was, up. Maybe she'd just pulled in and hadn't had a chance to shut it yet.

That had to be it.

Donnie scanned the property from tree line to tree line, then all the main house and the guest house he could see, but nothing except that open garage seemed out of place.

He got out.

34

Mom leaned forward: "Mr. Denton, are you telling us this…this *man* who's been running around in a chicken costume chopping people up…he's done it before?" Denton nodded, and Mom sat back with a puzzled frown. "Well, I don't see how that could be; judging by the circus this has—"

"Please, Mrs. Ross, allow me an opportunity to elucidate. First, however, I'd like to impress upon you all the absolute *need* for this information to stay out of the five o'clock news."

Angela said, "What do you mean?"

"I want an oath from each of you to keep silent concerning what you are about to hear."

Angela and Mom and I passed wary glances, but nobody said anything.

Denton snipped, "Let me put it another way: no promises to keep quiet means Mr. Ross goes back to Sheridan County. Immediately."

I said, "That doesn't give me much choice, Denton, but I agree."

Mom and Angela leveled dangerous scowls at the Senior Special Agent, but both promised to keep their mouths shut.

Chris was having none of it. "Why should I give a shit if Rossie rots in jail forever? It's where he belongs."

Denton turned to him. "You don't have to promise, Mr. Beaumont."

"I don't?"

"No, for I have every confidence that by the end of my tale, you will realize that you have no choice but to assist me in catching this scourge, this madman; and a significant percentage of that assistance—at least initially—will entail keeping close what I am about to share."

Chris sneered. "Yeah, well, we'll see."

Denton went on like Angela's brother hadn't opened his idiot mouth. "Yet I may be wrong, Mr. Beaumont, and if I am, and you hear me out and still choose to depart, I won't stop you."

Chris sat up straight. "I *knew* you couldn't hold me! I'm a tax-paying—"

"Yet if you take what you learn here to the media, I will dedicate my life to making your existence a misery—both personally and professionally."

Chris eyed Denton sideways for a long moment. "All right, fine, I'll keep quiet. You have my word."

"Thank you, Mr. Beaumont." Denton looked across the horseshoe; he spoke to all of us, but he pinned those frozen, calculating greens on me: "Please listen attentively; we have little time."

Denton talked.

We listened attentively.

God help us, we did.

35

Donnie unlocked the front door; cold, conditioned air washed against his fevered skin.

"Mom?"

No answer.

He bolted it and pocketed his keys, then started toward the back.

"Mom?" he called down the hall, but still no answer.

A flash out of the corner of his eye; their small flat-screen hanging opposite the plastic-covered couch was on, but muted. Leaving the TV on when nobody was in the room to watch was one of Mom's stupid pet peeves, and Donnie'd suffered her wrath for years until he'd learned to turn the fucking thing off; that was only one of her maddening peeves, like leaving the overhead light burning in his room, or drinking or eating anything on her precious couch (even with the fucking plastic); but she *especially* hated when the "idiot box" got left to blab to the air...

And there the damn thing was, closed-captioning blabbing away.

"Mom?"

Silence.

Her bedroom was down on the right, and his was on the left, directly across from each other. Her door was shut, but then so was his; hard enough to eek out any privacy with two people squeezed into a seven-hundred-square-foot guest house without leaving your door open for all the world to see your biz'ness. The half-bath they shared—Mom bitched about having no tub to soak in, but Donnie didn't give a shit—was further down on her side; its door was closed as well.

"Mom?"

Nada.

He walked down the hall, and only the whisper of his tennis shoes on the beige carpet and the steady hum of the air conditioning broke the stillness. He put his ear to her door, but didn't catch any of her patented raspy snoring.

"Mom?"

Nothing.

She must really be out. He raised his fist: *Whap whap whap.* "Mom?"

Silence.

WHAP WHAP WHAP WHAP! "Mom?"

Nothing.

Donnie swallowed, heart whamming so hard his fingers and toes felt all swollen and tingly. He tried the knob—unlocked—hesitated, then threw the door open.

36

"When the third nude and violated body was discovered, we understood we were dealing with a fiend."

Denton paused, as if making sure we were all paying attention. He needn't have worried; the dusty Injun was so still around our little group I clearly heard some G-Man way over in the foosball room talking on the phone about beware the fruit of the poisoned tree (whatever the hell that meant), and the laptops' key-clacks sounded like they were just down in Lane 7. Angela's big blue eyes were fixed on Denton, and she held my cuffed hands pressed against her flat stomach; the under-swell of her breasts caressed my knuckles as she breathed.

"That was in 1984," Denton offered, then paused once more, watching, waiting.

Mom just sat there with this big squint-frown…then her eyes shot wide and her mouth made a little o.

Angela said, "But Zane's only…" She gasped and glanced at me as nuclear cherry bombs went off in my brain:

I knew who had set me up.

I knew who the Chicken Man was.

Neither was Zane.

I leaned around Angela; Chief Rogers had one thick-soled cop boot propped on the opposite knee, arms folded across his chest, impatient and more than a little wry as he watched Denton.

Chris talked as he worked it out:

"'84? That's not possible. Rossie's my age, pushing thirty, but you say he's not the maniac who's chopping people up, and Zane's our age too, so…" Chris whipped his head around and stared at Denton. "Are you saying—?"

"Bob Jr. is the Chicken Man, Chris." Chief Rogers sounded as wry and as impatient as the rest of him looked: "This Traveler, too." Denton glared green death-daggers, but Rogers ignored him as he amended, "We're ninety-nine point nine percent sure, anyway."

Thunderous silence for maybe five heartbeats, and then all hell broke loose.

37

Mom wasn't in her room, but her queen-sized bed had been stripped to the bare mattress.

Frowning, Donnie stepped inside; both of the gigantor body-length goose-feather pillows she loved to snuggle with were also missing. When Mom washed the bedding, that included pillowcases, of course…but why the fuck would she take her big-ass pillows?

Donnie went across the hall and stuck his head in his room. "Mom?"

No Mom, but his bed hadn't been stripped. Mom usually did all the linen at once—usually? Hell, every stinking time—but not *this* time. He knocked, then opened the bathroom; she wasn't on the john or standing in the stall behind the flower-print shower curtain playing hide-and-seek with him. He checked the washer/dryer combo stacked in the corner (making an already cramped shitter-situation almost absurd), but no bedding. Mom always took the big stuff over to Mrs. Holly's, anyway, but it didn't hurt to…

Donnie snapped his fingers. *That's where she is!* And maybe while everything dried, she'd driven the old bat to Marcie's and they'd just gotten back—which explained the open garage. Mrs. Holly had required more and more such help over the past two years; even *he* drove her around sometimes, as much as he hated it, but Mom always reminded him when he griped that they rented this place for half what the old girl could get for it on the open market; helping around the yard or the garden or taking her to the grocery store or to the doctor or the dentist wasn't much of a price to pay, considering—and as he well remembered the succession of run-down trailer parks they'd been forced to live in after his dad left, Donnie knew she was right. He also had to admit Mrs. Holly wasn't all that bad as far as rich, paranoid old-lady landlords went; she gave *great* Christmas presents. It was just that Donnie was particularly bad at sucking ass, no matter how vital the cause.

Feeling better, he trooped back and clicked the set off (Mom had conditioned him well; he was like one of that Pavlov dude's trained mutts or something) and chucked the remote on the couch and went outside.

He crossed the sliver of manicured grass that separated Casa Donnie from Casa Old Bat and took a detour to peek into the backyard; the patch of garden was there, but the ladies weren't out toiling. Probably still inside, he decided, Mrs. Holly riding herd as Mom shelved goodies; the old lady liked her labels faced just so and everything in its exact, preordained place.

Donnie went back around front, hesitated, then bypassed the stone-paver walk to the front door and strolled into the open garage and stepped up to Mrs. Holly's Cadillac, all shiny and oozing money; the hated riding mower lurked off to the side, smelling like gas and grass and no ass, as usual.

Donnie gently placed his palm on the Caddy's hood.

Cool.

Cool? Hell, it was almost *cold*…but shouldn't it be hot, or at least warm, if they'd just gotten back? Donnie looked out the open garage and across the yard at his mom's Outback; maybe they'd taken her ride.

He mounted the steps with the anti-slip treads and the handrails and knocked on the glass-paned door leading to the utility hallway. "Mrs. Holly? Mom?"

No answer. He shaded his eyes and leaned in, but glimpsed only the red-tiled hallway and Mrs. Holly's monster kitchen at the end. He knocked and called again, more nothing, then tried the knob—unlocked. He swung it open and stepped inside.

"Mrs. Holly? Mom? It's Donnie!" Pause. "Hello?"

Silence.

Donnie shut the door and listened, hard, but the house was utterly still; he stuck his head in the utility room on the right, then entered and checked the washer and dryer, but no bed linens.

What the hell?

Donnie left the utility room and stepped into Mrs. Holly's big-ass motherfucking kitchen. The island had a full knife block and stools all around it and floating glass cabinets hanging above it with shelves stuffed full of delicate and expensive China; the thing covered more square footage than their entire kitchen over in the slave quarters—and Mrs. Holly rarely even *cooked* anymore!

He walked around the aircraft-carrier island and stopped when he could see into the wide-open, sunken living room:

No ladies.

Donnie glanced around nervously, then peered down the long, darkened hallway that led to the spare bedrooms and the late Mr. Holly's office, with the master bedroom at the end.

"Mom!" he shouted down that shadowy hall. "Mrs. Holly!"

Nothing. Maybe they'd boogied outside to do some grubbing just as he'd went to the garage. He crossed the living room's deep-pile carpet; it felt like walking on a giant marshmallow. He looked out the patio doors, but didn't see them, so he slid one back and stepped onto the new and still-fragrant cedar deck.

"Mrs. Holly? Mom?"

They weren't in the garden…so where the fuck were they? Their rides were present and accounted for, and Donnie knew damn well those broads wouldn't take off half-assing through the pines; they had to be here *somewhere.*

He went to the rail and cupped his hands: "MOM, MRS. HOL-LY, IT'S DONNIE! WHERE ARE YOU?"

No answer.

Then he sagged against the decking in pure relief; he even laughed a little. One of Mrs. Holly's rich-old-biddy homies must've busted out the rotary phone—half-blind Mrs. Stallingsworth, or that uppity bitch Mrs. Roundtree—and Mom got roped into chauffeuring them in their car on a round of rich-old-biddy errands. Donnie'd been coerced into that torture once—*once*—and if so, he felt sorry for Mom, but it explained everything…

He scowled uncertainly.

No, not everything: there was Mom not answering her damn phone; there was the open garage; there was Mom's stripped bed… and what the hell happened to her big pillows?

Donnie shook his head; he'd ask about all that weird shit when she got back. In the meantime, he'd buzz the po-po station again, try to catch that nosy, non-calling-back fuckwad Rogers.

He stumped over and dropped his ass into a wrought-iron patio chair, kicked his sneakers up onto the table with the folded "sun-brella" strapped to the pole, and dialed the non-emergency number from memory. *This time I'll make that fat bitch give me Chief Rogers' cell; fuck her, and fuck their "policy".*

Then he saw the motorcycle.

Or part of it, anyway; the bike was parked behind the metal shed that sat on the perimeter of the property, right at the edge of the pines; only a slice of black rear tire and the red brake light and the chrome fender and one orange turn signal were visible from where he was kicked back on the cedar deck.

Donnie's heart slugged ice-water through his veins as he dropped his feet and sat up, staring pop-eyed at that sliver of motorcycle.

"Indian Head Police Department, may I help you?"

Only a hiss came out.

"Hello?" Impatient. "If this is a prank, I'll have you know that—"

"I'll call you right back," he managed, then hung up and slowly stood and stuffed his phone back and floated over to the railing and unlatched and opened the gate, and then he hovered past the vegetable garden and up the slope across the grass, and then he drifted around to the back of the shed.

It was a black Harley Davidson with chrome dripping everywhere; it looked awfully familiar, too. Donnie flashed on the ZZ Top 'roid freak blating past Skeet's house—twice—and terror almost paralyzed him; his neck creaked with tension as he turned his head toward Mrs. Holly's oh-so-silent house:

"Mom," he whispered.

He stumbled around to the front of the shed and jerked the door open and pulled the light string. Mrs. Holly stored stuff like weed killer and rat bait and fertilizer out here, and also the gasoline cans for the mower and the garden tiller; his problem was that most of the tools that could double as weapons, hammers and such, were hanging over the workbench in the garage. But after rummaging with one eye kept on that ominously quiet house, Donnie finally came up with a big ol' nasty pair of turtle-head pruners and a short metal spike; he thought it was for staking weed barrier, but didn't give much of a shit.

"Mom," he whispered.

He yanked the string, then slammed the shed door with a clang; the latch didn't catch, and it swung open a little, but he didn't give much of a shit about that, either.

"Mom," he whispered.

Donnie slunk back across the yard with a snarl, improvised weapons clutched in his shaking hands, watching the open sliding-glass door intently. *Did I leave that fucker like that?* Yes, he remembered now; he'd come out onto the stinky cedar deck and called for them, leaving it wide-the-fuck open behind him.

He crept up the steps and around the patio furniture and leaned and peered cautiously through that opening:

"Mom? Mrs. Holly?"

Silence.

He moved across the shag—it still felt like walking on a marshmallow—and stepped up and out of the living room, and his gaze settled on the kitchen island; before, there'd only been a full knife block resting on that wide, sparkling surface, but now there were more things: things like a long, fake gray beard and a braided clip-on ponytail; things like a black half-helmet; and something else Donnie's frantic, despairing mind hardly registered…and then it hit him; crumpled nylon hoses covered with blue swirls and symbols.

Tattoo sleeves.

"*MOOOOOOOOOOM!*"

Donnie looked around wildly, then bolted down the hallway and threw open the first door on the right; spare bedroom, no Mom. Still screaming for his mother, Donnie did likewise with all the doors on both sides of that long, shadowy hall: another spare bedroom, a dusty sewing room that looked like it hadn't been used in years; same for the office with the bulky, stone-age monitor.

No Mom.

He panted in front of the last door at the end, the master bedroom; the smell told him what he would find behind it, and he squeezed his eyelids shut as tears tracked down his cheeks.

He turned the knob and pushed the door open.

Only then did Donnie un-squeeze his eyes, and the first thing that trickled through his bruised mind was that he'd found Mom's pillows.

Mr. and Mrs. Holly had enjoyed a king-sized four-poster during the latter years of their marriage, though it lacked a canopy. Donnie recalled when she'd hired someone to lower it; Mrs. Holly was afraid she would roll out of the ol' playground and break a hip. So now the four-poster hovered only twelve inches off the carpet, and Donnie's mom and Mrs. Holly were lying on that big, low-slung bed. They were nude. Their wrists had been tied with Mom's sliced-up sheets and then secured to kitty-corner posts, and their knees and shins and ankles had been bound together, wound around and around and around with twin masses of gray duct tape. Their hips were elevated by Mom's big-ass pillows, and they were pressed together down there, butt to butt, and…and…and there was something *shoved up inside them,* something long and angular and about the diameter of his calf. Donnie thought it was a spare corner post from when Mrs. Holly'd had her fancy new cedar deck put in…Mom was impaled on one end of that impossibly thick, splintery post, and Mrs. Holly on the other…blood, blood *everywhere,* covering Mom's goose-feather pillows and the sheets and comforter, and a lake of blood stained the carpet below the four-poster…blood had trickled out of Mrs. Holly's nose, and her eyes were glazed as she stared sightlessly at the ceiling, her fine silver hair unbound and hanging over the far edge, wrinkled mouth open in a silent shriek.

And Mom…

I never knew she had a yellow-rose tattoo.

Donnie staggered and dropped the clippers and the spike, holding himself up against the jamb. A clicking, buzzing racket was in his ears, and he hardly knew it was him screaming and screaming and screaming before something hard smashed above his right ear.

Hot agony filled his skull, and then, as he crashed face-first to the sticky carpet, the blessed darkness rose up and took it all away.

For a little while, it did.

38

I just sat there and let the uproar wash over me while Angela squeezed all the blood from my hands.

It was only Chris doing the yelling anyway, waving his arms and asserting he'd never heard anything more outrageous while listing all the charities R&R Investment Group generously funded: Make-A-Wish, Wounded Warrior Project, Habitat for Humanity, St. Jude's down in Memphis (along with at least a dozen other children's hospitals scattered around the country); basically, you name it and Bob Jr. forked it out for the worthy cause; not to mention all the good he'd done for Sheridan County and Indian Head, blah blah, how dare you suggest such an outstanding human being could be capable of chopping those kids up with an ax; Rossie was the only murderer Chris knew for certain, wonk wonk.

Denton eventually tired of it and nodded to Hawthorne, who grabbed Chris's trapezes and put the Vulcan nerve pinch on him; it didn't knock him out, unfortunately, but it made Angela's brother gasp and hunch to that side; most importantly, he shut his stupid yap.

I was grinning at him and Chris was rubbing his shoulder and glaring bloody murder back when Angela asked maybe the most important question:

"If you know it's Bob, why isn't he under arrest?"

"Many reasons, Ms. Beaumont, the primary example being we don't know his current location. Another is that the Chief is correct: we are only ninety-nine percent certain the Traveler, a.k.a. the Chicken Man," Denton's upper lip curled, "is Robert Richards Jr. He fits the Traveler's profile, however, so—"

"I *knew* it! You don't have any DNA or other hard evidence, just some 'profile'!" Chris flinched away and glared up at Hawthorne when he raised his freckled mitt in warning.

"As I was saying, he fits the profile. And let us clear the air a bit, shall we? I and my team are here for one reason: when events in Indian Head came to light, we recognized the correlation between the Traveler's paraphilia and that of this 'Chicken Man'." Denton turned and zapped Chris with the wintergreens. "And as for any 'hard evidence' we may or may not have linking any one individual to the Traveler or this 'Chicken Man'…I've stated I require your assistance to catch a brutal killer, Mr. Beaumont, and if you give me a chance, I will share what data I can, and hopefully that data will suffice in swaying you to facilitate my investigation. If not, then not, and we will proceed in our relationship along the parameters I have laid out. But in either scenario, there is *zero chance in hell* I will divulge all the details of my investigation to a civilian. Have I made the situation clear, Mr. Beaumont?"

"Yeah," Chris muttered, shifting on the seat and eyeing Hawthorne warily. "Crystal."

Mom spoke up. "Para…para*whatta?* Mr. Denton, I'd advise you to talk American if you want our help—or at least *my* help."

Denton pulled the little glasses off and pinched his blade of a nose with thumb and index finger, as if he was getting a whopper of a headache. *Good.* "Forgive me, Mrs. Ross, I tend to lapse into profiler argot; hazard of the profession, I fear." He hooked the glasses back on. "The word is 'paraphilia'. It implies a set constant of the perfect psycho-sexual experience." When Mom's irritated frown only deepened, Denton added: "Everyone has and ideal erotic milieu: person, place, mood, smell, position, what have you. Paraphilia refer to erotic scenes that are, shall we say, outside the norm, and frowned upon by mainstream society; asphyxiation and sadomasochism and the like. In the Traveler's case, however, we are alleging deviant paraphilia at the extreme end of the curve."

When we all just stared, Denton sighed: "To put it crudely, it's how a sadist gets his jollies."

That brought the silence again. Special Agent Denton unbuttoned the suit jacket and rested his elbows on his knees, yellow tie a cheerful vertical slash in the murky Injun.

"Please listen now, and when I have finished, mayhap each of you good people will be willing to assist me in apprehending a dreadful killer; a murdering, raping, torturing monster that has preyed upon the precious daughters, loving wives, beloved mothers, and treasured grandmothers of this great nation, from coast to coast and border to border, for three decades—and perhaps longer."

Denton droned uninterrupted, and what he had to snip almost made me sick; literally ill; like blowing-chunks-on-my-shoes kinda bad.

Raping and killing a woman is bad enough, but what this Traveler shit-heel does to get his rocks off…foreign objects, dear God, sodomy and vaginal rape with *foreign objects* until these poor women die from internal injuries…does one every three years like clockwork…bleaches and scrubs and discards her naked body, and the dump site can be just about anywhere…woman vanishes on one coast and then her corpse turns up on the opposite shore four or five days later. The feds thought the Traveler had been studying *them* long before they'd even caught a whiff of him; basically, he'd evolved even as they and the forensics had evolved, thus the body cleansing as well as the deliberate no-pattern of disposal sites.

He did the same with class and race—what walking-thesaurus Denton called "victimology"; most of these whack jobs had a preferred prey, but this fucker wasn't prejudiced: pretty black college girls, porcelain housewives, Asian secretaries, dirt-poor Indian res grade-school teachers, mustachioed Mexican cafeteria ladies, HR workers, toll-booth attendants, Yoga instructors; all fair game. He threw in a prostitute—the low-risk, ready-made prey most of these animals feed on—about once a decade, although the BAU profilers thought they were a calculated move, like everything else this bastard did.

"What about Tiffany?" I broke in. "Did he…?" I couldn't finish.

"You don't want to know, Jack." Chief Rogers' normally unruffled gaze was haunted. "Special Agent Denton can't tell you anyway, because he might compromise his investigation; she's at peace now, whatever happened. That's what's important."

I swallowed, hard. Poor Tiff.

A hot drop hit my forearm, then another. Angela sobbed, then released me to wipe her face; she kept her hands there, hunching and crying into her palms. Mom had both hands pressed over her mouth; the eyes over her fingers were wide with outrage as she stared at Denton like she was thinking of making him take it all back.

"I suspect this isn't a revelation to Ms. Beaumont," Denton said. "She found Mrs. Barbary's body and was ordered by Sheriff Neal to keep quiet about the details. Did you do so, young lady?"

Angela nodded jerkily into her hands and cried harder; Chris looked sick.

"Then you are to be commended. It is terribly hard not to reveal such horrors to close friends or family, if for no other reason than sharing brings comfort." Strange thing to say in such an icy voice; then the tender moment was over as he flashed the wintergreens around the horseshoe: "I trust the rest of you will display as much prudence while honoring your word."

I patted Angela's knee, cuffs clacking, then sat forward, drawing those cold lasers back to me: "But if this Traveler asshole really is the Chicken Man, and they both actually *are* Bob Jr., then it seems Bob doesn't give a shit about hiding anymore. I mean, I can't think of anything better to draw attention than wearing a giant chicken costume while chopping up a bunch of people with an ax. Can you?"

Angela's sobbing subsided as Denton eyed me speculatively across the horseshoe; he even wore a rueful little smile, now—although after talking about this sick shit, I didn't know how anybody could crack a smile, even a little one.

"He seems to have given up the 'Traveler' bit, too," I added, "what with murdering six people in one town and leaving the bodies here—and I guess he's also done with the killing-every-three-years thing, since all six were done in three days."

"Yes," Denton said, still with that questioning little smile; waiting to see what trick I would perform next: "It would seem that way, Mr. Ross."

I blinked. "Well, uh…" I one-eyed the others, but nobody threw me a life preserver; Mom did nod encouragingly, and Angela took my cuffed hands again and clutched them beneath her breasts. Rogers only looked at me deadpan; no help there. I scraped some gumption together and squared back on Denton: "And why the hell are we *here?* You know this place is owned by the killing machine you just described, right?" I gently shook free of Angela and rapped my cuffs on the plastic seat: "These are *his* chairs we have our butts parked on." I raised both arms and gestured grandly across the yellow-and-black-striped dimness: "Those are *his* lanes and gutters." I aimed one index finger over Denton's narrow, suited shoulder: "That's *his* foosball room you have your government 'bots doing government 'bot things in." I swung my arms the other way and spread my hands toward the front counter—as far as they would spread, anyway: "That's *his* trophy case—"

"I fathom your point, Mr. Ross. I daresay we all do. And as I already informed you out in the vehicle that transported you here—

of *course* we know the identity of the owner of this investment property. How could we not? And now I offer you an inquiry in turn." He spread his dainty little hands…but only so far, mocking me: "Why *not* the Injun?"

Why not the Injun? I could think of about ten thousand reasons why the fuck not the Injun, but before I could list any Special Agent Denton continued, still with that little smile; it was more of a condescending smirk now, and I was reaaaally not liking it.

"When Mr. Beaumont sought me out in your town's square—this would be directly after Sheriff Neil's caricature of a press conference—and proposed this property as a base of operations during our agency's hopefully short stay in this…quaint…municipality," I felt Angela stiffen, "I knew who employed him before he even opened his mouth. Of *course* I knew. So, with a small amount of noninvasive questioning, I discerned young Mr. Richards had *ordered* Mr. Beaumont to seek me out and make that offer." We all looked at Chris; he nodded shortly, scowling. "*Now*, Mr. Ross, having uncovered this fact, I utilized deductive reasoning to conclude that the senior Mr. Richards, wherever he is currently located, likely directed his son to *order* Mr. Beaumont to seek me out—and thus his proposal had a twofold purpose: mockery, and an attempt to sound me out as far as my knowledge of the true killer's identity. Thus it was that I *immediately* understood that to decline said offer would be to clue Mr. Richards to my suspicion…but to accept would keep him guessing as to the extent of my knowledge." Those pale eyes glittered behind the little glasses. "When I attend his execution, I will remind him of his overweening arrogance. But whatever Mr. Richards motivation, I determined that the *intelligent* course was to accept. And although the Injun is admittedly hygienically challenged, it provides the square footage and the parking we require—as no other local and currently unoccupied structures do,

I might add. So. Once more I put it to *you*, sir: Why *not* the Injun?" Silence except for the 'bots hammering on laptops: "No pithy response? How disappointing."

I opened my mouth, but before I could say anything about the supercilious pot calling the arrogant kettle black, Mom said, "What about bugs?" We all looked at her. "Not *bugs* bugs..." she waved her hands, frustrated. "*Bugs*. So he can hear what you're saying. He may have planted—"

"Well thought out, Mrs. Ross. Fortunately, we thought of it as well, and—also fortunately—we're the FBI, and we have access to the world's finest counterintelligence measures." When Mom just scowled, he sighed. "We swept the place from top to bottom, ma'am, and found no microphones or miniature cameras. Robert Richards Jr. has neither been listening to us nor watching us, nor is he listening to us or watching us at this moment." He stink-eyed me across the horseshoe again: "*Now*, Mr. Ross, as to your forthcoming and oh-so-insightful observations, the ones I can see building behind your teeth? Care to share?"

"Yes," I growled, then unclenched my aforementioned teeth: "Why the heck would Bob go after Angela? He was best friends with her dad, and she's known him her entire life. Hell, I bet he even offered her a job when she moved back." I got a sniffling nod in confirmation; Chris only sneered. *Prick.* "So why set out to kill someone he obviously still cares about? And while we're at it, you said he only kills *women*; better go tell that to Bill Napier and those two guys at the party." *God, Tiffany, you poor kid.* "I mean, I get setting me up; he hates me for Zack, and I don't think he liked me much even before that. And speaking of that, why bother framing me? Why didn't he just pick that ax up and come after me a long time ago?"

Special Agent Denton said nothing, only smirked, frozen eyes weighing and measuring and coming up short.

Asshole. "Also—and this is according to *you*, Denton—Bob's pretty much had the run of the country for thirty years while you FBI clowns have been sitting around with your thumbs up your asses." I was very happy to see that little smirk melt away. "Why would he shit in his nest now?"

Denton and Rogers exchanged an unreadable look before the Senior Special Agent pushed his wire-rimmed glasses up his sharp nose with the tip of one manicured finger. "Succinctly put, Mr. Ross." He cleared his throat. "However, let me refer you to the codicil I presented Mr. Beaumont." He speared me with the frozen-pond eyes: "Despite my need for your assistance, in no way, shape, or form am I obligated or inclined to open my investigation to an untrained civilian. I do believe, however, that I can address a handful of your concerns, though I doubt the answers will console—"

Chris suddenly spat, "I haven't heard a *single fucking reason* why I should believe Bob is a killer, and I better hear one soon or I really am leaving; I don't care what you tell your goons to do to me, Denton."

"Fair enough. And if I may implore you to pay close attention, Mr. Ross, I believe some of your inquiries are about to be fulfilled." He minced around in his seat to face Chris. "Allow me to commence with the profile, Mr. Beaumont. The Behavioral Analysis Unit believes the Traveler is a white male, late fifties or early sixties by now, and extraordinarily intelligent; he may be highly educated as well, although that is only conjecture. Whatever his perspicacity, he is physically powerful in the extreme; indeed, considering what has been done to some of these unfortunate women, he would have to be. We also believe he is the type of personality that would take exceptional care of his body, and would still, even at sixty, be an imposing specimen. Does that sound like anyone you are perhaps acquainted with, Mr. Beaumont?"

"Lots of people hit the fucking gym, Denton, but that's no reason to—"

"There is also the sheer *size* of the geographical area the Traveler claims as his territory; nothing less than the lower forty-eight and the District of Columbia. Only Alaska and Hawaii have escaped his depredations—so far as we know."

I frowned, doing the math, but Angela got there first.

"You told us he kills every three years, and that he's been doing this for thirty years; that's ten women, last time I checked. So how could…*God*, if he's killed in every contiguous state and the District of Columbia, that's *forty-nine women!* Is that what you're saying? *Forty-nine women!?*"

"If you'll recall, Ms. Beaumont, we conjecture the Traveler has been active for *longer* than thirty years; also, I believe I stated he discards a carefully prepared body every three years in such a location that it will inevitably be discovered."

We all stared at him.

Mom broke the horrified stillness: "He doesn't…he doesn't take little children, does he? I don't think I could *stand* it if he…if he did those things to…" Mom put her face in her hands. Angela let go of me and made her way across the horseshoe and sat and pulled Mom's head to her shoulder.

"We've never run across a juvenile-abduction case that fits the parameters we associate with the Traveler…but who can say?" The cold bastard let that hang there before he shook his head. "However, we do not believe the Traveler is interested in children. His prey are women. If indeed the Traveler is the Chicken Man, then at sixteen, Ms. Downing would be the youngest victim attributed to him—once again, that we are aware of."

Mom said, "Thank the Lord!" We all looked at her; she flushed. "I mean…you know what I mean," she mumbled.

"We know, hon." Angela patted Mom's shoulder, but her blue eyes almost crackled: "How can we not have heard about almost fifty women vanishing? This sick-o should've been splashed all over the news by now! By now? It should've happened *thirty years ago!*"

Before Denton could answer, Rogers said, "It's simple, Angela: The Bureau kept it quiet."

"Why in God's name would they do that?"

"Because no one likes to admit failure—especially if you work for the FBI. And unless I'm way off base, I'm guessing the BAU didn't even know this Traveler madman existed until he got tired of being ignored and started taunting them with bleached and scrubbed bodies. It's also likely it took them a few bodies to figure out they were from the same killer, so they weren't even sure he was real until…when, Denton? Early to mid-nineties? Sound about right?"

Denton didn't bother to answer, just pursed his lips and stared icy green death at the Chief.

"For twenty-plus years, they've quietly been trying to catch him; *over twenty years,* and all the while dozens of families lost wives, daughters, mothers, nieces, cousins, aunts, and grandmothers, and only a double handful ever got any explanation or closure; it was terrible closure, to be sure, but at least those few families aren't still agonizing in limbo, hoping against all reason she would turn up out of the blue one day."

Angela glared at Denton while her full mouth worked, but nothing came out. Mom gifted the Special Agent with the Scowl of Disapproval, the one that used to make me hop (still did), but all I could do was think about how I would feel if I was lucky enough to have a wife or a daughter, and then one day she vanished without trace or explanation, and how I would get through my day—day after day after endless day—if I was expected to soldier on without knowing.

And then I thought about what I would *do* to someone if I found out they'd known—or even *suspected*—what had happened to my wife or daughter, but had kept that information from me.

I shuddered.

Meanwhile, Denton and Rogers were engaged in a staring contest, although the Chief wasn't trying that hard; he looked about like he always did, calm and a little tired. Denton, however, was attempting to fry Rogers where he sat.

And then Angela found her voice.

"How can you be so cruel? HOW CAN YOU LET THOSE POOR PEOPLE SUFFER—"

"*Enough!* The decisions that I or my department or my agency have made regarding this case—*or anything else*—are not your concern."

"But they think there's still a chance—"

"*Your concern*, Ms. Beaumont, is deciding whether to assist our plan to catch this psychopath." He pinned that icy stare on me: "And to weigh the consequences should you not."

Denton should have been a pile of cinders on that hard-plastic seat, considering how Mom and Angela were looking at him, but I only said, "Speaking of plans, we still haven't heard how we can help catch this fucker."

Mom stirred. "Enough, Jackie. I've had all I can take from Christopher, and he's too big to scrub out his mouth, now."

"Yes, ma'am."

Chris said, "And I'm still not convinced it's Bob. So the guy travels; a lot of people travel, and it's part of his—"

Denton held up his hand and squeezed his eyes shut, like he still had that doozy of a migraine coming on. *Nice.* "You are correct, Mr. Beaumont, I apologize; we've wandered off course, and time is pressing." He opened his eyes and spoke to me. "Please let me finish laying out my arguments for Mr. Beaumont, and then perhaps I can share our plan with you, Mr. Ross."

"Go right ahead," I said, exchanging looks with Mom and Angela; they understood, I saw—and, like me, they didn't appreciate it much.

It's Chris he has to convince. He knows we'll do whatever the hell he wants just to keep me out of Neil's claws.

Denton faced Chris again. "You'll have to admit, Mr. Beaumont, that Robert Richards Jr. intersects with the salient points of the profile I've laid out for you—"

"I don't have to admit a goddamn thing."

"—but consider also what was done *with* and *to* the victims of the Traveler. Some were killed and discarded quickly, whether that was hours or thousands of miles later; some…some he took a considerable time with."

Chris broke the uneasy hush. "What are you saying?"

"As pervasive as the cliché of a 'soundproofed basement' is in our popular culture, we believe it is appallingly true in this case. Considering the perversities committed against a select few of these women, and considering the duration of starvation and torture revealed by their autopsies, it is obvious he has at least one safehouse where he can store someone—a 'soundproofed basement', if you will—and where he is comfortable leaving them constrained for extended lengths of time; with two of his victims, for over ten weeks."

Ten weeks. MORE than ten weeks. Two-and-a-half months plus tied or fucking chained up in the dark somewhere, and with only some evil bastard for company, an evil bastard who would come in where you were tied or chained to the wall or the bed or whatever and spread your legs, and then…

I pressed my face into my palms as the dusty Injun swam around me, thinking it entirely possible I would blow chunks on my shoes after all. But then Angela slid her slender arms around my shoulders, and I leaned into her, trembling and gasping in the clean scent of her hair, trying to get the ghastly plight of those women out of my mind; I knew those faceless, screaming women would haunt me for the rest of my life, though.

I do not want to hear any more of this twisted shit.

I managed a smile for her; she hooked a strand of golden hair behind her ear and smiled back from six inches away. *Good God, she's gorgeous.* She left her arms wrapped around me, but I didn't mind; over the years, I might've felt something better than her breasts pressed against my sore ribs, but right then nothing came to mind.

I looked around the horseshoe and found Mom watching me worriedly and both of us approvingly, but Denton hadn't paused for my bout of vertigo; he was still selling Chris.

"…that to enjoy the freedom of travel and to employ one or more—and we strongly speculate more; perhaps as many as half a dozen secluded and most likely soundproofed safe houses strategically located across the country—then that obviously implies whomever the Traveler is in the daylight, he is in possession of not-inconsiderable wealth, as well as expertise in real estate procurement."

Chris said, "So just because Bob made his money as a developer, and because he travels all over the country to scout his own deals, you've got him pegged as this…this monster?" He laughed. "Okay, then you need to haul in the whole real-estate mogul jet set that crisscrosses the American skies every damn day! Hell, I bet there's a bunch of 'em running around wearing panda costumes and hacking people up with machetes! This is so fucking *ridiculous!*"

"There is also for your consideration, Mr. Beaumont, the *way* Robert Richards Jr. travels, and it is certainly not in the 'jet set.'" Denton watched Chris coldly and confidently, waiting.

Angela's arms tightened, making my ribs talk, and her eyes shot wide; Mom got there a little slower, but then she clapped her hands across her mouth again: "Oh, my dear *Lord!*"

I felt as if Tweaker's hammer had connected with my temple instead of my forearm because I could see it now, too; God help me, I could:

Bob sniffs a hot deal and needs to head out pronto before some other bigwig swoops in, but he's afraid of flying, everybody knows *that*, so he zooms away in, say, that midnight-blue '69 hardtop Shelby, the one with the chrome side-pipes; the one I used to just about cream my Jockeys every time I saw it. And maybe he does some legit Bob-business and maybe not, but either way he has an excuse to be out roaming now, and another stable of vehicles waiting for him somewhere (or more than one, and probably all registered under shell corporations or dummy LLCs at that, both the stables and the cars; Bob would know how to set up all that gimmicky shit, that's for sure, and set it up right), and so he swaps the Mustang for some wet-work Corolla with a couple hundred thousand miles and does his evil shit, then discards the wet Corolla (the Traveler would know where to safely dispose of a car, you betcha) and grabs the Shelby again, or maybe just tools to another stable to pick up another classic, like that restored '71 GTO rag-top he had last summer…or maybe he just buys a new fucking ride. Screw it, he's rich as snot, why not?

Then, both righteous and evil shit accomplished, he bee-bops home in the new ride because hey, he's a wealthy prick and he pulls that bit all the time anyway, so nobody in good ol' Indian Head blinks fucking twice. And he's golden because there's no way he can be connected to the junker Corolla, and even if a witness comes forward out of the blue, the good people of Indian Head (especially the ones whose paychecks have his signature at the bottom) would line up out the door and around the corner and down the block to testify their beloved Bob Jr. wouldn't drive some piece-of-shit Corolla, let alone abduct some random woman.

Something else occurred to me: Was he truly afraid of flying? Maybe that's just a lie he'd started telling thirty or whatever years ago so he could have an excuse to do what he do; I'd sure as hell never heard of or seen Bob acting afraid of anything else, and I'd always kind of wondered at such a big man's one and highly visible flaw.

Ruse or not, it was perfect cover for a sick bastard like the Traveler.

Chris saw it too, I could read it in his face, but he'd always been stubborn. "So the guy doesn't like planes. So what? Lots of people choose to drive for—"

Denton steamrolled ahead, focused, merciless: "And there was his mother."

Angela, Chris, and I frowned in confusion, but Mom made a sound behind her hands and closed her eyes, as if in pain.

Angela glanced uncertainly from her to Denton. "You mean… are you saying his mother abused him?"

Chris scoffed, "I've never heard that."

Denton said, "You wouldn't have." He cleared his throat. "Mrs. Ross and the Chief and I are of an age to comprehend what I am about to say, but you three may have difficulty. Yes, Mrs. Emilia Leanne Salisbury-Richards ruled her only child and husband with an iron hand, but that was hardly uncommon back then; another tiny matriarchy thriving in a patriarchal, post-war society." Denton shrugged narrow shoulders. "Again, nothing singular; fodder for after Sunday services, I'm sure, but we suspect Mrs. Richards took it to a level that in this day and age may have resulted in her incarceration, and surely would have resulted in Robert Jr. being removed from the home."

I said, "So why wasn't he?"

"It was a different era, Mr. Ross; outside of metropolitan environs, social services were concepts in their infancy, and not yet in practical, practiced application—and if they were, certainly not functioning with any efficacy. Thus, such…unpleasantness…was handled within the family; or failing that, the church or social group." More narrow shrug: "Or not at all."

Angela said, "What did she do to him?" She sounded fascinated, and looked sick to her stomach…and, I thought, even a little sorry for Bob.

"As there were no police reports ever filed, we have only supposition birthed from rumor; however, Mrs. Ross *was* two grades above Robert Jr."

Every head swiveled to Mom; she dashed at her eyes with her fingers, then dropped her hands into her lap and sighed, "We…we all saw the marks. And he was always wearing a cast on some piece of him and wanting everybody to sign it. And some days—well, some *weeks*—he didn't show up to school at all. And despite his stories—he was always falling off his bike or out of the tire swing or off the barn roof or some other tomfoolery, he said—we all knew why: his mom was a mean old witch. The whole town said so, although she never so much as said boo to me; it was just known that she was…that way with him."

Angela was aghast. "And nobody did anything? What about his teachers, or the school counselor, or the principal?"

"Such things were handled quietly, dear." Mom's mouth twisted. "Or not at all, I suppose, like Mr. Denton said. We gossiped, sure, but we didn't stick our snouts in other people's business—or spread our own around, for that matter. Not like today! You've got thirteen-year-old girls splashing their lives all over the Facebooks or the Instant Grams or Chitter or the Good Lord knows what, and the federal government shoving their fingers knuckle-deep into every pie, states' rights and the Bill of Rights be damned!" Mom took a deep breath and gathered herself. "No, Mr. Denton is right; that was a simpler time. People handled their own affairs and kept themselves to themselves."

Chris was starting to look a little desperate. "But Bob *loved* his mom! You remember when she passed, don't you Mrs. Ross?"

"Yes, Christopher. We weren't invited to the service, but I recall that time well."

Chris blushed at that, but didn't let it slow him. "She was like eighty-something, and had been in a nursing home down in Sheridan for ten years, and the whole damn *town* turned out at Bob's house for the potluck after! And the funeral, *God!* They had to shut down the highway for two hours!" He looked at his sister. "Bob had us sit with him and Zane, right up front under the awning, like family. Dad didn't want to, but Bob guilted him into it. Remember?"

"I remember," Angela said quietly.

Denton twitched his eyebrows. "Does this poignant snippet have a point, Mr. Beaumont?"

"*Yes!* I've never seen Bob so brokenhearted, not even when he lost his wife or his—" Chris shot a hard glare my way. "Or one of his twins. And now you're telling me his mom abused him, and because of that he turned into a monster that…that rapes and kills…" He threw up his hands. "Might as well say he grew up in a 'dysfunctional family'—*as if there's any other fucking kind!*—and that he wet the bed! All these nut jobs do that, right, soak the mattress when they're not-so little? This is so *stupid!* Just because someone is abused as a kid doesn't mean they'll grow up to be a fucking *serial killer!*"

"You omitted setting fires and torturing small animals coinciding with the enuresis, but I happen to concur with the remainder of your statement, Mr. Beaumont." Despite all that "concurring" I could see impatience with Chris smoldering: "The vast majority of maltreated children transition to adulthood with no violence transference, and I am eternally thankful for their rectitude; if that were not the case, I'd be busier than the mythical one-legged man competing in an ass kicking competition. And as far as Mr. Richards showing untold sorrow at his mother's passing, there are two possibilities: it was an act, or genuine grief. As for the latter, it's not uncommon for victims to place their abuser on a pedestal and then simply convey their vengeance to others, usually of the same gender or social grouping, but I digress." He studied Chris without blinking: "Despite the myriad points at which Mr. Richards intersects with the Traveler's profile, I take it you're still not convinced, Mr. Beaumont?"

"Your summation of the situation is apt, Mr. Denton."

Denton didn't rise to the bait, only nodded. Then he turned and looked searchingly at Angela for some reason. And then he shrugged and stood and buttoned his suit coat:

"Inform them, Chief."

That's when I saw something I'd never seen before, something that made me more than a little uneasy; open anger flashed across Chief Rogers' face as he stared hard at the FBI Senior Agent: "You agreed now wasn't the time."

"I've changed my mind." Denton glanced at his watch; he still spoke to Rogers as if the rest of us had jumped off the edge of the universe. "Inform them, or I will. Afterwords, if Mr. Beaumont still does not wish to cooperate, then we will proceed without his assistance. Either way, I no longer have the desire or the time to advocate my case; I have an arrest to coordinate. Agent Hawthorne, with me. Agent Walters, continue to watch Ross."

From above and behind me: "Yes, sir."

Then Denton strode away toward the glowing foosball room, leaving us staring after him in the Injun's dusty dimness.

Arrest?

So if he's arresting Bob, what's he need us for?

Mom recovered first. "What in Heaven is it now, Chief?"

He didn't respond, just looked uncomfortably back and forth between Chris and his sister.

Angela said, alarmed now, "What is it? What's wrong?"

Chief Rogers was a study; finally he sighed and spoke a simple date:

"November 16th, 1997."

"What are you saying?" Angela's voice rose to a harpy's screech. *"What are you saying!?"*

Chris stuttered, "W-hat…? *W-hat…?*"

Mom had closed her eyes again, but her lips were moving in her agonized face; praying.

I was the slow one this time.

November 16th, 1997? What did some day in November almost eighteen years ago have to do with—?

"Holy shit," I whispered. "The accident."

Rogers focused almost thankfully on me. "Yes. The wreck that took Angela and Chris's mom, and Zack and Zane's as well; we now believe that 'accident' was no accident."

Chris lurched to his feet, almost stepping into the jagged hole where the ball rack had been. I lunged and grabbed his elbow before he could, handcuffs clicking and ribs screaming, but he just stared at me dumbly before making a halfhearted attempt to pull away.

"Let go of me. That's not…that's not possible," he told Rogers as I guided him to safety. "It *was* an accident. They ran off the road and flipped the car and broke their necks and died, which I guess was lucky for them considering how the car burst into flame and nearly incinerated their bodies! HOW THE FUCK IS THAT NOT AN ACCIDENT!?"

Angela quivered, watching Chief Rogers with her soul in her face. I couldn't take that, so I focused on Chris again, but he was almost worse; it was like the years had sloughed away and we were still eleven and sitting on the floor in my room after school playing DOOM 64 when Mom and Dad appeared in my doorway with the strangest expressions…

Rogers said, "Sit down and let me explain what we've dug up the last few hours." Chris just stared at him, wall-eyed and pole-axed, breath whistling. "Please sit down, son. You need to hear this."

Chris nodded like he was sleepwalking, then glanced at my hand on his arm; he snarled and jerked it away and collapsed into his lane as I settled back in mine, the years between eleven and almost thirty crashing down between us again. *Next time I'll let you break your ankle, shithead.*

Angela pleaded, "Tell us what you mean, Chief. Why do you think the wreck that took our mother wasn't an accident?"

Rogers began to speak.

39

Donnie swam up from the darkness when he felt twin jolts of fire in his shoulders.

Ow! What the fuck?

He opened his eyes…or thought he did; the black remained, so he blinked, and sure enough, his eyelids moved. Momentary panic took him. *Did I go blind?* But then he saw two dim strips of light lying along his cheeks and realized, no, he hadn't gone blind:

Someone had blindfolded him.

He was sitting with his legs sprawled—judging by the cold, squishy feel under his ass, most likely outside, on the damn ground—and something tall, narrow, and rough pressed along his spine. Someone had his arms pulled behind him, wrenching them around the narrow and rough something; that someone trussed his wrists together with what felt like a thin rope or cord.

"Hey," Donnie rasped in protest; his throat was so dry it hurt to talk. He fought to get his arms free, but whoever was back there didn't like that; they let go of the rope and grabbed his forearms and *jerked* him backwards.

Donnie screamed as his right shoulder tore; then the back of his head slammed into whatever he was leaning against and he sobbed and went limp. Someone let go of his forearms and resumed binding his wrists. Panting and not daring to offer resistance again, Donnie tried to will the agony in his shoulder and skull to subside while taking stock as best he could.

He was outside on the ground, so whatever he was leaning against was probably a tree. He'd deduced that because he was a smart motherfucker, and because pine scent was strong all around him, and he could feel the jagged bark scraping against the inside of his reversed arms and pressing into his back. Plus, there was a goddamn root knob jabbing into his butt cheek, and his right leg was going all tingly and numb. Maybe he'd taken one too many Deep Purple hits and passed out over at Skeet's and those asshole bikers had decided he really was a narc. *Shit.* But then his momentary alarm subsided in confusion. *No, Skeet went to work, and then I couldn't get Mom to answer her phone, and I…*

The dark flower of memory opened reluctantly in Donnie's mind, and it all crashed home.

"Mom," he whispered. That psycho had killed his mom and Mrs. Holly. And not just *killed* them; he'd violated them in a fundamental way Donnie couldn't imagine doing to *anybody*, even those evil, stuck-up twats he'd suffered through high school with.

And then the freak had snuck up and clocked him on the head and was now tying him to a tree.

This is sooooo not good.

Dude jerked the knots tight over and over, then grunted as he stood and came around and stopped somewhere off to Donnie's left.

Then he just…stood there and breathed.

Donnie explored with his fingers; the knots securing his wrists felt about the size of golf balls, and his hands were already tingling. Heart thumping, he stilled his useless fingers and listened to the crazy fuck just stand there. Was he waiting for Donnie to say something? *Okay, fine, I can do that, no problem. My mouth gets me into trouble most of the time; maybe this time it can bail me out.*

So he began to talk. His intention had been to plead for his life; you know, please-please-please don't chop me up with an ax, Mr. Psycho Nut Job, or shove something up inside me like Mom, I'm sorry I didn't put Jack's boots back in the toolbox like you paid me shit loads of bucks to do; like that.

Those would have been the *smart* things to say.

So what pops out of his idiot cake hole?

"You killed my mom, you sick fuck!" Tears streamed from beneath the blindfold as the realization struck home. *She's gone. She's really, really gone.* "You fucking *tortured* her, man! Why did you do that? God, what's *wrong* with you?" His self-preservation instinct finally kicked in and he clamped his teeth together and trembled, waiting for he didn't want to imagine what, but dude just stood there, breathing.

Then the *way* dude was breathing permeated through Donnie's terror; loud and labored, as if the whack job had just completed a marathon. *Well, he did just haul my ass out here.* A sudden thought deepened his dread: *Where the fuck is "out here", anyway?* Donnie strained his ears past his captor's heavy breathing (and his own panicky gasps), but all he caught was a light breeze shifting the needles above him and water bubbling over rocks somewhere off to his right. Now that he was aware of it, he could *smell* that water; he was so thirsty, that wet and stony scent was a torment.

Focus, shithead; you've got bigger problems than dry-mouth. No people, or traffic, just wind sighing through the boughs and that goddamn water and dude still just…standing there, huffing and rasping and watching him.

So, so not good.

And then the whack job spoke:

"Because I enjoy it."

That voice was hollow, as if dude had a pot on his head or something; it was also slurred enough Donnie wondered if the freak had tossed back a few before hauling him out to the deep woods.

That gave him a surge of hope—maybe the sick fuck would pass out and Donnie could get free somehow—but then…

Because I enjoy it? Is that what he said?

"What the fuck does that mean?"

Footsteps, closer, closer; the labored breathing came with them. Donnie pressed back against the bark, but there was nowhere to go; another grunt, and the breathing changed elevation.

Dude had squatted in front of him.

"I'm answering your first question, Donnie," the slurring, pot-on-his-head voice said conversationally from an alarming arm-length away. "I believe it was, 'Why the fuck did you do that, man?', or close enough. You were referring to the fact I tortured and killed your mom. And the answer is, because I enjoy it."

The little spit remaining in Donnie's mouth evaporated. He sat perfectly still as fresh tears leaked from beneath the blindfold and trickled across his cheeks.

Silence and silence and silence and more tears and more heavy breathing; then:

"The answer to your second question, 'What the fuck is wrong with you?', is complicated. I suppose it depends on who you ask."

"Wh-wh-what d-do you m-mean?"

"What I *mean*, Donnie, is that the federal agents hunting me could probably answer at length—if you're prepared to be bored out of your mind by psychobabble, that is." The slurring, echoing voice drifted closer and dropped to a mushy whisper; a fresh note of chilling glee laced the mush: "You could also ask your mom—or any other whore I've made acquaintance with over the years—and you'd hear another kind of biased answer. That's assuming you can raise the dead, of course. But, since you asked *me*, I'll just say I re-alized a long time ago that limiting my actions because of societal mores-of-the-moment is no way for a true man to live. A *true* man takes what he wants when he wants it, by force or by wits, and if I am anything in this broken world, Donnie, it is a true man."

Donnie couldn't help himself. "You're a sick, psycho piece of rapist shit, that's what *you* are."

"Rapist? No, no, no, Donnie, *no*." He sounded offended! "I wear gloves through the entire…process…that my whores and I get to know each other, and no part of my body touches theirs, or theirs mine." Donnie listened in amazement and growing dread; dude actually sounded *disgusted!* "No, Donnie, you don't understand me or what I do—and I can promise you won't have time to learn."

Donnie quit breathing.

Don't like the sound of that.

Dude grunted yet again as he stood up, and then Donnie heard him stagger before he caught his balance. *Maybe he really is drunk.* But Donnie didn't believe it; that entire calm, creepy conversation had been conducted as if they were sitting in a booth at Pat's on a Saturday morning, enjoying coffee and the obligatory Pat's post-stack peach pie.

Something's wrong with him, yeah, but he sure ain't drunk.

"Look, man, I'm sorry I didn't put the boots back in the toolbox. I, uh…" *I didn't want to*, he almost said, but the truth wouldn't work here. "I didn't have a chance! We were busy prepping, and the cops showed before I could make an excuse to go out back. I didn't even have time to grab a smoke!" Freak show said nothing, just rasped. "You, uh, you can have your thirty grand back; I didn't spend any. It's all still in the bag. You can have the boots, too. Just cut me loose and I'll tell you where they are, no harm no foul."

"I've already taken back the money, Donnie." The slur was suddenly so pronounced he was barely understandable; the freak seemed to realize it too, because when he spoke again, he articulated each word: "It was earnest money, deposited in consideration of services not rendered. I've got the boots as well, though their usefulness has passed." Ominous pause; then, angry, "You didn't honor our agreement, Donnie. You didn't keep your *word*."

"Hey, man, okay, I get it, I should've kept my end of the deal. I'm sorry! Okay? I'm sorry…"

"Yes, you are." Rapid footfalls; Donnie tensed, and then a gloved hand grabbed him by the chin and slammed his head against the bark. Pain exploded, but he fought as best he could, kicking out and screaming, "No! No!" That soggy voice growled, "Hold still!", and then Donnie discovered it wasn't a blindfold over his eyes; it was duct tape. The freak ripped it away and unwound it from the back of his head, then stepped back. But Donnie *still* couldn't see shit because the darkness had been replaced by the light; a flashlight shone directly in his eyes.

Squinting, Donnie tipped his head back until his aching noggin thumped bark and drank in a slice of heaven hashed by needles, sangria fading to eggplant, streaked with wisps of orange and pink and a glowing, dissipating contrail; the Bighorns lumped, of course, those mountains he'd tried so hard to get away from, blocking out half of the early yet ancient stars twinkling high above all this bullshit.

He was so lost in that amazing sky he hadn't realized dude had mushed something else until a gloved hand seized his face again and yanked his head back down.

"I said *look* at me."

Donnie cried and squinted, but only caught a hulking red and black shadow.

"I can't *see*," he sobbed.

The light fell away to point at a rocky and needle-strewn slope off to Donnie's left.

"Look at me," the deep, echoing voice slurred.

Donnie looked.

A whack job wearing the top half of an Elvis chicken costume loomed above him, black-gloved hand gripping his face, crushing his cheeks into his molars. That fat red comb dangled across that feathered forehead; those round black hipster glasses perched on the end of that hooked red beak, with no eyes behind the glasses; somehow that was the worst part, the no-eyes.

Donnie dropped his own eyes away, but turns out he was wrong; the zippers on the black motorcycle jacket should have been gleaming in the LED beam, but they shone a dull red. *Dried blood,* Donnie realized. *Mom's blood. And Tiffany's. And Mrs. Holly's. Holy fucking shit.* And the smell! Donnie crinkled his nose in disgust and horror; he'd caught that same stinging reek just before he'd flung open Mrs. Holly's bedroom door.

It was the smell of death.

The Chicken Man let go and stepped away, and Donnie dropped his chin to his chest and squeezed his eyes shut; he didn't want to see or smell anything else. He cried as the nut job just stood there and watched and breathed and stank.

"A man should keep his word," he finally said; a deep, hollow rasp. "That lesson would have stood you in good stead, had you been destined for a long life."

Donnie sobbed louder.

And then the Chicken Man strode away, fat red comb flipping to the other side of his feathered head, long tail swaying. The light went with him.

Pure panic seized Donnie. *Where's he going? To get the ax?* Despite his burning shoulder, he strained and yanked at his unseen wrists, but they were tied tight back there. *God, please help me.* Donnie had never been a religious cat, but right then he was willing to give it a shot. *Please, God.* He watched the flashlight bob and recede through the needles. *Where the* fuck *is he going!?* He searched frantically around in the darkness for something to help him, anything, and that's when he noticed the small clearing opening out in front of him; his sneakers were right at the edge of it. Starlight illuminated several low lumps littering the slope about fifteen feet away. *Fucking rocks.* Fucking rocks wouldn't do him any good.

Please, please God help me. Please.

A car door *ca-chunked*, rusty hinge squalling.

Donnie stared toward that familiar sound with fresh outrage. "That's my fucking car! The asshole stole my *car*, too!" Now that was just too much. His dome light glowed through the needles about fifty feet away as a red and black shadow dug in his back seat. He caught sight of a dim yellow square above and beyond his car, and then another. There was a house or a cabin back there! The mountains soared above the low, rectangular structure, stony heads crowned by stars. *Who lives there?* A firefly of hope, then it flickered and died. *It has to be him. Jesus, I'm screwed.*

Hinges squalled again, and the dome light went out as his Honda's door banged shut. The flashlight's beam sparkled as it swung through the needles and bobbed his way.

Donnie slumped, chin on chest, and waited. Fresh tears cut down his cheeks and dripped onto the front of his soiled Crazy's tee-shirt.

The footsteps and the harsh breathing and the light came closer, closer, closer…but then sheared away and stopped. Donnie raised his head cautiously; that nightmare silhouette hulked in the middle of the little clearing, holding the flashlight with the beam pointed at those rocks…no, not rocks; dirt mounds, four of them. But why dude was looking at piles of dirt, Donnie didn't know. Then he glimpsed what the Chicken Man now held in his other gloved hand; not the ax, like he'd feared. Whatever it was, it was small, and flashed red and brown at the edges of the beam.

What the fuck is *that?*

The Chicken Man swung around and faced him then, but kept the beam on the mounds…and Donnie saw what was crawling all over those shin-high piles.

Ants.

Each was near a quarter-inch long, and most were red with a large black butt segment hanging behind. Solid black insects mixed in, like raisins on a creepy-crawly cake, but whatever color, they ignored the light shining on them while bustling in and out of the holes near the tops of their mounds on urgent and mysterious errands.

The Chicken Man slurred hollowly from the darkness above the beam:

"See those big stingers, Donnie? Well, you probably can't from over there, but they burn like fire, which is why they're called Red Imported Fire Ants. They've been spreading north from Florida and Texas for years." He took the beam off the crawling mounds and shined it around the clearing. "They like open spaces with water nearby, and if I was a betting man, I'd say this nest extends far enough underground to enjoy some geothermal warmth. Yellowstone isn't the only hot spot in this state, just the best known." He put the light back on the squirming mounds. "The USDA informs us that even though they've been spreading faster because of the drought, they're not in Wyoming yet, just down in Colorado and over in Utah and out in California. They've even got a shitty little map on their shitty little taxpayer-funded website that shows their supposed 'maximum range', and our state isn't in it. 'Winters are too cold', they say. But that's our government; manages to screw up even the small things."

The freak came toward him then, doing something with the red and brown thing he'd gotten from Donnie's back seat; a ripping sound, the flashlight beam wavering wildly in the branches overhead, and then the Chicken Man was standing over him and Donnie saw what the red and brown thing was:

An open package of hot dogs.

The Chicken Man bent carefully at the waist and held them a foot from Donnie's horrified eyes, turning them slowly; *wanting* him to look at them, to see. "They like hot dogs, Donnie," he slurred gently. Then a deep chuckle echoed behind the mask: "They like steak better, but who doesn't? You should see what they do to a big, juicy rib-eye, how fast they take it apart piece by tiny piece and cart it off to their houses over there and down those holes, and all to feed their bitch-queen; that greedy, egg-swollen cunt's lurking down there in the dark somewhere, and she's welcome to it. But I won't waste a steak on a piece of lying trash who can't keep his word."

The flashlight lifted and then cracked down on Donnie's head. Pain exploded in his skull, sparkles swam across his vision…and then he was tasting and smelling hot dog. He coughed and spit, but the freak kept smashing a glove-full of squished hot dog in his face, rubbing and smearing. Donnie shouted and cussed and kicked, but the Chicken Man only dropped the mangled remains in Donnie's lap and moved around the tree and lathered fresh-smashed dog onto Donnie's arms and hands.

"I've learned my lesson! I'll keep my word! PLEASE!" He continued to scream and plead as the Chicken Man came back around the tree and stood there, looking at him and listening to him beg. After a minute he grabbed Donnie by the waist of his shorts and heaved, popping the button and ripping open the zipper, lifting Donnie while stuffing the remaining links into his underwear.

Donnie quit screaming when he hit the root knob with an "Oof!" He stared wide-eyed at the pink mass covering his crotch.

"No," he whispered.

The Chicken Man moved back toward the mounds. "Did I mention how aggressive these little bastards are, Donnie? They don't enjoy being fucked with. Kind of like me."

He bent at the waist again and with another grunt picked something up, a long, thick pine branch it looked like, and then he bounded forward and jabbed and whacked, destroying the mounds in seconds. A red tide boiled up, some insects racing along the stick. The Chicken Man banged it on the forest floor, then backed quickly toward Donnie while whacking the branch on the ground again and again.

"No," Donnie whispered.

"Fast little cunts," the killer in the costume slurred, flashlight beam bobbing wildly as he continued to smack the ground, still backing up. That red tide followed, flowing across the rocks and the dead and dried yellow needles, visible in the wild flashes of light.

"NO!" Donnie kicked and thrashed uselessly. "PLEASE, NOT THIS!"

The killer stepped backward across his flailing legs, still smacking at that tide with the branch, and Donnie tried to trip him, but he avoided it, stumbling and dropping the stick.

"Almost got me there, Donnie," he panted. "But that was your last move. Game over."

"OH MY GOD, PLEEEEEEEASE!"

"You should have kept your word."

The Chicken Man walked away, taking the flashlight and leaving Donnie in the dark.

But he wasn't alone.

A second later, the first ant found him.

40

Hawthorne and Walters gave me a lift to the Indian Head Police Station; nice of them, I suppose…not that any of us had much fucking choice in the matter.

Hawthorne drove, of course, and Angela and I took the second-row buckets; Walters once again parked his smug, shark-grinning ass on the third-row bench directly behind me—also of course. Mom sat next to him, dividing her worried frowns between the back of Angela's bowed head and the side of my face. Chief Rogers had pulled rank and snagged shotgun. Of course.

Working out the details for tomorrow's big show had taken until well after sunset, so outside the Suburban a starlit Wyoming sky framed slab-sided peaks, furrowed slopes glimmering in the moonlight; unfortunately, the long SUV had tinted windows, so the view was a muted glory compared to what it could have been had I been slated for a lesser G-ride—but hey, I was the famous feathered killer, so only the best to haul my celebrity kiester around. Damn skippy.

Lessened or not, it was a peaceful scene. The inside of the Suburban was quiet as well; however, if you were to mistake that calm for peace you'd be a moron with your head so far up your ass you could check yourself for tonsillitis.

I side-eyed Angela, not daring to turn my head, but her position hadn't changed; arms crossed, she hunched over her baggy purse, which she'd propped on her knees. Her face was stony despite the tears glimmering on her cheeks, and she glared without blinking through the back of Rogers' seat.

It hadn't only been the revelation about her mom that had put her in this state; Denton and Rogers had deigned to share their plan. The essence of the thing was simple, although its execution may not be as straightforward:

We're setting a trap for a killer.

I'm the big hunk o' cheese in that trap—not that I'd had much choice; Sheriff Neal's hospitality I can do without. Mom and Angela hadn't liked it, though, not one itty-bitty bit, and they'd liked it even less when they'd learned they would be hustled out of town and hidden somewhere so the Traveler didn't shove things up inside them until they stopped twitching and screaming; both wanted to be bait too, though it turned out each thought the other should be taken to safety. *That* had caused some tense moments, and the first of two female-only whispered conferences up by the Injun's empty trophy case. But they had come back arm-in-arm and announced that they were fine with being sequestered—as long as their conditions were met, first.

After that, things got ugly fast.

The women had only gotten their way with two of their demands—which, out of the multitudes they had made, was a piss-poor percentage. Their first victory had been the right to attend tomorrow's press conference, where I will be exonerated of the Chicken Man murders and released from custody in front of the entire world before Denton announces the arrest of Zane Richards, ostensibly for suspicion of those same murders. Mom and Angela absolutely *refused* to miss that.

Have to admit, I'm kinda looking forward to it as well.

The second win was Angela keeping her car. Denton wasn't going to allow it, then realized that since he'd already agreed the ladies could come to the show tomorrow, with everything else going on he couldn't spare the time or the manpower to fetch them in the morning and then drive them back; long story short, Angela got to keep her car. The rest, though, both small and large, the women had struck out on.

Angela hadn't been pleased with me bunking in the Indian Head PD drunk tank, either, but she hadn't thrown *nearly* as big a fit as Mom had; no, Angela had saved *her* fit to protest other injustices she felt needed redressing—like the fact they wouldn't let her confront the retired Wyoming Highway Patrol investigator currently dying of cancer in a hospice down in Sheridan; the man who'd confessed at his railed bedside that afternoon to being paid to falsify the report on the "accident" that had taken away her mother…

And protest it well, she had.

Wow.

I peeked at her out of the corner of my eye again; I hadn't known the human body could produce such sounds; even Chief Rogers had been taken aback by her raging screams. I had tried to restrain her, afraid she would attack Special Agent Denton with her small fists and bring an all-too-willing Hawthorne and Walters down on her, but she'd shoved me away with surprising strength. Only Mom could contain her, and pretty soon the second ladies-only conference ensued up near the Injun's barren trophy case, with much finger shaking and arguing back and forth to start, and then a bunch of hugging and crying on each other's shoulders; they were up there a long time, too, nearly thirty minutes. Whatever got said seemed to have calmed Angela, though; somewhat, anyway, enough that she stalked over to where I still sat at the end of Lane 14 like a one-eyed, handcuffed lump and kissed me and apologized for shoving me, asking how my ribs felt and had she hurt them? I lied and said no, she hadn't, and that they felt right as Saturday night.

Hours later, I continued to wonder at the sea-change that second confab had wrought in her; she was still spitting furious, that was obvious to everybody, but she was now also clear-eyed, and seemed very determined about something. Mom, on the other hand, had seemed sad, still did, and after giving Angela first crack, she hugged me a long time and told me, "No matter what happens, Jackie, I'll always love you."

"Okay, Mom," I'd replied, mystified, hugging her back as best I could with the cuffs. "Love you, too."

Headlights suddenly filled the Suburban.

Behind me, Walters announced, "Vultures're back."

Hawthorne replied, "I see 'em."

"Got three bogeys." More headlights flashed from a side street. "Make that four."

"I see 'em."

Walters groused, "Good thing. Thought you'd lost the useless pricks."

I had, too. We'd barreled out from the Injun's back lot and sped away before the crews set up at Pat's could react, although they'd belatedly given chase. The 'Burb's big-block V-8 had left their lumbering vans in its Detroit dust, though—which, while amusing, was bad for the "plan", because the freshly nailed-on first part of the "plan" was to draw the vultures away from the Injun so they wouldn't see the geeky fed leave in Angela's Camry. The crime scene tech would meet up with them later, after I had been secured in the clink, and then Walters and Hawthorne would escort my ladies to an undisclosed location—undisclosed to *me*, not them, which really chapped my ass. I'd argued that I, too, should know where Mom and Angela would be, but nobody, not even Rogers, had taken my side. "Need to know", they'd said, and evidently I didn't.

Hawthorne told Walters, "Easy, partner, we're almost there. We'll dump the package and the vultures'll circle it. They won't be our problem 'till tomorrow."

The 'package'. Great.

If I was the cheese, then Hawthorne and Walters and their SWAT buddies were the jaws that would snap on the psycho, ax-wielding rat—preferably before said cheese done got chopped up. The other four members of the team (I haven't had the pleasure, but I'm sure they're just as charming as Hawthorne and Walters) were currently surveilling Bob's lakeside estate (just in case), as well as tailing Zane. Hawthorn and Walters, along with Denton, would be the leads in Zane's takedown at his condo in the early hours tomorrow morning.

And would I have liked to be a fly on the wall for *that?*

Oooooh, you betcha.

So if I'm the cheese, and the SWAT assholes are the jaws, then I guess you could call Zane the insurance policy.

Can't say I was real surprised when Chief Rogers unfolded a government-issue laptop and pressed play and I sat there at the end of Lane 14 in the dusty and decrepit Injun and watched grainy black-and-white security footage of Zane parking his gleaming new truck in my gravel in the dead of Monday night and getting out and looking around furtively before spraying two vile slanders on the side of Crazy's. But I was sure as fuck angry about it, the amazing job Angela did to turn those hateful words into attractive advertisements notwithstanding. Darryl Wright had come through in spades while I'd been in Neil's puke-green pokey. He'd also had the good sense not to call Neil or the feds, but Chief Rogers—who had then taken it straight to the feds, but nobody's perfect.

Denton and Rogers' scheme is to use the indisputable evidence of Zane's petty soul as an excuse to arrest him—or more to the point, *announce* his arrest; coming on the heels of my exoneration, it should seem as if Zane is implicated in the Chicken Man murders, thus pissing Bob off even more and ensuring that he and his ax stick around for the festivities. They'll have forty-eight hours to charge Zane with something (which they won't do, even though I asked Denton straight out if that spoiled, date-raping cocksucker would pay for defiling my place of business, but the Senior Special Agent only told me in a voice even drier than usual to take the matter up with Sheriff Neil) before they have to release him, and in that forty-eight-hour window they hope to catch a by-then totally outraged Bob Jr. when he comes choppin' for li'l ol' free me.

That's their grand plan in a nutshell: keep the Traveler in a known location and pointed at a known target (me), and then catch him when he goes for it (me), because if it doesn't work, and Bob instead goes to ground somewhere (and since we're talking about a guy known as the Traveler, then who the fuck could even guess where *that* would be?), then the backup plan is to issue a BOLO and an APB and stick his mug on the Ten Most Wanted and tell the press and thus the world who the mad bastard in the giant chicken suit is.

That would no doubt work, eventually. In the meantime, though, how many women would die horrible, screaming deaths? This way the potential carnage is limited to a small geographical area, not to mention the target (me), and possibly the two most important people in my life…but sometimes sacrifices must be made for the greater good.

Or so preachith Chief Rogers and Special Agent Denton of the FBI.

Fuck me.

There's also a reporter from the Casper Star-Tribune in the mix, just to add spice. Chief Rogers evidently used him to unearth info on Bob when he'd first suspected Bob was the psycho in the feathery suit. That worthy scribbler had popped into the Injun like he owned the place while we were still hammering out the details for tomorrow's show, and he's apparently in the know about the true hunt for the Chicken Man as well as Bob's suspected role (although I wasn't clear on whether said worthy hack had been informed of the whole Traveler nightmare…but even without that, Denton's not happy about his involvement, not at all); so the forty-eight-hour window holds true for more than just charging that fuckhead Zane. It's for the hack too, because after a personal request and a grudging (extremely grudging) quid pro quo by Special Agent Denton for a sit-down interview for the forthcoming, behind-the-scenes piece, the reporter acquiesced to holding off submitting his Pulitzer-worthy (or so he hopes) story to his editor until Sunday night. Which means Denton has until then—roughly forty-eight hours—to capture the Traveler before all hell breaks loose.

All in all, it's shaping up to be an interesting weekend.

I braced myself as we whipped the wrong way around Indian Head's downtown square, tires squealing, and then Hawthorn glanced at Chief Rogers, where he sat calmly watching every traffic law on his town's books get pissed on.

"Agent Walters and I have to escort the women to safety, Chief, and pronto, so how 'bout it? You gonna tame the Fourth Estate for us?"

Rogers smiled wryly. "Special Agent Denton 'suggested' several statements for me to make on the off chance a microphone should be shoved under my nose."

"I bet he did." We flew off the square onto A Street, not bothering with piddling things like stop signs or turn signals; must be nice to be a fed.

Angela hadn't acknowledged any of this byplay, still hunched over her purse with that determined and fiery glare into middle-space, but she straightened and dashed her fingers across her cheeks and reached for my hand when we caromed into the IHPD parking lot and burled up to the front doors.

Hawthorn barked, "Everybody out!" as I squeezed Angela's hand gently and smiled. Her return squeeze was weak, and her answering smile was tremulous; I could see how much the effort cost her, but that only made it more precious.

Walters was already out; he yanked my door open. "C'mon, tough guy, you can play kissy face later—if you live long enough."

Angela clasped my hand tighter and clutched her purse strap in the other as Walters dragged us out; she glared hot hell, and for a second I thought she might brain him with her purse, but sadly she didn't. Behind us, tires squealed and reporters and camera guys piled out and bright-whites flooded the red-brick station:

"Jack!"

"Jack, why did you kill those kids?"

"Jack! Would you like to address your victims' families?"

Chief Rogers had climbed out the other side and was saying something about how I was to be housed here instead of Sheridan County because of security concerns (which was pretty much the fucking truth), and then we hustled inside, Mom following Angela with Hawthorne slipping in on her heels. He threw the bolt just as the hot light mounted on a shoulder camera speared through the blinds, throwing everything into stark, striped relief; Hawthorn sprang into action, bounding about and twisting the horizontal slats closed.

"Holy moley," said a voice behind us, and we turned to see Officer Tommy Toms standing behind the blue reception counter with his jaw on his chest and the brim of his frayed straw cowboy hat curled up on the sides; he eyed Angela and me holding hands, and way more than a touch of jealousy shadowed his face.

"Jack," he said. "Angie."

"Tommy," I replied, just like we were standing in line down at the Get 'n Go.

Angela said, "Hi, Tommy." Her cheeks held a slight flush.

Tommy had been after her since middle school, and when I'd heard he'd cranked up his pursuit again after she'd moved back from Chicago, I remember thinking he *still* didn't have a Crazy's Root Beer Float's chance in hell…but noting that redness, and the way she was suddenly shy about meeting my eyes, I wondered if he'd finally caught her.

Suddenly Tommy wasn't the only jealous one in the room.

None of your bucking fizness, my brain informed my idiot heart. *And you've got bigger things to worry about, Jackie boy, like staying un-chopped-up for the next forty-eight hours.*

Agent Walters gave me no more time to brood. "Officer Toms!" he snapped. "Lead us to your holding cell!" He held out his hand. "Better yet, give me those keys and point the way. Wouldn't want you to miss an important call."

Tommy snatched a jangling ring from his duty belt. "This way," he growled, stalking out from behind the blue counter and leading us down a beige cinder-block hallway, back stiff and curled cowboy hat riding high; the crown of that hat was about level with Walters' suited shoulder. Tommy isn't the sharpest tool, but he has his pride.

We passed the open door of Chief Rogers' small, cluttered office on the right, then made a left down a longer industrial cinder-block hall. Tommy unlocked a heavy steel door at the end and led us through. Walters grunted. Hawthorne whistled sarcastically. The IHPD drunk tank was a throwback to the days of floor-to-ceiling bars, with two walls of open bars and the other two comprising more beige cinder block. Two low, scarred wooden benches sat against those solid walls, with a lidless and rust-streaked steel toilet set into the corner between them. Very chic.

We bunched in the narrow gap between the bars and the cinder blocks, watching Tommy fumble with the ring before he opened the lock with a clank and swung the barred door wide. Walters pushed me inside, Angela letting go at the last instant as the door clanged between us. Tommy locked it, rattled the bars to make sure I wasn't going anywhere, then stepped back.

Hawthorne smiled around at the bare cell, then winked. "Sleep tight, tough guy." He headed for the open steel door and the industrial hallway beyond. Walters smirked me his best smirk, then followed. Angela and Mom stood on the other side of the bars and frowned worriedly in at me while Tommy pouted at Angela.

I wondered what the two women in my life saw; my chest felt tight, so I slowed and deepened my breathing and tried to smile reassuringly; antiquated or not, the IHPD tank is yet another concrete-and-steel box more than up to keeping my narrow ass caged until someone bothers to let me the fuck out again. It's only until the press conference tomorrow morning, true, but that's still eleven or so endless hours in the future. Eyeing Angela, I wondered if Tommy would let me enjoy a conjugal visit to whittle a few of those hours away.

Probably not. Might be fun to ask, though.

Tommy jangled keys, drawing all eyes. "All right, he's in there, let's go." He waved the ring, making as if to herd the women out. That elicited two dangerous scowls, but no movement. Then Mom stepped past him as if he didn't exist and reached for me. I held her awkwardly because of the bars, and because of the stupid handcuffs I would never be rid of. She sobbed into my chest while Angela silently cried with her. Tommy stood there uncomfortably. Finally, Mom pulled back and dabbed her face with her shirt hem.

"Be careful the next two days. Hear me, son? You be *careful*." Her sudden scowl was impressive. "I wish that Denton would have let you carry a gun."

"They weren't going for that, Mom, and you knew it."

She sniffed at me. "I did," she admitted, "but you get nothing in this world without asking, working, or fighting for it. I thought I taught you that."

"They were still never going to allow it. Besides, I'll have the SWAT team shadowing me. No man can ask for better protection." *I hope.*

Angela cleared her throat. We looked at her, and then we all looked at Tommy, who was staring at us in bewilderment. *Need to know.* I had a sudden hunch that, like me, Officer Toms hadn't been deemed worthy of being clued into every detail of Denton and Rogers' plan.

Mom eyed Tommy sideways. "Yes, well, look out for yourself anyway, son. I know you know how."

"Yes ma'am, I do. And I will."

"You better." Mom pulled my face down between the bars for a kiss, then dug some tissue from her tote and fixed her face as Angela twined her fingers into mine and buried her face in my chest between those same bars; she sobbed, trembling.

Tommy didn't like that. He stepped close, waving that ring again like a talisman—an impotent one. "Here, now! That's enough of—"

Mom replaced the tissue and smoothly took his elbow and guided him toward the open steel door: "How's your dad? I saw your mom down at the bank last Tuesday but didn't get a chance to gab with her. He still laid up with that broke foot?"

Tommy kept his possessive frown on us, but let Mom herd him. "Uh, yes ma'am, but he's gettin' 'round better. Doc Swanson sez—" He planted his cowboy boots as she tried to lead him into the hall. "Hey, she can't be back here alone with a prisoner! It's against regulations!"

Mom's fists flew to her hips. "Now, Tommy, those two have some things to work out, and they need a few minutes alone to do it."

"Well, they'll just have to *work them out* somewhere else. She can't—"

"How's that Becky Cummings? You two still hot and heavy?"

Tommy glanced guiltily at Angela before facing Mom. "We're not 'hot and heavy', Mrs. Ross. We're just friends, nothing serious."

"I saw you two snuggled in that booth in Pat's last weekend. Looked like 'friends' got left in the dust a long stretch back."

Tommy's face turned bright red beneath the straw hat. "Uh, well—"

Mom took his elbow again and tipped us a wink before leading him away between the cinder blocks. "You said your dad was getting around better? Shame that mare stepped on him. Must drive poor Susan crazy having him underfoot all the time. I'd know a little something about *that*, yes indeed I would."

Tommy's response was indistinct as they turned the corner down by Rogers' office.

Angela said, "She's something, isn't she?"

"Yes," I said. "Yes, she is." Then I arched the eyebrow that didn't hurt. "*Tommy?* Really?"

She gave me a guarded look from beneath those eyelashes. "It was way back in April, Jack, old news." I just stared, and she sighed with more than a tinge of exasperation. "What? He's good looking, he was available, and, well, I was lonely. It only happened once, anyway. I wouldn't see him again."

"Only once?"

Now her look said I was striding into dangerous territory. "Yes. I can handle dumb, and I can deal with a small penis, but both are a deal breaker." She freed one hand to poke me in the chest, carefully avoiding my right side. "At least he wasn't *married*."

She had me there. "True," I said. Then I started laughing, wincing as my ribs protested, but I couldn't seem to stop. Angela smiled weakly, but didn't join in.

"Poor Tommy."

"Poor Tommy," she agreed, then suddenly pressed her face between the bars again; my shirt started getting wetter. "Why didn't he *say* anything, Jack? He suspected all that time, and he never *said* anything! How could he cut us out like that?"

We sure weren't talking about Tommy anymore.

The bomb about Angela and Chris's mom had only been the first salvo. This MAJ. Dale Frisbee, WHP Ret., the investigator who had handled (or mishandled) the inquiry, had revealed Rogers wasn't the first person to come grill him about the "accident" that had taken Mrs. Beaumont and Mrs. Richards; he was just the first in about a decade. Turns out Angela's dad had kept after Frisbee for years until he finally gave up, although Frisbee told Rogers he wasn't sure the man had truly dropped it; Mr. Beaumont had just stopped pestering Frisbee.

That nugget had been a game changer, to say the least. I think even Angela harbored doubts until then, and Chris had been downright skeptical and not bothering to hide it; but when they'd heard their dad had been suspicious all along…hoo boy. It had finally brought a shell-shocked Chris over to Team Jack, but what upset Angela the most was that her dad had never shared his suspicions with his children.

Angela lifted her tear-streaked face to mine: "Chris and I always wondered why they were way out on Stagecoach Road that day when they were supposed to be Christmas shopping down in Sheridan, but now that I think about it, Dad never *once* offered an opinion when we brought it up, just got this tight look. Which means he suspected it wasn't an accident *right from the beginning!*"

"I'm sure he did," I said. "Your dad was one sharp cookie." Rogers and Denton thought Bob had killed his wife because she'd uncovered his shadow life as the Traveler; or maybe she'd only suspected; or maybe he'd just *suspected* she'd suspected. Whatever the case, with a man like Bob, the result had been the same. And obviously (or so shadow Bob would've thought), Mrs. Richards would share her horrific suspicions and/or discovery with her best friend, so Chris and Angela's mom had to be silenced, too.

"He should have told us, Jack! She was *our* mom!"

"You guys were just kids. He probably thought you had enough to deal with."

She shoved away from me and stepped back from the bars. I think she knew I was right, though, which is likely why she changed the subject:

"They should arrest that son of a bitch! Frisbee!"

"He's got three months to live, and that's if he's lucky." That got me another step away and an impressive blue glare for my trouble.

According to Rogers, Frisbee had been stuck in a financial crack eighteen years ago, what with three academically mediocre teenage daughters and little savings that hadn't been leveraged. So when someone contacted him anonymously with the offer of several extremely large cash payments for a creative writing assignment… yeah.

And the hard truth was, whatever he did or didn't write on a standard form wouldn't bring back the wives and mothers of the untimely bereaved. So Frisbee watched his daughters go to state colleges and graduate and get married and produce children and make him a happy, doting grandfather…but what he'd done lurked in the back of his mind, tainting all his good fortune. And when his wife of forty-three years died of the Big C four years ago, he'd thought of confessing, but wasn't sure anyone cared anymore. Then, last year, when the Big and Undiscriminating C knocked on his door, he'd resolved to tell someone, but then had second thoughts about leaving such a terrible last impression for his daughters and grandchildren.

Thus matters stood…until Chief Rogers popped up at his hospice bedside early this afternoon, asking pointed questions.

"He spilled it all after the third one," Rogers had confided to us in a low voice. "Easiest interrogation I've ever been a part of. I think it was eating at him worse than the cancer." That had brought no comfort to Chris and Angela, however. Matter of fact, I think that's about when the shrieking started.

It *still* hadn't garnered any sympathy for Frisbee in Angela's eyes; she spat: "I don't fucking care! They should arrest him anyway! *MY MOM WAS MURDERED AND HE COVERED IT UP!*"

Well, that was the end of our alone time. The whole gang trooped through the doorway, a satisfied Tommy leading a worried-looking Mom followed by smug Walters and leering Hawthorne; if he stared at Angela's ass any harder, it would catch fire. They were followed by calm-as-usual Chief Rogers, though by this point he looked as worn out as I felt.

Mom held a weeping Angela as Rogers coolly berated a stammering Tommy about leaving her back here with me while the two FBI Agents stood there staring in at me like wolves stare at a penned lamb—a lamb that had been fattened just for them.

The next forty-eight hours are going to be *so* much fun.

Things calmed after a minute, and Hawthorne was updating Rogers about the impending early morning sham arrest of Zane and leading the women in my life away when Angela suddenly turned and threw herself against the bars and clutched me almost desperately:

"I'll see you in the morning," she whispered. "I love you."

Then she was gone, and I stood there in my new cage with a stupid grin on my face as a huffy Tommy slammed the steel door and locked it with a clanking vengeance.

"I love you too," I said.

Ron shot the bolt and twisted the wand just enough to watch the two SWAT agents hustle the women into the Suburban. Reporters doing stand-ups scrambled clear as the black SUV powered away from the doors, swerving around the media trucks and out of the lot. A quick-reacting crew hopped in their satellite truck and gave chase only to slam on their brakes as another black Suburban with its headlights dark suddenly barreled down A Street and swung in front of the exit, effectively blocking anyone from following unless they drove over the sidewalk and curb.

After shouting at the unresponsive Suburban and a few meaningful hand gestures, that's just what the quick crew started to do, but then the blocking Suburban peeled away and flicked its lights on and raced after the first; Denton would run interference for Hawthorne and Walters when needed, giving them time and opportunity to get the women away. Two sets of ruby brake lights flared before the long SUVs veered off of W. A Street and vanished.

Ron shut the blinds on the frustrated media, then yawned and cracked his neck side-to-side; he was so tired he could hardly see straight, but this long day was far from over.

He went past his office and took a right into the supply room and opened the wall-mounted gun locker with his key and considered his options, then removed three Mossberg Tactical 12-gauge pistol-grip pump shotguns and a box of 00 Buck; they didn't have any tac ammo, so double-aught would have to do. Ron secured the locker and grabbed all both of the Indian Head Police Department's bullet-resistant vests from where they rested on a shelf, blew the dust off the top one, and carried everything up front.

Tommy was slumped in Mindy's chair, scowling at Jack in one of the three bulky black-and-white monitors built into the counter; the left-hand feed monitored the tank and the hall leading to it, and the other split-screens covered the station's doors, front and back, inside and out.

"Here."

Tommy's big eyes got bigger as he hesitantly took his vest and the Mossberg. Ron placed the shells next to Mindy's Dilbert mug and loaded his own shotgun and the spare. Tommy slowly followed suit; Ron could almost see the rust flakes falling out of his ears as the gears ground.

"So what's really going on here, Chief?"

Ron told the bare minimum; need to know. He laid the extra tac-gun and vest on the counter: "Bring Fleming in; these are his. Use your cell. We're still 10-21 until I say otherwise. When Ryan gets here, someone take the front door and the other the back; I don't care who's where as long as everyone stays alert. I'll call Pearce and Mosley in. If something comes up tonight, we'll send them out and keep Jack safe with just us three. And fire up some coffee, we'll need it."

"Um, don't *you* need a vest?"

"Need and have seem to be two different things at the moment. But don't worry, I don't plan on getting shot."

Back in his office, Ron used his own cell to roust his reserve officers, picturing (and in Amy Mosley's case, hearing) their wives' dismay as he issued marching orders just before bedtime on a Friday night.

On the way to the tank, Ron detoured to the break room and grabbed two metal folding chairs, then unlocked the holding area.

Jack lifted his battered face from the tank's floor; he still had his chest on the concrete and his legs spread at a torturous angle; that eye would go down by morning, somewhat anyway, but he would still sport quite the impressive shiner for the cameras tomorrow.

Jack took in the tactical shotgun with what Ron thought was appreciation, and then the folding chairs with what looked like speculation:

"Chief," he finally offered, guarded.

"Jack."

Ron set the tac-gun's butt plate on the floor, leaned the barrel against the cinder blocks, and propped the heavy door open with one unfolded chair. He straightened, still holding the other chair, but didn't approach the bars; Jack was innocent, but that didn't make him any less dangerous. Ron had seen how quick he was when he'd broken Dorsey's fingers. "Enjoying our luxury accom-modations?"

"Would it do any good to complain?"

"No."

"Well, it's better than Neil's shithole."

Jack sat up and folded his legs in, then kicked out, rolling smoothly to both feet without using his hands to push up from the floor; before Ron could even blink, the young man was standing calmly in the middle of the cell; he did wince and touch the floating ribs on his right side, though.

Oh, to be young again. "I could call Dr. Swanson, have him swing by and look at those."

"Nah. Denton's right, I'll live." He came to the bars and grasped them, handcuffs rattling. "I'm worried about Angela and Mom, though. Are you *sure* they'll be all right by themselves? I wish you'd tell me where they're staying."

"I still can't. And you still know why."

"And I still don't like it," Jack groused. "And I *really* don't like them being left alone 'till Sunday."

"Nobody does, but that's the way it has to be until reinforcements arrive."

"I guess."

Special Agent Denton now had a problem; with all the suspect Sheridan County jailers cooperating and demanding federal protection for their families, he was spread thin—or as Mary Ross put it, he had too much bread and not enough butter. Denton knew it too, and to his credit he'd stayed on the horn with D.C. until they'd sent him a dozen more bodies, along with a DEA K-9 team split away from an alphabet gang-bang just wrapping up a human trafficking and drug-ring operation in Phoenix.

Ron had also noted how Denton's pinched face drew even tighter after that call; apparently, his superiors believed he should've handled the situation with the resources at hand. Calling home for backup was a mark against him, and to a man like Denton, that consideration was everything.

"Don't worry," he offered. "Your mom will watch out for Angela." *And keep her in line*, Ron thought, but sure didn't add out loud.

Jack must've caught the undertone, though, because he flashed a wide grin: "Got a temper, don't she?"

Temper? That girl was hiding a live volcano under her beauty-queen pelt, although she had to be cut some slack because of the news she'd absorbed; still, Jack was in for a coaster ride with that one. Ron eyed that grin—it was almost proud—and refrained from offering a warning. *I'm too old to fall into that trap.* "Tired of those restraints yet?"

Jack wordlessly thrust his arms between the bars. Ron leaned the second chair next to the Mossberg, then pulled his key and held it up, but still didn't approach, not yet: "Will you behave yourself? If not, I can just leave those on. Won't hurt my feelings."

Jack looked pained: "C'mon, Chief, don't be like that. I'm a free man tomorrow, or close enough. Why would I screw that up?"

"Don't really know, son. Still don't understand why you'd make a boneheaded move like breaking Dorsey's fingers, but I sure know you did."

"I'll be a good boy from now on. Promise."

Ron grunted wryly. "Hold still."

Jack nodded his thanks and pulled his arms back, then massaged his wrists as he walked to the far bench and sat. Ron secured Walter's cuffs and unfolded his chair where he could see down the hall to his open office door, then almost fell into the thing; Lord, he was tired.

He looked up and found Jack watching him expectantly.

"Denton is a damn fool," Ron began.

42

Jack looked like he wanted to laugh, at first; then his bruised features stilled as he thought about it: "A pompous ass, sure…" he finally granted, "but a fool? The guy's pretty high up the FBI food chain, and they don't make a habit of promoting fools…at least I'd *hope* not."

"You'd be surprised." Ron stretched forward to ease the shooting pain in his lower back, then rested his elbows on his knees. "Remember what Denton said about the Traveler? The profile, specifically?"

"Sure, I guess."

"Tell me."

"Uh, white male, late fifties or early sixties by now; smart, and possibly highly educated, but no way to know that last for sure; physically powerful, and probably OCD about taking care of himself; rich as King Midas, with a job that gives him an excuse to hunt women across the lower forty-eight without arousing suspicion. Let's see…oh yeah, Mommy was a meanie ho. How'm I doin'?"

"Good enough. Now I'll rattle off another profile, and I want you to compare them. Ready?"

"Shoot."

"White male, twenty to forty years-of-age, menial or working-class job and existence; prior history of sexual crimes; most likely incarcerated during stretches of his life."

"Well," Jack said, frowning, "except for the 'white male', nothing syncs." He frowned harder, now directing it out between the bars at Ron. "And except for the sex crimes, you just described me, Chief—although I take exception to the 'menial' bit. I'm a 'working-class existence' kind of guy, goddamnit, and proud of it."

"Forget that," Ron told him, "and focus on all the ways the Traveler's profile differs from the profile I just gave you."

"I don't understa—"

"Because *the profile I just gave you*," Ron said, "matches ninety-nine percent of serial sex murderers ever caught."

"So Bob's in the 'One Percent'. We knew that already."

"It's less than one percent. I'm talking top-of-the-food-chain, to steal your figure of speech."

"What are you saying, Chief?"

"Remember when Denton touched on how the Traveler operates? The deliberate no-patterns with victims as well as disposal sites? The careful prep of the bodies to remove all evidence? How the BAU believes he's been studying them for decades, even keeping up with forensic advancements?"

"Sure, but—"

"Now compare the Traveler to, say, Angry Joe Schmo from Kokomo, who just got kicked after doing a solid fifteen for diddling a couple of little girls."

Jack made a face. "If I have to."

"Angry Joe's out in the world again, but the world doesn't want him; he can't find a job that's worth a shit because of his sheet, and everywhere he moves they put up notices, so the neighbors don't want him either, and watch him like hawks. So Joe's free, yes, but he's still angry, and now he's frustrated. But prison toughened him up, so he guts it out and lands a decent job and finds a fringe community that will accept him—or at least tolerate him. But Joe's *still* angry because he's going nowhere fast—the mean ol' world won't let him, or so he tells himself...and he's still got the taste."

"The taste for little girls?"

"Yes. And Joe sees them everywhere, Jack. *Everywhere*. No grown woman will have anything to do with him, not after finding out about his past, but let's say maybe he gets lucky and lands a steady… but then she leaves after she finds out—or just because she's tired of his bullshit." Ron shrugged. "Or maybe he lost his temper and punched out his asshole boss; he's still Angry Joe, remember. Whatever happened, it's a trigger—what Denton would term a 'stressor'—and Joe snaps."

"He wants a gun, but can't buy one because of his record, so he gets a serrated hunting knife from the outdoor store and some gloves and a ski mask. Then he spots some sweet blonde eight-year-old and her mom at the market a few days later and follows them home, maybe even cases the place once or twice to see if they have an alarm and to figure out which side of the house her bedroom's on. Then one night—"

Jack held his hands out, pleading: "I get it, I get it, he kills her. Jeez. I don't need every—"

"He rapes her and he kills her, yes. Maybe he snatches her and takes her somewhere he feels comfortable, a nest he's prepared, say. Or maybe he didn't think that far ahead and just does her right there on the pink My Little Pony comforter with the stuffed animals scattered all over; maybe he even kills her parents when her screams bring them rushing in."

"Chief, please, for God's sake—"

"Joe didn't *plan* on killing anybody—he's never done it before—but the frustration and the rage got the better of him and things just…spiraled. Who knows? But now she or they are dead and he thinks he's screwed…but the pigs don't show up with their blues strobing across his crappy yard; no bullhorns blaring for him to come out with his hands up, like he thought there would be—and Joe realizes he got away with it. And it was *easy*, Jack, so easy. Then comes the true payoff. Power."

"Power?"

"Power. Joe's been special but under-appreciated his whole life, but suddenly his hard work is in the papers and on the five-o'clock news, maybe even the national news, and everybody is talking about him even if they don't know they are. *Power*, Jack, and Joe's hooked, because that power—that feeling of his greatness finally being appreciated—is sweeter than all the booze and powders and pills in the world. And he wants more, he's gotta have more—but he *also* has to be smart, because this is the big time; this is the needle if he's caught, so Joe gets another job that's beneath him, but he shows up on time every day and smiles at his new asshole boss and cashes his check every Friday…but the whole time he's supposedly walking the straight-and-narrow, he's keeping an eye out for that next special little girl he'll make his and only his, forever his, and then he finds her and stalks her and strikes again: another little girl raped and murdered."

"And then another and another, and he's refining his technique now, getting smarter, using plastic ties on their little hands and feet and a gag and duct tape so they don't cry out when he lifts them out the window. He's also taking trophies; one of those macaroni bracelets they make in art class from one special little girl, maybe a stuffed bear from another, some bloody underwear or a fear-sweat soaked nightgown the next; he has mementos to his greatness now, a cash, something to remind him of his power; something to masturbate over between his special girls, because the heat is on; he's done four by now, and he's lying low because the community is up in arms and the pigs are swarming, desperately looking for him. But jerking off and sweet memories only satisfy for so long, so he spots and stalks and does another."

"But he makes a mistake with this one, or maybe with one before, because here they come: hard-eyed pigs in wrinkled suits and bad ties. And they're onto him, he can tell; he's registered in their goddamn sex-offender system, after all; they have his DNA on file in a damn government pig-bunker somewhere. But they don't know for *sure*, that's why they just want to talk, the stupid pigs, so he agrees to come down to the station without a lawyer because he *knows* he's smart and powerful, all the newspapers say so, and he's sure he can talk his way back out again."

"But Angry Joe soon discovers he's not as smart as he thought, or that they know too much, so he confesses—*brags*, even—showing the stupid pigs how powerful he is, how special. And then he pleads to avoid the needle and Angry Joe Schmo from Kokomo is back behind bars, where he belongs—*where he never should have been released from in the first place*, if you ask me, not that anybody is—and the nightmare is over. Until they let the next one out, an angry one with the taste."

Ron sat up and swiped sweat from his forehead with his uniform cuff.

"Are, uh, are you all right, Chief?"

"I've been doing this job too long," he said by way of answer; his back was still killing him, and now the metal chair had put his left leg to sleep. Ron stood and stamped his boot and flexed his tingling toes. "I suppose I don't have to tell you Angry Joe from Kokomo lurks below the ninety-nine percent line?"

"No," Jack said uneasily, "I get that. And I see what you mean about comparing Joe to the Traveler; it's like standing a gorilla from the zoo next to King Kong."

"Yes. Unlike Joe, Bob has no sheet, and neither his prints nor hair nor his DNA in the latter years ever landed in any database—and that's by strict design; way back when he started, Bob would have understood the value of keeping his aboveboard life squeaky clean." Ron grimaced and shook his head. "I saw a bumper sticker once. It made me chuckle until I really thought about it. It said, 'Serial killers drive the speed limit.' Bob obeys the limit wherever he goes, Jack, I have no doubt about it; strategy of that caliber, well, I doubt anything like it ever made the tiniest dent in whatever passes for Angry Joe's mind."

"And as for victims, Joe chose his pretty much at random, then hatched some rudimentary plan before he made his move a week or two later—likely less by the time they caught him, because by then the need to feel his power was too great. The Traveler's acquisition phase would be much, much longer—years, even—and—"

"*Years?* How the hell can you stalk a woman that long and not be noticed?"

"I didn't say Bob shadows her every footstep night and day. Maybe he notices her while developing property X—say she works at a restaurant near the job site, or at the corner gas station, or at a local bank he's dealing with—but however they cross paths, something about her catches his eye, just like Joe and his special girls. And also just like Joe, the Traveler has to have her—he *will* have her. But here's where Kokomo Joe and the Traveler part ways again, because unlike Joe, the Traveler has the discipline to wait before he eats his candy; so-called men like Joe, well, they gobble their candy right away. They can't help themselves."

"Bob Jr., though, marks this woman for later while keeping a careful distance—or if he's forced to interact with her, he makes sure he's only politely friendly or even neutral. But all the while he's finding out where she lives; what she drives; if she's married or has a boyfriend; kids or grandkids; if she has a dog; learning her friends, her patterns. We're all creatures of habit, Jack, and predators know it." Ron glowered with tired disgust: "And social media would've made it almost laughably easy for him the last few years."

Jack said, "So the apartment complex goes up or the golf course goes in or whatever, and then three or four or five years later Bob tells Zane and Chris and the rest of the flunkies that he's driving to whatever state on the east coast to scout some property and tools away in a Corvette, and at some point he switches cars and turns his phone off and hightails it to the *other* side of the country—"

"Where nobody suspects him to have a reason to be again and makes his long-anticipated visit to the unfortunate woman he marked out."

"And takes her to one of those 'soundproofed basements' Denton talked about, and…" Jack's Adam's apple bobbed, "does what he does. And she's never seen again—unless it's time to screw with the feds and dump another one."

"Right," Ron said. "That's the Traveler. Now go back to Kokomo Joe. With angry, confused, yet still-dangerous-to-little-girls Joe, the crimes were so unorganized that investigators had abduction, kill, *and* dump sites: a slam dunk." He lifted his left index finger out to the side, almost to the end of his reach; Jack's bloodshot eye followed it, then came back. "The Traveler, on the other hand, is a ghost. So for him, there are only abduction sites—and I'm guessing they only have a handful of those from the early years, before he refined his technique; the rest would simply be point A, where the woman was last seen, and point B, where she was supposed to turn up, and a likely route between, where she vanished without a trace."

"A *ghost?*"

"No wits, no scenes, no evidence: a ghost—a *deadly* ghost—that leaves bodies now and then, then fades back into the darkness. But now it's time for the ghost to remind the FBI he's still out there—remind them of *his* power—so Bob preps and discards another one." Ron still had his finger held out; he lifted his right hand to the side and popped its index finger up: "Dump site. And now we come to the girl in the rooster suit."

"The *girl* in the…?" Jack squeezed that eye shut. "Let me guess; she's not with us anymore."

"Her name was Miranda Leigh Keys, twenty-two years-of-age. Abducted outside her place of employment, Rocky's Rockin' Chicken, in Overland Park, Kansas, a 'burb of KC, in broad daylight; that was a little over three weeks ago, and her tortured, nude body was found in a cornfield in southwestern Iowa four days later; peeled her out of the suit and did her right there under the golden tassels." Ron drew his arms in, floating his fingers toward each other: "And now the BAU has something from the Traveler they've never seen before…"

Jack got there before Ron's fingers did:

"The kill site. But I don't get *why* that's special, Chief—you know, other than to Miranda's family; I'm sure *they* think it's special." The young man visibly took hold of himself: "What I mean is, she's just another body, right? So why would that make the feds go on point?"

Ron sat back down on the unforgiving metal chair; fell, really. "Because the Traveler finally broke his pattern. That told them something had changed, perhaps something significant."

Jack massaged his wrists, that eye far away, then slowly said, "You're talking about one of my many questions Denton never bothered to answer: why Bob stopped caring about being caught."

"He's sick—or at least that's the BAU's theory. I have to admit it fits. And they're not sure with what, but it must be bad. And that puts him on the clock. And *that* makes him even more dangerous— and that is far, far more dangerous than Denton told you."

"What do you mean?"

"Robert Richards Junior might be the deadliest man alive; he may turn out to be one of the deadliest that has *ever* lived."

Jack dropped his hands into his lap and leaned back against the wall. "Okay. I get it. You're trying to scare me so I'll take this situation seriously. Believe me, there's no need for the dramatics, Chief. I mean, the guy killed *forty-nine people*, fer crissakes, so of course I'm—"

"Special Agent Denton never confirmed that number; Angela threw that out there. Denton never confirmed it because he knows what I know; forty-nine is just scratching the surface."

"Just scratching the *surface?*"

"When all is said and done—when the Traveler is finally brought to ground and nearly four decades of Bob's business deals and movements crisscrossing the country are backtracked and matched with unsolved murders and missing persons reports…well, a *hundred* and forty-nine might be closer to the real number. Probably more. Perhaps many more."

Jack just stared, stunned; then that eye narrowed: "You said 'unsolved murders' and 'missing persons reports', not 'missing women'."

"When you consider old Bill and what he did to those two young men at the party, can you sit there and tell me with a straight face they were the first males he's murdered?"

"I guess not, but…Jesus Christ, Chief, a hundred and forty something murders has *got* to raise eyebrows at some point. How do you get away with that? And how the *fuck* did the FBI keep it quiet?"

Ron said, "As to the first, I'd say shoddy or lazy investigative work at the local level; most departments have little experience with these types of crimes, and even fewer resources, let alone the proper training. As for the FBI, how Bob operates gave them the opportunity."

"What do you mean?"

"The size of his hunting ground; that's a lot of jurisdictions that traditionally share little information—except with the FBI. And he's only dumped ten bodies, with a protracted interval between each; that gives people, even cops, the chance to move on. Sad but true, especially in big cities, where new cases keep driving the old down the pile. The main thing, though, is that the Traveler doesn't advertise."

"Doesn't *advertise?*"

"Most of these guys let their egos get the better of them: they call and harass their victims' families, or leave coded messages at the scene to taunt the cops, or even write letters to newspapers."

"That's right, Kaczynski did that, the Unabomber."

"Yes—speaking of egos; so have many others, and it almost always results in their capture. Not the Traveler. He's too smart."

"Right, smart…and they think now he's sick? Okay, I guess that fits…but why would he suddenly get sloppy, Chief? I mean, after decades of practice, he's got the program down, right? So sick or not, he could've done anything he wanted with the girl in the suit, anything at all, but he hauls her to some cornfield in bum-fuck Iowa and does his evil shit and leaves a big mess—"

The young man's throat seemed to constrict; Ron fisted a giant yawn away before it could bloom.

"He lured them here," Jack finally said, awestruck. "Chris spouted something at the powwow about DNA, but even if they have some, they don't need it; that's why Bob kept the goddamn giant chicken costume; he *wanted* the fucking FBI to follow him home."

"Yes."

"Denton knows it, too. That's why he brought Hawthorne and Walters and the other meatheads. But *why?* Why would Bob want them here, Chief?"

"I don't know, but the possibilities frighten me more than just about anything I can think of because he doesn't just want the FBI here; he wants the media circus; he wants the world's attention focused on Indian Head. Remember, above everything else, Bob's a planner; he may not have written a manifesto to the papers, but he's been taking bodies across state lines and forcing the FBI's involvement since the early '80s; demonstrating his power; *taunting* them."

"And now they're here, right where he wants them."

"Yep."

"Jesus," Jack breathed. "So if he truly is sick, then…then we're witnessing his endgame—witnessing, hell; we're stuck in the fucking middle of it! And li'l ol' me's not his only target."

"Bingo. And *that's* why Denton's a damn fool," Ron said. "He understands what the Traveler is better than anyone, but he's still arrogant enough to think this will all fall out his way." He casually glanced through the propped-open door then, letting his gaze trail down the hall, but glimpsed no straw cowboy hat lurking at the corner by his office; he refrained from looking up at the CCTV camera in the tank's corner; there was no audio, so Tommy could only watch them converse in black-and-white.

When he turned back, Ron lowered his voice: "There's something else."

"What?"

"Think those sniper rifles shoot big nets?"

Jack sat there staring at him without blinking that eye for at least thirty seconds before almost whispering, "They're not really interested in catching Bob, are they." Not a question.

"I have my doubts."

"So all that about capturing the Traveler and attending his execution, that was just so much of Denton's bullshit?"

"Or a smoke screen; or establishing plausible deniability; or however you want to term it. Think about what Bob *is*, Jack, about how he compares to the Angry Joe's of the serial-killer world. When this is all over, alive or dead, the Traveler will go right to the top of that terrible pantheon; there's never been one like him. Ever. We're talking urban legend come to life; we're talking sick-o online fan clubs; we're talking amateur sleuths following his trail all over the country, digging up who-knows-what horror—and likely trashing crucial evidence. We're talking *movie deals*, God help us all. And Denton knows all that. He also knows the BAU will look like utter fools, but if the Traveler's dead, at least they can salvage something, spin it how they want, because they'll be the only ones left to talk."

"But the *worst* that could happen is if the Traveler sat down for some creepy, strait-jacketed *60 Minutes* interview. I think they'd do just about anything to prevent that. And I think Bob knows it."

Jack stared for a long moment, then craned that eye down the empty hallway before leaning toward Ron and saying in a low voice, "Why are you telling me all this, Chief?"

"Because despite your many, many, many flaws—"

"Many?"

"Many. Despite those, I agree with Angela: You're a good man—or at least you're trying to be. That counts for something in my book. You're also one of my people, and one of my people is being used as bait…and do you believe the hunter is concerned with what happens to the bait?"

"No. As long as he gets the kill, who cares if the bait's taken?"

"Exactly."

Jack sat there looking a little dazed, as well he might; then he frowned and shook his head as if to clear the cobwebs: "Okay," he said, "but I *still* don't get why Bob would go after Angela if he cares about her. And why he'd go through all that trouble to cripple me instead of just killing me."

Ron yawned and scrubbed his face with both hands. "Maybe he sees her as a woman now, not a little girl; from what I understand about the Traveler's psychosis, that would be enough to flip his switch. As for crippling you, well…" Ron shoved to his feet, knees creaking, and picked up the shotgun. "Maybe we'll get a chance to ask him. But we'll have to survive the weekend, first. Speaking of that, Tom and Ryan are on the doors, and I'll make up a cot in here; you'll be well protected tonight."

"Really think he'll come after me in a police station?"

"Who knows? I intend to be prepared if he does, but there's only so much I can do; Bob's worth around four hundred and fifty million, and that means he has the resources to do nearly any damn thing he wants." Ron nodded at the wall behind the commode: "Including setting up out there at three in the morning with an RPG he snagged off the black market and blowing the back of this station to Pluto, us along with it."

Jack popped up and came to the bars, watching the back wall of the tank the whole way:

"Are you fucking serious?"

"As a colonoscopy."

"You sure know how to comfort a guy, Chief."

"Well, at least now you understand what you're up against."

"Yeah," Jack said. "Thanks. I think. Shit! Now I'm *really* worried about my dad."

Ron shook his head. "Harold will have to look out for himself 'till tomorrow; we've been over this."

"I know, but this talk of rocket-propelled grenades has me jumpy all the sudden."

"I was just throwing out worst-case scenarios—I hope. Bob knows by now that the attempt to cripple you failed, and that the feds took custody of you from Neil; he probably already knows you're here. But I'm with Denton on this: the real fireworks will start after tomorrow's presser and the announcement about Zane."

"All right," Jack said reluctantly. "Is Fleming still posting out by my place tomorrow?"

"Yes."

Eighty-five acres of dense, up-and-down scrub pines lurked on the mountainside above the Ross' property, and Ryan had hunted mulies out there every season since he was twelve. He would pack in a radio and a pair of night-vision goggles borrowed from the SWAT team, along with all the weapons he could carry, and set up in those trees with a good view of the house and barn and shed and wait for a killer.

But that was tomorrow.

We have to get through tonight, first.

Ron said, "Don't worry too much about your dad, Jack. Last time I saw him he was polishing his Springfield with two more rifles already cleaned and loaded and leaning against the wall behind that ugly green recliner."

"I know. Mom and Angela told me. They *also* told me about the cooler full of beer, and how he acted toward everybody."

"Yes." Jack's father had lived up to every bit of his reputation, and then some. "But it was worth it. I got to listen to Senior Special Agent Denton of the FBI try to convince Hank Ross to come in for federal protection; it was quite the conversation."

"I bet."

Ron grabbed up both chairs as Jack plopped on the floor (after giving the back wall another wary glance) and started what looked like self-torture to Ron, but was probably some sort of yoga.

"When's the last time you ate?"

"I had lunch at the nurse's station," Jack mumbled to the concrete. Then he sat up fast: "Why, Chief? You got a buffet in your pocket?"

"No, but by law I have to feed the drunks something. We've got microwave Beanie Weenies and some Mango Fruit Cups. Or if you don't like those, we've got Mango Fruit Cups and microwave Beanie Weenies."

"I'll take the first one. And thanks again. For everything."

"You're welcome." Ron let the door clang shut and redeposited the chairs in the break room; Beanie Weenies and Fruit Cups sounded good to him, too. *When's the last time I ate?* He couldn't quite remember, but it had to have been a stretch if those seemed appetizing.

Ron was passing his office when he spotted the hot-pink slip impaled on his message spike. He cradled the tac-gun in the crook of his elbow before snatching and reading, then frowned and walked back to the tank and unlocked the door. "Jack, question."

The young man was contorted like a pretzel, but he sat up alertly enough.

"Sir?"

Ron waved the pink square. "Don Straus keeps calling me. He's using the station's non-emergency number, but he says it's important. He wanted Mindy to give him my cell, but she wouldn't do it because I don't give out my cell, and he also won't say why. Any idea what's going on with him?"

Jack pursed his lips, then shrugged. "Nope."

"Hmm. At first I thought it was about his key to Crazy's. I took it to lock up after Rife's team was done. I left it here so he could swing by and get it from Mindy, but he went off on her when he called back this morning, saying it was something else—something he had to talk to me and only me about. He also said he had something to give me."

"Something to *give* you?"

"Any notion what that could be?"

"Not a one, Chief."

Ron held up the slip: "Called again late this afternoon. He hung up before Mindy could say three words, though, saying he'd call right back, but never did. So, no clue what all that's about?"

"No, sir. Donnie's always been a little…excitable, though. He's been acting even weirder lately, but I thought he was just screwing up his courage to tell me this would be his last summer at Crazy's." Jack squinted up through the bars at Ron with that one eye: "Speaking of clues, maybe that's it; maybe he thinks he found one that can help me."

Ron grunted. "A clue."

"Yeah, that would be like him. Maybe he'll tell you what it is when he calls back. And thanks for locking up Crazy's, Chief."

Ron waved that away as the door clanged shut behind him again. *A clue.* He could hear Pierce and Mosley and Fleming gabbing with Tommy up front. Time to get his officers positioned and Jack fed and him fed and ring Sheriff Mick Whitehorse down in Buffalo, give Mick heads-up on what was coming his way, then scrounge Jack a pillow and blanket and make up the cot; that faded cot was musty old Army surplus and about as comfortable as attending your ex-wife's latest wedding, but Ron didn't think he'd have trouble sleeping on it tonight. He certainly didn't have time to mess with Don Straus playing Hardy Boys. He'd get in touch with Straus tomorrow, after the presser, when he had time.

If he had time.

43

"God it hurts I'm sorry I broke my word GOD IT FUCKING *HUUUUUURTS!*"

Bob stood near the beat-up green Accord and listened to a liar's lamentation echo through the black woods; he nodded in satisfaction: There was a sharp lesson being learned back there, all alone in the dark.

"AAAAAAHHHHHHH IT HUUURRRRTS!" Spitting and frantic thrashing, then: "GET THEM OFFAME OH MY GOD OH MY GOD I'M SORRY PLEEEEEEEEE—OW! FUCK! *OW!*" More spitting and thrashing, then a pitiful wail: "*Pleeeeese get them offame!*"

Bob nodded again; his point was hitting home, and no mistake. "PLEEEEEE*AAA*SE!"

If the cheat was lucky, he would turn out to be allergic to fire ant venom, and would soon go into anaphylactic shock and pass out and die.

If not, he was in for a long night.

Bob shrugged out of the stifling costume, held it by a double handful of sticky jacket for a long moment, then tossed it aside; it hit the rock-studded slope and its eddying layers of dried needles with a feathery *fwump*; the thing had served its purpose.

"*AHGODITHURTSGETHEMOFFAMEGET-THEMOOOOOFF!*"

The deceiver's pain-wracked shriek crashed through the forest, but Bob wasn't worried about company; he owned this entire northwest quadrant, just shy of six thousand acres, and had protected it with vehicle barriers and posted NO TRESPASSING and NO HUNTING and WILL PROSECUTE signs and ringed it with security cameras, both dummy and real, long, long years ago; nobody came out here, not anymore.

But if for some reason somebody did…Bob pulled Old Bitch Barbary's Smith & Wesson from his back pocket and held it down by his leg:

Another corpse wouldn't matter much at this point.

Not a soul knew he owned this land, not even Zane. He'd bought it through an intermediary, then secured it under a dummy LLC, which itself was a subsidiary of a shell corporation; that had been not long after Zack's murder. Then he'd put on a big show, acting frustrated that the new owner wouldn't sell.

No one dared ask what he'd planned to do with it, though; they'd doubtless all thought he'd wanted to build another golf course or gated community and name it after Zack. He had a reputation, after all; a carefully crafted reputation.

"Pleeeeeeeeaaaaaaaseitburrrrrrrrrrrrrrrrns!"

Bob stretched a trembling, gloved hand toward Hawk's Point, less than half a mile to the south, where the rocky, Ponderosa-studded peninsula thrust into a shimmering cove:

As if he would ever defile sacred ground.

"Soon," Bob whispered to the shade of his murdered son, then stumbled up the three shallow wooden steps and across the split-railed porch and into his shadowed cabin.

"OHMYGODITBURNSGETTHEMOFFAMEPLEA-SEI'MSORRY*PLEAAAAAAASSSSEEE!*"

Bob set the Smith on the plank coffee table and stripped his gloves off, but didn't remove his sneakers as he lay down on the ratty old sleeper couch and laced his fingers over his chest; just a moment's rest, and then he'd get back on-plan.

"AAAAHHHHHHHHHHHHHHHH GOD IT HURRRRRTS!"

Dooming Jack Ross to his own fate, that of a sound mind trapped inside a broken, ruined body, had failed…but Bob hadn't given up on the idea quite yet; as those tricky, stubborn Japanese bastards liked to say: There are many paths to the top of Mt. Fuji. But that was for later; tonight, now that he'd dealt with the fraud, he had a long-postponed and much-anticipated visit to cross off his list.

Much anticipated.

Act, don't react, and continue to push the play; make those fools with the bold yet feeble yellow letters on their jackets react to *him*.

Keep it status quo, in other words.

"OHMYGODPLEASEI'MSORRYPLEASHEHELP-MEITHURRRRRRRRRRTS!"

A smile spread until it was a toothy, twitching blaze of white teeth in the dark; apparently, the liar wasn't allergic to fire ant venom.

"To bad," he whispered. "Should've kept your word."

"*AHHHHHHHHHHHHHHHHHHHHHHHHHHHHHHHHHHH-HHHHHHHHHHHHHHHHHHHHHHHHHHHHHHHHHHHHH-HHHHHHHHHHHHHHHHHHH!*"

Lying there in the screaming darkness, Bob grinned as he listened to a valuable lesson being taken to heart.

Saturday

44

Jezebel was barking.

Hank Ross snorted awake, and then adrenaline set fire to his bones as he realized what he was hearing. He sat up fast and kicked the footrest down, dumping the Pabst into his crotch and knocking over the Springfield .30-06 he'd leaned against the armrest. He cursed and caught it before it fell, then brushed ineffectually at his pants before snatching up the half-full can and slinging it into the corner; it hit the pile of crushed empties and scattered them. When the clatter died, Hank held his breath and strained his ears, but the damn dog had already quit yapping.

"Jezzie! What is it, girl?"

He sat poised on the edge of the recliner, rifle held across his chest with his finger resting outside the trigger guard, peering out through the mesh, more than half expecting a giant, feathered, ax-wielding freak to stalk across the circle of yellow illumination thrown by the yard light up on its pole.

Hank grinned fiercely.

If that was to happen, a certain freak would discover he'd brought his ax to a 7.62mm party.

He waited, but saw nothing and heard only crickets sawing out in the pines and faint stirrings from Fred White's cattle bedded down over on the other side of Jackie's barn. What the hell time was it? He looked for the moon, but its sharp grin had already set behind the Bighorns; late, then. He peered up at the stars through the screen and sniffed the night air, tasting its cool crispness (Hank Elmer Ross didn't need a damn watch or a cell phone to tell time, not like some city-lover), and decided it was close on three in the morning—the deepest watches. A time when honest men should be asleep and recharging their batteries.

Just like Hank had been busy doing.

"Jezebel!"

He waited some more, tense on the edge of the chair, surprised the little bitch didn't slink up the steps and grin at him shamefacedly through the screen—most likely she'd been barking at a fox or a blasted coon again—but…nothing.

"Goddamnit."

He stood, swaying as his right leg wobbled before he stiffened it; the fog of Pabst and sleep cleared, and as it went, Hank decided something about the tone of Jezzie's bark bothered him.

All dogs have different barks for different situations, and if you pay attention, they're easy to tell apart; Jezebel was no different, and Hank paid attention. She had her bark for when a strange car came down the driveway, and a similar if not-as-serious noise for when Jackie drove his Ford in, and another for critters such as coons and whatnot; her announcement of coyotes creeping up on her territory was a thing in and of itself, full of hate and fear, and unmistakable.

She also had a greeting for somebody she knew and liked: her happy bark.

It was that happy bark he could have *sworn* he'd heard…but maybe he'd dreamed it; he'd been sawing logs pretty hard. Hank thought back to those initial, half-asleep moments and realized something else:

Jezebel's barking had come from around the backside of the house.

He kept one gimlet eye on that circle of yellow light while he shouted off the side of the porch: "Jezzie!"

Hank waited.

Nothing.

That smart little contrary roly-poly bitch! She was usually good about coming at a fast waddle when called, but evidently not tonight; she'd been moping about since Jackie'd got his butt jugged in the hoosegow, true, but that was no excuse.

Hank called and waited again; no sign of her. *Goddamn mutt.* He glanced at the hated cane, where it leaned against the vinyl siding behind the recliner, then down at the Springfield nestled in his hands. He looked at the cane again.

"Fuck you, anyway," he told it, then limped toward the screen door.

That goddamn stroke had just about unmanned him, but his speech didn't slur anymore, and his leg was responding well to the physical therapy; that gook Physical Therapist slash Torture Master had even said so after the last session. Hell, at this rate, in nine months, a year at the outside, Hank Ross would be good as new—and everybody knew that was pretty damn good. He was going to snap that fucking cane over his knee and burn the pieces in the barrel out back when the time came to finally kiss it goodbye.

He reached out (not with the trigger-finger hand) and opened the screen, then went slowly down the steps and eased the door shut so it wouldn't bang. Hank peered around, listening hard:

Nothing but dark and crickets and cows.

"Jezebel!"

No answer.

Worthless dog.

Hank raised the Springy and beaded-up the blank wall of Ponderosa across the driveway; the old bolt-action and he went back to his secondary school days, and it still felt good in his hands, felt *right*. Hell, it felt better that nearly every woman he'd ever known, and it was surely less fickle—especially that faithless, nagging cunt he'd made the mistake of marrying.

Hank turned the rifle in his big, scarred hands, admiring it under the yellow gleam; he'd harvested over twenty mulies with this trusty girl, and without using any fancy scope; only four times had he shot more than once to bring a deer down, and those were because he'd been so schnockered he couldn't see straight.

Even so, he'd never had to shoot more than twice.

Iron sights were *fine* for a real hunter, just *fine*…but right then Hank would've given a lot for one of those new-fangled night-vision scopes; he knew those pines over there like he knew the feel of his own pecker, but that was in the daylight, and right that moment there could be anyone in there, looking out at him, studying him as he stood in the circle of light just like he'd been studying the Springfield.

Hank scowled at that dark green wall, then shouted, "Hey! Hey, you want some, *come on 'n get it!*" Only the crickets had anything to say. "Didn't think so." He hawked and spit, then yelled into the general night: "Jezzie, you stupid little twat! Where are ya?"

More nothing.

Muttering, Hank limped toward the corner of the front porch, intending to call down the side of the house for the damn dog again, when a sound froze him in his tracks—no, *two* sounds: a soft *thump*, followed by another, even softer *thump*.

Both furtive noises had come from around back.

Hank lurched as fast as his damn leg would let him lurch and pulled up and leveled the Springy down the narrow alley between his shop and the east side of the house. "Who's there? By damn, show yourself if you don't wanna eat a slug!"

No answer, and the warm glow of the back porch light showed nothing and nobody awaiting him at the end of the alley.

"Jezzie? That you, ya little bitch?"

Silence.

Hank advanced until he got to the rear corner, then poked one eye and the business end of the Springy around, but only the concrete stoop below his back door and his mud boots stacked to the side of the two wide, shallow steps, just under the roof eave, and his rusty-yet-trusty old Webber kettle grill on the other side and the depleted summer woodpile greeted him; the front edge of that shin-high stack of split logs was about twenty feet out from the stoop, and just visible in the glow.

"Jezebel?"

Nothing.

Where'd that goddamn mutt get to?

Hank eased around the corner, rifle up, ready and steady, and tested the doorknob with the non-trigger-finger hand; still locked. He'd secured both the cheap knob lock and the heavy bolt above it when he'd buttoned up for the night. Angus had been over, and they'd enjoyed a cold one or four while talking about—what else?—this crazy crap going on with Jackie and that whack-a-doodle in the giant chicken costume and the goddamn federals wanting Hank to hide behind their goddamn government skirts and Mary going off half-cocked and—

A scratching, scrabbling noise made Hank jerk around, and he lost his balance with a yell and sat down hard on the bottom step. Heart thump-whumping, he sighted from his sitting position, ready to unload…and beheld a fat momma coon sitting up on his woodpile, staring at him with her bandit face, triangle ears twitching; two half-grown spring kits stared past her bulk, eyes glimmering in the porch light.

"Goddamnit!"

Momma and her kits fled at his shout, ringed tails undulating, the scrabble of hard claws on wood sounding again as Hank struggled to his feet, cussing, and almost took a shot at them just because.

He rubbed his bruised tail bone as he limped back around the corner and up the alley, leg dragging, lower back on fire from compensating: "Jezebel, you stupid bitch! I don't know what you were barking at and I don't know where you're hiding and I don't care about either damn one! If you're smart, you'll stay there and keep your yap shut the rest of the goddamn night!"

Hank gimped back up the steps and across the porch, letting the screen door bang shut for all it was worth, and leaned the rifle against the wall next to the hated cane and threw back the lid on his Coleman and shoved his hand into the icy water and retrieved a fresh Pabst. He wiped it dry on his shirt and cracked it and downed half the can, belched, swiped his mouth with a forearm, slammed the cooler shut, belched again, then eased back into his recliner and levered up the footrest.

Hank crossed his ankles and scowled through the mesh at the night.

"Goddamn raccoons." Then: "Goddamn dog." A swig of beer. "Goddamn federals."

This was all the feds' fault; they had him jumping at shadows—*feathered* shadows, in this case. He'd sat right in this chair and cleaned his rifles and listened to that stuck-up, prissy little FBI Special Agent Denton tell him that this insane-o running around chopping up old people and kids was doing it to frame Jackie, and that when the killer found out the frame wouldn't fit, they thought the crazy bastard would come after the rest of Jackie's family, him included, as well as Angie Beaumont, seeing as how she was Jackie's main squeeze, now. Hank's faithless, wandering wife had stood right there next to said fed and called Hank a fool to his face when he'd refused to hide behind government skirts—or "come with us and talk about what we need to do", was how Mary had put it, but he could read the score:

Hank Ross didn't hide behind *any* skirts, government or otherwise, although he'd thought it was a good idea for the women.

Mary hadn't been the worst, though, because there High-And-Mighty-And-Too-Good-For-His-Shit-To-Stink Chief Rogers had been, standing behind Denton and his thugs in suits, watching. Hank took a deep draw on the Pabst, then crunched the empty and threw it in the scattered pile and retrieved another deliciously cold soldier from the cooler. He dried it on his shirt and opened it with a *hissst* and a crack and took a pull. Goddamn Rogers. Fuck him, anyway. Fuck 'em all, for that matter, especially Mary. *Holier-than-thou, ice-cold twat.*

And fuck Jackie's new squeeze, too, that fiery little Angie Beaumont. Standing there behind Mary, glaring at him with her blue eyes, the expression on her too-pretty face saying Hank Ross was a dog turd that'd had the gumption to stick to her high-dollar shoe—standing on his *own goddamn porch* and looking at him like that! Hank took another pull. *Stupid twat.* Back in the day, little Angie had been as sweet as gooseberry pie, always trailing those boys around, but she'd done growed into the woman Hank had always feared she would.

And now the little split-tail had her hooks set hard into Jackie.

Hank grinned reluctantly. No doubt those hooks were as soft and as warm as they looked—but hooks like those were the hardest to get shunt of. Jackie was in for a rough go, no question, but in between driving him crazy and making him miserable, Hank figured his son's shriveled little cock would be deliriously happy.

Hank's grin fell into his wide lap.

Jackie.

Speaking of someone who looks at me like I'm dog shit…

He hadn't truly believed Jackie'd killed those kids, let alone that old bitch Barbary or that sot Bill Napier, but the boy needed to be taken down a peg—and the *look* on Mary's face when he'd told that FBI man about the day Jackie had gotten out of prison, and that yes indeed, he did think Jackie was capable of killing them…

Woo boy, *that* had been worth all the bother since, and then some.

Hank stared out at the spot under the light pole where he and his son had had their little "talk" (as Jackie called it); a fight should be two men duking it out until the weaker man stayed down. *That* was a fight, by God, and Jackie *had* slugged him in the jaw (the boy didn't lack for toughness; Hank had seen to that himself), and he sure enough hit like an ornery mule kicked, but all that other sneaky bullshit just wasn't fair; tripping a man, and when Hank tried to get up, throwing him back down by his wrist and holding him there so that he would've had to rip his own shoulder out if its socket just to get free—and *then* the damn boy had twisted his arm up behind his back and rolled him face down and actually *sat* on him before leaning down and whispering in his ear that he would kill Hank if he ever even thought about touching his goddamn holier-than-thou mother again.

Hank took a pull of Pabst. The boy just didn't understand: women needed correcting now and again. Hell, this whole *generation* didn't understand; Oprah and that cunt-licker Ellen and all those other commie liberals out in Hotel California had brainwashed 'em into thinkin' you weren't supposed to ever lay a *finger* on a woman, let alone a hand; you were supposed to *talk* to 'em. But Hank had figured out long ago that if a woman got you talking, she could convince you of damn near anything—especially if she was sharing that thing between her legs with you; access to *that* thing weighted a lot of arguments.

Hank yawned and scratched his cheek. His own daddy had corrected his momma so much she'd served them dinner at five-thirty every night 'cept for Sundays, and it was never late. Ever. Not even by a minute. It was always good, too. That woman could *cook*, by God—not like Mary, who could barely fry an egg. Hank's momma had kept her eyes on her plate and hadn't said ten words in forty years, neither; just the way it should be…

Hank suddenly scowled; something was niggling at him worse than raccoons or dogs or Mary or even pansy-ass federals; this "frame" bullshit Denton had tried to sell him made no sense. Only two men on the planet hated Jackie enough to pull something like that—and one was Zane Richards. Hank snorted a laugh. Zane didn't have the balls or the heart. Slip some sorority skirt a Mickey and pump her dry? Sure, that was in a coward like Zane's wheelhouse, you betchya…but mincing people with an ax while leaving clues pointed straight at Jackie?

No way, not Zane.

Bob Junior, now…

Hank took a long, thoughtful drink of his Pabst, then yawned even wider and set the can between his legs and settled back into the recliner with a sigh; Bob was a cat of a different stripe. Robert Richards most definitely had the sack—Bob's momma had seen to that—but *would* he?

Hank didn't think so, and for one simple reason: too much to lose.

His nose dipped, and his eyes fluttered closed. All that money, not to mention the biiiiiig reputation to maintain…Hank snickered without opening his lids; to a man like Bob, that last was the most important…and even if it worked, *still* too much to lose if he was ever found out…hell, *everything*…no, Bob may hate Jackie's guts, but he would never do something like this…had to be someone else…a stretch in the clink would do that boy good, take him down a notch or three, give Hank a chance to set things straight with Mary; that damn woman needed correcting like no other…

Hank's chin thumped on his broad chest, and he slept.

Time passed.

Hank's head lolled, and his raspy snores drowned out the crickets sawing in the pines across the driveway. The Pabst tilted in his crotch, spilling amber liquid on the already damp spot, but he didn't stir, not even when the front door opened softly beside him.

Heavy boots clumped as Jezebel trotted to the screen door to be let out. The rusty spring creaked, and she went with a wag, then stopped on the top step and peered back through the screen, tail still going.

The boots clumped over beside Hank…and he smacked his lips and cracked bleary eyes.

Then they shot wide.

"What are you…" He saw the ax. "Whoa, what the—!" Hank struggled to sit up, fumbling behind him for the Springfield, which fell over with a clatter as the ax swung down, and Hank yelled as he lifted a hand in pitiful defense.

The blade sheared through three of his fingers, digits flying away as the stubs squirted blood onto the wall behind him, and the hated cane. Hank screamed as the ax kept going, shearing through his right clavicle with a crunch. More blood spurted, a river of blood, an ocean of blood, and the ax head was jerked free to rise and fall again and again and again and again and again and again and again and again and again.

Out in the yard now, Jezebel resumed barking. She still sounded happy.

45

I stood next to Chief Rogers and waited for the show to start.

I wasn't cuffed. Instead, my thumbs were hooked jauntily in my back pockets as Special Agent Denton prepared to step to the podium. Only a single, lonely microphone decorated that lectern today; no line of blocky, unsmiling chaps wearing grim suits and uninspired ties lurked off to the side, either; Denton had no intentions of duplicating Neal's farce. Indeed, he'd only given the media about twenty minutes' notice, and that calculated brevity had led to disgruntled yet intrigued reporters scrambling to jam shoulder-to-shoulder onto the once-green grass of Indian Head's town square.

A satellite truck screeched to a stop out on A Street and a statuesque redhead piled out and waved urgently for her cameraman to set up; counting the tardy arrival, there were now over two-dozen television cameras pointed at me. Most of the pack held microphones or digital recorders or old-fashioned pens and spiral notebooks at the ready as well, and at one point or another all of them had stared at my eye as I had stared out at them; the swelling had gone down, and I could see out of it again (which was nice), but it had blackened gorgeously overnight.

I bet all those worthy scribblers had noticed my state of uncuffedness, too, and I was enjoying that—both their noticing, and the fact of it.

You betchya I was.

Three faces in that sea didn't belong to reporters or cameramen; Mom and Angela stood at the edge of the crowd off to my right, but I hadn't acknowledged them, conscious of Denton and Rogers' warnings not to single them out just in case Bob or the Chicken Man or the Traveler or whatever the fuck the psycho was calling himself today was watching. I thought that caution unnecessary, perhaps dumb even, especially if Bob really was the Traveler; he would go after the women in my life whether I waved at them or not. But I kept my yap shut and did as they said because the arguments, stupid or not, of people who hold your life in their hands swing mucho weight.

The third non-reporter face belonged to Miriam. She lurked on the other side of the crowd (thankfully), way off to my left, flashing that little glossy quirk that promised things—things of which I was all too aware that Miriam could deliver—but after one glance earlier I hadn't bothered to acknowledge her again. I just hoped Angela didn't notice her standing over there. Or that glossy quirk.

That would give the reporters something to write about.

Denton finally motivated his prissy behind up to the podium and adjusted the mic down; he stood ramrod straight, chin raised, the gleaming bald spot on the back of his head straining toward the blue heavens.

"My name is Special Agent Denton of the Federal Bureau of Investigation. There will be no questions taken this morning. I am here to announce that Jonathan Eugene Ross will not be charged with six counts of murder."

A murmur arose, although not a surprised one; they had indeed noted my blessed and uncuffed state. A female voice shouted, "Who's the killer, then?", and then another woman, somewhat snarkily, "No questions this morning? What about after lunch?"

True to his word, though, Denton disdained to answer; the man's a big believer in disdain, I've noticed. "Mr. Ross has been released on his own recognizance, and with my personal apology for both the tarnishing of his name, and the inconvenience and heartbreak that his premature arrest has undoubtedly caused his family."

That felt good. He was laying it on a little thick, and there sure as fuck hadn't been any apology (personal or otherwise, from anybody, let alone Denton), but it still felt good.

Boy, did it.

Shouted questions, but Denton simply raised his manicured hand until relative quiet descended. "I am also here," he said, placing that sculpted hand back on the podium, "to announce that the FBI has taken into custody one Zane Zachary Richards, age twenty-nine."

The murmur swelled to a roar that could've been boiled down to: Would Zane be charged for the Chicken Man murders? Denton just stood there like a prissy little cold-eyed suited statue, and eventually the squall died out as they realized the G-Man meant what the G-Man said 'bout no questions.

"As yet, Mr. Richards has not been charged with any crime, although I expect that to change come Monday morning," he lied. A renewed avalanche of shouts, frustration ringing loud and clear: "And now, Mr. Ross will issue a statement."

That shut them up; all eyes and cameras swung to cover me. Denton and Chief Rogers gave me warning looks as Denton stepped back, and both were easy to read: Stay on script. Don't fuck up.

I walked over and adjusted the mic back up; the speakers propped on the gazebo railing behind me thudded and whined.

Don't worry, Jackie boy, it's only the entire goddamn universe watching.

"Hello," I said, feedback blasting again as my amplified voice flooded the square.

Nobody said hello back; I didn't hear any crickets, but there *were* birds chirping; I cleared my throat and tried again: "First, I want to express my gratitude to those of you who never doubted my innocence. Thank you. Your belief kept me going."

More chirping, two or three fleeting (extremely fleeting) shame-faced looks, and one discrete cough, but most of the Fourth Estate gathered before me were impassive bordering on impatient; they wanted me to get on with it, and they had also never questioned my guilt for a nanosecond—the bastards.

Thank you, Mom. Thank you, Angela.

"Second, I'm inviting you all down to my place, Crazy's, for a Free Cheeseburger Giveaway. It's in honor of our great nation's founding, and the amazing rights and freedoms our forefathers secured for us, freedoms we enjoy to this day. It's also to celebrate other, newer-found freedoms."

That got a few laughs, although mostly I saw bemused outrage that I would attempt to profit from this situation. *Fuck 'em.* "Just give me a few hours to get set up and open, say five o'clock. That free cheeseburger thing is only good for tonight, by the way."

And then I was pummeled with shouted inquiries, and none were about free cheeseburgers; most had to do with Zane and whether I thought he was the killer in the feathered suit; a handful had to do with my eye and how I'd come by it in the Sheridan County Jail, and if I would file a civil suit against the county and Sheriff Neal; boy, did I want to crack my teeth on *that* one, but somehow I kept it zipped.

"Thank you again, and I hope to see you all down at Crazy's."

And with that I walked slowly (sauntered, really, but who could blame me?) back over next to Rogers.

That didn't deter them, of course; they hadn't earned the right to stand out there by being shy or retiring, and not a single, stinking one of 'em enjoyed being stonewalled by the FBI, let alone some piss-ant convicted man-slaughterer slash burger flipper…but we all have to deal with little disappointments in life, don't we?

It had been Denton's notion to invite the world to Crazy's and then set an ambush for the Traveler there. He'd brainstormed it in his pointy head last night and seemed to think it was the best idea since oral sex. The gist was that Bob would be so furious over the twin outrages of A: me being set free, and B: Zane getting his date-raping ass arrested, that he would immediately come slavering after me at work, gobs of witnesses or no gobs of witnesses, and then Denton could scoop the Traveler up with cameras rolling and slap some cuffs on him (or rather, considering what Rogers had more than hinted at last night, put a bullet in Bob's head) and jet back to D.C. for a quick promotion ceremony. Walters and another of the SWAT boys had already set up in the woods behind Crazy's, with another camped out at Darryl's Shell across the road. The other three were around the square somewhere, eyeballs peeled and fingers hovering near their triggers—or at least I fucking hoped so.

Chief Rogers didn't believe it would be that simple, however, and had made his opinion known; his objection had been dually noted and dismissed. As for me, I thought choosing your ground and letting your enemy come to you was a proven tactic…but would Bob—aka the Traveler; aka the super-duper planner himself—act that reckless, no matter *how* pissed he was?

Didn't think so.

But I'd kept my pie hole shut for two simple reasons: one, nobody gave a damn what I thought. And two, this was a chance to salvage the holiday week. I mean, if a guy can't capitalize on some free promotion while the whole fucking *world* watched, what's the point?

By then most of the print Fourth Estate had given up yelling at us and had scurried off to churn some hot copy, and all the TV talent had spread out and were jabbering earnestly into camera lenses while I fretted over how many people would show up at Crazy's this evening, and how I would feed them when they did. Metro doesn't come 'till tomorrow, and we're already low on supplies, even with what I bought from the Sam's on Thursday. *Shit.* Employees might be helpful, too; I needed to call Donnie and Miguel and make sure they could work tonight, and that they were both okay with being potential casualties if Bob actually did drop by.

I wasn't too worried about Donnie; with all the excitement, I figured he would have to be beaten away with a stick. I was less sure about Miguel; he was illegal, and the last thing in the world he wanted was the world's attention. Maybe Walters would strap on an apron and a hairnet and flip some burgers in the dungeon; I pictured Hawthorne wearing a Crazy's tee-shirt with the sleeves rolled up to display the waxy guns, giving people the dead-eye as he handed ice-cream cones out the pick-up window, freckles shining in the sun.

Now that *would be something to see…*

"Jack? Care to join us?"

Chief Rogers, amused at my space-out, gestured politely for me to walk ahead of him; anytime we went anywhere in a group, the Chief always trailed the pack. Always. I think he did it so he could keep an eye on everyone, me probably most of all. I glanced over and found Denton and all of Rogers' officers looking at me either impatiently or quizzically, waiting for me to join them around the backside of the gazebo, ostensibly out of the media's view.

Flushing, I did just that until we stopped in a little choreographed congregation with four of Indian Head's finest facing outward at the cardinal points while pretending they were doing no such thing. Tommy even had his hand on his gun like a white-hat gunfighter ready to throw down on a no-good hombre in the dusty street until Rogers muttered something to him in passing and he took it off with a sheepish grimace.

Denton and Rogers and I huddled with our heads together as the Senior Special Agent snipped, "Good job, Mr. Ross," and I wanted to inform him that sarcasm was the lowest form of humor, but before I could he added: "Now hopefully we can bring this farce to a conclusion by this evening."

Rogers said nothing, and loads of it, but that was enough to spark those frozen greens from me to the Chief. Denton opened his mouth angrily, thesaurus-bending venom ready to spew…and Mom and Angela bustled around the gazebo and I was enveloped in joyful tears and hugs and kisses. Tommy spared me one sullen glance, then kept doing his job to the best of his limited ability. Officer Fleming raked his gaze across Angela, and I could tell what *he* was thinking, even though his blue eyes gave Denton's green a run for lead in the Iceberg Follies.

And then the kisses stopped and the two women in my life jumped on me with all four dainty feet:

Mom: "You look tired. Did you sleep *at all* in that awful cell?" I fibbed and assured her that I had indeed slept and slept fine, but she only snapped, "Don't lie to me, Jackie!"

Angela: "I still want to help at Crazy's tonight." I told her no way José, again, but she kept arguing for it even though Denton and Rogers came in on my side, again, just like this morning on the phone; speaking of tired, Angela looked it, with sagging shoulders and bags under her eyes, as if she hadn't had a lick of shuteye; couldn't sleep for worrying about me, knowing her.

Mom: "Did you *eat* something, at least? You've lost weight, and you were already too skinny!"

Angela: "You'll need me, especially if you guys are as busy as I think you will be."

Mom: "Jonathan Eugene! Did you eat last night? And what about this morning? A good breakfast is—"

"Jesus Christ, Mom, yes, Chief Rogers fed me dinner *and* breakfast, and no, Angela, you're not helping at Crazy's. You're going back to wherever you guys stayed safe and stay safe again, end of discussion."

Four small fists were planted on four hipbones.

Mom: "Don't you *dare* take the Savior's name in vain! Not where I can hear it!"

Angela: "Where do you think I'll be safer, dummy? With your mom, or with you and a professional SWAT team?"

"I think anywhere not near me would be a helluva lot safer than standing *beside* me, especially if—"

That's when Miriam swayed around the gazebo.

Well, shit.

Her dark hair was pulled into a simple ponytail today, secured high on the back of her head with a perky, bright-blue scrunchie; the combination made her look ten years younger. She wore a blue sleeveless button-down top, her khaki shorts were tight (real tight), and her legs were smooth and muscular and nut-brown above simple white Nike running shoes and ankle socks; in short, she looked completely edible.

There was a charged silence as Miriam wound her way through the officers; all four watched her, not their surroundings…not that I could blame them; even Chief Rogers pursed his lips and gave her the once-over.

She stopped in front of me, which put her right next to Angela, whom she didn't even so much as glance at; apparently, as far as Miriam was concerned, Angela was a space rock on Jupiter.

"Hello, Jack. Congratulations. I never doubted you for a second."

"Uh, hello. And, um, thanks."

Angela stared at the side of Miriam's face with this…speculative look, as if my former lover were a mildly surprising and thus somewhat interesting phenomenon; that changed in a hurry when Miriam patted my chest.

"You're welcome," she purred.

Something ugly flickered in Angela's eyes then, and I shot my arm between them, but Mom moved faster, tugging her away while gifting Miriam a flinty look of her own before leading Angela up into the gazebo where they sat knee-to-knee on the octagonal bench; Mom whispered and whispered, but Angela never took that hate-filled, unblinking stare from Miriam.

Great.

"Jack? Are you coming over tonight?"

"I don't think that would be a good idea."

Miriam shrugged, which did nice things to the cleavage peeking over her shirt button. "Your loss. If you change your mind, you know where I'll be." She went up on tip-toe and pecked me on the lips, then undulated away, pausing to smile up at Officer Fleming and pat *him* on the chest.

There were a lot dumber things in the universe than my sudden surge of jealousy, but right then I couldn't think of any. We all watched her sway back around the gazebo, and then a dry snip dropped me back into reality:

"As entertaining as observing your personal life devolve before our very eyes is, Mr. Ross, I have business to be about." Denton shot a frozen glare at Rogers. "Since it seems Sheriff Neal has not only failed to attend our little gathering, let alone bothered to send Mr. Ross's pickup as requested, I trust you will provide Mr. Ross transportation to the Sheriff's impound?"

He walked away, not bothering to wait for an answer.

Rogers' tone was decidedly dusty when he said, "Need a ride, Jack?"

"Apparently."

"Jackie."

I turned around and found Mom behind me. Angela was still up in the gazebo, still sitting on her section of octagonal bench.

The fury she'd displayed toward Miriam had evaporated; she was slumped forward, hands dangling limply between her knees, staring across the square toward City Hall, but I don't think she saw it.

"Jackie! I'm speaking to you!"

"Is she okay?" I started toward the gazebo. "I need to tell her I didn't want or ask for that kiss. Miriam just—"

Mom seized my elbow with surprising strength and swung me back around. "She knows. Just give her a minute. She had a rough night."

"Was she up worrying about me?"

"Yes," Mom said. "Now listen: we're going out to check on your father, and I believe Officer Flemming will accompany us and then follow us back to…to where we stayed. Is that right?" That last was directed at Rogers, who nodded. Flemming gave me a friendly smile, then faced forward again; I tried not to glare at his back. "Jonathan Eugene, *are you listening to me?*"

"Sorry, go ahead."

"I *said* we're going out to check on your dad. I need to make sure the fool remembered to take his blood-thinner medication, and that he has food to eat, not just beer." She sniffed. "I bet there are crushed cans *all over* that porch. I'll make sure he remembered to feed Jezzie, too, and pick out a few outfits while I'm there."

"All right," I said, enunciating and trying not to be obvious about throwing my voice toward my crotch: "I'm riding with Chief Rogers down to the Sheridan County impound to get my truck, then I gotta call Donnie and Miguel to make sure I have help tonight."

I hadn't gone insane (at least not yet); they'd stuck a pencil-eraser sized microphone underneath my zipper first thing this morning, and I had been instructed to say what I would do—and where I was going to do it—out loud to ensure my protectors had both the time and the opportunity to protect me; I felt like some bad-boy idiot in a soap opera standing around in an empty room talking to the air about my evil plans. "I'll swing by the Sam's Club while I'm down there, make sure we don't run out of burgers and buns and cheese tonight."

Mom patted my cheek, then pulled me into a hug. "Well, whatever you do, you take care of yourself. Hear me?"

"Yes, ma'am."

And then Angela was there. Mom drew Chief Rogers away to give us privacy—as much privacy as you can get with the government listening through your crotch, anyway. She didn't say anything, just enveloped me; I hugged her back, hard, and when she lifted her head from my chest, I said, "I didn't want that to—"

She pressed a finger over my lips. "I know it was her. Don't worry about it, Jack, already forgotten."

The *look* on her face…well, I wasn't about to call her a liar. "If you say so."

"I do." She eyed me critically, then stood on tip-toes and fixed my hair to her satisfaction; she even licked her thumb and smoothed my eyebrows. Angela then considered my lips, licked the *other* thumb, and wiped (scrubbed) at the spot Miriam had graced. Then she planted a big wet one on me. "There. Did your mom tell you where we're going?"

"To check on Dad."

"And you still won't let me help at Crazy's tonight?"

I sighed. "You'll be safer—"

She pressed her finger over my lips again. "It's okay, Jack, I understand. Let's just make sure you stay safe and that we do what we have to do to get this mess over with, because you and I…" She glanced down significantly (she knew about the crotch mic), "still have your ears to discuss."

I was suddenly ready to get this mess over with, too. "That should be an interesting discussion."

"Oh, it will be, I promise." She patted my chest in the same spot Miriam had. I didn't think it was an accident.

Mom collected Angela then, and they and Officer Fleming were off. He trailed my ladies, and he gave me another smile before they rounded the gazebo, checking out Angela's ass the whole way.

Prick.

The Chief and his remaining officers and I then fiddle-farted around for a few minutes, giving the SWAT team time to get organized, and then we walked to Rogers' cruiser. A handful of media types jumped us, but Tommy and the other two ran interference like wide receivers blocking down-field. Then we piled in and I decided it would be good to see my old truck again, and to drive myself somewhere instead of sitting in the back of a cop car or a damn Suburban.

We were ten minutes from the impound when we got the call about Dad.

Ron hovered near the backside of the woodpile and watched FBI criminalists snap pictures of bloody boot prints with their government-issue iPads. The techs started to compare something on their screens, then remembered he was there and moved away and stood shoulder to shoulder with their backs to him.

Whispering, pointing, head-shaking, and then one, a skinny woman with poofy dark hair, knelt and measured the depth of a print with a ruler about the size of an old-fashioned mercury thermometer; the three egg-yolk yellow letters on the back of her dark blue tee-shirt stretched across the knobs of her spine. She tapped a note out on the pad, started to say something to her coworker, noticed Ron watching again, then stood and whispered in the other technician's ear; he nodded without looking at her and tapped out a note on his own pad.

Ron grimaced. They'd been chatty enough earlier, but then Denton had noticed and shut the cooperation down. His left eyelid fluttered before he got it under control; he was becoming weary of Very Special Senior Special Agent Denton of the FBI.

Ron shook Denton off with an effort, and was adding what he'd just seen to his tally on the current state of affairs (and not liking the sum, not at all), when his cell rang, his friend tone, and sure enough, when he pulled it out he saw Mike Smithers' name;

there was no picture. There was no picture because Ron was old, and he didn't share this "cell phone" generations' obsession with attaching photos to every damn thing in creation.

"LT, how are you?"

Mike cleared his throat. "Good, Chief. And you?"

"Good."

"Haven't by chance caught a whiff of Sheriff Neil up that way, have you?"

A surge of something unpleasant shot through Ron, but he kept it nonchalant: "Should I have?"

"Well, considerin' that nobody's heard from 'im all damn day, and that he's not answerin' his cell or house phone or email, and that nobody can find 'im down here even though they've been lookin' all over Sheridan and hell and back, I figured checkin' ta see if anybody'd run across him up there would be worth a shot."

"I guess it goes without saying that someone's been out to his place?"

"Right, and it also goes without sayin' that he wasn't there, but his county truck was. Four of his deps finally got their asses in gear and took off for Caddo Springs 'bout fifteen minutes ago. Neil bought a cabin and a coupla acres out there three or four years back, so they're holdin' out hope he's there…although why Neil wouldn't tell anyone he was takin' the day off, or that he was goin' to his cabin, or the tiny fact that it's after lunch now and he *still* won't answer his goddamn cell…hell, Chief, nobody's mentionin' any o' *that* shit."

"I see."

"Yeah."

That Sheriff Neil had skipped the press conference where Jack Ross would be exonerated had surprised exactly no one; that Sheriff Neil also wouldn't let any of his people attend said conference had surprised the same number, so when Neil and his boys hadn't turned up this morning, nobody had given it much thought—except to send up thanks.

This shined a different light on Neil's absence, however.

Mike sighed like a hurricane gust in Ron's ear: "We're in the middle of the fuckin' shit storm now, ain't we, Chief?"

"I'm afraid it's just cranking up, Mike." Denton appeared from around the front of the house, cell phone pressed to his ear, face and posture even more brittle than usual. "I think the word's spreading. Gotta go, LT, call me if they find him."

"Will do, Chief. Keep yer head down and yer wits sharp."

"You do the same."

Mike laughed. "I'm not the one out swimmin' with the damn sharks. All of *mine* 're stuck in cages." He hung up.

Ron lowered his phone at the same time as Denton. The federal agent had come around on the opposite side of Hank's tool shed and now stood glaring across a trail of evidence markers leading from the back steps and across the yard and into the pines; he jabbed a finger toward a spot near his shiny wingtips and snapped, "Agent Dexter, has this data been cataloged?"

Poofy-hair blinked and looked up from her iPad. "Uh, yes sir."

Denton strode through, mashing a neon-green marker without looking at it or seeming to notice; his steaming eyes had never left Ron. "This changes nothing. The plan *will* go forward."

Ron simply nodded. Denton had said the exact same thing when he'd been looking at the red smear behind the gore-spattered screen; the smear that was all that remained of Hank Ross.

Ron walked away, cutting wide around Hank's shed, heading for the barn.

"Where do you think *you're* going?"

"To talk to Jack. I have a question for him." *And I need to make a call I don't want you to hear.*

"Tell him what I told you! Neil changes *nothing!*"

"Yes, sir." Ron managed to keep his eyelid from fluttering until he got out of Denton's sight, but it was a near thing.

When he rounded the shed, he stopped and surveyed the porch that stretched across the front of the small white house; drying blood still glopped on the inside of the screen in many places, and was splattered in loops and swirls on the white vinyl siding above the maroon recliner—a maroon recliner that had been a green recliner—but at least all the bits and pieces had been scraped together and hauled away.

Two techs in full-body suits were taking a smoke break over underneath the light pole; they'd removed their shoe booties and gloves and clear-plastic face plates, though their hair nets remained. One attempted to light his smoke; the tip trembled so badly he had to chase it with the flame for at least three seconds before he succeeded.

Ron still held his phone. He glanced back to make sure Denton hadn't followed, then peeked down the alley between the house and shed; all clear.

He rang Sheriff Whitehorse down in Johnson County.

Mick sounded busy and put-out, but he answered Ron's questions—and then he had questions of his own, of course, the main one being why the hell Ron was grilling *him* when checking up on the women had been Mick doing him a favor in the first place.

Ron thought about what he'd just learned, adding it to the tally, still not liking it, then said: "Can't talk right now, Mick; got the G all over me. But I'll fill you in as soon as I can."

"That's a buncha crap, Chief, but whatever. Got my own fish to fry, so I'll be seein'—"

"Wait a sec, I've got another favor to ask." He told Mick what he wanted.

"Are you fuckin' serious? Is there somethin' goin' on with these women I need to know about?"

"Just set it up. I'll tell you why later."

"Shit, Chief, you're gonna owe me for this."

"I know."

"I ain't jokin'. And I'm talkin' introduce-me-to-my-future-ex-wife kinda owe."

"I'll see what I can do."

Ron hung up and made his way to the barn's red-and-white double doors, ignoring the lineup of curious, cud-chewing cows gathered at the fence attached to the far corner, along with their fragrance. He knocked on the left-hand door and the dog barked furiously from the other side.

There was no human answer.

He knocked again, sharper, and once more Jezebel sounded off, but this time Ron heard, "Come in!" from a hoarse female voice.

He pulled open the wide, heavy door and stepped inside accompanied by a blazing slant of sunlight and beheld Jack sitting cross-legged on the plank floor with the dog in his lap; when Ron met her eyes, she showed her sharp little teeth and growled.

Jack gently bopped her on her graying nose with one finger and whispered, "No, Jezzie." She licked his hand and wagged her tail and growled at Ron again. A green towel lay on the planks by Jack's knee—a damp and bloody towel; when they'd arrived, a tech was just finishing collecting evidence from the pads of her feet; she'd started to clean the rest of her then, but Jack had insisted on wiping his father's blood from his dog himself.

Ron raised his gaze.

The women were in the leather recliner, over between the television and the ladder to the loft. They were twined like cats, with Mary's head resting on Angela's shoulder. Angela was stroking the older woman's hair, and their faces were haggard and tear-streaked; Mary turned hers away, sobbing anew, but Angela watched him back steadily.

"Jack, I need to talk to you."

"So talk."

"Outside."

The young man just kept petting his dog; long, slow strokes, from bent ears to stubby tail.

"Jack."

"Say what you have to say, I'm busy." Long, slow strokes: "You're a good girl, Jezzie," he whispered. "*Such* a good girl."

Wag-wag, lick-lick; another look up at Ron and another raspy growl.

His cheeks puffed as he blew out a slow breath, and then Ron walked out; he left the door standing open.

He waited by the corner of Hank's shed and thought about the state of things; he still wasn't a fan. The smokers had suited up and gone back inside and two more had taken their place at the base of the pole, although these appeared to be non-smokers. Ron was still thinking and watching them converse in tones too low to make out when he heard Jack admonish Jezebel to stay, and then the barn door *whammed* and clattered shut; moments later Jack appeared at his side, face discolored marble as he stared at the blood congealing on the screen. Ron watched him; there was a constant flow of anger running through Jack now, but other than that dangerous current, there had been no trace of grief for his father.

"It's okay to cry, son."

"If you say so. Why the hell are we out here?"

Ron just shook his head. "Sheriff Neil is missing."

"So?" When he didn't respond, Jack faced him: "You mean *missing* missing?" Ron nodded. "So much for Bob waiting to see what happens at the press conference. And so much for Denton's grand plan—*your* plan, too, I might add! Dad should've never been left here alone!"

"Staying was Hank's choice. You know that."

Jack scowled, then changed the subject. "You didn't have to drag me out here to tell me about Neil. Mom needs me right now, and—"

"It wasn't only that. Come with me."

He led Jack around the open front of the shed and past the woodpile to the back stoop. Denton and the two techs from earlier were over by the eastern tree line now, talking to the three agents who had trailed Hank's killer out to the road.

Denton saw them at the same time, and Ron could feel the frost from two hundred feet away; he said something sharp to his fellow suits and stalked towards Ron and Jack.

"What the fuck is *his* problem? And why are we back here?"

"These." Ron indicated the bloody boot prints on the steps. There were five total; three dark and distinct prints coming down; a partial on the sill, and one full on each step. There were two more that were not-so distinct—less blood; these led up the steps and into the house. A small set of bloody paw prints to the right of these tracks also led up to the door.

"So?"

Ron walked out into the yard, staying well to the side of the neon-green markers. Jack went with him, arms crossed, jaw clenched.

"Jezebel was outside when your dad was killed. When the deed was done, the murderer walked through the house and exited the back door. Jezebel ran around from the front, probably through the alley between the shed and the house, but it's hard to be sure because no blood on her paws yet and her prints were everywhere already." He pointed at a batch of evidence markers, neon-orange instead of neon-green: "This is where she started to follow the killer. They stopped here," he indicated a jumble of markers a few yards further out, orange and green mixed, "and then they turned around and went back to the house and the killer put the dog inside and shut the door. The question is why: Why not just do away with her?"

"Who the fuck knows? Maybe Bob's a dog lover." Jack paused then, eyes narrowing, standing perfectly, utterly still, not even seeming to breathe. Then, quiet: "Why are you showing me this, Chief?"

Before Ron could answer, a dry whip-crack came from behind:

"Well, well, well, why didn't someone tell me it was Amateur Sleuth Day? I would've had my team pack their junior science kits. Why is Mr. Ross here, Chief? Why isn't Mr. Ross preparing for tonight? Did you *inform* Mr. Ross about Sheriff Neal? Did you *explain* to Mr. Ross that Neil doesn't matter, and that the plan to catch the Traveler *can* and *will* go forward?"

"Fuck you, Denton. And fuck your so-called plan. It stinks almost as much as you do."

"Why do you continue to allow this civilian to contaminate my crime scene, Chief?"

"Do you know why you both stink? Because you're both pieces of dog shit, that's why, and *don't talk over my head like I'm not fucking standing here!*"

"Chief, inform Mr. Ross that life is fleeting, and therefore I endeavor to converse with individuals who are worthy of conversation."

"You conceited bastard! Dad just got chopped into a pile of *meat*, and all because of your crappy 'plan'! He should've never been left here alone!"

"I offered your father the opportunity to come with us and he declined, and therefore I refuse to indulge in remorse for someone who brought their demise upon themselves through what I surmise as nothing more or less than sheer, pigheaded stubbornness."

Jack's nostrils flared, and Ron thought there might be real trouble then—the kind that would necessitate the SWAT team breaking cover in order to save Denton's bacon—but that's when his and Special Agent Denton's cell phones rang near simultaneously.

They checked the numbers; Mindy was calling Ron from her cell, and the only reason he could think why is that they'd found Neil and she'd heard about it.

Which meant that someone had already put it out on the box.

Which meant the media hounds would be all over it.

He and Denton looked at each other. "Neil," Ron said. Denton nodded curtly, then walked to the other side of the woodpile to take his call.

He took his own where he stood, but Mindy surprised him; she wasn't calling about Sheriff John Neil, and as he listened, Ron understood he'd made a terrible mistake.

47

I meandered back to my barn, so much in a daze I hardly spared a glance for the smear on Mom and Dad's porch—the smear that used to be my dad.

I stumbled to a halt near my front door and tried to call Donnie again, but the same thing happened that had happened the ten other times I'd tried to call him; the same thing that had happened when Chief Rogers tried. Even Denton had given it a whirl, his attitude shouting that the results *should* and *would* be different if the FBI made the call. But even the power of the federal government backed by Denton's monster ego couldn't change the fact that every call went straight to voicemail, like Donnie's phone was turned off.

Turned off, or dead.

I could sense Hawthorn and the other SWAT pricks out in the trees, listening through my crotch with their federal ear-buds, patiently waiting for a giant chicken to stroll up in broad daylight and brain me with an ax. Maybe they'd even shoot him before he brained me, but at this point I wasn't holding out too much hope.

Where were those assholes when Dad needed them?

Oh yeah, that's right, they'd all been *busy*. And I know Dad had refused to go with them to the Injun, but Denton still could've and should've put somebody out here last night. But the goddamn High and Mighty Federal Agent would never admit it, and for one simple reason:

Nobody cared.

Nobody gave shit one about a half-crippled, wife-beating sot, and they sure as *hell* didn't care when he got chopped to bits—no one but me and Mom, anyway, and despite all the histrionics, I wasn't sure how she truly felt. She'd been busy making plans to leave him, as I recall, and now she'd been freed from all that bitter drama, not to mention saving money on a divorce lawyer.

And how much did *I* care?

Just off the top of my brain I could remember wishing my father dead at least two dozen times, but those fantasies had always involved a big heart storm or a backhoe slipping out of gear on the job or something of the like—something sudden; something sent by fate or the gods or whatever; something that would finally free us from him with no guilt attached.

But to have him taken like *this*…

No. Not like this.

And then there was Tiffany, with her entire, amazing life spread out in front of her, just waiting for her to snatch it up…and now Donnie, who'd become my friend over the past three seasons; Donnie, only nineteen, but smart-as-hell nineteen, who couldn't shut up about the glories of structural engineering and how he was going to, quote: "make a fucking mint" fixing America's crumbling infrastructure…

And their only mistake had been to apply at Crazy's.

Their only *crime* was knowing *me*, Dad included.

I faced the high, bumpy slope to the east, letting my gaze roam up and across those dark-green needles, and reached down and tapped my zipper three times, imagining the sound that would emanate from their ear-buds: a scratchy yet hollow *thud thud thud*.

"Hey fellas, tell ya what; this fucker shows up, do me a favor and go take a nap or a dump or something and *let him come*. I'll settle this myself. Hear me, assholes? I'm fucking serious. And tell Denton he's an arrogant cocksucker and that I'll kick his ass when this is over."

There was no answer because the mic at my crotch wasn't a receiver, only a transmitter, but I was aware of them laughing as I shoved my phone in my pocket and turned the handle and jerked the heavy door open, sunlight spilling into my kitchen. Jezzie was right there to greet me, and I bent and scratched her ears, but her short tail stopped wagging and her liquid eyes lost their happy shine as she caught the vibe; she whined and squirmed under my hand and licked my fingers, giving comfort.

"You're a good girl, Jezzie."

I stood and beheld Angela down the wall to my right, standing in front of a bookshelf with one of my unused cookbooks open in her hand—the Korean again. I guess she really likes Korean. She'd been quiet most of the day, busy dealing with Mom, but I'd felt her watching me; her blue eyes were now soft with sympathy, but there was a question in them, too. I remembered Chief Rogers' insistence we talk outside; she would be wondering what he'd wanted.

I opened my mouth to tell her…and then closed it again because I wasn't sure what to say. So Bob had put the dog inside instead of hacking her into little doggy bits; I didn't know *why*, but I was grateful. He was a nut anyway, and there was no figuring what one of those would do, so why bother with "why"? But Chief Rogers had thought it was important enough to drag me out there and show me…

I blinked and came back as Angela shelved the cookbook and walked toward me. "Jack, what's wrong?" The dog saw her coming and waddled forward. Angela squatted and scratchy-scratched her, still looking at me; Jezebel turned under her hands, grinning her toothy grin, tail going and going hard.

I watched them together as the toilet flushed and water ran in the sink and the towel rack squeaked, and then all three of us turned as Mom opened the bathroom door; she'd washed up and brushed out her hair, but fresh grief had plowed new furrows into her face.

She took one look at my expression and said, "For Heaven's sake, Jackie, what is it *now?*"

I told them.

Mom gasped and tented her mouth and nose with her fingers when I related the few (thank God) details I'd learned about how Steve Baxter had found Donnie's mom and Mrs. Holly, and Angela stood and hugged me hard when I told them Donnie was missing and that his phone was dead and that by this point he was presumed to be in the same condition.

"Steve freaked and called 911, and I guess the media was sitting on the police band because now they're swarming out at Mrs. Holly's place. It's only a matter of time before they sniff out Dad, too. Chief Rogers is taking it all pretty hard." I paused. "Or at least I think so. Difficult to tell with him."

Angela said, "What do you mean?"

"Donnie's been trying to get a hold of Rogers for the last two days, but he always used the non-emergency number to the police station, telling Mindy that he wanted to talk to the Chief, so at first Rogers thought Donnie wanted the key to Crazy's back. Then yesterday Donnie apparently cussed out Mindy, saying it wasn't about Crazy's when she told him Rogers had left the key for him, and that he wanted Rogers' cell so he could call him directly. She wouldn't do it because the Chief doesn't give out his number, and Donnie wouldn't tell her what it was all about, only that he had to talk to the Chief and *only* the Chief—oh, and that he had something to give him."

"Donnie had something to give Chief Rogers? What was it?"

"He never said. Rogers asked me about it last night but I just sort of shrugged it off and said Donnie maybe thought he knew something or had something that could help me…but, I mean, what the hell could a nineteen-year-old *kid* know about the Traveler?" I grimaced. "Chief Rogers and that creep Flemming just tore out of here for Mrs. Holly's place. Denton and most of his team did the same. Before he left, Rogers told Mindy to issue a BOLO for Donnie's Honda. He was on the phone with Neil's second in command, too, some guy named Willis, but they're all bent out of shape down there now that Neil's gone missing. Rogers also said something about securing a warrant to track Donnie's cell, but he didn't think it would be possible to get it until Monday, what with it being the weekend and everything else going on."

Mom said, "The *Sheriff's* gone missing?"

"Oh yeah," I said. "Forgot to tell you about Neil." No way I could pull off heartbroken, not for Neil, but I managed somber as I relayed what Rogers told me, and about how that puke Denton had been insistent Neil changed nothing for us three or his precious "plan".

I ended with a heavy, "Bob's been a busy boy."

Angela's arms were still wrapped around me, and her tired, wary eyes searched deep into mine. "So they think Bob got Donnie and Donnie's mom *and* Mrs. Holly *and* Neil last night, as well as your dad?"

I shrugged. "That's the current theory, but who really knows? Denton sure as hell doesn't." I moved my crotch away from hers reluctantly, but I wanted Hawthorne to hear—to hear, and to pass it along: "For all *Denton* knows, Neil turned his phone off and is sitting in an Indian casino somewhere, playing blackjack and pouting about my release. Denton doesn't know *shit*. All *Denton* knows is that the plan to trap the Traveler will go on as scheduled, no matter what. Speaking of that…" I let go of Angela and unlimbered my phone. "I need to call Miguel and make sure he can work tonight, although without Donnie…" I blinked and cleared my throat.

This time it was Mom who gifted me with a feel-better hug. Angela gave her some room, then sat on the floor to pet Jezzie. I hugged Mom back with one arm and dialed Miguel's number, but got only a voicemail box that my cook hadn't bothered to set up, so I couldn't even leave a message. I tried again, same, then again; still no answer and no voicemail, so I tapped out an extra-long text explaining the situation. Mom kissed me on the cheek and went into the kitchen and got the makings together for a round of green tea.

It was a pain in the butt, that long-ass text, but I wanted Miguel to be aware of the risks involved; he had a wife and four kids.

I finished and waited, but got no response. I sat on the floor and scratchy-scratched one end of the dog while Angela did the other, Jezzie squirming between our hands, reveling in what I was sure was her version of doggie heaven. Mom got three steins out of my cabinets and filled them with ice and a tea bag each and poured the bubbling water in as the ice crackled and popped. She stooped, then stirred in yellow stuff for us and honey for Angela and added a handful of fresh cubes and brought all three steins over and sat on the floor nearby and handed us our tea.

"Thanks, Mom."

"Yes, thank you, Mary. This'll hit the spot."

"You're welcome, children. Now be quiet and drink up and let's enjoy this moment of peace while we can."

"Yes, ma'am."

"Yes, ma'am."

We sat on my floor and drank tea and scratched the dog as Mom stared hollow-eyed into space, tea forgotten on the floor beside her knee while outside the techs that remained scraped up what remained of Dad.

Still no Miguel.

A quiet dread filled me as I pulled my phone back out.

Angela read me. "Do you think…? Oh no, those sweet little kids! Do you really think—?"

"God, I hope not," I began, but that's when Miguel texted me back. I read, and Mom came back from wherever she'd floated off to and watched along with Angela; they saw my expression.

"What?"

"*What*, Jackie?"

"My cook just quit, that's what. Says he and Maria are taking the kids and heading north." Mom just nodded, but Angela raised a golden eyebrow: "I close Crazy's after Labor Day, and Miguel rolls up to Washington for the September apple harvest and comes back. It's early, but this time they're *all* going, and even though Miguel didn't say adiós, I'm pretty sure it's implied." I shoved the phone away. "The kids were born here—well, the youngest three were—but he and Maria are both illegal, and I guess all the authority types spooked them. And all the dying." I sighed, then straightened my spine and slapped my knees. "Well, so much for Denton's plan. Ain't no way I can run Crazy's by my lonesome." I leaned back and double-tapped my zipper: "What about it, Hawthorne? You up to flippin' some burgers?"

Mom said, "Stop antagonizing those brave men, Jackie. They're out there to protect you," but her heart wasn't in it; she wasn't even looking at me. She and Angela were eyeing each other, and then they nodded in sync and faced me, fixed features and determined body language shouting they were settling in for a long fight, but it was one they meant to win.

I got there a little late, as usual, but I got there:

"Hunh-*uh*," I said. "No way. You guys are going back to wherever you were last night, end of discussion."

But of course it wasn't. I'm sure Hawthorne and those other dickheads had a good chuckle while listening to the women in my life shoot down every logical argument I could muster, along with some illogical ones. Mom finally routed me with, "Agent Denton will stick you in Crazy's for bait whether you have any help or not, and he sure won't give you people he can't spare, so Angie and I are *it*, buster."

"We can help you, Jack. Let us. Please."

Mom added, "And I need to do something with myself. If I have to go back to that hotel room and just sit around…" she shook her head as my ears perked; I'd figured they were in a hotel somewhere, but this was the first confirmation. "No," Mom continued, "I *need* this, Jackie, just like Angie did the other day, after she found poor Jess. And you close at nine, so it's not like we'll be at Crazy's the whole night."

"All right," I sighed. "But Denton won't like it."

Mom's face went all stony and cold, like I'd seen so few times in my life.

"Good," she said.

48

So that's how I found myself flipping Crazy's CLOSED sign to OPEN at five o'clock on a blazing-hot July Saturday afternoon.

We normally open at eleven, so we were only six hours late (or two-and-a-half *days* late, if you counted from when Neil had arrested my innocent ass on Thursday morning—and I did), but the people sweating in a line that stretched across the sweltering gravel and through the packed cars and trucks and SUVs almost to the highway didn't seem to mind either the heat or the late start.

I slid the window open. "Welcome to Crazy's. How may I help you?"

I took the brunette reporter's order and answered her inane questions while some guy stood off to the side with his shoulder-mounted camera and filmed it all for the inquiring masses.

No, I had no comment on the murder of my father. Would she like two orders of Large Freedom Fries to compliment her two Free Freedom Cheeseburgers? No, my mother had no comment either. How about an Extra Large Crazy Coke Float? No, I had no comment on the grisly death of Sheriff John Neal. No, I had no comment about the rampant speculation spreading online that Zane Richards had left even *more* bodies in his wake before his arrest, and that heaps of corpses were just lying around, waiting to be discovered. That would be two Free Freedom Cheeseburgers, one with mustard and onions and one with ketchup and pickles. Your order number is one-oh-one, come to the pick-up window when your number is called. Please step aside so the next person can… How did my father's murder make me feel? How the hell did she *think* it made me feel?

"Please move out of the way, ma'am."

The brunette gave me frustrated, but she and her camera mule moved to the edge of the awning's shade and conferred in low voices before walking out into the sunshine, where they set up for a shot with Crazy's and the line of people in the background.

I faced the next person, a tourist. The people behind the tourist chattered and preened as they took selfies or filmed themselves being filmed or texted their family and friends or updated their social media, informing all and sundry that they were on the Teee-Veeeee!

Woo fucking hoo.

"Welcome to Crazy's. What can I get for you?"

Mom placed two cheeseburgers in the dungeon window and Angela stalked behind me and grabbed them and stacked and squirted the requested condiments and wrapped-and-bagged and snatched down the mic: "Order number one-oh-one is ready!", but the reporter and her sidekick didn't bother to acknowledge their free food. Angela tossed the bag on the shelf beside her without looking and muttered, "Bitch!" but thankfully she'd already released the button.

"Welcome to Crazy's. How may I assist you on this fine, fine day?"

After the fifth order, I asked Angela to take over while I cobbled a sign out of a flap of cardboard box and a black permanent marker and taped it in the glass above the mesh. It said **Limit 2 Free Freedom Cheeseburgers per customer, and only with minimum purchase of $1!!** That got some grumbles as the news was passed back, and a third of the line melted away and drove off, but the remainder constricted like a hungry snake and kept coming.

"Welcome to Crazy's. Beautiful evening, isn't it? That's right, great day to be alive and free. How may I help you?"

Sheriff Neal had been found by a gaggle of wannabe cowboys vacationing at a dude ranch; they'd stumbled upon him while out on a guided horseback ride…or what was left of him. Information had been sketchy—the mainstream outlets were refusing to report the grimmer details—but it had been confirmed by several reputable sources that Neil's hands and feet had been removed and the stumps cauterized with a handheld propane torch before he had been crucified between two jackstraw pines. Alive. Neil's hands and feet were still missing, which made me wonder about the fate of the hat and the mustache.

It also made me wonder, rather uneasily, what they'd found too offensive to report.

"Welcome to Crazy's. How may I serve you?"

They'd caught wind of Dad around the same time, mid-afternoon, so between him and Mrs. Holly and still-missing Donnie and Donnie's mom and Neil, only a half-dozen vultures had bothered to flap on down to Crazy's for that all-important sound bite from the falsely accused and the newly exonerated. We'd just finished straightening the mess Rife's team had made and were stocking for five o'clock when they'd gathered at the windows and shouted their insensitive questions in at me…

And then they'd recognized Mom.

One male reporter made the mistake of asking her if she felt that helping her son profit from innocent people's murders—one of which just-so happened to be her husband's—was ethical. After Angela and I dragged Mom back inside and calmed her down and the reporter stopped running, I went out and gathered them around me and told them I would grant each an individual interview—if they came back at five and stood in line and ordered something. That had caused more than a few splutters, but I only informed them nothing was free and went back inside.

"Welcome to Crazy's. What do you want?"

So far only the brunette had taken me up, but I had seen another television crew roll in behind the brunette, and from the reactions of the people still broiling in line out past the vehicles, I knew they had set up somewhere out of my sight and were busy doin' their reportin' thang without botherin' to talk to little ol' me. *Good.* I also saw a fine-looking blonde across at the Shell, holding a phallic microphone while yapping her head off to a camera, so I figured the brunette would be it as far as order-window interviews went. That was also good; it meant fewer Free Fucking Freedom Cheeseburgers that I would have to hand out, for one thing.

"Welcome to Crazy's. Let me take a wild guess: Two Free Freedom Cheeseburgers and a small drink, right?"

Despite my sign, the line kept replenishing itself, and my earlier fear about running out of supplies was more and more likely to come true…but I wasn't giving much of a shit because I'd realized how bad of an idea this had been—and not just about giving food away or that Bob wouldn't show up and try to kill me because he was plum tuckered from torturing and murdering half the town last night; no, this had been a bad idea for one horrible, awful, terrible reason:

Crazy's was haunted.

I'd thought I was losing it when I'd first noticed our ghostly visitors earlier that afternoon. I was busy peeling and slicing the big sweet Texas yellows I always ordered for the rings when I caught a whiff of cigarette smoke drifting in through the propped-open back door, and I actually had to check myself before I called for Donnie to get his ass back inside to help. I must've turned pale, too, because both of my ladies asked me if I was all right. I told them I was just peachy, but two minutes later I caught a swirl of dark hair out of the corner of my eye and almost turned to look; I'd glimpsed that glossy flow over behind the ice-cream cooler…or had I?

Now I wondered: If I *had* looked, would I have seen the misty form of a sixteen-year-old girl with big dark eyes and a taut body, plum nails flying as she texted her BFF? Maybe, maybe not, because maybe Crazy's was now truly haunted and maybe it was all in my head…but either way, I couldn't take being reminded of those great kids every time I turned around.

I was in front of the dungeon window, wrapping and bagging free cheeseburgers when my hands paused, and I sighed.

"What is it, Jackie?"

Mom stabbed a filled ticket on the spike and stretched tip-toe to snatch the next one off the wheel; she held the new order in one hand as she used my grill spatula to flip a done patty from the hot side to the warm and cheesed it, all without looking as she peered out at me with a mother's concern. Sweat streaked her worn face below the hairnet, and my heart suddenly ached at what I was doing to the two people I loved the most—and all to keep my selfish dream alive. Oh, we were supposedly helping to catch a madman, but I knew the reason *I* was here.

Mom had two-dozen patties going, keeping ahead of the crush, as any grill man worth his salt would. I pulled the ticket off the spike and stapled it to the bag and handed it all to Angela, then stepped into the dungeon and squeezed behind Mom and checked the box of 80/20 patties; it was a sixty-count box, and it was less than half-full. I carried it to the walk-in and felt the blast of cold air envelop me as I set the box on top of five more just like it—you know, except they were full.

I went back out into the heat and shut the heavy steel door with a clank. Someone tapped on the order window and said something, but we ignored him. Someone else, a woman, the owner of the bag in Angela's hands, bent over and shaded her eyes and peered in at us, but we all just stood there staring at each other.

"I can't do this."

My ladies didn't reply, just watched me with pity.

"I keep seeing Tiff and Donnie…" I cleared my throat and dashed at my eyes with a sleeve. "We'll serve what's on the grill, then that's it. If someone wants to *pay* for a chili dog or a chicken sandwich or a Crazy Float or whatever, we'll serve them, but I'm closing this place down at seven o'clock. You guys look exhausted. You need to go back to your hotel and get some rest."

"Jack—"

"Son—"

"I can't do it anymore." I went to the order window and the douche bag who was still tapping and threw it open. *"What?"*

Mid-forties, taller than me, medium build, glasses; he opened his mouth angrily and then reconsidered when he took in my expression. "I…I just wanted two Free Freedom Cheeseburgers with mustard and pickles only, and, um, I guess two Extra Large Crazy Root Beer Floats. If that's okay."

"Fine." I scribbled it out and rang it up and he paid with a credit card; he looked relieved when he hurried over to stand at the back of the line that had grown in front of the pick-up window. "Next!"

When the allotment of cheeseburgers was up, I ripped the sign down and told the freeloader behind the freeloader at the window the bad news, and soon the line was much shorter and my lot almost empty.

Just the way I wanted it.

Three minutes after the sign came down, the tall, lean form of Agent Walters appeared at the back of the much-shortened line. I almost didn't recognize him in cheap black sunglasses and blue polyester trunks and a white wife-beater and green flip-flops. He was even carrying a Styrofoam six-pack cooler by its red handle; the beach-bum SWAT Agent.

When he got to the front, he flipped the glasses onto his hair and hissed through the mesh: "What the *fuck* do you think you're doing, Ross? You're supposed to stay open 'till nine, so *stay* fucking *open* 'till *nine*. You can't just change the plan on the fly! Agent Denton said—"

"Screw Denton. Bob won't come after me here; too many witnesses. But tonight, when he thinks I'm alone? That's got a better shot. You know it. Hawthorne knows it. Hell, *everybody* knows it except Denton. The plan will only change insofar as the time I close up shop, seven instead of nine; the girls will still need to be followed back to wherever you have them stashed, and I'll still go straight home and go to bed with a big target painted on my back."

Walters glared, then straightened and glared some more. Then he flipped the cheap shades back onto his nose. "Write me a ticket," he growled.

I scribbled something and handed it out and told him his number and he threw a ten-spot through the window and stalked away without waiting for any pretend change and went to an older-model black Toyota Tacoma with jacked-up suspension and *sweet* mag wheels and climbed in and slammed the door. I didn't bother to call his number, and four more freeloaders got their food and went away and Mom and Angela watched me with sympathy and Tiff went back over and hid behind the ice-cream cooler and Donnie punched me on the shoulder and called me the Mack Daddy Jack before Walters reemerged from the Tacoma and flapped over to the pick-up window in his silly green flip-flops; he'd lost the little cooler, but he was carrying his ticket. Angela slid open the window and handed him a grilled chicken sandwich and a large Dr. Pepper as he said, "Seven o'clock." He took the grub from her, and I felt almost relieved when he looked her up and down and grinned like the wolf he was.

Almost.

He flapped back to the Tacoma and peeled gravel as he sped back up toward Indian Head and probably my place on the other side; setting up. Or maybe he was preparing to follow the girls;

could be either, but nobody was very fucking likely to inform me. Why tell *me* anything? It was just my life and the lives of the two people I loved the most in all the world, that's all.

The line dwindled and vanished as the golden sun dropped behind the pines to the west, long, jagged shadows stretching across to the Shell, the mountains glowing high above it all like the promise of a better day. Mom and Angela were quiet as we cleaned and shut everything down and then stocked out of sheer, dumb habit. Tiffany stayed just as quiet as she swept her station, and Donnie went out back to smoke as I flipped the OPEN sign to CLOSED. Maybe for the last time.

My ladies took turns hugging me before they left, Mom telling me, "Don't rush into any decisions, Jackie." Angela only whispered, "I love you," but that was enough.

I didn't see anyone follow Angela's white Camry up the mountain, good guys or otherwise. I waited around for five minutes, then locked up and lowered the boards over the windows and locked them too, then stood in the gravel and stared at Crazy's as the shadows deepened around me, remembering all the waves as well as all the good times; the jokes and the laughs, and those that had laughed with me: Jen and Donnie, Miguel and Tiffany. All gone, now. Some were dead, some were only missing and *presumed* dead, and some were…well, just gone. Gone out of my orbit and out of my life; gone for good.

Gone.

I turned and crunched toward my truck.

"See ya, bitch."

I rumbled up and through Indian Head and to our place on the ridge as the light was dying, although the snow-filled saddles high above continued to glow spectacularly. I didn't see anyone following me, and I sure hadn't seen anyone bolt out of the pines behind Crazy's and jump in a concealed car and speed ahead, but I knew Hawthorne and his team would already be watching from somewhere; those guys were good, I had to admit.

I bumped down the drive and emerged from the needles to a silent house and barn and shed, the school-bus yellow crime-scene tape still wrapped all the way around the house like a giant ribbon around a macabre present; even Dad's tool shed and the woodpile were wrapped. I turned my truck off and got out and looked over at the porch, at the rust-colored splotches that still stained the inside of the screen, and then I realized someone had hauled away Dad's old recliner—for evidence, I suppose.

The place was eerie, especially compared to the bustle of earlier; even the steers were missing. Fred White had shown up not long after we'd learned about Donnie and moved them to another pasture, sheepishly offering his condolences to Mom and I after telling us he didn't want the herd to get stressed from all the hubbub.

The creepy-crawlies were just stealing over me when Jezebel barked from inside my barn. Her waddle was urgent as she shot past me with an accusatory look, then took care of business out at the edge of the yard before bouncing back, tail going so hard it was probably stirring up dust down in Sheridan.

"Hey, pretty girl!"

I bent to scratch her while casting another uneasy glance at the porch; Crazy's wasn't the only haunted house, now. Maybe Dad was sitting in there, kicked back in a misty recliner, dripping Pabst clenched in big fist, watching me through the splotchy screen; if I'd heard a breathy yet contempt-filled "Man of the house!" echo across the yard right then, I wouldn't have been too surprised.

I looked away from those dark-and-I-sincerely-hoped-empty recesses and stood up hurriedly. *Jesus Christ.* "Come on," I told Jezzie. "Let's go inside. Good girl wanna treat?"

She should've gone nuts at the T-word, but she just stared toward the shadowy mass of trees across the driveway with her ears laid back, sniff-sniffing, then started yapping.

I said, "That's just some friends." *Sort of.*

Rrrrrrrrrrrrowl, rowl, rowl!

I had to speak to her sharply, and then she slunk after me and went to her bed by the stove and put her chin on her paws and watched me move around the barn, stuck in full-doggy-pout mode until I'd fulfilled the T-word promise. Then I scratchy-scratched her and told her she was a good girl and grabbed my biggest knife from the knife drawer and climbed the ladder.

I really, really, really wanted to tell those SWAT dicks to have a nice, comfortable night, and that I hoped they'd packed in toilet paper (needles not being an optimal choice for such business), but I somehow didn't as I put the knife on the nightstand and carefully removed the eraser-sized microphone as per instructions and placed it next to the knife and got undressed and flopped face-first into bed and buried my nose in my pillow and inhaled the faint trace of Angela that still lingered, drawing it deep, hoping that if I actually survived the weekend that somehow that incredible, tantalizing scent would turn out to be a promise of magical things to come.

More fool me.

49

Miriam ran the tortoise-shell brush through her hair one hundred times, switching hands every ten strokes, turning this way and that to admire her body in the full-length mirror, taking pride in her full—natural!—breasts and trim tummy and nicely rounded ass above lean-yet-muscular legs.

And why *shouldn't* she feel pride? She'd worked damn hard for this body—and she worked harder every day just to keep it. She turned again and paused, posing; all the sweat and sacrifice: Pilates for an hour in the morning before Doug and the kids even woke up, followed by an hour on the treadmill or stationary bike every evening, followed by thirty minutes of power yoga; all the plain yogurt and brown rice and unseasoned chicken breasts and kale and every other tasteless thing she ate, and all the pizza and bacon cheeseburgers and ice cream she didn't.

She *deserved* a little pride!

Miriam placed her brush on the dresser and faced the mirror full on and tossed her head, spreading her hair across her shoulders. She touched the tip of her right nipple with her index finger, then pinched it, rolling it between thumb and finger as she let her other hand slide down her stomach…then reached lower and slipped two fingers inside, maintaining the pressure, fingers plunging, breath coming faster and faster.

She paused as he stirred and then sat up on the bed behind her. She waited, breathing hard, and then he got out of bed and came up behind her and kissed her on the side of the neck, sliding his own hand down to replace hers, rough fingers working, working, and then he straightened and his rock-hard cock slid up inside her.

She braced her hands on the wall on either side of the mirror and alternately watched her breasts sway and his handsome face turned up toward the tray ceiling in ecstasy as he pounded her, and then he grabbed a handful of her hair and yanked her head back, just like she liked, and she was feeling something, yes, he was finally going to make her come, *yes*…and then from downstairs she heard a loud *thud*, and then a softer *thump*.

"Wait!" she told him. He kept thrusting into her and moaning and pulling her hair. "Ryan! Stop! *Stop*, damn it!"

He paused, still deep inside her, and opened his pale blue eyes and scowled at her reflection. "What's wrong?"

"I heard something."

"I didn't." He let go of her hair and reached his long arms around and cupped her breasts, cock now sliding slowly in and out, in and out.

"Stop!" Miriam bumped him back with her ass, and he grunted as he slid out of her with a wet sound. She faced him, and the sight of a fully erect man who was also standing was as comical as ever; her smile was rueful as she quick-stepped across the room and opened the top drawer of her jewelry hutch and pulled out her SIG Sauer .45 1911 Scorpion.

His eyes widened appreciatively. "Nice. Know how to use that?"

"Doug taught me." Miriam racked a round, noting that his cock was wilting already as she padded to her bedroom door and put her ear to it.

"It was probably that schizoid cat. Come back over—"

"It sounded bigger than the cat."

She grasped the knob, and he said, "Wait," and moved to his clothes and lifted his gun belt from the pile and took the strap off his holster and pulled his service revolver, a Smith & Wesson .38; a good, dependable weapon, but Miriam would take her Siggy any day of the week. He popped the cylinder and checked the load, then closed it with a flip of his wrist and gently took her hand off the knob.

"Let me go first," he whispered.

Miriam moved aside; he *was* the cop.

Ryan opened the door and stepped into the hallway, Miriam on his heels, Sig held at her shoulder in a double-handed grip, barrel pointed at the ceiling; ever since the Fourth, when those kids had died and that terrible cell-phone video got shared around the world, Miriam had been keeping her pistol close. Doug had called and had made her promise to do so, but she'd already resolved to keep it near, even carrying it in her purse when she went to work at her dress shoppe; she'd never felt the need before, but that grainy, jumping video had given her the jim-jams.

They crept down the stairs, bare feet making no sound on the carpeted risers, nude reflections overlaying the framed pictures that angled down the wall to their left; Miriam and Doug, or her and Doug and the kids, or just the kids; Casey and Heath, then little Queen Lacey all by herself, cuteness oozing, then all three.

Ryan was near the bottom when another soft *thump* came from the direction of her kitchen.

They froze and held their breath and strained their ears, but only the steady hum of the fridge came to them. After a few seconds they kept going, then stopped on the final two risers and listened again...and then before he could react she flicked her safety off and slipped by him and swung around the corner, .45 out and ready in a two-handed shooter's grip, trigger finger resting outside the guard:

Her kitchen was empty.

Ryan pushed past her, sparing her a sullen glance as he covered the living room with his weapon, and then the dining room, and then the laundry room, finding them all empty. He straightened and lowered his gun…and then Hobbes, who had apparently been lurking in the dining room, jumped up on the counter through the service window.

Ryan started back, half raising his weapon again before catching himself.

"Christ!"

Miriam burst into laughter.

Ryan glared, and Hobbes, her big, mopey, scatter-brained, fuzzy faced Persian, jumped back through the service window with a startled trill.

"You think that's funny? I almost shot your damn cat! *Speaking* of the damn cat, I *told* you that's what you heard, that stupid fucking cat!"

"I'm sorry for laughing," Miriam said…but she wasn't, not really. Ryan was sooooo full of himself all the time (Mr. Big, Bad Police Man, he was, even though he was really only an also-ran junior officer in a tiny, also-ran town), and it was nice to see him jump—not to mention taken down a peg.

Miriam put the Siggy's safety back on and checked around more thoroughly, making sure Hobbes hadn't knocked something over in his nocturnal feline wanderings; nothing. She went back down the hall and past the stairs and checked the front door; locked. She went into the formal dining room, saw Hobbes up on the oval, eight-person table busily grooming himself, and walked over as he stood and arched his back, purring and turning under her hand while she stroked from fuzzy ears to long, fuzzy tail.

"Did you do something, big boy, hmm? You makin' messes again?", but he just went back to grooming, pink tongue rasping on smoke fur. Miriam walked to the door to the garage and checked it; still locked. She looked out through the glass panes, past her white

Escalade where it sat in the rolled-up garage; Ryan's Indian Head Police cruiser was parked brazenly in her driveway, blue light-bar glowing softly in the muted yellow radiance from the front porch; it was so, so nice not to have to skulk around anymore, now that she and Doug had come to their agreement.

Ryan moved up behind her and pressed his flaccid penis against her bottom and bent down and breathed, "I *told* you it was the stupid cat," as he nibbled on her earlobe, service weapon held out to the side. "Besides, nobody's gonna do anything with a cop car sitting out there."

She turned and took him in her hand, stroking. They kissed, tongues swirling, and then she pulled away and said, "Don't you have to go on duty soon?" and ducked under his arm and crossed the kitchen and bounded up the stairs; the sooner he left, the sooner she could finish herself off—and think about who she *really* wanted to think about. And that person was not Officer Ryan Flemming.

By the time he arrived upstairs she was already lying back on the pillows, legs spread and playing with herself, but not in any urgent way. He stood in the doorway, limp now, face equal parts irritated and amused. Then he snorted and went to his clothes and picked up his gun belt and sheathed his weapon and buttoned the holster, then began to dress, still watching her as she slowly swirled her middle finger and plunged it in; swirl, plunge, swirl, plunge.

When he was dressed, he continued to watch in silence, pale eyes drifting from her face as she watched him watch, down the contours of her body, to her finger as it worked, and then to the SIG .45, which she still held down by her leg in her left hand, resting it on the satin sheets.

He spoke while watching that finger. "So that's it? Wham, bam, thank you, Officer?"

"Did you expect something else? You know I'm married, and that we're just having fun. Don't get all sanctimonious on me now, Ryan."

He looked her in the eye: "Well, I'm sorry I'm not him."

Her finger paused. "Doug's a good enough husband, and he's great with the kids, but you shouldn't—"

"I didn't mean Doug."

Miriam blushed and turned her head away; she'd cried out Jack's name the first time they'd done it. They'd ended up in doggie style, and just as she was about to come, it had slipped out. Ryan had pulled out of her abruptly, and Miriam had thought he would be mad, but he was only getting off too soon—as usual. He'd said nothing about her slip then, or during the second time, or the time before the mirror, but obviously he'd noticed—noticed, and not forgotten.

Ryan was still just standing there, watching her…and suddenly Miriam didn't like his pretty-but-frozen eyes on her. She closed her legs and grabbed the sheets and covered herself.

"Don't you have to be at work?"

He chuckled. "Thanks for the fuck, Miriam. Maybe we'll do it again sometime. Then again, maybe we won't. I'm thinking it's time to move on to someone else—someone more my age, say."

"*Leave*, Ryan. Now."

"Maybe I'll hook up with Angie Beaumont. She'll chuck Ross to the curb eventually, and she doesn't have a husband and three kids—not to mention all those stretch marks…"

Miriam twisted up to her knees, sheet still wrapped around her. "*Go!*"

"See ya around." He walked out.

Seething, she listened to his heavy cop-boots thump on the carpeted risers, and then she left the SIG on the bed and scrambled to the door with the sheet still wrapped around her: "And don't come back! We're *through!*"

"Whatever," came his reply, and then the door from the kitchen to the garage opened and closed.

Miriam dropped the sheet and pounded down the stairs and *flew* into the kitchen just as headlights shone through the panes. She flung open the door and stood there, turning slightly, letting the light bathe her; letting him see what he would never see again.

He paused to take her in, then just shook his head before backing the rest of the way out.

Miriam watched him drive away, then punched the button and the garage door churned down. She slammed the interior door, fists clenched in fury.

How *dare* he!?

She took several calming breaths, then glanced down at her naked body; she worked so *hard* to keep it healthy and in shape, to keep it toned and attractive, but she'd given natural birth to three kids—three beautiful, wonderful, amazing kids—and that meant she had stretch marks. She would never be able to work them off, either, not all the way, and short of plastic surgery she would never be rid of them. Miriam *refused* to let anyone cut on her, though, and certainly not for such a vain, shallow reason…

Not yet, anyway.

She sobbed quietly for a time before dashing the tears away with her fingers. It wasn't Ryan she was crying over, and she knew it; it wasn't even her hated stretch marks.

It was Jack.

Jack, and Angie Beaumont.

Those two were together tonight, Miriam just knew it; after being freed from jail for a crime he didn't commit, where *else* would he be but making love to his beautiful girlfriend? Miriam's teeth clenched; his *young* and *gorgeous* girlfriend. Angie Beaumont was so beautiful it made Miriam's *toenails* ache!

And there Miriam had been today, at the square, making a fool out of herself, pursuing Jack like a love-struck schoolgirl—something she hadn't been in a long, long time.

Men chased *her*, not the other way around!

But Jack was different. Even three years ago, when she'd first brought him to her bed, it had been *her* convincing *him* (he'd been reluctant, spouting some nonsense about her being a married woman), and after they'd made love that first time…

Miriam's skin flushed at the memory.

He'd broken it off after only four months, though, when he'd met Jenifer, and she still remembered her shock; men didn't call the shots, not with *her*…but again, Jack had always been the exception. During that four months, Miriam had been with no other man—well, besides Doug, and he didn't count. And then, when Jack and Jenifer had finally broken up, she'd waited and waited and waited for him to come back to her, stupid pride convincing her that *this* time she would make sure things were different; that *this* time *she* would call the shots. And then, when she finally realized he was never, ever going to call her, she'd subsumed her pride and went to Crazy's…but she'd been too late. That blonde beauty-queen bitch Angie Beaumont had already staked her claim.

Miriam sighed.

Yes, Jack was different. She'd never met a man so flexible, or so strong, or so attentive. Or so *enthusiastic*. The recently departed and not-missed-at-all Officer Ryan Flemming was good in bed, and he usually (when her head wasn't filled with Jack Ross, anyway) made her come at least once, and sometimes even twice…but he was no Jack.

Not even close.

Miriam shuddered softly, feeling the wetness seeping between her legs, and then flashed across the kitchen and up the stairs, ready to climb back in bed and lose herself in memories of Jack and Jack's tongue and Jack's lovely, amazing cock…

She stopped.

Hobbes (or Sir Hobbes Kitty, Esquire, as her giggling, then-young children had named the tiny gray meowing puffball Doug had brought home) was crouched in the upstairs hallway with his back to her, fuzzy ears standing at attention as he peered around the jamb and through the open doorway into her bedroom, long-haired tail snapping side-to-side.

An uneasy jolt went through Miriam. She whispered, "What is it, Hobbes?"

He glanced back at her with his vivid and inscrutable cat-eyes, then stood and padded off down the hall before vanishing into the guest bathroom with a flick of that tail.

Miriam stared after him, then moved to the doorway and cautiously looked in, but saw nothing out of the ordinary: There were the sheets tangled on the floor, where she'd dropped them in her fit of pique; there was her Siggy, still lying on the bed, the round, black hole at the end of the barrel just peeking at her past the edge of the comforter; there was her purse and her iPhone on the nightstand, under the lamp where she always left them; there was the lingerie she'd been wearing when she'd met Ryan at the door, the one-piece Doug had bought her last year, a cream silk number that felt like heaven against her skin and slipped off like a dream; there was her tall jewelry hutch and the door to the bathroom, which was open; the lights were off, and its recesses were full of shadows.

Miriam looked down the hall toward the half bath, where Sir Hobbes Kitty, Esquire had vanished:

"Weird cat."

She went over and picked up her pistol and ejected the chambered round onto the comforter, then popped the clip and thumbed the bullet in and shoved it back before replacing the gun in the top drawer of her hutch. Miriam still wanted to finish herself off while thinking about Jack, but first she needed to pee. She walked into the bathroom and flicked the light on, then froze in shock.

SLUT was scrawled in angular, gashing red letters across her vanity mirror. Her Rapturous Red lay on the counter before the mirror, crimson stick twisted out, golden cap off.

Shock was turning to alarm when the bathroom door swung violently shut and out stepped someone wearing a black ski mask and black gloves, someone who had been hiding in the angle behind the door. Miriam had time to register a claw hammer before it sailed toward her head. She ducked, and it bounced off her shoulder before clipping her above the ear. She stumbled against the counter and slid to her bottom, catching herself with one knee twisted under and the other leg sticking out. She raised an arm in defense as the second swing arced down, and Miriam felt and heard both bones in her forearm snap like twigs.

She yowled at the fiery lance that raced down her arm and across her shoulder to her neck before exploding into her brain. And then the hammer head struck the crown of her skull with a *thock!* that she felt in both big toes before darkness swept up out of nowhere and took her away.

Miriam woke with blinding light shining in her eyes. She rolled her head to the side and groaned and tried to shield her face with her hand…and the pain in her shattered forearm flared so hot she screamed.

Her arms wouldn't budge; they were also extended over her head, and something bound her wrists together; her legs were spread wide open, and she couldn't move them, either. She squinted and tried to focus on the multiple lights hovering over her, but her vision was strangely doubled; she finally figured out it was the chandelier in her dining room; it had been turned up high and was blazing into her face.

I'm lying face-up on my own polished-oak table. Worse, she'd been *tied* face-up on her own table. And then she realized something even more terrifying:

She wasn't alone.

Miriam raised her head, agony erupting from a point on top of her skull, and regarded the doubled, wavering figure between her feet. The intruder still wore the black ski mask and still carried the now-bloody hammer in one gloved hand, but there was something new in the other hand.

Miriam focused on it with difficulty.

It was her big pepper mill, the foot-long ceramic she never used because it was too fancy for everyday wear and tear; she kept the whole set stuck up in one of her kitchen cabinets, and she hadn't even thought about it in two years.

The masked figure standing between her feet held the long mill up for her to consider. Miriam licked dry lips and croaked, "What… why are you?…" but that's when the intruder bent and shoved the pepper mill inside her.

She shrieked as the grinder handle tore its way into her, and then convulsed and screamed louder as it was pushed deeper, all the way in. Her blurry attacker left the pepper mill stuck inside her and clumped around to her head and looked down at her and listened to her scream.

The hammer slowly raised high.

"*No*," she wailed, "*my kids, please, you can't—!*"

The hammer head crashed between her eyes, crushing her skull and snapping her neck. Darkness swept up out of nowhere again and carried Miriam off, but this time it did not let her go.

Sunday

50

I've had it too easy, that's the problem.

Dawn was a pale rumor as Bob took 15 down to CR 161 and made the turn, sleek red '76 Stingray's pop-up headlights glowing like monster eyes, yellow beams sweeping across rank upon rank of tall Ponderosa pine.

Soft. That's what I've become, soft and spoiled.

He'd set the stage and then brought them all here to his town—brought the whole *world*—and he'd thought he could control the situation, just as he'd done for decades, both in his true life *and* his false.

I was wrong…

…though the FBI's play with his surviving twin wasn't exactly what you'd call a shock, and stank of desperation; Bob wondered idly what PC they would concoct for Zane's arrest—or perhaps Zane, being the hotheaded idiot he was, had done something foolish enough that they hadn't had to invent anything; no matter either way, because Bob had countered the move with one call from a fresh phone, which he had then destroyed.

Bottom line, Zane was out of harm's way now, and Bob could proceed with his plan for those oh-so-smart men with the three pathetic letters on their jackets.

This new player, though, the one that had entered the game late by killing Hank Ross, piggybacking on and thus *hijacking* Bob's own efforts…whoever they were (and "they" could have been any number of people; Hank Ross had been a stubborn and contrary man—the *best* that could be said about him—and over the years Hank had made almost as many enemies as Bob had), they had opened his eyes to the truth. And the truth was, in trying to engineer his will down to the last component, he'd gotten too cute; there were too many players now, too many personalities making decisions that had nothing to do with his desires.

So.

Time to simplify.

Black suede creaked against the gaudy crimson-leather steering-wheel cover as his hands tightened in rage; he'd wanted poetic justice. He still did. Jack Ross should share Bob's terrible fate—*would* have shared it if his plan had been executed properly. But Neil had failed him. Well, the Sheriff had paid for that, paid in full. And Bob had another regret besides letting Zack's murderer off easy.

Angie Beaumont.

The little slut had escaped him. *No one* escaped him! Several had tried, and a bare handful had succeeded, if only temporarily; a twitching grin appeared as he recalled one such instance: He'd gone to collect a whore he had marked out, but in the intervening months she'd acquired a new beau; no matter, he'd easily dealt with such twists before, but that evening the beau'd brought a dog, a big Irish wolfhound-looking mongrel that had sniffed out Bob where he'd been hiding; what's more, the new beau had been armed, concealed carry, and Bob had to flee into the trees behind the whore's property with bullets whizzing over his head.

But Robert Richards Jr. played a long game; he'd kept tabs from afar as the "hero" had been lauded for saving his woman from a burglar or a home-invasion rapist or worse (Bob's grin twitched wider: *much* worse), noting when they inevitably split shortly thereafter, noting when the whore had married the next new beau and had whelped a brat by him and then divorced him and married the next and had squirted out a couple *more* brats, just like the whore she was. He'd kept up with the "hero" as well, who had married and fathered children of his own, noting when the hero moved four states away for a new job.

And then, eight years ten months and twenty-six days later, Bob had finished his interrupted program, collecting the hero first, then the whore, bringing them together again at one of his special places…and it was a shame, really, because those two might have been meant for each other:

Their screams had blended quite beautifully.

No one escaped him…but little Angie Beaumont might go down in history as the first *and* the last, because although he played a long game, time was working against him, now; the stage was set, events were rushing to a conclusion, and his enemies were all around him, hunting him, waiting for him to make a mistake. He had to keep pushing the play, keep them off balance and guessing until it was too late; a true man acts, he doesn't react.

In other words, Bob just might have to swallow his regrets and let the whore live and simply kill Jack Ross.

If so, then so be it; he could both live *and* die with that; he would not whine or complain. He would *not* be spoiled; Bob would be grateful for the opportunities his plan had brought within his grasp, and then he would seize those opportunities and crush them.

Resolved anew, he gassed it, throaty V8 speeding him along the dirt road and sending dust billowing into the needles on either side;

just before the first rise, a bump of ridge that would hide him from the highway, he checked the rearview and side mirrors to make sure no one had made the turn behind him:

Beyond the dissipating dust-haze, the long, pale finger of road was empty.

Satisfied, Bob fishtailed the 'Vette as he popped over the rise and sped down the grade, the lonely dirt road spearing deeper and deeper into a miles-long wooded cut; there was nothing down here but pines and the occasional hunting cabin and what he had come to destroy.

Bob checked his mirrors again and saw only the huge Wyoming sky as it opened up with the sunrise, pale blue slashed with pink, spreading to forever over a tunnel of dusty white and green. He tilted the rearview down and turned his head side to side and checked his caked-on rouge and cobalt blue eyeliner—perfect— then snugged his outrageous honey-blonde wig, making sure the seams were tight; he pursed his lips, checking the Ruby Red.

Good to go.

Bob blew himself a kiss, then tilted the mirror back.

His hand trembled as he grasped the shifter knob, but even a reminder of the damn disease couldn't spoil his mood, because today his false skin would shed, and for the first time in his life he would be free—free to show the entire world who Robert Richards Junior truly was.

He would likely die today as well; Bob had resolved himself to it. He was looking forward to it, even. What he *hadn't* resolved himself to was living the remainder of his amazing, extraordinary life out as an invalid while his still-brilliant mind squirmed like a rat in the sinking ship that was his body; better to go out in a blaze of glory than that.

Better *anything* than that.

Bob saw the narrow track up ahead and slowed and made the turn, then slowed the 'Vette further as this new "road" roughened, the chrome side pipes on the classic car dragging and scraping as he see-sawed over rocks and through deep erosion cuts; the Stingray was an integral part of his last disguise—the final disguise in a long, long history of disguises—and he didn't particularly give a damn if it got banged up. But he couldn't afford to high-center the thing and get stuck way out here.

Bob pulled over, needles scraping, and shut the grumbling motor off and grabbed his camp shovel and a satchel he'd prepared and opened the door and set them out, then turned sideways and grasped the roof and struggled to pull himself up and out of the low-slung car.

He made it, then slammed the door with a bang and started walking, flower-print dress swishing around his smooth knees; this morning there had been one last shave to go with the final disguise, but he'd foregone the damn high heels. He was done with those, thankfully; he'd certainly worn his share.

Bob reached his destination and caught his breath, then cautiously stepped out and glanced around, but the endless, slanting clearing was empty except for giant metal-frame towers marching up the ridge to his right and down to his left, the humming, crackling lines themselves, and a double handful of low scrub pines. The young trees' crowns were still well below the bottom rail of lines, but Bob knew the power company would soon send men and trucks out to chop and mulch them away; no rogue conifers would be allowed to interrupt service to their paying customers, not if they could help it. Bob had used that diligence a handful of times over the years, when he'd wanted a whore's body found.

Today he had other business.

He made his way to the nearest tower's base as it loomed over him like a giant kid's giant Tinkertoy and stopped next to a thick concrete support pillar and unfolded the metal camp shovel and unearthed a shallow hole right up against the plug—on the *inside* edge, away from view of the trees on either side. Details. Never forget the details, even on what might be his last day.

Shallow or not, he was sweating and trembling by the time he lowered the satchel and snugged it against the plug, then filled in the hole and oh-so-gently tamped it down and refolded the shovel and walked back to the Corvette.

Inside, Bob pulled out the phone he'd chosen and flipped it open and made sure it would turn on when needed and that it was fully charged and that it had service and then turned it off again. Details. He checked his makeup in the mirror and found his sweat had made it run, so he cranked the V-8 and flicked on the AC and lifted his cosmetics' bag out of the passenger floorboard and fixed his face, reflecting that after hundreds of disguises he probably knew more about makeup than most whores he'd met.

He put the kit back in the floorboard and then stared up at the line tower where it soared above the jagged forest and realized he would regret not seeing it teeter and fall when he called the other cheap phone in the satchel; it would be quite the sight, but if he was going to seize any opportunity that arose from the chaos he was creating, he would have to keep a laser focus on his purpose.

Bob backed the Corvette out too fast, scraping and banging the side pipes again, still not giving much of a damn. He had five more satchels to place, more utilities to interrupt and more chaos to seed, and then a drive back across Indian Head to where he would wait in his blind for his efforts to bear fruit.

He smiled, Ruby Red lips twitching:

And then Jack Ross would die.

The second and third satchels went just as smoothly; the second he buried directly on top of the main underground phone and cable line that connected Indian Head to the rest of the world, and the third he tossed over the security wire that surrounded the small, fenced-off area that protected the base and workings of the cell-phone tower on Ranch Ridge Road.

The second tower, however, the one they'd built way out on Crowley Ridge Lane, and where he'd intended to place his fourth satchel, is where things got interesting.

He slowed the battered and dusty red 'Vette as he saw a company truck parked at the base of the second tower. The two-door white generic Chevy pickup sat with the driver's door open, the chain-link door in the fenced-in area at the base of the tower also open, and as he made the turn and stopped behind the Chevy, a woman with a company logo decorating her shirt and baseball cap that matched the one stenciled on the truck's door stepped out of the protected area.

Mid-thirties, attractive in a spare way, with short dark hair nesting out from under the company cap; pale-blue button-down work shirt tucked into blue jeans; tool belt encircling her slim hips and steel-toed boots and no wedding ring. When she saw Bob in the wig and dress behind the Corvette's wheel, she planted her fists on her hips above the belt and frowned, obviously wondering what this silly blonde bitch thought she was doing.

Bob took in her short hair and mannish aspect; perhaps she was a lesbian. He'd taken three of those over the years, the first out of sheer curiosity; she'd been a professed man-hater, and while that had certainly made things lively for a time, in the end she'd died screaming and begging just like her cock-loving sisters.

Bob threw open the Stingray's door and swung his smooth legs out, then gathered the floral-print dress around his knees primly before using the door and roof edge to pull himself up and out.

Her eyes went round as she took in what she probably still thought of as a woman…and then her dark eyebrows made a V over her nose as she considered the black gloves, and then the black Nike running shoes that clashed so horribly with the swishing dress.

"What…?" she began, then seemed to misplace her thought-train, jaw hanging slightly.

Bob grinned as he slammed the door; too bad she would never see him in high heels. He'd been told it was quite the sight. He started toward her, stumbling before catching his balance, and her face took on a tinge of alarm as she backed away, saying, "Wait a minute, you can't come in——"

He used a falsetto to throw more confusion on her as he swiveled his upper body and pointed down the road, back the way he'd come: "Can you help me? I got turned around and now I'm lost. Where exactly *am* I?"

The woman paused just inside the open chain-link door; it and the fence protecting the cell tower had an orange-mesh visual barrier woven into the links. She started to answer…then got a good look at his eyes; fear spread over her finely drawn features, but by then it was too late. Bob lunged, grabbed her, then lost his balance and fell, bringing his full weight down on her as they crashed inside the fence.

She fought like a tiger, cussing and spitting and biting, but even with the damn disease slowing and weakening him, she had no chance.

Bob slugged her one last time, then staggered to his feet and scooped her up and deposited her against the inside of the orange fence. He went out to the company truck and shut the door, glanced up and down the deserted two-lane blacktop, then retrieved old bitch Barbary's Smith & Wesson from the 'Vette before going back in and shutting and locking the gate behind him.

Bob stripped her bare and bound her to the inside of the orange fence with black electrical tape and a bright yellow extension cord he'd found among the woman's own tools, and as he did, he thought about how fate and luck seemed to be with him today. He didn't believe in any so-called God—good, bad, or otherwise, not in this random, catch-as-may-can world—but he *did* believe in fate and luck.

Fate had seemed to be telling him that after his orgy yesterday and last night, his work was finally done, and that the only task left for him was the destruction of his enemies. That was regretful—he *so* enjoyed his work—but all good things come to an end, even for one such as him. But now luck had interceded and here he was, a nude slut spread out before him once again, maybe for the last time.

And if fate and luck stayed with him on his final day—his first *true* day—then would he perhaps have the chance to rectify other regrets?

Only the unspooling of the day would tell.

Bob brought his mind back to the task at hand as the lesbo snapped out of it, shaking her head to clear the cobwebs, staring first with disbelief at her own nudity and spread legs, and then twisting to stare at the bonds that held her wrists and ankles to the links above her head, and then at last up at him from between her knees, dawning understanding and growing horror infusing her bloody and puffy face. He searched through the woman's tools again before finding what he needed, ignoring her pleas and tears and then shrieks as she saw what he held.

If this *was* his last whore, he resolved to make her his masterpiece.

Bob bent to his work.

51

I slept like a baby-lad, one with a tummy full of mother's milk and a dry diaper. The only thing that woke me up was Mom calling at six minutes after six because she'd figured to hear from me already, and she was right; normally I would've been up by now and wailing on my bag or practicing kata or cranking out push-ups or stretching or all of the above, but I had conked out hard last night.

I know, I know: How on Earth *could* I? After all, my dad had been finely minced only steps away from where I'd slept, and my young employee and friend was missing and presumed dead, and my mother and whatever the heck you classified Angela as were busy hiding from a psychopath that wanted to shove stuff up inside them until they stopped twitching, and I'd just given up on my business and perhaps my dream, and I was being babysat by a bunch of sneaky, muscle-bound assholes with big guns who were also not thrilled with their charge—oh yeah, and I had the serial-killerest of all serial killers after me, a guy that made Jack the Ripper look like a slow intern.

But even with all that, I'd managed almost ten hours of sound, dreamless sleep—something I hadn't accomplished in weeks, if not months. Maybe crashing in my own bed instead of a jail-house rack or on that damn torture-bench in the IHPD drunk tank had something to do with it. Probably so.

Mom had stopped talking.

"Wha—" My jaw creaked with a Gigantor yawn. "What did you say?"

"I *knew* you weren't listening to me! I saaaaid, you had me worried *sick* when you didn't call! For all I knew, that maniac had gotten you, too!"

"C'mon, Mom. Hawthorne and Walters and the rest of the gang have been outside all night—and for all *I* know, Bob showed up and they bagged him and nobody bothered to wake me up and tell me." I paused at another thought, one that wasn't so swell: maybe the Traveler had killed all my protectors and was at that very moment standing outside the door with ax raised, just waiting for me to bee-bop on out.

"Don't be flip with me, Jackie! I won't stand for it!"

"Yes, ma'am."

She sucked a deep breath and puffed it out. "I'm sorry, son. I was just worried when you didn't call. Hold on, Angie wants to talk to you."

And just like that, I was conversing with my sorta-kinda girlfriend:

"Hi."

"Hi."

"Is, uh, is Mom okay?"

Angela hesitated, then said, "Just a sec." She said something to Mom, then a door opened and closed before she continued in a hushed and overly patient tone: "No, Jack, she's *not* okay; she didn't sleep much. Neither of us did."

"Is she upset about Dad?"

"What do *you* think?"

I pulled the phone away and looked at it before pressing it back to my ear; it seemed Mom wasn't the only one who had woken up on the wrong side of the hard-ass hotel bed this morning. "Forget I asked." I reluctantly climbed out of my own warm, soft bed and did a big yawn-stretch. "Listen, I gotta let Jezzie out and make sure all my guardians are still kicking—" I reached down and tap-tapped the tiny microphone, where it lay next to my big butcher knife on my nightstand. "You boys alive out there?"

"Jack, stop. They're out there for *you*."

"They're out there because they were ordered to be, and because they're paid to follow orders. You sound like Mom." I slipped on boxers before I tweezed the mic between thumb and index finger and shot down my ladder and made my way to a grinning, wagging Jezzie, who was already waiting by the door. That was reassuring; if someone really had been lurking right outside, ax in feathered hand, Jezebel would have been barking and growling and going bonkers.

Or at least I sincerely fucking *hoped* so.

Angela said, "I sound like her because she's right; you need to stop baiting the SWAT team."

My own irritation flared. "Hey," I said, "ya know what? Gotta be the best bait I can be and all that, so I guess I'll talk to you on the flip side—"

"Jack…" Then she sighed. "I'm sorry. I know I'm being a bitch, but your mom…" Her voice dropped even lower. "She jumped all over me this morning when she realized I hadn't woken her up when you didn't call. I guess I'm just channeling some of her mood."

"It's all right," I said, even though it really wasn't. I turned the handle and pushed open the door and Jezebel scooted out as I poked one eye around the edge…but no giant chicken with an ax; that's generally a good thing, and this morning's lack of such was even better. I stepped into the predawn, the Bighorns shouldering into the pink-tinted gray, and did a slow toe-touch, loosening the ol' spine one, protesting, vertebra, at, a, time.

"Jack? Still there?"

I rolled back up, spine re-stacking and realigning; it was an agreeable sensation. "Yeah, sorry. I just let Jezzie out, and now I'm in the yard, trying to wake up a little." I looked over at the house, and then at the porch, and then at the maroon smear that used to be Dad.

My jaw clenched as I turned away.

Jezzie was by the fence on the other side of my truck, butt tucked and going in circles, so I turned away once more, this time out of courtesy, and scanned the slope crammed with Blackjack and Lodgepole and Ponderosa pine. They resembled an army of spiny toothpicks, but I could spot no movement beneath their spread of needles; all quiet on the western front.

I raised the mic. "Mornin', boys. Any big, baaad chickens come scratching last night? Everybody comfy out there?" I reached up and over and grabbed my head, pulling it to the opposite side, stretching my neck and one hellishly tight trapezoids muscle.

Angela sighed again. "Jack…"

"I'll stop." *Maybe.* "I'm just funnin' with 'em, anyway." I switched the phone and mic to the other hand and stretched the opposite way.

"It's not that," she said. A pause, and then, forcefully and in a rush: "I want to see you."

I stopped pulling on my head. "You mean today?"

"Yes."

"I don't think—"

A *thunk*, and a piece of my barn spun away. I ducked instinctively as the *crack* came just behind it, and then I heard Jezebel yelp and glanced over in time to see brown dirt and yellow needles kick up in three different spots around her as three more *cracks* echoed from beyond the tree line, and then another *thunk* and *crack* and a second piece of my barn flaked away—this time just over my head.

"*Shit!*"

"What is it? What's wrong?"

"Uh, nothing." *Jesus.* I whistled for Jezzie, and she had a hunted look as she waddle-zipped back inside. I followed and slammed the door and locked it. "I'm pretty sure Hawthorne and Walters and the rest of the boys are still out there," I told Angela.

"Why?" she demanded. "What happened?"

"Nothing happened." I placed the microphone on my kitchen island and backed away from it. *Fuck me.* "You said that, uh, that you wanted to see me today? I don't think that's a good idea. I mean, helping at Crazy's yesterday was one thing, but if you and Mom come out here, Denton will give birth to a calf—an *elephant* calf."

"Jack—"

"Hold on." I scooted up the ladder and turned and stood at the loft's lip and watched the tiny gadget uneasily; I could still see it, so maybe *it* could still see *me.* I know they'd said it was just a microphone, but what if they'd lied? The feds had all the cool tax-payer-funded toys, after all.

"Still there?"

"Yeah." I ducked further into my loft, just in case. "The plan was for me to 'act normal' and draw Bob to me, and for you and Mom to stay wherever the hell *you* are and be safe—and don't forget, reinforcements are arriving this morning. You guys will finally get your minders, so you'll have to wait for them."

Then I winced:

Should've picked another word, Jackie boy...

Angela repeated it: "*Minders.*" Deep, *deep* breath: "I know what the 'plan' is, but I don't care; I want to see you. I *miss* you."

"Angela..."

"I want to stay with you."

That gave me pause. "You mean...?"

"Yes," she said. "That's what I mean."

"Er, don't you think that'll be kinda awkward? You know, with Mom here and all?"

She sounded amused when she said, "It'll just be me. Mary said she wanted to stay; like I told you, she didn't sleep well, and she needs to rest." Then, a whisper: "We've been cooped up together for going on four days, and we both need a break. *I* need a break. So, what do you say I come over and we talk about those ears?"

A thorough ear-discussion sounded better than just about anything I could think of, other than having Tiff and Dad and Donnie back…

Donnie. I felt like I'd been punched in the liver. Had they found him yet? Maybe they had last night and I just hadn't heard.

"Angela," I began gently, "we need to stick to the plan, so we can keep you and Mom safe, but when this is over—"

"That's just it! What if it never ends? What if Bob goes to ground in Amsterdam or Singapore or Timbuktu? Your Mom and I are going to get our *minders* today, but what if we end up having to keep those 'minders' for weeks, or even months? We—and you, for that matter!—could end up in protective custody for *years!*"

I thought that was going a little far and said so, then added, "Rogers told me…well, he told me about some stuff Friday night, stuff Denton didn't bother to share with everybody when we were at the Injun, and, uh…"

"What 'stuff'? What are you talking about?"

"Just, you know, stuff." No *way* was I going to inform her that the T-Rex of serial killers might be after her; things were tense enough already. "And I don't think Bob has years or months to wait; he might not even have *weeks*."

"What are you babbling about now?"

Babbling? "He's sick, so that means he's—"

"Sick?"

"Yeah, sick. Maybe *bad* sick—or at least that's the theory. Remember when I asked Denton why Bob came out of the shadows now, when he'd been doing so well? You know, killing all across the country while the FBI clowns didn't have a clue and all that?"

531

"Yes. And I remember Denton glaring a hole through your head."

"Yeah, well, fuck him. But do you also recall how he didn't answer?"

"You're right," she said slowly. "And Bob sick would explain some things…a *lot* of things, really, if the diagnosis was terminal…" Her voice hardened. "But right now, for you and me, that doesn't matter; I still want to see you."

"You don't know how much I want that too, but—"

"'But' nothing, mister! I want to see you, and I want to make love to you." And then her voice took on a husky quality that made my palms sweat even as my mouth went Sahara-dry. "I'll just come out and say it: I want to *fuck* you."

I swallowed. Twice. "God, I want that too, b—"

"Don't you *dare* say 'but' again! Not after I just acted like a brazen hussy! I've never done that for anybody…well, not in a long time…" My eyebrows twitched at that, but her voice gained steam again: "My point, Mr. Stubborn Jack Rossie Ross, is that you're not thinking this through!"

"What do you mean?"

"We considered the possibility of the Traveler going to ground and us having to waste away in protective custody until they catch him, right?"

"Well, *you* di—"

"Now take it the other way: What if he succeeds?"

"You mean…"

"Yes! What if he kills you? Or me? Or both?"

My soul just about shriveled up and blew away at the thought of Angela in the Traveler's sadistic hands. "I won't let that happen to you, I promise."

"Oh? And how will you keep that promise if you're there and I'm somewhere else?" I didn't reply because she had a point. "And don't forget the 'minders'; if the plan doesn't work and that reporter's story lands Monday morning, then maybe Denton will decide to spirit us somewhere far away until this ends, one way or the other; my point, Jack Rossie Ross, is that *today* might be our only chance to be together for a long time." She paused, and then said it, voice vibrating with feeling: "Maybe *ever.*"

She was scoring left, right, and up the middle, now—boy, was she—but...

Then, eager: "I've got an idea."

"Angela—"

"Just listen! Why don't you and I meet at Pat's for Sunday brunch? That way Denton can just send my 'minders' across the street; your mom's will have to drive dow—uh, drive to where we're staying, but they were going to do that, anyway. Then we'll head back to your barn and we'll have the SWAT team outside, *plus* whoever they send with me! None of those jerks, including Denton, can say no to *that!*"

"That sounds great except for one problem."

"What?"

"I'm supposed to stay here and draw Bob—"

"No, you're supposed to 'act normal'; hanging out there all day wasn't mentioned—not that I ever heard, anyway. Is that what Denton and Rogers told you to do?"

"Well, no, but—"

"There you go; you're just supposed to 'act normal'—and what, I ask you, is more 'normal' in Indian Head than taking your girl to Pat's? All the locals will be there, even with all this crap going on—and you *know* the place will be open. Pat wouldn't close on Sunday for a nine-point earthquake; it's her 'money' day. You know *that*, too."

"Yeah," I said, then gave in. "Okay, but let's make it a late lunch instead, say one o'clock. That way the place will have cleared out a bit, and we can—"

"Ten o'clock," she countered firmly, "and brunch, not lunch; I can't wait that long to see you."

"All right," I said, capitulating completely, "ten and brunch." A nice, long ear-discussion is a powerful persuader. "But Hawthorne and the boys will probably know what we're doing in here." And then I remembered the goddamn microphone: "*And* hear," I said, reminding her about it as well.

"So? *Let* them hear. Let them listen to the *whole thing*, I don't care!"

My eyebrows shot up, way up, but I managed a skeptic-sounding, "All right." Maybe Angela was an exhibitionist. That had possibilities, yes indeed it did, even though normally I was a private person with stuff like that; Jen had once gone down on me at a Sonic, but I'd been nervous about getting caught the whole time—and that had been at night, and *after* the car hop had brought our food.

And then Angela said something that made me forget all about that long-ago Sonic interlude:

"Jack?"

"Yes?"

"They'll hear me without the microphone. I guarantee it."

"Oh," I said, and blinked.

"That okay with you?"

"Okey dokey by me." I glanced at my watch. "Crap!"

"What?"

"It isn't even six-thirty yet. This morning is going to *crawl* by."

She chuckled, low and throaty. "Patience, big boy." Then: "Okay! I'll tell your mom what we've planned—"

"You'll what?"

"Don't be a dolt! I'll tell her I'm meeting you for brunch at Pat's and picking up my 'minders' there."

"Oh."

"But she's not dumb, you know. She'll figure out the rest."

"I, uh…"

Angela laughed. "You're sweet, Jack Rossie Ross. I'll see you at ten, bye."

"Wait! You've still got my Colt, right? Make sure you bring it." She had a longer drive than normal to get to Pat's—exactly how long I wasn't sure, but I did know it was a helluva lot longer than the one from her dad's house to Pat's; that meant all kinds of evil opportunities for Bob, if he was looking for her car. And I was sure he was. "And make sure Mom keeps that Glock Walters gave her handy."

A touch of irritation marred her sweet voice. "I will and she will, you can count on it, but I'm pretty sure Bob doesn't know where we are. If he did, we would have filled his sicko ass with bullets by now and this crap would be over."

I smiled a little; I couldn't help it. "Guess you're right."

"Of course I am. Now let me off here; I need to shower and get ready for you. I'll see you at ten, Mr. Jack Rossie Ross." She paused. "And then…"

I could feel her smiling; I know *I* was smiling. "And then…"

"Bye."

"Bye."

I sat on my bed for a minute, letting my blood cool, then shimmied down the ladder and bounded over to the kitchen island. Jezebel raised her head from her paws, silvery eyebrows bunched, but I only grinned at her as I snatched up the tiny microphone:

"Yo Hawthorn, you down for some brunch?"

52

I rumbled out of the driveway at 9:20 on the dot.

I was going to be way early; it only takes ten minutes to drive down to Pat's from our place up on the ridge. But that was with sane traffic, and I wasn't sure what the heck I'd find in town today, what with it being the first day of a new week after an admittedly memorable Fourth of July holiday week. Angela was right, though: crazy crap or not, it was still Sunday, and that meant Pat's would be packed with locals, so popping in early to lay claim to a booth sounded like a good plan to me; attempting to cuddle with Angela while perched on stools at the front counter didn't seem like something I wanted to try.

I hadn't driven half a mile when an all-to-familiar Suburban powered up behind me and then slowed a scant four feet from my trailer hitch. A trio of square-jawed, unsmiling men wearing baseball caps and dark sunglasses and loud Hawaiian shirts were perched inside like floral-shirt-wearing gargoyles. Walters was driving. The gargoyles didn't talk, just watched me out the windshield.

So much for hiding.

Forget, for a moment, the G-ride; those guys looked like tourists about as much as I resembled a theoretical physicist. Bob would have to be blind *and* stupid to miss them, but maybe Walters and his gang were tired of squatting in pine resin and just wanted a chance at a little action. I didn't see the freckly and much-loved presence of

Hawthorne back there, or the other two, but I'd given them plenty of notice, so they'd likely already clicked their heels together and materialized at Pat's in time to establish a perimeter.

I jabbed the radio and listened to about three seconds of an REO Speedwagon tune I'd heard ten zillion times and then dialed it down to the classic country station. The fed-bots stayed exactly four feet behind me as I sang along with Dandy Don Williams' "Lord, I Hope This Day Is Good" (amen) and rolled my Ford through town and arrived at Pat's without incident.

I lucked out; a spanking new Volkswagen Beetle was backing out of a spot way in the back, hard against the tree line, just as I pulled in. I looked for Angela's car as I negotiated my way through the packed lot, but I didn't see it. I'd meant to beat her here, so I wasn't *too* worried…but boy oh boy, would I be glad when she had her very own bots: big, unsmiling men with guns and dark shades and off-the-rack suits who would stare at her ass, no doubt, but who would also put slugs into anyone who tried to hurt her; they could stare at her ass all day long as long as they kept her safe.

Walters and the other two refugees from Maui hadn't been as lucky, so they simply pulled to the end of the row nearest Pat's etched-glass front doors and sat there staring at me.

Well. Guess a night in the pines made the G-man grouchy.

I hopped out just as the Tacoma that Lake Bum Walters had been driving yesterday turned in from Third and stopped by the Suburban. I almost didn't recognize an unshaven Hawthorne with a blue bandanna folded over that red hair and a purple tie-die tee-shirt that was even more obnoxious than the Hawaiian shirts polluting the Suburban. A lit cigarette dangled out of the corner of his mouth, and he had one eye squinted against the smoke.

Hawthorne and Walters had a brief exchange that involved a bunch of shooting me tight-lipped looks, and then Walters powered the Chevy out of Pat's and across Third, where the matching Suburban controlling access to the Injun hurriedly reversed out of the way. Walters sped around back as I counted five fresh G-rides parked below the chalky mural; the back lot was probably pretty darn packed with black-on-black Suburbans as well.

The gang's all here.

So Angela and Mom would get their minder-bots. Finally. The suited fed pulled his Suburban back across the entrance and then sat there, stone-faced; ecstatic over his parking-attendant assignment, for sure.

Hawthorn took the initiative from Walters and parked at the end of the first row, thus creating his very own spot before hopping out and slouching toward Pat's, in character with bandanna and cig and tie-die shirt—and the raggedy-edged cutoffs and the rope sandals I now saw. His forearms and neck and face were browned (or in his case, reddened), but his legs and feet were blinding, and he didn't so much as glance at me as he plucked the smoke out of his mouth and used the metal rail by the two front steps to delicately detach the cherry and twist it out with the ball of his foot before saving the half-smoked cig in the pack; in character. He flap-clanged up the steps and yanked open the right-hand door and disappeared inside.

I hadn't spotted the last two of the six-pack, but maybe they were already in there chowing down; either way, Angela and I would have company for brunch.

I shrugged—the more the merrier—and headed toward those metal steps myself…then slowed when I caught sight of a dusty Indian Head PD cruiser near the end of the third row and wondered who it had transported to the party: Rogers, or Tommy, or even that jerk-off Flemming; perhaps, if we were lucky, it had brought all three.

Out fucking standing.

And then I clanged up the steps and opened an etched-glass door and stepped into the familiar and comforting environs of Pat's—

And froze.

Normally on a Sunday morning (or any morning), Pat's is filled with the aroma of fresh-brewed coffee and crisp bacon and maple syrup as well as the low murmur of conversation punctuated by the scrape of knives and forks across plates and the clink of spoons swirling inside coffee cups. You could also bank on Mike the Cook rasping from the kitchen's service window as he informed Daisy or Sara of an, "Order up!"

Not today, though.

The tantalizing scents were still floating around, reminding me of just how long it had been since I'd graced Pat's, but all sound had ceased when I'd stepped inside; every soul was staring at me except for Hawthorne, who had squeezed onto a red stool at the counter and was just now being served a cup of steaming java by Sara. I glimpsed Chief Rogers way in the back, shoehorned into a corner booth. He had a steaming cup of his own resting in front of him, along with his cell phone and a battered notebook and a red pen; so that answered that.

Rogers lifted his chin and met my eyes over the silent throng, then nodded to the empty seat across from him, requesting that I join him—except by that stony expression it wasn't a request.

Great.

Motion and sound resumed as I picked my way down the aisle, stopping and exchanging words with a bare handful of locals, every one of whom just so happened to be friends with my mom. They offered heart-felt yet hesitant condolences on my dad, and I under-stood completely; I myself still had mixed feelings about that. The words had to be said, though, and I appreciated every sentiment.

The rest either turned away coldly (part of the vast majority who were serfs to the Richards' family, or not exactly die-hard fans of the Ross clan; or both) or stared curiously if they were a tourist; a half-dozen of that ilk even raised their goddamn phones and took my goddamn picture, like I was some kind of useless "reality" star or YouTube celebrity…which, come to think of it, I kinda was. It had only been four days ago that the world thought me a costumed mass murderer, and less than twenty-four hours since it had learned I wasn't, so I guess I would have to live with this nonsense until the next flash-in-the-pan came along and drew the mob's attention.

Double great.

I'd almost made it to Rogers when Daisy caught me.

"Rossie!"

Faces swiveled back to me from all across the diner as she plunked the tub of dirty dishes she'd just bussed out of a booth onto the edge of another booth table, this one occupied by a family of tourists. They stared at it bemusedly as Daisy caromed into me, enveloping me in a fierce hug, her big, soft breasts spreading across my chest.

"Hi, Daisy. You're looking good."

It wasn't quite a lie; our families had known each other for a long, long time, albeit loosely; Dad and Daisy's great-grandpa, Sam "Smitty" Smith, had been drinkin' buddies back in the not-so-good ol' days, so we'd played together as little kids. Once we got older, Daisy and I had enjoyed an on-again, off-again thing for a couple of years—if you can call getting lit and screwing in the front seat of my truck after Friday night football games a "thing". Daisy had been an early bloomer, and when I hadn't been available some Friday nights, she'd readily replaced me with another football player (or more than one sometimes, if small-town rumor could be believed; I, for one, did. Daisy had always been a…free spirit, shall we say, when it came to men).

Anyway, she *did* still look good in a healthy-big-girl-with-a-pretty-face kinda way…but compared to how she'd looked in high school, before the rest of her caught up to those breasts?

Yeah.

Daisy squeezed until my sore ribs gave a shout. "You're sweet. And I *knew* you didn't do it!" She pushed back and swiped sweaty brown hair out of her eyes, then gripped my forearms with her thick, strong hands. "I *told* everybody! I said, 'Rossie wouldn't kill those kids, they've got the wrong man, he's innocent!', but nobody would listen!" Then she giggled. Daisy had always been a giggler, which was one of the many reasons we'd never gotten serious. I don't do giggling. "Willie was so *pissed!*"

"I bet."

Willie's the guy Daisy had settled down with—or settled *for*, which was probably closer to the truth. Either way, Willie didn't like me much. Willie was also a sometime sawmill worker and full-time lush who had managed to convince a doctor (and more importantly, the Social Security Administration) that he had fibromyalgia and at least two other big-word diseases that prevented him from holding a steady job, so between his fat disability check and Daisy's tips, they made do. They also had three kids now, one of which we were all fairly certain was Willie's; none of them were mine, which was the important...

Chief Rogers watched me over Daisy's wide shoulder, and what I observed in his normally placid face, I didn't like. I attempted to disengage from Daisy so I could slip by (around) her, but "try" was the operative word; *crap*, she was strong.

She un-clamped one forearm and brushed her fingers under my eggplant eye. "You poor baby. And your dad! I was soooo sorry to hear about Hank."

"Thank you."

"How's your mom holding up?"

"She's making it. I think she'll be all right."

"Good." Then Daisy yanked me closer, splaying those breasts against me again. "Call me tomorrow, I'll make it aaaall better. Willie's goin' fishin' for a whole week, and Grammy will have the kids. You still have my number?"

"Uh, yeah," I lied. So ol' Will was goin' fishin', huh? And with debilitating fibromyalgia, no less; the wonders of modern medicine never cease.

She pouted up at me. "That's what you *say*, but you never call!"

The tourists with the tub of nasty dishes fermenting under their noses were starting to look a mite piqued. "Excuse me," the blonde mother of the two young kids said to Daisy. "Would you mind—?"

"In a minute," Daisy said without turning. A few other tables with empty coffee cups were growing antsy as well, but Daisy kept her grip on my forearms and those breasts pressed hard against me. Sara squeezed by carrying a coffee pot while balancing platters of scrambled eggs and hashbrowns, all while sparing her idle coworker a hateful glare.

"Call me this time," Daisy purred. "I *promise* you won't regret it."

"We'll see. But right now—" I managed to free my arms and backed away until our bodies separated; it took some backing. "I think Chief Rogers wants to talk to me…" I glanced around, frowning; the place was bursting at the seams, but I didn't see Pat or her husband, Jerry.

Pat and Jerry lived in a trim log house attached to the property they'd built their livelihood on; their cabin was set out in the pines a couple hundred feet beyond where I'd parked my Ford. That meant they were nearly always present and accounted for on Sundays, mornings especially, Jerry helping Mike crank out orders or doing dishes or manning the register up by the doors, Pat helping the girls serve when they got slammed or jawing in a booth with locals whose families she'd known for thirty-five years when things were calmer, that mass of not even close to natural honey-blonde hair shimmering in the light slanting through the railcar diner's plate-glass windows…

But *this* Sunday morning?

No Pat and no Jerry.

I surveyed the place twice, just to make sure, then glanced at Daisy, who had finally snatched her tub from in front of the indignant tourists.

"You guys are getting your butts kicked," I told her. "Where's Pat and Jerry?"

She flounced by me and held the full tub on her hip with one mighty arm as she *whapped* me on the butt with her free hand. That got some laughs from the locals (and some outraged goggle-eyes from the tourists, along with giggles from the tourist's kids), but Daisy just kept rolling, raising her voice to cover the growing distance between us: "Mike tried to call 'em this morning when they didn't show to open but they ain't answering their cells. The car's gone, too. He figured they tied one on down at the Horse Palace and they're still passed out in their room."

That elicited a round of wryly agreeing nods from the locals as Daisy turned and backed through the swinging porthole doors. She shouted, "I figured he figured right!", which got more laughs. She winked at me before she vanished into the kitchen.

Man, I thought. *Things will sure be interesting around here after Angela shows up…*

"Jack. I need to talk to you."

Rogers.

I slid in across from him. "'Sup, Chief. I'm meeting Angela for brunch, so when she gets here we'll snag our own booth; no offense, but I think I'd rather sit with her." He only stirred his coffee and stared at me without blinking from the other side of the vintage red Formica-and-chrome table. A leaden dread filled me. "What is it? Did you find Donnie? You did, didn't you." I didn't bother to inquire if Donnie was still alive.

He set the spoon aside and sipped, cop-eyes flickering about, checking the people sitting in the red booths on either side and then down the bustling aisle; satisfied we weren't being eavesdropped on, he set the coffee aside before speaking in a low, tired voice:

"We haven't found him yet, but we won't give up until we do. *I* won't give up. But Zane was transferred to Sheridan County custody last night."

"Oookay," I said, searching his face and really not liking what I was seeing. "Does that change anything as far as the plan goes?"

"Not particularly. He'll still be released Monday with no charges filed whether we get Bob by then or not. Del Peterson, the Sheridan County Prosecuting Attorney, suddenly started making noises yesterday about the 'jurisdictional issues' in Zane's arrest, so Denton agreed to let Zane stew in the county jail for the next couple nights. Del is Bob's man, root, shoot, and bough, so not much of a surprise."

"So if the plan's still on track, what's the problem?"

"Other than some two-thousand-dollar-an-hour suited shark holding forth outside the Sheridan County jail and proclaiming our corruption and Zane's innocence to the world, all while grabbing himself some face-time and his high-rolling Cheyenne firm some free advertising? Nothing. That's where all the journalists got to this morning, by the way." Rogers caught my expression. "What, didn't notice the missing scribblers?"

"I noticed," I said defensively, although I hadn't noticed shit because I hadn't had much room in my head for anything but the impending ear-discussion.

Rogers didn't call my bluff, just sipped his coffee while watching me over the rim. "Well," he said, "that's where they all are." He set the cup down again, leaving his index finger hooked in the white ceramic loop. "I was over at the Injun and heard you were coming here, and I wanted to have a quick word with you." Pause. "But I didn't cross the street to talk about reporters, or even Donnie and Zane."

There was a heavy vibe hanging over our corner booth now, and I wasn't digging it, not in the least, so I just sat there and watched him watch me and waited for the other shoe to drop.

"Miriam Jacobson is dead," Rogers finally said, never taking his eyes from mine. "That's not general knowledge, so keep it under your hat for now."

I grabbed the edge of the table and squeezed my eyelids shut. "I should've thought about...*damn* it!"

"Keep your *voice down*."

"I should've known Bob would go after her," I whispered, agony and guilt shooting through me. "He would've heard about our...our friendship, and he..."

Miriam.

So full of fire, of life...and those three beautiful kids. I hadn't known them—I *couldn't* know them—but she'd talked about them, and it was obvious that even if she didn't love Doug in the traditional sense, she'd treasured her family...

Chief Rogers' voice, from the other side of the galaxy:

"Get a grip, son. I need to tell you something important, and you need to listen."

I opened my eyes. He watched me as he sipped his coffee; his other hand now rested on the closed notebook.

I spoke carefully: "So Miriam getting murdered by the Traveler wasn't what you came to tell me, either?"

I could see the man taking my measure, see the caution—and that caution made *me* cautious:

What the hell is going on?

At last Rogers said, "I never stated the Traveler killed Miriam, Jack."

53

A bizarre species of aching relief surged through me; I'd seen Miriam naked many times, but I couldn't even begin to imagine the twisted shit the Traveler was into being done to her.

I didn't *want* to imagine it.

"Okay," I said. "But if he didn't kill her, who did?"

"Perhaps the same person who chopped your dad to smithereens." Rogers took another sip of coffee while watching me over the rim.

I stared at him as the cash register dinged and banged and then Mike rasped: "Daisy! You got orders up! I'm goin' out back for a cig! First one I've had all damn mornin'!" The porthole doors boomed open and then clacked together as Mike the Cook left for his much-needed cig.

Finally, I said, "What the fuck are you talking about, Chief?"

He flipped his ragged notebook open while leaving it flat on the table, scanning and turning several pages before placing his index finger on a sentence containing a set of numbers written in black ink; the numbers had been underlined twice with dark, heavy strokes.

"One point four centimeters," he announced without looking up.

"What the hell does that mean?"

He fast-flipped to another page, finger moving until it found more numbers; these were scribed in red ink and circled: "Point six centimeters," he read, then turned two pages and put his finger on yet another set of figures, once again in red ink; these were circled *and* underlined with twin red slashes. They were written on the last page in the notebook that had been used; the rest were clean and blank. Waiting.

"Point five centimeters," Chief Rogers said, then shut the notebook and sipped his coffee.

"Why are you reading off a bunch of metric measurements? And are you saying that somebody other than the Traveler killed Dad? That's insane. Who else would—"

"Keep your voice down," Rogers commanded; several heads had turned our way; two had even poked above the frosted-glass partition beside us. "Those measurements represent the depth of boot prints," Rogers replied softly once inquiring minds had gone back to their respective conversations and the heads beside us bobbed back below the partition, becoming ghostly outlines once more.

"Boot prints?"

"Boot prints. The first measurement, one point four centimeters, is the average depth of multiple prints measured around the Beaumont property, as well as Mrs. Barbary's. The second measurement, point six centimeters, is from a print found at your place; out back by the woodpile, to be specific."

"Okay."

"The third, point five, was taken from a print found in Miriam Jacobson's azalea bed earlier this morning."

"So maybe the soil moisture or aggregate or both are different in different locations," I heard myself say, "and the depth of a print can vary just by the way or how fast somebody strides. And if they stood in one spot for a long time, that would—"

"All true," Rogers broke in, "but none of it would account for almost a centimeter's difference. The only thing that explains such a large discrepancy is that someone lighter—someone *significantly* lighter—wore the boots for the second and third measurements. And it's not just the print depth, Jack. It's the boots themselves."

"*Now* what the hell are you talking about?"

Rogers set his coffee cup on the slate-white napkin again, where it began making another creeping brown ring, and laced his fingers over his ugly notebook. "I'm talking about Schallamach patterns."

I wasn't familiar with that exact term, but I'm not dumb; I understood where this was headed, and I didn't like it. I didn't say anything, though, just sat there and felt a black fissure open inside me.

At my stony silence, Rogers' face didn't change, but his hazel cop-eyes sharpened on me before he continued: "Schallamach patterns are used to identify individual footwear, and the boots that made the prints at Angela's place and at Mrs. Barbary's and at…well, Special Agent Denton hasn't seen fit to share the evidence gathered by Sheriff Neal or Rife's team with me, but I'm assuming at Bill Napier's place, and behind the lawyer's estate, and at the Simkins' lake house. Point is, they'll all match because they were made by size-12 Red Wing Heritage Model 8146 Moc Toe Lug Boots that have been worn enough to put a star on the right heel. It's likely from a sharp rock—or, considering what you do for a living nine months out of the year, a screw or a nail; whatever scored it, it was distinctive as well as deep, and located the same place in every print, just at the edge of the instep side of the heel. The prints cataloged at your place and at the Jacobson's, however, appear to have been made by new boots—or new enough; somebody roughed them up to hide the newness, and they did a decent job, but none of those prints have that star on the right heel."

"Wait, *my* boots? The ones the FBI confiscated from my barn?"

"They never—"

"So you're saying Bob ganked my boots, wore them to kill people, then snuck back into where I fucking *live* and put them back?"

"They—"

"That's the nuttiest shit I've heard yet! I mean, I know he's the big, baaad super-planning Traveler and all, but he's not a fucking ninja! There's no *way* he could've—"

"Let me finish! I'm trying to tell you that the feds never found your boots."

"They don't have them?"

"No."

"Well, if they're not around to compare, how can you know any of those prints were made by *my* boots? You're also 'assuming' the prints at old Bill's place and at some fucking lawyer's estate and at the house where Tiff was killed match the others, but what if they don't? You can't just jump to conclusions like that!"

"I'm not jumping to anything." The Chief unlaced his hands and jabbed his pointer finger straight down at the scruffy notebook. "I logged my own observations after the Barbary house, and while I was at the Beaumont's. And before Denton shut them down, I talked to the feds working your place; the impressions found at the Jacobson residence this morning only confirmed my suspicions. And once the feeb techs make their 3-D casts and get them under the scope and compare them side by side with the casts made by the state rats, I'm confident those suspicions will be confirmed; that star on the heel and print depth are just two of the multiple differences they'll find, I'm thinking. They call them 'characteristics'…" Rogers scratched his cheek. "Or 'randomly acquired characteristics', maybe…" He waved the scratching hand in dismissal. "I don't care what they call them as long as they don't screw it up and a judge rules it all admissible at trial."

Judge. Trial.

Those words seemed to echo in the darkness eating away inside me, making it spread faster.

I rallied, though; I didn't have a choice. "But my boots are still MIA," I pointed out.

"True."

"So you are still very much 'assuming' that *any* of those prints match them! And that means you have to find them and make the comparisons *before* you can state this bullshit as fact! So? Where are they, Chief? Where's my Red Wings?"

Rogers watched me, face still, eyes hard and unblinking, then clicked the red pen on and opened the ratty notebook and flip-flipped until he marked a spot on a writing-filled page with that finger again. He spoke while reading: "You stated on the morning of 05-7-2015 while being questioned at Crazy's, your place of business, by Special Agent Steven A. Rife of the Wyoming Division of Criminal Investigation that your work boots could have been in two locations: the toolbox located behind the cab of your F-150, or the armoire in your bedroom." The Chief looked up. "Could they be somewhere else?"

"No. I don't *keep* them anywhere else."

He stared at me unblinking for another long moment, then made a big and deliberate red check by where his finger rested, clicked the pen off and tossed it back on the table, closed the notebook with a dry rustle, then picked up his coffee and sipped.

"In that case, I have a theory."

"A theory."

"Yes."

"Well, let's hear it."

A tinge of sadness entered those eyes, but it barely made a dent in the steely determination shining from them: "Don Straus."

"Donnie? What about him?"

"He's been tossing money around these past few weeks, and since I was pretty sure you hadn't doubled his pay, I thought he'd thrown in with his buddy, Skeeter Rumpke. Skeet's been dealing pills and weed and coke for some biker wannabes that live over the ridge from his place, out in the county. I've been keeping an eye on them, along with Neil's drug guy, Lt. Gary Watson. Gary even contacted the DEA, but since these guys weren't associated with any of the mover-and-shaker gangs, the feds took a pass. We've been planning to take them down when we had enough to make it worth the DA's time, so I stopped Donnie a little over two weeks ago and gave him a friendly heads-up that he needed to hang out with somebody besides Skeeter. I don't think he appreciated my efforts, but I had to try; the wannabees may be small-time to the feds, but they're enough trouble to drag a young man like Donnie down with them. Skeeter's surely headed that direction."

"But you no longer think that?"

"No. Now I think Bob contacted Donnie somehow and offered money to steal your boots—probably a great big chunk of money; enough to blind even a smart guy like Donnie to the consequences, at least temporarily." Rogers sipped his coffee, cop-peepers peering at me unblinking over the rim; "Had Donnie ever been in your toolbox? Would he have known you kept your boots there?"

"Yeah, I guess…but how did *Bob* know? And before we go too far down this rabbit hole, this is still just a theory; you don't know this happened for sure."

My argument for argument's sake sounded hollow even to me, but Jack Rossie Ross doesn't go down without swinging; nevertheless, that black chasm was opening wider and wider.

"As for Bob, I'm starting to appreciate how long and how carefully he's planned this." Rogers' tone seemed deliberately light, but those unblinking eyes now held a deadly promise, forecasting an interesting conversation should the Chief ever get the chance to discuss the current situation with Bob Jr. "And, yes, it's still just a theory—but it's looking more and more likely to pan out considering I dropped by Rufio's down in Sheridan last night and talked to Skeeter Rumpke and learned that Donnie has indeed been throwing wads of cash around, cash supposedly received from his biological father, who supposedly contacted him out of the blue because he'd suddenly had an attack of guilty conscious." The Chief flicked impatient fingers. "But Skeeter didn't buy that and neither did I, so I tracked down Donnie's dad; he's had zero interaction with Donnie or his mom for fifteen years." Sip. Watch. Weigh. "And Skeet told me something else. He said Donnie had been acting weird—scared, even—since your arrest. Thursday night's also the first time Straus tried to contact me at the station, saying he had something to give me.

Sip. Watch. Weigh.

"So…what? After Thursday, Donnie suddenly realized the shit he was in and tried to make it right?"

"Or cover his ass as best he could. I think he'd gotten the boots back somehow and was supposed to put them back in your toolbox, but after your arrest—and Tiffany's murder—he got cold feet. And then the Traveler killed him for it. Donnie's mom and Mrs. Holly were just a bonus."

"Again, this is still all just a 'theory', though, right? I mean, you don't have my boots—or Donnie, for that matter—to prove it."

"What would have been the perfect nail in your coffin, Jack? Footwear that likely had blood from at least four different victims on them—perhaps all six—sitting right there in your toolbox to be found when the authorities opened it up because the perpetrator of a massacre had been seen on home security footage getting into a F-150 that could have been a twin to yours, right down to the tire-make? Neal wouldn't have needed anything else. And I doubt Rife would have, either."

"Yeah." No arguing that. And even though I still didn't like it, not at all, it made a certain grim sense; Donnie *had* been acting strange—well, strang*er*—for the last few weeks, and just because I'd thought he'd been gearing up to tell me this would be his last season at Crazy's didn't make me right.

And then there was the money.

Donnie was in college, but on scholarship, and thus just scraping by. Would a poor university kid jump at a big ol' wad of cash to steal his boss's boots, especially if he thought those boots wouldn't be used for any nefarious purpose? And then scramble to make it as right as he could when he discovered different?

Would *I*, say, have stolen Tuc's boots from his toolbox if offered enough money—as long as I thought there wouldn't be any harm to it?

You bet your everlovin' ass I would've.

Jesus. Jesus, Donnie…

"Jack."

"What?" I replied, lips numb.

Rogers hesitated, watching me—and was that *sympathy* on his face, now? Nah, surely not—then visibly made the decision to continue: "And I know the Sheriff of Johnson County." It came out as a sigh. He picked up the coffee again as he leaned back and sipped, watching me over the rim. "His name's Mick Whitehorse. Mick's a friend, and when two ladies that you might happen to be acquainted with were going to be staying by themselves down in Mick's jurisdiction for a couple of days, I asked him to keep an eye on them—two eyes, if he could spare them. Mick's a good guy, and even though his men are already spread thin—Johnson County covers a lot of territory—he agreed. And while I didn't go into specifics as to *why* I wanted these two particular ladies checked on, Mick's no dummy, so I figure he understood it had something to do with the madness we're dealing with up here."

I didn't want to hear another goddamn word.

Not a single.

Fucking.

Word.

"Chief—"

Rogers was unrelenting: "So I gave him the ladies' description as well as the plate number of Angela's Camry and he said he'd instruct the man that had the duty in that part of the county Friday night to do a drive-by welfare check on a certain pair of ladies staying at a certain hotel in Buffalo."

"Let me guess," I said, voice wooden even though I was trying like hell to make it sarcastic. "Angela's car wasn't there."

"Oh, it was there, all right." He flipped the notebook open to the last page again. "One Cpl. Stanton logged in his duty report that at 0009 hours a white Toyota Camry with the correct Wyoming plate number was parked at the hotel in question, so he took no further action and drove on and finished his shift at 0200. Mick runs three shifts: ten to six, six to two, and two to ten." Pause. Sip. "Cpl. Stanton was second shift."

Rogers watched me. Waiting.

I didn't want to ask, goddamnit, truly I didn't.

I asked anyway.

"What did the third-shift guy report?"

"She's a woman. Her name is Sgt. Wicks, and she's the lone female deputy in Johnson County. Gotta be tough as nails to swing that weight, believe you me. Mick confirmed as much, said she's his best deputy as well, and the nicest and sweetest person you'd ever care to meet…until you piss her off, then watch out. The nickname her fellow deputies grafted to her is Wicked Wicks, and as soon as she clocked in that morning, Wicked was called out to assist at a multiple-vehicle accident with injury, suspected DUI. By the time that wrapped it was past 0400, so she swung by a certain hotel in Buffalo and checked to make sure a certain white Toyota Camry was where it was supposed to be."

"It wasn't there?"

"Not a trace," Chief Rogers confirmed. "Sergeant Wicks parked and logged it at 0423, then called Mick on his cell, as per instructions. Mick said he was in the middle of fuzzily telling Wicked to roust the night manager and find out what room the women were registered under when the white Camry in question pulled in and out stepped two ladies, one older and one younger. They were toting multiple plastic Wal-Mart bags, and when Mick told Wicked to ask the ladies where the hell they'd been, there was an…exchange, shall we say, between the three that…well, let's just say it got a little testy."

"Testy?"

Rogers consulted the notebook. "'Testy'," he confirmed. "Sgt. Wick's own word." The Chief's finger drifted down the page. "Wicked also states that the two women seemed agitated at being 'checked up on', and then they carried their items into Room 3B and slammed the door in Sgt. Wick's face." Rogers' finger moved again. "This was at 0437. Mick was unsure whether to call and update me, but seeing as how the two night-owl ladies in question seemed unharmed, he decided to send Wicked back on patrol and go back to bed."

Rogers closed the notebook and leaned back and sipped.

Watching.

Waiting.

He was waiting for naught, however, because I was done asking questions. I only wanted to curl up in the booth and take a nice, long nap until this mess was done and over, like Rip Van Winkle: just wake up twenty years later or whatever and the whole sordid deal would be flushed down the Toilet o' Time. I'd have a way cool beard by then, too.

Rogers spoke into the thorny quiet:

"When things didn't add up with your dad, I called Mick and learned all this. That was just before I showed you how the killer had turned around and put Jezebel inside the back door." More silent thorns; Rogers' face tightened. "Let me ask you a question, Jack. Where did you buy your boots? Was it at Wal-Mart?"

I didn't answer because if I was done *asking* questions, then by God I sure as fuck wouldn't *field* any. Besides, I hadn't bought those Red Wings. Mom had bought them for me three years ago, when she'd seen I'd needed new boots:

She'd picked them up at Wal-Mart, now that I think about it.

The Chief sipped and watched me, waiting, but I only glared back while wishing he would just say it; wishing this was all over; wishing for Sara or Daisy or *somebody* to get their asses in gear and bring me my own cup of coffee so I could lean back and sip and stare at Rogers over the rim. What I got instead was a disappointed grimace from the Chief and then more shit I definitely didn't want to hear:

"I changed things up last night. I asked Mick if he could put sticky eyes on the ladies in question, follow them if they went on another early morning 'shopping' jaunt. He wasn't happy about it, and he was even shorter on manpower Saturday night than usual because one of his deputies took off that morning for a week-long second honeymoon—one of those last-ditch, save-the-marriage deals—but he agreed. Mick ended up taking the job himself, as a matter of fact. He drove his personal vehicle and rented a room at a no-frills motel down and across the way."

Rogers paused there, studying me, but there was no disappointment now; now it was the clear-eyed caution of a cop sitting across the table from what he believed to be a dangerous ex-con:

I was now watching *him*, you see…

…and as for why he was bothering to tell me all this, I didn't need to ask. I knew. Oh, I suppose if I *did* ask, he might spout some horseshit about me being one of his people again, or that I was a good man (or at least trying to be). But then again, considering those hard, unblinking cop-eyes probing into mine, he might just tell me the truth. And the truth was, Rogers had come across the street to feel me out to see if I'd known what shenanigans my ladies had been up to—maybe even facilitated them somehow.

My insides clenched, but I didn't let the pain show; I just kept watching him. Waiting. He'd gotten the right read—I hadn't had a clue until now—but they still clenched; his instincts could've been off (unlikely, but they could have been), and if they *had* been, I knew without a single fucking shred of doubt that I would already be handcuffed in the back of his cruiser out there, on my way to another play date with the concrete and steel.

The Chief never took those unyielding eyes from mine as he set his coffee on the folded napkin again, but this time his right hand slipped off the table and dropped casually onto his brown-uniformed lap…or perhaps not-so casually; his matte-black Kimber was down there, hanging off of his right hip.

I didn't acknowledge the move. I just stared across the table at him. Watching. Waiting. There was something dying inside me; I wasn't sure what: my hopes and dreams for the future, perhaps. Whatever it was, I could feel it slipping off and going away from me. Dying. I didn't acknowledge the hollow space it left, the one rapidly opening up inside me; the black hole; the dead space; the crevasse. I just kept watching Rogers, waiting; waiting to hear what else he was going to tell me so I could eventually do something about it.

"So there Mick was," Rogers continued, right hand resting still as a winter snake below the edge of the red-Formica table, "ready to stay and watch or roll with them if they ventured out again. But then the ladies got lucky." Pause. "Or perhaps Miriam Jacobson and her kids got *un*lucky."

I tensed at that, and his right shoulder twitched, but we stayed locked eye-to-eye:

"All was quiet until 2217," Rogers went on, "and that's when Mick got a call-out on a domestic outside Kaycee, way down toward the south end of his county; a hostage situation: a battered wife had finally had enough and had tried to leave with the kids, and her husband had threatened to kill her and the kids and then himself if she did. Then he proceeded to beat the living shit out of her and the neighbors heard her screaming and the kids crying and called the cops, and when the officers arrived, he threw the couch across the front door and threatened to kill them too if they showed their nosy-pig faces in his house."

"Well, that's an all-hands-on-deck deal if there ever was one, and Sheriff Whitehorse dropped his surveillance of a certain pair of ladies like the sideshow and waste-of-time he probably thought it was and rolled with the rest of his people. By the time the woman was dead and the shell-shocked kids were in county custody and the piece-of-shit was handcuffed in the back of a squad car and on his way to be booked for murder and about sixteen other charges, it was after three in the morning, so Mick left his chief deputy in charge at the scene and headed back to his motel and looked across the street." Pause. Sip. "What do you think he saw then, Jack?"

I watched him and waited.

Rogers' right hand slid a fraction of an inch closer to his hip, but that was all before he continued smashing my world to bits:

"He saw a white Toyota Camry parked in the same spot it'd been parked in when he rolled out to the DD at 2219."

Something must have shown on my face then, because Rogers shook his head. "Don't get your hopes too high. Mick's a good cop as well as a good man, and that means he's diligent, dedicated, and thorough—everything Sheriff Neal wasn't. Mick didn't choose that motel just because he liked the mini-fridge; he chose it because he'd helped the owner install a new security system three years ago, after the night clerk had been pistol whipped and robbed by a no-count drifter who was later caught in Idaho. Mick had the owner readjust one camera to cover his competitor across and down the street because being the good, thorough cop he is, he didn't trust that nothing would happen to pull him away, and he wanted a backup."

Pause. Sip.

"What do you think that video showed, son?"

I'm not your fucking son, I wanted to say, but didn't.

I only watched him and waited.

"At the time stamp of 2247, it showed a younger woman with short blonde hair and an older woman with long, gray-streaked brown hair leave 3B and speak for a moment, then embrace before the older woman walked to the white Camry, got in, and drove away. The blonde watched her leave, then entered 3B again and shut the door."

My vision collapsed to a white-hot pinpoint. There was a roaring in my ears, and I felt my fingers gripping the edge of the table again, so hard my knuckles cracked.

Through the roaring, I heard Angela's voice from the phone this morning: *"Your mom didn't sleep much last night. Neither of us did."*

Inquired I: "Is she upset about Dad?"

"What do you think?"

And then, like the drowning man I was, I grasped desperately at anything I could reach. "Denton! Does *he* know about this? I bet he doesn't! That's why nobody *else* has said *shit* about centimeters, or my boots, or fucking *stars* on the heel, or—!"

"He knows," Chief Rogers cut in; his left eyelid beat out a quick tattoo before he reached up and smoothed it away. "He knows," Rogers said again, softer: "Or at least he suspects. But he doesn't care. Denton cares about parading the Traveler's bullet-ridden corpse in front of the media and his bosses." Rogers shook his head, as if he couldn't credit what he was saying about a fellow law-enforcement professional. "But let me tell you something."

"What?" I gritted.

"*I* care, and I won't stop until—"

Sara materialized at the end of our booth. "Sorry about the wait, but we're slammed." She pooched out her lower lip and puffed away a strand of limp blonde hair that had fallen across her forehead. "Guess Daisy told you why, too—you know, in between molesting you and slapping you on the ass…" She finally picked up the vibe; her attention flicked uneasily between the Chief and

I; our eyes were still locked. "Uh, do you want coffee and water as usual, Jack? I guess you don't need a menu… Chief, do you need a refill?" Nobody said shit, or even looked at her. Sara shifted from foot to foot, then stuck her order pad and pen in the pouch on her red apron before peering closely at me. "Are you all right? You look like you're about to puke."

"I'm fine," I lied, finally tearing my gaze from the Chief's. "And I have a…a friend coming, so I guess I'll wait 'till she gets here."

Sara's smile was a lopsided razor as she glanced over at Daisy. "*She*, huh? This should be fun…but if Pat were here like she was *supposed* to be, I wouldn't have to put up with this crap." She flounced away while yelling over her shoulder: "Let me know when your *girlfriend* gets here, Jack!"

I swear Daisy's ears swiveled like radar dishes before she turned her face away from the coffee she was refilling and glowered at me.

I turned back in time to witness Chief Rogers lift a hip and pull his leather wallet out and slap a couple bucks on the table before draining his cup and setting it on the bills. He slipped his phone into his uniform shirt pocket and hooked the red pen next to it, then grabbed up his damning little raggedy goddamn notebook before beginning his slide out of the booth, saying to me, "Denton's big powwow is about to start, and I need to get over there and see what sort of FBI fuckery is on the menu for today before I tell them what I've—"

"Chief, please." I held out my hand, and he stopped his slide with one leg hanging in the aisle, gazing at me with iron-eyed impatience.

"All this shit you're telling me…I'm trying to wrap my head around it, but I just can't." He nodded, accepting that. "You're not saying anything outright, though." It wasn't quite a question, but Rogers nodded again. "Does that mean you're not a hundred percent sure?"

He levered up out of the booth and folded the notebook lengthwise and shoved it into his back pocket. "Not yet, but I'm only getting started. And when I arrive at where the evidence appears to be taking me…well, you need to steel yourself for whatever I find when I get there."

The Chief hesitated, watching me, weighing me, then reached down—with his left hand, I noted—and gripped my shoulder and squeezed. He let go and turned away, but stopped short when he saw who was making his way down the aisle between the booths. I stared as well, along with all the locals:

Mike the Cook had left his kitchen.

Mike the Cook (his last name's Dumont…I think) is almost as much of an Indian Head institution as Pat's, and his talent on the burners is surely a prime explanation for the diner's success. The only reason Mike ever left his tiny but fragrant kingdom was to operate the cash register (which pissed him off no end) or slip out back to grab a cig—which was why I and the locals and even the unflappable Chief Rogers were staring.

Mike's a wide guy, and after he turned sideways and squeezed his hanging belly by Daisy's rump, he stopped in front of Rogers and snatched his limp, sort-of-white chef's hat off and offered his big, square, fire-scarred right hand; the insides of the ends of the first two fingers on that hand were stained an ugly yellow-brown from nicotine.

"Chief, can I talk to yas for a sec?"

Rogers pumped the hand and let it go. "What is it?"

"Well, it's like this," Mike began, then related to Rogers the story Daisy had already told me about the tardy and assumed-to-be-hung-over Pat and Jerry.

Rogers appeared to be growing more than a wee bit impatient until Mike added, "An' that's just what I thought, ya know, that they'd roll in eventually, all red-eyed but ready ta sling chow, ya know, like they do sometimes, although I ain't never had 'em not answer their damn phones, 'specially after ever'body done got these blasted cells…" Mike cleared his throat at the Chief's expression. "My point bein' is that I just popped out back for a coupla drags, ya know, real quick-like cuz I got orders pilin' up, and I spotted that red 'Ray sittin' in their driveway and I thought, 'hallelujah, they're back, we can get some goddamn help over here', an' I whipped out my own cell and tried to call both of 'em again but even though there sits that fancy damn car, they still ain't answerin'. I stepped over until I wuz under the boughs and looked yonder, but I di'n't spot no lights gleamin' in the house, neither. Somethin's wrong, Chief, I know it. They ain't never acted like this afore. I wuz wonderin', ya know, if ya wasn't too busy, if you could pop over there and check on 'em. I'd mosey over m'self if I didn't have all these good people's eggs…Chief?"

But Rogers had stopped listening; Mike could see it as easily as I could. The Chief had also gone perfectly still at some point during Mike the Cook's rambling soliloquy, his hazel eyes sharp and alive on something that wasn't in the diner with us.

"When's the last time you saw them?"

"It, uh, well, it wuz late yesterday evenin', ya know, after we shut 'er down, and they wuz tellin' me they might shoot down to the Horse to pull the arm on them bandits, ya know, like they like to do…"

Mike trailed off again, but not because Rogers wasn't listening. Mike had stopped talking because Chief Rogers wasn't around to hear it any longer.

I slid over and stood up out of the booth, heart larruping and blood throbbing in my ears, as I watched Rogers blow past Mike and go around Daisy in a flash and zip past Sara, who squawked and dropped a plate. It shattered with a pop, shards of heavy white ceramic and chunks of yellow yolk and strings of hash browns scattering around people's best Sunday shoes, but nobody paid any attention because they had all seen what I had seen: a police officer moving like the wind with his gun drawn.

Some had stood up like me, so they also had a good view as Rogers ran up behind Hawthorne where he was slumped over his coffee at the front counter and grabbed his purple tie-dyed shoulder and whispered something in his ear. Hawthorne yanked his shoulder free and said something sharp back, but Rogers only grabbed him again and said something else. This time it must've been above a whisper because the guy seated next to Hawthorne jerked his head around in astonishment, but by that point Hawthorne was up and moving himself, a gleaming semiautomatic appearing as if by sorcery in his freckled mitt as he and Rogers stood at the window by the server station and craned their necks to peer through the fifty yards of Ponderosa separating Pat's from Pat and Jerry's cabin.

Well, that second gun did the trick.

People surged out of booths, clutching cell phones and purses and car keys and crying children. A woman screamed, a man ranted at Rogers, wanting to know what was happening as Mike bellowed at everybody to get out of his way; he had somethin' burnin' on the grill, ya know. But the Chief ignored the spreading bedlam while conferring with Hawthorne, who nodded and made his semi-auto vanish beneath the purple tie-die. And then I witnessed a remarkable transformation as Hawthorne visibly got back into character before pushing outside and slouching down the steps. I watched out the window as he meandered to the Tacoma, kicking his rope-sandaled feet, not looking toward the trees and Pat and Jerry's cabin just visible through the sun-dappled green shadows beyond. He flipped out a Zippo and lit a smoke, and when he cupped his palm to shield the flame, I could see his lips moving.

And that's when Angela turned off Third and drove slowly past Hawthorne while frowning at him in puzzlement, as if she recognized him but couldn't place from where. She found a spot that had opened up in the row one over from mine and got out of her Camry just as Hawthorne jumped in his Tacoma, lips moving frantically now as he stared across the road toward the Injun, but I only had eyes for Angela. Her sunglasses were perched on her hair, and she'd slung her purse strap over her right shoulder. She was wearing white shorts and white-leather platform sandals; her sleeveless top was pale green and low-cut, hair done nicely and makeup just right.

In other words, she looked utterly mouth-watering…but my stomach gave a lurch and sickening roll at the sight of her.

Damn Rogers!

I didn't have time to agonize over it, though, because that's when everything went straight to hell.

54

It was the day Jack Ross would die, and Bob was ready to get on with it. But first, the real him would be birthed in fire. Such a grand entrance into the world would befit a man like him—a *true* man, one that was actually worthy of the designation.

He watched his enemies gather, their tiny images jumping as he held the Bushnell military-grade binoculars to his eyes in one shaking hand and the burn phone in the other, flipped open and ready, prepared to dial the numbers that would lead to Jack Ross's death, and so much more…but something held him back; some intuition—some hunter's instinct—told him to wait just a little longer, even though the agony was terrible now that he was at the end:

At the beginning.

And so he waited, poised to die, to be born…and then an IHPD radio car came around from the Injun's back lot, Chief Ron Rogers behind the wheel. Rogers stopped to speak to the fed who was controlling access from Third; a moment later, the black SUV reversed out of the way. Instead of turning left toward the square and the courthouse and the police station, however, Rogers looked both ways before crossing Third and pulling into Pat's and parking before getting out and striding inside.

Bob lowered the binoculars as he considered how to respond to this new development:

No mistakes now, Robert, not this close to the end; to the beginning…

His feet moved before he was aware of where they were taking him, the hunter's instinct propelling him out of Pat and Jerry's dining room and through the vaulted living room and past what remained of Pat and Jerry.

Jerry was intact except for the mouse under his eye. Bob had given him that to quiet him down, and Jerry was still duct taped to the dining room chair Bob had placed in the center of the room, facing the river-rock fireplace so Jerry could better watch the action. The rope-and-leather gag he'd been forced to put on the man was still crammed between his teeth, but Jerry's head lolled to the side; he'd died of either a massive aneurysm or a stroke—didn't matter which—while screaming and begging for Bob to stop:

For the love of God, please stop.

Bob hadn't stopped.

Pat herself still dangled like a Christmas stocking from the heavy cedar mantle, wrists and ankles bound above her head, long, fake-blonde whore's-hair now shriveled and blackened up past her bare shoulders, blistered and fire-scarred scut and butt still hanging over the bloody and blackened and shit-stained ring that was all that remained of the smaller fire he'd built underneath her on the flagstones, just out from the big blaze in the hearth; that small fire and the fireplace implements he'd left in the hearth-blaze until they were glowing a beautiful yellow-orange-red had been all the tools he'd needed to accomplish some special work here last night, special indeed…and having Jerry as a witness had added just the right touch.

Yes, fine work.

Those well-used tools, now covered in glazed grume to their handles, were discarded haphazardly across the ruined carpet. Bob barely noticed the charnel-house reek (he'd smelled worse) as he kicked one out of his way, only stumbling once as his finely honed hunter's instinct carried him into the kitchen and to the window over the sink. He kept himself carefully back and didn't disturb the slit between Pat's ugly yellow curtains as he scanned with the high-powered glasses, waiting…

And then he understood that his power was waxing on this last day, his first true day, because Jack Ross pulled into Pat's lot and stepped out of his piece-of-shit Ford.

Bob's blood sang even as his soul raged at the sight of his ultimate enemy, the one he would kill today; but he only watched and waited: something…yes, those men in the Suburban and the Toyota. But that wouldn't be all of them. He probed the shadows under the pines near the house, then patiently searched the woods between the cabin and the railcar diner's parking lot and soon spotted them: two men in needle-and-cone studded ghillie suits toting high-powered automatic weapons, barrels made long by sound suppressors.

Bob swiveled the glasses back in time to witness the Suburban cross the street and join his enemies at the old bowling alley and the man from the Toyota get out and slouch into Pat's; he'd affected a disguise, but Bob could have taught him a thing or two about those. He kept the binocs pinned to Jack Ross, snarling unconsciously until he, too, was in, and then Bob found the men in the camouflage suits under the trees once more.

Endless minutes passed as he watched his enemies and hovered on the edge of being born; the pain was excruciating, but fresh plans formed and were discarded and replaced before he settled on a way to—

And then a white flash drew him back, and he watched through the binocs as Angie Beaumont parked her Camry and stepped out, and Bob knew for sure then that fate and luck were with him on his last day, his first true day, because now he could have everything he'd ever wanted.

His finger shook as he started dialing, face twitching with unbridled joy:

It was time to be born!

"Stop it, Spank."

Drug Enforcement K-9 Agent Phil Boding pulled back on his partner's lead, but Spankey continued to strain toward the shadows filling the head of the dusty lane, long Sheppard nose first sniff-sniffing and then huffing air out, as if he didn't like what he smelled, huge, pointed ears at full mast. A growl abruptly vibrated from his broad chest, toenails clicking as he scrabbled for purchase on the smooth wood.

"Spank, stop!"

The dog rumbled deeper, a full-out war-growl now, and then he barked once, a sharp report that stilled conversations as faces rotated toward them from all across the bowling alley.

A tick of silence, and then a cold, clipped voice behind him: "Is there a problem, Agent Boding?"

Phil raised his own voice to answer, but for his partner's sake he modulated his tone: "No, sir. Spankey's just smelling rats or something." He pulled on the lead again, sharper this time, and the ninety-five pound black-and-tan German Sheppard stopped straining toward the dark end of the lane and looked over his furry shoulder at Phil reproachfully.

Phil whispered, "Cool it, okay?"

Spank grinned toothily, waved his long, curved tail like a hairy flag, then turned and barked furiously at the pin-setter end of

Lane 8, where he and Spank now stood near the people end, and where some fool had ripped out the seating and the old ball-return machinery.

Phil stepped further away from the gaping hole near his feet and snapped, "*Down*, Spankey!" The big dog dropped to his belly. "Stay!"

His partner spared Phil another hurt glance before staring off into the dark once more, cone ears erect, long, ultra-sensitive nose sniffing and huffing, a low growl again issuing from deep inside his chest; at least he'd quit raising hell.

That voice spoke from behind: "Control your animal, Special Agent, or I will order you to tie her outside for the duration of the upcoming briefing."

"He," Phil said.

"Pardon me?"

"Spankey's a male dog, sir, not a female. He."

Utter stillness; someone coughed over by the comm station, a stifled laugh.

From behind, that voice again, and this time it was deceptively soft: "I don't care if that beast is a hermaphrodite, Special Agent Boding, as long as it does not disturb the briefing I am about to conduct. Are we clear?"

"Yes."

"Yes, what?"

"Yes, *sir*, Special Agent Denton."

"Thank you. And see that you remember it or I may have you tied next to her."

The voice waited to see if Phil had any response to that. When it was obvious he didn't, it resumed conversing at normal volume with a circle of FBI agents and newly arrived DEA agents and a gaggle of lab techs that even now kept to themselves awkwardly; everyone had gathered up by the abandoned front counter, shooting the breeze and comparing notes before this so-called briefing that was supposed to start any minute. There were even a couple uniformed badges back there, local yokels who'd somehow managed to crash the party; one had a fucking straw cowboy hat clamped on his head, fer crissakes.

Phil had checked them out a few minutes ago, and the city boys' faces had been stone, exuding confidence, but their shifting feet and nervous eyes gave them away; they looked like seventh graders who'd mistakenly wandered onto the neighboring high school track and now prayed the bigger kids wouldn't notice them.

He sensed a presence at his shoulder before he heard a low, "Christ, Philly, go easy with this peckerwood. If he knows half the big bugs he's rumored to know, he's nobody to screw with."

Phil said, "I don't care how much juice he pulls, he's still a little asswipe. And I *am* taking it easy, Witty. I didn't sic Spank on the fucker, did I?"

DEA Special Agent Jason DeWitt said, "Now *that* would be somethin' ta see."

"Yes, it would." And it would almost be worth losing his job and going to jail to see it, too, although that would also mean losing Spank forever, so it wasn't going to happen.

Phil didn't turn his head to look at or speak to the new arrival at the end of Lane 8; Phil had never taken his eyes from the shadows where his partner still stared avidly, growling with his coal-black ears sticking as high as they would stick. At some point during the conversation with Denton, Phil had also been aware of three well-built guys wearing loud Hawaiian shirts trooping through the plywood-encased back entrance, and despite those ridiculous shirts, their gaits and their postures and their buzz-cuts and their hard, confident faces said they belonged; must be part of the SWAT team Phil had heard guarded whispers about when they'd arrived (whispers that had occurred well out of Denton's presence); the SWAT team staking this ex-con that some psychopath apparently wanted to ream with an ax.

Those boys gotta love that shit. All that training, and now they get to use it to babysit some smart-ass convict.

Phil grimaced.

And here he and his DEA brothers were, fresh off completing the mission in Phoenix and being thrown into the fucked-up mix. *Hooray.* Those whispers had indicated he and his brothers were also destined to pull guard duty, but for the con's mommy and girlfriend (who, if the whispers were true, was some hot-as-hell ex-beauty queen; Phil would believe that horseshit five minutes after he'd seen her and not before), not the con himself—thank God for small favors.

Guard duty might be the destiny laid out for his non K-9 brothers, but Phil had a hard time seeing it for him and Spank; Denton might be a well-connected cocksucker, but Phil doubted the man was stupid enough to not utilize the resources at hand—and you didn't rise to Denton's level if you were stupid. That meant only one thing: Phil and Spankey would soon be tracking some crazy bastard through the pines—a crazy bastard with an ax, no less, not to mention one wearing a giant chicken suit.

This just kept getting better and better.

Well, when they cornered the nut job (and they eventually would; he and his good boy Spank always got their man), he would be dammed to hell before he let Spank off his lead and anywhere near that ax, he didn't care what Denton ordered. Phil was carrying the cure for crazy on his right hip—ten of them, in fact, one in the chamber and nine in the clip—and when they had the fuck-nut cornered, he intended to *use* that cure; screw letting Spank get split like firewood because Denton wanted this jack-off captured alive.

Witty moved up beside him, Styrofoam cup of steaming coffee in one hand and the other shoved in his front pocket. "What the hell's wrong with 'im? Is it rats, like you said?"

"I don't know," Phil answered slowly, staring off into the murk, where he could just make out the square hole at the head of their lane, like a giant, cold fireplace in a long row of giant, cold fire-places; a hole where ten gleaming pins used to sit waiting for some moron who had nothing better to do with his precious time on Mother Earth than to roll a sparkly fucking ball toward them and try to knock them down. *God, I hate bowling.* "He's encountered rats before, but I've never seen him act this way. Maybe he just doesn't like this place. I know *I* don't." He dropped his voice. "Or this as-signment. This has humongous balls-up written all over it, you ask me." Not that anybody was.

"Amen, brother. But so what? We go where they send us." Witty was peering down at the dog; his cup shone incandescently in the light streaming from the com room. Witty waved his coffee at the scars crisscrossing Spankey's starboard hip—the lattice of silvery scars that were glowing through the tan and black fur; glowing almost as bright as the cup: "Poor guy, that had to hurt. Where'd he get 'em again?" He leaned down, squinting in the gloom. "Iraq?"

"I wouldn't—" Phil started to say, but by then his warning was unnecessary. Spank's eyes had rolled back, and his black upper lip had lifted to reveal impressive canine teeth; his strangely plaintive growl morphed into a raspy snarl that vibrated his whole body.

Witty froze with a sick look, then leaned away slowly and took a long step back. "Jesus," he breathed.

"Told you he knows when you're looking at them, and he doesn't like it. He's sensitive." Spank dismissed the strange human that had ventured too close and went back to growling toward the murk at head of Lane 8.

Witty snorted a laugh, but it sounded strained: "Whatever you say, but that's bullshit. Ain't no way a dog could know that. So where'd he get 'em?"

"You'd be surprised what they know. And remember. 'Specially Spank here, he's smart. And it was Afghanistan; Helmand province, to be exact. Big IED. Went off under their MRAP, so Spank didn't have a chance to sniff it out. His former handler got it worse; lost two fingers and the thumb on his right hand, and he's now tooling around on two prosthetics courtesy of Uncle Sam and Mr. Walter Reed."

"That's gotta suck," Witty opined, then took a sip of his java. "MWD, huh? Which branch, Jar Heads or Rangers?"

"Marines. We get the ones they retire, like my good boy Spank here, and then we retrain 'em to find the goodies and chase down dopers instead of bombs and dune coons. Some of 'em are kinda messed up, though, and even the ones that are salvageable have to learn a whole new set of commands because the military uses different ones, battlefield shit, so ninety-five percent of 'em don't cut the mustard. My good boy Spank here cut it, though, damn straight he did, and he's one of the best. I'd put him up against any—"

Spankey suddenly stood up and barked at the darkness at the head of Lane 8.

Phil gaped down at his partner, frozen in shock; Spank had only once before broken a "stay" command in their two-year-plus partnership, and that had been to take down a doped-out mex tunnel rat who had mistakenly thought he could brain Phil with a dirt-caked crowbar while Spankey looked on.

Witty muttered, "Jeez-*us*, must be some rat," then scuttled off as that voice from behind cranked up again:

"Special Agent Boding! I thought I told you to control that animal! Do I have to make good on my threat?"

"No, sir! I've got him under control!" Phil pulled hard on Spankey's lead, whispering, "Goddamnit, Spank, down! *Stay!*"

Spankey dropped back to his belly, once more giving Phil a reproachful look as that voice snipped closer: "Perhaps I didn't make myself clear, Special Agent Boding. I will *not* allow that animal to disturb—"

And then Spankey surged back to his feet, breaking stay a second time, but instead of straining against his lead and barking, he immediately sat on his haunches facing down Lane 8. He looked over his shoulder at Phil again, but this time that look wasn't re-proachful; *this* time it was proud, as if Spank had done something he felt should earn praise from his partner.

Phil's body went ice cold.

Denton was closing in: "*Special Agent Boding!* Are you listening to me? I said take that filthy animal and yourself outside! Agent DeWitt can inform you of your duties, but right now I want…"

Phil tuned Denton out; a hot flush had replaced the ice as he slowly bent and unhooked the lead from Spankey's harness, whis-pering a command to his partner as he did. This command wasn't one of the DEA's. *This* command was one a friend and fellow K-9 handler from the Marines had told him about over cold brews while speculating on how much Spankey remembered from his time in the 'Stan:

"Seek it, Spank! *Seek-seek-seek!*"

The dog didn't power toward the dark at the end of the lane, though, as Phil had expected. Instead, he trotted forward, head and tail erect, nose leading as he sniff-sniffed, toenails clicking on wood.

"*What do you think you are doing, Special Agent?* Secure that animal immediately!"

Spankey dropped his nose and crossed two gutters and a lane divider into Lane 9.

"Do you understand me, Special Agent Boding? I said—!"

"Be quiet. Something's not right." Out in the lanes, Spankey crossed back into Lane 8 and moved further away, then abruptly circled back, crossing into Lane 7 briefly, tail wagging.

A double handful of flashlights clicked on as men moved through the gap in the low wall and gathered to watch, beams lancing through the murk to highlight and follow Spank as he sniff-sniffed his way down Lane 8 again. An FBI suit Phil hadn't been introduced to said, "What the hell's he smell out there?"

"I *ordered* you to secure that animal, Special Agent Boding!"

Denton grabbed Phil's shoulder, attempting to spin him around, but Phil shrugged the smaller man off without thought and watched as his partner abruptly sat down again, this time in the middle of Lane 9, nose pointed at an angle that had him facing the pin-setter end of Lane 10. His K-9 partner then looked over his shoulder at Phil, long pink tongue hanging and curling and dripping spittle as he panted; that look begged praise for a job well done.

All the spit in Phil's own mouth turned to dust.

"*Sir!*" Someone called from back near the front counter, and several beams swung away from Spank, responding to the urgency in that voice: "Agent Hawthorne's calling in! We have a situation, sir!"

Denton said, "In a second, Special Agent Walters!" and grabbed Philly once more, rougher this time, seizing a handful of his black DEA tee-shirt that had K-9 Officer emblazoned across the chest and back.

Phil ripped free and reached one arm behind and shoved Denton away.

Gasps as the SAC stumbled and fell to the floor, but Phil still didn't turn. Someone helped Denton up, and then that voice came again, frozen now: "I hope you enjoyed that, because you can kiss your career in the Drug Enforcement Agency goodbye, Boding. I'll also make sure you lose whatever pension you have vested, and—"

"Sir! *You need to hear what Hawthorne has to say, sir!*"

Phil had stopped listening to all of it. Instead, he listened to a muffled ringing coming from out in the lanes near his partner.

It was muffled, Phil realized, because it was coming from *beneath* the floor.

Spankey heard it too, and after cocking his head, he stood up and backed away, barking savagely.

Phil turned at last and screamed, "GET OUT!"

They all stared at him, the suits from the FBI and his brothers and the techs and the two yokels. A dozen flashlight beams swung to cover him.

He squinted against the lights, waving his arms franticly: "GOD DAMN IT, *LISTEN TO ME! EVERYBODY GET OUTSIDE RIGHT NO—*"

56

The shockwave hit first, shattering Pat's windows and rocking the railcar diner on its foundations. And then the clap of thunder came; it left my ears whining and my vision shivering.

I caught my balance, winced, then reached back and fingered a long sliver of non-tempered plate-glass sticking from the meaty part of my shoulder; I yanked it out and dropped it tinkling and bloody to the floor just as a hailstorm of bricks pounded the diner, taking out the few windows that had survived the initial shock, a burst of rusty brick-dust blowing inside, coating the tables and booths and everyone still lucky enough to be upright in them. Outside, car alarms blared, punctuating the terrified screams filling Pat's.

Seconds.

Beside me, a man, one of the tourists, stared across the booth at his blonde wife; she was slumped over her short stack (the lady had preferred blueberry syrup, I saw), bleeding from a shank of glass jutting from her right eye; the left eye was a gorgeous gray-green, and already dimming. His shrieks merged with his kids' screams and added to the chaos as shell-shocked mothers clutched crying children and a man shouted hoarsely that his granddaughter needed an ambulance, somebody please call an ambulance.

Seconds.

Angela.

I peered through a jagged hole in the parking lot side of Pat's, a hole that used to be a window, finding Angela's car but not Angela… and then I spotted Hawthorne. He was out of the Toyota, standing by the tailgate, staring across Third toward the Injun…and his *expression*. Yikes. I'd never seen one like it, on any face, and I hope like hell I never see it again: pain and shock and fear and rage all dolloped onto a heavy slice of awe spread across all those dusty freckles made for one ugly picture.

And then I forgot about Hawthorne as a distant *boom!* came to my still-ringing ears, followed by five more in measured succession; the power in Pat's flickered and died after the third, plunging us into semi-darkness and eliciting more screams.

Out in the lot I saw Angela stagger to her feet next to a black extended-cab Dodge Ram pickup two over from her Camry and I almost slumped to the glass-strewn tiles in relief. She was covered in brick dust and she had a bloody scratch on her cheek and her hair was mussed and she was now barefoot; she clutched one white platform sandal in one hand and her purse in the other. The second sandal was nowhere to be seen; the sunglasses were also missing in action.

"Angela!" I shouted through a glass-toothed hole, leaning over the red booth seat, ignoring the dead man lying in it with blood all over what was left of his face.

Seconds.

"*Angela!*"

She heard me that time and turned dazedly and peered through the billowing dust, putting one hand to the cut on her cheek and looking at the blood on her fingers and then absently wiping them on her shirt while searching for me again; I waved, arm jerking back and forth, and she spotted me:

"Jack!"

I booked it toward the front door, going around people when I could and sort-of-gently easing them aside when I couldn't; Angela was definitely in shock, and she might be more injured than she looked and just didn't know it yet. Chief Rogers was still up by the waitress' station; he appeared shaken for the first time in my experience, but otherwise unhurt—

I skidded to a halt and stared down at Daisy.

A foot long glass-lance had transfixed her neck; blood still spurted from both ends, runnels of red combining into a glistening pool beneath her head, gumming her long hair to the floor. Her pretty brown eyes were open and fixed. I squatted and brushed her bangs away from her forehead, remembering those Friday nights long ago, and after, how sometimes she'd tell me she loved me. Maybe she really had.

I closed Daisy's eyes before standing up and shoving through the coughing throng; they were coughing, I realized, because smoke poured from Mike's kitchen, a foul-smelling cloud spreading just below the hammered-copper ceiling.

And just as I'd finished processing *that* fun fact, I remembered Pat's was all electric except for the burners and the grill and the big over/under oven. They ran off the giant propane tank outside, the one Pat and Jerry had put in for Mike twenty years ago because he'd insisted, "Gas tastes better, ya know." Whatever the hell that meant.

And of course that's when I realized that if the shockwave had damaged the lines back there as much as they'd pulverized the annealed-glass windows, then we might all be about to learn what it was like to live as a piece of toast.

I brushed by Chief Rogers without a word and was halfway out the door when he grabbed me: "Don't go out there!" Back in the kitchen, a smoke detector chose that moment to add its pulsing wail to the party; panicked shouts greeted it.

"Angela," was all I replied before ripping free and stepping out…

And then froze, gaping:

The Injun was gone.

A towering mushroom cloud and a fiery crater were all that was left of the old bowling alley—except about half the front wall, the one with the giant mural I'd so loved as a kid. Now that painting was distorted as well as faded, peace-pipe smoking Injun only half there and dancing squaws bulging. As I watched, stunned, that wall crumbled outward in a shower of blackened bricks, completing the Injun's destruction and putting to rest a ghost from my childhood.

The G-rides closest to the Injun were tipped over on their sides; two were on fire, black smoke pouring up to merge with the sky-mushroom. The remaining rides in the front lot had only suffered shattered windows and dents from the blast and the bricks; with all the smoke, I could only assume the vehicles parked in back were in a similar sorry state; the lucky parking-attendant fed-bot climbed slowly out of a battered and brick-covered Suburban and stood and stared in disheveled wonder.

Then Angela screamed my name. She was still standing by the Dodge, still barefoot but now with both sandals dangling from one hand and her purse hooked back over her shoulder.

"Are you okay? Are you hurt?"

"I'm fine!" She shouted, then started toward me as I started toward her…and Chief Rogers lunged out the door and grabbed me again, much harder this time.

"You shouldn't be out here!" He had a hold of me with one hand; in the other rested his matte-black Kimber .45, and it was pointed past my shoulder at the pines looming behind my Ford.

"I have to make sure she's all right!" I told him as a coughing, crying, bleeding throng streamed past us and down the steps and into the lot.

The Chief shot a hard glance at Angela, who was now fighting her way upstream towards us: "My rover is charging out in the city ride, and my cell's not getting any bars," he said. "I'm sure everybody else's is the same, but I can use Pat's land line to call for backup. I hope." He glanced over his shoulder. "I'll shut the gas off in the kitchen and kill that damn smoke detector." He shoved me stumbling down the steps. "Grab her and come back inside!" He scanned the pines again, weapon up and ready, then darted back in after the last of the shell-shocked patrons had pushed out of the cracked doors.

I glanced at those trees as I ran to Angela; I saw nothing but needles and the sun-dappled darkness beneath them and the wood-brown and stone-gray outline of Pat and Jerry's cabin and the red-and-chrome flash of Pat's Stingray sitting in the driveway.

And then I enveloped Angela in my arms. She was unhurt except for that scrape on her cheek, and also one on her elbow and knee, I now saw; she must've been thrown to the pavement by the blast.

She pulled back and looked at the blood covering her forearm and hand and cried, "You're hurt!"

"Just a piece of old window glass," I told her. "There are people inside who got it worse, and most are never leaving the diner. Not on their feet, anyway." I looked down into those amazing eyes…

And the conversation with Rogers came flooding back.

She must have seen something change. "Jack? Why are you looking at me that way?"

I opened my mouth…and then two men dressed head to toe in camouflage with pine branches strapped to their arms and legs and pine cones glued to their helmets burst out of the woods and double-timed it across Pat's lot to Hawthorne, who had recovered enough to shout orders. They carried sound-suppressed automatic weapons along with a bevy of other goodies; the silenced barrels of the sniper rifles strapped to their backs stuck up behind their helmets. Beneath those helmets, I saw tears glistening on their war paint as they gazed across the road; more to the point, I saw the faces *beneath* those tears, and I felt a chill; people died when such men wore that face.

One of the camo guys reluctantly trotted our way on Hawthorn's barked order, but Hawthorne and the other guy were already sprinting across the road, grabbing the stunned parking attendant as they went—going to look for survivors, I suppose; I thought them overly optimistic.

Angela had turned to watch with me. "They're all gone, aren't they," she said, voice raised to carry over the car alarms but somehow still soft.

"Yes."

Behind us, Chief Rogers opened the cracked right-hand door and poked his face out, a dank cloud of burnt eggs and charred hash browns escaping into the blue above his head; I belatedly realized the smoke detector had quit blaring.

"I turned the gas off," he hiss-shouted, "but Pat's phone is dead. I'd wager all the land lines are." He shot a wary look toward the trees that walled the other side of the lot. "Get her in here!"

I propelled Angela up the steps. "You stay here and let Rogers protect you. I'm going across the street and see if I can help." Perhaps I was an optimistic soul as well.

"No!" she protested, grabbing me on the diner's glass-strewn threshold and looking up at me with those eyes. "You stay with me and let Rogers protect us both! There's nothing you can do over there!"

Then: "Get inside!", and I whipped around to find the SWAT agent in the pine-cone studded ghillie suit, the one Hawthorne had ordered back, shoving through the awe-struck crowd that had gathered to stare across the road. "*Get inside,*" he yelled again, waving the sound-suppressed barrel of his weapon at the doors beside us; his upturned black-and-olive green face was a mask of rage.

And then a *crack!* from the woods, and that face below the helmet exploded sideways, splattering teeth and blood onto the side of Pat's before the rest of him collapsed at the bottom of the steps.

Angela screamed. I think I did too, but then Rogers dragged us both inside. So I didn't see the beginning of the firefight, but I heard it as I stumbled and fell near the front counter with Angela on top of me; the unfortunates caught out in the crossfire wailed pathetically.

I gently pushed Angela off and crawled into a bloody booth and poked one eye above a jagged sill and caught the end of it; a dark figure lurked near my Ford, bursts of automatic-weapon fire flashing from those green and gold shadows like tree-lightning as it fired toward Hawthorne and the two agents across the road—or what was left of them.

I think they'd turned back at the shot that had killed their team member, but by then it had been too late; the other camo guy was down for the count, and the parking bot took at least four rounds to the chest and neck and face as I watched, dancing and twitching back across Third before crumpling in a bloody heap. Hawthorne returned fire before getting raked across the legs. He dragged himself to the closest ditch, taking cover as more rounds sparked behind him; he'd left a red trail on the pavement, I saw, along with his pistol.

The firing from the trees stopped.

The people out in the lot were still screaming, and Angela had slipped her platforms back on before making her way to another blown-out window two booths away to catch the show. Rogers had his Kimber up and ready as he watched out a triangular hole in the shattered front doors. At least the smoke had dissipated; a benefit of all the windows being permanently—

Bob Jr.'s voice called to us from the woods.

Now, at first, what that salesman's baritone had to say hardly registered because I hardly *recognized* it; oh, it was still deep and self-assured to the point of arrogant, oh yes…but it was also mushy and slow. And the effort he was putting into speaking—into *enunci-*

ating—came through clearly. So did the frustration; it sounded like Bob had knocked back a few before heading out to do his evil thing and now regretted it.

Mushy or not, effortful or not—*drunk* or not—that deep, confident voice cut above the din, easily carrying to us in the diner:

"Chief, I see you there! Grasp your weapon by the barrel, push it out slowly and throw it off to the side, then bring my son's killer and his whore out!"

Rogers cursed under his breath and ducked back as that strange/ familiar voice spoke again: "Throw the weapon away and bring them out, or I'll mow these sheep down one by one!"

Wails and sobs from the lot; I peeked out again. Most had hunkered in place when the short-lived firefight had broken out, but some were jammed beside or even crammed under vehicles; wherever they'd sheltered, they all stared toward a spot near my pickup, faces twisted in fear.

A darker shadow moved over there before that sloppy voice called again: "Do as I say, Chief, or they die!" More wails, punctuated by a few strident screams. "And then I'll reduce that building to scrap with all three of you inside it!"

Sobbing children. Two or three more screams. Maybe four.

"One minute!"

"We have to go out there," Angela said to nobody in particular; she sounded both resolute and absolutely terrified. "He'll kill them if we don't."

"He'll kill them anyway," I told her. "Probably right after he does us."

Before Angela could respond, Rogers said, "Not necessarily." The Chief was back to peeking out the little window to the left of the waitress' station; somehow, out of all the windows in Pat's, it alone had survived intact. He turned then and squatted with his back to the coffee machine; an unopened pack of industrial-sized bleached filters rested on a chrome shelf just past his ear. "He could've shot us as easily as that agent, but he didn't. And that means he wants something."

"Yeah," I said, "me dead. And as slowly and painfully as possible."

"True. But he's demanding both of you. And that means if we play our cards right, we may survive this."

It took a second, but I got there:

"Hunh *unh*. No fucking way, not gonna happen; she's staying in here."

We both looked at Angela.

She swallowed. Twice. But she said, "I can't just sit here and listen to him execute those people. Can you?"

"No, but I'm not about to let him hurt you either, so the Chief and I will—"

"He'll kill you as soon as he sees I'm not with you!"

"Maybe, but if—"

"Thirty seconds!"

Chief Rogers said, "She's right; we all go. If we don't, he'll slaughter those people. *My* people. I won't let that happen." I saw no fear in his face, only resolve. He stood, then yanked up a baby-shit-brown uniform pant leg and unstrapped a small semi-auto from a black Nylon ankle holster and tossed it to me.

I caught the hold-out weapon. It was a Beretta .32 Tomcat; compact but deadly. "You've got one in the chamber and six in the clip," he told me. "I'll draw his fire, and you put him down."

Then he looked straight at Angela; his cop-eyes blazed with suspicion, and that left eyelid was going like mad. She visibly recoiled from him. "As for *you*, young lady..." He controlled himself with an obvious effort. "Do you still have Jack's .45?" She nodded, face half defiant and half uneasy as she unsnapped her purse and dug around and then held up my Colt. "Well then," he told her, "I recommend readying yourself to use it. And in whatever manner you see fit; if he kills us, he won't shoot you, but I guarantee you that before the end, you'll wish he had."

Then I said, "No," and tossed him back the Tomcat. "*I'll* draw his fire. This is all about Zack, anyway—and me, I guess—so you'll both just have to save me."

Angela slid out of her booth and duck-walked across the shattered glass and the trampled eggs and a flattened and bloody bacon slice and the wide, still form of Daisy and clutched me, short nails biting the tender inside of my left wrist and forearm:

"*Please* don't do this!"

"It's the only way to save everybody," I told her as a mushy monster shouted from the woods one last time:

"Ten seconds before these people die, Rogers!"

Angela spat, "Everybody but *you!*", and I had no answer.

"Let's do this," the Chief said calmly as fresh screams rose from outside. He shoved the Beretta into his right front pocket, then bent and yelled out the triangular hole in the glass: "We're coming out!" He grasped the big Kimber by the barrel and stuck it into the smoky sunshine, waggled it so Bob could see, then chucked it off to the side; I heard it clatter against a metal railing.

Angela searched my eyes fiercely with hers, then *threw* my arm away and stood and shrugged her purse strap off her shoulder and let the bag drop to the bloody floor without so much as a glance. She ripped her green shirt loose from her white shorts and stuffed the Colt's barrel down the back, hammer now sticking up along the knobs of her spine.

She tugged her shirt down to cover it, and Rogers pushed open the shattered left-hand door and we stepped out: the Chief first, a determined-looking Angela right behind, and me last.

God help us, we really did.

57

We stopped just outside the door and stood in a little line: Chief Rogers on the left, Angela in the middle, and me on the right; I immediately pressed against the rail, getting as far away from her as I could just in case Bob really did open up as soon as he saw me. But no gunshots came; people had finally shut their damn car alarms off, too, so only ominous silence greeted us—you know, other than the terrified sobbing from those sheltering wherever they could, along with the occasional child's whimper.

I glanced up. The mushroom from the Injun had spread, bringing twilight to Indian Head before lunch. To the northwest, I saw two more dissipating, albeit less-apocalyptic mushrooms. I did some fast calculations and realized they marked where the new cell phone towers stood—or rather, *had* stood. Off to the southeast I saw another mushroom near where the HV transmission lines that supplied Indian Head with juice ran up the mountain, and another beyond it that marked I didn't have a clue what; something that wasn't there anymore. Two more had bloomed over town, one in the direction of the square, and another on the northeast side, where all the recent growth had been; their 'shrooms had already mingled with the Injun's, adding their bit to the spreading gloom.

And then that voice spoke from the dappled darkness near my Ford at the far corner of the lot:

"Good," it slurred in tones of deepest satisfaction.

"Here we are," Rogers agreed. "Now let these people go, Bob. They don't have any part in this."

A deep chuckle: "Did those oh-so-smart fools across the road share my identity with you, Chief? Those burnt corpses with the three pathetic letters on their charred jackets?"

"They didn't have to," Rogers replied evenly. "I suspected you when I saw the frame around Jack. But I was certain when I learned what Bill Napier did to you and those other boys." Heavy pause. Then: "And what your mother did. Is that why you rape them with whatever's to hand, Bob? Because that's what she did with you?"

No response; the quiet emanating from those gold-and-green shadows was deathly.

Angela's slim eyebrows drew together as she leaned sideways and mouthed, "What did old Bill do to him?", but I just shook my head because I was watching a mom and her little girl out in the parking lot, both with long, dark hair. The girl was five or six. They were huddled beside a maroon Chrysler 300 parked one row closer to Pat's than mine, and unfortunately for them, they were the nearest souls to the psycho lurking in the shadows. The mother gathered her whimpering daughter into her lap, shushing and soothing and rocking her, and at that moment her eyes found mine over her little girl's head; the desperation in them cut like a blade.

Chief Rogers broke that dangerous hush, tone still conversational: "Where's Don Straus, Bob? Is the boy alive?"

Angela drew a sharp breath and clutched my arm, quivering. I did a bit of quivering myself; if there was even the slimmest chance Donnie was still breathing somewhere…

"It's a possibility," that voice allowed. Angela clutched me harder, but my flickering hope for Donnie guttered out as Bob added, "But if you cared for the liar at all, you'll pray he's dead by now."

Tears glistened on Angela's cheeks as she pressed her face into my arm. I fought my own tears as I gently held her:

Peace out, Donnie. We'll hang in the next round.

Chief Rogers simply nodded, as if that had been no more than he'd expected. "And what about Councilman Starkly? Any chance he's still alive?"

Another pause, and this one had a considering feel to it; then: "None. Fred is most assuredly dead. And good riddance."

Chief Rogers just said, "All right," then glanced across Third, toward what used to be a bowling alley…and what I glimpsed in that brief moment made my breath catch; his tone had been conversational throughout, even nonchalant:

Nonchalant didn't match those eyes, though; not even close.

"Let these people go, Bob, then put down the weapon and surrender to me, and I'll make sure you live to see a trial; after what you've done, I can't guarantee the FBI will do the same. And they're on their way, Bob, swarms of them. *All* of them. There will be no escape for you, not now. Not after this."

Silence.

"Surrender, and you can be the centerpiece of the Trial of the Century, Bob." Chief Rogers slowly descended the steps and moved to his left, arms out and hands up, even turning his right hip toward the pines, presenting that empty holster, showing he posed no threat, and I understood what he was doing; I also approved: Over there, if Bob shot him, the rest of the people cowering in the lot, as well as Angela and I, would be out of the line of fire—at least initially.

And then Angela and my Colt could end this nightmare.

"Think about it," Rogers continued as he stopped next to the last vehicle in the line closest to Pat's, a bright-red convertible VW bug that reminded me heartrendingly of Tiff. The Chief still had his arms out and hands up: "The Trial of the Century, Bob. I know someone crowns one of those every other year, but this truly would be it, with every eye on you, every ear and mind filled with tales of the Traveler's exploits. You can make them understand your greatness at last, just like you've always wanted. But that can only happen if—"

"The 'Traveler'? Is *that* what those fools named me? It would be just like them, to use something so simple to quantify a force beyond their comprehension." Silence. Then: "Still, I have to admit a part of me approves: the *Traveler.*"

The skin on the back of my arms prickled in hard gooseflesh; that voice had quickened in…not excitement; more a vile species of prideful vindication.

"Yes," Rogers answered, tone betraying nothing, eyes gleaming with the same revulsion crawling through me. "And if you surrender, you can make everyone understand—"

Angela and I jumped, and I instinctively pulled her behind me as the lot full of prone, bleeding, and terrorized people shrieked and gibbered anew at flashes of white fire beneath the needles, *blam-blam-blam-blam-blam*, five rapid-fire shots only, from what sounded like a heavy automatic weapon, the long side of Pat's behind Chief Rogers dimpling with five fresh holes; Rogers, to his credit, barely flinched.

When the screaming petered out, that voice slur-snarled from the shadows near my truck: "So. Smart. You think you're *so smart*, Chief, just like those crispy fools across the road: Saying my name over and over to soothe me, like I was some out-of-control headcase. See that smoke plume to the south? The one hovering over the square? That's your police station; the one to the northeast is what's left of the new fire station. And that moron Toms and your other second-rate officer, Flemming? They were over at the Injun. *Were.* All of which means no one is coming to save you, Rogers. And except for a twist of luck, you would have already joined them in hell. I've been three steps out in front of you all along, just like

I've been ahead of the FBI from the very beginning! And *me?* The Traveler? *Surrender?* There will be no surrendering. Not *this* glorious day! Not *ever!*"

This time there were way more than five shots; the green shadows on the passenger side of my Ford inverted, revealing a large figure dressed in gray and black camouflage and wearing black gloves as rounds ripped the convertible bug to smoking pieces. When the fusillade stopped, screams became whimpers as the reek of spent fireworks drifted through the needles like rancid fog.

"If you—"

Pow! Pow! Pow!

The maroon Chrysler 300 sheltering the brunette mom and daughter suddenly sported a hole in the windshield, a flat front tire, and a hole in the grille; the mom and daughter proned themselves on the rough pavement and mewled in terror as more screams and shouts rippled through the smoky air.

"Defy me again, and the next two will be for this whore and her whelp, the little whore-in-training. Do you understand, Chief?"

"Yes," Rogers said. "Then what do you want from us?"

"Not you," Bob mushed from those shadows. "*Them.*"

And then I felt him look at me; I literally felt it, like an evil, insane weight pressing against my face.

Not a pleasant sensation.

"Hello, Jack."

"Hi, Bob. So, what can we do for you today?"

"What I *instruct* you to do, smart ass. And what I told the Chief goes for you and Angie; defy me just once, and these two die. Then the rest of the sheep." He let the fresh round of moans trail away. "Do *you* understand?"

"Yeah, got it."

"What about the little slut? Didn't hear her."

From behind my shoulder, rich with suppressed fury:

"Got it."

"Good." The world held its breath. Then: "This is what will happen now: Give Angie your keys, Jack; we'll take your piece-of-shit. She will walk to me while you, Jack, and you, Chief Rogers, stay exactly where you are, like good little boys. Then Angie and I will drive to—"

"N—!"

Pow!

The round whined as it skipped off the asphalt next to the mom's head before plunking into the side of a smoke-gray Nissan Altima with Nebraska plates. She shrieked and clutched her daughter and curled into the fetal position with her back to the madman hidden in the tree line.

Bob waited for relative quiet again before saying, "That was close, Jack. You almost sealed her fate." From the shadows, I heard the mechanical music of an automatic weapon's slide rack. "Send the Beaumont whore to me now, or you'll watch them die."

It felt like red-hot iron hooks had been inserted into my brain, my soul:

Barbed hooks.

"I'm not telling you no," I began carefully. "I'm not, so don't shoot them. Please. But we all know what you'll do to Angela; I love her, and I can't let that happen to her."

From behind, slender arms squeezed gently.

"How sweet." I felt that hot, loathsome gaze crawling on me. "And on any other day, you'd be right. But I need her to bring you to me, because it's *you* I will kill this glorious day, Jack. Before I do, though, I'll break you with my bare hands. It will be a slow, painful process, I promise. Your little slut can watch. She'll remain unharmed as long as you meet us at Hawk's Point in one hour, and then face me, man to man. Rogers can bring you and keep everyone away until we're finished—and you better pray to whatever god you believe in that he *does* keep everyone away, Jack, and that we settle our business uninterrupted, or she'll die begging and screaming, just like all the rest."

"You…you want to *fight* me?"

"What, afraid of an old man? I'm not Zack; I can handle a punk like you. Trust me. But if somehow you *do* beat me—which you won't—but if you do, you can have her back, untouched and unharmed. You have my word. And unlike your friend, Donnie the Cheat, I keep *my* word."

This was nuts; he sounded sincere. I didn't believe him, though—and I don't think anyone within earshot did, either; could the Traveler restrain himself from doin' what he do to a young, beautiful woman he held captive, even if for only an hour?

Not a chance.

"I…I can't. I love her, and I…" *Shit!* "I can't let…"

The universe had gone utterly still.

Then that deadly, slurred, insane voice:

"Are you defying me, Jack?"

The mom uncurled and looked at me over her daughter's quivering shoulder; her flowing hair had yellow needles caught in it, and her shining dark eyes were beyond desperate as they pleaded with me.

Oh God…

And then Angela stepped around me and spoke in her clear, sweet voice:

"I'll go to Hawk's Point with him."

58

"No."

I'd blurted it, consequences and horror-stricken shrieks from Pat's lot be damned…but there were no shots from the piney shadows as Angela faced me and laid her index finger over my lips, just like she had that Fourth of July morning on my barn floor, right before our first kiss.

"I have to," she told me. Those eyes were huge and blue and scared and determined. "He'll kill them if I don't."

"But—"

The finger pressed harder, shushing me. "I love you, Jack Rossie Ross."

"I love you too," I managed to choke out past the finger, then dug in my pocket and reluctantly handed her my keys.

Angela plucked them from my hand with a smile…and if there had still been any birds around, they would've all been knocked kersplat from the sky.

She started to turn then, but I reflexively clutched her arms; I couldn't let her do this.

Then that voice: that arrogant, hateful, triumphant, mushy voice; I was getting reeeeally tired of that voice:

"Let her come to me, Jack, or you know what will happen."

No shrieks from out in the lot this time, only whimpers.

So I let her go; it was the hardest thing I've ever done in my life, but I let her go.

Angela patted my cheek and went sedately down the steps… and then paused there next to the fallen SWAT agent, blonde head tilted as she listened along with everyone else to the siren that had suddenly started wailing in the distance; it sounded like a fire truck to me, but everyone out in the lot perked right up; rescue from this nightmare was a possibility, after all…

Angela's right heel twisted outward, tapping and nudging the dead man. Only my eyes dropped to what that shapely, platform-sandaled appendage was trying to show me; a tan camouflage Nylon holster, semi-automatic pistol resting within; its grip stuck out beneath the holster's mottled strap like a charcoal-colored promise.

I lifted my gaze and found Angela giving me a smile over her shoulder. But no birds would ever fall out of the heavens for *this* smile; in fact, they might just fly away faster. She glanced significantly across the road before weaving through parked vehicles, sumptuous tan legs scissoring, green top billowing, revealing her narrow waist and trim stomach as well as the varnished grip and the burnished hammer of my .45 edged up along her spine.

I cut my gaze toward the destroyed Injun and immediately spotted what she had:

Hawthorne.

I'd thought the man dead, but a crimson trail marked where he'd dragged his once-blinding legs out of the ditch and over to his most-definitely dead SWAT teammate and secured the .50 cal rifle. He was now using its butt and one spotted forearm to grimly drag himself further out into the Injun's lot. I didn't get why for a second, and then I did; he needed a better angle for a shot on the madman lurking in the tree line across the road. As he crawled, something dangled and bumped along at the end of his left leg. I'm pretty sure it was his foot.

Then that goddamn voice again, speaking to Angela:

"Don't stop there," it mush-commanded. "Come in here, to me, or they die."

Angela had made her way through the brick-covered cars and the cringing people and was now standing near the tailgate of my Ford, sandaled feet spread wide, small fists balled tight and hammered down on her hipbones as she faced those green shadows; my keys were still clenched in one hand.

"Then shoot them! I don't care!"

"Oh shit," I whispered while sidling down the steps as quickly as I could sidle; the dark-haired little girl screamed and clutched her mother.

Angela didn't seem to notice—or care. "I have a question," she told the needles to the right of my pickup, "and I'm not moving a step further until I get an answer!"

I held my breath, waiting for the green lightning, waiting for the dying, but there was only the Injun crackling across the street and the siren warbling steadily closer; I watched Angela in profile, her fiery determination and seeming lack of fear, and could only shake my head.

And then: "One question," that voice slurred. "I answer, or not. Then you step in here with me. You ask two questions, you don't come to me, they die. Agreed?"

"Agreed!" Then, a whiplash: "Did you kill my mother?"

Silence.

Oh shit oh shit oh shit. I bent and popped the camo holster strap and removed a government-issue Glock .9mm and then stood back up, holding the pistol behind my right leg, hoping Bob hadn't noticed me disappear behind the cars and then reappear again; evidently not because there was only that pregnant crackling-and-siren-laced quiet.

Chief Rogers noticed, though; he'd stood by the ripped-apart bug this whole time, as still and as silent and as eerie as a cigar-store cop. When I straightened with the Glock, he came alive enough to look over at me, and in his hammer-hard face I saw the warning, and the message:

Not yet, it said.

Not yet, but soon.

And then, from that green-and-gold tinted darkness came a single word, heavy and slurred and final:

"Yesh."

Angela's full lips trembled. Tears dripped from her chin. "*Why*, Uncle Bob? She was my *mother!* And *Chris's* mother! And your *best friend's wife!*" She dashed a forearm across her streaming eyes. "You killed Aunt Susan, too, didn't you? *Zane and Zack's mom!* You killed them *both!* You doomed the four kids you supposedly cared about most in the world to growing up without their *mothers!* Was it because they discovered the truth about you? Was *that* the shitty excuse you had for killing my *mother*, you sick son of a bitch? And all this…this…*shit?*" She violently circled the hand with my keys in it over her head: "You did all this, hurt all these people, just because Zack died? What happened to Zack was an *accident*, Uncle Bob, and Jack already paid for it! And all of this…this *crap*, this hurting people, won't bring him back! God, what the fuck is *wrong* with you?"

Bob had said one question and that was way more that two—plus a few not-so-flattering statements thrown in—so again I waited for the green lightning, for the dying…

A shadow moved forward, needle-laden branches swaying, parting, the shadow becoming something more than a shadow, an apparition, and then it resolved into a big man dressed shoulder-to-toe in black-and-gray Arctic camouflage carrying an honest-to-God AK-47, barrel pointed at the ground and banana clip curving beneath its right forearm; the wooden butt was tucked tight into its left armpit and the shoulder strap dangled near its knees; there was even a fucking bayonet jutting out under the long barrel. That apparition stopped at the edge of the pavement near my Ford's front right quarter panel, facing Angela, revealed at last, and I found myself staring in both fascination and revulsion.

I hadn't seen Bob up close in years, for obvious reasons, but he still had a full head of hair and his asshole twins' vivid green eyes, although instead of jet black his hair was now solid gray and sticking up in wild tufts, as if Bob couldn't be bothered to take a break from his evil schedule for personal grooming. He was even bigger than I remembered, too, with a deep chest and massive arms; his face was still handsome, with a square, cleft chin, straight nose, and thin lips, but that's where my memory and the current monstrosity facing Angela parted ways; that face sagged now, and twitched, and even from fifty feet away, I could see the AK tremble in his black-gloved hands.

Then I blinked.

Twice.

Bob wore makeup.

I blinked a few more times, sure my mind had taken a wee little break in the stress of the moment, but nope: Bob was wearing electric blue eyeshadow and black eyeliner and red, red lipstick, and there were spots of rouge high on his cheekbones. His lipstick and lip liner had smeared, giving his mouth an insane-droopy-clown vibe on one side; throw in the Arctic getup, and he looked like a transvestite polar-bear hunter having a really bad day.

But beneath the makeup, beneath the rage, beneath the insanity, I saw a flash of something human; I saw regret and sadness as he looked at the woman standing before him, the woman that used to be a little girl he'd dandled on his knee. But mostly what I saw was iron resolve and utter weariness, as if Bob didn't have much left to give but was going to give it, come what may.

And then Bob Jr. looked across the top of the dusty and brick-festooned cars and SUVs and trucks and a sample of his cowering victims at me, and that face twisted with something beyond hate and rage, something beyond human, and I saw him for the first time; for the last time:

I saw the Traveler.

"Accident?" he snarled. "My son's death was no accident! Zane told me! He was there that night! He saw what you did! And Jack knows it! He knows he got off easy! *Accident?* My son was MURDERED!"

I kept my face carefully neutral as I felt Chief Rogers look over at me again.

The Traveler turned that twitching green gaze on the young woman standing before him, tears streaking her cheeks, gorgeous, anguished…but there was no regret in those blazing eyes now, no sadness, and then I understood something terrible:

Angela would never get her answers.

The AK came up fast, and I screamed "Watch out!" as I sprinted between the parked cars, jumping over huddled people as the Russian assault rifle shouted *blam-blam-blam-blam-blam-blam-blam*, screaming incoherently as I racked one in the chamber and started firing, *pow-pow-pow, pow-pow-pow, pow-pow-pow,* certain I would see Angela cut to pieces like the VW, still screaming and firing as I ran around the last car, almost crying with relief as I caught sight of Angela with my Colt up and firing as well, her face twisted with her own hate and rage, stumbling sideways to shelter on the other side of my truck. The Traveler staggered as three of my shots hit home, and at least four of Angela's, but he was so big and so strong and filled with so much vitality and so much hate he somehow stayed up…and that's when my heart plunged into my shoes, because I saw that beneath the bullet-torn Arctic getup, Bob was wearing a fucking bulletproof vest!

Jesus Christ! Shit!

He snarled as he swung the AK my way, insane-droopy-clown face twisted into something beyond nightmares…but just as the barrel leveled on my chest he seemed to leap sideways and slam against my truck, the assault rifle dropping from those shaking hands to clatter at the edge of the asphalt.

Hawthorne.

It hadn't been a head shot, though, and again the vest had saved Bob; but vest or no vest, he'd be feeling that .50 cal bullet.

I wasted no more time in regret. I just leveled the Glock at his big fat evil head and pulled the trigger.

Click.

Aw, hell.

Time slowed. Bob raised his black-gloved right hand toward me while still leaning drunkenly against the quarter panel of my Ford, a gleaming revolver with a six-inch barrel pointed straight at my heart. But then his mad-dog eyes jerked past me as I dove behind the front bumper and Angela screamed and that revolver spoke twice, *Boom!-Boom!*, but neither blast covered up the four clean *pop-pop-pop-pop's* from behind me:

We'd forgotten about Chief Rogers.

I guess he'd moved up when I'd rushed forward, watching as Angela and I emptied our guns ineffectually, watching as Hawthorne's shot hit the vest, and then he'd used my truck as a screen and had taken his shots—and Chief Rogers hadn't missed: two to the Traveler's throat and two to the Traveler's face. The revolver clattered next to the AK as Bob flopped onto the dried needles piled at the edge of the lot, what was left of his skull coming to rest near my front passenger tire.

Angela and I stumbled around to the other side of my pickup and stared down at him.

Then she glanced behind us: "Oh my God!"

I turned and discovered that the Traveler hadn't missed, either.

Chief Rogers lay on his back, hold-out Beretta near his out-flung right hand, surprise on his face as he stared blank-eyed up at the umbra of black smoke spreading across his town. Both of the revolver's rounds had hit true, shredding brown uniform and pale flesh alike; one was a clean heart-shot. I figured the Chief had died instantly, and with little pain…but really, that was just hope.

Then, bedlam.

Some people scrambled to their vehicles and slumped against them, crying and shaking and hugging each other; some just lay there on the needle-strewn asphalt, weeping. Some tried to drive away and were blocked by a fire engine that had arrived and slewed to a stop crooked out on Third unnoticed by me sometime during the shooting; it had BECKTON scrawled in gold letters on its side. The stunned Beckton firefighters in their full gear and yellow helmets were just straightening from behind the long truck, where they'd taken cover.

I took a deep breath, then glanced over near the maroon 300, at what was left of the dark-haired woman and her little girl, my stomach and heart and soul twisting:

The Traveler had done exactly what he'd said he would.

Rot in hell, asshole.

Angela turned my face away, whispering, "Don't. Don't look." She was crying, and I discovered that I was crying, too. I clutched her, and she wrapped her arms around me, squeezing me just as tight.

She whispered, "Is it over?"

I considered what to say to that; she must've felt the tension because she raised her head from my chest.

"What is it?"

I looked down at this stunning, vibrant woman in my arms, and I knew I had a choice; all life comes down to choices, and now I had to make one, and fast, because I had about seven seconds, eight tops, before the whole shebang would be wrenched from my hands.

I thought carefully but quickly, then made my decision.

"Hold on," I said, then gently pried my keys from her fingers.

Angela frowned and said, "What are you doing?", but I didn't respond because I was busy peeking over cars; most of the survivors appeared to be weeping over dead loved ones or quietly celebrating being alive and were paying zero attention to us; out on Third, two of the fire-boys were hooking up a long canvas hose to the hydrant, although I didn't know what good that would do considering how much (or little) of the Injun remained. One firefighter had come onto the lot and was ministering to an injured victim. Another had ventured out into the Injun's lot and had squatted beside Hawthorne, who was face down and motionless next to the .50 cal, which was still propped on its shooter's biped. As I watched, the first responder pulled two fingers away from Hawthorne's neck and shook his head. More sirens warbled and screamed, closing fast:

Police sirens.

"Jack?"

I stared down at Chief Rogers for about three nanoseconds—there would be no turning back from this—then, careful not to touch him, I slid the folded notebook from his back pocket and went to my truck, Angela now silent and watching me with an unreadable expression. I opened the door and slid the bloody notebook under the bench seat and locked the door and eased it shut again.

I walked back over to Angela, her summer-sky eyes intent on my face, and then I handed her my keys back and wrapped her in my arms. She put a palm on my chest and pressed me away while looking at Chief Rogers. She turned her head the other way and looked at my truck. Then she looked back up at me, and I saw something ooze across her features, just under the skin—something dark. And then it was gone, vanishing into the depths once more.

But that was all right. Something dark was inside me as well, swimming just under the surface, waiting for an excuse to come out and play; I accepted her darkness because she had accepted mine. Maybe it wasn't just Angela and I. Maybe that same darkness lurked inside all of us, waiting for the right—or wrong—circumstance to appear, to have an excuse to rear its ugly head into the light; patiently waiting for its chance to come out and play.

Waiting.

Angela's ripe mouth pursed thoughtfully as the bones of the Injun smoldered and the survivors in Pat's lot moaned and wept and out on Third St. the sirens screamed. She spoke for my ears alone:

"What about your mom?"

"What about her? Oh, by the way, we need to sit down and have a talk about Schallamach patterns sometime."

Those eyebrows drew together. "What are Schallamach patterns?"

"Exactly. You guys need to be more careful."

Soft: "Like you were with Zack?"

I didn't answer, and in that moment of knowing stillness between us Angela peered deep into my skull, using first one eye socket and then the other as a window…and it seemed to me she found something in there, something she'd been seeking; she pressed her body to mine fiercely, molding us together, making us one.

"Now it's over," I said.

About the Author

Edward Rand is an American novelist and short-story artist. He wears other hats, such as Dad, zealous reader of great writers, (former) ne'er-do-well, dedicated martial artist, Stoic, dog and cat fanatic, and smarty britches. He loves talking about himself in the third person, too, so he's really getting a kick out of this.

Discover Edward's other work and sign up for his sporadic newsletter, wherein he gives away the short stories he writes just because at bloodchucklespress.com.

Rabid readers and their oh-so-opinionated opinions are the lifeblood of indie writers and publishers (traditional publishers as well, though they don't like to admit it). So however you felt about this book—love, hate, or meh—please compose an honest review wherever you purchased it.